THE
DREAMING

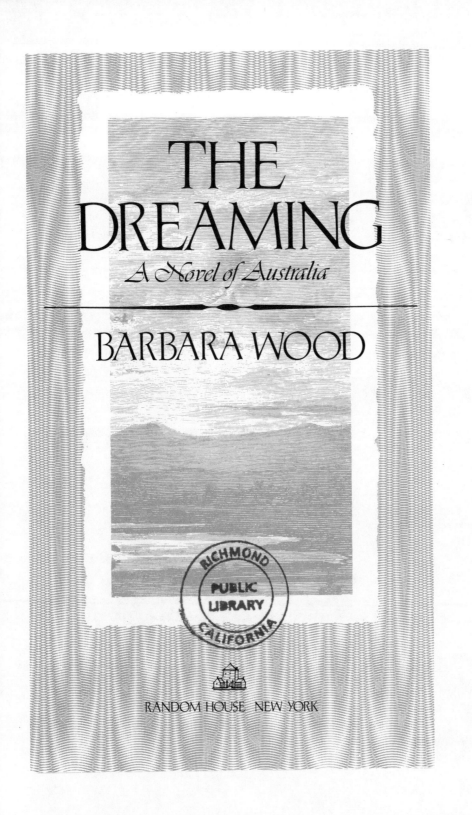

THE DREAMING

A Novel of Australia

BARBARA WOOD

RANDOM HOUSE NEW YORK

Library of Congress Cataloging-in-Publication Data
Wood, Barbara.
The dreaming : a novel of Australia / Barbara Wood.
                    p.   cm.
               ISBN 0-394-56592-4
   1. Australia—History—1788–1900—Fiction.   I. Title.
PS3573.O5877D7   1991   813'.54—dc20   90-52883

Manufactured in the United States of America
2 4 6 8 9 7 5 3
First Edition

Book design by J. K. Lambert

This book is dedicated with love
to my brother, Richard.

Special thanks go to some special folks Down Under:

To Chris Bennett of Newstead, Tasmania, for his careful research, meticulous notes, interviews, tapes, and patient answers to a thousand queries. And also for knowing the Western District so well.

To the Lewandowski family, also of Tasmania, for their support and confidence in me, and especially for their indefatigable and always cheerful efforts to obtain obscure source material for this book.

To Mr. and Mrs. Peter Cameron of the Western District, Victoria, for giving me a window into life on a sheep station.

To Lucy Lewandowski-Porter for her wool samples, spinning-wheel instruction, and particularly sensitive insight into the spirituality of Aboriginal women.

And lastly, but not leastly, to L and B Research Consultants, whose motto is "Our Business is History."

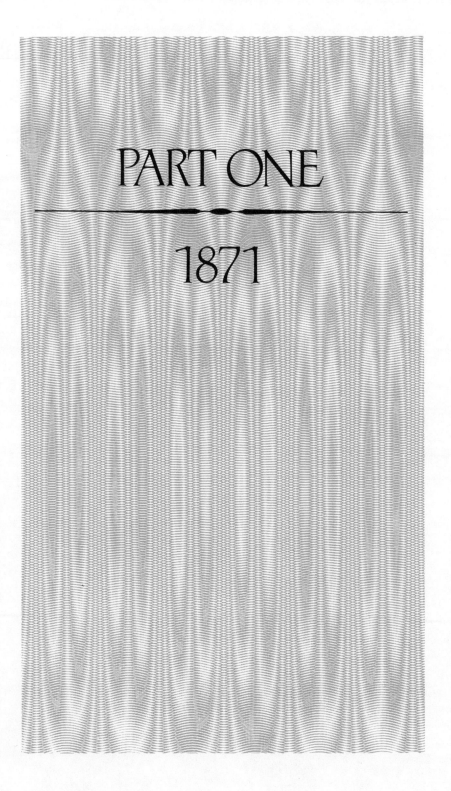

PART ONE

1871

CHAPTER 1

J oanna was dreaming.

She saw herself leaning on the arm of a handsome young officer, grateful for his support but otherwise immune to his solicitous attentions. She was oblivious also to the British soldiers, standing erect in their smart uniforms, and to the ladies, elegant in their gowns and bonnets. Officers on horseback raised their sabers in salute as the two coffins were lowered into the graves. Joanna was aware of only one thing: that she had lost the only two people she loved, and that, at eighteen, she was suddenly alone in the world.

The soldiers lifted their rifles and fired into the air. Joanna looked up, startled, as the clear blue sky tore apart. Through her black veil she saw the sun, which seemed too large and too hot and too close to the earth.

As the commander of the regiment began to read the eulogy over the graves of Sir Petronius and Lady Emily Drury, Joanna gave him a puzzled look. Why wasn't he speaking clearly? She couldn't understand what he was saying. She looked around at the people gathered to pay their final respects to her parents, and noticed that they ranged from servants to the highest army officials and royal elite of India. None of them seemed to find the commander's speech muddled or out of the ordinary.

Joanna sensed that something was terribly wrong, and she was suddenly afraid.

Then she froze: At the edge of the crowd was a dog—the dog that had killed her mother.

But the animal had been shot! Joanna had seen a soldier kill it! And yet here it was. Its black eyes seemed fixed on her, and when it made a move in her direction, Joanna tried to scream, but could not.

Then the dog was running toward her, it lunged, but instead of attacking, flew straight up into the sky and burst into a thousand hot white stars.

The stars swirled overhead like a brilliant carousel, overwhelming her with their beauty and power.

And then the stars began to form a shape across the sky, a long and winding celestial highway paved with diamonds. But it wasn't exactly a road; it moved.

And then the road became an enormous serpent, slithering across the heavens.

The diamond-bodied serpent began to uncoil and slide toward her. She felt the cold heat of star-fire wash over her. She watched the massive body grow and grow, until she saw in the center of its head a single, brilliant fiery eye. As the snake's jaws opened, the blackness inside was like a tunnel of death that was about to engulf her.

She screamed.

———

Joanna's eyes snapped open, and for a moment she didn't know where she was. Then she felt the gentle rocking of the ship, saw in the dim light the cabin walls around her. And she remembered: She was on board the SS *Estella*, bound for Australia.

She sat up and reached for the matches on the small table by her bed. Her hands shook so badly that she couldn't light the lamp. Drawing her shawl around her shoulders, she got up and made her way to the porthole; after a struggle, she managed to get it open. She felt the cold ocean wind on her face, closed her eyes and tried to calm herself.

The dream had seemed so real.

Taking deep breaths, and drawing comfort from the familiar sounds of the ship—the creaking of the rigging, the groan of timber—Joanna slowly brought herself back to reality. It was only a dream, she told herself. Just another dream. . . .

"Are dreams our link to the spirit world?" Joanna's mother, Lady Emily, had written in her diary. "Do they carry messages, or warnings, or the answers to mysteries?"

I wish I knew, Mother, Joanna thought, as she stared at a vast ocean that stretched away to the stars.

Joanna had thought the stars over India were powerful and overwhelming, but she decided that they were nothing compared to the formidable display in this night sky. The stars were grouped in ways she had never seen before. The reassuring beacons of her childhood were gone, and new ones winked down at her. Because this was the Southern Hemisphere.

Joanna thought about the dream she had just had, and what it might possibly mean. That she should dream of the funeral was understandable, and perhaps even of the dog. But why a star-serpent, and why the terror? Why had she felt the serpent was about to destroy her?

Just weeks before her death, Lady Emily had written in her diary: "I am plagued by dreams. One is a recurring nightmare, which I cannot explain and which terrifies me beyond endurance. The other dreams are strange visions of events that are not frightening but which seem unbelievably real to me. Could these in fact be lost memories? Am I somehow remembering my childhood at last? If only I knew, for I sense that an answer to my life lies in these cryptic dreams. An answer that must soon be found, or else I shall perish."

Joanna was startled out of her thoughts by sounds drifting in from over the water—a man's voice in the darkness, calling "Stroke, stroke, stroke," accompanied by the sound of oars dipping into the water. And then Joanna remembered that the *Estella* was becalmed.

"Never seen anything like it," the captain had said only the day before. "In all my years at sea, never been becalmed at this latitude. Can't explain it for the life of me. Looks like I'll have to put men in the longboats and see if we can pull us out of it."

And Joanna felt her fears rise again.

Back in Allahabad, in the sanatorium where she had spent some weeks recovering from her parents' unexpected deaths, Joanna had dreamed that this would happen.

Why? she wondered, as she shivered beneath her shawl. Could whatever haunted my mother and finally destroyed her be pursuing me out on this ocean?

"You must go to Australia, Joanna," Lady Emily had said, hours before she died. "You must make the journey you and I were going to make. Something is destroying us, and you must find its source and put an end to it, or else your life will end as mine is, prematurely, without anyone knowing why."

Joanna turned away from the porthole and looked around the tiny cabin. As a wealthy young woman, she had been able to afford quite adequate accommodations for herself for the long journey from India to Australia, and she was grateful; she would not have wanted cabin companions. She needed to be alone now, with her grief. She needed time to try to unravel what had happened to her family, and to her; to understand what was taking her to the other side of the world, to a land about which she knew so little.

She looked at the papers lying on the small writing desk, papers that pertained to a legacy from long ago, from grandparents she had never known. She had been working at deciphering them, just as her mother had tried to understand their strange meaning. Her mother's diary, too, lay on the desk—Lady Emily's "life-book," filled with her dreams and fears and her own futile attempts to understand the mystery of her life: the lost years of which she had no memory, the nightmares that seemed to foretell a frightening future. And there was a property deed, also part of Joanna's legacy from her grandparents. No one knew where the land was that was mentioned in the deed, or why Lady Emily's parents had purchased it or whether they had ever lived there.

"But I sense very strongly, Joanna," Emily had said toward the end of her life, "that the answer to everything lies in the place located on that deed, named Karra Karra. The property is somewhere in Australia. Possibly it is the place of my birth. I do not know. Sometimes it has occurred to me to wonder whether the woman who haunts my dreams is there, or once was. It is conceivable my own mother is still there, still alive—although that is unlikely. You must find Karra Karra, Joanna. For me. To save yourself. And to save your future children."

To save myself, to save us all from *what*? Joanna thought.

There was also a letter on the desk—an angry letter, saying, "Your talk of a curse is an affront to God." The letter was unsigned, but Joanna knew that it had been written by her Aunt Millicent, the woman who had raised Joanna's mother, Emily Drury, and who had refused to speak of the past, it terrified her so. And finally, there was the miniature of Lady Emily, a beautiful woman with sad eyes. How did these pieces fit together in the puzzle of this woman's life? And, Joanna wondered, into that of her own destiny as well?

"I have no idea why your mother is dying," the doctor had said to Joanna. "It is beyond my knowledge, my capabilities, to understand. She is not ill, yet she appears to be dying. I believe it is an affliction of the spirit rather than of the flesh, but I cannot explain why, or imagine what is the cause."

But Joanna had an idea. Several days before, a rabid dog had made its way into the military compound where Joanna's father was stationed. It had cornered Joanna as she had stood, frozen with fear, tensing for an attack. And then Lady Emily had stepped between her daughter and the dog, and just as the animal sprang, a soldier had fired a rifle, and the dog had fallen dead at their feet.

"Lady Emily seems to have all the symptoms of rabies, Miss Drury," the doctor had said, "but your mother wasn't bitten by the dog. I am mystified as to why she should have such symptoms."

Joanna returned her gaze to the porthole, and looked out again over the dark ocean. She heard men in boats trying to pull the steamship through the night as if it were a gigantic, sightless creature. And she thought of how her mother had lay dying, helpless against the power that was killing her. And how, just hours after the death of his beloved wife, Colonel Petronius had put his service revolver to his head and pulled the trigger.

"Strange forces are at work, my dearest Joanna," Lady Emily had said. "They have claimed me, after all these years. They will claim you. Please . . . please, go to Australia, find out what happened, stop this poison . . . this—this curse, from harming you."

Joanna thought of what her mother had told her long ago. "A sea captain brought me to Aunt Millicent's cottage in England when I was four years old," Lady Emily had said. "I had been on his ship, coming, apparently, from Australia. I had very little with me, I didn't speak. *I couldn't.* I can only believe that whatever it was that happened in Australia, which I have never been able to recall, must have been somehow, quite literally, unspeakable. Millicent said it was months before I said anything to her at all. Joanna, it's important to know why, and what happened to our family in Australia."

And then, just over a year ago, when Lady Emily had celebrated her thirty-ninth birthday, she began to have the dreams, which she believed might actually have been memories of those lost years. She had described them in her diary: "I am a small child being held in a young woman's arms. Her skin is very dark, and we are surrounded by people. We are all waiting in silence for something. We are watching the opening of what looks like a cave. I start to speak, but I am told to remain silent. Somehow, I know that my mother is about to come. I want her to come. I am afraid for her. The dream ends there, but it is so vivid, I see things in such detail—I can feel the heat of the sun on my bare body. I cannot help but wonder if it is a recollection from my years in Australia. But what does it mean?"

Joanna looked up at the collection of stars known as the Southern Cross, the tip of which pointed the way to Australia, which lay just a few days away. She was determined to get there and to find answers. As she had sat at her mother's bedside, watching the beautiful Lady Emily die of a mysterious illness, Joanna had thought: It is over now. Mother, your years of nightmares, of nameless fears, are gone. You are at peace.

But when she was in the sanatorium, she had been visited by a dream: She saw herself on a ship in the middle of the ocean, and the ship was becalmed, her sails drooping lifelessly from the yards, the captain telling his crew that water and food rations were dangerously low. And in the dream, Joanna had somehow known that she was the cause of these events.

She had awakened in terror to realize that whatever it was that had haunted Lady Emily all her life had not died with her. It now belonged to Joanna.

As she listened to the sailors straining at their oars in the darkness, trying to draw the *Estella* out of the calm, Joanna was gripped with a new sense of urgency. It couldn't be a coincidence—her dream, and now this becalmed ship. There was something, after all, to the mysteries that had so haunted her mother. Joanna, looking out into the night, tried to imagine the continent that lay only a few days away—Australia, where secrets of the past and of her future might be waiting.

"Melbourne! Port of Melbourne! Prepare to disembark!"

Joanna stood out on the deck with the rest of the passengers, watching Melbourne Harbor draw close. She was in a hurry to be off the ship, to get away from that small cabin. She looked past the crowd gathered on the dock to meet the ship, lifted her eyes to the city's skyline a short distance away. She wondered if, out there beyond the buildings and the church spires, somewhere in the heart of a country that had for thousands of years known only the nomadic Aborigines, she would find the answers her mother had been looking for.

As the gangway was raised and the ship's officers gathered to say good-by to disembarking passengers, Joanna gripped the rail and looked up at the sky, overwhelmed by the light. It was like no light she had ever known—not the hot, musky sunlight of India, where she had grown up, nor the soft misty light of England, which she had once seen as a child. The sunlight of Australia was broad and bold and clear; it was almost aggressive in its brightness and clarity.

She saw a group of men, laborers judging by their clothes, hurrying up the gangway. Once on deck, they began seizing luggage and anything they could lay hand to, promising the disembarking passengers that the job of carting their bags would cost only a penny or two. A young black man approached Joanna. "I take for you, miss," he said, reaching for her trunk. "Only sixpence. Where you want to go?"

She stared at him. It was her first encounter with an Aborigine, a race she had heard so much about all of her life. "Yes," she said after a moment. "Please. Just down to the dock."

As he gripped the handle on the end of the trunk and began to lift it, he smiled at Joanna. And then his face changed, and he gave Joanna a long look; his eyes flickered, he dropped the trunk and turned abruptly away. He reached for a wicker basket which an elderly woman was struggling with. "I carry for you, lady?" he said, and moved off along the deck, away from Joanna.

A ship's porter came up, bearing a trolley. "Shall I put your trunk ashore for you, miss?" he asked.

"What was that all about?" she said, gesturing to the Aborigine.

"Don't take it personal, miss. He probably decided the trunk was too heavy. They don't like hard work. Here, I'll just cart this down to the dock."

She followed the steward down the gangway, glancing back to see if she could see the Aborigine. But he seemed to have vanished.

"Here we are, miss," the porter said when they were on the pier. "Is anyone meeting you?"

She looked at the crowd amassed on the dock, people who were waving excitedly to arriving passengers, and she thought of the entry in her mother's diary: "Sometimes I wonder, is there any chance that members of my family are still alive somewhere in Australia? My parents?"

Joanna handed the porter a few coins and said, "No. No one will be meeting me."

As the crowd jostled around her, she forced herself to think what she should do next. First she would have to find a place to stay, and a way to manage on her allowance; it would be two-and-a-half years before she would come into her inheritance. And she would need to find someone to help her locate the property her family owned, someone knowledgeable about the Australia of thirty-seven years ago.

Suddenly, Joanna was aware of a commotion behind her, a voice shouting, "Stop! Stop that boy!"

As she turned, she saw a small boy darting through the crowd on the deck of the ship. He looked to be four or five years old, and he was flinging himself first in one direction, then another, a steward in pursuit.

"Stop him!" the steward shouted, and as people grabbed at the child, he twisted around and ran down the gangway, flying past Joanna.

She watched him run blindly, his skinny legs in short pants frantically pumping up and down. As the steward reached him, the boy threw himself flat and began to bang his head on the pier.

"Here, here!" the man said, grabbing the child by the collar and shaking him. "Stop that!"

"Wait!" Joanna said. "You're hurting him."

She knelt next to the squirming boy and saw that he had cut his forehead. "Don't be afraid," she said. "No one is going to hurt you." She opened her bag, took out a handkerchief and patted his head gently. "There now," she said, "this won't hurt."

She looked up at the steward. "What happened?" she asked. "He's terrified."

"I'm sorry, miss, but I ain't no nursemaid. He was put aboard back at Adelaide, and someone had to keep watch. He's been belowdecks for the past few days, and he's been nothing but trouble. Won't eat, won't talk . . ."

"Where are his parents?"

"Don't know, miss. All I know is, he's been a lot of trouble and he's getting off here. Someone is supposed to be coming for him."

Joanna noticed that there was a one-pound note pinned to the boy's shirt, and a piece of paper that read ADAM WESTBROOK. "Is your name Adam?" she asked. "Adam?"

He stared at her but did not speak.

The steward started to unpin the pound note. "I reckon this is due to me considering all the trouble he's been."

"But it belongs to him," Joanna said. "Don't take it."

The steward looked at her for a moment, taking in the pretty face and the voice that sounded as if she were used to giving orders. Recognizing the expensive cut of her clothes and the first-class sticker on her trunk, he decided she must belong to someone important. "I reckon you're right," he said. "I don't dislike kids, mind you. It's just that he was such a handful. Cried the whole time, threw fits like this. And he wouldn't talk, wouldn't say a single word. Well, I have to get back to the ship." And before Joanna could say anything more, the steward disappeared into the crowd.

Joanna looked carefully at the boy, at his pale, fragile face. It occurred to her that if she were to hold him up to the light, she would be able to see right through him. She wondered why he had been all alone on the ship, and what terrible pain or unhappiness had driven him to injure himself.

Then Joanna heard a man say, "Pardon me, miss, but is this Adam?"

She looked up to find herself staring at an attractive man with a square jaw, a straight nose, sun-creases around smoky-gray eyes.

"I'm Hugh Westbrook," he said, removing his hat. "I've come for Adam." He smiled at her and then dropped down to one knee and said, "Hello, there, Adam. Well, well. I've come to take you home."

Without his hat, Joanna thought she could see a resemblance between the man and the boy—the same mouth, with a thin upper lip and a full lower one. And when the man gave the child a serious look, the same vertical furrow appeared between his eyebrows that was etched between the boy's.

"I reckon you must be kind of scared, Adam," Westbrook said. "It's all right. Your father was my cousin, so that makes us kin. You're my cousin, too." He reached out, but Adam shrank back against Joanna.

Westbrook was holding a packet wrapped in brown paper and tied with string. He began to open it, saying, "Here, I've brought these for you. I thought you might like to have some new clothes, the kind we wear at Merinda. Did your mother ever tell you about my sheep station, Merinda?"

When the boy didn't speak, Hugh Westbrook stood up and said to Joanna, "I bought these in Melbourne." He unfolded a jacket, which had been wrapped around boots and a hat. "The letter wasn't specific about what he might need, but these will do for now, and I can get more later. Here you go," he said, and he held the jacket out to Adam. But the boy let out a strange cry and covered his head with his arms.

"Please," Joanna said, "let me help." She took the jacket and guided the boy into it, but it was too large, and Adam seemed to disappear.

"How about this, then?" Westbrook said, but when he put the bush hat on the boy's head, it covered Adam's eyes and ears and settled on his nose.

"Oh dear," Joanna said.

Westbrook turned to her. "I hadn't thought he would be this small. He'll be five in January; I'm not used to children, and I guess I overestimated things." He gave Adam a thoughtful look, then said to Joanna,

"I envisioned a boy who could take care of himself. I haven't a notion of the needs of a boy this small, and at the sheep station we're out working all day. I can see that Adam is going to need a lot of attention."

Joanna looked down at the child and inspected the cut on his forehead. "He's in such pain," she said. "What happened to him?"

"I don't know exactly. His father died several years ago, when Adam was a baby. And then his mother died recently. The South Australia authorities wrote me saying that Adam had been suddenly orphaned, and asked if I would take him, since I was his nearest relative."

"The poor boy," Joanna murmured, resting her hand on Adam's shoulder. "How did his mother die?"

"I don't know."

"I hope he didn't witness it. He's so young. But something seems to have left a terrible mark on him. What happened to you, Adam?" Joanna said to him. "Tell us, please do. It will help if you talk about it."

But the boy's attention seemed to be focused on a towering crane that was lifting cargo onto a ship.

Joanna said to Westbrook, "My mother was hurt when she was very young. She witnessed something terrible, and it haunted her all her life. There was no one to heal her, no one to help her understand the pain and give her the love and kindness she needed. She was raised by an aunt who lacked affection, and so I believe the wound never healed. I believe the memory of that childhood event actually killed her."

Joanna placed her hand beneath Adam's chin and lifted his face. She saw pain in his eyes, and terror. It's as if he's living a nightmare, she thought. As if we are all part of a bad dream.

She bent down and said to the boy, "You're not dreaming, Adam, you're awake. Everything is all right, really it is. You are going to be taken care of. No one is going to hurt you. I have bad dreams, too. I have them all the time. But I know that they are only dreams and that they can't hurt me."

Westbrook watched Joanna speak soothingly to the boy, noticing how her slender body arched gently toward Adam—like the eucalyptus that grew in the outback, he thought—and when he saw the calming effect she was having on the boy, he said, "Thank you for doing what you did, it was kind of you to help. You must be anxious to be going. If there is someone here to meet you, they'll be looking for you, Miss . . ."

"Drury," she said. "Joanna Drury."

"Are you here on holiday, Miss Drury?"

"No, not on holiday. My mother and I planned to come to Australia together. We were going to look into some things about our family, and also for some land she inherited. But she died before we left India. So I have come on alone." She smiled. "I've never been to Australia before. It is a bit overwhelming!"

Westbrook looked at her for a moment and was surprised to see something spark suddenly in her eyes, and then vanish. And there had been something behind the smile, and he recognized it as fear. When he heard the restraint in her voice, as if she were saying something quite ordinary while holding back a secret, he realized he was very intrigued.

"Where is this land you're looking for?" he asked. "I know Australia pretty well."

"I don't know. I believe it is near a place called Karra Karra. Do you know it?"

"Karra Karra. Sounds Aboriginal. Is it here in Victoria?"

"I'm sorry, I just don't know."

Westbrook looked at her for a moment, then said, "I know a lot of people in Australia. I would be glad to help you find your land."

"Oh," she said. "That would be very kind of you, Mr. Westbrook. But you must be in a hurry to take Adam home."

As he watched her brush a stray hair from her face, he was struck by the delicacy of the gesture. He looked over at the men gathered around the gangway, ogling the female passengers. Some of the men held signs that said, WIFE WANTED. MUST COOK and NEED HEALTHY WOMAN, MATRIMONY IN MIND. A few of the bolder ones called out to the disembarking women. Westbrook suddenly pictured Joanna all alone in Melbourne, a rough frontier city where men outnumbered women four to one, and where she would be defenseless against the more ruthless types.

"Miss Drury," he said, "may I ask where you will be staying in Melbourne?"

"I suppose I shall go to a hotel first, and then look for a boarding house or an apartment."

"It occurs to me, Miss Drury, that perhaps we could help each other. You need help in getting acquainted with Australia, and I need help with Adam. Might we make a bargain? You help me with Adam for a time, help us get him settled in, and I'll get you going on looking for this Karra Karra. It wouldn't be for long, I'm getting married in six months," he said. "My station, Merinda, isn't fancy, I imagine you're used to far finer places. The house is mostly a veranda and a wish. But you and Adam can have it to yourselves, and I'll see that you have everything you need. I want the boy to get off to the right start with me, and he seems calmer with you."

When she seemed uncertain, he added, "I can understand your hesitation, but what do you have to lose? The bargain will be, come and take care of Adam for six months, and I'll help you look for whatever it is you're looking for. Australia covers three million square miles, most as yet unexplored, but I know a certain amount of it. You can't do it on your own, you'll need help. One of my friends is a lawyer, and perhaps I could ask him to look into the property you inherited. Please think about it, Miss Drury. Even come for a month, get us going, and I'll help you get started on the matters you mentioned. I promise you, nothing improper will occur. Think about it while I go and get the wagon."

She watched him disappear into the crowd, then she felt a small hand slip into hers. When she found Adam's large gray eyes studying her, Joanna considered this unexpected turn of events. She thought of everything she had sacrificed to come here, everything she had left behind: her friends in India, the cities she knew so well, the culture she had grown up with, and finally the handsome young officer who had stood with her at the funeral and who had asked her to marry him. And she felt suddenly homesick. Now, as she watched the crowd on the pier disperse to waiting carriages, wagons and horses, saw the heavy traffic on the street that led into Melbourne, as she thought of being alone for the first time in her life, among strangers in a strange country, she thought of how easy it might have been to stay in India, but for her mother's request.

Then she found herself thinking of the young Aborigine who had come aboard the ship a few minutes earlier, and the strange look he had given her when he had taken hold of her trunk. And she remembered that she really had had no choice but to come to Australia.

She thought of Hugh Westbrook, and was surprised to realize that what she mostly thought was how attractive he was. He was good looking, and he was young—around thirty, she judged. But it was more than that. Joanna was used to spit-and-polish uniforms and a rigid correctness in manner. Even the marriage proposal from the young officer had come stiffly and politely, as if he had been following protocol. That young man, Joanna knew, would never have dreamed of addressing a lady he had not been formally introduced to. But Westbrook had seemed relaxed and comfortable, as if following his own rules, and Joanna found that she liked it.

He had said he would help her find Karra Karra. She knew she was going to need someone's help, and he did say he was familiar with

Australia. Should she tell him, she wondered, the other part of it—about the dreams, how bad things seemed to follow them? No, she decided, not now, not yet. Because not even she understood the dreams, was not even sure they existed, except in her imagination.

When the memory of the young Aborigine on the ship came back again—how he had looked at her and then abruptly turned away—she pushed it out of her mind. Also her dream, subsequently fulfilled, of a big ship becalmed. And she focused on what Hugh Westbrook's sheep station might be like. Did it sit upon rolling green pastures like the sheep farms she had once seen in England? Was it shaded by oaks, did sparrows chatter in a garden behind the kitchen? Or was Hugh Westbrook's home different from any farm in England? Joanna had read as much as she could about this curious continent of Australia, where there were no native hoofed animals, no large predatory cats, where the trees did not shed their leaves in autumn, but their bark instead, and where the Aborigines were said to be the oldest race on earth. And she was suddenly curious to see it all.

"Well, Miss Drury? What do you say?"

She turned and looked at Hugh Westbrook. He had not replaced his hat, and she saw the rough way his hair lay on his head. She had grown up among pomaded men, officers who kept their hair slicked down; Westbrook's fell this way and that, longish and wavy, as if he had given up on a comb and let the hair go the way nature meant it to.

She felt Adam's small hand in hers, and thought of how desperately this child had banged his head on the ground, as if to drive out unspeakable memories. So she said, "All right, Mr. Westbrook. I'll come for a little while."

His smile was one of relief. "Do you want to stop in the city for anything? You might want to send a letter to your family, tell them where you will be?"

"No," she said. "I have no family."

As Westbrook loaded Joanna's trunk into the wagon, she went through a smaller bag, took out a bottle and a clean bandage, and patted some lotion onto Adam's wound.

"What is that you're putting on Adam's head?" Westbrook asked.

"It's eucalyptus oil," Joanna said. "It's an antiseptic and it hastens healing."

"I didn't know there were eucalyptus trees outside Australia."

"A few have been imported to India, where I lived. My mother obtained the oil through a local chemist's shop. She used it in many of her remedies. One of her talents was medicine, healing."

"I didn't think anyone but Australians knew about the healing powers of eucalyptus oil, although credit has to be given to the Aborigines. They were using eucalyptus in their medicines centuries before the white men came here."

As the wagon pulled away from the pier, away from the crowds and the *Estella,* Joanna thought of what she might find somewhere in these three million square miles. She thought of the mysterious young black woman who had haunted her mother's dreams, and of the grandparents who had come to this continent over forty years ago. She thought of dreams and nightmares and what meanings they might hold, and she thought of returning to the place where it had all begun, where her mother's fragmented memories abided. Something had been started there that must be ended.

Finally she thought of the man at her side and the hurt little boy, people who had suddenly come into her life. And she was filled with a sense of wonder and fear.

CHAPTER 2

Pauline Downs couldn't wait for her wedding night. While the seamstress put the last few pins into the elegant peignoir, Pauline turned this way and that, admiring herself in the full-length mirror. She could barely contain her excitement.

Just wait until Hugh sees me in this!

It was the very latest style—only as old as the weeks it had taken for the pattern and fabric to make the voyage from Paris to Melbourne. The material was a creamy champagne-peach satin, trimmed with Valenciennes lace and the kind of tiny buttons only the House of Worth could produce. The peignoir seemed to spill over Pauline's slender body, outlining the full breasts and smooth hips, and the way it pooled at her feet made Pauline, who was tall, look even taller. It had taken her weeks to arrive at just the right design for what she would wear on her first night alone with Hugh Westbrook.

The peignoir was only part of the enormous trousseau she was preparing for her honeymoon. Her bedroom suite at Lismore, her home in the Western District, was cluttered with bolts of fabric, fashion magazines, patterns and gowns in various stages of completion. And they were no ordinary gowns; Pauline did not consider herself an ordinary woman. She made certain that, despite being on the other side of the world in a colony whose fashions were usually a few years behind those of Europe, her bridal wardrobe was going to be in the latest style.

How delicious, Pauline thought, as she looked around at the dresses she would be wearing when she was Mrs. Hugh Westbrook. The tedious old crinolines were finally being done away with and a whole new style was emerging. She was dying to show off this radical new invention called the bustle, and the daring tied-back skirts that lifted the hems inches off the floor. And the fabrics! Blue silks and cinnamon satins, waiting to be seamed and bowed in black or gold velvet, with white lace to set off the throat and wrists. How perfectly they complemented her platinum hair and blue eyes. Dress was one of Pauline's passions. Being in the forefront of fashion helped her to forget that she wasn't in London, but in a colonial backwater named Victoria in honor of the Queen.

Pauline was a member of Victoria's rural gentry, having been born and raised on one of the oldest and largest sheep stations in the colony. She had grown up in pampered luxury; her father had called her "princess," and he had made her brother Frank promise that, when the elder Downs was gone, Frank would keep his sister in a life of continued comfort and ease. Now she lived on a twenty-five-thousand-acre sheep station, alone with Frank in a two-storied mansion with a full staff of servants. Pauline's days were spent fox hunting and at weekend parties, holiday balls and social fetes, much as they would have been if she lived on a wealthy country estate in England. Frank and his sister were the trendsetters for the upper crust; they set the standards by which others of their class lived. Pauline firmly believed that despite the fact that one lived in the colonies, or perhaps *because* one lived in the colonies, it was important not to let oneself "go bush."

The only unfashionable thing Pauline had done was to remain unmarried at the age of twenty-four.

Not that she had not had opportunities for marriage. There had been many hopeful suitors, but they had mostly been men who had gotten rich quickly from sheep or gold, the rough sort who had made their fortunes in the outback and who had come to Victoria's grazing district to playact at being lords of the manor. A few were even wealthier than her brother. But she believed they had no manners or breeding, they gambled and drank beer straight from the bottle, they spoke atrociously; they had no respect for class. Worse, they had no ambition to improve themselves, nor saw any reason to do so. But Hugh Westbrook was not like that. Even though he, too, had come from the outback, had made a small fortune in gold and was now the sort of grazier who rode out with his musterers and drove his own fence piles into the ground, in many other ways he was different. There was something about Hugh that had drawn Pauline to him the moment she had met him, ten years ago, when he had purchased the Merinda property. Pauline had been only fourteen years old then, and Hugh, twenty.

It wasn't just Hugh's good looks that she had fallen in love with. She believed there was more to him than muscles and an attractive smile. For one thing, he was honest, a word that failed to describe most of the men in the outback. And she felt there was a special kind of strength to him, a quiet strength, not the sort one saw in the brag and swagger of the other bushmen. Hugh seemed to Pauline to have a strength that was deeply anchored, steady and sure, a strength that made her see not so much the man he was today, but the man he was going to be.

When Hugh had purchased Merinda there had been nothing there but a squatter's shack and a few diseased sheep. With his own hands and a strong will, Hugh had started out alone, struggling to build Merinda into a station worth being proud of. Ten years ago, Frank had estimated that the young Queenslander would sell out before the year was over. But Hugh had proven Frank and the rest of the graziers wrong. And now, there was no doubt that Hugh Westbrook was going to go even farther.

We will go far together, my darling, Pauline thought. And that was what excited her most about him: When other people looked at Hugh they might see his calloused hands and dusty boots; when Pauline looked at him she saw the refined gentleman he was someday going to be—that she was going to make of him.

"That will be enough for now," she said to the seamstress. "Go take a rest and have a cup of tea. And would you please tell Elsie to run my bath?"

For a long time Pauline had kept secret her hopes about Hugh Westbrook. While Western District gentry had expected her to marry someone of her own class—someone rich and cultured—Pauline had been determined to marry Hugh. She had managed to see him at every available opportunity: at the annual graziers' show, at barn dances and social events on the various stations, at the races and in her own home, when Hugh had come to discuss sheep farming with Frank. Each time she saw him her desire had grown. Sometimes he would appear unexpectedly, riding up on his horse, smiling and waving, and she would feel her heart jump. And afterward, Pauline would lie awake, imagining what it would be like to be his wife, to be in his bed . . . .

She could not say exactly when she had known she was going to marry him, but her careful and subtle seduction had spanned nearly three years, drawing Hugh into a mutual flirtation that had left him believing it was he who had pursued her. Pauline knew what moonlight did to her hair, so she arranged walks in the garden with Hugh on such nights. She was aware of the handsome figure she cut when she was at the archery range, so she made sure Hugh attended events in which she was competing. When she discovered that he had a passion for Dundee cake and egg curry, she cultivated a taste for them as well. And when Hugh had said that his favorite poet was Byron, Pauline had devoted days to familiarizing herself with his works.

Finally, Hugh began to talk about marriage. He turned thirty, and started to say "when I'm married," or "when I have children of my own." That was when Pauline knew the time was right. But other women had their eyes on Hugh, and although Pauline knew he felt something for her, she had as yet received no commitment from him. And this was when Pauline's secret was born.

She had done something that, if it were known, would have shocked local society. She had proposed to Hugh. While her friends would declare such an action demeaning to a lady, that no man was worth such a "low" step, Pauline had regarded it as a practical move. Time was passing, and various women in the district were inviting Hugh for tea or to go riding, and paying attention to him at local events. It had been simple expediency that had driven Pauline to invite Hugh on a picnic by the river, on a day that dawned with the promise of rain. They had gone riding together and had lunched by the river on egg curry and Dundee cake, talking about sheep, about colonial politics, the upstart Darwin and the new novel by Jules Verne, when, as if Pauline had orchestrated it herself, the rain clouds burst. She and Hugh had had to run for cover under the nearby trees, but not without getting wet and stumbling on the ground and holding onto each other because they were laughing so hard. And Pauline had said, "You know, Hugh, we really should get married," and he had kissed her, hard and passionately, and with an explosiveness, Pauline would later think, that dimmed the brilliance of the lightning breaking around them. There was only the one kiss, but it had been enough. Hugh had said, "Marry me," and Pauline had won.

But once they were officially engaged, Pauline had discovered that pinning Hugh down to a date had been like trying to trap a willy-willy, a whirlwind. His sheep station always came first: the wedding couldn't be in the winter because of crutching—shearing the tails and hind legs of ewes who would soon be giving birth, to keep them as clean as possible—or in the spring because of lambing and shearing; the summers were busy with dipping and breeding, and the autumn—

But Pauline had pointed out that autumn was the least demanding season on sheep stations, and they had settled upon a March wedding.

Everything had been going according to plan until the letter arrived from the South Australian government informing Hugh about Adam Westbrook, the child of a distant relative.

Suddenly Pauline saw a flaw in her vision of their future together. She and Hugh would not be free to enjoy each other, they would not be free to be lovers, wild and impulsive and uninhibited. They would start married life already burdened with a child—another woman's child. And Pauline did not like to think of what Hugh might be bringing back: some half-wild, obstreperous creature. "He's not your responsibility," she had said, instantly regretting her words, because a flash of anger had come into Hugh's eyes. Pauline had quickly reassured him that she would welcome the boy, while in her heart she was dreading it.

She wasn't ready to be a mother—she wanted to get used to being a wife first. There were certain sacrifices involved, she knew, and a way of life that often meant placing the other's needs before her own. Pauline had no idea of how one went about being a mother. Her own had died years ago in an influenza epidemic that had swept across Victoria, also taking Pauline's two sisters and younger brother. Pauline was raised with her surviving sibling, Frank, by their father and a succession of governesses. She had no idea how it was between mothers and children; she especially had no idea of what it was like between mothers and daughters. She wanted a daughter; she often imagined teaching her to ride and to hunt and to be "special." The teaching and molding of a daughter, Pauline often thought, must be very rewarding. But the feelings that passed between mother and daughter—the love and devotion and duty—seemed quite beyond her understanding.

"Your bath is ready," Pauline's maid said, interrupting her thoughts.

After a tiring yet exhilarating day spent over patterns and fabrics and standing still while her two dressmakers worked with pins and scissors, Pauline decided to enjoy a long, indulgent soak. She was a sensual woman; she enjoyed the kiss of pearls at her throat, the brush of a feather boa on her bare shoulders, the luxury of satin sheets and soft lace nightgowns. Textures gave her pleasure; even the hardness of gemstones in their silver and gold settings brought joy to her fingertips. There were few sensations she denied herself, or had not experienced. Frank was wealthy enough to provide his sister with champagne from France, and their dining table was always graced by the finest foods. Pauline spent hours at her grand piano, delighting in Chopin and Mozart. She also rode hard at hounds, taking the most perilous fences and ditches, relishing the sensation of controlling the horse, of flying through the air, of daring the fates. There was little, at twenty-four, that Pauline Downs had not indulged herself in, with the exception of one supremely cardinal pleasure: She had yet to be intimate with a man.

As Pauline luxuriated in the hot water, slowly moving the sponge over her body, she glanced in the steamy mirror at the reflection of Elsie, her lady's maid, laying out fresh undergarments. The girl was English, young and pretty and, Pauline knew, was walking out with one of the grooms who worked in the Lismore stables. As she watched the maid leave the bathroom, Pauline wondered what Elsie did with her young man when they were alone.

And suddenly she felt a pang of envy.

Looking at herself in the mirror, at the face she knew was beautiful, and framed in thick blond waves, she thought: Pauline Downs, daughter of one of the oldest and wealthiest families in Victoria, envious of her maid!

But, it was true.

Did they make love, she wondered, Elsie and her beau? Did they run into each other's arms every time they met, and then hurry away to some private spot where they embraced and kissed and felt the heat and hardness and softness of each other's bodies?

Pauline closed her eyes and sank deeper into the hot water. She moved her hands along her thighs, feeling the ache again, the ache that was becoming almost a physical pain, the wanting, the desire, the need to have Hugh Westbrook make love to her. She fantasized about their wedding night, she relived their one kiss on that rainy afternoon by the river, and recalled how his body had felt against hers, and the promise it held for future lovemaking.

Soon now, she thought. A mere six months away, and she would be in bed with Hugh, and she would know at last that ecstasy she had for so long dreamed about.

When the bedroom clock chimed the hour, Pauline suddenly realized it was getting late.

She was determined that her wedding was going to be like no wedding the Western District had known, and so she had asked Frank, who owned the Melbourne *Times*, to use his influence in trying to persuade a world-famous opera singer to sing at the wedding. Pauline would not settle for an Australian. No matter how perfect the voice, a colonial would still reduce the wedding to a colonial event. But the Royal Opera Company was scheduled to perform in Melbourne in February, and Dame Lydia Meacham, an Englishwoman known from Covent Garden to Leningrad for the purity and excellence of her voice, was coming with them. Pauline had informed Frank that her dream would be to have Dame Lydia sing at her wedding.

Frank was not keen on the idea, not being overly fond of the Royal Opera Company in the first place. "They look at us as if we're an unwanted stepchild," he always complained whenever the company made the long journey from England down to the Australian colonies. "They come here with their fine airs and jumped-up ways and act as if they're doing us a big favor," Frank would say.

But how else could it be, Pauline wondered, with the colonies so far away?

It made her recall how she had felt, years ago in England, when she had attended her first dance. What a near disaster it had been! How hopelessly out of fashion Pauline had felt, with the other girls at the London Academy marveling that she would show up wearing such an out-of-date dress. And then, seeing her puzzlement and dismay, telling her that it was all right, that she had, after all, come a long distance. They had treated her in the patronizing manner she had finally learned to expect in England whenever someone discovered where she was from. People had called her and her brother "colonials" and they had seemed not to take them, or where they lived, seriously. Those girls had not meant to be cruel—they had merely expressed an honest disregard for someone who came from so far away and from a group of colonies to which English people gave little thought, and which, when they did think of them, they regarded as backward and provincial.

That had been when Pauline was sent to London for her "coming out." Well-to-do colonial girls always went "home" for schooling—"home" being England. Even Pauline's mother, who had been brought up on a farm in New South Wales, had made the voyage to Britain when the time came. And Pauline planned to do the same when her own daughters came of age, to have them "come out" in England, as was the proper thing to do.

As she stepped into the towel Elsie held for her, Pauline thought: Frank will be back any time now. She couldn't wait to hear his news. Had he been able to engage Dame Lydia for the wedding? Because everything must go perfectly: the wedding, the reception, the honeymoon. Her life.

Pauline smiled as her thoughts returned to Hugh and their wedding night, and how she hoped to make it a night of surprises for both of them.

"Frank!" John Reed said as he joined his friend at the bar in Finnegan's pub. "When did you get back?"

Frank had to look up meet his friend's gaze. Reed towered over him, as most people did. "Hello, John. I just got back today. I thought I'd stop and have a drink before going home." And before, Frank added mentally, facing Pauline with the bad news. "How are things over at Glenhope?"

"Couldn't be better. I'm expecting a good clip this year. Any news on the inland expedition?"

When Frank had purchased the ailing *Times,* it had been merely for the sake of diversion, a hobby. But it had soon evolved, some of his friends believed, into something bordering on obsession, as Frank grew increasingly determined to build it into a newspaper to rival any in the colonies. The *Times* was thus far still small, but it was growing, due mainly to the imagination and energy of its thirty-four-year-old owner. Frank was constantly seeking new ways to increase the paper's circulation, and so when he heard that the *New York Herald* had sent a man named Stanley to Africa to search for the missing Dr. Livingstone, Frank had come up with the idea of outfitting an expedition into the Australian interior, the great heart of the continent called the Never Never, to see what was there.

Many men had tried to traverse the continent from south to north, trekking from Melbourne or Adelaide in the south, northward to the Indian Ocean. But always they were stopped by a vast expanse of waterless salt flats and furnace-like temperatures. Those who ventured into that hell never came out alive. Frank believed that somewhere beyond the dancing heat lay a great inland sea, and he had used his own money to outfit a ten-man, sixteen-camel team in the hopes of finding it. The expedition was taking along an enormous boat, hauled on sleds, in the hope of reaching that sea, and in exchange for Frank's financial support of the expedition they were going to name the sea after him, should they find it.

The *Times* published periodic updates on their progress as they sent telegrams along the way; but the expedition had not been heard from in some time, and speculation was running high that they, like others before them, had perished in the Great Desert.

"Do you reckon we've lost them?" Reed said.

Frank had grown up hearing stories about the Aborigines, who were said to inhabit that formidable, unexplored region—fantastic tales about songlines and Dreaming Sites, where magic and miracles were a daily occurrence; legends of ghosts and ancestors who grappled with mythical beasts like Yowie the Night Monster and the Rainbow Serpent. The stories were too incredible for a white man to believe, and yet, Frank had always argued, they must have some basis in fact. If Aborigines were surviving in that wilderness, then it was possible that white men could survive, too. "We'll hear from them, John," Frank said. "Don't you worry about that."

Reed took a long drink of beer, then said, "So, what do you think of the new barmaid?"

Frank had noticed her when he first came into Finnegan's. The pub was located on the edge of Cameron Town, where the main street joined the country road known as the Cameron Highway. Frank had been surprised, when he had ridden up in the late afternoon, to see so many horses and gigs tied up in the yard. Finnegan's was a quiet pub, being more expensive than its competitors; it catered to a genteel crowd; wealthy graziers and cattlemen gathered here to drink in peace and quiet, whereas Facey's, the workingman's pub across the street, did a more voluminous trade with station hands and shearers. Finnegan's yard was rarely crowded, but, on this late October afternoon, it was. And Frank was further surprised to find, when he walked in, that there wasn't an available seat in the place.

"It's because of her," Reed said, jerking his head toward the barmaid who was pouring whiskeys at the other end of the bar. "Started working here six weeks ago. Old Joe Finnegan's been doing a brisk business ever since."

Frank studied her, a mildly attractive woman in her late thirties, not slender, in a rather plain dress that clearly wasn't designed to excite the male imagination. When she handed over the drinks and took the customers' money, Frank saw none of the usual barmaid flirtation; in fact, from what Frank could see, there didn't appear to be anything striking or unusual about her.

"She's the reason for the crowd?" Frank asked.

"Her name's Ivy Dearborn," Reed said. "She draws people."

"What do you mean?"

"When she isn't serving, she does sketches. See that pad and pencil by the cash register? Watch. Pretty soon she'll pick it up and make a drawing of one of the patrons."

"And they pay her?"

"Oh no, she doesn't do it for money, and you can't ask her to do your picture. It's her choice. And you never know who she's going to do, or what kind of a picture it'll be. She does caricatures, sometimes not very flattering ones. She says she draws people as she sees them. You should see how she did me! A fat, lazy-looking koala bear!"

Frank laughed. "So she draws the truth, eh John?"

"Don't speak too soon, my friend. She's been doing you."

"Me!"

"I noticed she's had her eye on you ever since you came in."

Frank had been aware of very little beyond the whiskey before him. The expedition was on his mind, the possibility of its fate, and then there was the news he had to tell Pauline. And finally he couldn't stop thinking about running into Hugh Westbrook, in Melbourne, and meeting that girl Hugh said was going to help him take care of the boy. The young woman had asked Frank about a deed that she thought had titled her grandparents with land thirty-seven years ago. Although he had been unable to tell her if the deed was still valid, she had piqued Frank's interest. He was always looking for a good story to spice up his newspaper, and so he was wondering now if there was a story in that girl and her old document.

"Go on," Reed said. "Ask Ivy to show you the picture she did of you. Aren't you curious to know how she sees you?"

Frank could already guess how she would draw him; he had no illusions about himself. He knew what he looked like: short, with a receding hairline, and a face that women rarely glanced at twice. Once before, when he was younger, he had had a caricature done of himself at a carnival, and the artist had depicted him as a strutting cockatoo with a cigar in its beak.

Reed went on: "She's single, has a room at Mary Smith's boardinghouse, and although every man in the place has asked her out, she won't go. I asked Finnegan if he was having her on the quiet, and he swears not. Their relationship is strictly business, he says. I can't imagine who she's saving herself for!"

Frank watched as the woman went to work on the sketch pad, her pencil flying. Her look was one of complete concentration, with none of the coyness that meant she was hoping for a tip. She seemed to be absorbed in the drawing.

Finally she finished and handed the sketch across the bar to Paddy

Malloy, the man she had drawn. Everyone gathered around to see, and suddenly, there was shouting: "Look what you've done to me! This is an insult! An outrage!"

"Good Lord," John Reed said. "What do you suppose she's done with the poor old fellow?"

Frank and John went to join the circle that had gathered around the irate Irishman. "I won't stand for this!" he was shouting.

Frank looked over the man's shoulder and saw that the barmaid had done a drawing of a tall bird, a crane, wearing a bowler hat and a monocle in one eye. The bird strongly resembled Malloy.

"Aw, go on, Paddy," one of his friends said. "She didn't mean anything by it."

"I want her fired!" cried the Irishman. "I want this woman out of here this instant!"

"Now now, Mr. Malloy," Finnegan said as he came up, drying his hands on his apron. "I'm sure Miss Dearborn intended no harm. It's all in good fun."

"So help me, Finnegan, if you don't fire this—"

"Calm down, Malloy," Frank said. "Where's your sense of humor? You have to admit there's a resemblance."

"Oh you think so, do you? Let's see how you like it when the shoe is on your foot." He picked up a pile of papers from the bar and started to go through them. "I'm sure I saw her doing one of you," he murmured. "She's been doing all of us."

Frank looked at the barmaid, who appeared to be neither amused nor upset over the situation, and then he found himself wondering how she kept all that beautiful red hair piled so neatly on top of her head without having it come tumbling down. Her eyes met his, and Frank felt his cheeks grow hot. He suddenly didn't want to see the sketch she had done of him. "Let it go, Malloy," he said, and he started to turn away.

But John Reed, laughing, said, "Come now, Frank, be a sport. Let's see what the lady sees in you."

Someone at the back of the pub made a wisecrack, and everyone laughed. Then a somber Scotsman named Angus McCloud said from his solitary place at the other end of the bar, "The lass probably only needed a half a sheet of paper to draw you, Downs!"

Finally Malloy said, "Here we go!" and in the next instant his face fell.

Frank didn't want to look, but when he saw Malloy's expression, and noticed how the others, too, fell silent, he took the sketch and stared at it.

"Crikey, Downs," someone said. "That *would* look like you—if wishes came true."

Frank had never seen such a flattering likeness of himself. It was his face, and yet it was not. Ivy had captured his eyes perfectly, but she had worked some sort of subtle magic on the hair and chin. Why, Frank couldn't help thinking, he was almost handsome!

He looked up at Ivy, who was busy wiping down the counter, and then back at the sketch. Suddenly aware of the silence in the pub, Frank cleared his throat and said, "I don't see what you're all upset about, Malloy. The lady is clearly very talented."

Malloy threw down his sketch, and went back to his drink, and the other men drifted back to their tables, their places at the bar, their conversations. When Frank picked up his whiskey, John Reed nudged him and said, "I take it she's picked you."

But Frank didn't know what to think. He sipped his drink and tried to concentrate on what he should he do next, if anything. First of all there was Pauline, and the news he dreaded having to tell her, about seeing Westbrook, and the pretty nursemaid Westbrook was bringing home; and about the boy, Adam; and how, in a few days, all the tongues in the western district were going to be wagging about all this. And then he tried to think about the expedition and whether or not he should consider sending a rescue party after them.

But in the end his thoughts returned to Ivy Dearborn and what she could mean by that flattering sketch she had made of him.

"Miss Downs?" Elsie said, coming into the bathroom. "Excuse me, but Mr. Downs is here."

Pauline reached for her dressing gown. "Thank you, Elsie. Tell him I shall be right out."

Frank looked around his sister's room as he poured himself a drink. It looked as if a lady's trunk had exploded.

There were clothes everywhere—gowns and dresses draped over chairs and sofa, frilly and lacy objects scattered all over the Turkish carpet, feminine ribbony things hanging everywhere. It was her trousseau, he knew, for her honeymoon with Westbrook. The bill from the dressmaker was going to be fantastic, but Frank decided that if it made Pauline happy, he wouldn't say anything about it.

When Pauline emerged from the bathroom, Frank smelled her before he saw her; fragrance and hot steam preceded his sister's entrance. And then when he saw her he thought as he always thought,

my God, but she's beautiful. But that was because Frank had a weakness
for tall women. Like that barmaid at Finnegan's, whose actions he was
still turning over in his mind.

"Frank, darling," Pauline said, gliding toward him and kissing him
on the cheek. "I hope you have good news for me."

That Pauline was going to marry Hugh Westbrook made Frank very
glad, among other reasons because she would be the one wife in all of
Victoria who could be certain that her husband was faithful to her.
Hugh Westbrook was no womanizer; he was known, in fact, for having
only one great passion in his life—Merinda.

"It took some diplomacy and the promise of the best orchestra Melbourne has to offer," Frank said, "plus an outrageous fee. But your wish
has been granted. The letter finally arrived from London—Dame Lydia
has agreed to sing at your wedding."

"Oh Frank! Thank you!" Pauline said, hugging him. "Now everything will be perfect. How on earth am I going to wait six months!"

Frank laughed and shook his head. Pauline was going to have no
trouble occupying her time until the day of the wedding. The Melbourne Cup race was coming up, which meant the Governor's Ball and
lots of parties and several hunts, immediately after which came Christmas and the annual ball the Ormsbys gave at Strathfield, which always
demanded every minute of Pauline's time. And then there was the New
Year's midnight masquerade Colin and Christina MacGregor gave at
Kilmarnock, which was usually followed by summer picnics and excur-
sions to the sea.

Pauline went to her dresser and began to comb out her hair. "I
invited the MacGregors to dinner tonight, Frank. I hope you'll join us
instead of hurrying off to your men's club."

"I thought you didn't like the MacGregors."

"I don't. But they have the station next to Merinda, and they will be
my neighbors, so I thought I had best start cultivating their friendship.

"Speaking of Merinda, Pauline," Frank said. "I ran into Hugh as I
was leaving Melbourne."

Pauline turned and looked at him. He noticed how just the mention
of Hugh brought color to her cheeks and a sparkle to her eyes. "Oh
Frank! Tell me he's on his way home!"

Frank envied Westbrook; he doubted that the mention of his own
name had ever affected a woman so. He found himself thinking of that
flattering portrait; why had she done it, when she had done comical
ones of everyone else? He had tried to talk to her before he left Finnegan's, but she had been busy serving a demanding crowd, and Frank

had known that Pauline was waiting for him. "Yes, Pauline," he said. "Hugh is on his way home."

"Then he should be back tomorrow. I'll plan a picnic—"

"He probably won't be here for another two or three days. I was traveling alone on horseback, but Hugh is coming in a wagon. And with the child."

"Oh," she said. "So the boy did come."

"Yes." Frank looked down at his drink. The child had seemed a little strange, Frank thought, and there had been a haunted look in his eyes. "There's something else."

She looked at him. "What?"

"There was a woman in the wagon, too."

"A woman?"

"Yes. Hugh hired a sort of nanny off one of the immigrant ships. To care for the boy."

Pauline stared at her brother. One of the reasons Hugh had given for insisting on a long engagement was that Merinda was unfit for a woman in its present state; he had said he wanted time to make it suitable for Pauline. But now he was taking another woman to live there!

After a moment of jealousy, Pauline reminded herself of the immigrant women she had seen, and how many of them were grateful just to have a roof over their heads, no matter how crude that roof might be.

"I know what you're thinking, my dear," Frank said. "But you only have yourself to blame. If you had offered to take care of the child yourself, Westbrook wouldn't have been forced to hire a nanny."

"You're right, of course. And anyway, this might be a blessing. After all, we'll have someone to look after the boy when we go on our honeymoon. Remind me, what is the child's name?"

"Adam," Frank said, turning to the liquor tray to refill his glass.

As Pauline watched her brother, she realized he seemed preoccupied with his whiskey; he was avoiding looking at her.

"Frank," she said. "What is it?"

"What is what?"

"Frank, I can read you like one of your own newspapers. There's something more. What is it?"

"Well," he said, turning and looking at her. "You're going to hear about it sooner or later, so I'd rather it came from me. The nanny— she's young."

"Young? How young?"

"Oh, you know, I'm not good at judging ages."

"How young, Frank?"

He shrugged. "Well, not quite twenty, I'd say."

"So she's a girl?"

"No, not a girl, Pauline. A young woman."

"I see." Pauline carefully set her hairbrush on the dressing table. "What does she look like?"

"Well, she's, ah, not quite what you might expect. I mean, she doesn't look like an immigrant girl. She's very well dressed, for one thing."

"Go on."

Frank took a sip. "And some people might say she was pretty."

Silence descended over the gowns and laces and bolts of fabrics. "Some people," Pauline said. "What about you? Did you think she was pretty?"

"Well yes," Frank said. "I suppose."

"Would you even say she was beautiful?"

When he didn't reply, Pauline said, "I see. What is her name?"

"Joanna Drury."

Joanna Drury, Pauline thought. Young and beautiful Joanna Drury. Traveling for days in a wagon, alone on the Melbourne Highway with Hugh.

Pauline felt a cold chill run through her body.

"Well then!" Frank said, putting down his glass. "I'm ready for a bath and a change of clothes. I hope you'll forgive me, my dear, but I'm not up to facing the MacGregors for dinner tonight. Colin is such a bore with his constant talk about his lineage, and all poor Christina ever does is sigh. Do you mind?"

But his sister wasn't listening.

"Anyway," Frank said as he walked to the door. "I'll be out for the evening. I told John Reed I'd meet him at Finnegan's . . ."

Pauline didn't even hear the door close behind him. She was staring at herself in the mirror, and she was thinking: Frank is right. This is all my fault. I am responsible for the fact that Hugh hired a nursemaid. Well, I can also be responsible for seeing that she leaves. I shall tell Hugh that I want the child to come and live with me at Lismore until the wedding. And that, therefore, he does not require the services of a nanny.

CHAPTER 3

T here's a place up ahead where we'll stop for the night," Hugh said, as the wagon rolled along a road shaded by eucalyptus trees. "I hope you don't mind camping out. There aren't many inns along this road, so most people just set up camp."

It was late afternoon, and Melbourne seemed very far behind them as they rode in the country silence past green fields and farmhouses and great flocks of sheep with newborn lambs. It was October, and the plains of Victoria were alive with spring. Hugh had filled the past few hours since leaving the city telling Adam about Merinda, the new home he was going to, a sheep station in the Western District of the colony.

"Sheep are what is going to make these colonies great, Miss Drury," he said. "The world needs wool and mutton, and we can provide all that it can use. If we work together—the colonies, I mean. We need to find ways to make the Australian colonies the first in the world in wool production. And I have an idea of how to do it."

Joanna noticed that Adam was starting to get sleepy; she was glad they were going to be stopping soon.

"Only a small part of this continent is inhabited, Miss Drury," Hugh went on. "Just the coastlines. The rest, the interior, is too harsh, too defeating, so it's going to waste. I've been working on a plan to produce a new breed of sheep, one that can live in that kind of country. If I'm successful, then we can make use of that wasteland, and run millions of sheep on it."

Joanna noticed that Hugh spoke slowly, with pauses between his sentences, his words measured. There was none of the hurry to get something said, the way Joanna had heard people speak at the social clubs on the military outposts in India. She thought of Hugh West-brook as a man who had never had to compete for a chance to talk; he hadn't known crowds. The pauses between his phrases reflected a life of solitude. "You sound very determined, Mr. Westbrook," she said.

"I am."

Adam suddenly sat up and pointed. There were people in the road directly ahead, some on horseback, some on foot. There was shouting, and fists were being waved.

"What is it, Mr. Westbrook?" Joanna said. "What do you suppose is happening?"

Hugh snapped the reins and when they drew up at the scene, they saw a man on horseback raising a whip and threatening to "beat the life out of the whole lot o' you!"

Hugh got down from the wagon and called out, "Hoy there. What's the trouble?"

Joanna realized that the men on horseback were white, while those on foot were black. Aborigines. They were poorly dressed, and she guessed that they were a family, for there was an elderly couple, some men and women, and a few children; they were carrying blankets and bundles on their backs.

The man with the whip was saying to Hugh, "They tried to rob us! Flagged us down and asked for handouts, and while we weren't look-ing, had their kids try to steal from our packhorses!"

"No, boss," said the eldest of the group, an old man with a white beard and eyes so deeply recessed beneath heavy brows that they could not be seen. "Not true," he said, shaking his head. "We don't rob, we don't steal."

"I *saw* you, old man!" the one on horseback said. Then he turned to Hugh. "Gotta watch 'em every minute. Steal you blind, they will."

As the arguing continued, Joanna felt the eyes of the Aboriginal women on her. They seemed to stare so intently that she became suddenly uneasy.

Finally the men on horseback spurred their horses and rode off, while the Aborigine elder said to Hugh, "That one a liar, boss."

"Maybe so," Hugh said. He looked at the family huddled close together, at their cast-off clothing, the children clinging to the women's dresses. "Do you have anything to sell today?" Hugh asked. "I could use some good baskets. Or maybe possum-skin blankets."

"No blankets, boss," the old man said. "No baskets." The women were whispering among themselves, and the elder turned to them, then turned back and said, "My wife. She say she can tell your fortunes."

"Yes," Hugh said with a smile. "All right then." He reached into his pocket and brought out some coins.

The oldest of the women stepped up to the wagon, looked carefully at Joanna, and then stared hard. She held up her hands and said something in a language Joanna didn't understand.

"What is she saying?" Hugh asked the old man.

"She say there is something about your missus. Shadows be around her. Shadow of a dog. Following your missus. She say she see the shadow of dog there, behind your missus."

Adam glanced around, but Joanna froze. The recurring nightmare suddenly came back to her—the nightmare from the ship, the dog, the funeral; the serpent made of stars.

"May I ask her a question?" Joanna said. "I'd like to know if she can interpret dreams."

"Dreams are an important part of their beliefs," Hugh said. "What do you want to know?"

"What does it mean to dream of a serpent—a giant serpent?"

When Hugh turned to repeat the question to the old man, the elder suddenly threw up his hands and said something Hugh did not understand.

"What is it, Mr. Westbrook?" Joanna asked.

"I'm afraid we've broken a taboo. They're not allowed to talk about the Serpent."

"I don't understand. *What* serpent? Wait, please don't let them go! I want them to explain something to me."

Joanna watched the old man quickly gather the family together and guide them off the road and into the trees. The old woman looked back once, and then she was gone.

As Hugh climbed back up into the wagon and took up the reins, he said, "I'm sorry, Miss Drury, but there are just some things the Aborigines won't talk about."

"She knew something," Joanna said. "I wonder what."

Hugh gave Joanna a puzzled look, then said, "Miss Drury, you're trembling. Is something the matter?"

"That old woman knows something about me. I could tell by the way she looked at me. She knew about the dog that nearly killed me and that somehow caused my mother to die."

"I don't think so," Hugh said. "She said she was telling your future. There must be a dog in your future."

"No," Joanna said, as the wagon moved along into the twilight. "I know what she was referring to." The shadows, Joanna thought. What do they mean?

She turned to Hugh and said, "What is significant about serpents?"

"Well, there's something called the Rainbow Serpent, and it's part of their mythology. I can't tell you much, except that the Rainbow Serpent is a creature of destruction. I believe the Aborigines feel it is something to be very much afraid of."

"Rainbow Serpent," she murmured, thinking of the references to dreams about a "colored snake" in her mother's diary.

"What was the fight about just now, Mr. Westbrook? Why were those men so upset with these people?"

"They claim the Aborigines were trying to steal from them, but I doubt that they were."

"But one of them was going to whip the old man. Why?"

"Unfortunately, some white people are afraid of the Aborigines. They think they have special powers—supernatural powers. And so they fear them."

"And *do* they have supernatural powers?"

"Some people believe they do. I don't know. I've seen Aborigines do extraordinary things." Hugh guided the two-horse team along the country road. "Who's to say why? White men weren't even *in* this part of the country as little as thirty-five years ago. We hardly know the race that lived here for thousands and thousands of years before we came. Some of us have made friends with them. I have an Aboriginal girl, Sarah, working at my station—she helps Ping-Li in the cookhouse, and does the laundry. And I have Aboriginal stockhands; they're good workers. And then there's Ezekiel, who's older than time and remembers when his people had never set eyes on a white person. We get along, most Aborigines and myself. But I have to admit that I don't understand them as well as I do white men."

What had the old woman seen, Joanna wondered, when she looked at me? "Where are they going, Mr. Westbrook?" she said. "The old man and his family?"

"Nowhere, really. They're just wandering out of instinct. Now that their land has been taken up by white settlers, the Aborigines don't have anywhere to go. I've heard that this road used to be what they called a songline. Maybe that's why we ran into them here."

"A songline?"

"I'm not sure I can explain it to you," he said. "Songlines are part of the Aborigines' sacred lore, their beliefs. It's taboo for them to speak about sacred things, especially to a white man, and so there is little we know about them. But as near as I can determine, songlines are like invisible tracks. They mark the routes the Aborigine ancestors walked, thousands of years ago, and on up until fairly recently—thirty-five years or so ago, anyway, even less in some parts. Songlines are sort of like invisible roads, crisscrossing the continent. Apparently way back the ancestors walked all over Australia, and as they walked they sang out the names of everything they encountered. They believed they were singing the world into existence. The Aborigines believe that song is existence—to sing is to live. And that is why, too, to the Aborigines, everything in nature is sacred—rocks, trees, waterholes. Even," he said, leaning toward Adam, "*even* little boys who won't talk!"

Adam gave Hugh a wary look, and then a shy smile.

Joanna watched the countryside slowly surrender to the night, and with twilight came a strange kind of silence, a settling of the world. Joanna wondered about the Australia of those far-off times. *Was* there something from back then, some ancient magic embodied in her, in her family, as her mother had seemed to believe?

Joanna's grandparents had been here at just about the time Hugh Westbrook said the native people had begun to lose their ownership of the land. Had an elder, much like the one she had just encountered, spoken some sort of curse on John and Naomi Makepeace and their three-and-a-half-year-old child, Emily?

She tried to imagine what kind of invisible lines the ancients might have walked, what kind of songs they might have sung. She thought of her mother being born here, living here as a child. She thought of the Aborigines they had just passed. Perhaps it had been a person like one of them, thirty-seven years ago, who had taken the child Emily to the authorities, and put her on a boat for England. Had it been the woman who kept appearing in Lady Emily's memory-dreams?

They must have still had dignity then, those Aborigines of her mother's childhood. But the natives she had just seen appeared to be a sad and dejected group, moving slowly along out of instinct, with nowhere to go, no destination—on the move because of some vague dream, an inherited compulsion that, Joanna now speculated, might be not unlike the compulsion that had brought her here. The compulsion that had pressed her mother to want to return to the place where she was born, in the hope of retracing the patterns of her life. Her own family's songline, in a way.

Joanna peered ahead into the darkness, and saw the thin ribbon of road disappearing into it. She imagined that this road might become her own songline, and wondered: If she followed it far enough, would she come to the end—and to the beginning?

They set up camp at a site called Emu Creek, where other families had pitched tents and lit campfires. A smoky pall hung over the campground; children laughed and ran about, and the aroma of coffee and bacon filled the air.

"Who are all these people?" Joanna asked as they sat beside their own fire, waiting for the tea to boil.

"A lot of them are shearers," Hugh said, stirring the tea in what he had called a billycan. "Shearing season is about to start and the gangs are on the road. The rest are families headed out to farms in the west and up north." Joanna looked around in wonder. The night air seemed to pulsate with life, its rhythm invading her and sharpening her excitement. So many people on the move!

Hugh found himself noticing how pretty Joanna looked, how gracefully her body leaned toward the fire, and he was surprised to realize that he was comparing her to Pauline, the woman he was soon to marry.

He looked over at Adam, who was exploring the perimeter of their tiny camp. "The boy seems to be a little better now," he said to Joanna. "I just hope this journey won't be too hard on him. It'll take us four or five days to get to Merinda, depending. I'll make a bed for you and Adam in the wagon, and I'll sleep here by the fire."

"There is something strange about his not speaking," Joanna said. "He hasn't said a word since we left Melbourne. It's as if he has withdrawn inside himself and is hiding there, with a secret that he can't bring himself to tell. If only we knew how his mother died. Perhaps it would explain his hysterical episodes, and why he won't talk."

Hugh looked at Joanna and he wanted to say: You have secrets, too, which you aren't telling.

"Tell me about this place you're looking for," he said. "You said it was called Karra Karra."

Joanna reached into the bag that she had set by her feet, and brought out a yellowed piece of paper. "This deed is very old," she said as she handed it to him. "Unfortunately, the ink has faded. We weren't able to make out when and where it was signed."

As Westbrook looked the paper over, he could make out certain phrases: —"Two days' ride from . . . and twenty kilometers from Bo— Creek." There was an illegible signature and an official-looking seal. At some time in its history, the paper had been exposed to water; the date of the deed was nearly obliterated. "It's impossible to tell from this document where the land might be," he said. "But you say it's near a place called Karra Karra. That is most likely an Aboriginal place name, and a lot of those names have been changed over the years, some of them so long ago that the original names have been lost."

"I shall find it somehow," she said, as she rolled up the paper and replaced it in her bag. "I must."

The tea was boiling, and as Hugh poured it into two enamel mugs, he said, "I can't help feeling, Miss Drury, that this Karra Karra means something more to you than just being a piece of land you've inherited."

She called to Adam that he would have to go to bed soon, then she said, "Yes, I think it might be a lot more than just that, Mr. Westbrook. It might be the place where my mother was born. That was something she wanted to find out all her life. My mother and father were the only family I had, so it's important to me to do those things for her that she was not able to do."

Westbrook tasted his tea. "My mother died giving birth to me. After that, it was just my father and me. We were rootless, we never had a home. We traveled around the outback taking jobs where we could, moving from town to town like forwarded letters. He died when I was fifteen. A horse threw him, he was killed instantly. We were on our way to a shearing job. I buried him under the only tree for miles around. And I've been on my own ever since."

He paused, took a sip, and said, "That's why I told the authorities in South Australia that I would take Adam. A child needs a home, a family."

"He's lucky to have you, Mr. Westbrook," Joanna said.

Hugh looked at Joanna for a moment, seeing moonlight reflected in amber eyes, then he said, "What did you want to ask the old woman back there about a giant serpent?"

"It has something to do with my mother." Joanna found herself reaching into her bag again and bringing out a book. "My mother had nightmares, and often they were about a giant serpent. One of the strange things is that after her death I too began to dream of a monstrous snake. It's all recorded in here."

She handed the book to Hugh, who opened it to the front page. He read the inscription: "To Emily Makepeace on the day of her wedding, from Major Petronius Drury, her loving husband, July 12, 1850."

"It's a kind of memory book," Joanna explained. "My mother started it as a diary, but then she thought that if she recorded her dreams, and any memories, however brief, that came back to her, she might be able to work out the blank places in her life. And also the—"

Hugh looked up from the book. "And also the what?" he said.

"I don't know that you want to hear about it. I'm afraid it's going to sound so odd."

Hugh smiled and said, "Go ahead."

Joanna spoke more quietly. "My mother believed that there was some sort of a . . . curse on her family. She had no proof of it, it was just a feeling she had."

"What sort of a curse?"

"I don't know. *She* didn't know. But she thought it might have been Aboriginal."

Hugh stared at her, then said, "Please go on."

Joanna spoke hesitantly, telling him about the rabid dog that had come into the military compound where they were living, and how Lady Emily had stepped in to save Joanna from its attack, how a soldier had killed it just in time. And then how Lady Emily had developed the fatal symptoms of rabies a few days later. "She believed right until the end that it was the curse that had done it—a poison, she called it."

"A poison? Why a poison?"

"I don't know. She said she had dreamt it. She also believed that the curse had been passed on to me."

"Do you believe that?"

"I don't know what to believe, Mr. Westbrook. But I can't shake the feeling that . . . something, I don't know what, surrounds me. Maybe it's just some kind of bad luck, or whatever you might call it."

When he gave her a dubious look, she said, "The ship that I came out on was becalmed, in a place where the captain said it had never happened before. We were stopped for days on the ocean, Mr. Westbrook. Our water supply was threatened."

"So? These things happen."

She sighed and said, "Yes, I know. And I know it sounds outrageous. But I had a dream, back in India before I left. I dreamt it all—what was going to happen. And it turned out to be exactly like the dream."

"Well, that's odd, but it does happen sometimes. I don't see why you need to think you were the cause of it. Miss Drury, did you know at that time that you were coming to Australia?"

"Yes."

"Then perhaps what you had was a nightmare that's quite common to people who are about to travel. A lot of people are afraid of sailing. Ships are lost at sea rather frequently; it's a dangerous way to travel. Your mind was worried, that's all."

"Most people dream of shipwrecks or drowning, Mr. Westbrook. Not of being becalmed."

He flipped through the diary, and noticed that some of the earlier pages contained recipes for medicines and remedies. "Your mother appears to have known a lot about medicine," he said.

"We moved frequently; my father was an officer with the British army. And very often we found ourselves in places where there was no doctor. My mother learned from the local native healers, she read books, she taught herself. She took care of my father and me, our household servants, and sometimes even wounded soldiers."

"How did she become interested in healing? Was her father a doctor?"

"No, I think he was a minister. A missionary, actually, to Aborigines somewhere here in Australia."

"I see," Hugh said. Noticing that her cup was empty, he said, "Here, let me refill that for you." When he handed the cup back, he said, "So that's why your mother thought the curse, or poison, was Aboriginal— she lived among them for a while, as a child."

"She suspected that she might have, but she couldn't remember— except perhaps in her dreams."

"Maybe that's where she inherited her interest in healing—from the Aborigines. They were a very healthy race when the white men first came here. They knew how to take care of just about any ailment. In fact, you told me your mother used eucalyptus oil in her remedies. Until very recently, the eucalyptus tree wasn't even found outside of Australia."

Just then Adam came over to Joanna, and Hugh said, "Speaking of which, Adam doesn't look too well. What's the matter, son? Does your head hurt?"

Joanna put her hand on the boy's forehead and discovered that it was hot. "Do you have a headache, Adam?" she asked, and when he nodded, she said, "I'll give you something that will make you feel better." She took a small ivory box from her bag, and when she opened it, Hugh saw an array of tiny bottles. Joanna poured a few drops from one into the rest of her tea for Adam. "What's that?" Hugh said.

"It's willow-bark extraction. It will ease his pain and reduce the fever. He must have banged his head very hard on that pier. Here you go, Adam. Drink this down, and then to bed with you."

After Adam was settled and asleep in the back of the wagon, Joanna said, "Has he always had trouble talking?"

"I don't believe so. Whenever Mary wrote to me, she always said Adam was a happy, healthy boy. But the authorities in South Australia said he was mute when they found him, and they were unable to get him to speak."

"We have to encourage him to talk about what happened. But slowly, in his own time. Could we possibly write to the authorities for more details about him? Perhaps if they can tell us what happened, we might be able to find a way to help him over it."

"I'll send a letter as soon as we get to Merinda."

"It is kind of you to take Adam, Mr. Westbrook. I think that, even more than most children, he will need a strong sense that he belongs somewhere."

"When his father died, I wrote to Mary, inviting her and the baby to come and live at Merinda. But the farm had been Joe's dream, she said, and she wanted to keep it going. I sent her money, but perhaps I should have done more."

"Well, you're helping her now. You're taking care of her son, and I'm sure she is somehow aware of it."

"Perhaps. The Aborigines believe the dead are always with us. They go back to the Dreaming, but they are still with us."

"The Dreaming?"

Hugh picked up a stick and stirred the embers. "It's a concept white men have little understanding of, myself included."

Joanna stared at him; she thought of one of the memory dreams her mother had described in the diary: "I dreamt again about waiting at a cave. I am small, I am being held in someone's arms. I see women emerging from a dark red mouth. Is it the cave? They are dark, they are carrying things, they are singing. A white woman appears, and I realize it is my mother. She is naked; how pale her skin is, compared to the other women. I call to her, but she doesn't look at me. She has a strange expression on her face, and I am suddenly very afraid."

What was this, a dream or another buried memory, or both? Joanna wondered. Why had her mother cared enough to write it down?

Hugh was saying: "As nearly as I can judge, the Dreamtime, or the

Dreaming, is what the Aborigines call the distant past, when the first people walked the earth and sang everything into creation. Their spirituality is very earthbound. From the earth we come, by the earth we are sustained, and when we die, to the earth we return. To wound the earth is to wound ourselves. That's why the Aborigines never developed farming or mining or anything that altered the environment in any way. They were not just part of nature, they *were* nature."

"Mr. Westbrook," Joanna said, "*do* they have the power to put a curse on someone? Can they destroy someone that way?"

"Let me just say that they have a certain power, and they certainly might put a curse on someone. But I'm not sure it would matter, unless that person believed that it did."

"Then the way to be safe is simply not to believe in it?"

A spark suddenly exploded in the fire and shot up into the sky.

"You don't really believe there is a curse on you, do you?" Hugh said quietly.

"I don't know," she said. "I know it must sound terribly farfetched. But I have to find out. Mr. Westbrook, we saw Aborigines begging in Melbourne, and we have seen them on the road since. Are there any left who still live the way they used to? The way they did even thirty-five years ago?"

"You want to know if the Aborigines at Karra Karra still have the power that's frightening you."

"Might they still be there?"

Struck by her intensity, Hugh said, "I believe, Miss Drury, that the Aborigines who live in the outback practice the old ways. But they are many miles from here, deep in the interior, which is a great big inhospitable desert. How they live today is anyone's guess. There are probably over a million square miles that remain to be explored. There could be all kinds of things out there that we don't know about." He smiled and said, "But I don't think you're cursed, Miss Drury. I really don't."

She looked up at the sky, at the unfamiliar stars, and wondered if Karra Karra was near or far, and whether she was going to find it, and how, and when. And she thought of her mother, tormented and fearful all her life, finally believing she was being stalked by some terrible Unknown, and succumbing in the end to a lingering death at a young age. Joanna's throat tightened, and she suddenly felt afraid and alone.

When Westbrook saw how the firelight glowed on her face, the tension in her posture, he thought she looked very young and very beautiful. He searched for something to say, then began to recite softly:

"Behold the cheery campfire,
    A light of glitter and gleams,
And the camping ground so crowded
    With tents and men and teams;
And weary jests are driven
And the favorite songs are sung,
And harmony is given
    Through strength of heart and lung."

Joanna looked at him and smiled. "That was lovely," she said. "Who wrote it?"

"I did. It's something I do to pass the time as I'm watching over sheep."

Their eyes held across the dying campfire, and then Joanna looked away. She reached for her shawl and drew it around her shoulders. "Are autumn evenings always this chilly here?"

"This isn't autumn, it's spring."

"Oh yes, of course. I'd forgotten. It's strange to think of October as springtime. . . ."

"Don't worry, Miss Drury," Hugh said. "We'll find some answers for you. After all, we made a bargain. Pretty soon we'll be at Merinda, and we can start working on your problem then. In the meantime, *I* don't believe in curses or the Rainbow Serpent, so you're safe with me."

CHAPTER 4

F or as far as you can see," Hugh said, "all this is Merinda."
Joanna was spellbound; it was as if she were gazing out over
a sea of green, fertile pastures, gently rising and falling beneath
the cloudless sky. A fresh wind blew, snapping her skirt and the
brim of Hugh's hat. Overhead, a wedge-tailed eagle rode air currents,
and in the distance smoky mountains rose up, their summits curiously
curved like a row of waves, as if the mountains had once been an ocean
rolling to shore, but were now frozen in stone.

"Merinda's only five thousand sheep on seven thousand acres now,
but it will grow," Hugh said.

"Why is your station called Merinda, Mr. Westbrook?"

"Merinda is the Aboriginal name for this place. It means 'beautiful
woman.' "

"Was it named for a beautiful woman, do you know?"

He looked at Joanna and saw that in the sunlight her amber eyes
darkened to a deep honey color. And the thought flashed into his mind
that the beautiful woman was here, now. "No one knows," he said,

"although there are legends. The story goes that a long time ago, perhaps in the Dreamtime, there was a young woman named Merinda. She was a song-woman, which meant she kept all the songs and song-lines of her clan. Everybody in a clan knows some of the songs, but only a song-woman or a song-man knows all of them, because to know all of them is to possess the clan's power. The legend goes that one day a member of a rival clan across the river decided to steal Merinda's power, so that he could drive away her people and keep the good hunting and fishing grounds for himself. He kidnapped Merinda and tried to force her to tell him the songs. But she refused, and died without uttering a sound, leaving her people safe."

"Did that happen here?"

"According to the legend, she died somewhere in this area."

"What happened to the Aborigines who used to live here?" Joanna asked.

"They died off, mostly. When the first settlers arrived, the local natives thought that they were only passing through, that they were searching for their homeland. But when the white men stayed and began pushing the Aborigines off their ancestral land, fighting broke out, and it was very bloody. If anything was stolen from a white man's farm, he and his neighbors would ride out and slaughter the first blacks they came upon, whether they were the guilty ones or not. And then the Aborigines would retaliate by burning the farm, murdering the white man's family, and destroying his stock. There was wholesale slaughter—entire tribes were massacred by white men who claimed to be defending their land. And then the natives who had managed to survive began to succumb to diseases their bodies had no immunity against—smallpox, measles, influenza. It's estimated that within the first few years after the convicts arrived, thousands of Aborigines died of illness alone."

In a short time, Hugh added, with their families and tribes broken up, the Aborigines began to lose their sense of unity, their culture. They started hanging around the settlements, expecting handouts. They developed a taste for alcohol. The children began to beg; the women became prostitutes.

"As a result," Hugh said, "the ancient knowledge is vanishing. With the breakup of the tribes, the young Aborigines have no way of learning the customs and laws of their ancestors. If this keeps up, then someday their culture will vanish altogether."

Joanna looked at the green pastures bordered by hedges and fences stretching to the base of the mountains, with stately old trees and tall

eucalypts dotting the plain, and great flocks of sheep ebbing and flowing over the landscape. "It's hard to imagine that a place so beautiful
as this," she murmured, "could have been the setting for tragedy." And
then she wondered, did the Aborigines her mother perhaps once lived
with suffer a similar fate?

"Where is your homestead, Mr. Westbrook?" she asked.

He pointed and said, "There, at the end of that road. Do you see the
buildings through the trees?"

"Yes, I see them."

And all of a sudden, Adam, who was standing between them, cried,
"Farm! A farm!"

Hugh and Joanna stared at him. "Why, Adam," Joanna said, taking
him by the shoulders. "You spoke! You *can* talk!"

"Farm!" he said excitedly, pointing. "A farm!"

"Well, well," Hugh said. "Not a sound out of him in five days, and
now all of a sudden—" He laughed. "I reckon the way to keep him
talking is to get him to the homestead."

Merinda's homeyard was enclosed by a collection of ramshackle buildings, which seemed to have been built with whatever materials were at
hand—some of the structures were made of bush timber and weather
boards; others, of stone—and they appeared to have been put up at
various times, following no method or plan. The yard was filled with
noisy industry, men on horseback shouting and whistling frightened
sheep into pens, while sheepdogs raced back and forth yelping.

As Hugh drew the wagon to a halt, a man came riding up. "Thank
God you're back, Hugh!" he said. "We've got some serious troub—"
He looked at Joanna and stopped.

"This is Miss Drury, Bill," Hugh said, as he got down from the
wagon. "She's going to take care of the boy for me. And this is Adam.
What's the trouble?"

The man stared at Joanna for another moment, then said, "We've
found a lice infestation among the wether flocks."

"But those animals were clean when I left!"

"There's no doubt about it, Hugh. The animals have the distinctive
sores, and the wool has been affected."

"When did you discover it?"

"About five days ago. Stringy Larry thinks the lice might have come
in with those merinos you brought from New South Wales last month.
But I'm not so sure. I inspected those animals myself, Hugh, and I'd
swear they were clean. I can't imagine what's caused this."

Hugh signaled to a boy who was shoeing a horse in front of the stable. "How widespread is it?" he asked Bill.

"I can't tell yet. If we're lucky, it's only the wethers."

"That's still at least a fourth of the wool clip. What about the in-lamb ewes?"

"Stringy Larry and his men are inspecting them now."

Hugh mounted the horse the stable boy had brought up. "Is there any chance of salvaging the infected wool before the shearers get here?"

"I wouldn't bet on it."

Hugh turned to Joanna, who was still sitting in the wagon with Adam, and said, "This is Bill Lovell, my station manager. I'm sorry, Miss Drury, but I have to go and inspect the sheep with him. There's the house over there. You and Adam go ahead, and get settled in. I'll have a couple of the men bring your trunk inside. If you want something to eat, just ask Ping-Li in the cookhouse."

Joanna started to say something, but Hugh turned his horse and galloped out of the yard.

"Well, Adam," Joanna said, lifting him to the ground, "it looks as if—"

"Sheep!" he cried suddenly, pointing to a pen where some men were wrestling with a ram.

"Yes, Adam, sheep," she said, thrilled that he had spoken again, and anxious to keep him talking. "But those men won't want you getting in the way. Let's go and see the house, shall we?"

Holding Adam by the hand, Joanna walked across the yard toward the cabin Hugh had pointed out. As they walked past the stable, a young man in a leather apron stopped in the middle of shoeing a horse and stared. Another man crossing the yard glanced toward Joanna, looked away, and then suddenly stared back at her.

As they approached the cabin, which Joanna saw had been crudely made of logs and bark, Adam suddenly became animated. He pulled on her arm and pointed past the house, saying, "River! River!" She looked toward the trees beyond the north end of the yard, through which Hugh and the station manager had ridden, and she thought she glimpsed, through a wooded area, the flash of water.

"All right, Adam," she said, delighted that he suddenly seemed so happy. "Let's go and see what it's like."

They followed a path that wound behind the cabin, across a grassy field and into the distant woods. As they made their way through the trees and came into a clearing, Joanna looked around in wonder.

She and Adam had arrived at a place where a stream branched off the river and meandered into a large, placid pond. The air was filled with a symphony of sounds: water gurgling in the creek, a cool wind rustling the branches of acacias and eucalyptus, the whine and buzz of insects in the spring air. Joanna felt as if she were standing in Eden; there was beauty all around her. Majestic old Red River gums cast orange and white reflections on still water. Wattle trees were exploding in thousands of bright yellow flowers. A black-and-white honeyeater, its face streaked with brilliant blue feathers, was perched on a decayed branch, cocking its head from side to side.

Joanna thought: What a wonderful place.

She recalled a tea plantation in India she had once visited with her parents. The main house had been set apart from the work center of the plantation—far away and high on a hill, protected among trees and lush green grass. How unfortunate, she thought, that Merinda's house wasn't here, by the river, instead of in that noisy, muddy yard.

She heard a splash and, in the next instant, Adam broke away from her and ran to the pond. He dropped down to the ground and plunged his hands into the water.

Joanna hurried over. "Be careful," she said. But to her surprise, Adam was laughing. "Platypus!" he said, splashing his hands in the water.

Joanna looked at the boy in astonishment, as the laughter transformed him. There was a hint of color in his cheeks, and the shadows seemed to have faded from his eyes.

"Platypus!" he said again, as the mirror-like surface of the pond rippled, and out climbed a strange-looking animal that appeared to be a cross between a beaver and a duck.

Adam squealed and clapped his hands, and Joanna thought: This place is magic.

"Miss Drury! What are you doing?"

She turned and saw Hugh standing behind her, frowning. "We wanted to see the river," she said.

"Miss Drury, I'm afraid it's dangerous down here by the billabong, especially if you don't know your way through these woods."

"Billabong?" she said, looking around.

"Billabong. The Aborigines' word for a pond."

"Oh," said Joanna. Then, "This is a beautiful place."

"Yes, it is. I'm going to build the house here—we're standing approximately where the front door will be. The rest will go back as far as those ruins. But we haven't started on it yet."

"What will the house be like?" she asked, keeping an eye on Adam as he pulled off his shoes and socks and paddled at the edge of the water.

"I thought it should be Queensland style, but Pauline, the woman I'm going to marry, has her heart set on a house she saw in a magazine. She read a story about reconstruction in the American South, now that the war is over, and she fell in love with a picture of a large white-columned house called Willows Plantation, in the state of Georgia. Luckily, I was able to find an American architect in Melbourne who is familiar with the style."

"It sounds lovely," Joanna said. "You must be very excited."

"Yes," Hugh said. He stared at Joanna. There was something about the way the sunlight seemed to be gathering around her. She was still neat after five days of travel, although a few wisps of brown hair had escaped their pins. He realized he wanted to say something to her, but he didn't know what.

Joanna walked toward a cluster of waist-high rock walls, tumbled and broken. "What is this place?" she asked.

"Those are old ruins. People lived here many years ago, there was a settlement."

"Is this one of the sacred sites you told me about?"

"Maybe. We're not sure. Only the elders—the song-men—can look at a rock or a tree and determine whether it was created by a Dreamtime ancestor."

"If it were, would that make this place holy?"

"It depends on what you call a holy place. Aboriginal sacred sites are more than just holy places, Miss Drury. The Aborigines believe that everything that ever happened on a particular spot is still there, still happening. To disturb it would be to disturb the past."

"And that land over there," she said, pointing across the river. "Does that also belong to Merinda?"

"That's the start of Colin MacGregor's property," Hugh said. "It's called Kilmarnock, it's the next station over."

"It's all so green and lovely—" Joanna stopped and stared. There was a man standing among the trees a short distance away, silent and unmoving, watching her. "Mr. Westbrook, who is that over there?"

Hugh looked through the trees. "That's Ezekiel. He's the old Aborigine I told you about. He works for me sometimes. He's one of the last of his generation. He remembers what it was like here before white men came. If you want to know anything about the legend of Merinda, he would be the one to ask."

Joanna stared at the old man standing on the bank of the river, looking as if he had just materialized out of the reddish-brown clay. He wore trousers and a shirt but no shoes, and his white hair and beard nearly reached his waist. He was too far away for her to see his eyes, but she could feel them on her.

She turned to Hugh and asked, "Why is he staring at me that way?"

"He isn't used to seeing a woman at Merinda. And we are standing very close to these ruins. He tends to be very protective of the old sites."

Joanna was struck by the old Aborigine's gaze, and the uneasy feeling it gave her.

Just then Adam came running up. "Look!" he cried, and he opened his hands and held out a grasshopper.

"Yes, isn't he a handsome fellow," Joanna said, turning her back on the man in the trees, and trying to shake off the strange feeling she had. "Can you say grasshopper for me, Adam?"

As Hugh watched Joanna, he thought of his youth in the outback, its solitary existence, where a man could go for weeks without encountering another soul. When he purchased Merinda, at the age of twenty, he had had no time for social life, he had thrown himself into building up the station. In all those years, he had known only the intimacy of such women as those who worked at a house in St. Kilda. And then Pauline had come into his life, a woman like no other he had ever known, and whose passionate kiss one rainy afternoon had awakened him.

Hugh looked at Joanna and thought how beautiful she looked, how capable she seemed, and yet how vulnerable, too. He thought of their past few days together on the road, and the nights at various camps, and he was startled to realize that he was mildly depressed to see their journey end.

He also realized that, after inspecting the sheep with Bill Lovell, instead of his first thought being of Pauline, of going over to Lismore where she was waiting for him, he had thought only of looking for Joanna.

"It's getting late," he said. "I'll take you and Adam to the house."

"Let the grasshopper go, Adam," Joanna said, and as they started to walk back to the homestead, she looked back at the river, where the old Aborigine, Ezekiel, continued to stand and stare.

The cabin was plain, as Hugh had warned, consisting of little more than a fireplace at one end, a bed at the other, with a table in between. But Joanna didn't mind. It would do for the short time she was going to be here.

Hugh left her and Adam there, explaining that he had more flocks to inspect, after which he was going to ride over to Lismore. Joanna unpacked her trunk with Adam's help, and then settled him down by the fire with the stuffed animal she had inherited from her mother, a funny-looking toy made of kangaroo fur, which was one of the few things Lady Emily had brought out of Australia with her when she was four years old. A station hand whose nickname was Stringy Larry came in with bathwater and wood for the fire, explaining with a laugh that he was called Stringy Larry not because he was tall and thin but because he had once tripped over a string that was stretched between two fenceposts, falling facedown in the mud. Joanna gave Adam a bath, and they ate the dinner that had been sent over from the cookhouse—a generous meal of lamb chops, peas, fresh bread, and custard, accompanied by a pitcher of milk, and a pot of tea for Joanna, so welcome after food cooked over campfires.

Finally, Adam was asleep in the bed, which he would share with Joanna tonight, another bed being promised for tomorrow. He lay curled on his side, his arms around the stuffed animal Joanna's mother had christened Rupert.

It was late, night having settled over the homestead, and a light spring rain was beginning to patter on the iron roof. Joanna had changed out of her traveling clothes, bathed, put on a fresh nightgown and combed out her long hair. Now she turned to the things she had placed on the table, where an oil lamp gave off a warm, reassuring glow.

She opened the small bundle which the steward had given to her on the dock, when he had left Adam with her, saying that it had been put aboard with the boy in Adelaide. Joanna had expected to find shoes inside, a toy or two, but to her surprise, the wrapping, which looked like a piece of blanket, fell away to reveal a black leather Bible, an ivory comb, a folded handkerchief and strangest of all, a printed tea towel from Devon, England, that had never been used. Joanna opened the Bible and saw four entries inscribed on the "Family Record" page. The first read: "Joe and Mary Westbrook, wed on this day, September 10, 1865." The next was: "Born January 30, 1867, Adam Nathaniel Westbrook." The third entry: "Died, Joseph Westbrook, July 12, 1867, of gangrenous injuries." And the last: "Died, Mary Westbrook, of pneumonia, in the month of September, 1871."

Someone had wrapped a thin, gold wedding band in a handkerchief and tucked it inside the Bible.

Joanna looked at Adam, whose closed eyes flickered in restless slumber, and she thought: This is all he has to remember his mother by—a ring, some dates in a Bible, a Devon tea towel and an ivory comb.

She picked up her own mother's diary and held it for a long moment before opening it.

There was comfort in feeling the familiar rich leather binding between her hands; she imagined that it was almost alive with the currents and tides of her mother's lifetime. The diary also contained Joanna's life, her past. And she thought now about those years when she had been so happy, when, as a child, she had lived in an enchanted world of make-believe and innocence, when she had thought of her mother, Lady Emily, as a fairy princess, as pale and delicate as the white peacocks that strutted on the immaculate lawns of the viceroy's mansion, and she had imagined that her father, the colonel, in his tall white helmet and dashing uniform with brass buttons and his polished boots, was the man who commanded all of India. He was gallant and true, like the heroes in fairy tales, and what had been even more wonderful in Joanna's young mind was that he had been passionately in love with his wife.

Petronius Drury had grown up among a class of people who believed in being guarded in speech and actions, in which there were rules to follow and where propriety was insisted upon, even between married couples, and the love he bore for his wife was legendary. Joanna had many times overheard remarks while she was growing up: "Lucky Emily, Petronius so devoted to her . . . Never looks at another woman . . . If only my Andrew were like that."

Which was why, Joanna believed, her father had been unable to go on living after Lady Emily died.

Joanna opened the diary and read by lamplight.

The pages covering the early years were filled with excitement and beauty, descriptions of balls at palaces and the visits of Indian princes. There were recipes for herbal remedies, and passages where Lady Emily became more philosophical. When she was twenty-four, she had written: "If you must, you can." When she was thirty: "Optimism empowers." There were remarks on fashion—"British ladies have taken to wearing saris over their hooped skirts."—and customs—"I felt sorry for the poor young bride who spoke out of turn to the senior officer's wife." But there came a day, after Lady Emily had been recording in the book off and on for almost nine years—thirteen years ago—when the tone of the writing suddenly changed.

It was the entry marking Joanna's sixth birthday, and Lady Emily had written, "Joanna turned six today. We had a lovely party, twelve children and their parents." It was then that she had begun to write about the nightmares.

"The nightmares have returned," Lady Emily had written on the next page. "I have not dreamed these dreams since I was a child. I had thought I was free of them forever, but now they have come back— wild dogs are chasing me, a great serpent with rainbow-colored scales is trying to devour me. Petronius says that I wake up screaming. If only I could remember! I sense that what is contained in my father's satchel might be the key to the answers, but I am afraid to open it. Why?"

As Joanna read, the fire hissed. Adam cried out once in his sleep, and then was quiet.

Then, an entry from nine months ago: "Strangely, the shock of our encounter with the rabid dog has made me remember things," Lady Emily had written. "The name Karra Karra runs through my head like a melody. I feel a tremendous significance linked to it. Was I born there, perhaps? Is that where my parents' land is? There is another name, too—Reena. I wonder, could that be the young Aboriginal woman I remember holding me in her arms? But there is something else, the strange feeling associated with Karra Karra—that I was supposed to have gone there long ago, but that my path was diverted.

"I sense that a secret is locked away somehow in my mind," Lady Emily had written later, after she had fallen ill. "I cannot shake the feeling that something was hidden, and that I must unearth it. But I cannot remember! The doctors say there is nothing wrong with me— but there is. Something is poisoning me, and I am powerless against it. And I fear for Joanna, too."

In the days that followed, before Lady Emily grew too ill to write, she filled the diary with her obsession that "another legacy" awaited her at Karra Karra, something which she was under compulsion to claim. She was obsessed with the growing fear that something was trying to destroy her, something from the past. In the last entry, Lady Emily wrote, "I no longer fear for my own sake, but for Joanna's. I believe that whatever is now claiming me does not end with my death. I am frightened that my daughter will inherit it, too."

Suddenly, there was a sound at the window. Joanna looked up, startled, and saw a face, dark-skinned with large eyes, peering into the cabin. Joanna stared for a moment, then, realizing that it was a young Aboriginal girl, she got up and went to the door. But as soon as she opened it, the girl turned and ran down the veranda steps.

"Wait!" Joanna said. "Please, don't run! Come back!"

She dashed out around to the side of the cabin, where the girl had disappeared, and ran straight into Hugh.

"What—" he said, catching her as they stumbled.

"Oh, Mr. Westbrook! I'm sorry! I didn't see you!"

"Miss Drury," he said, laughing, "don't you know it's raining out here?"

They hurried back into the shelter of the veranda, and Joanna said, "I'm sorry for running into you like that, but I saw someone at the window, a girl, looking in. I wanted to talk to her, but she ran away."

"That was Sarah," Hugh said. "The Aboriginal Mission near Cameron Town hires their girls out to the big houses in the district to learn domestic work. Sarah's fourteen, and I imagine she is very curious about you. I'm sorry if she startled you. I was just coming by to see if there is anything you need." He suddenly realized that she was in her nightdress, and he felt a shock rush through him, a swift, startling stab of desire.

"Adam and I are fine, Mr. Westbrook," Joanna said, also suddenly aware of how she was dressed. "Will you come inside?"

"I can't, I'm on my way to Lismore. I only just now finished inspecting the stock."

"And how are the sheep?"

He looked away, stunned by the arousal that had so quickly and unexpectedly gripped him. "I'm afraid it's bad," he said. "The success of a sheep station depends upon the yearly wool yield, and a widespread lice infestation would mean financial trouble. We can't determine the cause. It came on so suddenly. What's really puzzling is it seems that only Merinda is affected."

He didn't tell her the rest—that old Ezekiel had approached him out in the field where he was inspecting the stock, and had stood around until finally Hugh had asked him if he wanted something. Ezekiel had warned him then, saying that he saw bad luck around Joanna; he couldn't, or wouldn't, explain why.

Hugh thought of how her body had felt a moment ago, when she had run into him. "I'll have one of the men take you into Cameron Town in the morning to buy some clothes for Adam," he said, "and anything else you need. I have accounts at several shops. I'll give you a letter of introduction to a lawyer there, who's a friend of mine. He could look at your deed, and see what he can do to help you." He looked again at Joanna, at the way her long brown hair lay against her back, and a strange ache grew deep inside him. He felt as if he had suddenly been caught off balance. He wanted to leave, and yet he didn't want to. "I would go into town with you myself, but I'm needed here at the station."

"I understand," she said. "Thank you."

"Are you and Adam fixed all right in there? I know it's rough—"

"We're fine, thank you."

"One of the men will bring in another bed tomorrow. And I'll take you around the station. We've got some baby lambs that I'm sure Adam would like to see."

He paused, and looked into her eyes, struggling against his newly born desire, denying it, pushing it away. He thought of Pauline, who was soon to be his wife, and how passionately she had declared her love for him. He said, "Good night," and forced himself back into the dark and the rain.

Joanna watched him go, then she quietly closed the door.

She looked first at Adam, then she returned to the table and the puzzle she was trying to solve.

Thirty-seven years ago, her mother had been taken away from her parents and delivered to an aunt in England, possessing only a fur toy and a leather satchel. The flight had apparently been in haste, which indicated danger. And as the satchel had been sent with her, it meant someone had thought the contents were worth saving. Joanna undid the silver buckles, and took out a sheaf of papers.

All Lady Emily had been able to learn from her Aunt Millicent was that she had been picked up by an English sea captain when a merchant marine had passed her on to him in Singapore. Of that long journey, Lady Emily recalled nothing. Her earliest memory was of playing in Aunt Millicent's garden. She had been unaware of the existence of the satchel until Millicent had given it to her, on the day she married Petronius. Emily had seemed to remember it instantly, or rather to recognize its significance, and the sight of the satchel had so struck her with dread, that when she had taken it with her to India as a bride, she had hidden it away.

Joanna stared at the hundred or so pages spread before her. They were covered with writing, but it was like no writing she had ever seen. It wasn't English, it wasn't even a proper alphabet, but row upon row of cryptic symbols . . . .

What were these papers, she wondered, and why had they been entrusted with a little girl who had been taken away from her parents? More significantly, what could these papers have to do with Australia, and with the journey Lady Emily had wanted to make? Was there in here, somewhere among all these strange symbols, an explanation of her fears, of her dreams of wild dogs, of snakes, of the past and the future?

Joanna slowly went through them, but found only page after page of mysterious symbols. Whatever this was, it had been written in some sort of code. But whose code, what code, and why?

She was too sleepy to think.

She dimmed the lamp and got into bed, taking care not to waken Adam. When she laid her head on the pillow, a familiar scent instantly brought Hugh Westbrook to her mind, and she realized that it was his scent that she had caught, in the pillow—the sharp smell of shaving cream, and the gentler fragrance of hand soap, mixed with a trace of tobacco and wool and something else. She was startled by her reaction to such intimacy—to be sleeping in his bed—and she realized that it suddenly excited her, to be lying here, where Hugh normally slept. A strange new feeling swept over her, one she had never experienced before, or perhaps only fleetingly, when she had danced in the arms of the handsome young officer.

She tried not to think about Hugh, about the way the furrow between his eyebrows deepened when he was concentrating, making him look even more attractive. Or about the way he would laugh unexpectedly. Or the habit he had of frequently removing his hat and running his hands through his hair. Or the feel of his hand holding hers when he had helped her down from the wagon. And their encounter of a short while ago, when she had run into him and he had caught her.

She had been sleepy when she had gotten into bed, but now she was wide awake, her body betraying her, her thoughts on Hugh, as she wondered what it would be like to be with him now, in this bed.

She forced herself to remember that he was going to be married soon, that she had come only to help Adam get adjusted, and to establish a place from which to begin her search. She knew she must not allow herself to think of Hugh Westbrook in that way. She concentrated on her reasons for being here: to find her inheritance, to seek out the legacy her mother had believed awaited her at Karra Karra, to put an end to the dreams.

But, in the end, though she tried to focus her thoughts on these things, her mind and body brought her back to Hugh, and the desire she felt for him.

CHAPTER 5

"Vilma Todd is boasting that she is going to ruin you, Pauline," Louisa Hamilton said, as she stared enviously at Pauline's hair.

Pauline Downs looked at her friend's reflection in the glass behind her, and laughed. "My dear Louisa, Vilma Todd hasn't the courage to challenge me."

They were sitting in Pauline's bedroom, and as Louisa watched the maid arrange Pauline's hair, she raised a hand to her own elaborate coiffure, as if to reassure herself that it was still there.

The latest fashion was to wear one's hair in a complicated knot that projected an astonishing twelve inches straight from the back of the head, so that one's hat was tilted forward, almost down to the eyebrows. But few women had enough hair of their own to create such a knot, and so they padded their chignons with hidden cages and cushions. Louisa Hamilton was lucky; her husband was rich enough and generous enough to provide her with a real hairpiece, which a reputable importer had assured her "did not come from the head of a dying hospital patient or destitute street woman as so many do, but from the head of a young novice entering a Catholic convent." Louisa's mammoth chignon was her pride and joy, but her pride was short-lived when she watched Pauline's long, platinum tresses flow like ribbons through Elsie's hands, reminding Louisa that every strand of that pale blond hair was Pauline's own.

Louisa felt a second stab of jealousy when Pauline was helped out of her peignoir and into the hoops and bustle and petticoats that were to go under her dress. Louisa could remember when her own waist had been as slender as Pauline's, seven years of marriage and six children ago. But now, at the age of twenty-five, she was matronly plump, and she had to resort to excessive corseting and, occasionally, morphine, to dull the pain of tight lacing, in order to have any sort of waistline at all.

As Elsie fastened the many tiny buttons down the back of Pauline's dove-gray silk dress, Louisa caught a glimpse of herself in the mirror. She wanted to hurl something at what she thought she saw—a typical fat grazier's wife, a useless woman with no purpose in life other than to spend her husband's fortune and produce babies. She felt instantly guilty; her thoughts horrified her.

"I've heard, Pauline," she said, turning away from the vision in the mirror, "that Vilma Todd has been in training all winter. I should think you might be a *little* nervous."

"The day that I am intimidated by someone like Vilma Todd is the day you can bury me, Louisa. She won't stand a chance against me on the archery range. I have held the undefeated title for four years, and I intend to make it five."

Pauline was secretly pleased that Vilma was going to compete against her in the summer archery trials. She was an excellent archer, and Pauline already knew about her intense training. It promised to be a delicious contest. Competition brought no pleasure if the opponent was no match; for Pauline, the greater the skill of her competitor, the greater the joy in the sport.

"I don't know how you do it, Pauline," Louisa said. "I get nervous if I enter one of my cakes in the baking contest of the Annual Graziers' Show. And if I were ever to win, I think I should have to retire to my bed for a week!"

"Competition makes one feel alive, Louisa," Pauline said, as she inspected herself in the mirror. "Winning is everything, it's the ultimate stimulation. Any fool can be a loser, any fool can walk away from a contest. To win is to validate one's existence."

Pauline sometimes thought there was something sexual in competition, whether it was competing against other people, as she did, or against nature, as Hugh Westbrook did. It was, in fact, Hugh's intensity and fight that had attracted Pauline to him in the first place, when she had seen that not even numerous setbacks could deter him from establishing Merinda. His determination to succeed was exciting. Pauline had always known that she could only love a winner. She liked to think that while other people got drunk on wine, she got drunk on victory.

Even the small victories, she thought, arranging her hat on her head. Such as changing Hugh's mind about the nanny he had brought from Melbourne. She had offered to bring the boy to live at Lismore, but Hugh had said he preferred the arrangement the way it was. He could be stubborn, Pauline knew, but she also knew that she would have her way in the end. One way or another, Miss Drury was going to go.

When Louisa suddenly sighed, Pauline looked at her and said, "I have the distinct feeling, Louisa, that you did not come here this morning to tell me about Vilma Todd. What is it?"

"I've caught you at a bad time, Pauline. You're getting ready to go out."

Pauline motioned for the maid to leave, then sat down next to her friend on the bed and said, "Tell me what's the matter, Louisa. Perhaps I can help."

"You can't help," Louisa said as tears rose in her eyes. "I . . . I think I'm pregnant."

"Louisa dear! That's nothing to cry about."

"Isn't it? I only just gave birth to Persephone and now I am in that way again! You don't know what it's like, Pauline. You know nothing of bedroom matters."

Bedroom matters, Pauline thought—something she was very much looking forward to experiencing. She thought again of Hugh, how he had appeared unexpectedly three nights ago, after his trip to Melbourne. She had only just taken him into the parlor and closed the door when he had suddenly drawn her into his arms and kissed her, impulsively and ardently. Pauline had reeled both from the unexpectedness of it, and from the intimate nature of the kiss. If Hugh had not remembered himself, they would have gone on, and Pauline would not now still be facing the delicious mystery of the wedding night. But although Hugh had behaved like a gentleman, Pauline had sensed the sexual tension in him, the coiled energy that had caused him to pace back and forth in the parlor. He had excited her more than ever before.

"You just don't know what it's like," Louisa said, as she dabbed her eyes with her handkerchief. "Miles is so demanding. Do you know, Pauline, that there are times when I pretend to be asleep at night so that he will leave me alone."

"Louisa, I had no idea. Can't you speak to him about it?"

"Talk to him? Pauline, Miles won't discuss sheep breeding in my presence, let alone our own personal matters. He is very correct, you know."

"Yes, I know," Pauline said, wondering why her vivacious friend had married such a stiff, stuffy man. When Miles Hamilton had kissed Louisa at the altar, seven years ago, Pauline had thought he looked as if he were eating a lime. Pauline could not imagine him being demanding in the bedroom.

"I'm so unhappy, Pauline. I don't know if I can keep going like this."

Pauline was beginning to wish Louisa hadn't come to see her. She disliked emotional displays, considered them to be in poor taste. "My dear Louisa," she said. "You must learn to take control. Crying isn't going to help your situation."

"You can say that now, Pauline. But wait until after you're married. It will be different then."

"I have no intention of allowing my life to change simply because I am married. I intend always to be in control, married or not. And that is how you should start thinking. Surely there is a solution, Louisa. If you can't talk to Miles, then assert yourself. Move into another bedroom. Plead fatigue or ill health. You can take control, Louisa. Just decide to try."

Louisa wrung her handkerchief as her eyes darted around the room. Finally she said in a voice that was nearly a whisper, "I have tried to take control. Pauline . . . I've done a terrible thing."

When Louisa said nothing more, Pauline finally said, "My dear, you know that whatever you say will not go beyond this room."

Louisa went to the window and looked out over gardens that were acclaimed by everyone as the most beautiful in Victoria. A hundred acres of orchards, lawns, lake and deer park surrounded Lismore's Tudor-style mansion. The house was set so far away from the working heart of the sheep station that from here you could see nothing of the sheep business, allowing you to believe that you were at a manor house in the English countryside. From where she stood, Louisa could see the flagstone terrace where Pauline and Frank held garden parties. Nearby were a croquet lawn and an archery range. Beyond were the servants' quarters, woodshed, laundry, and extensive stables for horses and carriages. Louisa knew that a staff of fifty took care of the house and grounds for Frank and Pauline, while many more worked the station. Lismore was like a small town, complete with store, blacksmith, wheelwright, veterinarian and housing for both permanent and transient workers. It was one more thing for which Louisa envied Pauline.

Would Pauline understand? Louisa wondered. Could a woman who had led such a sheltered life possibly begin to imagine what she was going through?

Louisa also knew that Pauline was spoiled. The elder Downs, who had worked many years ago back in England as a stable boy, had often spoken of the bitterness and frustration that had marked those boyhood years, when he had been kicked like a dog, or whipped for no reason, taking abuse from rich men because he was powerless to defend himself. Pauline's father had sworn, with every stroke of the lash, that someday he, too, was going to be rich and rule over other men. So he had come to the colonies and had built up a prosperous sheep station on 25,000 acres of lush grazing land in the western plains of the Australian colony of Victoria. Then he had built a house that was a copy of the half-timbered Elizabethan manor house where he had worked as a stable boy, sending to England for the finest furniture, carpets, chandeliers and paintings to fill it. No expense had been spared, and his two children, Frank and Pauline, shared in that reward.

And so Pauline moved in a world of richness and elegance. The rooms to which Louisa had been brought made up Pauline's private suite—a bedroom, sitting room, dressing room and personal bathroom. Louisa remembered when this last had been installed, and the talk it had caused around the district. The architect who had built Lismore had fascinated the local people with descriptions of Pauline Downs's amazing bathroom. At a time when even the richest home did not have indoor plumbing, Pauline had insisted upon having pipes installed and a flushing toilet and a sunken bathtub built right into a room off her bedroom! Louisa often thought it was like something out of Cleopatra's palace. And how typical of Pauline, too, to go against convention: Everyone knew that sitting in a tub was bad for the health. Doctors, in fact, advised against immersion bathing, citing that not even the Queen herself bathed more than twice a year. But Pauline boasted that she sat each day in a tub of hot water, and thought it was the most healthful practice in the world.

Could such a pampered woman, Louisa wondered, have the slightest notion of the torment she was going through? Louisa was torn. She had to talk to someone about her problem, and Pauline, although she might not understand, was nonetheless a woman whom Louisa knew for certain could be counted on to keep a secret.

"I paid a visit to Doc Fuller in Cameron Town," she said at last. "I asked him for advice. I'd heard that there are . . . ways to prevent these things from happening. Winifred Cameron told me that women in Europe have found a way to keep from getting pregnant. But it's all very secretive. It's against the law to write or talk about such things. But I thought that Doc Fuller, being a physician . . . I thought he might know and might tell me."

Pauline stared at her. "And did he?"

Louisa shook her head. "He lectured me about God's laws and wifely duties, and then he threatened to tell Miles about my visit. But I cried and begged him not to, and finally he said he wouldn't, so long as I gave up this foolish idea of trying to prevent further pregnancies. He made me feel wretched, Pauline."

"What are you going to do now?"

Louisa turned and looked at her. "There's a new doctor in town, David Ramsey—"

"Yes, I heard about him from Maude Reed. She says he's very good."

"He's young, Pauline. I thought a young man might have a more liberal mind. I'm going to go to him. I'll beg him for the information if I have to. I'll offer him money, whatever he wants. I'm not going to give up. I don't want to end up like my mother did. She died giving birth to her eighteenth child. She had only just turned thirty-nine, you know."

"Yes, I know," Pauline said, wondering if there really were ways in which a woman could control her fertility. She had never thought about it before; she had always pictured her future as Mrs. Hugh Westbrook, surrounded by an army of beautiful, perfect children. But the producing of those children—childbirth itself, and the attending unpleasantness of pregnancy, such as physical discomfort and gaining weight, to say nothing of the limitations pregnancy put on what a woman could do—Pauline had never given these much thought. But now she did, and she was intrigued. A new challenge faced her, because she had no intention of being encumbered and kept from engaging in her favorite activities, such as riding, hunting and archery. Most especially she did not want to end up like Louisa and so many of the other young wives in the district, who had given up their youth and who were prematurely old because of being unable to control the timing of their pregnancies. Whatever those special secrets of the European women were, Pauline was determined to learn them.

"I'm sorry, Pauline," Louisa said. "I didn't mean to come here and spoil your morning. But I've been so wretched that I needed to talk to someone."

"It's all right, Louisa, I understand. I'm glad you told me. When are you going to see Dr. Ramsey?"

"I'll have to wait until I have an excuse to go into Cameron Town. I'll wait until Miles is busy with the wool baling." Louisa sighed again. "Now I must be getting back to the children."

"It's such a lovely day, Louisa. Why don't you come to Kilmarnock with me? I'm going to pay a call on Christina."

"Thank you, but I'd rather not. Kilmarnock is so gloomy. And poor Christina. I know she can't help it, but she is tiresome. I can't imagine why you would want to go there."

"The MacGregors are going to be my neighbors in a few months, I want to cultivate their friendship."

"And that husband of hers! Colin MacGregor is so cold, and he's so tedious about his peerage. He never passes up a chance to remind you that his father is a lord."

As they went out into the hall, Louisa said, "By the way, what do you think about the nanny Hugh brought from Melbourne?"

"I have no opinion at all. I haven't met her."

"I can imagine what she's like. We hired two of our downstairs maids straight off an immigrant ship, and they didn't know a fork from a spoon. And talk about no manners! Still, they're better than employing Aborigines."

They reached the downstairs foyer and Louisa caught a glimpse of herself and Pauline in a full-length mirror. She felt another stab of envy. She had never seen the new bustle-style dress before, and she thought it very becoming on someone tall and slender like Pauline. Louisa wondered if the new fashion might improve her own image. She was beginning to detest the cumbersome crinoline that billowed around her like a big brown cloud.

"But still, Pauline," she said, "if I were you, I would be burning with curiosity. I should think you would want to go to Merinda and see what she's like."

Pauline already had an idea of what Miss Drury was like. Frank had said she was pretty; no doubt she was a daughter of the lower classes, hoping to find a rich husband in the colonies. In Pauline's opinion, Australia was overrun with such women. "To go to Merinda," she said, "would be to ascribe a significance to her that she does not have. She's a hired nanny, nothing more. And only a temporary one at that. Once

Hugh and I are married, I intend to replace her with someone more suitable."

"Older, you mean," Louisa said.

Pauline laughed. "Definitely older!" she said.

As they waited for their carriages, Louisa said, "I wish I were strong like you, Pauline. Nothing frightens you, does it?" She pointed to the glass case where some of Pauline's trophies and awards were displayed.

Pauline smiled, determined that her private fear would not surface. She knew that people thought of her as a woman whom nothing intimidated. She hunted wild dogs and rode spirited horses. The sudden appearance of a deadly tiger snake one day during a lawn-tennis party had sent other women running, but Pauline had killed it with an arrow. Even Frank regarded her as having a hard shell. "If you were ever pitted against an African lion, Pauline," he once said, "I wouldn't put my money on the lion!"

But there was, in fact, one creature on earth that did frighten Pauline, and she kept that fear a secret.

"Here's your carriage, Louisa dear," she said. "Please let me know how your visit with Dr. Ramsey turns out. I might find myself needing such information myself someday."

Louisa said, "Thank you, Pauline, for letting me talk. I do feel better, and I will let you know what Dr. Ramsey says."

They stepped out into the bright sunlight. "If you run into Vilma Todd," Pauline said, "please tell her that I am looking forward to seeing her on the archery range, and that I would love to put some money on the contest, if she is amenable to a friendly wager."

"Wager? Did I hear something about a wager?" Frank said as he came down the stairs. "Hello, Louisa. Leaving already? Give my regards to Miles."

Pauline stared at her brother. It was not yet noon, and here he was dressed in a black frock coat and starched white shirt, and carrying, of all things, his top hat and cane. In the middle of the day, during shearing season!

"Frank, what on earth has gotten into you?" she said. "In all the years that you have been running this station, I have never known you to be anywhere but in the paddocks during shearing. Napoleon's army couldn't drag you away from Melbourne during the rest of the year, but come shearing, you're out there watching the shearers like a dingo watching a wallaby. And now, four times in a row, you are all dressed up and about to go out in the middle of the day. Where are you going, Frank?"

"I have business in town," he said, pulling on his gloves, "and it is none of your concern."

"I see," she said. "So it's a woman then."

When he started to protest, Pauline held up a hand. "I don't want to hear about it, Frank. Enjoy yourself. Just don't whine at me when the wool clip comes up short, or if you don't get a good price from the wool brokers. I'm off to Kilmarnock."

"Good God, why?"

"I'm doing it for Hugh. It's important that he start to establish his position in the district."

As Frank watched her go he realized that, for the first time in his life, he envied his sister. She had the man she wanted, while at thirty-four Frank had yet to find a woman to whom he could be devoted. Although it was not for lack of trying.

That first night at Finnegan's, when the barmaid had done the flattering sketch of him, Frank had gone back and offered to escort her home. To his surprise—after all, he was a rich man—Miss Dearborn had declined. The next night he had asked her if she would like to go for a carriage ride. Again, to his astonishment, she did not accept. The third night he offered to take her out to dinner. But she said she was not hungry. So he had decided that he didn't want her after all. Who was she, a barmaid, to be so choosy! He hadn't gone to Finnegan's last night, and he was proud of himself for it. But when he awoke this morning, he found himself unable to stay away. He would have lunch at Finnegan's, he decided, before getting over to the shearing shed.

He wasn't going to give up. One of these times he was going to discover the one thing that Miss Dearborn could not resist. And then he would have her, the only man in the Western District to do so.

———————◆———————

The big, castle-like house at Kilmarnock had many rooms, but there was only one which young Judd MacGregor was afraid to enter. He believed it to be haunted.

Kilmarnock sheep station, situated between Merinda and Lismore, covered 30,000 acres. The house, built of bluestone, was meant to be a replica of Kilmarnock Castle in Scotland. It was massive, with turrets and battlements and tall narrow windows protected by iron bars. All that was missing was a drawbridge, although the illusion of a moat had been created by a deep bed of flowers encircling the house. It stood in the middle of vast lawns and was protected from the winds off the plains by towering eucalyptus trees. A strangely brooding sight for the first-time visitor, the house at Kilmarnock was both magnificent and foreboding. The interior continued the old world theme, with walls of dark wood, heavy Gothic furniture, and imported suits of armor standing guard. Its purpose was to create an ambience of feudalism and lordship, and anyone passing between Kilmarnock's massive doors and into the darkly paneled foyer, where crossed swords and medieval tapestries hung on the walls, could not help thinking of Colin MacGregor as the laird of his castle.

The room that six-year-old Judd MacGregor was afraid to enter stood behind a heavy door with a stone arch. Ghosts dwelt in that room, he was sure of it. Whenever Judd had to go there, he avoided looking at the waxy-skinned faces peering down from their places on the walls—austere men and women trapped between gilt frames, people long dead who seemed to look upon the living with jealous eyes. There were also ghosts who could not be seen, whose troubled spirits hovered around objects in a glass display case: a silver snuffbox, a pair of glasses, a bull's horn. And Judd knew the stories of all of them.

The first had belonged to fourteen-year-old Mary MacGregor, who had been beheaded for having hidden Bonnie Prince Charlie at Kilmarnock Castle. She had received as a reward a lock of his hair, which she kept in the silver snuffbox. The pair of spectacles had been worn by Angus MacGregor, the boatman who had taken Bonnie Prince Charlie to safety, and who had later hanged for it. Finally there was Duncan, the fourth chief of Kilmarnock, who, back in the fourteenth century, while out on the road, was confronted by a mad bull. Armed with only a dirk, he slew the beast and cut off one of its horns.

The room contained stranger things still, which had come not from Scotland but from here in Australia. They were weapons of war and magic, and Judd knew that they had once belonged to Aborigines, and that they contained great power, because old Ezekiel, the black tracker, had told him so. The spirits of slain animals, Ezekiel had explained, lived in the wood of the spear, the boomerang, and the possum-skin drum. But most powerful of all was the *tjuringa*, which, Ezekiel had said, contained someone's soul. Judd was afraid of the *tjuringa*, and he never walked near it, in case the soul should reach out to grab him. But Judd's father was proud of these possessions, and he brought visitors into this room, which was his study, to boast about his collection.

Judd stood there uneasily on this October afternoon, and tried to pay attention while his father talked.

Colin was telling his son about the heroism of a MacGregor at the Battle of Culloden: "There was Robert MacGregor, cornered and without a weapon, who seized the shaft of a wagon and killed eight of Cumberland's men before he himself was killed. And you'll go there someday, son. I'll show you the place where Duncan, the fourth chief of Kilmarnock, slew a wild bull and cut off its horn. This horn, Judd," Colin said, showing it to the boy. Colin handled it proudly; for centuries young MacGregors had had to prove their manhood by draining this horn filled with claret. And the MacGregor coat of arms had a bull's head and the motto "Stand Fast."

But Judd wasn't sure that he ever wanted to go Scotland. His father had described Scotland as a place of mists and monsters that lived in the lochs, of the restless spirits of Celtic chieftains, and of seals who turned themselves into women to bewitch innocent men.

Worst of all, there were the ghosts and ghoulies which Judd decided must be very populous in Scotland, because his grandmother, Lady Ann, had sent him a sampler from Kilmarnock Castle in Scotland, which read: "From ghosties and ghoulies, and things that go bump in the night, may the Good Lord protect us."

While Colin told his son about the great clan battles and the brave chiefs who had resided at Kilmarnock Castle for seven hundred years, Judd's eyes strayed to the open window, where sunshine pierced the branches of elms and alders. He wanted to be out there, on the open plains beneath the hot sun, where the kookaburra laughed and kangaroos seemed to sail in great arcs against the sky.

Colin didn't notice his son's distraction. He was thinking of his ancestral home, the island of Skye in the Inner Hebrides, the "mild winter isle," fifty miles from tip to tip, where Bonnie Prince Charlie had once found refuge before leaving Scotland forever. It was the isle of red deer and golden eagles, and deep woods and clear streams; of the thrush singing after sunset, and bats winging from a haunted church; Skye, stern and wild, a land of heather and bracken and springy turf; of granite peaks, snow-water lakes and inland bogs, and sea inlets that were deep, like fjords. And of Kilmarnock Castle, a large and formidable fortress stronghold on a rocky promontory, home of MacGregors since the eleventh century, when Scotland had been called Caledonia.

Colin often dreamed of home, where the white-tailed eagle soared upon a six-foot wingspan, and a mythical prehistoric monster swam the cold, dark depths of Loch Kilmarnock. Colin longed to speak Gaelic again, "the language of the heart," and to watch the winter mists gather around the austere summits of the Black Cuillins.

Colin had left home when he was nineteen, twenty years ago, and he and his father, Sir Robert, had argued over the issue of clearances.

The elder MacGregor had wanted to evict tenant farmers to make room for wool and mutton production, while young Colin had sided with the ousted farmers. Colin had lost, and had passionately vowed never to return. But finally he had gone back, eight years ago, homesick for Skye. His father would not receive him, but his mother, Lady Ann, had treated Colin kindly, and had sent him away with the heirlooms that now adorned his study. Colin did not consider the journey a waste, since now he possessed the treasures of his heritage, and also because he had brought home a bride.

Colin stared at his son and thought, how like Christina he is. With each passing year, Judd MacGregor grew more and more into the image of his mother. He had her sun-white hair, the periwinkle blue eyes, the delicately clefted chin. Colin saw nothing of himself in the boy; there was no sign of Colin MacGregor's jet-black hair or dark, hooded eyes. And Judd's little-boy lips were already full and pouty like Christina's, his chin soft and rounded like a cherub's, whereas Colin's mouth was a thin hard line, his jaw prominent and square.

"Some day, son," Colin said. "You are going to be the laird of Kilmarnock. When my father dies, I will become the laird. But after me, comes you. And you will inherit all this."

But Judd wasn't sure he wanted to inherit "all this."

There was a knock at the door, and the butler appeared. "Dr. Ramsey said you may go up now, Mr. MacGregor."

Father and son went upstairs, and when they entered the bedroom, Colin went straight to Christina and sat on the edge of the chaise lounge. "How are you feeling, my dear?"

Christina was reclining against satin pillows with a fox fur blanket over her legs. The curtains were drawn against the sunlight; but the glow from the oil lamps illuminated a pale complexion and blond hair. "I feel fine, darling," she said. "I'm not ill. I'm just going to have a baby."

Colin looked at David Ramsey, who, with his reddish hair and lanky frame, looked too young to be a physician. "How is she, doctor?" Colin asked.

"Your wife has what is called an incompetent cervix, Mr. MacGregor," Ramsey said, as he folded away his stethoscope. "Which means that her womb might not be able to support a baby. I could operate, but sometimes surgery triggers a miscarriage. I recommend complete bed rest, limited activities and absolutely no stress."

Although the diagnosis sounded alarming, Colin found it reassuring nonetheless. There was comfort in scientific facts, as opposed to old

Doc Fuller's attribution of Christina's previous miscarriages to full moons and goosedown in the pillows. Colin was glad now that he had taken John Reed's advice and sent for David Ramsey, for all his youth and recent graduation from medical school.

Colin took his wife's hands and searched her face. After eight years of marriage, she still possessed the enchantment that had won him over one magical evening in Glasgow. Colin was beside himself with worry. This dangerous pregnancy had not been his idea. After giving birth to Judd, Christina had suffered two miscarriages and one stillbirth. Against Colin's better judgment and fears, she had persuaded him to let her try again for a child. He prayed now that he would not regret it.

The butler came in, bearing a card on a tray. "You have a caller, madam," he said, handing the card to Christina.

"No," Colin said. "No callers."

"Oh, but Colin dear, it's Pauline Downs. I would love to see her."

"It's all right, Mr. MacGregor," Dr. Ramsey said. "Your wife can have visitors, so long as they don't tax her or excite her."

"You must take care of yourself and the bairn," Colin said to Christina. "I could not bear to lose you. Without you, Christina, my life would not be worth living."

Pauline came in then, and saw Colin kiss his wife, and heard him say to her, "When you're well enough, my love, I'll take you and the bairns home for a visit. We'll see the moonlight on the heather, and we'll stay at the inn where we spent our first night together as husband and wife." Pauline thought: It will be like this with Hugh and me.

"Pauline," Christina said. "How nice of you to come. Please sit down. Have you met Dr. Ramsey? Dr. Ramsey, Miss Pauline Downs. Colin, will you please ring for tea?"

"I hear Westbrook has got himself a son now, too," Colin said to Pauline as he went to the bell pull. "Still, it's not the same as having your own, is it?"

Pauline didn't care for Colin MacGregor, but she conceded that he did have the darkly handsome looks of a Celtic highlander. She knew several women in the district who had expressed the secret desire to know him "better."

"Speaking of Hugh, have you seen this?" Christina said, as she handed a newspaper to Pauline. "You must be very proud of him."

Pauline had already seen the poem that Frank had printed on the front page of the *Times*. It was Hugh's latest ballad, "Droving Days," which he had published, like the rest of his poems, under the pseudonym "Old Drover":

> The dust is blowing in the Southern Land,
> The dust that follows ten thousand head,
> Over the black soil, over the sand,
> Over the ridges red.

Hugh is too modest, Pauline thought, I must convince him to publish under his real name.

"How are you feeling, Christina?" she said. "I heard from Maude Reed that you've been having morning sickness."

"And afternoon and evening sickness!" Christina said with a smile. "But I'm feeling better today, as I was just telling Dr. Ramsey. This was sent over yesterday." She handed Pauline a small stoppered phial.

Pauline uncorked it and sniffed the aromatic decoction it contained. "Chamomile?" she said.

"And black horehound and meadowsweet," Dr. Ramsey added, "with a touch of cloves. A rather effective remedy for morning sickness."

"Who sent it?" Pauline said.

Christina handed her the note that had accompanied the phial.

Pauline stared at it. The writing clearly belonged to a lady, and it was signed, "Joanna Drury, Merinda."

"Miss Drury certainly has an impressive familiarity with herbs," Dr. Ramsey said. "I encountered her the other day at Thompson's chemist's shop in Cameron Town. She was buying such a variety of things and in such large quantities that I asked her what she planned to use it all for. She told me that she keeps a supply of everything on hand, should the need arise. Apparently her mother had been something of a healer. Maude Reed was in the shop, telling Winifred Cameron about Mrs. MacGregor's morning sickness. Miss Drury must have taken it upon herself to have this decoction sent over."

"And I feel so much better," Christina said. "I must thank her."

"I'll be glad to take a message to Miss Drury for you, Mrs. MacGregor," Ramsey quickly offered. "I'll be passing by Merinda tomorrow, on my way to Horsham."

"Phoebe McCloud told me that Miss Drury was hired by Hugh Westbrook to take care of the orphaned boy he inherited," Christina said. "What is she like, Dr. Ramsey?"

"What is Miss Drury like?" he said, and Pauline noticed how he blushed.

As she listened to David Ramsey speak rather self-consciously of the "lovely and ladylike Miss Drury," Pauline looked at the note. She read again the correct salutation and closing, the perfect spelling and punctuation, all written in a delicate hand.

The butler appeared again with another calling card. "Miss Flora McMichaels to see you, madam," he said.

"This is too much," Colin said.

But Christina asked the butler to bring Miss McMichaels in.

Feeling suddenly disconcerted by this new information about Joanna Drury, Pauline turned to David Ramsey and said with a smile, "How do you find life in the Western District, doctor? After Melbourne, we must seem very dreary."

"Hardly dreary, Miss Downs! Since my arrival five weeks ago, I have barely had a moment to myself. Especially now, during shearing. We learned about shearing accidents in medical school, of course, but I had no idea what a dangerous occupation it really is."

A large woman entered the room, in a crinoline so wide that it threatened to knock over several small tables that were standing about. "Christina, my dear!" she said as she glided to the chaise longue with her hands extended. "I heard from Maude Reed that you're not feeling well. We can't have that, can we? I've brought you just the thing."

Pauline watched as Flora McMichaels placed a wicker basket on the floor and began to produce jars and tins, and cakes wrapped in cloth. "You must keep up your strength," Miss McMichaels said, but Pauline noticed that she kept her eyes on Colin while she spoke.

Pauline felt her uneasiness grow. Flora McMichaels, who was a bit too loud and who was obvious about her infatuation with Colin, was the embodiment of Pauline's secret fear—the one creature in the world who frightened her. It was not so much the woman herself that Pauline felt threatened by, but what she stood for. People regarded spinsters as unfortunate women who had somehow failed to get themselves a man. They were condemned to lives of loneliness and secondary status, to become the maiden aunts whom every family supported with begrudging charity.

Pauline didn't like being around such women, they disquieted her, their very presence a reminder of how unpredictable life can be—and how unjust. No woman asked for such a fate. Pauline knew that Flora McMichaels had once been a very pretty and lively young woman, engaged to be married to a well-liked young man from a good family. But Flora lost her fiancé in a hunting accident on the eve of her wedding, and now, thirty years later, she was privately referred to by her friends as "Poor Flora."

Such a fate, Pauline knew, could strike any woman at any time, and she would be helpless to prevent it. As she watched Flora McMichaels smile coyly at Colin, Pauline thought of desperate women, and she wondered if Joanna Drury was such a one. Miss Drury was living at Merinda, in Hugh's cabin. "I've moved into the bunkhouse," Hugh had told Pauline. But that brought little reassurance now.

And then Pauline remembered how agitated Hugh had been the night he had returned from Melbourne, three days ago, talking about a lice infestation in his best wool producers, and the possibility of financial problems. Pauline hadn't thought anything of it at the time, but now she was hearing it in a different way: Hugh had almost seemed to be warning her that he might not be able to build the house.

Pauline realized the mistake she had made, that she had been complacent when she should have been vigilant. Suddenly Joanna Drury was no longer a hired nanny; she was an opponent.

"The real reason I came by, Christina dear," Pauline said suddenly, interrupting the talkative Flora, "is to invite you and Colin and Judd to a party I am giving next week for Adam, the little boy Hugh has taken in. I thought it would be nice to introduce him to the Western District, and let him get to know us, and us get to know him."

"How lovely," Christina said. "And how kind of you, Pauline. The poor child must feel very lost. Colin dear, we must see to it that Judd makes friends with Hugh's boy. And where is Judd? Where is my baby?" Christina said. "Come here, darling."

Judd left his place in the corner and buried himself in his mother's embrace. He knew she must be very sick, because of the careful way everyone was treating her.

"Yes," Pauline said, as the idea rapidly took shape in her mind. "It will be a garden party. I plan to have clowns and a magician, and Adam can make friends with the other children." And he will have presents to open, Pauline decided. He will be given his own pony and cart, he can have all the sweets he wants and I'll prepare a room for him at Lismore and fill it with toys. When the time comes to leave, he won't want to go back to Merinda. He'll want to stay at Lismore with me.

And the services of Joanna Drury will no longer be required.

CHAPTER 6

Something strange was going on, Joanna was certain of it. She had come out onto the veranda and found a cluster of feathers, carefully tied together with string, lying in front of the door.

This was not the first time such a thing had happened. In the two weeks since she had arrived at Merinda, she had come across strange objects: shiny river stones placed mysteriously on the outside windowsill; wild flowers lined up on the top step of the veranda; and, two days ago, a circlet woven from river grass and human hair hanging on the front door. And now these feathers.

Who was placing these things here, and why?

She looked around the busy yard, where frightened sheep were being funneled into chutes that led to the shearing pens. The noise and the smell were almost overpowering.

The shearing gang had arrived the day after Joanna had come to Merinda, and she had discovered that these three weeks each November were the reason for everything else that went on at a station throughout the rest of the year. This was when the sheep were shorn, and the wool was shipped to England. Shearing season meant late nights and early mornings, hard work and stolen sleep, food grabbed on the run and a suspension of all activities until the shearing gang moved on and the wool was shipped to the harbor. In all that time, Joanna had seen Hugh only when he had come by the cabin each night to ask how Adam was doing, and to make sure that she and the child were comfortable.

Joanna stood on the veranda, and studied the feathers she had found in front of the door. They were cockatoo feathers, a lovely delicate pink with a hint of yellow at the tips, and they had been carefully tied together with a thin strip of bark. There were three of them, just as there had been three river stones, and three wild flowers. There was no doubt about it—someone had gone to the trouble of collecting them, and then placing them where they would be found. But who was doing it, and for what reason?

As she puzzled over it, she watched Adam run about chasing chickens. The scab was gone from his forehead, and there had been no more fits, no repeat of the head-banging episode. To a stranger, he might in fact appear to be a normal, healthy boy. But a stranger didn't see the torturous way Adam sometimes looked when he was trying hard to say something; a stranger didn't see the way the child suddenly fell into silence, just staring; a stranger wasn't awakened at night by Adam crying out in his sleep.

Watching him run made Joanna think of the toys that lay neglected in the cabin. She had bought them from Mr. Shapiro, the old peddler who made regular rounds through the district with his colorfully painted wagon drawn by an ancient horse named Pinky, and who sold everything from calico to "genuine Arabian perfume." Joanna had mainly bought items for the cabin—a hooked rug, a ceramic teapot, curtains for the window—but she had also bought a kite and a ball. To her surprise, Adam received them with indifference; and then she realized that he was unused to toys, that he had, in fact, never had any toys before. He preferred to play with nature. He paddled in the billabong, and spent hours watching the platypus skim the bottom for food. He carried Rupert around a lot, but the ball and the kite lay untouched. Joanna had tried several ways to reach Adam, to find the key to his private torment, but she had so far been unsuccessful. When she had shown him his mother's Bible and wedding ring, he had burst into tears.

Joanna was anxious to hear from the authorities in South Australia. She was hoping they could tell her something that would shed some light on what had wounded him, for then she might know how to heal him. She thought again of her mother, and wondered if Lady Emily might still be alive today had someone long ago been able to help her face what it was that had damaged her, and coax the pain out of her.

Joanna was looking for other letters in the mail as well.

On the morning after her arrival at Merinda, she had written to the governments of the six colonies into which Australia was divided, requesting information on missionaries named John and Naomi Makepeace; she had also asked that maps of the colonies be sent to her. She had taken the deed to Hugh Westbrook's lawyer in Cameron Town, but all he had been able to tell her was that, until they knew in which colony the land was located, there was no way of finding out where the land was, or if the deed was even legal.

She was also watching for an envelope bearing the postmark of Cambridge, England.

One of the entries in Lady Emily's diary had been written eight years ago, when Joanna had accompanied her mother on a visit to England. Lady Emily had written: "Although Aunt Millicent refuses to speak of my parents, so deep is her grief over losing her sister, I have nonetheless learned a few things from her neighbor across the green, Mrs. Dobson, who knew Millicent and my mother when they were girls. She mentioned a name—Patrick Lathrop—and she seemed to recall that he had been a good friend of Father's from school. Perhaps if I can locate Mr. Lathrop, I might be able to find out where exactly in Australia I was born, and what my father was doing there."

As far as Joanna knew, her mother had never followed up on Lathrop, but Joanna had thought it a piece of information worth pursuing. Knowing that her grandfather had attended Christ's College, Cambridge, from 1826 to 1829, she had written to the university two months before she left India, giving as her return address General Delivery, Melbourne. And the Melbourne postmaster knew that she was now residing at Merinda.

She was puzzling over the cockatoo feathers she had found, when she saw a sudden movement in the shadow of the shearing shed across the yard.

She realized that it was Sarah, the young Aboriginal girl who worked at the homestead. She was standing very still, staring at Joanna the same way Ezekiel had stared at her by the river two weeks ago. The fourteen-year-old watched her now in the same unsettling way the old man had. Joanna did not think the girl was simply curious, as Hugh had suggested; she had the impression that Sarah was wary of her, was assessing her.

She had caught Sarah spying on her before, at unexpected moments. Joanna would feel that she was being watched, and she would look up to see the girl there. Joanna had tried to talk to her, tried to make friends, but Sarah always turned away. "She speaks English," Hugh had told Joanna when she had asked him about the girl. "Not very good English, but enough to make herself understood. I imagine she's mystified about you. I don't think she's had much contact with white women outside of the Aboriginal Mission, where she grew up."

Joanna thought Sarah pretty, with high cheekbones and large, almond-shaped eyes. She wore her hair long and straight; it was a shiny mahogany brown, as dark as her skin, and she wore ordinary dresses, but no shoes. Why did she seem to be spying? Joanna wondered. Why was there an attitude about Sarah of watching and waiting? Was she responsible for the strange objects Joanna had found on the veranda?

Bill Lovell, the station manager, suddenly appeared across the yard at that moment, with something in his arms. "Hello," he called. "I've brought something for the boy."

Joanna had seen little of Bill in the two weeks since her arrival, but when she did encounter him, he was always friendly. He had the white hair and weathered skin of a man who had spent all his life in the sun; his blue eyes were bleached, as if from having continually squinted over great distances.

When he stepped into the shade of the veranda, he unfolded the burlap sack he was carrying and Joanna saw a pair of tiny brown eyes blinking up at her. They were set in a soft, furry face that had an impossibly big nose, a white fuzzy chin and outlandish ears. She was spellbound; she had never been this close to a koala before.

"I found it upriver, lying on the ground," Bill said. "I'd say it's about eight months old, not quite mature yet. There was a dead female nearby, I assume it was its mother. She had been shot, probably by a hunter using koala bears for target practice. I thought the boy might like him for a pet."

"Adam," Joanna called. "Come and see what Mr. Lovell has brought you." She looked over at the shearing shed and saw that Sarah had gone.

"They're a nuisance, really," Bill said. "As I'm sure you've heard."

"Yes, Mr. Lovell, I have heard!" Everyone's sleep was being disturbed these days by the koalas. It was the mating season, and all through the night the bellowing of the males and the wailing call of the females kept everyone awake. Hunters were encouraged to kill them. "But still," the station manager said, "I couldn't just leave him there for the dingoes."

"Here you go, Adam," Joanna said, as she placed the animal in the boy's arms. "Be very gentle with him, he's only a baby."

"Ko-la!" Adam said with glee.

"No, Adam," Joanna said. "It's ko-ah-la. Can you say koala?"

Adam's eyebrows drew together and the furrow between them deepened. "Ko-ah-la," he said.

"The word koala is Aborigine for 'doesn't drink,' " said Bill. They're not really bears, you know. They're silly creatures, too. All they do is hang in the trees all day, getting drunk on eucalyptus juice. And they were made wrong. Their pouches don't open at the top like a kangaroo's, but at the bottom."

Joanna laughed. "I should think that would be most inefficient for a tree dweller! We'll build a pen for him," she said. "I'll give him water and"—she looked at Bill—"what do koalas eat?"

"Well, they don't drink water. And they only eat the leaves of certain gum trees. But we can manage something."

"Oh, you've hurt your hand."

"A sheep tried to bite me," he said. "It's nothing."

"Let me take care of it for you. Adam, would you please go into the house and fetch my healing kit? And can you bring me a basin of water as well?"

"Please don't trouble yourself, miss," Lovell said, as Joanna peeled away the handkerchief that was tied around his hand. "It'll be all right. Stumpy Larson poured kerosene on it."

Joanna laughed. On her first day at Merinda, she had found a bottle of kerosene in the cabin with a label on it that said, "Just whack it on everything."

"This needs something more, Mr. Lovell," she said.

"Please call me Bill."

"All right, Bill. You must be one of the few men around here who doesn't have a nickname!"

"Australians are fond of nicknames. It's the rare man who doesn't have one."

Adam came back carrying a basin of water and the healing kit. As Joanna washed Lovell's hand with soap and water, and then applied a salve to the bite, the boy stood beside her, taking things out of the box and handing them to her.

Bill watched Joanna wrap the bandage, and then he looked at her bowed head and the glossy brown hair that threw back auburn glints in the sunlight. He reckoned it had been a while since he had given much thought to a woman—not since Mildred died. But he found himself curious about this young girl Hugh had brought home. And he wasn't the only one who was curious about her. Bill would swear he had never seen so many combed heads and freshly shaven faces come out of one sheep station bunkhouse in the morning. And there was that young doctor, David Ramsey, who had come by a few times. He was always on his way somewhere else, and had just dropped by "to see if everything was all right." Bill wondered what the young man's intentions were toward Miss Drury, and was surprised to find himself feeling jealous. What, after all, could the young lady possibly see in an old brumby like himself?

"You certainly have a nice touch, Miss Drury," he said as he flexed his bandaged hand.

"I just wish the other men would let me take care of them. I've tried to help with some of the injuries around here but they run away!"

"The men don't like to show weakness in front of a woman."

"Well, it's silly to risk bleeding to death until Doc Fuller or Dr. Ramsey can be summoned! Please keep the wound clean, Mr. Lovell. Animal bites can be tricky." She handed the leftover gauze to Adam and showed him how to roll it up and put it away. "How is the wool clip, Bill?" she said. "I haven't seen Mr. Westbrook to ask."

"I'm afraid it isn't good. Lice is bad for the sheep, makes the wool break apart easily. Hugh's down at the washing right now, and he doesn't look too happy."

Joanna looked toward the trees clustered at the river's edge, and a poem came to her mind:

> Amid life's hurley, hubble-bubble,
> Two things stand alone:
> Compassion in another's trouble,
> Courage in your own.

Joanna had found it written in an awkward hand on the inside cover of a book she had come across in the cabin. The author's signature was beneath it: "Hugh Westbrook, aged seventeen."

She had discovered Hugh's books on her first morning at Merinda. They stood in a small collection on a wooden shelf—old, well-thumbed volumes of poetry, history, farming and fiction. There were works by Trollope, Thackeray, Dickens, and even the Brontës. Every one of them appeared to have been read many times; some had underlinings and pencil notes in the margins. In the book titled *Sheep Farming and Wool Growing*, Joanna had found a collection of old and yellowed newspaper and magazine clippings, articles with such headings as "The

Breeding of Subterranean Clover," and "The Application of Scientific Principles in Wool Production." The dictionary was very worn, as were the world atlas and a history of the Australian colonies.

As she had gone through them, Joanna had come to learn something more about the man who owned Merinda.

"I never went to school," Hugh had told her when they had spent the night at Emu Creek. "We never stayed in one place long enough. My father and I had to keep on the go if we were going to find work. It was an old hermit woodsman, up near Toowoomba, who taught me my first letters."

Hugh's modest collection of books had told Joanna the history of that boy's road toward self-education. In *Jane Eyre*, for example, nearly every page had words underlined, clearly to be looked up in the dictionary. Two dates were written inside the cover—July 10, 1856, and June 30, 1857—which Joanna had assumed indicated the dates on which he started and ended this book. Hugh had been fifteen years old and it had taken him nearly a year. But *A Christmas Carol* had taken him only from August 1860 to October of the same year; he had been nineteen then, and only a few words were underlined—clear evidence of his progress. And while the notes written in the margins of the history book, first opened in 1858, were full of misspelled words, the notes written in the sheep-management handbook were nearly perfect, with better penmanship. The date in that book was September 1867—four years ago.

As Joanna had handled the books, she had a strong sense of seeing Hugh Westbrook's life unfold before her. She saw the illiterate boy struggling to print letters facing the right way—many a "b" had an erasure and the ghost of a backward "b" underneath it; then the teenager, hungry for knowledge, his head bent as he pored over the world atlas—a town on the map of Queensland had been circled and a star drawn next to it; Joanna wondered what had happened there that made it special to him. And finally she had seen the man, confident and sure of himself, assimilating the knowledge of "scientific" farmers in faraway England, printed in the humble pages of outback newspapers.

And then there were the poems written on scraps of paper, some in pencil, some in ink, some with words scratched out, a few whole and flawless as if the entire piece had flowed in perfection. Hugh had written ballads about Australia's outlaws, known as bushrangers: " 'I'll fight, but not surrender,' said the wild colonial boy." And poems about shearers: "They work hard and they drink hard, and they go to Hell at last . . ." And about the outback, where "Rugged old she-oaks sigh in the bend/O'er the lily-strewn pools,/Where the green ridges end."

And there was the ballad of "The Shearer's Widow," which Joanna had discovered was not about a woman whose husband had died, but whose husband had "hit the wallaby track" in search of shearing jobs—gone for half the year, returning home penniless.

"I'm sorry Mr. Westbrook is having problems," Joanna said now.

"In all the years I've known Hugh—and that's a fair number—I've never seen him look so discouraged."

After Bill left, Joanna showed Adam how to clean the instruments in the healing kit, and put them away. "You must be sure to put everything back where it was," she said, "and that way it will be there when you need it."

They both looked up when they heard a voice call from the yard. "Finish putting the things away," Joanna said to Adam, and she walked out of the veranda into the sunlight.

"Hello," she called when she saw Constable Johnson come riding up. This was his fourth visit in the past two weeks, and when he said, "I knew I would be passing by Merinda, Miss Drury, so I thought I would bring your mail for you," she was not surprised, because he had said the same thing the previous times.

"Thank you, Mr. Johnson," she said. "That's very kind of you." Joanna noticed that he was wearing his uniform for the first time, and she wondered if he was going somewhere on an official errand, as he was rarely seen in the stiff black tunic with shiny brass buttons. When he swung down from his horse, she noticed that his boots were highly polished, and the badge of office on the brim of his hat flashed back the sunlight. She also detected the fragrances of cologne and hair oil.

"It's a lovely spring day, isn't it, Miss Drury," the young policeman said as he handed her the mail.

"Indeed it is, Mr. Johnson," she said, and she quickly looked through the envelopes. Her attention was caught by two return addresses: one was from South Australia, the other from Cambridge University in England.

Adam came out at that point; Constable Johnson turned and said, "Hello, son," and the boy started to scream.

———————————————

Joanna tried not to drive too quickly; she didn't want to alarm Adam. After she had calmed him down a bit, holding him and keeping him from hurting himself, she had suggested they go for a ride in the wagon. She had realized she needed to get him away from the yard, and from Constable Johnson.

Now they were riding through beautiful countryside, following a small, noisy flock of ewes and lambs. Joanna looked at the boy. His eyes were still swollen from crying, but his attention was caught up with the business of nature all around him. When she had asked him what had frightened him, he had closed up like a flower.

Finally they came to a bend in the river where they were met by an extraordinary sight.

A monstrous machine resembling a locomotive engine stood on the bank, belching black smoke and churning great wheels, which in turn were connected by leather belts to smaller wheels attached to what looked like a large, square water tank. Steam spewed from the top of the tank, while boiling water poured from conduits at its base. As Joanna brought the wagon to a halt, she stared in amazement at the bleating sheep being pushed into the river and goaded toward the water tank by men with sticks. The animals were then plunged into a steaming pool, where men standing inside tarred barrels vigorously scrubbed them; and when the sheep came out on the other side, they were soaking wet but beautifully white and clean.

She saw Hugh standing at the river's edge, his hands on his hips and a scowl on his face.

"Hello!" she called.

He turned, and a vision flashed in his mind of how she had looked on that first night, when she had run out of the cabin after Sarah had startled her, and he had caught her briefly in his arms. Despite his efforts to forget it, the memory stayed vividly in his mind: the nightgown, the shiny hair flowing over her shoulders and breasts. How soft she had felt, how warm in his arms.

And suddenly he was remembering something Bill Lovell had once said years ago, when Bill had had too much to drink. "Now take the woman I used to be married to. She never did like me to touch her. Was always grateful when I did it fast and got it over with. Women are like that. They're not like men. It repulses them. Can't imagine why God made the two sexes so different. How does He expect the human race to keep going?"

And then another voice, that of Phoebe Ferguson, who ran the establishment down in St. Kilda, whispered in his mind, "Most of my customers, if you can believe it, Mr. Westbrook, are married men. I don't get many single gents like yourself. Husbands come here to get what their wives won't give them. High-class ladies, in particular, don't enjoy the bedroom."

Hugh thought of Pauline, and the way she had responded to his kiss two weeks ago. He knew there would be no reluctance with her. And then he found himself wondering about Joanna.

"Miss Drury," he said. "What a pleasant surprise." He held out his hand and helped her down from the wagon. And then he saw that, although she was smiling, there was worry in her eyes. "Is everything all right?" he said.

"Adam had a terrible fright a short while ago."

"Oh?" Hugh looked at Adam, who was staring at the chaotic scene in the river. "What happened?"

She described the sudden hysterical fit. "It was worse than the one he had on the pier. And I think it was caused by the sight of Constable Johnson."

"How can that be? Adam has seen Johnson before."

"Yes, but not in his uniform. And this came today," she reached into the pocket of her skirt and drew out the letter from the South Australia authorities who had taken charge of Adam. She had managed to read it while driving out to the river; the rest of her mail she had left at the cabin. "They say that a gold digger found Adam. He told the authorities that he had gone to the farmhouse hoping for a handout, and had heard a child screaming. He saw the child there with a dead woman, and so he went into the nearby town and got a policeman to help. When they went into the farmhouse, they found Adam alone with his mother. Apparently she had been dead for quite a while."

"My God," Hugh said, looking again at Adam, who appeared to be mesmerized by the wool-washing machine.

"He must have been crying for days," Joanna said. "And I think that that is somehow the cause for his speech problems now."

"And being frightened of Johnson," Hugh said. "Of course—police in uniforms no doubt took him away from his mother." Hugh went to the wagon and said, "I hear you had a scare this morning, Adam. Well, don't you worry, no one's going to take you away. This is your home from now on. We're mates, aren't we?"

Adam looked at him.

"Come on, come see how we wash the sheep." Hugh held out his hand and, after a moment's hesitation, Adam took it.

They walked to the water's edge, and as the boy watched in wonder at the workings of the machinery, Joanna said to Hugh, "There was something for you in the mail also, Mr. Westbrook—a parcel from the Cameron Town Book Emporium."

"Oh yes," he said, keeping his eye on the sheep going across the river. "Well, you can open that one, Miss Drury. It's really for you."

"For me!"

When Hugh said nothing further, Joanna thought of a book she had found in the cabin—a history of the Australian colonies from 1788 to 1860. In it was a map of the continent of Australia, showing a massive island at the bottom of the world, with towns and settlements scattered along its coastlines. But at the center of the map lay a great blank called the Never Never. This was the silent, mysterious heart of Australia, an unexplored center that had no rivers mapped out, no mountains marked, no landmarks identified; it was just a vast, unknown land that, according to the book, no white man had ever seen. What was there? Joanna had wondered when she had looked at it. What strange world or undiscovered races and cities existed there, at this moment, unknown to those who lived on Australia's coasts?

And recalling it now, she found herself suddenly thinking of the secret heart of Hugh Westbrook. He seemed to Joanna to be like that formidable Never Never—unexplored, enigmatic, unpredictable.

"This is a new process for washing wool," Hugh said after a moment, as if suddenly self-conscious. "We used to send the fleeces just as they were, right off the sheep's back, to the textile mills in England, and they did the washing. But we discovered that we get more money for our wool if we wash it ourselves before we ship it."

"Mr. Lovell said you aren't happy with this year's wool clip, Mr. Westbrook."

"I'm afraid lice got into my best wool producers. As you can see, the wool is brittle, the fibers break up in the water. Those fleeces will be useless when we shear. Five thousand useless fleeces, and a year's profit, literally down the drain."

Joanna had learned in the short time she had been here that a grazier's whole life—his money, his reputation—lay in his wool. Each December, right after shearing, a grazier did not rest until the massive bales were purchased by the Melbourne wool brokers and shipped off to the Lancashire mills, making him one year richer. But, as Joanna saw the fleece fall apart in the water, she realized that Hugh had reason for being discouraged.

Then she saw something that caught her attention—a yellowish foam collecting on the banks. Going to the water's edge, she knelt and scooped the waxy residue into her hands. "Mr. Westbrook," she said, "what is this?"

"It's what is washed out of the wool—grease, yolk, dirt—"

"And lanolin?"

"Yes, lanolin."

"The medical men of India prize lanolin very highly," she said, as she studied the substance on her fingertips. "They say it is absorbed by the skin faster than creams or oils, thereby making it an ideal vehicle for medicines that cannot be taken by mouth. My mother used lanolin in many of her remedies. But unfortunately it was very expensive; we had to import it from England. And here it is, just lying on the river bank! May I collect some?"

"Take all you want. I have no use for it." He picked up a billycan. "Here. You can use this."

"Would you like to collect it for me, Adam?"

The boy reached eagerly for the can.

"Let me show you how. Just skim the surface—yes, slowly, like that."

As Joanna watched Adam fill the can, she laughed and said, "When I think of how carefully my mother measured out her lanolin! Do you know, Mr. Westbrook, that we sometimes paid as much as a pound for a jar of lanolin one fourth the size of this can? And here it is, free for the taking."

"There!" Adam said, holding up the filled can.

"Once I get the impurities out," Joanna said, "and separate the lanolin from the wax, I shall have a fortune's worth!" She looked down at the waxy foam that was breaking away from the river bank and being carried off downstream. "It seems such a shame to let the river carry it away."

"This is the first time I've used this machinery," Hugh said. "Up until now, I've always sent raw fleeces to England. I hadn't thought of doing anything with the residue."

Joanna stared at the river for another moment, then she said, "Did you know, Mr. Westbrook, that Mr. Thompson, the chemist in Cameron Town, charges ten shillings for an ounce of lanolin?"

But Hugh was already deep in thought, watching the waxy foam break away from the river's edge and swirl downstream around the bend.

The afternoon was hot and still, and while Adam napped in the cabin, Joanna sat on the veranda, going through the mail Constable Johnson had brought, while Bill Lovell constructed a small cage for the orphaned koala.

The first of the letters Joanna opened was from a government office in the Queensland colony, but it contained none of the expected maps or information, just a brief letter saying, "Please remit sixpence for the topographical survey, and twopence to look up the records of the Makepeaces."

The second letter, from Cambridge University, however, was more promising. Patrick Lathrop, the letter said, had attended Christ's College from 1826 to 1830. "The last the university heard from him," the letter added, "was in 1851, when Mr. Lathrop sailed for California. The address we had for him at that time was the Regent Hotel, in San Francisco."

Joanna frowned. That was twenty years ago. But still, it was something to go on, because if he was indeed a close friend of her grandfather's then he might know where in Australia John Makepeace had gone to serve as a missionary.

The last item was the parcel from the Cameron Town Book Emporium, which was addressed to Hugh Westbrook and which he had told her to open. When she tore away the brown paper and string, she found a book titled: *Codes, Ciphers, and Enigmas*. She stared in wonder as she flipped through pages filled with codes and alphabets, and realized that Hugh must have ordered it for her, to help her decipher her grandfather's notes. "We made a bargain," he had said that first night at Emu Creek. And Joanna knew then that the book was going to be very special to her.

"Listen," said Bill Lovell suddenly. "Someone is singing."

Joanna looked up, and she heard a girl's voice, a melody . . .

Then she saw Sarah standing across the yard in the shadow of the shearing shed. The shed was empty and silent, as were the pens and the yard; shearing was done, the gang had moved on, and the heat of the day pressed down upon a deserted, almost lifeless homestead.

Sarah was standing near the same spot Joanna had seen her in that morning, but now she was singing a high-noted melody, repeating it over and over, in words Joanna could not understand. And as she sang, she kept her eyes on Joanna.

"Bill," Joanna said, suddenly uneasy, "how did Sarah come to be here at Merinda?"

"We took her in because the director of the Aboriginal Mission, Reverend Simms, asked us to take her. He said she was in danger of losing her soul."

"What do you mean?"

"Well," he said, looking across the dusty yard at the girl, "apparently they caught some of the old women performing an initiation on her. Simms intervened and got her out of there. One of the purposes of the mission is to train the young Aborigines to white ways, to keep them from learning their tribal customs."

"What sort of initiation?"

"I don't know, really. It's all very secretive, taboo. It has to do with teaching the young ones the laws of the clan, the ways of the Ancestors, the songlines, the mythology of their race. When an Aboriginal youngster is initiated into the clan, he or she is considered an Aborigine for life, and the missionaries don't like that, because then the Aborigines are difficult to control. If, however, the young ones are deprived of the initiation, then they aren't accepted by the clan and they turn to the white culture for help, for identity."

"How cruel," Joanna said.

"The missionaries mean well, Miss Drury. I believe they are acting on good intentions, believing they are making a better life for the Aborigines. But unfortunately, some missionaries themselves also fear the Aborigines. They believe the natives have a dark, evil side to them that has to be kept suppressed."

Joanna watched the girl. Sarah had long, slender limbs and skin that glowed in the sun. Her hair, fluid and silky, made Joanna think of a waterfall. The melody she sang was quite lovely, with a haunting refrain.

"And are the Aborigines happy at the mission?" Joanna asked Bill, thinking of her grandparents.

"I couldn't say," he said. "With many natives it's hard to tell what they're thinking. In some ways, the white man has brought improvements to the Aborigines' lives, but in others, there have been great losses. When the young ones are raised outside of the tribes, they lose their cultural identity. They are no longer accepted by their elders, but then they aren't accepted by white society either."

The old Aborigine, Ezekiel, came to Joanna's mind then, and she wondered what he thought of Sarah, half-Aboriginal, half-initiated, working on a white man's sheep station. Ezekiel also sometimes worked for Hugh, Joanna knew. But what did he really think of white men, and the new race that had invaded his land?

"What is she singing?" Joanna said.

"I would guess, Miss Drury, that she's telling a story. Most Aboriginal songs tell a story. It's their equivalent of books. I recognize a few words." He paused and listened. "She's talking about sheep—sheep losing their fleeces."

Joanna was spellbound as she listened to the song fill the still afternoon air.

"Bill," she said, unable to take her eyes away from Sarah, "I've been finding unexplainable objects around the cabin." When she described them, he said, "They sound like Aboriginal magic. And judging by the way the girl is singing, I'd reckon she's the one who put them here."

"But what do they mean? What sort of magic?"

"I don't know. Something Sarah learned from the elders at the mission, I suppose. Sarah isn't a full-blood, she wasn't raised with a clan. We were told that her mother was a full-blood, but her father was white. However, she obviously learned something from the old ones at the mission before Reverend Simms was able to get her away from their influence."

"What sort of things were they teaching her, do you suppose?"

"Well, when I was a boy in the outback—which is more years ago that I care to think about—the Aborigines were still living the same way they had when the first white men came here, a hundred years ago. And I remember that they still held *corroborees*—dances—when they sang their magic songs. There were songlines then, and a belief in the Dreamtime, and they didn't have any concepts of stealing or property ownership. No one had personal possessions, and everyone was part of the land. Everything was shared. Whenever a family had a stroke of luck, such as killing a large kangaroo, everyone ate well. And nature was allowed to regenerate. They never drank a waterhole dry, or hunted an area until there was no wildlife left, and when they did kill an animal, they asked its forgiveness first. And," he added, "they practiced a very powerful form of magic. I imagine that was what they were teaching Sarah."

Joanna thought of her mother being here as a child, and the Aborigines she might have lived with. And the poison—the magic—that might have come from them, and destroyed her.

And Joanna felt the familiar sense of foreboding come over her again.

"The song that she's singing, Bill, is it good magic or—bad?"

"What were those things again that you said you'd found? Well, as I recall, cockatoo feathers, especially the pink or yellow ones, were generally used as protective magic."

"Protective magic! What do you mean?"

He shrugged. "It's my guess the girl's trying to protect something from something."

Joanna stared at Sarah for another moment, and then she remembered a passage in her mother's diary. "I have had a dream about the past again," Lady Emily had written. "At least, I think it might be the past. I am a small child, and I am with a dark-skinned woman—

the same woman who appears in my other dreams, the one I think might have been called Reena. We are hiding behind some rocks—we are afraid. I see her brown hands doing something with feathers, and she is singing."

Joanna went cold, despite the warmth of the day.

"Bill," she said, "are you telling me that Sarah thinks we're in need of some kind of protection here?"

He looked at the eucalyptus twig in his hand, which he had been trying to coax the koala to eat. He didn't say anything. He didn't want to upset her by telling her old Ezekiel had for some reason taken a dislike to her and was telling Hugh that her presence here was bad for Merinda. Hugh had ignored the old man, and so Ezekiel was starting to tell the Aboriginal station hands that there was bad luck here. Bill didn't know exactly what it was Ezekiel had against Miss Drury, but he knew that the old man had influence over the highly superstitious stock hands—enough to make them so nervous that they might leave. And Hugh couldn't afford to lose them right now. They were among his best workers, and he needed them.

Sarah stopped singing then, and, to Joanna's surprise, walked across the yard and stood at the bottom of the veranda steps. Adam appeared suddenly in the cabin doorway and, when he saw her, he ran down to her. He tried to speak, saying, "Um." She gave him a curious look, then she reached out and placed her hand on his head. *"Wandjitnup,"* she said.

Joanna quickly stood. "What are you doing?"

Bill said, "Don't worry, Miss Drury. Sarah won't hurt the boy. That's their way of acknowledging a child with affection—placing a hand on his head."

Joanna was further startled when Sarah knelt down and, looking at Adam, said, "You don't speak good. Like Sarah. Maybe we teach each other good whitefella English, okay?"

Then she looked up at Joanna and smiled.

CHAPTER 7

F rank Downs has recently obtained a map, Miss Drury, that we can look at," Hugh said to Joanna as he guided the wagon onto the main road. "He tells me it takes up nearly an entire wall, and it is the most comprehensive map of Australia that he has ever seen. Karra Karra is bound to be on it."

Joanna had not expected to be invited to the party Pauline Downs was giving for Adam; she had been surprised when Hugh asked her to go. "Adam will want you there," he had said, "and it will give you an opportunity to talk to Frank, meet other people who might be of help. But I think that if anyone is likely to help you in your search, it's Frank."

And so they rode through the hot November sun, past newly shorn flocks of sheep grazing in fields that were starting to scorch. Adam rode in silence, sitting between Hugh and Joanna in the wagon. He was wearing brand-new clothes, and his hair had been slicked down. It had been explained to him where they were going and why, but Adam had not understood. What was a party, and why was it being given to him?

Hugh was also wearing his best clothes: a handsome dark-brown suede jacket over a white shirt with no tie, dark brown pants and boots polished to a sherry-colored shine; the familiar bush hat on his head. And Joanna was wearing a yellow satin dress with a matching yellow hat.

They had left Sarah at home; the question of bringing her had not even come up, though Sarah was already proving to be a good companion for Adam. A bed had been fixed up for her on the veranda, and Joanna had altered two of her own dresses to fit the girl. Sarah had begun to help take care of the cabin and to collect wild herbs and roots for Joanna, but mostly Joanna was training Sarah to look after Adam. She was patient with him, taking him into the woods and telling him stories about the animals that lived there—myths such as "How the Koala Lost His Tail," and "Why the Tortoise Has a Shell." She encouraged him to talk, to take his time and try to repeat words after her; although his progress was slow, he was starting to improve.

Joanna often caught the girl staring at her, and although Sarah always smiled and talked and seemed interested in Joanna's knowledge of healing, she remained an enigma. Joanna had hoped to learn about sacred Aboriginal things from Sarah; she had asked her about the singing, and the objects she had found at the cabin door—had even asked her what she was protecting Joanna from—but so far Sarah either did not understand or pretended not to understand Joanna's questions. But there was a dignity about her, and she seemed to have a special knowledge of natural things, such as knowing that it was going to rain even when the sky was cloudless.

"Pinky!" Adam cried suddenly, pointing.

Coming toward them down the road was Mr. Shapiro's gaily painted wagon, swaying and creaking, with pots and pans clanging on the sides. Pinky, the old horse, came to a halt alongside Westbrook's wagon before Mr. Shapiro reined her in.

"Good day to you, sir," the old peddler called, tipping his battered hat. "What a lucky coincidence to run into you like this. I was just on my way to Merinda. Here you go, Miss Drury," he said as he reached inside his coat. "I've brought you your mail."

"Thank you, Mr. Shapiro," Joanna said. Since there was no postal service in the Western District, bringing mail to one's neighbors was a courtesy practiced by everyone. Joanna read the address on the envelope. It was from the Church of England Mission headquarters, in Sydney—a response to her inquiry about her grandparents.

After Joanna had received letters from the various colonial governments requesting money, she had sent off the required fees, and now anxiously awaited the arrival of maps and records. She had also written to all the missionary societies she could locate. So far, five had replied: None had any record of the Makepeaces.

"Here you go, Adam," she said, handing him the envelope, as she usually did. "Would you like to open it for me?"

"Off to a party, are you?" said Mr. Shapiro. "I've seen others on the road. Must be big goings-on over at Lismore. There'll be lots of food, I reckon. And plenty of beer, too."

He smiled shyly, as if suddenly embarrassed by himself. No one knew Mr. Shapiro's story—he seemed to have been a part of the Western District since anyone could remember. People guessed his age at somewhere between seventy and ninety, and he spoke with traces of an accent. He didn't have a lucrative trade, and often he had to resort to asking for food, but he was known for his kindness. There were rumors of a wife and baby, long ago in the old country, who had been murdered by soldiers.

"Mr. Shapiro," Hugh said, "what kind of flowers are those?" He pointed at the bouquet in a bucket on the seat next to the old man.

"They're English primroses, Mr. Westbrook. Fresh out of Widow Barns's garden this morning, in payment for some thread."

"How much do you want for them?" Hugh asked, reaching into his pocket.

Mr. Shapiro's clouded eyes widened behind his thick spectacles. "For you, Mr. Westbrook, twopence."

"Here's threepence for your trouble, Mr. Shapiro. There you go."

The old man looked at the coins in his hand. Then he closed his fingers around them and said, "God rewards a generous man, Mr. Westbrook." Shapiro took up his reins and moved on.

Hugh passed the flowers to Joanna and took up his own reins. "They're for you," he said.

She looked at him.

"Hair, Joanna." Adam pointed to her head.

"All right," Joanna said, a little confused by Hugh's unexpected gesture. She handed the bouquet to the boy, taking the tiny flowers from him one at a time and tucking them into her chignon.

When she was finished, Adam handed her the opened envelope and she read the brief letter enclosed. To her disappointment, the people at the Church of England headquarters in Sydney said that they had no record of the Makepeaces having served in any of their Australian missions.

"Is it good news?" Hugh said.

"I'm afraid not. My grandparents apparently did not serve with the Church of England missions." She folded the letter into her purse. It would be put with others, in a growing file.

As they rode along the country lane, Joanna glimpsed homesteads through the trees, and Hugh told her their histories. Just a generation ago, he explained, the landscape through which they were riding had been as mysterious and unknown to Europeans as the landscape of the moon. When the first explorers reported what they had found here and the news reached England, where there was no "new" land, where it was all owned already and jealously guarded by an old aristocracy, there had been a great migration to the Australian colonies. They had come from England and Scotland and Wales, the Camerons and the Hamiltons and the MacGregors, with their broods of children and their threadbare dreams. They had fought the native Aborigines who had lived here for thousands of years, and pushed them away or killed them off; they cut down the forests and dammed the streams; and they introduced sheep and wheat. They had become rich. They had built mansions and their wives wore expensive gowns; they had formed hunt clubs and private gentlemen's clubs and forgot or lied about the fact that they had once been coal miners and street sweepers.

Now they lived on impressive-looking estates with impressive-sounding names, like Monivae and Barrow Downs and Glenhope, houses built in Georgian and Elizabethan and Gothic styles, some designed to reflect the country of origin of the owner—such as Kilmarnock's Scottish castle—others to showcase the taste of those who lived there, as in the Mediterranean "villa" that sat on Barrow Downs, and the vaguely Moorish curiosity Hugh said was inhabited by a branch of the Cameron family. No two houses in the district were alike, Joanna discovered, but all, in their way, looked as if they belonged someplace else in the world.

Even the gardens, what she could see of them, seemed to be made up of trees and flowers imported from England or Scotland or Ireland. She glimpsed rabbits and deer, which she had learned from Hugh were not native to the Australian continent, but had been brought over from Britain. There were birds, too, starlings and sparrows and goldfinches, which Joanna knew were not native to Australia. It struck her that the people living on these magnificent estates seemed determined to create the illusion that they lived, not in Australia, but in Suffolk or Yorkshire or Cork.

And Lismore, Joanna saw at last, was no exception. As Hugh guided the wagon off the main road and down a drive lined with elms, Joanna saw up ahead an English manor house that reminded her of the stately homes she had seen near Aunt Millicent's village. A formal English garden was laid out in front, and gardeners toiled with rakes and clippers and hoses in an attempt to keep the lawn an English green as it baked beneath the Australian sun.

There was a line of carriages in front, and Hugh maneuvered the wagon into a place among them, handing the reins to a boy who had come running up. They followed a flagstone path to the rear of the house, and came upon a vast, green lawn, where a party was in progress.

There were so many people scattered over the lawn, sitting at tables or standing beneath shady trees, drinking and eating and murmuring quietly among themselves, with children of all ages running about, that Joanna realized most of the wealthy families of the district must be represented here. Long, food-laden tables covered with white cloths were attended by uniformed maids. Thick cuts of beef and lamb sizzled over five large outdoor grills, and huge kegs of beer and wine filled an endless supply of glasses. Adults played croquet on one lawn, badminton on another, and for the children, there was a miniature merry-go-round driven by a donkey. Musicians played beneath a striped canopy. Joanna thought it looked more like a small fair than a garden party.

When she saw a beautifully dressed woman come toward them, she guessed that she must be Hugh's fiancée. And she did not look at all as Joanna had imagined. Unlike her brother, whom Joanna had met briefly in Melbourne, Pauline Downs was tall, with thick blond hair, and she was dressed, despite the heat, in a striking green velvet gown and matching feathered hat.

"Hugh darling," she said when she came up, taking his arm and kissing his cheek. "We've all been anxiously awaiting your arrival. Everyone is eager to meet your little boy."

"Pauline," he said. "I'd like you to meet Joanna Drury."

Joanna felt cold eyes meet hers. "How do you do?" Pauline said, then she bent down and said, "And you must be Adam. How do you do?" She held out her hand. "I'm going to be your new mother. What do you think of the party, Adam? All this is for you."

When Adam drew back, Joanna said, "Say hello, Adam. And give Miss Downs your hand." She nodded and added gently, "Go on, it's all right."

Pauline slipped a hand through Hugh's arm and said, "We must find Frank, he has been anxious ever since he received a telegram from

Melbourne. It seems your lanolin venture is going to prove very profitable."

"We have Miss Drury to thank for that," Hugh said. "It was her idea."

"Really?" Pauline said, her smile turning hard. She glanced at Joanna, her eyes flickering to the primroses in Joanna's hair. "How nice," she said, and turned her back. "Come along, we have to introduce Adam to his new friends."

A large man with a ruddy complexion suddenly appeared, saying in a booming voice, "There you are, Westbrook. I've been wanting to talk to you about that new wool-washing machine. I hear it's—"

"Not now, John," Pauline said. "Hugh is mine today. I want you to meet Adam, he's the guest of honor, you know."

As Hugh said, "You're welcome to come over anytime and take a look at the machinery, John," more people came up, asking to hear about Westbrook's latest innovation.

Joanna watched Hugh and Adam become the center of attention, with Pauline at their side. And suddenly she realized she had made a mistake in coming. Clearly she was out of place here, and not welcome.

She walked among the guests, who either did not acknowledge her or gave her curious looks, until, remembering the map Hugh had spoken of, she decided to go into the house. She entered the kitchen, which was crowded with maids and chauffeurs, who seemed to be having a small party of their own. They fell silent when she came in, and looked at her oddly. An older woman in a stiff black dress with a ring of keys at her belt, said, "May I help you with something, miss?"

Joanna saw how the others stared at her; one man even stood up and put his jacket on. Joanna said, "No, thank you," and quickly passed through and entered the house. As soon as the kitchen door closed behind her, the laughter and talk resumed.

Joanna found herself in a dark hallway, with rooms branching off either side. She walked down it until she came to an open door, and when she looked inside and saw shelves of books from floor to ceiling, deep leather furniture and a Turkish carpet, she realized she had found the library. Then she saw the map.

It was as Hugh had described it—a map of the entire continent of Australia, showing the coastal towns and cities and settlements, and the great blank in the center, which was over a thousand miles across. Joanna was suddenly excited as she examined it, hoping to see place names that might resemble Karra Karra, or the "Bo— Creek" that was written on the deed. She studied particularly carefully harbors and rivers where her grandparents might have landed, hoping that they had not traveled too far into the interior. But she found nothing even close to what she was looking for. She stared at the empty space in the center, where there were no names, rivers, landmarks indicated, as if a vast cloud engulfed it, hiding what lay below. Karra Karra could be somewhere in there, she thought disappointed.

When Joanna stepped back from the map, her gaze fell upon the desk below it, and she saw a piece of paper covered in familiar handwriting. It was a poem, written in pencil on the back of a dry-goods-store receipt. Joanna knew by now that Hugh wrote at odd moments, when he was inspecting fences, or mustering sheep, and that he wrote on whatever paper was handy. She realized that this must be his latest ballad; it was titled "The Swagman."

As she read it, the door to the library opened, and someone walked in.

"There you are, Miss Drury," Hugh said. "I've been looking for you. I see you found the map. Did you find anything on it?"

"I'm afraid not."

He saw what she had in her hand. "My poem. What do you think of it?"

"It's lovely," she said. "But I don't fully understand it. What, for instance, is a swagman?"

"Swagmen are men who roam the outback with all their belongings wrapped up in a swag—a blanket carried on their backs."

"And 'waltzing Matilda'?"

"Matilda is another word for swag. Waltzing Matilda means carrying the swag, or, in other words, vagabonding about."

"Why is it called that?"

"I have no idea. It goes back to the convict days."

They stared at each other across the sunlit library. Then Hugh said, "I've just been talking to Frank, who told me some good news. The day after you came down to the river, I began to wonder if there might not be a market for the lanolin that we wash out of the fleece. I discussed it with Frank—he knows every businessman from Adelaide to Sydney. He contacted two pharmaceutical companies that expressed an interest in our offer. They say they'll buy all the lanolin we produce!" He paused. "So I will have a profit this year after all. Thanks to you, Miss Drury."

Joanna was suddenly struck by how well Hugh fitted into these elegant surroundings. The homely cabin and muddy yard of Merinda seemed to have nothing to do with this tall man in the handsome suede jacket. She realized that here was a side of him she had not seen before—the gentleman grazier. And she thought: This is the kind of house he should have, this way of life.

"Shall we rejoin the party?" he said.

Hugh held out his arm and Joanna slipped hers into it.

"How is Adam getting along?" she asked as they left the library. "I was afraid that so many people might frighten him."

"Well, he really doesn't seem to know what to make of it all."

Out in the hall, Joanna noticed something she had not seen earlier—a curious painting hanging on the wall. She stopped and stared at it.

It was no ordinary painting done on canvas or wood. It looked like a large piece of tree bark on which concentric circles and wavy lines, clusters of dots and rows of dashes, had been painted.

Seeing her looking at it, Hugh said, "That's a bark painting. Frank told me once he bought it from an old Aborigine who came from one of the northern tribes."

The more Joanna stared at it, the less chaotic it became; shapes started to emerge. She could make out a human face; a woman with large breasts and a man with exaggerated genitals; a kangaroo with a baby in its womb; something that might be a tree, and clouds and a river, and finally, she saw something large and grotesque encompassing it all—a serpent, Joanna realized, that appeared to be about to devour everything.

"It's frightening," she said, stepping back.

"I guess it was meant to be frightening. The old man who sold it to Frank claimed it was a painting of something called a poison-song."

She gave Hugh a startled look. "A poison-song!"

"It was a way of punishing someone. The Aborigines had very strict codes of conduct, and anyone who broke one of their many laws and taboos was condemned to death. One way to die was by being 'sung.' Do you see the figures in the center of the painting? They represent all of creation—the humans and the animals, the trees and the rivers, the clouds, and so forth. And this figure, around the edge, is the Rainbow Serpent which is about to devour them all. A song-man or song-woman would be able to look at this painting and chant the poison-song that goes along with it. And they believe that whoever they 'sing up' will die."

Joanna felt herself go cold. "And *do* they die?" she asked.

"I've heard of stories in which they did. Poison-songs are known to be very powerful magic. The thing is, once a man has been 'sung' he can't reverse it. There is no medicine that can cure him, because doctors are helpless against the power of singing."

She looked at Hugh. "Could this be," she said, finding it difficult to speak, "could this be the poison my mother was afraid of? Had she heard a poison-song being sung—over her grandparents, or even herself, maybe? Was that what she witnessed as a child, what she could never remember? Mr. Westbrook, could a poison-song have killed my mother?"

"Oh, I doubt it, Miss Drury. You said she was very young at the time. She could hardly have understood what was happening."

Suddenly, Joanna remembered her grandfather's notes. "What if my grandfather recorded a poison-song? What if he sent it out of Australia with my mother, not realizing what he was doing? What if those papers I've been trying to decode are the poison-song that killed my mother?"

"Miss Drury," he said, "it's all superstition. Surely we're too civilized to believe that a song can kill someone." But even as he said it, Hugh heard the hollowness of his own words. His years spent in the outback, when very often his only companions were tribal Aborigines, had taught him that there were powers and mysteries that defied rational, or "civilized," explanations.

And then he was recalling the argument he had had two days ago with Ezekiel. The old Aborigine was claiming that Joanna should leave Merinda. "I see spirits around her, boss," Ezekiel had said. "She got strong power, strong magic. She upset the balance. The Ancestors tell me in dreams: make the girl go."

When Hugh had again told the old man that he was talking nonsense and that he didn't want to hear any more about it, Ezekiel had said, "Your mob got lice, boss, no wool clip. More bad things coming." And now apparently Ezekiel was telling the native station hands that they were working a bad-luck station. So far, four of Hugh's best workers had taken off, and the rest were getting nervous.

When he saw the fear in Joanna's eyes, how she stared at the painting, he suddenly realized that he couldn't let her find out what Ezekiel was saying, that he would have to keep the old man away from her. "Miss Drury," he said, touching her arm, "let's go and see what Adam is up to, shall we?"

When they stepped into the sunshine, Joanna was momentarily blinded, and she put her hand over her eyes. She was still seeing the painting in all its grotesque beauty. She couldn't get the images out of her mind, or the words "poison-song."

Pauline came to claim Hugh and as Joanna watched them walk across the lawn, she heard someone say her name.

She turned and saw Dr. David Ramsey coming toward her. He was wearing a dark green frock coat and black cravat; he was bareheaded; his hair shone red-gold in the sunlight.

"Miss Drury, how nice to see you here," he said.

"Hello, Dr. Ramsey."

"How are you? And how is Adam doing? Have you been able to get him to talk a little more?"

"Yes, a little," she said, searching the crowd for Adam, and seeing him with a group of children.

"Unfortunately, we know so little of the human brain, but surely your kindness and patience will help. He is lucky to have you, Miss Drury. Come, let's have a glass of champagne."

As they started across the lawn, Ramsey said, "I have been reading Darwin's *On the Origin of Species.* Are you familiar with it?"

"I haven't read it," Joanna said, suddenly feeling that she was being watched. "But I know about it. I believe my grandfather, whose whereabouts I am seeking, was at Cambridge at the same time as Darwin."

She looked at the people scattered around the lawn, sitting in chairs, or standing in groups. No one was looking at her, and yet she had a very strong feeling of being watched.

"I envy Mr. Darwin," Ramsey was saying. "It must be wonderful to know that you're actually making history. There is so much going on in science and medicine today, so many discoveries, so many great men. Pasteur, Lister, Koch—they will be remembered. My ambition, Miss Drury, is to make that kind of contribution to medicine."

And then she saw Ezekiel standing at the edge of the garden. He wore the familiar tattered shirt and dusty pants, and he stood so still that he could have been a statue, except that his long white hair and beard stirred in the breeze. He was watching her the same way he had watched her before, down by the river.

"Are you all right, Miss Drury?"

"Yes," she said, smiling. "Of course. Doesn't the sun feels good?" She turned away from Ezekiel's stare and saw that Adam was the center of attention in a small circle of people. They were making a fuss over him, and trying to put a party hat on his head.

"I wish they wouldn't crowd around Adam like that," Joanna said. "He still doesn't trust people, or crowds. Who is the pretty little blond boy talking to him?"

"That's Colin MacGregor's son, Judd, and that's Colin standing behind him. His father is some sort of Scottish noble."

Joanna looked at the darkly handsome man who was overseeing the boys' shy attempt to become friends. "Oh yes, Christina MacGregor's husband. And how is she?"

"If she's careful, she'll carry the baby to term. By the way, do you see that rather imperious lady over there, the one in black, who appears to be holding court?"

Joanna saw a woman of imposing stature, wearing a voluminous crinoline and dominating a circle of women who were seated on chairs and drinking tea.

"That's Maude Reed," Ramsey said. "She is what you might call the matriarch of the district—eight daughters, twenty-three grandchildren, and an odd number of great-grandchildren with, I believe, three more on the way. Mrs. Reed is the wife of that man over there, John Reed," Ramsey said, pointing to where Hugh was standing with Frank Downs and the large man who had met them when they first arrived.

Joanna saw Hugh glance in Ezekiel's direction, and then she saw him scowl suddenly. While David Ramsey continued to tell Joanna about the other guests at the party, she watched Hugh walk across the lawn, and go up to the old Aborigine. She couldn't hear what they were saying, but she thought Hugh looked angry. Ezekiel's face remained impassive; but he was shaking his head and gesturing.

"Dr. Ramsey," Joanna said.

"Please call me David," he said.

"David, do you see that old man over there?"

"Yes, Ezekiel. People around here use him as a tracker when they go hunting."

"Does he live here at Lismore?"

"Oh no, no one knows exactly where he lives. He just appears now and then, and people hire him. We don't know where he goes in between tracking jobs. Why?"

"Why is he staring at us?"

"I imagine he's curious."

Joanna saw how Ezekiel's face remained expressionless while Hugh was clearly angry. She wondered what they were arguing about; if it was because of her. She remembered the poison-song painting again, and the dreams. And her cold feeling returned.

"I was wondering, Miss Drury," Ramsey said. "Might I have your permission to call upon you sometime? I mean formally. For instance, there is going to be a Christmas Eve ball at Strathfield. You would do me a great honor if you would accompany me to it."

"I'm afraid I don't know if I shall be able to go. It might be better for me to be with Adam then."

"Well, perhaps a picnic some Sunday?"

Joanna looked into his pleasant face, at the green eyes framed by red-gold lashes, the splash of freckles across his cheeks, and she was struck by how young he seemed, although she judged he was at least five years older than she.

Then she saw Hugh returning to the party, and Ezekiel walking away through the trees. When Joanna saw Pauline go up to Hugh and slip her arm through his, she heard herself say, "Yes, David. A picnic sounds very nice."

Suddenly, Adam screamed. Joanna ran to him and took him in her arms. A man dressed in a clown suit was saying, "I didn't do anything. I was just trying to make the boy laugh."

"Oh, Adam," Joanna said. "It's all right. It's all in fun."

"Well really!" said Maude Reed, who came up with a swishing of her enormous crinoline. "Why would a great grown boy like that be afraid of a clown?"

"He doesn't understand," Joanna said. "He doesn't know about parties or clowns. He'll be all right though, won't you, Adam?"

"Miss Drury is right, Maude," another voice said, and Joanna turned to see Pauline coming through the cluster of people. "Come on now, Adam, let's have some ice cream. I'll bet you've never had ice cream before, have you? Miss Drury, would you care for something to eat?"

They walked to the buffet tables where cakes and puddings, salads and cold meats, cheeses and fruits were being overseen by servants, while chefs carved hams, roast beef, and venison. After giving Adam a dish of ice cream, which he tasted tentatively, and then began to eat in earnest, Pauline said, "Will you try some of this pudding, Miss Drury? I'm told it's made from a recipe that is uniquely Australian— something the convicts invented, I believe. Hugh tells me you're from India. Victoria must seem very alien to you. I have heard that India is so"—she paused—"well, so *barren*. Are you sure you will fit in here? After all, you will find life quite different in Australia. We of the Western District aren't like other people. It is always difficult for outsiders to adjust. Sometimes they simply cannot."

Pauline spooned small amounts of potato salad, chilled oysters, and slices of cold roast beef onto their plates.

"There was a young woman not too long ago," she said, "who came out from England. She was very much like you, in fact, young and inexperienced. She married one of our local graziers and she lasted exactly one year. She found she hated life here and went back to England on the very next boat."

"I am only temporarily in Victoria, Miss Downs," Joanna said. "I came to Australia to look into some things about my family. And I believe I have inherited some land."

"Indeed?" Pauline murmured. She saw that Adam's bowl was empty, so she set the plates down and said, "Come on, Adam, there is something I would like to show you. You, too, Miss Drury."

The three went into the house. "I am told that environment is so important in raising a child," Pauline said as they mounted the grand stairway. "I am only too familiar with the cabin at Merinda, very unsuited for a child. And that yard! You must agree that it is not the best place for a young person."

"Adam is used to living on a farm," Joanna said.

"Yes, but he won't be living on one any longer. As soon as Hugh builds our house, Adam will be living a more genteel way of life. Here we are." She opened a door and stood aside.

Joanna and Adam looked into a child's bedroom, with a canopied bed and dresser, flowered wallpaper, and sunlight streaming through the high dormer window. It was filled with toys—stuffed bears, wooden soldiers, a train set, an easel and paints, a rocking horse—everything a child could want.

"I bought these things myself," Pauline said. "Everything you see in here, I chose especially for Adam." She bent down and said, "What do you think of your new room, Adam?"

Joanna looked around the room. She wondered how the boy would adjust to such confinement, after so much freedom by the river.

"I want us to make friends as soon as possible, Adam," Pauline said to him. To Joanna, she said, "He will stay here at Lismore beginning today. He won't go back to Merinda after the party."

"But Mr. Westbrook said nothing to me about this."

"Hugh doesn't know yet, but he will agree with me. Adam and I must have some time to get used to each other."

"I understand that," Joanna said. "But Adam has had a lot of changes in his life recently. He has suffered a terrible loss, and other things we don't know about."

"Yes, I know. Hugh has explained everything. I intend to hire a private tutor who will give Adam lessons in how to speak properly. Would you like that, Adam?"

Joanna was horrified at the thought of Adam being kept in a schoolroom. And then another emotion gripped her as well: possessiveness—not only of Adam, but also of Hugh.

They returned to the buffet table, where Hugh and Frank and John Reed were helping themselves to English trifle and strawberries. "I tell you, Hugh," Reed was saying, "it's madness to think you can develop a breed of sheep that can be run in parts of Queensland and New South

Wales, which are frankly too hot and dry to run sheep. It's been tried, and no one's been successful so far."

Hugh said, "I intend to succeed."

"You Queenslanders are a stubborn lot."

Hugh smiled and said, "To be a Queenslander is to be a survivor."

John looked at Frank and said, "You've been awfully quiet today, Downs. That's not like you."

"Just have a few things on my mind, John." Frank had wanted to invite Ivy Dearborn to the party today, but Pauline had said no. Ivy was still refusing to go out with him, which baffled him, because she had put his picture up on the wall at Finnegan's. He didn't blame her for wanting to protect her reputation; he suspected she wanted to be treated respectably, not the way barmaids were usually treated. So what could be more innocent and respectable than a party for a little boy? But Pauline had been adamant about it, and Frank had backed down. If he had insisted and brought Ivy to the party, Pauline would have made her miserable, and then Frank might lose his chances with the woman altogether. But he was not giving up. The more she turned down his invitations, the more attractive she became. Frank found himself revising his initial impression of her as being rather plain and no one special. During the past weeks, on his frequent visits to Finnegan's pub, Frank had discovered that Ivy had a subtle attractiveness; she was desirable by virtue of being unavailable. But Christmas was coming, and he suspected that the right gift would win him some time with her.

John Reed said, "I say, Hugh, I saw you talking to Ezekiel a few minutes ago, and you didn't look pleased. What's the old devil up to now?"

Hugh looked at his drink and said, "Just sheep business, John."

"I think you should know, Hugh," Frank said, "that I overheard some of my station hands talking about Ezekiel going around saying that Merinda's come into some bad luck. What do you make of that?"

"I don't make anything of it," Hugh said, glancing at Joanna. "I had the bad luck to have a lice infestation just before shearing, I imagine that's what he's referring to."

"Oh, Miss Drury," Frank said to Joanna. "I hope you remember me. We met briefly in Melbourne. What did you ever find out about that deed?"

"Of course I remember you, Mr. Downs," she said, and then she told him about her visit to Hugh's lawyer in Cameron Town.

"Yes, he's right," Frank said. "Until you can determine which colony the deed was granted in, I'm afraid you've got a worthless document on your hands."

Joanna thought of her grandfather's coded papers, and the very strong possibility that the key to what she needed to know was contained in them. But the book Hugh had given her—*Codes, Ciphers and Enigmas*—had proven to be of no help. Whatever code the papers had been written in, it was not a commonly known one.

"Let me see what I can do," Frank said, as he took a small notepad out of his pocket. "As anyone will tell you, I love a mystery. If you will permit me to run a small item on this in my paper, maybe someone will read it and . . ."

Joanna watched as he wrote, and when she saw the lines and squiggles, she said, "What is that you are writing, Mr. Downs?"

"It's called stenography. I require everyone on my staff to know it."

"Stenography?"

"Yes, or shorthand, as some people call it. It's a way of writing rapidly by using symbols and abbreviations. There are various types of shorthand; this particular system was invented by a man named Pitman back in 1837. As you can see, it is very efficient. It enables a reporter to get a complete story down. Martin Luther wrote all of his sermons in shorthand, you know."

"May I?" Joanna said, and Frank handed the notebook to her. She drew the symbols she had come to know so well, symbols that had eluded even the detailed *Codes, Ciphers and Enigmas*. "Mr. Downs, would you happen to know this code?"

He looked at it, and said, "This is no code, Miss Drury. This is another form of shorthand. And it looks vaguely familiar, although I am not sure where I have seen it."

"Mr. Downs," Joanna said, excitement creeping into her voice, "my grandfather left some papers that were written in this shorthand. I believe that if I can translate them, I will be able to find out where my grandparents lived and where the land is that was deeded to them. Would you happen to know how I can find out which shorthand system his was?"

"I have a book on various shorthand systems that you are welcome to take home, Miss Drury. I also recommend that you write to the Shorthand Society of London, and send them a sample of it." Frank returned the notebook to his pocket and said, "I'll run your story in the Monday edition. Your identity will be kept a secret, of course. I'll simply state that if anyone has information regarding—what was their name?"

"John and Naomi Makepeace. They were here from 1830 to 1834, at a place called Karra Karra."

When Pauline noticed that Adam was looking sleepy, she said to him, "Why don't we go up to your room and you can take a little nap?"

Hugh said, "What room is that, Pauline?"

When she explained, Hugh said, "The boy's not staying here. He's going back to Merinda."

"But this is a much better place for him, darling."

"Merinda is his home, and that is where he is going to live."

"I think we should let Adam choose where he wants to live."

"We will not let the boy choose. He goes back to Merinda."

Pauline smiled graciously. "Well, all right, darling. After all, four months isn't very long. And then I shall be his mother."

As they left, with Hugh carrying the sleeping child, and a footman carrying the presents Adam had received, Joanna realized she was exhausted. The vision of the bark painting hung over her, as well as worry for Adam, and the fear of Pauline's cold manipulation. And she realized she was filled with an emotion she had never felt before—jealousy.

CHAPTER 8

Adam looked at the picture Sarah had drawn, of a bird in flight, and tried to describe what he saw. But when he put his lips together, the words would not come out. He said "W—" and gave up in exasperation.

Sarah gave him a long, thoughtful look. "Why don't you talk, little boy?" she said. "What spirit holds your tongue?"

He looked at her with apologetic eyes, and Sarah put her arm around his shoulders. "It's all right," she said.

They were sitting on the veranda, having their morning English lesson, which had been Sarah's idea. But it hadn't been as easy as she had thought it would be. Adam's difficulty in speaking wasn't the same as her own, which was the result of having lived at a Christian mission among Aborigines who couldn't speak English. Sarah knew that she would eventually speak as properly as Joanna, but Adam's problem, she had realized in the short time she had been trying to help him, stemmed from other, mystifying causes.

Adam looked at the picture again and tried very hard to form the words. He wanted to please Sarah. She was kind, and she never scolded him for not being able to say things. He wanted to say them; he even knew what it was he was supposed to say. But he couldn't get his mouth to work. It was just like the time when—

But he didn't want to remember. Something had happened, and he had tried to talk, but the words wouldn't come, and policemen in uniforms had gotten impatient with him, and Adam had cried, and they had gotten angrier, and then they had taken him away and put him alone on a ship.

He tried again. "Wallow," he said. "Swallow!" He looked at Sarah. "Swallow," he said, pointing to the picture.

"Yes," she said, hugging him. "Very good. Now tell me where the swallow is going—"

Suddenly, she froze.

Out in the yard a collie lay in the dust, swishing his tail at flies. It was a languid December morning, hot and somnolent, the earth dry in summer's fierce power. Sarah looked at the sky, and sent her thoughts up, trying to feel out what it was that had just come to her. She turned her gaze to the fields that stretched far away from Merinda to the eastern horizon. She thought: Something is happening.

"Sarah?" Adam said.

She looked at him; his voice had sounded too loud. Something was wrong, she could feel it.

"Sarah," Adam said, tugging at her skirt.

She closed her eyes and searched inward.

This had happened to her before, warnings suddenly sounding in her mind. Back at the mission, Old Deereeree, one of the women elders, had told Sarah that it was because someday she was going to be like her mother, who had had the Knowing.

But Sarah's "knowings" were often frustrating, incomplete; they were vague and unspecific. Old Deereeree had said that it was because Sarah's initiation had been interrupted. If she had been allowed to be fully initiated by the women elders, then her Knowing would be sharper and clearer, as her mother's had been. And so now, as she sat in the shade of the veranda, looking at the strange light around the yard and the buildings, Sarah did not know what it was she was sensing. Only that it was urgent. And that it had to do with Joanna.

Sarah thought about last night, how she had been awakened suddenly by a cry. She had peered through the window and had seen Joanna sitting up in bed, shaking. Sarah had remained there, watching Joanna pace back and forth in the darkness as if trying to drive away a bad memory. She had seen fear on Joanna's face, and she had wondered if Joanna had had a nightmare, and what it had been about.

"Adam," she said, rising and taking his hand. "Let's go for a walk."

As they headed toward the trees by the river, Sarah tried to measure her fear. Was this a real "knowing," or was it just her own apprehension about Joanna's visits to the ruins?

There was so much Sarah wanted to understand. If only she could talk to Old Deereeree. But Reverend Simms had forbidden Sarah to see the women elders. Old Deereeree knew everything. She would be able to tell Sarah how and why Joanna was different from other white women. Sarah had known that Joanna was different the first night she came to Merinda and saw her with the book, which Joanna read every night and sometimes wrote in.

Could it be that Joanna was a song-woman; that her mother had been a song-woman? Sarah knew that the book, which Joanna called a diary, contained the songs of Joanna's mother. Joanna read them every day, and Sarah believed she did this to keep her mother's Dreaming. That was how it would have been for Sarah, if she had finished her initiation—she would sing her mother's Dreaming, and add songs to it of her own, as Joanna was adding her own songs to the book, to be passed on eventually to her daughters. Of course, Sarah and Joanna had never talked about it. Joanna had never actually said that the book was her mother's Dreaming. But Sarah knew.

She wondered if Joanna had also inherited her mother's powers. She seemed to know which plants healed, and which were deadly. She could feel a person's wrist, and tell if the heart was strong or weak. Joanna had taken Sarah down to the river, and she had shown her the herbs and flowers growing there that drove sickness away. Was that not power, Sarah wondered, a very special power?

Sarah knew that her own mother had had the special powers of a song-woman, and she often sensed that she might have them too. But so far they were only whispers, like something brushing against her in the dark, and she wondered if, since she wasn't initiated, her powers would never be fully developed. They were supposed to come when a girl arrived at womanhood, with her first bleeding. But so far they had not.

When Sarah and Adam reached the trees, they slowed their pace.

"Sarah—" Adam began.

But Sarah put a finger to her lips. "Shh, you must be quiet."

She removed the shoes Joanna had given her, and crept barefoot into the woods. She found Joanna near the ruins, sitting on the ground beneath an ancient gum tree. Sarah saw that she was writing in her mother's book. Sarah remained very still, and watched.

"I have exhausted Mr. Downs's book on shorthand," Joanna wrote, unaware of being observed, "and there are no systems that remotely resemble the system my grandfather used. I have written to the Shorthand Society in London. I suppose that if I could find Patrick Lathrop, there is a chance that he might be familiar with this peculiar shorthand. I need to find a key to my grandfather's life, and therefore to my mother's. I had a terrible dream last night, about the frightening bark painting I saw at Lismore. I awoke in fear and could not get back to sleep. It was a strange dream—I was standing at a cave; I was naked, and Mr. Westbrook was walking toward me. I felt intense desire for him. I wanted him to take me into his arms. But then a serpent appeared—the one in the bark painting—huge and monstrous, and I realized that it was going to kill Mr. Westbrook. I tried to cry out, to warn him. But I had no voice. I tried to run toward him, but I couldn't move. I woke then, badly shaken, and consumed by a feeling of dread. Was the dream a premonition, like the one about the *Estella* being becalmed? Is my presence here at Merinda somehow a threat to Mr. Westbrook? If only I could find the source of this trouble!"

Joanna had received letters from the other colonies, with maps and reports from the Records Offices, but the maps, although highly detailed, had shown no place called Karra Karra, and the records officials reported that they had no evidence of the Makepeaces having ever lived in that particular colony. Now Joanna tried to concentrate on the elusive Patrick Lathrop, her grandfather's classmate at Cambridge.

She resumed writing: "Mr. Westbrook has offered to contact a Mr. Asquith, who works in the Office of Aboriginal Affairs in Melbourne. He says that it is possible that a man closely associated with the governing of the natives might have some knowledge of them. I had hoped that Sarah could be a source of native information, but she remains reticent on the subject of her people. I do know one thing: Sarah grows increasingly disturbed by my presence here at the river. I think perhaps she does not like me to come to this spot by the ruins. I still catch her spying on me from a distance. Last night, when I awoke from my nightmare, I felt her watching me from the window. I wanted to talk to her about the dream, ask her about the meaning of the serpent, the cave. But then I would have had to describe the rest of the dream to her, about my desire for Hugh Westbrook."

Joanna looked up through the trees, and she could just see, between the cluster of twisted trunks streaked gray and red and pink, the sweeping plains of Merinda, yellow now beneath the scorching sun. She searched every rise and fall of that grassy sea, taking in the solitary Murray River gums dotting the landscape, the flocks of grazing sheep, the occasional rider on horseback, and she wondered if Hugh Westbrook was out there. The nightmare came back to her again, in all its intensity—the fear and the sexual longing.

Joanna was troubled that her desire for Hugh was continuing to grow. The ache never left her, it was like an all-consuming hunger in every part of her body—in her heart, her fingertips, her thighs—the need to touch him, to feel him. She recalled how she had thought him attractive when she had first seen him on the pier, two months ago. Now she was struck by how much more handsome he had become; she would find herself studying his face, the line of his jaw, the straightness of his nose, and she would feel her passion deepen.

Was she endangering him by staying at Merinda? she wondered. Had the dream last night been a warning that something bad was going to happen? Should she leave? She had heard that Ezekiel was going about saying that she was bad luck for Merinda, and that because of her some of the Aboriginal stockmen were leaving. Joanna had only agreed to come here to help Adam; she didn't want to be the cause of trouble. She recalled the dark look she had seen on Hugh's face when Bill Lovell had reported two more Aboriginal station hands gone. Hugh had said nothing about it to her, but when she thought about the day of Adam's party at Lismore, when she had seen Hugh and Ezekiel apparently having an argument at the edge of the garden, she wondered if she really was bringing bad luck to Merinda.

But where would she go?

She thought of Dr. David Ramsey, who had said, "I had the opportunity to work with the new Nightingale nurses, Miss Drury. And they are indeed elevating nursing to a very respected profession. It would behoove a physician like myself to have such a woman as his partner. And I was thinking, Miss Drury, that with your knowledge of natural remedies, and mine of medicine, you and I could make a considerable team."

A kookaburra laughed suddenly overhead, startling her. Joanna looked up to see a sharp eye glinting down at her.

She thought again of Hugh, and how he had appeared the day before, when he had ridden into the yard. She wondered what it would be like to be married to such a man, to know that when he came home at night, he was coming home to her.

She heard a noise, and looked around. She held her breath and listened, searching the clearing. She could see only the trunks of old eucalypts, shedding their white-and-gray barks, and the moss-covered Aboriginal ruins. She had a strong feeling of being watched.

A kind of unearthly stillness seemed to have fallen over the glade. Even the gurgling water in the stream seemed muted. A family of salmon-pink cockatoos fluttered about in the branches overhead, yet Joanna didn't hear them. She was aware only of the golden sunlight dappling the leaf-covered ground, and the thumping of her heart.

"Who's there?" she called out.

There was no reply.

"Sarah?" she called in a louder voice. "Adam?"

No response.

Joanna moved forward a few steps. She saw no one, yet still she felt someone was there.

"Who are you?" she said. "Please."

Then there came a rustling beyond the trees, followed by a queer-sounding footstep.

Joanna frowned. It hadn't seemed like a human sound.

She continued forward through the trees, cautious, listening. She paused and gazed ahead, seeing before her only the rolling plains of Merinda, an ocean of yellow summer grass stretching away to the mountains. She looked to the right, toward the homestead buildings, and then to her left, where she saw—

Joanna caught her breath and stared. "Hello," she said.

Two large brown eyes, heavily fringed with lashes, blinked at her.

"Hello," Joanna said again, transfixed. She had never been so close to a kangaroo before.

It was a large, blue-gray doe, almost as tall as Joanna, and she stood just a few yards away, resting back on her tail and hind legs, with her arms crossed over her chest. Peeking over the lip of her pouch was the face of a baby kangaroo, what Joanna had heard called a "joey."

They stood frozen, staring at each other. Joanna was afraid to move, afraid she might send the animal away. She was spellbound to be so close, to see in such detail the gentle colorings, the soft grain of the fur, the twitching whiskers. She looked at the joey. He was huge and seemed barely to fit inside his mother's pouch. She watched in fascination as the pouch rippled with his movements, as if he were cramped and ready to jump out.

"Aren't you lovely," Joanna said.

The kangaroo blinked, then turned, languidly fell onto her front paws and loped off toward the billabong. Mesmerized, Joanna followed.

The doe made her way slowly toward the creek, her enormous legs sweeping up and down, carrying her and her heavy burden along. When she neared the water's edge she paused. Joanna walked around her, staying well away, and watched as the kangaroo did a strange thing. She bent low to the ground, as if to graze, and reached down to the joey. The pouch seemed suddenly to give way, and the baby kangaroo came tumbling out.

Joanna stood motionless as she watched the joey wobble around on ungainly legs. The doe hovered protectively over her young, watching its every move. It bent down, trying to graze on the marsh grass, and fell over. It got up again, but didn't seem to know how to coordinate its cumbersome tail with its legs. The joey looked at Joanna, but remained very still.

Joanna smiled. Plucking a handful of the rich grass, she held it out. She took a step toward the joey, and then another. She came close enough to touch it. She dropped the grass and stepped back. The joey looked at it, then he nibbled it.

Finally the doe made a series of gentle clicking sounds, and the baby came to her. She licked his fur and scratched him between the ears, and helped him climb back inside the pouch. Then the kangaroo fell onto her front paws and loped away through the trees.

Joanna watched them go, unaware that other eyes, hidden behind the trees, were fixed on her.

Sarah, wide-eyed and trembling, still holding Adam's hand, slowly backed away.

When Joanna saw Hugh in the yard, saddling his horse, she came down the veranda steps.

"I'm leaving for Melbourne now, Miss Drury," he said, as he strapped saddlebags to the horse. "I'll be back in two weeks, in time for Christmas. Is there anything you need from the city?"

She hesitated. She wondered if she should talk to him about leaving Merinda. Last night's dream continued to trouble her, her fear that it might be a premonition. But she said only, "No, thank you. I can't think of anything."

"I'll stop in at the city library and see what I can find. There is also a legal firm there I have dealt with before, I'll ask them about your deed. Will you be all right, Miss Drury, here alone?"

"I'm hardly alone, Mr. Westbrook. I have Adam and Sarah, and Mr. Lovell." She looked around. "Bill, have you seen Sarah?"

"Not since this morning, miss."

Joanna frowned. "She's never disappeared for this long before. I wonder where she's gone?"

Adam came running down the veranda steps. "Joey! Saw a joey!"

Hugh caught him up and swung him in the air. "What's this about a joey?" Hugh said.

"We saw a baby kangaroo down by the river this morning," Joanna said.

He looked at her. "All by itself?"

"Oh no, with its mother."

"I hope you didn't get too close."

"Very close, as a matter of fact. I gave the baby some grass to eat."

He stared at her. "Miss Drury, you could have been killed. Did the mother see you?"

"Oh yes. And she did a curious thing. She let the joey out of her pouch, and then she took him back in, although he seemed far too big."

Hugh exchanged a glance with Lovell. "You saw a joey being born?"

"Oh, he wasn't being born, he was quite grown."

"Miss Drury, kangaroos are born twice. The first birth is the same as for other animals, but then the joey stays in the pouch for about eight months of suckling. When the mother decides he's ready, she lets him out of the pouch and helps him into the world a second time. You witnessed that second birth."

"Did I?" she said.

"I saw it, too!" Adam said.

Bill scratched his head and said, "I don't reckon I've ever met anyone who's seen that. And I know men who've witnessed some strange sights."

Hugh scowled and finished strapping down his saddlebags. "I don't want you doing things like this again, Miss Drury. When a kangaroo feels threatened, it will attack. Especially a mother with a baby. Those hind legs can be lethal."

He looked at her; she had come outside without her hat. He smiled and said, "Just promise me you'll be more careful."

She stood back and watched him ride off.

Bill Lovell removed his hat, wiped the inside with a handkerchief, replaced it on his head and said, "Well, I'd better get over to the stable, I've got a mare about to foal. If you need me—"

"Foal!" said Adam. "Let me see!"

"I don't know—" Joanna began.

"It's all right, Miss Drury, let him come and watch. Come on then, Adam. Would you like to come, too, miss?"

"Yes, of course. Let me go and get my hat."

Back inside the cabin, Joanna paused. The way Hugh had looked at her when she had told him about the kangaroo . . .

A shadow suddenly filled the open doorway, and Joanna turned. "Sarah!" she said. "Where have you been?"

"Come," the girl said, taking Joanna by the hand. "Come with me."

"What is it?"

As they went past the stable, Joanna called to Bill that she would be back in a few minutes.

When she and Sarah came to the Aboriginal ruins by the river, Sarah sat down, and gestured for Joanna to sit with her.

"I saw you," Sarah said after a moment. "I saw you with kangaroo and joey."

"Yes, I know," Joanna said. "Adam told me. Sarah, why did you bring me here?"

"There is something I must tell you," the girl said. "Whitefella never see joey being born. Kangaroo-spirit never allow whitefella to watch. Only people of the Kangaroo totem. This place is sacred to Kangaroo Dreaming."

Joanna looked at the stately Red River gums, the pearly surface of the billabong. She felt her surroundings shift. Something had happened—was happening.

"You come here, to this forbidden spot, many days," Sarah said, "but you don't die. You watch joey being born, and you don't die. You walk on this spot, and Kangaroo is not angry. You have great magic, great power. You belong to Kangaroo Clan."

Joanna stared at the girl. "But I'm not Aboriginal, Sarah. How can I belong to the Kangaroo Clan?"

"Kangaroo-spirit come to me in a dream, tell me you have Kangaroo Dreaming. Tell me to tell you about your Dreaming. You must know your Dreaming."

Joanna looked at the girl. "But I wasn't born in Australia," she said.

Sarah closed her eyes, seeming to turn inward. Then she said, "All people have totems. Whitefella, too. The kangaroo gives you your sign. You see joey's birth. You are special to Kangaroo Dreaming."

Sarah opened her eyes, and said, "Do you know . . . where is your songline?"

"My songline? I don't know. I don't think I have a songline."

Sarah said, "Everyone has a songline. Where is your mother's songline?"

"I don't know," Joanna said. "Somewhere here in Australia? Why do you want to know?"

"Because you are following a songline. That is what brought you here."

"I'm not even sure what a songline is, Sarah. How can I be following it? Explain songlines to me."

Sarah said: "This place belongs to Kangaroo Dreaming. Kangaroo Songline runs through Merinda from there. . . ." She pointed northward. "From far away. In the Dreamtime, Kangaroo Ancestress traveled from great distance to come here, and she goes on, and she dies somewhere over there." She pointed southward. "That is what a songline is. It is a spirit-line, it is time-line. It is now-and-yesterday-line."

Joanna stared at the girl. "Sarah, how do you know that the Kangaroo Songline comes through here? I don't see anything."

"Look," Sarah said, pointing to a grassy hillock farther upriver. "That is where Kangaroo Ancestress slept. Do you see her great hind legs, her long tail, her very small head?"

Joanna squinted. At first she couldn't see anything, but then she thought she could just make out the outline of a kangaroo in the hill—or imagined that she could.

Suddenly, the girl began to chant.

Joanna said, "What are you doing?"

"Singing. We will sing up Kangaroo Dreaming."

"I don't understand."

Sarah drew in the dirt with a stick—lines and circles and dots. She said, "This is the songline of the Kangaroo Ancestress. She comes from here, you see? And she goes there. Do you see?"

But Joanna saw only lines and circles and dots.

The girl's voice wove a spell; the heat of the afternoon lay heavily upon the woods. Joanna began to feel herself become disembodied; the trees and river began to seem illusory. Something dream-like was settling over her. Sarah seemed somehow to grow old before her. She sang words that Joanna didn't understand, in a rhythm that invaded her; she felt it in her veins, she saw it behind her eyes, old words, older than time, chanting, telling, singing up the past.

Joanna closed her eyes. She felt hot, heavy. She felt as if she moved in a dream. Suddenly, she saw raw red mountains and fire spewing up from the earth, and birds in flight in great massive flocks, and human silhouettes, tall and strong against the sky, loping across a bleak landscape, spears thrust up, arms swinging down in an ancient cadence. And then: gigantic creatures, leaping in graceful bounds across the scene, with great hindquarters and small heads—kangaroos in huge numbers massed across the land, blackening the horizon, sweeping, vaulting across the flat red plains. And the human figures, following, watching and revering.

The afternoon sun beat down through the trees; flies and mosquitoes filled the air with buzzing and droning. Joanna tried to keep her thoughts clear. How am I able to see these images? she wondered. And then she was recalling a passage in her mother's diary, another of the perplexing memory dreams: "I dreamed last night of kangaroos, great herds of them sweeping across a red plain. The red mountain is there again, the one that visits me in other dreams. And I see the dark outlines of people against a red sun. Could I possibly have once witnessed such a fantastic scene?"

When Sarah was finished singing, Joanna said, "What can you tell me about the Rainbow Serpent?"

Sarah said, "The Rainbow Serpent is very powerful—belong to women's secrets, to women's Dreamings."

"Do women have separate Dreamings?"

"Yes," Sarah said. "Women have their own songlines—more powerful than men's, because we have life in us. I can tell you this, Joanna, because you are a woman. Boys have many trials before they become men. They suffer cutting and bleeding. But girls do not, because life is already within them. They become women on their own." She paused, then she looked at Joanna and said, "My mother was a song-woman. She kept women's secret myths and rites, and she sang women's ceremonies. If the white man had not come, I would be a song-woman, too."

"Are you also a member of the Kangaroo Clan?"

"No," Sarah said. "My ancestor was the Fur Seal, and so I have the Fur Seal Dreaming, which is far from here. Someday I will follow my songline. I will walk in the Ancestor Tracks and find my Dreaming."

"You say your ancestor was the Fur Seal," Joanna said. "Do you mean that you are descended from a fur seal?"

Sarah smiled and said, "In the Dreamtime, the first Fur Seal ancestor sprang from the southern waters. She sang herself into existence, and then she sang the islands and the rocks into existence. She taught her children the Fur Seal Song. The song was passed on, from generation to generation. The same song, down through time, and it came to me."

"But," Joanna said, "why aren't you a fur seal now?"

"Because we changed. We came up on the land and slowly we became human. But my Dreaming is still Fur Seal, even though I am human. Do you know Ezekiel, the old tracker? He has the Emu Dreaming. And Old Deereeree at the Mission, she has the Cockatoo Dreaming. We come from these Ancestors. Ezekiel may never eat emu or wear emu feathers. Old Deereeree may never eat cockatoo. And I may never kill a fur seal, or eat her flesh, or wear her fur."

Joanna grew thoughtful. "I'm sorry," she said, "but I still don't understand what the Dreaming is."

"The Dreaming," Sarah said, "connects us to mothers who came before us, and to daughters who have yet to be born. My mother sang me her Dreaming, just as her mother did before her, and all the way back to when the Ancestors sang the first songs. I will sing to my daughters my Dreaming, and so they will be connected through me to all their previous mothers, all the way back to the Fur Seal Dreaming."

Joanna said, "That is not the way it is with my people. My mother never sang me her Dreaming."

Sarah smiled. "But she did. You have your mother's Dreaming. It is in the book you write in."

"You mean her diary?"

"Yes, it is her songline. And you put your songs into it. You continue her Dreaming. You must prepare this for your own daughter."

Joanna was spellbound. When Hugh had explained songlines to her, she had imagined that they were physical things, like roads carved through forests and marked with signposts. But she was beginning to understand that they were far more—that they could be something as simple as a diary, or letters exchanged between a mother and her daughter. Songlines were the passing along of spirit and wisdom and feelings, like soul-links. Lady Emily had once observed in her diary, "When I write about my mother, I feel as though she is with me, alive still, even though I can't remember her." And Joanna began, for the first time, to understand the meaning of "singing up creation."

"Where is your mother now?" she asked Sarah.

"She ran away from the mission, to go to her clan. But a song-man said she had told whitefella our secrets, so he sang her bad magic."

Joanna stared at her. "Do you mean a poison-song?"

"Yes."

"And . . . did she die?"

"I don't know. Maybe she will come back. Song-women do."

"Sarah," Joanna said slowly, "my mother spoke of poison. I wonder if perhaps she died because of a poison-song. But it would have been sung to her mother, I think—not to her—to my grandmother."

Sarah said, "Grandmother spirit is very powerful."

"When you look at me, Sarah," Joanna said, "do you see bad luck around me? Do you see a poison-song?"

"Wait," Sarah said suddenly, holding up her hand. She looked around, and then slowly got to her feet. Joanna also stood, and saw Ezekiel coming through the trees. He was carrying a boomerang, similar to the ones Joanna had seen hanging in the study at Lismore. He came up to Sarah and said, quietly: "Taboo."

Then he turned to Joanna and said, "Go away. This place is not for you. You hear taboo things. You bring bad magic."

Sarah said, "No, Old Father, it is not taboo," and there was a flicker of surprise in the old man's eyes.

"You speak taboo things, child," he said.

Joanna saw that Sarah was shaking; and there was a look of both fear and defiance in her eyes. She also saw by the way Ezekiel was looking at Sarah that he was not used to being defied.

"Bad things come now," he said, and although Ezekiel didn't raise his voice and his face was mask-like Joanna sensed his anger, and his own special fear. Joanna thought that he was all the more formidable for his quietness.

He looked at Sarah and Joanna for another moment, then he continued on into the woods.

CHAPTER 9

C hristmas! Pauline thought. A time for gifts and carols, for friends and mistletoe and spiced wine. A time, she thought as she smiled at her reflection in the mirror, for seduction.

She looked again at the clock over her bedroom fireplace. It was eight-thirty, and Hugh had said, before he left for Melbourne two weeks ago, that he would pick her up at nine o'clock tonight for the Christmas Eve ball at Strathfield. She had received a telegram from him three days ago, when he had left Melbourne. He would be at Merinda now, getting ready.

Just as Pauline was getting ready.

She couldn't stop smiling at herself in the mirror. Hugh was going to have a surprise. He did not yet know it, but Pauline had decided that tonight, and not a night three months from now, was going to be their wedding night.

She was wearing the peach-satin peignoir that was part of her trousseau. Her ball gown was still laid out on the bed, the bustle and petticoats still hanging in the wardrobe.

The plan to seduce Hugh had come to her that morning, when she had wakened to sultry December sunshine. She had lain in bed, awash in a sea of perfumed satin sheets, savoring the after-effects of an erotic dream she had had about Hugh. She had ached for him, wishing he were in bed with her, wondering how she was going to last another three months until her wedding day. And it was then that the idea had come to her. The answer was simple: She wasn't going to wait.

But there was a dispassionate, pragmatic side to her reasoning as well. Pauline had decided that Joanna Drury was a real threat. She couldn't stop thinking about how Joanna had looked at the garden party. Those primroses in her hair! What an unsubtle ploy! Pauline thought. But a clear sign that Miss Drury was out to get Hugh. Pauline had decided then to wage a real campaign against her. After tonight, after her seduction of Hugh, Pauline's victory would be guaranteed

It was hot, the air heavy with the perfume of gardenias and mimosa. Pauline felt the satin whisper against her bare skin. She moved her hand along her thigh, and thought about her plan. The servants had all been given the night off, with the exception of Elsie, her lady's maid, who was in on the conspiracy. When Hugh arrived, Elsie was to bring him upstairs. He would be expecting to find Pauline in her gown, ready for the ball. Instead, he would find her just as she was now, seductively dressed, ready for his embrace. It was going to be perfect. He would not be able to resist; and afterward, Hugh would be hers forever.

When there came a knock at the door, Pauline gave a start. She looked at the clock again. Hugh was early.

But it was Frank, dressed in evening clothes. "I just came by to say good-night. I'm off to Finnegan's."

"You're not going to the ball?"

"I have other plans. There's going to be a private party at Finnegan's. Just us bachelors," he said with a wink.

Pauline knew what her brother was up to. She had seen the diamond bracelet he had secretly purchased and wrapped in gold paper. "It sounds like a rather dreary way to spend Christmas Eve," she said in a teasing tone.

Frank said, "You never know," thinking about the private room he had reserved at the Fox and Hounds Inn. His plan was to wait for a discreet moment to give Ivy Dearborn her Christmas gift. And when she saw it, she would be unable to resist his invitation to a late-night supper.

He looked at Pauline. "I thought you were expecting Hugh at any minute. Why aren't you dressed?"

"You will be here for Christmas dinner tomorrow, won't you?" she said, ignoring his question. "Surely even Finnegan will want to spend Christmas Day with his family."

"I'll be here," Frank said as he went to the window and looked out. The glass, imported from England, was old and splintered the hot moonlight into tiny prisms. He wondered what Miss Dearborn was doing for Christmas dinner. Where did barmaids go, on such days?

"What do you know about her?" Frank had asked Finnegan a few days ago. "Where did she come from?"

"Don't know," Finnegan had said. "She just showed up one day and said she needed a job. Now, any woman can work a bar, Frank. And I saw that she was no beauty, and I know my customers like to look. But she showed me some drawings she had made, and I saw potential in that. I'm glad now that I hired her. She's cheerful and works hard, hasn't had a sick day in four months, and she's not the sort to give my place a bad name—not like Sal over at Facey's, with her fifteen-minute bed in the back room."

They had had the conversation on the day Frank had gone into the pub and had been shocked to see Ivy with red and swollen eyes, as if she had been crying. He had been further surprised to find himself suddenly full of rage—against whomever or whatever had hurt her, and rage, too, at his inability to help her.

As he surveyed Lismore's gardens bathed in the light of the December moon, Frank realized that he felt sad, an emotion he rarely experienced.

"What is it, Frank?" Pauline said. He heard the swish of satin, and felt her hand on his shoulder. "Something is troubling you. Is it the expedition?"

That was part of it. Frank had received word the day before from the rescue team he had sent in search of the expedition that had hauled a boat to the Never Never. They had found all members of the expedition dead, with the exception of one man, who appeared to have gotten away. Apparently they had been massacred by Aborigines, and Frank felt responsible. The expedition had been his idea, funded by his money. Now he vowed personally to take care of the men's widows and families.

"You'll send another expedition, Frank," Pauline said, "and next time they'll be successful. They'll find the inland sea, and they'll name it after you."

"Not with the Aborigines out there, we won't."

"Why did the blacks kill them?"

"Apparently they walked on a sacred site or something."

"That will all end. Such incidents are becoming rarer and rarer. Someday soon, the whole continent will be safe for white people."

"Yes," Frank said. "But at what expense?"

Pauline looked at her brother. "Frank," she said, "you're in a strange mood. What is it? It's not just the expedition that's on your mind, is it?"

Why couldn't he get anywhere with Miss Dearborn? And why did he care? They exchanged words over the bar; she laughed at his jokes. And sometimes, when he took a glass from her, their fingers touched. Why couldn't he get her out of his mind? Why couldn't he go back to Melbourne, where he should be right now, and take care of his newspaper? Frank had had plenty of women in his time, and he didn't fool himself, he knew it was his money they were attracted to, and not him. But Miss Dearborn seemed attracted to neither.

Was there perhaps a husband somewhere? Was she a runaway wife? Was Dearborn her real name even? He thought again about her tear-stained face, how she had smiled, trying to hide a pain that he could only guess at. It infuriated him to think that perhaps one of the patrons—one of his own friends—might have insulted her. What had someone done or said to make her cry?

Suddenly he was thinking of the diamond bracelet in his pocket. When he had bought it he thought it was beautiful, a compliment to Ivy. But now it seemed to be too much, too gaudy, and so obvious in its purpose that it might seem an insult to her. What on earth had he been thinking! He couldn't possibly give her such a thing—out of the blue like this.

"Pauline," he said, turning. "What do women want?"

Her eyebrows rose. "The same thing men want, I suppose. Happiness, success—"

"No," he said, walking away from her. It was nearly time to be getting over to Finnegan's, and he suddenly no longer felt he had anything he could offer to Miss Dearborn that she would accept. "I mean, supposing you were a woman who had nothing. What would you like to receive as a gift?"

"If I had nothing?" she said. "Then I would want everything!" When she saw his scowl, she said more gently, "Women don't really want *things*, Frank. If a woman cares for you, she'll want only you."

But he had been offering himself to Ivy for three months, and so far she had not accepted.

Pauline didn't know much about her brother's latest interest, but she was beginning to see that it was more than his usual passing flirtation. She was sorry to see him so distressed when she was so happy with Hugh. "What do you know about her?" she said.

"She's a barmaid."

"Then give her the one thing other men won't give her."

"What's that?"

"Respect."

Frank stared at his sister. He thought about the diamond bracelet, and the private room he had reserved at the Fox and Hounds Inn. And then he remembered something about Ivy: she always wore a small gold crucifix around her neck. Suddenly he knew what he was going to do.

"Thank you, Pauline," he said, kissing her cheek. "And a Merry Christmas to you. Let's hope both our Christmas wishes come true."

Pauline laughed as she closed the door behind him. She had no intention of depending upon wishes. Tonight she was going to make sure her dream came true.

Hugh was only a mile from Merinda, riding through the moonlit countryside, when he saw something at the side of the road that made him draw his horse and packhorse to a halt.

Mr. Shapiro's wagon was tilted in a ditch, with Pinky still harnessed to it, calmly grazing. Hugh looked inside, but the old peddler was not there. He looked around at the fields that lay like platinum counterpanes over the landscape. There was no sign of Mr. Shapiro.

As he mounted his horse and continued on his way, Hugh made a mental note to send word to the constable in Cameron Town.

When he arrived in the yard, finding it deserted and still, he glanced toward the cabin, where golden light spilled from its only window. He hesitated, then decided to go on to the bunkhouse and bathe and change for the Strathfield Christmas ball before letting Miss Drury know he was home.

He had the bunkhouse to himself. The station hands had either gone to a Christmas party at Facey's on the highway, or home to families. Hugh took care in dressing. One of the purposes for his trip to Melbourne had been to stop at a tailor's and pick up evening clothes he had been measured for months ago. Pauline had been with him; she had chosen the cloth and the cut of the suit, and the red satin lining for the opera cape. When he was dressed, and he saw himself in the mirror, he was struck with the feeling of looking at a stranger. How curious it was to see himself in such an outfit, complete with silk top hat and a black-pearl stick pin, also picked out by Pauline.

As he gathered up the parcels he had brought from Melbourne, he remembered Mr. Shapiro's wagon at the roadside, and wondered where the old peddler had gone to.

Inside the cabin, Joanna was preparing a Christmas cake, while Adam and Sarah sat at the table, making drawings. When Mr. Shapiro the peddler had stopped at Merinda a few days ago, he had complained of a headache and Joanna had given him some willow-bark tea. In return, he had given Adam and Sarah a paint box, and Sarah was using the watercolors to help Adam. The window was open to the warm summer night, and the aroma of spiced cider filled the air. As Joanna stirred dates and nuts into the cake batter, she first listened to Sarah go over words with Adam, and then she looked at the door, anticipating Hugh's visit. She had heard him ride into the yard a short while ago; she expected to see him at any moment.

"That's a nice farmhouse you paint," Sarah said to Adam. "You put people in it now."

But Adam said, "No. No people."

Joanna glanced at the door again, both anxious to talk to Hugh and fearful of it. Since the encounter with Ezekiel by the river two weeks ago, and the nightmare about the poison-song painting that hung in the hall at Lismore, Joanna had wrestled with the idea of leaving Merinda. Her feeling of dread was growing; she sensed that something bad was about to happen.

Finally, there was a knock at the door. Joanna paused to dry her hands, and to try to hide her nervousness before seeing Hugh.

"Hello," he said, standing on the threshold with packages in his arms. "Merry Christmas."

Joanna stared at him. She had never seen him dressed this way. The top hat and opera cape made him seem taller, more broad shouldered. The black tail coat and striped trousers gave him a worldly elegance and sophistication. His handsomeness caused her almost physical pain. How could she possibly leave?

"Hello, Mr. Westbrook. Welcome home."

He couldn't take his eyes off her. She was wearing a pale pink gown with an apron over it. Her sleeves were rolled up, there was flour on her hands, and her cheeks, he noticed, burned hotly. He thought that she had never looked more beautiful.

Adam suddenly said, "No, no," and quickly removed something from the table. Joanna smiled and said, "May we step outside, Mr. Westbrook?"

After she closed the door behind them, she said quietly, "Adam has made you a present, and he doesn't want you to see it yet. I must warn you, you might not be able to identify it. It's a pipe holder."

"But I don't smoke."

"He saw it in a magazine, and he decided you must have one. He's worked on it all day. How was your journey, Mr. Westbrook?"

"I stopped by the Land Office in Melbourne, and gave them the details in your deed. I thought that if the land is in Victoria, they might be able to locate it with the few clues the deed provides. We should be hearing from them in a few weeks. Unfortunately, inquiries at the library didn't produce any results, but I did leave a request to forward any information that might come along about a place called Karra Karra."

"Thank you," Joanna said. "I appreciate everything you've done." She wanted to say more, tell him about her apprehensions and her fears, and that she had been thinking about leaving. But she didn't know how to begin.

"How is Adam?" Hugh asked.

"He's talking a little more. Sarah is very good with him. But we still can't get him to talk about his mother, or what happened."

"I'll be taking him to Lismore tomorrow for Christmas dinner."

"I had thought you would."

"What about you, Miss Drury? What will you do?"

"Dr. Ramsey is coming to have Christmas dinner with me. I assumed it would be all right."

"Of course," he said. He was aware of moths flitting against the lantern, and mosquitoes whining in the heat, and of Joanna's perfume.

"I bought Adam a present in Melbourne. Here," he said. Joanna took the parcel, and when she unwrapped the sacking, she saw a handsome, shiny brass spyglass, the kind mariners used.

"And this is for the girl, for Sarah," Hugh said. It was a scarf, embroidered with flowers. "I'll leave these here on the veranda. You can give them to Adam and Sarah in the morning." He reached into his pocket. "And this is for you."

Joanna lifted the lid of the small box and found a pair of delicate blue earrings nestled on a bed of velvet.

"The stones are lapis lazuli," Hugh said. "I guessed at the color. I was trying to match the blue in the brooch you often wear."

They were beautiful, and a perfect match for the brooch.

"Thank you," she said. "They're lovely." She was aware of Hugh's nearness. She wanted to put her arms around him and kiss him and tell him that it was the most beautiful present she had ever received, and that she loved him.

"Wear them tomorrow," he said.

Joanna looked at the box in her flour-dusted hands, and she thought: These are not meant to be worn for Dr. Ramsey, or for any other man except you.

"I have a present for you, too," she said, and she went inside the cabin, returning with a parcel wrapped in string and brown paper. When he opened it, he stared at the contents.

"It's for your poetry," Joanna said.

Hugh ran his hand over the rich leather binding, which was intricately tooled, the word "Journal" stamped in gold leaf on the cover. He opened the book to blank pages that were creamy white and waiting to be filled. "It's beautiful," he said, thinking of the ballad he had begun on the road to Melbourne:

> The trail is long and the dams are dry;
> The burrs are clinging to raw, red feet;
> Under the imminent brazen sky
> Hovers a haze of heat. . . .

He had written it on the back of a sales receipt. He could transfer it to this book.

"So," he said. "Merry Christmas, Joanna." He wanted to say: David Ramsey is in love with you. He wants to marry you.

And he was astonished at the wave of desire that swept through him. While he had been gone these past two weeks, he had not been able to get her out of his mind. Joanna had appeared to him, in his solitary thoughts on the road, as a mercurial figure, part girl, part woman. He hadn't been able to fix her in his mind; the vision of her had changed from second to second, as if he couldn't capture her. But here she was now, filling the outlines he had carried in his mind. All of a sudden, words came to him: "She traversed the great swelled seas/To this golden land . . ."

"I'll be leaving then," he said, thinking, Pauline will be wondering where I am. "By the way, a Mr. McNeal will be coming by day after tomorrow. He's the architect who is going to build the new house. Construction will begin on New Year's Day. It should be ready to be moved into by the time of the wedding."

Yes, Joanna thought. The wedding, the new house. Pauline . . .

"Mr. Westbrook, before you go, there is something I must talk to you about."

He was surprised by the sudden seriousness in her tone. "What is it?"

She felt her heart race. "Mr. Westbrook, I'm thinking of leaving Merinda. I think I should go."

He stared at her. "What are you talking about? What do you mean, leaving?"

"I heard you ride into the yard just a short while ago, so I assume you haven't spoken with Bill Lovell yet. Mr. Westbrook, while you were gone, the rest of your Aboriginal stock hands left. It's because of me, isn't it?"

He gave her a startled look. "Why on earth would you say that?"

"Sarah told me that Ezekiel has been telling the station hands that I'm bad luck for Merinda, that something terrible is going to happen here if I stay. And on the day you left for Melbourne, I encountered Ezekiel down by the river." Joanna briefly described the incident.

"I told Ezekiel to stay away from you."

"It's not his fault, Mr. Westbrook. You can't be angry with him because of his beliefs. His people were here first. He's only trying to defend something important to him. This is all a part of what brought me to Australia, to try and find the ancient way of life that used to be here, that has affected my family, that is affecting *me*. And part of it has to do with what Ezekiel sees about me. I can't ignore it. I have to figure out how to understand it and come to terms with it. I don't want to go, but I think there will only be more trouble if I stay."

"Surely you don't believe the nonsense he's spreading, do you? You don't honestly believe in things like bad magic!"

"It doesn't matter what I believe, it's what he believes. And he's got the men who work for you believing it, too. If I go, they'll come back—"

"No," he said. "You're not going. I won't allow that old devil to dictate to me how to run my station."

"But your workers—"

"I'll hire more." He suddenly took her by the shoulders. "Miss Drury," he said. "Joanna. Don't let Ezekiel frighten you. He won't hurt you. He's harmless really—"

"But it's not just Ezekiel," Joanna said. "The day I arrived at the harbor, a young Aborigine came on board to carry baggage. If you could have seen the way he looked at me—I think he was afraid of me. And I had a dream, a nightmare, about you . . . about us. It was so real, and it has stayed with me ever since—a feeling of dread, that something terrible is going to happen. Hugh," she said. "I'm afraid. I'm frightened for Merinda, for you, for Adam, and for myself. There is another world here, which we can't see, but which I am starting to feel. My mother felt this, too. She lived thousands of miles from here, but she believed the forces had their roots here, from somewhere in Australia. The Aborigines believe in supernatural powers, they believe in poison-songs and magic. How can we say they're wrong? How can we know?"

"I'm not going to let you leave, Joanna, not like this. Anyway, where would you go?" His grip tightened on her shoulders and he brought his face close to hers. "You must stay, Joanna. Say you'll stay."

Suddenly, they heard footsteps, someone hurrying across the yard. Matthew, one of the stableboys, ran up the stairs and said, "Mr. Westbrook! Come quick! Mr. Lovell's sick!"

Hugh went with him across the yard, and Joanna went into the cabin for her healing kit, and then followed. They found Bill lying in bed in the station manager's shack.

"How long has he been like this?" Hugh asked.

Matthew's eyes were large and dark. "I dunno, Mr. Westbrook. We ain't seen him for a couple of days. We didn't think nothing of it. Thought maybe he'd gone Christmas visiting somewhere."

"Bill?" Hugh said. "Can you hear me?"

"Hugh . . ." he moaned. "Hugh, it's just a summer cold."

"May I?" Joanna said. She sat on the edge of the bed and studied Lovell's face. Then she felt his forehead, and the pulse at his neck.

Bill's eyes fluttered. "Hello, Miss Drury," he said thickly.

"Are you in pain?" she asked.

"Yes—in my gut."

"When did this start?"

"About a week ago . . . headache, sore throat . . ."

"Why didn't you tell someone?"

He smiled. "Thought it would go away."

"Just lie still, we'll take care of you."

They went outside. "It's outback fever," Hugh said. "I haven't seen a case of it in a long time, but I recognize the signs."

"I'm not so sure," Joanna said. "I seem to recall something . . . I don't know. Normally, a fever is accompanied by a rapid heart rate. But Mr. Lovell's pulse is strangely slow. If only I could remember . . ." And then she said, "I'm sure my mother's book has something about this."

She went to the cabin, and was back a moment later. "It happened when I was very young," she said, as she flipped the pages of the diary. "An epidemic of some sort at the cantonment where my father was stationed. My mother recorded it, and she remarked on the strange pulse—Here it is." Joanna read for a moment, then she handed the diary to Hugh.

"Mr. Lovell has the classic symptoms," Joanna said as Hugh read Lady Emily's account of the epidemic. "Symptoms such as those are not found in any other disease."

"Typhoid," Hugh said, closing the book. He turned to the stableboy and said, "Saddle up a horse. Find Dr. Ramsey. Tell him it's urgent. If he isn't at home, try Strathfield. He'll be attending the ball. And hurry!"

"If this really is typhoid," Hugh said to Joanna, "then we have a serious situation on our hands. And we will have to act quickly."

"Mr. Lovell's fever is high," Joanna said. "But I think it will go higher. I must try to bring it down."

While Joanna went back to the cabin for a basin of water and towels, Hugh removed his cape and top hat and draped them over the end of Bill's bed. He sat next to his friend and said, "What's this all about, mate?" lapsing into the accent of his boyhood. "Feeling lonely on Christmas, and wanting a bit of attention?"

Bill smiled, but he was clearly in pain.

Joanna returned and placed a cold wet towel on Bill's head. She and Hugh regarded each other across the bed. He saw the fear in her eyes, and a look on her face that seemed to be saying, *I knew this was going to happen . . . .*

David Ramsey finally arrived, dressed in evening clothes. "Hello, Joanna. Well, Bill," he said, removing his top hat. "I'm told you're not feeling well. Let's take a look. Do you think you can hold this in your mouth?" Ramsey slipped a thermometer between Bill's lips, then he lifted up Bill's shirt and examined his abdomen. There were clusters of pink spots on the pale white skin. When Ramsey gently pressed down, Bill cried out. Finally he took the thermometer from Bill's mouth and read it by the light of the oil lamp.

"It's typhoid all right," he said as he and Hugh and Joanna went outside. "Jacko Jackson found Mr. Shapiro, the old peddler, dead in one of his fields. It looked as if he had had been crawling to get help."

"Do you think we might have a serous outbreak on our hands?" Hugh said.

"It's possible. I suggest we proceed as though we do."

"Tell us what to do."

"First, quarantine Bill. Don't let anyone near him, except for those who are taking care of him. No one knows what causes typhoid or how it is transmitted. But I am a believer in the new germ theory. Experiments with certain diseases have shown that isolating the infected victims can stem the spread of the disease. We don't know why exactly, but it seems to work."

"And what about Bill? Will he be all right?"

"There is no cure for typhoid. All we can do is make him comfortable and keep him fed and well hydrated. Above all, we must keep his fever down. If there are no complications, he should come out of it in about two to three weeks. But I have to warn you—there are frequently complications with typhoid. One of them is pneumonia, the other is perforation of the intestines, which leads to peritonitis. And neither can be cured.

"You'll want to watch the rest of your men closely. Keep an eye out for headaches or backaches, loss of appetite. Abdominal pains follow soon after, with distention. Joanna, I will leave this thermometer with you. It's one of the new ones—it only takes three minutes. As for nursing the sick—"

"Don't worry, David. I know what needs to be done," she said. "It's here in my mother's book."

"We'd better get to work then," Hugh said. "I have a feeling that by tomorrow we are going to have more cases of typhoid than we can handle."

As Dr. Ramsey rode out of the yard, Ezekiel stepped out of the shadows, listening.

CHAPTER 10

Joanna sat up through the night with Bill Lovell. After Hugh and the stableboy had undressed him and wrapped him in a wet sheet, Joanna stayed with him, changing the wet cloths on his head, giving him sips of water and checking his temperature every half hour. One of the station hands, returning after midnight from an evening of Christmas celebrating at Facey's, remarked upon the impropriety of a girl sitting up with an undressed man. But when he saw the seriousness of Bill's condition, he made no further comment.

In the meantime, Hugh had changed from evening clothes into work clothes, and made a round of the district, stopping first at Facey's to collect men who were sober enough to ride. They went armed with information Joanna and Dr. Ramsey had provided: a list of the disease's symptoms, precautions to take to prevent it and how to take care of the victims should it strike. They fanned out over the countryside, stopping wherever there was habitation, rousing people and warning them of the possible outbreak of typhoid. Hugh went first to Strathfield, where the Christmas Eve ball was in progress, and spoke briefly to the gathered guests, advising them to go home; then he rode to Lismore, where he spoke to a startled Pauline. It was not until he was riding away from their brief visit that he realized she had not been dressed for the ball.

The dawning of Christmas morning saw twelve new cases of typhoid, two of them Merinda men.

The station hands were moved out of the bunkhouse, and Joanna supervised its conversion into a hospital. The mattresses were removed from the beds and distributed to the men who chose either to sleep outside or in the shearing shed. She warned them not to drink well water or river water, only boiled water, and that upon the first appearance of a symptom, they were to report to her. The bunk beds were covered with mattresses of sacking stuffed with eucalyptus leaves, which could be easily removed and burned, with fresh ones ready to go in their place. Buckets of quicklime were placed by the door, with which to wash down the walls and floors at regular intervals.

Bill Lovell was transferred to the bunkhouse, where Joanna could watch him along with the new cases. He was screened behind a curtain, and someone sat with him at all times.

And Sarah, who thought these precautions weren't enough—the disease seemed, after all, to have started at Merinda—gathered protective stones and feathers, and quietly placed them around the cabin.

Hugh returned at noon on Christmas Day, exhausted and hungry, but refused to sleep until he had made sure all the homesteads had been warned.

"Maude Reed has the symptoms," he said as he ate. "Down near Mount Rouse I found an entire family sick with it. I left Stringy Larry there to help however he could. If it becomes an epidemic," he said, "we'll have to find some way to get food and water to all those people."

Joanna said, "You and your men should be all right if you wash your hands immediately after you leave an infected house. Don't eat or drink anything while you are there. According to my mother's diary, the physicians in India believe that typhoid is not carried on the air or spread by a person's breath. If you follow precautions, you should be all right."

Before Hugh left again, he looked at Joanna and said, "Are *you* all right?"

"Yes."

"It isn't your fault, Joanna," he said quietly. "Things happen. And people can also have premonitions about them. But you aren't the cause of any of this. Promise me you'll take care of yourself and Adam."

Hugh rode off to the east, where small farms were spread over many miles, while Joanna appointed one of the station hands to organize the men into collecting eggs, and boiling and bottling water in case they were needed. Then she concentrated on taking care of her three patients, enlisting the help of the two stableboys.

Frank Downs came to Merinda to join Hugh in his rides around the district. They went with eggs and boiled milk, Joanna's willow tea, and instructions on caring for the sick. The families were spread over two thousand square miles, with only two medical doctors to serve them.

But Frank stopped first at a modest clapboard house that stood on a tree-lined street at the edge of Cameron Town.

During the Christmas Eve party at Finnegan's, Frank had watched other men try to give Ivy Dearborn expensive gifts, and Ivy had politely refused them. But when Frank had said to her, "Would you like to attend Midnight Mass with me tonight?" she had said, "Yes."

They had listened to the service, and sung the Christmas hymns, and then they had ridden through the countryside in his carriage. Frank had wanted more, but he knew not to press for it. He and Ivy had talked about cricket scores, and the Melbourne Cup race results, the weather, and the end at last of the Franco-Prussian War in Europe. And when he had returned her to the boardinghouse, and asked her if she would care to go on a picnic with him, she had accepted.

The picnic was planned for this weekend. But now everything had changed.

Frank pushed past the landlady, who said, "No gentleman callers, this is a respectable house," and took the stairs two at a time. He knocked on Ivy's door and began to speak before she had it all the way open. "There's been an outbreak of typhoid," he said. "I want you to stay here. Don't go to Finnegan's. Don't leave this house until the danger has passed."

He took her hand and squeezed it. "I'll be back to check on you."

Three days later, typhoid fever was being reported from everywhere within a radius of eighty miles from Cameron Town. No one knew what had brought it.

Panic swept through the Western District. No family went untouched by the disease. At Monivae, nearly the entire servant staff succumbed, and it was left to the mistress of the house and her two daughters to nurse them. At Glenhope, Maude Reed burned with fever while John Reed protected himself with large quantities of whiskey. At Strathfield, candles were lit and the Ormsbys knelt in the family chapel, saying the rosary around the clock. At Kilmarnock, Colin MacGregor locked the doors, closed all the windows, and turned away visitors, believing, as most people did, that typhoid was carried on the air.

When Dr. Ramsey and Doc Fuller were unable to answer frantic summonses, people turned to Joanna Drury. "She cured my children of a summer fever," Winifred Cameron said to her friends. "And look what she did for Christina MacGregor's morning sickness," Louisa Hamilton said, adding silently: Maybe I could have been relieved of these swollen ankles if I hadn't listened to Pauline.

They went to Merinda to seek Joanna's advice, and using her mother's diary as a guide, she instructed them to keep the patients' fevers down by constant sponging with cold, wet sheets; to administer plenty of fluids and only liquid food; to watch the abdomen for rigid distention; and to boil all water and milk before drinking it. The wind, she reassured them, did not bring typhoid, and fresh air in the sickroom would be beneficial.

Dr. Ramsey's buggy was a constant sight on the country lanes. He went where he was summoned, diagnosed typhoid, administered digitalis injections to those with failing hearts, left nursing instructions with those who were still well, and departed feeling helpless and impotent. In the face of such a disease, he saw that a medical man was no more effective than an ordinary person. For all the boiled water and gentle nursing care, the epidemic was spreading. Doubts began to settle into his mind.

When he arrived at Merinda, nine days after Christmas, he found Joanna in the bunkhouse, supervising the nursing of ten very ill men.

David paused in the doorway to watch her. As Joanna gently propped a man up to give him something to drink, Ramsey thought that even though she looked tired and worn, her hair escaping its bun and her dress covered in a sackcloth apron, she was still beautiful. "Larry!" she called, when the patient began to toss in delirium. "Please help me with Johnno."

A moment later, when the sick station hand was quiet again, Joanna looked up and smiled at Ramsey.

"Hello, David," she said, coming up to him and sweeping a strand of hair from her face. "How are you?"

"I'm fine, Joanna. And you? How is Adam?"

"He's fine, thank God."

"Joanna," he said. "I need to talk to you."

"Very well. I have to check on the water situation in the cookhouse. Will you walk with me?"

"I'm not sure we're doing the right thing, Joanna," Ramsey said as they crossed the sunbaked yard. "The way we are nursing the patients now, they have the fever for three weeks or more. This brings them to such a debilitated state that even when the typhoid has passed, they are so weak that pneumonia sets in. And then they surely die. Unless, of course, they don't die of peritonitis first because of a perforated intestinal ulcer. It is the duration of the disease, Joanna, that kills people, not the typhoid itself. If only we could rid the body of it more quickly, if only we could cure typhoid almost as quickly as it strikes."

"I know of no such cure, David."

"I have been working on one, Joanna," he said. "I read recently that medical men in Europe are experimenting with a new treatment for typhoid—disinfecting the intestinal tract with frequent doses of iodine and carbolic acid."

"But those are poisons."

"Only if given in too-large doses. Frequent purgings will clean the typhoid microorganism out of the bowel, and the patient will recover. It makes sense, doesn't it?"

"Have these medical men had much success with this treatment?"

He frowned. "It's still highly experimental. There have been some successes, but there have also been deaths."

"David, I think I prefer to take care of patients according to my mother's experience. Nursing and constant vigilance."

But David was thinking of Edward Jenner, the developer of the smallpox vaccine, and Théophile Laënnec, who had invented the stethoscope, and Rudolf Virchow, the first man to demonstrate that disease came from microscopic cells—all men who had contributed to medicine. David Ramsey wanted desperately to join their ranks.

The epidemic worsened. The one priest and three ministers in the district found themselves busy with burials and grieving relatives, but the churches were strangely empty and silent. Isolation, everyone had been told, was their salvation.

But even those in self-imposed prisons, such as the Ormsbys at Strathfield and the MacGregors of Kilmarnock, were not safe from the disease. Closing windows and shutting doors did not keep out the dreaded typhoid. It lurked in the water they drank, in the food they ate, and they had no way of knowing that something so tiny as to be invisible could deal such a deadly blow. Dr. Ramsey tried to warn people about microorganisms, but how could anyone be afraid of something they could not see?

When Christina MacGregor complained of headaches and a sore throat, Colin rode into Cameron Town and wakened David Ramsey out of a stolen hour of sleep.

"Keep her fever down with constant sponging," Ramsey said, after examining her. "Give her as many fluids as she can tolerate. And it is too hot and close in this room. Open the windows, let fresh air in. If she worsens and I am unavailable, Joanna Drury at Merinda knows what to do."

Christina was in her eighth month of pregnancy. "What about the baby, doctor?" MacGregor said.

But Ramsey could not predict.

Hugh and Frank continued to ride over the countryside. They helped farmers bury wives and children; they brought isolated shepherds who had fallen ill back to Merinda's makeshift hospital. Joanna watched over the constant spongings, the feedings, the changing of the eucalyptus pallets. She passed among the beds, measuring temperatures with the thermometer David Ramsey had given her, taking care to disinfect it with alcohol between patients. The fevers climbed steadily; the pulse rates slowed; the rose spots appeared on swollen abdomens; men tossed and turned, burning in delirium.

And the epidemic continued to spread.

Ezekiel stood as silent and still as the eucalyptus trees around him, watching Sarah perform her daily ritual down at the river. Since the day sickness had come to Merinda, the girl had come every morning to the billabong, to sing over objects she brought from the house: a comb, a handkerchief, a Bible. These were possessions, the old man knew, of the people Sarah lived with, and she was using them in her magic to protect the three white people from the illness. Ezekiel watched her every day; and every day his bewilderment grew. The girl was a contradiction: She spoke whitefella language and wore whitefella clothes, but she practiced blackfella magic.

And he wondered: Why would a girl whose ancestors had been taken away from her, whose tribe had been scattered, and whose songlines had been defiled want to protect the people who had done those things?

Sarah sat back when her song was done, and pushed her long hair away from her face. She stared at the homestead through the trees, looking at the bunkhouse, where sheets soaked in disinfectant hung over the doorway and windows. She believed that a terrible poison was at work there, a poison that needed to be fought with more than disinfectants, with magic as well. And yet she was afraid that her own magic was not strong enough. She needed help.

I'll go to the mission, she thought. I'll talk to Old Deereeree and ask her to teach me a song powerful enough to fight the poison-song on Joanna.

Sarah suddenly stiffened. The old man was back, watching her; she could sense him behind her. It was four weeks since she had stood up to him in this very place; Sarah had been troubled by the incident ever since. She had been raised to respect elders, to address them as "Old Mother" and "Old Father," and to defer to their wisdom, their judgments. But Ezekiel didn't understand about Joanna. Sarah wanted to give the elder the respect he deserved, but he made her angry.

"You break the taboo, Old Father," she said now, without turning around. "You watch women's ritual. You walk on woman's Dreaming Site."

"I break no taboo," he said, coming through the trees. There was anger in his voice; he wasn't used to being stood up to by young females. In the old days—

Sarah rose and faced him. "This is woman's Dreaming," she said. "The Kangaroo Ancestress spoke to Joanna here."

A look of doubt flickered in his eyes. Then he said, "She brought sickness to Merinda."

"No, Old Father. Blackfella magic brought sickness here. She has a poison-song on her."

He stared at Sarah, and she read the conflicting emotions on his face. She said, "Joanna is a song-woman."

"But she is whitefella!"

"But she is a song-woman all the same."

Ezekiel looked away, his keen eyes peering at the woods around him from under heavy brows. He consulted the air and the sky, and his own wisdom, and finally he shook his head, and said, "I don't understand. I think the Dreaming may be coming to an end."

"No, Old Father," Sarah said gently. "The Dreaming will always be here. Joanna has powers. But she has blackfella poison-song on her, too."

"Do you see this poison-song?" he asked.

Sarah had to shake her head. "No, she told me. A poison-song on her mother, on her grandmother."

"She *says.*" He shook his head again. Finally he said, "We wait and see." And he turned and walked away.

———————————— • ————————————

When Joanna came out of the cabin, she paused and looked past the yard, over the blistering plains. She had not seen Hugh for days, she couldn't sleep; she had nightmares of people falling ill, of Hugh ill and alone, far from any house. She thought of him making his way to one of the many shepherd's huts that dotted the landscape, and lying there, burning in delirium and pain.

She knew he rode to Lismore every day. "Pauline has organized the women," he told Joanna. "They're donating sheets and bedding, collecting eggs, boiling water and putting it into bottles. The men pick up supplies at Lismore and take them to the outlying farms."

She looked for him now, then she went across the yard to check with her "nurses." Fevers were still climbing, and pulses continued to slow down. One man was recovering, and two others were past the stage of delirium. For those, Joanna would be vigilant against pneumonia. The bunkhouse was thick with the smell of disease and disinfectant, the day was hot; flies settled everywhere. The eucalyptus pallets became soiled very quickly and had to be changed constantly. At times Joanna felt like giving up. She was reminded of the final days of Lady Emily's life, when she lay weak and dying, and Joanna had nursed her. Those same feelings of frustration and hopelessness, of despair and anger, threatened to overwhelm her.

She went to look in on Bill Lovell. It had been three weeks since the night of Christmas Eve, and according to Dr. Ramsey, and to her mother's diary, the disease should have run its course, and Bill should be better. But when Joanna came around the curtain that screened him off from the others, she received a shock.

"Matthew," she said quietly to the stableboy, who was washing down the floor with quicklime. "Go at once and find Dr. Ramsey. Hurry. Tell him to come immediately."

She returned to Bill's bedside. She could see from the pulsing of his closed lids that his eyes were moving rapidly. His face was ashen.

Joanna picked up her mother's diary, and it fell open to pages she knew by heart. But she read it again, as she might a Bible, finding solace in the familiar words, and seeing in them also an exact chronicle of her own current experience: "We are in the third week of the epidemic," Lady Emily had written. "Jaswaran is tireless in his care of our patients. Major Caldwell died during the night. Petronius is with his widow now. I fear that this dreaded typhoid might be with us always. I worry for little Joanna's sake. Am I doing the right thing by keeping her here with me? Would she be better off if I sent her away?"

Joanna closed her eyes and thought of Adam, who seemed so frail when she tucked him into bed every night; and also of Sarah, who, although strong, might not possess a natural resistance to white man's diseases. Every night Joanna prayed for guidance, as she asked herself the same questions that Lady Emily had asked. And when Joanna opened her eyes and continued to read the diary, she read the same conclusion she herself had come to: "But where would I send Joanna, who would take care of her as well as I can?"

Joanna closed the book and held it between her hands. She felt suddenly close to her mother, as if Lady Emily were there in person, guiding Joanna. And then she recalled Sarah's words: "The diary is your mother's songline."

David Ramsey walked in then, his red-gold hair plastered to his head with sweat, his jaw showing a growth of beard. It took only a brief examination of Bill Lovell for him to say, "I'm sorry, Joanna. It's peritonitis."

"What can we do for him?"

David wanted to shout that, if only he had had to courage to try the experimental cure, Bill might have been saved. "There is nothing any-one can do for him," he said in a weary voice. "Keep him half-sitting, give him nothing by mouth except for a few tiny sips of water. The end will come soon."

"Will you stay for a while, David?" she asked.

He saw the sorrow in her eyes, and he wanted to take her into his arms; he wanted to ride out of the Western District with her, and take them both far away from all this disease and death and hopelessness. "I'm sorry," he said. "There are others who need me."

"Yes, of course."

She found Matthew behind the shearing shed crying, because he had overheard the conversation. "See if you can find Hugh," she said gently, laying a hand on his shoulder. "He should be with Bill now."

Hugh rode into the yard a short while later, looking exhausted and beaten. His gray eyes had taken on a hunted look from what they had seen. He had found entire families down with the typhoid, mothers and fathers and children, lying on mattresses, eaten with fever, dehydrated, delirious, with no one to take care of them or bury them. In one case he had found a ten-year-old boy—himself hot with fever and thirst—trying to sponge fevered faces.

Whenever Hugh returned from riding around the district, he was always fearful of what he might find—Joanna down with the typhoid, or Adam. He wanted to stay with them, protect them. But he was needed elsewhere, and what, after all, could he do if he stayed? At times he was nearly paralyzed with feelings of rage and helplessness, and with memories of himself as a fifteen-year-old boy burying a father under the only tree for miles around. There had been no minister, no mourners, no coffin even, just the old blue blanket that the elder Westbrook had slept in for many a star-washed night.

He hurried into the bunkhouse and went behind the curtain where his old friend lay. Joanna stood up. "Did Matthew tell you—?"

"Yes," he said, sitting down and looking at Bill. Hugh saw the pall of death that had settled over those sunbaked features. "Hello, Bill," he said.

Unfocused eyes gazed back at him. "G'day, Hugh," he said. "Have we reached Coorain yet?"

"Almost there, Bill."

"Good," he said. "My droving days are done, Hugh. I want to settle down. Maybe have a small run, a few sheep . . ."

He rambled for a while about the past, speaking of men long dead and outback towns long since deserted. Toward midnight, his focus sharpened and he spoke in a nearly normal voice. "Keep writing those ballads, Hugh," he said. "Don't let Australians forget what they once were."

He died during the night. Hugh said, "He was like a father to me," and Joanna comforted him as he cried.

———————————————————

Pauline removed the thermometer from beneath Elsie's arm and read it. It was not one of the new thermometers, such as the one Dr. Ramsey used, but one of the old kind, that measured the body temperature in the armpit, and took twenty minutes to register. But it was accurate nonetheless, and Pauline saw, on this stifling January day, that her maid's temperature had gone up another degree.

Drawing a towel out of a bucket filled with cold water, Pauline wrung it out and sponged Elsie's face.

"Miss Downs," the young woman whispered. "You shouldn't be doing this."

"You've taken care of me," Pauline said gently. "Now I shall take care of you."

"How is my Tom?" Elsie asked, referring to the young man whom she loved and for which Pauline had once envied her maid. Tom had died the day before.

"He's fine," Pauline said.

"Why doesn't he come to see me?"

"He's helping Mr. Downs take supplies around the district. Just lie quietly, Elsie. Everything is going to be all right."

Pauline put the towel back into the bucket and drew out another one. She wrung it out and pressed it along Elsie's feverish shoulders. She stared at the girl's death-haunted face and thought: How quickly and easily life is taken from us. She was struck again by the frightening unpredictability of fate, and it made her think of Miss Flora McMichaels, who had not asked to be widowed before she was even wed, thirty years ago.

Leaving Elsie in the care of another maid, she went back out to the lawn where the women were making up hampers of food, and sorting and folding sheets to be delivered to afflicted families.

"Where is Winifred?" she said, looking around.

Louisa put a hand to her lower back and grimaced. She was five months pregnant. "She went home. Little Timmy has fallen ill."

Pauline looked over the operation on the lawn. Each day, there were fewer and fewer of them to do the work. Everyone was either sick, or nursing loved ones. She thought of Hugh; she wondered where he was, if he was still well. She felt her nerves growing tight, the very blood in her veins seemed to race with tension. Elsie's Tom, only twenty-six years old and as healthy as the horses he took care of, dead in ten days.

She looked at the bottles lined up on the table, glinting in different colors in the sunlight—milk bottles, beer bottles, bottles that had once contained medicine. They had been rounded up and brought to Lismore, where they had been washed and boiled and were now waiting to be filled with sterilized drinking water. Pauline rolled up her sleeves and, despite heat and fatigue, got to work filling them.

Louisa looked up and saw a woman hovering at the edge of the garden.

"I'll go and see who it is," Louisa said.

"Is there something I can do for you?" she said to the woman.

"Are you Miss Downs?"

"I am Mrs. Hamilton. That is Miss Downs over there. Who are you?"

"My name is Ivy Dearborn. I would like to help."

Louisa looked at her, taking in the conservative dress and the bright red hair swept up under a modest bonnet. Louisa knew who she was. She had overheard her husband mention the new barmaid at Finnegan's. "I'm sorry, but we have enough help."

Ivy looked at the tables piled with food and bottles and sheets, and she saw that there were not nearly enough people to manage it all. She looked at Pauline, so tall and beautiful, not at all like Frank. She pictured the man she had thought about all these months, ever since the night she had sketched him. She recalled how she had watched for him, hoping he would come into the pub, wanting to accept his invitations, but afraid to, because of what had happened to her before. And then the invitation to go to church, and Ivy had allowed her hopes to soar—dashed now, in the bright daylight of reality.

"I see," she said, and went away.

When Louisa returned to the table, Pauline said, "Who was that?"

"No one," Louisa said. "Just a barmaid. She wanted to help."

"And you sent her away?"

"We don't need her kind here."

"Louisa, this is my house, and I say who will be admitted and who will not." She rolled down her sleeves and prepared to go after the woman.

But before she could do so, a man whom she recognized as a footman from Kilmarnock appeared. "Mr. MacGregor wants you to come right away, Miss Downs."

Pauline called for her carriage and rode to Kilmarnock, where she found Colin at Christina's side; she was delirious and bright red with fever. The little boy, Judd, stood whey-faced in the corner.

"I can't find Ramsey anywhere," Colin said. "And the woman who was taking care of Christina fell ill this morning. Will you watch her for me? I'm going to ride over to Merinda and fetch Miss Drury."

Pauline was shocked by the way he looked. Colin MacGregor was always so robust, and impeccable in appearance. But this man was far too thin and pale to be the boastful next laird of Kilmarnock. "It's better if you stay here, Colin," Pauline said. "I'll go and fetch Miss Drury."

Hugh rode into Merinda's silent and deserted yard, jumped down from his horse and went into the bunkhouse, where he found Joanna drawing a sheet over the face of one of the station hands. She looked at Hugh, dark circles under her eyes. Her dress seemed to hang on her. She said, "Hugh," and then she collapsed.

He carried her across the yard to the cabin, laid her on the bed, looked at her.

"Joanna," he murmured, touching her face. Her eyelids fluttered. She breathed deeply. She was asleep.

He continued to watch her. She was beautiful, but she was so fragile; he thought her skin looked as if it was stretched too tightly over her bones.

Pauline stood in the open doorway. She watched them for a moment,

Hugh bent over Joanna, a look of concern on his face. "Is she sick?" Pauline said.

He looked up. "Pauline," he said in surprise. "No, but she's exhausted. She desperately needs to sleep."

"Colin MacGregor is asking for her. Christina is gravely ill."

"Tell him Joanna will come in a little while, after she's had some sleep."

Pauline looked at the way Hugh was bent over Joanna, the way his eyes were fixed on her. She turned and left.

When she was back at Kilmarnock, in Christina's bedroom, she said to Colin, "Miss Drury will come later."

"Why can't she come now?"

Pauline hesitated. She couldn't get the image out of her mind, the way Hugh had sat by Joanna's side, the way he had gently touched her face. So Pauline said, "She's busy taking care of the station hands," and was amazed at how easily the lie had come to her.

When Christina died three hours later, taking with her the unborn child, Colin clutched his wife's body, sobbing. Six-year-old Judd, who was still standing silently in the corner, knew that the thing he had always dreaded had finally happened—his mother had joined the ghosts in his father's study.

———————— ◆ ————————

Joanna awakened to the sound of someone knocking at the door. It took her a few seconds to struggle out of her deep sleep, and when she tried to sit up, she found that she was very weak. She looked around the cabin and realized that it was late afternoon. She tried to remember how she had gotten here. And then it came to her: she had collapsed in the bunkhouse.

When she heard the knocking at the door again, she said, "Who is it?"

"There's a message for you from Dr. Ramsey, Miss Drury," said the person on the other side. Joanna recognized the voice of one of the station hands.

"Just a minute, please," she said. She couldn't remember when she had felt so weak.

When she opened the door, the station hand held out a letter; a messenger from Cameron Town had just brought it, he said.

The note was was from David Ramsey's landlady, saying that the doctor had fallen ill and was asking for her.

"Tom," Joanna said to the station hand, "would you please hitch up the wagon for me? I have to go into town."

"Mr. Westbrook's out with the wagon, miss."

"Then have one of the stableboys saddle a horse for me, please. Do you know where Sarah and Adam are?"

"The little boy's in the cookhouse helping Ping-Li, and the girl said she had to run an errand."

Joanna washed her hands and face, and combed her hair, and started to feel a little stronger, although still exhausted. Wondering what errand Sarah had gone on, she wrote a note, saying where she was going, and left it on the table.

She rode as swiftly as she could in the gathering twilight, and when she arrived at Ramsey's boardinghouse, she found him in bed. The room was filled with the smell of disease and death. She took one look at Ramsey's face, and knew by the blue lips and strange pallor that he was in the grip of an illness other than typhoid: He had taken poison—the experimental "cure." Bottles of carbolic acid and iodine stood on the nightstand.

She sat at his side and placed a damp cloth on his forehead.

The landlady stood in the doorway, wringing her hands. "I didn't know what to do," she said. "Him being a doc and all."

Ramsey opened his eyes, looked at Joanna and smiled. "I had the symptoms . . . that last day I saw you, Joanna," he said, speaking with difficulty. "When . . . I diagnosed Bill Lovell's peritonitis. I knew I had the typhoid."

"Shh," she said. "Don't talk. I'll take care of you."

His head rolled from side to side. "No, Joanna," he said. "I know what I have done. I knew . . . all along that I couldn't experiment on others. I had to try the cure on myself first." He lifted a hand toward the bottles of poisons. "I . . . wanted to make a contribution to medicine. I wanted to be like Jenner and Pasteur. But . . . these don't work, Joanna. All I have done is kill myself. I'm sorry I failed . . ."

He died with his eyes still open. Joanna gently closed them.

She rode slowly back down the country road toward Merinda with the image of David's face before her. She felt lifeless inside; as dead as the men she had seen carried off by the typhoid. Night was rapidly approaching, but she was unaware of it. She felt the weight of all those lives on her shoulders. What did she have to do with all these things that were happening? Was the old Aborigine Ezekiel right? If she had never come here, would this disaster never have occurred?

She began to feel dizzy; she remembered that she had not eaten since the day before. She peered ahead at the darkening road and tried to get her bearings. How far was the Merinda homestead? She knew that the road curved southward before turning northward again to Merinda, adding extra miles that she wasn't sure she was up to traveling. She looked at the fields to her left, which lay in the last pale glow of dusk, and she tried to estimate how much light remained.

Her dizziness increased; she felt light-headed and weak. She was suddenly afraid that if she stayed on the road she might not make it to Merinda. Her best hope, she decided, was to cut across the fields and head straight for the homestead.

She spurred the horse into a gallop, and soon was riding swiftly over fields of dry grass. It felt good to be going so fast, to be moving, to be doing something. She thought of David and began to cry.

Finally, she saw the lights of the homestead up ahead through the trees. She made the horse go faster.

When Joanna had decided to take the shortcut to Merinda, she had not calculated the river being in the way, and so when the horse saw the water at the last minute, and suddenly reared, she was taken by surprise. She lost her grip and was flung from the saddle. She gave out a cry, and fell to the ground.

———

Adam was frightened. He had been helping Ping-Li in the cookhouse, where Sarah had told him to stay while she paid a secret visit to the Aboriginal Mission. He had been told not to go to the cabin, because Joanna was sleeping and he mustn't disturb her. But when Ping-Li had fallen asleep on his cot in the cookhouse and Adam had gone to the cabin, Joanna wasn't there—no one was there. He had gone to the bunkhouse, but a station hand had told him to stay away, because there was sickness inside. And now it was night and he was alone.

He didn't like being alone. It made him think of the other time he had been alone, and he didn't like to think about that, he *would* not. He wouldn't let it come into his mind when it tried to, or when Joanna or Sarah tried to coax him to talk about it. He would not think or speak about it. But now he was frightened, and it was just like that last time, when he had come in from outside and found Mama lying there looking so white, and he had tried to wake her up and she wouldn't, and he had tried and tried to get her to wake up, calling to her over and over, and his panic had turned to terror when he had realized she had gone to sleep and was never going to wake up again.

Adam looked around at the silent yard and wondered if Sarah and Joanna were down at the river. But when he reached the woods, he found no one there, and his fear grew; he had never been here at night before.

And then he saw a horse on the other side, saddled but without a rider. He splashed across the narrow part of the river, and when he saw a figure, a woman lying on the ground nearby, he was suddenly back inside the farmhouse and the bad thing was happening all over again. "Mama!" he cried, running to Joanna. "Mama, wake up! Don't sleep! Mama, Mama!" He tugged at her, but she did not respond.

He tried to think. He should go for help. He should run and get somebody. But he was too afraid. He threw himself down and banged his head on the ground. "No, no, no!" he cried, feeling helpless and terrified. "Mama! Wake up!" He buried his face in his hands and sobbed. He was a bad boy; he couldn't wake Mama. He couldn't move, or go for help. He just stayed there and cried.

Finally, the crying subsided and he looked at Joanna again. Her eyes were closed, her hair was spread on the grass.

And he realized: This wasn't Mama.

He got to his knees and said, confused, "Joanna? Joanna, wake up. Please wake up." He shook her shoulder. "Wake up now, Joanna."

He stood up and stared down at her, gripped with terror and indecision. He looked over his shoulder and saw the lights of the homestead. He looked at Joanna again. He didn't want to leave her, he was afraid to leave her. But if he didn't go for help, then she might go to sleep forever. The way Mama had.

He turned and ran.

"Help, help, help," he called as he ran into the yard. "Help! Joanna's hurt! Joanna's hurt!"

He ran up the veranda steps, but there was no one in the cabin. He ran to the cookhouse; a pot bubbled on the stove, but he could not see the Chinese cook anywhere about. "Help, help," Adam cried as he ran to the bunkhouse. He stopped at the blanket-covered doorway, the smell of carbolic stinging his nose and eyes.

Then he turned and ran out of the yard and down the drive toward the main road.

———

Hugh was glad to be nearly home; he couldn't remember when he had been this tired. Sarah rode silently at his side; he had picked her up along the road. She had said that she had gone to the Aboriginal Mission, hoping to visit Old Deereeree, only to be told that the old woman had died of typhoid.

"I'm sorry, Sarah," Hugh said now, sensing the magnitude of her grief. "I'm sorry about Deereeree."

"She was old," Sarah said, but nothing more, because it was taboo to speak of the dead. Sarah knew that she would carry Deereeree's death with her, and think about it, for the rest of her life. And the fact that all the old woman's secrets, her magic, her songs, and the wisdom of her ancestors had died with her.

"Hello," Hugh said, "who's that up ahead? Why, it's Adam!"

He brought the wagon to a halt and jumped down. "What is it, Adam? What's the matter?"

"Joanna! Joanna's hurt!" Adam cried. "Back there! At the river! She fell off a horse! She won't wake up!"

Hugh drove the wagon as fast as he could, going off the drive and plunging across the fields. When they reached the trees, he jumped down and ran the rest of the way. "Joanna!" he called. "Joanna!"

Then he saw the horse grazing, and when he reached Joanna, she was sitting up and rubbing her head.

"My God, Joanna," he said, falling to his knees.

"The horse threw me—"

"God, Joanna," he said again. And then he took her into his arms and kissed her, and drew her tight against him.

She put her arms around him, held him, and kissed him as urgently as he had kissed her.

He took her face in his hands and saw the tears.

"David's dead, Hugh," she said. "This is all such a nightmare."

He helped her to her feet, and they held on to each other for a long moment.

Then Adam came up and said, "Are you all right, Joanna? I was so scared. You wouldn't wake up. Like Mama. But it's all right now, isn't it? I brought help, didn't I?"

"Yes, Adam," Joanna said, suddenly feeling alive as she held on to Hugh, no longer weak or exhausted, but feeling his strength, and never wanting him to let her go. "You did just the right thing."

CHAPTER 11

Sarah collected her stones and feathers and bracelets made of human hair, and took them down, again, to the river. Her magic had worked, the typhoid was gone. And although many in the district had died, Joanna and Hugh and Adam had been spared. Everyone was saying that it was Mr. Shapiro who had brought the disease to western Victoria, but Sarah believed that a poison-song was part of it, too. She believed this because her singing seemed to have sent it away. And now the objects of ritual had to be buried, because they were powerful; they had lives of their own, and must be shown proper respect. As she dug into the soft clay of the bank of the billabong, she sang one last song. But this was a song of love.

Sarah had seen the love that had been growing between Hugh and Joanna, and the love they both shared for the little boy who had been so wounded, and who was now starting to heal. But Hugh was getting married, and Joanna had said she must leave. But it was wrong for Joanna to go, Sarah thought. She belonged here. Her songline had brought her to this place.

The song Sarah sang was a powerful one. She had learned it from her mother long ago, before her mother had gone into the desert, never to return. Sarah sang it to bring Hugh and Joanna together.

When she had buried all the things, making sure they wouldn't be found, she sat back and realized the old man was again standing among the trees. He was holding a boomerang, the kind that rich people came to the mission to buy, to hang on the walls in their houses, and for an instant Sarah saw him as a ghost. Ezekiel wore the shirt and trousers the mission had given him, but around his head he wore a hairstring headband, and she could see on his bare arms the old tribal scars that had been etched into his flesh many years ago.

He came through the trees toward her, now that her ritual was over and it was not taboo to approach. Sarah rose and stood respectfully. They looked at each other in the dappled sunlight of the clearing.

Sarah said, "There is strong magic here, Old Father. There is song-woman magic, and there is poison-song magic. They are at war. I need your help."

He looked at the boomerang in his hand; it was the "killing" kind, not the "returning" kind. He had carved it himself, long ago, its body engraved with the magic symbols of his youth. As Ezekiel contemplated it, he thought about what it might mean that he had done more thinking in the past few weeks than he had for most of his life. He had watched and waited, as he had told Sarah he would, and he was still baffled. Nothing was simple any more. In the old days, there were rules governing everything, such as the law that determined when a mother-in-law may speak to her son-in-law; the law that said while a son is undergoing initiation, his mother must speak a special language; the law that dictated who sat where around a campfire, who would carry water. And in those days, before the coming of the white man, everyone knew the laws, they respected the laws; the world was orderly, chaos was avoided. Now the laws were breaking down, people were forgetting the old order, and elders like Ezekiel no longer had the answers.

He had wrestled within himself about the white woman at Merinda. He had watched her, feared her, and had been confused and impressed by her. Now he considered what Sarah had said about her. He had seen how Joanna had worked magic, saving men from the sickness, even herself and Hugh, whom Ezekiel respected and admired and considered a friend.

"Why do you sing the love-song?" he asked.

"To make Joanna stay. She went away this morning. Hugh must bring her back."

When Sarah resumed her song, Ezekiel sniffed and looked up at the sky. Love-singing was women's magic; he didn't know about it. Maybe it worked, maybe not. He thought for a moment, then he turned and moved off through the trees toward the main road. Love-singing might be strong, he decided, but the elders knew that sometimes magic needed to be helped by human intervention.

Hugh and Pauline walked among the headstones, placing flowers beneath familiar names: Bill Lovell, David Ramsey, and countless others named Cameron, McClintock and Dunn. Pauline paused before the stone marker that said only "Baby" Hamilton—January 22, 1872. Louisa had not come down with the typhoid, but the stress had brought on premature labor. As Pauline placed some flowers on the small grave, she wondered if Louisa had been able to learn the secret of birth prevention from Dr. Ramsey before he died.

Pauline was not dressed in full mourning, as many of the women visiting the cemetery were, but in gray edged with black, out of respect for others. She and Frank had escaped the epidemic. Although, she realized, her brother had been in a way touched by the typhoid: Miss Dearborn had disappeared. Frank had spent days searching for her, believing in the end that she must have died of the typhoid. He was back in Melbourne now, back to the business of running his newspaper, putting time and work and distance between himself and painful memories.

As Pauline walked among the graves, her arm through Hugh's, feeling the cleansing February sunshine on her, she thought: We must turn our faces to the future now. We must put tragedy behind us and carry on with the business of living. But the subject of the wedding, which was only a month away, had still not been brought up.

She fanned herself and said, "My, but it is hot today. I hope it won't be this hot for the wedding!"

"Pauline," Hugh said.

She felt it coming; it had been coming for days; she wanted to ward it off, keep it from being brought into existence. "Let's get away from this dreary place, darling," she said. "Let's go for a ride in the mountains. They look so cool and green."

"Pauline," Hugh said. "We have to talk."

So here it was, the thing she had been running from ever since the afternoon she had gone to Merinda and found Hugh with Joanna in the cabin.

"Don't sound so serious, darling," she said with a smile. "I think this dreadful cemetery has spoiled your mood. Why don't we go to the Fox and Hounds Inn, and have a cold—"

"Pauline," he said. "You have never known me to be anything but honest with you. And I have to be honest with you now. It's about Joanna Drury."

"Please don't," she said.

"It wouldn't be fair to you to enter into our marriage by keeping the truth from you. It would be dishonorable, and a poor reflection upon my high regard for you."

Pauline stiffened. "You're going to tell me that you're in love with her."

"Yes."

She turned cold blue eyes upon him. "And do I take it then that you intend to keep her on to take care of Adam?"

"No. That would not be fair to any one of us. Joanna is going away. She has her own life to lead, and you and I have ours."

"Then why did you have to tell me about your feelings for her?" Pauline cried.

"Because the truth is there; because you know it anyway. I could not become your husband knowing that you and I had kept this truth unacknowledged."

Pauline's jaw was tight as she looked at him and said, "And what about me? Do you love me?"

He looked at her—she was so beautiful, so elegant. But he was thinking of Joanna, of kissing her, and the passion that had shocked them both. He took Pauline's hands between his and said, "I respect you and admire you, Pauline. I have the highest regard for you."

"But you don't love me."

"I'm very fond of you, Pauline."

"Hugh!" she said. "I want you to love me!"

She turned away from him. Why couldn't they have left this a dark little secret between them? What would have been the harm in that? She could have gone on pretending, and perhaps in time she could have come to believe that he loved only her. Perhaps in time he would have.

She felt rage welling up inside her, and she recalled how she had seen Hugh with Joanna, how tenderly he had touched her, how his eyes had lingered on her face. And Pauline wanted to shout at Joanna, Go away! You don't deserve him! You haven't earned him! You haven't loved him since you were fourteen. You didn't put your arms around his neck and kiss him when you were sixteen years old and he had won the grand trophy at the Graziers' Show. You didn't cry for days when you were seventeen and Hugh was brought home from a hunting accident, his face white as death, his shirt covered with blood. You never stood at the sidelines of a horse race, praying with all your might that Hugh would win. I did all those things! Hugh is supposed to be mine!

"You told me this," Pauline said in a controlled voice, "because you want to cancel the wedding."

"No, Pauline. That was not the reason."

"But it's what you want, isn't it?"

"No. And what I want is not the issue here."

"God, Hugh, I don't want a martyr for a husband! I don't want to marry you under such conditions—just because you're an honorable man!"

"Pauline," he said. "I will be a good husband to you. I will give you a good life. I will always be faithful to you. I promise that."

Pauline closed her eyes and thought: But you don't love me!

"And when will the hate and the resentment begin?" she said. "As soon as the minister pronounces us husband and wife, I will look at you and wonder at what moment, and in what circumstances, you will look at me and hate me. For not being Joanna."

"I will never hate you, Pauline."

"Then you will grow bored with me, and that would be worse!"

Pauline thought of her love for this man, of the planning she had done to claim him for herself. The picnic in the rain, her proposal to him. She thought of the campaign she had waged against Joanna Drury, to make her feel unwelcome here, to drive her away. Pauline looked back and saw how coolly and logically and with what determination she had run her race, and now she looked at Hugh and realized that although she had won his loyalty, his honor and affection, and would even win his name, she had not won the man himself. In the end, it was an empty victory.

"Hugh," she said. "I want you to want me. To marry me because you want to, unconditionally and willingly and out of love. Not out of some noble sentiment, but because you desire me as much as I desire you."

"I can't give you that right now, Pauline."

"Then I think we should call off the wedding," she said.

When he didn't say anything Pauline felt something stab deeper into her heart.

Why was love so hard? she wondered. There was Colin MacGregor, locked away in his castle, grieving for his dead wife. And Frank, how furiously he had searched for the woman called Ivy. And now . . .

"It isn't just Joanna," Pauline said, instinctively protecting herself. "There are other problems as well. The house isn't built, and I cannot bear the thought of living in that cabin. You don't want to live at Lismore, you want to be right there at Merinda, overseeing everything. And I realize now that no matter how I have tried, I . . . I just can't warm up to Adam. He doesn't like me much, and I don't want the burden of a child right now, especially another woman's child."

"Now who's being noble?" Hugh said.

She tipped her chin. "Grant me the privilege of ending this with dignity and in good taste, Hugh. We should deserve that at least."

"Are you sure about all this?"

No, she cried in her heart, I'm not at all sure about all this! I want you to take me into your arms and say you love me and that you will marry me no matter what I say. "Yes," she said, turning away from him. "This is best."

When he reached for her she said, "Please Hugh, if you don't go now, then we will not have such a dignified finish, but rather a scene that we will both later regret."

"Let me take you home."

"I'll walk, it isn't far, and I have a lot of thinking to do. Plans will have to be canceled, explanations made . . ."

She removed her engagement ring and started to hand it to him, but he said, "Keep it, Pauline. We are still friends."

Tears, like diamonds, glittered in her eyes as she walked away. She realized the enormity of her loss, she saw everything that was never going to be hers: the feel of Hugh's body making love to her, placing their first child in his arms. Pauline saw two futures, the one that could have been hers but which would now be Joanna Drury's, and the one that might be hers now—a future of long, empty years filled with loneliness and regret, as she became a hard, embittered woman who measured every man she met against Hugh Westbrook, and found each one lacking. A woman, she realized as the tears held, who was going to be like "Poor Miss Flora," pitied by her friends because she had been "passed over."

But such was not going to be Pauline's future, because there was a third alternative; and as it began to form in her mind, her sadness hardened into a new resolve; she turned her eyes eastward, toward Kilmarnock. And she thought of the handsome Colin MacGregor, locked away, and grieving over the loss of his wife, Christina.

"My dear Mr. Westbrook," Joanna wrote. "By the time you receive this letter, I will be on my way to Melbourne."

She paused and looked at the overland coach that was getting ready to leave. She was sitting outside the Fox and Hounds Inn with other passengers waiting to board the coach; the luggage was being strapped on top. Joanna's trunk had gone on first.

She resumed writing: "Since we both knew that I could not stay at Merinda once you were married, I decided to leave now, and spare us a difficult farewell. You have your new life, and I must get on with my purpose for coming to Australia. Perhaps I was not responsible for the things that happened at Merinda—the deaths of good people—but I know that I am caught up in forces beyond my control. I made a promise to my mother, and I owe it to my future children to find out what plagues our family, and somehow seek to disempower it."

She paused again, thinking about Hugh—of when he had found her by the river and taken her into his arms; the life and heat that had suddenly surged through her body; the kiss, the kisses. How strong she had felt at that moment.

And she thought: I came here not to fall in love and put down roots, but to claim my legacy, to find Karra Karra, to put to rest the demons that pursue the Drury women.

She tried to focus on what she was going to do next. Five months of searching had not brought her any closer to Karra Karra or the mystery of her grandfather's papers. She had heard from Mr. Asquith, the gentleman who had been appointed to the Board of Aboriginal Affairs, and whom Joanna had hoped might know about the natives, give her some information. But Mr. Asquith, it turned out, was a banker, who had been appointed for political reasons, and who had never even visited an Aboriginal mission or reservation. The Land Office in Melbourne had likewise been unable to help. There was not enough information on the deed, they had told her, for them to locate the land. She had received no response from Patrick Lathrop in America, who might have once known her grandfather.

Joanna had to begin all over again, searching for new clues, new signs that would put her on the right path.

She continued to write: "It is with great sadness that I leave Merinda, Mr. Westbrook, but my reason for being there—to help Adam—no longer exists. He is on the way to recovery. On the night you found me by the river, and you explained to Adam that he was not responsible for his mother's death, that he could not possibly have saved her, I saw the healing begin. Sarah will help him through the rest of it. And you and Miss Downs.

"I will never forget the time I spent at Merinda; I will certainly never forget you. I wish you health and happiness for all your days."

"All right, miss," the coachman said, "we're ready to go now."

Joanna sealed the letter and dropped it into the postbox at the coach stop. Then she took a seat with the other passengers, and as people waved good-by, the drivers picked up the reins and the coach lurched forward.

While the other passengers introduced themselves and remarked on what a hot summer it was, and what a blessing it was that the typhoid was over at last, Joanna stared out the window, saying a silent farewell to the familiar countryside, knowing that she might never see it again. And she thought: Maybe someday, years from now, I'll come back, and see how Adam has turned out, and what became of Sarah. And Hugh.

But the coach was stopping unexpectedly. They heard voices outside, and one of the passengers said, "A latecomer." And an elderly woman said, "Oh dear, we've no room."

They were startled when the door was suddenly opened, and Joanna saw Hugh standing there, looking furious. "I met Ezekiel on the road. He told me you'd left. Joanna, you were leaving without saying good-by."

"Hey there, mate," one of the drivers called out. "We've got to get going."

"I thought it would be best," Joanna said. "What you would prefer."

"Good God, if it hadn't been for Ezekiel, I would have missed you! Joanna, come out of there. You can't leave." To the driver he said, "Fetch Miss Drury's trunk down, please. There's been a mistake."

"But Mr. Westbrook—" Joanna began.

"I won't let you go, Joanna," he said. "Not like this. I want you to marry me. I love you."

She felt the eyes of the other passengers on them. "I don't understand," she said. "Miss Downs—"

He held out his hand. "Come back to Merinda with me, Joanna. Please."

"But we agreed . . . I mean, the trouble—"

"Joanna, for God's sake. Whatever it is, we'll fix it. I love you, Joanna. I love you and I can't live without you. I need you. Adam needs you."

"Yer holding up the coach, miss," said one of the drivers. "Either yer coming with us or you ain't, but make up yer mind. I got a schedule to keep."

She looked at Hugh's outstretched hand, and at his handsome face. She slipped her hand into his and stepped down to the ground.

She started to speak, but he drew her into his arms, and kissed her, and she put her arms around him and kissed him back.

PART TWO

1873

CHAPTER 12

A stranger was walking through the trees. Sarah remained hidden as she followed his progress along the river bank. When he stopped, she stopped; when he walked, she walked, like a shadow. She had never seen the man before.

She had come down to the billabong to harvest dandelion roots for Joanna, and she had glimpsed the man at the water's edge—a man strangely dressed. His trousers were made of buckskin, his shirt was of white linen, with billowing sleeves. He wore no jacket and no tie, and he was bareheaded. Sarah saw light-brown hair that was almost as long as her own, tied at the nape of his neck in a ponytail. He was carrying a large, flat book, and he stopped every so often to write in it. She saw that his hands were long and slender. A gentleman, she decided.

He paused to inspect a tree, squinted up at the sky between the clustered branches; then he wrote something down. Sarah saw a bright, metallic flash on his right wrist.

Her body was tense; the man didn't belong here. This spot was special to women—to Joanna, and to herself. They grew their herbs here, and it was where they talked and learned from each other, and exchanged women's secrets. Joanna told Sarah about the greater world, where ships sailed on vast oceans, and military men danced correctly and stiffly with beautifully dressed young ladies, and Sarah told Joanna of the ancestors' beliefs, and how they had created the world.

Sarah thought of this place too as her initiation site. Reverend Simms had interrupted her initiation by the old ones at the mission, and so she had not completed learning the secrets, but she learned other secrets now, about life, and just as sacred. "When you put this seed into the earth," Joanna had told her, "and you add water and sunshine and love, it will grow, just as a human being grows." Sarah's people had never put seeds into the ground; they had not made plants grow. This was magic—good magic.

And now, on this March day when summer was giving way to autumn, a strange man walked over their ground. Sarah felt uneasy; she had a feeling she couldn't put a name to. Perhaps it was because he was a man.

He might bring bad magic to this place; he might disturb the song-line. Now he was dangerously close to the sacred ruins. Sarah realized she would have to stop him.

She watched as he walked past the billabong. His tall, thin body was briefly silhouetted against the opalescent surface of the water. And now he was headed toward the ruins. Sarah crept along softly, her eyes never leaving him. When he stopped at the edge of the old ruined walls, she stopped too.

At the sacred stones, he dropped down on one knee; he reached out to touch them. Sarah cried out.

As Joanna stared at the drawing of the Rainbow Serpent, she felt a chill go through her. It looked exactly as her mother had described it in the diary—the giant snake that had haunted her dreams. To look at such a grotesque and frightening creature, and yet feel such familiarity with it, disturbed Joanna. The snake's one sharp eye seemed to be staring at her, mocking her, defying her.

"I know you're interested in Aboriginal things, Mrs. Westbrook," Mr. Talbot, the owner of the Book Emporium, said, "and so whenever I come across something I think you might like, I set it aside for you. This book is rather rare, you know, and quite fascinating, I think."

Joanna read the title: *My Life Among the Aborigines,* by Sir Finlay Cobb. It had been written in 1827, just forty years after the first white men set foot in Australia, and three years before her grandparents had arrived. "Yes, Mr. Talbot," Joanna said, staring at the disturbing image of the Rainbow Serpent. "It looks very interesting indeed."

She couldn't stop looking at the serpent's mesmerizing eye. She suddenly realized that, for some reason, the single eye of a serpent had figured largely in her mother's dreams—not just in the nightmares but, surprisingly, in the memory dreams as well. "I see my mother coming out of what might be a cave," Lady Emily had written, "and in the next instant, a giant snake bursts out of the cave, and its single eye terrifies me. Strangely, the woman who is holding me is not frightened. And the dark-skinned people all around me seem to be happy."

"Mrs. Westbrook?" Mr. Talbot said. "Do you wish to buy the book?"

"Yes," she said, handing it to him and reaching into her purse. As she did so, she placed her other hand on her abdomen, and thought of the new life there. She was going to have a child. Her joy was immense, but it was shadowed by the fear of her mother's legacy.

A year and a half had passed since the *Estella* had been becalmed, and then had sailed into the port of Melbourne. Joanna and Hugh had been married for a year, and Merinda was prospering, yet she was as intent as ever upon solving the mystery of her family's past, of finding the land that had been deeded to her grandparents. But so far she hadn't been able to learn much: People had responded to the inquiries Frank Downs ran in the *Times*, but always there was a problem—the dates were wrong, descriptions of the Makepeaces were inaccurate, and there were suspicious offers, the information being for sale. No communication had come from the Shorthand Society in London, so that Joanna doubted they would be able to help her. A visit to Farrell and Sons, cartographers, in Melbourne had shed no new light on the landmarks mentioned in the deed; and the government land survey offices to which she had written had all responded the same way: They needed more information.

But Joanna knew she had to persist, especially now that she was going to have a baby.

And perhaps her diligence was beginning to be rewarded at last. She drove the wagon as quickly as she could, anxious to get home to Hugh, the newly purchased book tucked in her shopping basket along with Merinda's mail—which finally included a letter from Patrick Lathrop in San Francisco. Joanna wished she could make the horse go faster, that she could reach Hugh faster. It was now painful for her to be away from him, she felt such a deep sense of connection when they were together. She was anxious to show him the letter from Lathrop, and the promise that it seemed to hold, that her search might soon be over. "I believe you knew my grandfather," she had written to Lathrop in letters sent over a period of months. She had not lost hope that he might still be alive, that one of her letters would reach him. And certainly the letters had never been returned. And here, after so long, was a response from him.

She steered the wagon into the yard, and looked anxiously around. Adam was where she had left him that morning, helping Matthew in the stable. Adam was six now, and anxious to be part of everything that went on around the station. Seeing no sign of Hugh or Sarah, Joanna went into the cabin.

A series of unexpected turns over the past year had delayed the building of the new house by the river, and so they still lived in the log cabin in the homeyard, but rooms had been added to make it more comfortable; the inside walls were plastered; there was more furniture. Joanna was eager to move her family away from the dirt and flies and odors of the sheep yard, down to where the air was clear and fresh and healthful. And that move was coming soon. Hugh had made an inspection of his ten thousand sheep and declared that, come November, they should have their best wool clip and lanolin production ever. And then they would start to build their fine new house.

Joanna set her basket down and lifted out the book she had just bought. It was subtitled: "The True and Detailed Account of a White Man's Sojourn Among the Savages of Australia." She trembled to think of what it might contain. Perhaps there was a mention of the red mountain in her mother's dreams, or possibly a description of the worship of the Rainbow Serpent, or even an explanation of poison-songs, and why they were sung. Because Joanna had come to believe that one of her grandparents, or both of them, might have done something taboo and been punished for it.

Tucking Lathrop's letter into her pocket, she went outside to find Adam, and then to look for Hugh.

The man looked up and saw the girl standing there, half in shadow, half in sunlight, brown and still and silent like the trees around her.

"Hello," he said, smiling, but Sarah simply stared at him.

He stood up and brushed off his knees. "This is a beautiful place," he said. "Do you live here?"

Sarah continued to stare.

"Did you plant this garden?" he asked.

Amid the native plants that grew along the billabong—the creeping buttercups and bluebells, the mock-olive bushes and tree ferns—Joanna and Sarah had planted exotic plants such as dill, cayenne and rosemary, which Joanna had told Sarah possessed healing properties. She also grew rare ginger, farther along the river, where a modest waterfall in the embrace of sunbaked boulders created the necessary humidity. The ginger was a short distance away from the ruins, but Sarah now realized she could smell the heady fragrance of its late-blooming blossoms.

She noticed that the man wore a beautiful bracelet worked in heavy silver and inlaid with turquoise; she had never seen a man wear jewelry before.

He squatted down and inspected a plant. "Goldenseal," he murmured. "The Indians in America use it to cure stomach ailments." He looked over the garden. "This looks like a healing garden. Are you a medicine woman?"

Sarah's eyes flickered over his head, and he looked back and saw the homestead through the trees. "The owner of this garden lives there?" He smiled. "At least I know you understand what I'm saying. My name is Philip McNeal," he said. He held out his hand, but Sarah remained frozen.

He took in the deeply set eyes, the reddish-brown hair hanging long and silky, the bare feet and the dress that had clearly once belonged to someone else but which had been altered to fit her. She didn't seem to be afraid of him, or shy, but there was something distrustful, wary, about the way she stood there. A wild girl, he thought, whom someone was perhaps trying to tame.

When he took a step toward the moss-covered wall, Sarah stiffened. "You don't want me there, do you?" he said. "This is a sacred place, isn't it? I know a little about that. I'm a great respecter of sacred places."

He saw that although her look remained wary, it held a spark of interest. "You remind me of a young woman I once knew," he said. "She was a Navaho, an American Indian. I was injured and she took care of me. Her name was Pollen on the Wind. I've been trying to read the marks on these stones. Do you know what they mean? Pollen on the Wind lived near a canyon where there are ruins like these. They were said to have been inhabited by a race called the Anasazi, which is a Navaho word meaning 'ancient alien ones.' They left markings similar to these."

He moved his arm and noticed that her eyes followed his wrist.

"I see you like my bracelet," he said. He took it off and showed it to Sarah. "It's Indian. Go ahead," he said. "Take a closer look."

Sarah suddenly stepped back. *"Tjuringa,"* she said.

"So," he said with a smile. "You *can* talk. I don't know what a
... *tjuringa* is. This is just something I wear to remind me of someone
special. It tells a story—see? There's a rainbow at the top, and a snake
at the bottom. The snake was Pollen's personal totem."

Sarah stared at it, her eyes wide.

"Tell me about this place," he said. "I really would like to know."

Sarah looked away, across the river, at tawny plains glowing in late
summer light.

"I'm asking you things I'm not supposed to, aren't I?" McNeal said,
putting the bracelet back on his wrist. "Pollen was a little like that. Her
people had been fighting the white soldiers for many years, until they
were finally forced to take a long walk across the desert and live in a
place that was not their ancestral land. Pollen didn't trust me at first,
but later she did. My government thought that her people should learn
to live in proper houses. I'm an architect. That was what I was supposed
to do for Pollen's people—show them how to build white men's
houses."

Sarah kept her eyes on the man. She realized that he was beautiful,
despite the slightly crooked nose which she decided must have been
broken once. There was a softly nasal quality to his voice, and he spoke
of things she had never heard a white man speak of before—totems and
clans, sacred places and rainbow serpents.

"Sarah," she said softly.

His eyebrows rose. "Is that your name? Sarah? It's a very pretty
name. If you live here, then I know we'll become friends. I've been
hired to build a house here."

A look of uncertainty crossed her face, but before he could say
anything, there was the sound of footsteps approaching, and, turning,
he saw a young woman coming toward him, leading a small boy by the
hand.

"Hello," she said. "You must be Mr. McNeal. How do you do? I am
Joanna Westbrook." They shook hands, and McNeal realized Hugh
Westbrook's wife was younger than he had expected, a few years
younger than himself in fact, and very pretty. Her eyes, he saw, were
the color of amber, and her rich brown hair was swept up from a
slender neck, revealing a pair of bright blue earrings. She wore a pale
green dress with a brooch at her throat.

"I see you've already met Sarah," Joanna said.

"Yes," McNeal said. "She seems not to want me to be here."

"This place is special to her people, Mr. McNeal. Sarah lives with
us, at the homestead."

"Sarah's my friend," Adam said, and McNeal laughed and smiled at the boy. "Lucky you," he said.

"This is Adam," Joanna said, and Adam stared at McNeal. "Why do you have long hair?" he asked.

McNeal laughed and said, "I learned to wear my hair this way when I lived with some native people in America. I learned a lot of things from them." He glanced at Sarah. "Why are these ruins sacred to Sarah, Mrs. Westbrook?" he asked.

"The Aborigines believe that the Kangaroo Ancestress came through here in the Dreamtime, and that she sang this place into existence. Her spirit is here still. No one but a member of the Kangaroo Clan can walk here."

"These are a very spiritual people," McNeal said, looking at the silent girl.

He glanced around at the heavy old gum trees reflected on the shimmering surface of the pond. "Your husband told me he wanted me to build your house here. What would happen if I did?"

"What do you mean?"

"Would it cause problems? I mean, do the Aborigines put up a fight when their sacred sites are disturbed?"

Joanna recalled again what Farrell, the cartographer, had told her: "The name of Karra Karra could have been changed years ago. Today it could be Johnson's Creek or New Dover. You could pass right through it and never know it was the place you were looking for."

"They did resist, I'm told, years ago," she said. "But they were no match for European guns and horses."

McNeal said, "There are wars going on now where I come from, too. Tribes such as the Sioux, the Navaho, and the Apache are fighting white soldiers for the right to hold onto their land. They are terrible, bloody battles, with heavy losses on both sides."

"Yes," Joanna said. "We have heard about them."

McNeal looked at Sarah, and then said to Joanna, "What would the Aborigines believe would happen if we built a house here?"

"Since apparently this site lies along a songline, the Aborigines believe that to change the songlines is to change Creation, because to desecrate a sacred spot is taboo. It is to uncreate the world."

"To uncreate the world," Philip McNeal said, thinking of the day he had said good-by to Pollen and her people, knowing even then that he would never see her or her world again.

"Does this river ever flood, Mrs. Westbrook?" he asked, looking around to see if there might be an alternative building site.

"I don't know, we'll have to ask Mr. Westbrook. I came to Australia only a year and a half ago."

"May I ask what brought you here?" he asked, wondering about the relationship between this poised young woman, the boy, and the half-wild Aboriginal girl.

"My mother died two years ago," Joanna said. "In India. She died of a spiritual affliction." Joanna paused, thinking of the poison-song. "She believed that that affliction somehow was mine as well. I came here to find out, and to heal myself."

"Is that why you have created this healing garden?"

"These herbs heal the body, Mr. McNeal. The healing I seek is more complicated, I'm afraid. Partly, it has to do with a place."

"A place?"

"It's a place called Karra Karra—or at least I think so. My mother believed it was a place that held a key to things. But I haven't found it yet."

"Is it a sacred site?"

"I'm not sure. Possibly."

"Why is it so hard to find?"

Joanna thought of the gentleman she had met in Melbourne last year, a scholar from England who had spent five years studying the Aborigines. "If Karra Karra is the name of a sacred site," he had told her, "then you might never find it. I've learned that to speak of a sacred site to a white man is taboo. You might in fact meet an Aborigine who knows the whereabouts of Karra Karra, but he won't tell you."

Philip McNeal now said, "Maybe Karra Karra isn't a real place at all, Mrs. Westbrook. Maybe it's a state of mind. Or a philosophy."

"What's that?" Adam said, pointing to the silver-and-turquoise bracelet.

"Adam," Joanna said.

"I don't mind. Here, Adam," McNeal said, handing him the bracelet.

Through the trees Joanna saw Ezekiel standing on the other side of the river. She had gotten used to his appearing suddenly near here, to stand for a while and stare, and then to disappear just as suddenly. He had not spoken to her since the day by the river, when he had walked up, carrying a boomerang. But she knew from Sarah that the old man was no longer so opposed to Joanna's being at Merinda. Joanna sometimes had the strange feeling, when he was watching her, that he was guarding her.

"There is the gentleman you should ask about Aboriginal culture, Mr. McNeal," Joanna said, and the architect looked over at the old Aborigine, standing like a statue on the river bank. Then he said,

"Maybe Sarah can explain these things to me. The people I lived with, the Indian tribes in America, centered their lives on songs. They would sing a song that went on for hours, or even days. Their songs were everything to them—their history, their art, their religion. The Song of the Coyote is actually made up of over three hundred songs."

"What's a coyote?" Adam asked.

"A native wild dog of America. Smaller than your dingoes."

Joanna felt a sudden chill. One morning the previous week, when she had been down here working in her garden, she had looked up to see a dingo moving through the trees. It had stopped and looked at her, then moved away, but what had startled her, and what she remembered most vividly now, was the terror she had felt upon seeing the dog. She had realized with a shock that she had inherited her mother's excessive fear of dogs.

"What brought you to Australia originally, Mr. McNeal?" she said.

"I suppose you might say I'm looking for something, too. I went to a college in the East in America, where I thought I would learn everything there was to know, but I came out realizing that I didn't know much of anything that was very useful. My father died in the war, at a place called Manassas, and my mother was never able to accept it. I wanted to know why things like war happen. I wanted to know why the world was the way it was. I traveled around America looking for answers, and I stayed for a while with the native people. And then I left and came here."

He glanced toward Sarah, who was inspecting the bracelet with Adam, then he said, "I'm afraid we have a problem, Mrs. Westbrook. I've spent the morning looking over your land here by the river, and where these ruins are is the best site for your house. Clearly the people who lived here long ago knew that, too. The ground is too sandy and marshy everywhere else, and there is danger of the river flooding. You and your husband might be forced into making a choice—build here, or up there where you are, at the homestead."

Hugh had news for Joanna, and he had ridden home fast. But as he dismounted, he heard someone call his name. Squinting in the glare of the March sunshine, he saw a familiar figure riding up. It was Jacko, the man who owned a 7,000-acre run to the northeast of Merinda.

"Can I have a word with you, Hugh?" he said.

Hugh was hot and tired, and anxious to see Joanna. "What is it, Jacko?" he said.

Jacko swung to the ground, a portly man who sweated in the heat of late summer, and said, "It's about the maid, Hugh. I came over to ask if you would give the job to my Peony."

"Maid?"

"I was in town this morning, and I heard from Poll Gramercy that your wife is going to be hiring a maid to help around the house, now that she's going to have a baby."

Hugh stared at the man.

"Peony's a good girl, Hugh," Jacko said. "She mightn't be bright, but she's honest and she's quiet. And well, she's eighteen years old now, and I don't reckon any man is going to want to marry her. The missus and I worry about Peony's future. What do you say, Hugh?"

Hugh barely heard what Jacko said. His mind was racing back over recent days, recalling Joanna's morning indispositions, a special look that he would catch on her face, and her exceptionally cheerful mood as she left for Cameron Town.

He brought himself back to Jacko. "You said you heard this from Poll Gramercy?" The Widow Gramercy was the local midwife.

"I hope you don't mind my coming to you like this, Hugh. I knew that once the word was out you'd have an army of girls begging for the job. And my Peony, well, she's—"

Jacko's voice faded as Hugh stared at the cabin. So Joanna had paid a visit to the midwife.

"Will you think about it, Hugh?"

He looked at Jacko. Everyone in the district knew about poor Peony Jackson, about how while Jacko's wife had been plowing a field she had gone into labor two months before she was due. She had been all alone, with no way to send for help, and it had taken her almost a day and a night to deliver the baby on her own, it being her first baby and Sal being only seventeen. Everyone had declared that the baby couldn't possibly survive, but it did. And Peony had grown up to be a nice girl, quiet and obedient, except that she was a little simpleminded.

"I'll talk to my wife about it, Jacko," Hugh said, "but I suspect Peony can have the job. Now, if you don't mind—" Hugh started to walk away.

But the man remained where he was, shooing a fly away from his face. "I was wondering, Hugh," he said after a moment, "if you had heard about the trouble I'm having."

"I've been out working the far paddocks. What's the trouble?"

"My mob's been infected with the scab. I won't have a wool clip this year."

Hugh was stunned. He knew Jacko had been struggling to make a go of his run; such a loss could mean his ruin. And Jacko had six kids, with a seventh on the way. "I'm sorry," Hugh said. "I didn't know."

"I'd swear it's that bastard MacGregor behind it," Jacko said as he pulled out a handkerchief and wiped his sweating face. "He's been after my run for a long time. I'd lay odds that he got some bad sheep mixed in with my mob somehow. Remember Rob Jones, who used to have the run the other side of me? It was MacGregor who saw that he went bankrupt. I can't prove it, but Rob sold to MacGregor and now that bastard wants my run as well."

"But what makes you think Colin MacGregor's behind it?"

"Because he sent his agent to me with an offer of a loan. It's obvious what he's up to, Hugh. If I accept his money, and then something happens next year and I still have no clip, he'll take my station."

Hugh looked into Jacko's broad, honest face and felt like swearing. He thought of how Colin MacGregor had changed in the year since the death of his wife and unborn child. He seemed to have become consumed with hate and vengeance. And with greed—he was buying up all the land in the district, using ruthless tactics if necessary. It was as if he had abandoned all conscience and ethics, and the other graziers were starting to raise eyebrows. Hugh suspected MacGregor had his eye on Merinda.

"I don't like to see any man driven off his land, Jacko," Hugh said. "Tell MacGregor's agent you don't want his deal. I'll lend you the money."

Jacko stared at him. "You'd do that, Hugh? *Can* you?"

Hugh thought of the house they were about to start building, and the expensive new stud ram he wanted to bring in, the wells he wanted to drill. And now . . . a baby on the way. But he had inspected his sheep and it looked as if this year's clip was going to be good. "Don't worry, Jacko," he said. "I'll manage something. And come shearing time next year, you'll be taking wool to Melbourne with the rest of us."

As Jacko rode away, Hugh went up the veranda steps and into the cool interior of the cabin. Joanna was not there, but her hat and shopping basket lay on the table, along with the weekly newspapers and journals she always picked up for him.

When he went back outside, he saw someone else riding into the yard, a young man named Tim Forbes, who hired himself out as a delivery boy and messenger in Cameron Town. He had been riding hard; Hugh saw the postal sack on the back of the horse. "Special parcel for you, Mr. Westbrook!" he said. "Here y'are. Gotta have ya sign for it."

Hugh signed, and was handed a square box, wrapped in brown paper and twine. He looked at the parcel and saw that it was addressed to Joanna. The sender was the lawyer in Bombay who sent her quarterly allowance to her. He hurried down to the river, where he found Joanna near the Aboriginal ruins with Adam and Sarah, and the architect from Melbourne.

"Daddy!" Adam cried, running to Hugh. Then, "What's that?"

"It's something for your mother. Hello, Mr. McNeal," he said, as they shook hands. "I see you found us all right."

"Your wife and have I just been discussing the site for the new house."

"Before you say anything further, Mr. McNeal," Hugh said as he slipped his arm around Joanna's waist, "I want to tell you that when you and I met over a year ago, I had said that I wanted something American, southern plantation style you called it, with columns and gables. We've changed our minds. My wife and I want our house to be Australian, suited to this climate and environment. We don't want a house that tells people where we've come from or where we'd rather be, but where we are."

When he saw McNeal frown, he said, "What's wrong?"

"Hugh," Joanna said. "There's a problem."

When she had explained about the sacred site, Hugh said, "But this is the only place we can put the house. There's a solid rock foundation here, good drainage and no threats if the river flooded."

"But this is a Dreaming site," Joanna said. "It's sacred."

"But Joanna, the Aborigines don't live here any more. They don't even come around here. They've forgotten this place, Joanna. They're forgetting all their Dreaming sites. And we have to build our house somewhere. We can't go on living in the cabin."

When he saw the distressed look on her face, he turned to Philip McNeal and said, "What do you think?"

"I don't know, Mr. Westbrook. It's possible that an alternate site might be found. I'll have to do some soil testing, see where you've got sand, where you've got clay, check the water levels, that sort of thing. If you're not set on the American-style house, then it's possible I can design something that will solve the problem." He smiled. "It's a challenge, but that's what I like. If you don't mind, I'll look around some more."

"Of course."

McNeal struck off through the trees, back toward the river, and after hesitating a moment, Sarah and Adam followed.

"Hugh," Joanna said, "where did the parcel come from?"

He turned to her with an anxious look. "What did Poll Gramercy say?"

"How did you know I went to see Mrs. Gramercy! Oh Hugh, I wanted it to be a surprise."

"Believe me, Joanna, I'm surprised. What did she say?"

"Mrs. Gramercy confirmed it. We're going to have a baby."

Hugh took her into his arms and kissed her. "What do you want it to be, a boy or a girl?" he asked.

"I hope it's a son for you," Joanna said. "But I'm wishing for a daughter. I've always wanted a little girl."

"I fancy a girl, too. I never had sisters, I never knew my mother. I've always thought how nice it would be to have a daughter."

He kissed her again and held her close, this marvel of a woman who had come so unexpectedly into his life a year and a half ago and turned it around. He thought of the ballad that he was writing, inspired two Christmasses ago: "She traversed the great swelled seas/To this golden land . . ." It was the longest ballad he had ever written, it was nearly finished, and now suddenly, the title came to him: "The Dreaming— For Joanna."

"Tim Forbes just brought this for you," Hugh said as he handed her the parcel. "It came by special post."

"It's from Mr. Drexler," she said in surprise, and began to work at the twine and sealing wax.

"And now for my news," Hugh said. "Joanna, do you remember my telling you about a man I met in Melbourne, when I took the last clip to the harbor? A man named Finch?"

Joanna searched her memory, then she remembered: Back in November, Hugh had spoken about meeting a Mr. Finch, who owned a special kind of ram. It came from a French strain, Hugh had explained, called a rambouillet, and it possessed the characteristics he had been looking for to crossbreed with his merino ewes in the hope of finding a strain of sheep robust enough to suit the arid plains of Queensland. But the ram had not been for sale.

"I got a telegram from Finch today. He has decided to go back to England, and he's offering to sell me the ram," Hugh said. "It's a magnificent animal, Joanna, big and rugged, with a deep frame and long-stapled wool. Finch said it yields a fleece weighing twenty-five pounds of unwashed wool. Think of it, Joanna. If I can combine the best characteristics of that ram with my best merino ewes, then we could be well on our way to creating a breed that can be run all over

Queensland and New South Wales! I've dreamed for so long of creating a new breed that now that I almost have it in my hands, I can't let it get away."

"Of course not!" she said, feeling his excitement. "How soon can we have it?"

"I'll have to leave for Melbourne at once. Finch has given me first chance at it, but there will be other buyers." He fell silent and looked at her. "So," he said, "we're going to have a baby." He laughed. "A fine thing, a man learning about his wife's pregnancy from another man."

"Whoever wrapped this parcel," she said, trying to break the string, "never intended for it to be opened."

"What do you suppose Drexler has sent you?"

"I can't imagine. And it cost him a lot for the special handling. Look at these stamps." Other than the quarterly check that came from Drexler's Bombay office, Joanna received no communication from the lawyer. But she did expect to hear from him in a year, when she turned twenty-one and came into her full inheritance.

"Oh, Hugh," she said, remembering Lathrop's letter and reaching into the pocket of her skirt. "This came today, from Patrick Lathrop—the man mentioned in my mother's diary."

While Joanna persisted with the uncooperative twine, Hugh opened the letter and read: "My dear Miss Drury, I write to you in response to your several communications to me. Forgive the lateness of my reply, but I have been away. As I travel a great deal, my permanent address in California is here at the Regent Hotel. I can always be reached through Mrs. Robbins, the proprietor, should the need arise.

"Yes, I was a classmate of your grandfather's at Christ's College in Cambridge, during the years of 1826–1829. We were both there to prepare for Holy Orders in the Church of England. I recall John and his bride well. I was the best man at their wedding! Naomi so sweet and so much in love. John so zealous and anxious to get on with his work. But he did not go to Australia as a missionary, Miss Drury. And his papers are most assuredly not sermons."

"Not sermons," Hugh said. "Then what are they, I wonder?"

He continued to read. "John never finished his schooling at Cambridge," Lathrop wrote, "having discovered that he had no taste for the religious life. In fact, I rather suspected your grandfather was something of an agnostic, although he never admitted it. Rather than preaching the Bible, he was far more interested in proving it. And as I recall, he was particularly interested in the account of Eden.

"He had a theory that God, being disappointed in Adam and Eve, decided to create a second Eden in another part of the world. John believed he would find that second Eden in Australia. When he read accounts of a primitive people being found at the Sydney Settlement, people who did not read or write, who knew not the wheel, who went about unclothed, and who did not even grow their own food, he had thought this was the second Eden, from which the original parents had *not* been expelled. John's theory was based on the fact that the Australian Aborigines fear and revere the serpent, and that therefore they would not have been tempted by it to eat from the forbidden Tree of Knowledge. I do not know if John was ever able to prove his theory.

"You wrote of your grandfather's papers, Miss Drury. Perhaps they are his observations of the people he studied."

Hugh turned to the second page. "You say that they seem to be written in a kind of code," Lathrop wrote. "Several of us used shorthand of one sort or another for taking notes during lectures. I had my own system, invented by myself and not very good. I recall that your grandfather's was very efficient. Perhaps if you sent me a sample of it, I could translate it for you.

"I regret, Miss Drury, that I am unable to supply you with the more precise information which you requested in your letter—specifically, where in Australia your grandparents traveled to. But I do recall one fact that might be of some help. I saw them off on the day they sailed, forty-three years ago, in 1830. I remember that their vessel had a rather exotic name. The name itself I cannot call to mind, but I do remember that it was some sort of mythical beast. Alas, I cannot recall their port of disembarkation, but perhaps if you can identify their ship, you can determine where they went ashore."

"Mythical beast!" Hugh said.

"Perhaps a unicorn," Joanna said. "Or a sea serpent. Hugh, there must be records somewhere of ships arriving at Melbourne or Sydney. I'll go to Melbourne with you," she said. "We'll search the records for a ship with this kind of a name."

"I'll ask Frank Downs to help us. He has friends all over the city."

"Hugh, I simply *cannot* get this package open."

"Here, let me try." He broke the twine, peeled away the paper and wax, and handed the box back to Joanna. Inside, she found a smaller box nested in straw, with a letter on top.

She read the letter, then said, "Oh, Hugh! I'm to receive my inheritance now! Mr. Drexler says that since I am married I don't have to wait until my next birthday. And it's such a large amount. What shall we do with it?"

"It's your money, Joanna. Your parents meant for you to have it. What do *you* want to do with it?"

She thought a moment, and said, "I'd like to use it in my search for Karra Karra. My mother would have used it for that purpose. And the rest of it I would like to put away for our daughter, for her future."

"What's in the box?"

"I don't know, Mr. Drexler says only that it is something my parents placed in his safekeeping. He says he doesn't know what its value is, but that he suspects it might be considerable."

Joanna lifted the smaller box out and removed the lid. She stared for a moment at the contents. Then she brought it out and showed it to Hugh.

When he saw the gemstone that nearly filled the palm of her hand, he said, "It's an opal—a fire opal. You can tell by the way the red flashes seem to follow the sun when you turn your hand. Fire opals are very rare, Joanna, and quite valuable."

Joanna was mesmerized by the stone. It was about as large as an orange slice, irregularly shaped, and the colors were dazzling: Set in a wine-yellow sea were vivid green and red flames that danced like fire, and which did indeed, as Hugh said, seem to follow the sun when the stone was turned. "It's beautiful!" she said. "Where do you suppose my parents got it? Could it have come from Australia?"

"I've heard of opals being found in New South Wales, but nothing like this. It might have come from Mexico, that's where the big opal mines are."

"The flames in the center appear to be moving. And the colors, Hugh! What makes it do that?"

"I don't know."

"It feels warm. Here." She placed it in his hand.

He shook his head. "I don't feel anything. It just feels like a rock." He gave it back to her. "You didn't know your parents had this?"

"I don't recall them ever mentioning it," Joanna said as she stared at the flashing red heart of the opal. She couldn't take her eyes from it.

Philip McNeal appeared then, with Sarah following a short distance behind, holding Adam by the hand. "I think I've found a solution to your problem, Mr. Westbrook," he said. "The soil looks good over there. What we can do is sink deep footings, about five or six feet below the level of the river, and pack them with concrete. We can raise the foundation of the house and reinforce it with a concrete bunker. If you still have trouble when the river floods, we can take care of it with a coffer dam. But I'm afraid it's going to be costly, and it will take a lot longer to build. However, if you're still interested, I think I've found the site for it, if you would care to come with me and take a look." He turned to Joanna and added with a smile, "I know it's all right to build there, Mrs. Westbrook, because I walked all over it and Sarah didn't say a word."

As Joanna and Sarah walked in silence to the homestead, Sarah turned and looked back at Philip McNeal.

CHAPTER 13

Your old adversary Vilma Todd has been seen riding with Colin MacGregor," Louisa Hamilton said as she watched Pauline take aim at the distant target and let loose her arrow.

Bull's-eye.

"Indeed?" Pauline said as she reached into her quiver, drew out another arrow, nocked it on the bowstring, took careful aim and let fly. Another bull's-eye.

"Well done, Pauline!" Louisa said. "That gives you six hits at thirty yards, the record score for the Western District Archery Club!"

Pauline was shooting on the private archery range at Lismore, while Louisa watched, sitting on a chair beneath an umbrella, sipping lemonade. "It must be wonderful," she said, "to be so skilled. I do envy you."

Pauline cast a glance at her friend. Pauline knew that Louisa had always envied her; but that envy had of late been tempered with a tinge of gloating. The whole district seemed to be infected with it. Pauline knew what her friends thought of her: that she had been passed over for a nursemaid! It didn't matter that both Pauline and Hugh had told everyone that it was Pauline, not Hugh, who had called off the wedding. And it didn't matter that Joanna Drury hadn't in fact been a nursemaid but rather the daughter of a knight. Pauline's reputation had suffered.

"What was I saying?" Louisa said. "Oh yes, Vilma Todd and Colin MacGregor. They've been seen on four separate occasions. People are speculating on the possibility of their getting married."

"Is that so?" Pauline said, as she waited for the groom to remove the arrows from the target. She had already heard about Vilma Todd and Colin MacGregor, and it didn't worry her. Nor did it worry her that several young ladies in the district, younger than herself, had set their sights on the handsome and eligible Colin, now that the customary year of mourning for Christina was over. Neither was Pauline concerned with the fact that despite her own carefully planned campaign to win Colin MacGregor, he had, for his own reasons, rejected her. She would have him in the end. She was determined.

When the target was clear, Pauline took out another arrow, raised her longbow, sighted down the shaft and let go. This time the arrow went slightly off the mark.

She sensed her friend's smile from beneath the shade of the umbrella. Ever since Hugh had married Joanna Drury, a slight air of superiority had crept into Louisa's attitude, but Pauline chose to ignore it. Let Louisa and the rest of the district think what they liked, Pauline thought as she drew out another arrow and loosed it on the target, ninety feet away, hitting another bull's-eye. They would not remain smug for long. What they didn't know, and what her young and pretty competitors for MacGregor did not know, was that Pauline held a secret card, one that should assure her of victory.

She knew two things about Colin that no one else knew. The first was that he would never love anyone again. She had been in the room with him the night Christina died, and she had seen what the tearing away of her life had done to him. The other girls in the district might delude themselves into thinking they could get Colin to fall in love with them, but Pauline knew that he would never allow himself to love another woman. And Pauline had another advantage: She, too, would never love again. And so it would suit her if Colin did not fall in love with her. She wanted only his name, his wealth, the position of a wife and, like Colin himself, children.

"You know that Colin MacGregor *will* marry again, Pauline," Louisa said. "He told Mr. Hamilton that he's not going to send his son away to school when the time comes, but rather he will keep him at Kilmarnock. So the boy will need a mother."

Louisa watched her friend carefully for a crack in that cool façade.

Pauline's body was perfectly straight, disciplined; whenever she shot during public archery tournaments, Pauline was always praised for her "impressive form and figure," as Frank, in a moment of brotherly adulation, had reported in an edition of the *Times*. "Miss Downs, winner of her sixth Championship Cup, struck the spectators with amazement and awe, she seemed a modern-day Artemis." Louisa thought that if Pauline was troubled by the fact that she didn't stand a chance of snaring a man everyone knew she was after, she was skilled at hiding it. To Louisa she appeared to be as in control as ever.

"Even though he's been seen with Vilma Todd," Louisa continued. "I'm putting my money on Verity Campbell. After all, Verity is only nineteen years old, while poor Vilma is nearly twenty-four. A man with a mind for starting a family wants a young wife."

Pauline, who was facing her twenty-sixth birthday, let fly another arrow.

Another bull's-eye.

"I was talking with Mrs. Gramercy the other day," Louisa said. "She said that Maude Reed is having female trouble . . . ."

While she talked on, it occurred to Pauline that it had been over a year since Louisa had lost her baby during the typhoid epidemic, and that she had yet to get pregnant again. Pauline wondered if Louisa had in fact found out about the secrets of birth prevention.

"Poll Gramercy told me something else," Louisa said, carefully watching Pauline. "Joanna Westbrook is pregnant."

"Yes," Pauline said. "I know."

Pauline needed to concentrate to maintain control over her next shot. The news of Joanna's pregnancy, when she had heard it, had sent her into a cold rage, making her wonder what madness had driven her to commit that selfless act of letting Hugh go. It must have been the atmosphere of sickness and death, she decided; in the midst of so many new graves, Pauline had felt a rare and strange nobility of spirit. But she would not allow herself to live with regret. Regret, in Pauline's mind, was a waste of time and it got no one anywhere. Hugh was married; that was that.

But was he happy, Pauline wondered, with his little English bride?

"I understand," Louisa said, "that Angus McCloud has been calling on you."

Pauline sighed and, lowering her bow, signaled to the groom to bring her a glass of lemonade.

She thought of the men who had started paying attention to her, as soon as news of her break with Hugh was known in the district. They came with airs and promises, they came in all sizes and shapes and ages, most of them wealthy and all of them boring. There were times when Pauline would much rather not have to get married at all; she cherished her independence. But she hated the fact that society marked an unmarried woman as a failure—one who had not been up to the competition. And, too, she was lonely. What was she now to do with her life?

Pauline thought of Colin MacGregor. Everyone knew about his desire to have more children, more heirs. The sudden loss of Christina and the baby had made him fanatical about Judd; he realized his feelings would have a bad effect on the boy, and he was terrified that he would lose his only heir. The noble line of MacGregor had to go on, and so there was this competition to see who would get him.

And Colin was a choice prize to win. Even though it was apparent that Colin didn't consider Pauline a candidate, she was making her plans. She didn't want this target to escape. And this involved the second of the two secrets she knew about Colin, the other thing that no one else knew.

The thought of him excited her. Colin was a man with power; he knew how to use it. And if people were saying that he had been on a rampage lately, was becoming ruthless and unscrupulous, buying up land, Pauline decided perhaps that was the way of the future. Only the strong could be victorious. Men of weak will and faint heart did not become rich, they did not build empires. His strength and power aroused her. What would it be like, she wondered, to be made love to by Colin MacGregor? To be in bed with him, to feel his arms around her, his body against hers.

She suddenly turned away from the target. It was time, she realized, to play her hand. "You will forgive me, Louisa, but I have to run."

"Oh?" Louisa said, searching Pauline's face. "Can I give you a ride in my carriage?"

"I'm afraid we're going in opposite directions, Louisa dear. But you stay and finish your lemonade. I know how sensitive you are to the hot weather."

A few minutes later Pauline was mounted on a handsome dapple-gray named Samson, riding away from Lismore. She gave the horse free rein and soon they were galloping over the grass-carpeted plains, with Samson flying over hawthorn hedges and wooden fences, his hooves thundering through clumps of scarlet honeysuckle, past stands of blackwood trees and she-oaks. Cockatoos flew up out of gum trees to flutter startled in the sky, their hundreds of coral pink bodies etched against the blue. Pauline thought of Colin MacGregor as she rode, as she felt the horse's massive body move between her legs, and she held tightly to the reins and controlled him.

———————————————•—————————————————

"Shoot her!" Colin shouted. "Shoot her, I said!"

Judd struggled to take aim, but he was shaking so badly that he couldn't control the rifle.

"Damn it, Judd! Shoot!"

Judd pulled the trigger and the shot went wild, ricocheting off a rock and sending the big kangaroo to flight.

Colin cursed under his breath. The animal had gotten away, again.

"I don't know what gets into you, Judd," he said, shaking his head as he tramped over the dry grass toward his son. "We've been after that doe for weeks. You couldn't have asked for a better shot at her. And you let her get away."

Judd didn't say anything, he just stood there with his rifle in his hands, staring at the spot where the kangaroo had been. Now all he saw were grass and shrub and wild flowers.

"Ah well, at least we got these. Not bad for a morning's work." Colin gestured toward a large pile of kangaroo carcasses heaped under a gum tree, but Judd stared at them despondently. They were all different sizes and colors, but mostly they were young ones, with the kind of soft gray fur and big, deer-like eyes that made him loathe kangaroo hunting.

"All right," Colin said to the men who were standing near the pile. "Set fire to it. We've done enough for today."

And that was the worst part of it for Judd—they weren't killing the animals for meat or fur, but just for the sport of it. Judd recalled how it used to be, in the days when his mother was still alive. Visitors would come to Kilmarnock, and there would be a big hunt and maybe four hundred kangaroos would be slaughtered, then left behind in a fiery heap. Sometimes the fire would be started while the animals were still alive, and you could hear them screaming as you rode back to the homestead.

"Don't be upset, Judd," Colin said. "You can't win every time. At least not yet. You'll get better at it. And next time, I'll wager you'll get that doe. It looked as if she had a joey in her pouch. That would be a double trophy!"

But Judd was upset, and for reasons his father didn't suspect, and so he couldn't help the tears from coming. Finally he dropped his rifle and sobbed into his hands.

Colin was on his knees at once, taking the nine-year-old into his arms. "That's all right, son," he said. "I know how you feel. I was frustrated, too, when I was your age, and my father took me out shooting and I wasn't as good at it as the men were. But you're only a boy yet. You'll be a marksman someday, I promise you. Come on, then, stop the crying."

Little Judd gulped back the sobs and then ran his hand under his nose.

"That's better," said Colin. But when the boy wiped his hand down his pants, Colin MacGregor frowned. "Where's your handkerchief? Here. Use this on your nose, not your hand, you know."

And when Judd, taking his father's handkerchief, said, "Aw, bugger it," Colin's eyebrows shot up. "Where did you learn language like that?"

"It's what the stockmen say."

"Well, you're not a stockman and you're not to use such words. Do you understand?"

As Judd nodded dumbly, Colin said, holding his son by the shoulders, "Listen. Someday you're going to be the laird of Kilmarnock. You're going to be a lord and a gentleman. Gentlemen don't use words like that."

Colin studied Judd's face—so like his beloved Christina's—and thought once again: This boy needs a mother.

It was a brutal fact that had to be faced, much as Colin loathed the thought. It had been fourteen months since Christina's death; it was time to be thinking of remarrying. He couldn't risk losing Judd, and find himself with no heirs. Colin refused to believe that all his hard work would be for nothing.

When young Colin MacGregor had arrived in Australia to find no established ruling class and no peasantry, just a hodgepodge of social strata with no clearly defined top or bottom, he had known that an aristocracy would eventually emerge. He had built his castle as a vanguard of civilization in a rambling half-tamed place and as a reminder to those of common blood that a true lord was living among them. He had worked hard to give Kilmarnock a name that meant power and influence, a name, Colin sincerely believed, that made the ordinary man proud to live near him. A name that needed to be carried on.

He took Judd's hand and led him to the refreshment tent. Colin towered over the servants and grooms, a tall, aristocratic man elegantly dressed in a cableknit sweater, tweed jacket, and moleskin trousers tucked into shiny black boots. There was no dirt on Colin MacGregor, no mud or dust marring his perfection. The working of the station he left to his agents, while he himself engaged in more gentlemanly pursuits.

He accepted a whiskey from one of the grooms and turned to see his manager, Locky McBean, ride up, removing his hat and twisting it in his hands. Colin didn't like the man, but he was necessary, and he did as he was told without asking a lot of questions.

"I'm afraid I've got bad news, Mr. MacGregor," he said. "It's about Jacko Jackson."

"Well? What is it?"

Locky's eyes slid to the liquor cart, rested there for a moment, then came back to his employer. "Jacko's sheep have got the scab all right, and there won't be no wool clip this year." Locky looked at the cart again, licking his lips.

"And?" Colin said. He knew that other graziers, such as Westbrook and Frank Downs, drank with their station hands and allowed other laxities in propriety, but he did not drink with his overseer. "Get on with it then," he said. "What about Jacko?"

"He turned you down—your offer of a loan."

Colin said, "But how can he? There isn't a bank in the colony that will lend him money."

"Well, sir, it seems that Hugh Westbrook will. Jacko got the money from Westbrook."

Colin's face darkened. When Westbrook had first appeared in the district nearly twelve years ago, Colin MacGregor and the rest of the graziers hadn't thought he would survive. But Westbrook had surprised them all, not only by surviving, but by making a success of a run that had known only bad luck. Now Merinda was growing into a prosperous and desirable station, and it occupied one of the best stretches of river frontage, with excellent grazing grass and plentiful wells.

It wasn't fair, Colin thought, that Westbrook should prosper so, while Christina lay cold in her grave.

"All right," Colin said, dismissing the overseer. He stared into his whiskey, then glanced up to see someone riding across the plain. A woman. She was not riding sidesaddle, but the way a man rode, which could only mean one person: Pauline Downs.

Colin suspected that Pauline considered herself a likely choice to be the next Mrs. MacGregor. He recalled the last time he had paid a visit to Lismore, to discuss with her a certain five thousand acres of woodland that lay along the southern base of the mountains. It was a piece of property that had been in the Downs family for thirty-three years, ever since the elder Downs had bought it when he had first carved out his domain in the Western District back in 1840. It was considered useless by most men, being unsuitable for grazing, having a poor water supply and unable to support wheat or other crops. But it had one thing in its favor that made it priceless to Colin: It stretched along the northern boundary of Merinda.

Colin recalled now how happily Pauline had first greeted him, using her best charms and wiles, and then how abruptly her manner had changed when he had told her the purpose of his visit. Pauline had turned cold and had archly informed Colin that she didn't know if her brother would sell, and that she wasn't sure she would want him to.

Colin had once briefly contemplated the idea of considering Pauline for marriage, but after assessing her character—the streak of independence, the fiercely competitive spirit—he had decided that it would be a mistake. Colin wanted not so much a wife and partner as a mother for his children, and he wanted to make sure that the next Mrs. MacGregor would be compliant, obedient and fertile. Above all, it was essential that she made no demands of him and that, outside of the bedroom and nursery, they had little to do with each other. Pauline Downs did not fit into this picture.

"Good day, Mr. MacGregor," she said, as she rode up. "I trust I am not intruding?" She looked at Colin standing tall and erect in the sunshine, his black hair stirred by the morning breeze. She was surprised to feel a stab of sexual desire.

"You're not intruding at all, Miss Downs. I am just ridding the countryside of vermin. Would you care to join me? I've brought along extra rifles."

"Rifles aren't necessary," she said, gesturing to the bow that rode across her saddle.

"Come now, Miss Downs," Colin said. "Bows and arrows aren't the weapons for a real hunt."

"I can hit anything with an arrow that you can with a bullet."

He smiled. "Very well then, how about that tree over there? Would you say it's perhaps a hundred feet away? Can your clever arrow hit it?"

Colin watched as she got down from her horse, selected an arrow and sighted her bow. The way she stood in the morning sunlight, in a long dress with a tight bodice and voluminous skirts, her full breasts counterbalanced by a bustle, and a feathered hat sitting on her platinum curls, her left hand stretched before her clutching the longbow, her right arm pulled back behind her ear as she took aim—it reminded him of a poem he had once read: "Cold Diana, Huntress of the Moon, Slayer of the Stag, Eternal Virgin . . ."

He knew that Pauline's appearance was deceptive. Tall and slender, with fair skin and a decidedly feminine air, Pauline made people think she was delicate in the way fashionable women were supposed to be. But Colin knew that Pauline was a strong woman, in body as well as in spirit. Not everyone was aware that she used a man's longbow, and that she pulled forty pounds.

As he watched her release the bowstring, sending the arrow shooting straight and sure to the target, Colin realized that there was something sexual about the way Pauline handled that bow and arrow, with her back so straight, her shoulders square, her chin even with her left shoulder. She struck him as being a woman made for the bedroom.

As Pauline selected a second arrow from her quiver and prepared to shoot again, Colin said, "It seems unfair competition, Miss Downs, to hit a target that doesn't move."

Pauline whipped around, bow held before her, string pulled back behind her ear, arrow aimed directly at Colin. He gave a start, then he laughed. "Can you hunt with that primitive apparatus, Miss Downs? Or do you only go after trees and haystacks?"

She relaxed the bowstring and lowered the bow. "There is nothing I cannot shoot with this, Mr. MacGregor," she said.

"But is it as good as a gun?"

"Do you wish to put it to the test?"

He grinned. "There's a blue-gray doe that's been sighted by the river, with a joey at foot. I've promised her to Judd. He's nine years old now and has yet to make his first kill. Would you like to join us? Or perhaps you're not so sure about that bow and arrow."

"On the contrary, Mr. MacGregor, I am very sure of my bow and arrows. I should be only too glad to demonstrate what a hunting arrow can do."

The party was headed toward the river, Pauline and Colin in the lead, with Judd on his pony between them. Grooms followed, bearing blankets, picnic baskets and guns. Lastly came the old Aboriginal tracker, Ezekiel, who rode bareback.

"By the way, Mr. MacGregor," Pauline said, "are you still interested in those five thousand acres?"

"Has your brother decided to sell them?"

Frank didn't know anything about it yet, but Pauline knew he wouldn't object. The land was useless to him, and if selling it made Pauline happy, then he would agree to it. "I'm sure he can be persuaded," she said.

"When can I meet with him to discuss the terms?"

"Frank is too busy with his newspaper to bother with something like this. You can deal through me."

"What are the terms then?"

"I don't know yet, but I'm sure you and I can come to some sort of agreement."

He gave her a look, but said nothing.

"How old is Judd now?" she said. "Nine, did you say? You'll be sending him away to school soon."

"I've decided not to send him to school. I want to keep him with me."

"Poor child, such a difficult age for him to be without a mother. There is talk around the district, Mr. MacGregor, about you and Vilma Todd."

"The people of this district seem to have nothing better to do with their time. To set the record straight, Miss Downs, I am not thinking of asking Miss Todd to be my wife. Nor Verity Campbell, whom I'm sure you have also heard linked with my name."

"You plan not to remarry then?"

"I have every intention of it. But I plan to marry out of the district."

While he talked about the various candidates he was considering, daughters of substantial Melbourne men, Pauline felt her self-assurance suffer a tremor. But then she remembered what she knew about him, what none of the hopeful young ladies in the district knew—that on the night Christina died, Colin had sworn revenge against the man whom he blamed for the death of his wife and unborn child: Hugh Westbrook. Joanna had not come when summoned; Colin blamed that on Westbrook. Since then, Pauline had watched Colin and she had witnessed his growing obsession with ruining Hugh. She knew that that was what was driving MacGregor in his determination to buy up so much land: to ultimately seize Merinda and destroy the man he had convinced himself should suffer for Christina's death. The fact that he might actually succeed didn't trouble Pauline. Hugh was a competent adversary; he would put up an excellent fight. Pauline thought it would be interesting to see the competition between the two.

She thought again of the five thousand acres that abutted the northern boundary of Merinda. She alone knew why Colin was anxious to get his hands on it. Revenge, she thought, was a powerful instrument. And if she played her hand skillfully, she could use it to her own advantage as well.

As they came to the river, a pair of plovers, nesting nearby in the ground, flew up excitedly, circling and diving at the intruders, screeching in their peculiar way. Ezekiel took the lead, guiding his horse along the river bank, examining the ground. Colin followed close behind, with Pauline and Judd. It was quiet by the water's edge, the air smelled of loam and decay. Dark shadows lay pooled between the massive trunks of Red River and ghost gums. The horses picked their way carefully among the debris, avoiding fallen logs rotten with termites, and snake holes. A male emu, crouching on a nest of freshly laid eggs, lay with his neck stretched out on the ground and hardly stirred as the horses' hooves passed nearby. Overhead, a pair of pink-gray galahs squabbled around a nesting hole.

"She been here, Mr. MacGregor," Ezekiel said quietly, pointing to fresh kangaroo spoor. "Not long ago. This morning, maybe. Got joey with her, too."

Colin nodded and turned in his saddle to look at Pauline. Her long-bow lay across her saddle, the quiver of arrows was strapped to her back. They had agreed that they would both try for the doe, Colin using his gun, Pauline her bow. But the joey, Colin had said, was to be left for Judd.

They crossed the river at a shallow point and followed it only a short distance before the tracker led them off along a smaller creek. Ezekiel raised his hand, bringing the party to a halt. Then he slid down from his horse and got on his hands and knees to examine the ground. The others waited in silence.

Ezekiel knew this area well. He had lived as a boy in a small settlement farther up the river with his extended family, who had numbered nearly thirty. In the years since, Ezekiel had seen his kin die from white man's diseases or get slaughtered by white men wanting this land. Now he was the only one of his family left.

"Well, boy?" Colin said finally. "What do you think?"

Ezekiel got to his feet and frowned. "I think that blue-flyer go through them trees there, Mr. MacGregor. But old Ezekiel don't go in there."

"Why not?"

"Taboo ground, Mr. MacGregor. Belong to Emu Dreaming. Bad luck if we go in."

"Stay here then. Judd, follow me."

They picked their way through the trees, still on horseback, until they came to a small clearing. Then they dismounted, left the animals with a groom and continued their silent exploration on foot.

Pauline walked with her bow ready, a hunting arrow, with its deadly barbed tip, slack against the bowstring.

Colin heard a sound, stopped suddenly and looked around. Judd, not paying attention, bumped into his father and received a reprimanding look. The three listened, holding their breath.

"Over there!" whispered Pauline, pointing. She raised her bow and took aim.

The doe, her blue-gray fur looking smoky in the autumn light, rose up from her grazing and stared at the hunters. Nearby, the joey was munching on the river grass.

Colin raised his rifle, but Pauline was already loosing her arrow.

The doe quickly thumped one of her great legs, and the joey, hearing the alarm signal, looked up in time to see his mother spring into the air and catch an arrow in her flank. She fell to the ground, kicking wildly. And then she was up again, hopping, with blood streaming down her thigh.

Before Pauline could take aim with a second arrow, Colin's rifle went off and the doe flew out backward. The panicked joey hopped frantically toward its mother, then swung about on its tail and darted in another direction.

"Shoot, Judd!" cried Colin. "You've got a clear shot. Do it now!"

Judd froze, and shook so badly he couldn't keep the gun still.

"*Now!*"

Judd tried to follow the frightened joey with his gun. He felt sick. He started to cry.

"Damn it, boy!" shouted his father. "*Shoot!*"

Judd pulled the trigger and fell down, stunned by the report.

"You got him!" Colin cried, as he ran to the dead kangaroos. "This is the doe we tried to get last spring, Judd! I told you she had a joey in her pouch." He put his boot on the doe, grasped Pauline's arrow, and pulled it out. Tossing it to her, he said triumphantly, "I believe you have lost the contest, Miss Downs!"

But Pauline was helping Judd to his feet. "Come on," she said gently. "You're all right."

But the boy was weeping uncontrollably. "Poor little joey!" he cried. "Poor little joey!"

Colin said with annoyance, "Come here, Judd."

The boy didn't move; his shoulders heaved.

Having heard the shots, the grooms came running through the trees. "Good shot, sir," one of them said, a man who got down on his knees, took a knife out of his belt, and proceeded to hack off the kangaroos' tails.

"Judd," Colin said in a significant tone. "Come here and claim your trophy."

But the boy held back, sniffing and gulping down his sobs. "Go on,

Judd," Pauline said, giving him a gentle push. "Do as your father says."

Judd finally walked stiffly forward, his blue eyes wide with horror. When he saw the bloodied tails come away from the lifeless bodies, he spun around and threw up.

"Come here, son," Colin said as he reached out for the joey's tail. "This is your first kill. It's something to be proud of."

When he took Judd by the arm, Pauline said, "Colin, wait," knowing what he was about to do.

But she was too late. Colin smeared the bloody tail over Judd's face and hair.

The child screamed.

"What's the matter with you?" Colin shouted as he tried to hold on to the wriggling body of his son.

"He's frightened," Pauline said. "Leave him alone."

"Frightened! Damn it, Miss Downs, I was blooded when I was seven years old, and I wasn't frightened!"

"He doesn't understand! He doesn't know what you're doing!"

While the grooms exchanged anxious glances—when their boss got mad everyone suffered—Ezekiel watched. He had seen this ritual before, this cutting off the tail of someone's first kill and smearing the blood on them. It was an old tradition, one of the graziers had once explained to Ezekiel, brought over from the old country, although there it involved an animal called a fox. It was one of the few white man's rites that Ezekiel thought made sense, although they always forgot to ask the animal's forgiveness just before they killed it. No Aborigine would think of overlooking such an important formality; it brought bad magic.

Judd kicked and screamed until finally he was free, and he ran away from his father and was caught up in Pauline's arms. "There, there," she said, trying to calm him. "It's all right. It happens to everyone their first time. It won't ever happen again."

"Stop mollycoddling him," Colin said. "How do you expect him to grow up and be a man if he doesn't start learning now? Stop crying, Judd!"

"Shouting isn't going to help, you'll only make things worse. Can't you see how upset he is?" She stroked Judd's hair and said, "There, there, it's all right. We'll go back now."

She delivered Judd into the care of one of the grooms, who washed his face.

Colin came up to Pauline and said, "Forgive me for shouting at you, Miss Downs. I worry for Judd's sake. He must learn to take care of himself. If I should lose him—"

"He'll be all right, Mr. MacGregor."

She turned her face into the wind and shaded her eyes. "Is that Merinda property over there? Have you heard, Mr. Colin, that Hugh's wife is expecting their first child?"

She saw Colin's face go hard.

"I shouldn't be surprised," Pauline said with a laugh, "if in a few years you had a whole brood of Westbrooks for neighbors! Hugh is doing quite well, I hear. He's even started to build a big house down by the river. And apparently he's come by an extraordinary ram that he claims will create a sturdy new breed of sheep. Who would have thought it, Mr. MacGregor, when Hugh first came to the district all those years ago?"

She saw where his gaze was fixed: on the stretch of land at the foot of the mountains, the five thousand acres that embraced Merinda's northern border. As she started to walk away, Colin suddenly took her arm and said, "Miss Downs. You said your brother was willing to sell that land to me."

"Well," she said. "Perhaps not *sell* exactly."

"What do you mean?"

She looked over at Judd, who seemed to have already forgotten his fright. "He's better now," Pauline said. "He just needed a gentle touch."

After a moment, Colin said carefully, "You were right when you said Judd needed a mother, Miss Downs. And I have been giving it a great deal of thought. Perhaps in fact it wouldn't be fair to the boy to bring in a stranger. He needs someone he is already comfortable with."

"He knows Miss Todd and Miss Campbell."

"Yes."

Pauline turned her eyes to him. She watched the breeze stir his black hair as he searched for the right words. "I was thinking, Miss Downs, perhaps Judd would prefer that I marry someone more like you."

"Like me?"

He glanced toward the mountains, toward prosperous Merinda, where he envisioned Hugh Westbrook enjoying a happy life with his bride. "Would you consider it?" he asked.

And Pauline smiled. "Perhaps," she said.

CHAPTER 14

M y dearest sister," the letter read. "After five months at sea, we have arrived at the Sydney Settlement at last. Words cannot describe the horrors of our voyage. Miss Pratt and myself and two other ladies were jammed into a cabin measuring seven feet by nine; we slept in bunks too narrow to hold us, and three would have to step outside while one dressed. The ship's only two water closets for over two hundred passengers were alongside our cabin, and they stank abominably. Many of the migrants on board possessed no change of clothing; we swarmed with lice, and the ship was infested with rats. Eight children were born during the voyage; five died."

Joanna looked at the rain washing gently down the window of her hotel room. She could make out the halos of gaslights in the street, and hear the creak and rattle of carriages hurrying by, the horses' hooves clip-clopping on the pavement. It was cold outside, but her suite at the King George Hotel was warmed by fires that burned in two large fireplaces, one in the bedroom, the other in the sitting room where she sat, watching the rainy, dying day outside. She had been at work since early that morning, sorting through the boxes of papers Frank Downs had sent over from the *Times*. They were a curious mélange of documents, deeds, notices, private letters, receipts, bills of lading, old yellowed newspapers, and even diaries and one ship's log—all dating as far back as 1790. They were being collected and catalogued by the staff of the *Times*, in preparation for a special book Frank was going to bring out, a "scrapbook" commemorating Australia's centenary, which would take place in four years. He had placed them at Joanna's disposal when she had told him about Patrick Lathrop's letter, and his reference to a ship bearing the name of a mythical beast. "Aussies love a mystery," Frank had declared when he had brought the boxes to the hotel. "And your family's story, my dear Joanna, is certainly a mystery. If there is anything in here that leads you to Karra Karra and you finally do find it, it will make a good yarn for the *Times*."

Joanna felt that it was more serious than "a good yarn," but she was grateful for Frank's help, and she liked the fact that Frank Downs possessed such enthusiasm for his young country. "A lot of people don't realize it, Joanna," he had told her, "but Australia exists only because America broke away from England. Up until 1776, England sent her unwanted criminals to the American colonies. But once that door was closed, they had to find another dumping ground for her outcasts. Australia was the choice, and here we are." The book was going to begin, Frank had said, with the discovery of Australia by Captain Cook. When Joanna had remarked that she wondered if the Aborigines had been aware that they and their land were being "discovered," Hugh had said, "Invaded is more the proper word for it."

Joanna thought of Sarah, and wondered what she was doing at that moment. Keeping an eye on Philip McNeal and his work crew down by the river, Joanna suspected. She had noticed Sarah's growing attraction to the American, how she was always somewhere near where he was working.

The clock on the mantel chimed six, reminding Joanna of the hour. Hugh had gone out that morning to arrange for the transport of his new ram, which he was calling Zeus, to Merinda, after which he had said he would stop by the house of a Miss Tallhill, with whom he had left Joanna's deed and a sample of John Makepeace's shorthand. He had also gone to a gemstone expert to see if they could determine the value of the fire opal she had inherited. Joanna expected Hugh any moment; they were going to meet Frank for dinner in the hotel dining room.

She looked at the letter she had just read. It was dated 1820, and it was signed by a Miss Margo Pelletier. Joanna wondered how Frank had come by the letter, and she wondered about Miss Pelletier, what had made her leave England, and what had become of her.

Joanna picked up a piece of paper entitled, "To the Advocate-General, George Fletcher Moore, Western Australia, 1834, A Report on the Conditions of the Aborigines in the Colony." She read: "The blacks are a singular race of beings, possessing none of the rudiments of civilization, having neither house nor home, worshipping no God, fearing no devils, glorifying in massacre, totally without morals or conscience whatsoever, and who do not cherish the land as a white man will."

Joanna's hours of work had so far produced no mention of a ship named for a mythical animal, or any clue that could lead to solving the puzzle of her family's past. She had hoped to find mention of a red mountain, or even of a white couple living with their child among the Aborigines. The book she had purchased at the Book Emporium, *My Life Among the Aborigines,* had provided no useful information.

She opened the last of the boxes and lifted out a hand-lettered notice that read, "Who ever stole My Horses Sunday last is gone to get found and He's gone to be sorry That He Did It." There was a hole at the top, where the notice had been nailed to a tree.

Finally, she picked up a brittle copy of the Sydney *Gazette,* dated 1835.

"Public Notice," it read. "The vessel *Nimrod,* Captain White, arrived Sydney Harbour on Saturday from London, Plymouth, Tenerife, and the Cape, bearing a cargo of copper, tools, cloth, carriages, mail, and agriculture supplies, plus a complement of passengers. Owners Buchanan and Co. respectfully inform the Public that the *Nimrod* will set sail one week hence for England, and will accommodate twenty paying passengers."

Did such a notice as this still exist somewhere, Joanna wondered, announcing in 1830 the arrival of the ship *Minotaur* or *Cyclops* or *Pegasus,* bearing cargo and a complement of passengers? And was there among those passengers a man named John Makepeace, with his young wife, Naomi?

And where, on this great, vast continent, had they first set foot on land? "You won't find any records of a ship docking at Melbourne in 1830," Frank had warned her. "At that time, Melbourne didn't even exist. There was nothing here except Aborigines." That left Sydney and Brisbane in the east, Adelaide in the south and Perth in the west.

Joanna was determined not to give up hope. She thought of the letters she would write to the addresses of shipowners Frank was going to provide her with, inquiring about a ship named for a mythical beast and whether a couple named Makepeace had sailed on it. If she could just find that, then she felt she might be able to locate where her grandparents had gone to, and where her mother had been born. And then she could get on with resolving the past, and the dreams that continued to haunt her, her fears that her unborn child would inherit them.

Miss Adele Tallhill's soft voice joined the whisper of the rain beyond the windows as she said, "The study of this deed, Mr. Westbrook, provided me with hours of enjoyment. It was rather like solving a puzzle. And I am happy to report that I was successful in deciphering some portion of the writing."

Hugh and Miss Tallhill were sitting in her parlor, warmed by a roaring fire, a tray of sherry and biscuits on the table between them. The room was cluttered with bric-a-brac, and the air was pervaded with the heavy scent of lavender.

Hugh had brought the deed and a sample of John Makepeace's shorthand to Miss Tallhill, an invalid lady confined to a wheelchair, who lived with her parents and who earned a modest living with her calligraphy. She received commissions to write personal letters, inscribe diplomas and invitations, and create fancy love notes. She was also known around Melbourne for her expertise in handwriting analysis.

Hugh glanced discreetly at the clock over the fireplace. He was due back at the hotel and he was anxious to give Joanna his news. After making arrangements for transporting his new ram to Merinda, Hugh had stopped at the office of Buchanan and Co., a major shipping line, and there he had learned that they owned two ships named the *Pegasus* and the *Minotaur*. The clerk offered to write to the Buchanan and Co. headquarters in London for information on their histories.

He had also taken the fire opal to a dealer in precious gems, to have its value assayed, and possibly to determine where it had come from. The man had not been able to guess the country of origin, or its market value. But he had offered to buy it from Hugh for a considerable price.

"What were you able to decipher, Miss Tallhill?" he asked.

She looked at her visitor, guessing that he was in his early thirties; he had smoky gray eyes and an attractive vertical furrow between his eyebrows. There was a faintly pleasant fragrance about him which she realized after a moment was the scent of lanolin. She had encountered it before in sheepmen; it seemed to get under their skin. And there was a robustness about him that one often found in men from the outback. But from there she saw that he differed with other men of his kind; he was mannered and possessed a polish that she rarely saw in country men.

She laid the deed before him and pointed with a long, delicate hand. "I concentrated first on this passage here," she said, "Two days' ride from something unreadable, and twenty kilometers from what looks like Bo— Creek. Let me show you how I finally worked them out." She produced a sheet of paper that illustrated how she had solved the puzzle. "You see on the deed this swirl here, and this line here. I traced over the words as best as I could, following the lines that are discernible. I then wrote them different ways, as you can see on this paper, filling in the illegible parts with letters, altering them in various ways until a feasible word came clear. Here, Mr. Westbrook, this is the letter 't'. This looks like an 'l,' but when written so, it makes no sense. But if you assume that letter to be an elongated 'e,' then we have a real word."

Hugh compared the experimental samples against the faded writing on the deed. "The first word, Mr. Westbrook," she said, "is Durrebar."

"Yes," he said, nodding. "I can see that now."

"The second example proved to be a little more difficult, but I was in the end able to work it out. Bowman's Creek. Here is how I arrived at it." She brought out a second sheet of paper covered with various words and spellings.

"There is no doubt in my mind, Mr. Westbrook, that this is a deed to land located two days' ride from Durrebar, which I suspect is an Aboriginal place name, and twenty kilometers from a place called Bowman's Creek."

"Yes," Hugh said excitedly, "Of course. Were you able to discern in which colony this deed was issued?"

"I'm afraid I was not. It is apparent that the document was exposed to water at some time. The official seal and date are nearly washed away. I scrutinized them most carefully, Mr. Westbrook, but I cannot make them out. And, as you can see, the signature is illegible."

"Bowman's Creek and Durrebar," Hugh said, anxious to get back to the hotel and Joanna. "I can't thank you enough, Miss Tallhill."

She smiled. "Anyone could have done it, really. It just takes time and patience, and as you can see, Mr. Westbrook"—she laid a hand on one of the wheels of her invalid chair—"time is something I have in abundance."

"Were you able to do anything with John Makepeace's shorthand?"

"I have studied it, Mr. Westbrook, and you are correct that it is shorthand. But I have so far been unable to break the code. If you would care to leave the paper with me, I will devote more time to its study. I can send my findings to you through the mail."

When he tried to pay Miss Tallhill for her work, she refused, saying, "It was my pleasure. And we are not finished yet, Mr. Westbrook. I shall commence to study the shorthand at once."

After he left, she wheeled herself to the window, parted the drapes and looked out at the rainy street, watching him get into a carriage. Miss Tallhill was amazed at how much Hugh Westbrook had reminded her of her beloved Stephen, who had left twenty years ago for the gold fields, and never returned. Adele had never given up hope that he would come back to her someday.

She wheeled herself away from the window and back to the fire. "Hysterical paralysis," the doctors had said. "There is nothing physically wrong with your legs, Miss Tallhill. You can walk if you want to."

But that was nonsense. What did medical men know of afflictions that had their deadly roots in the heart?

Yes, she thought with a sigh. Mr. Westbrook had reminded her so of her dear Stephen. And that was why she had been unable to send him away with nothing. She couldn't have stood to see the disappointment on that face that was so like Stephen's, if she had told him the truth: that she hadn't been able to make anything out of the words on the deed and that probably no one ever would. Bowman's Creek had a realistic sound to it, and what harm, after all, if she had made it up, and Hugh Westbrook believed there was such a place? What did it matter that Durrebar was her own invention? His smile had been just like Stephen's.

———————————

Mystery, Frank Downs thought as he looked out over the city of Melbourne. That was what this country was all about—mystery. As he stood in his tower high above the city, looking out over the rooftops and bridges and factory chimneys, Frank envisioned the great outback that sprawled in the distance. So many stories out there, he thought, so much adventure and excitement. That was why he had gotten into the newspaper business, in order to be close to the pulse of this mysterious continent. Frank knew what people wanted, they were passionate for a "good yarn." From outback campfires to Melbourne drawing rooms, nothing satisfied an Australian more than a good story. And the

Times provided those stories. Now that education was compulsory in the colonies, Frank saw in the next two decades a whole new generation of readers, people who were going to be young and schooled and hungry for entertainment. And the Melbourne *Times,* under the energy and creative thinking of Frank Downs, was going to bring it to them.

Frank had purchased the paper seven years ago for two thousand pounds. And he had used tricks to salvage it and turn it into a popular newspaper. He was an innovator. When he had taken over the *Times*, he had discovered that it was the last paper to come out with the news. Knowing that in order to survive he would have to find a way to get the news out on the streets before his competitors did, Frank came up with the idea of sending reporters on fast boats out to intercept incoming sailing ships, where they purchased English newspapers from passengers and crew. The reporters then raced back to the city to get out a hastily printed "extra," an edition that carried news brazenly copied word for word from those English papers. When his competitors began doing the same thing, Frank again came up with a new idea. He sent reporters to Adelaide to meet the ships that stopped there before coming to Melbourne. Those men would hurriedly read the papers from England, and then telegraph news stories to the *Times.* Soon, the other newspapers also had reporters in Adelaide. And when Frank thought of contracting with the postal service to deliver the *Times* free to rural customers, shipping editions out by train and the fast coaches of Cobb & Co. and thereby tapping into the news-hungry countryside, the *Age* and the *Argus* followed.

Frank's success was evident in the Times Tower, the tallest structure in Melbourne. It rose a monumental five stories above the dirt streets and, with gaslight glowing in every window, it stood over the city on this misty April night like a beacon. Frank's office was on the top floor. His colleagues had laughed when he had first installed himself here, "up with the cockatoos," they had said. Everyone knew that the higher floors of a building were the least desirable, because who wanted to climb all those stairs? Men in substantial positions, such as Frank's banker friends, always had offices on the ground floor; it was folly to go *up* in a building! But Frank, always intrigued by novelty, had made a great spectacle of opening the brand-new building and carting his friends up to his office in a steam-powered elevator!

Now, as he stood at his window, Frank imagined the machinery of his paper throbbing beneath his feet. Steam-powered presses thundered day and night, while nearly a hundred hand compositors worked at their racks, laboriously setting tomorrow morning's stories in long metal columns. The editorial offices bustled with activity as messengers came running in with reports from Parliament, from police stations, from the harbor, while an enormous clock, set high on the wall and watching the harried staff like a single eye, ticked away the minutes over a sign that read: THE *Times* NEVER SLEEPS.

He looked at that clock, and realized he should be getting to the King George Hotel, where he was meeting the Westbrooks for dinner.

Joanna Westbrook, he thought, now there was a mystery! He sometimes felt he was as eager as she to find out what strange and violent thing had taken place thirty-nine years ago at a location called Karra Karra. What sudden and terrible calamity had befallen a young white man, his wife and their small daughter? What was the curse, or poison-song or whatever it was, that had haunted Emily Makepeace for the rest of her life, and the dreams about the Rainbow Serpent? And how had that young couple managed to live with a race that had only just become aware of white men?

Stories were always surfacing about a "wild white man" or a "wild white woman" being discovered living among the natives. Australia's brief history was full of such tales. Even now, rumors were circulating about a "wild white man" having been found living with a tribe in western Queensland. Frank wondered if it could be the missing member of the ill-fated expedition of 1871. A police expedition had found him living with Aborigines near Cooper's Creek, and he claimed to be that missing member. The man was also saying that it was not the Aborigines who had killed the members of the expedition, but that the men had fought among themselves over the issue of turning back. The police were bringing the man to Melbourne, and Frank was going to interview him personally.

As Frank was about to leave the office, his secretary came in, carrying an envelope. "Mr. Downs," he said. "This just came for you."

It was from his lawyer—the contract turning five thousand acres of land over to Colin MacGregor.

Frank was glad his sister was getting married at last. Although he might have chosen someone other than MacGregor for her, the fact that she was so happy made him happy too. And so when she had asked if he would make a wedding gift of the five thousand acres to Colin, Frank had been unable to refuse. He couldn't imagine what MacGregor would want with the land—it was quite useless. But Pauline was pleased and that was all that mattered. Ever since she had broken off her engagement to Westbrook, Frank had feared she was committing herself to a life of spinsterhood. But everything had, in fact, turned out well for all parties concerned.

Now if only, he thought, he could do something about his own situation.

In the year that he had been living in Melbourne, ever since the typhoid epidemic, Frank had made the acquaintances of various young and eligible women. But he had found himself unable to go beyond a polite friendship with them, and he rarely saw a woman after two or three meetings. He just couldn't seem to get interested.

Frank had thought about Ivy Dearborn occasionally, and the mystery of her disappearance continued to bother him. After searching the Western District for her, he had placed a notice in the *Times*, similar to the ones he had run for Joanna asking about Karra Karra. But no one had come forward with information.

Perhaps she had died of the typhoid after all, he told himself again as he stepped into the elevator that everyone else refused to ride. Or perhaps she had gone back to England. Whatever had happened, Frank was determined to put her from his mind. He had other things to think of now.

CHAPTER 15

There is a beautiful place," Sarah said, "which no one sees. A valley filled with green grass, trees, streams. It is the valley where the Moons live." She was telling a story as she worked at the stove, making tea for Philip McNeal and Adam. She spoke softly: "The Moons are very happy in their valley, but sometimes the Moons, they get restless. They explore the sky when night comes. But only one Moon goes at a time. Now, the Moons, they don't know a giant lives on the other side of the mountains. And what happens is: That giant, he catches each wandering Moon, and every night cuts a slice out of it until there is only a sliver left. Then he chops up the last slice and scatters the pieces so that they become stars. And then . . ."

McNeal and Adam waited. When Sarah didn't say anything more, Philip said, "How does the story end?"

Sarah thought a moment, then said, "I don't remember."

"It's a good story," McNeal said. "You know many good stories. Perhaps you should write them down."

Sarah shook her head. "Taboo to write them," she said.

Philip watched her as she worked, tall and slender at fifteen, with long bones and dark skin. He wondered what she was going to be like when she was a woman. Then he thought of Pollen on the Wind, and his nights and days with her. Was she, too, he wondered, like Sarah, starting to forget the myths of her people?

Aware of his eyes upon her, Sarah concentrated upon measuring the tea into the teapot. Thunder cracked in the distance. She looked toward the window and frowned. Bad magic tonight, she thought.

As if he read her thoughts, Philip said, "We've had storms before. It'll be all right."

But Sarah shook her head, and frowned.

"Do you think tonight will be worse than others?"

Sarah didn't know how she knew. Sometimes she just knew things. Like the times when she would recall an Aboriginal story or myth, and she couldn't remember actually hearing the story from the elders at the mission, and yet she knew it all the same. Like the story of the Moons. She couldn't recall Old Deereeree at the mission ever actually telling it to her. But how else, Sarah wondered, could she know it? And sometimes she saw visions, quick flashes in her mind of people, events, scenes that made no sense. She knew they weren't memories—at least, not her own memories. And there were moments when Sarah just knew something, like the time she had told Joanna that the leaf of the wild geranium stopped an insect bite from stinging, and Joanna had said, "Who taught you that?" But Sarah had not known.

At times these half-memories frightened Sarah. They seemed to take over; she had no control of them. At other times, she drew comfort from them, knowing in some deep part of herself that they were part of her heritage.

She wished she could go to the mission and talk with the elders. She had gone back a few times, leaving without telling Joanna where she was going, cutting across the countryside to avoid the main road, and skirting the town so that she wouldn't be seen. She would sneak into the mission compound and seek out the elders, and they would talk for a time, until it became too dangerous—if Reverend Simms found Sarah there, he would be angry with the old ones.

It was getting hard to visit the mission, harder for Sarah to maintain a link with her people. Old Deereeree was dead, and the others were afraid of punishment if they were caught teaching the old ways. So that now, when Sarah made her way to the mission, she was met with fearful looks and silence.

It frightened her. She didn't want to lose touch with her people.

Already, she was starting to forget many of the stories. She wasn't sure of all the rules and taboos. She needed the elders to guide her. Sometimes she sat and listened to old Ezekiel, but he belonged to a different Dreaming, and he was a man; he could not teach her women's secrets. More and more, Sarah wished she had been initiated into her clan.

She heard Philip McNeal moving around the cabin. He spoke quietly to Adam, leaned into the fireplace to add logs, checked the shutters over the windows against the rising wind. She liked the American; she felt calmed and reassured whenever she was around him. She wondered if she could tell him about her fears, about the poison-song that followed Joanna, the bad magic that might have brought typhoid to Merinda, that might now be bringing this storm that somehow frightened Sarah; she felt that it was going to be unlike any other storm.

McNeal came and stood next to her at the stove, and watched as she worked. "Americans don't drink tea," he said quietly. "Mostly they drink coffee. Do you know what that is?"

Sarah spooned tea into the teapot and said, "No. I don't know coffee."

She was conscious of every detail of him—the soft laugh, the relaxed and easy way in which he stood next to her. "Pollen on the Wind was like you," McNeal said. "She knew things. She couldn't explain it. She said it was her ancestors talking to her. But she said it felt more like a memory. And she sometimes had premonitions. She could tell when something was going to happen. Is that how it is with you, Sarah?"

She looked at him. Yes, she thought. That is how it is.

Thunder rolled in the distance, and McNeal, looking at the window, said, "Perhaps you're right, Sarah. We might be in for a bad night." He looked at her. "I'm going to go down to the building site and send my work crew home. You know that it will be bad for them if I don't, don't you?"

She regarded him with a steady gaze.

And what else, he wondered as he reached for his jacket, do you know?

———————— • ————————

As Joanna drove the wagon into the farmyard, she looked at the distant mountains, a curious blue-green at this late afternoon hour, with clouds gathering at their summits. An unusual light seemed to cover the sky; the air felt strange, as if the barometric pressure were rapidly dropping. A storm was coming.

She had ridden into Cameron Town to see if there was a letter from the shipping company that owned the *Pegasus* and the *Minotaur*. She had also been hoping for a letter from Patrick Lathrop in San Francisco. But there was only one letter—from Aunt Millicent. Joanna had gone alone because of the weather, and the trip had taken longer than she had expected; the hour was late, the sky looked threatening. She searched the deserted yard. Normally the men would be down the road at Facey's pub, or in their quarters, drinking and talking. Tomorrow was Sunday, and Hugh always gave his men Saturday afternoons off, the only grazier in the district to do so. But she heard no voices coming from the men's quarters, no sounds of Jew's harp and banjo. And she saw no horses in the stable.

"What's going on, Matthew?" Joanna asked the stableboy who took the wagon from her.

"They've all gone to the paddocks, missus. Mr. Westbrook says we might have a thunderstorm. Makes the sheep nervous. Sometimes they bolt."

Joanna looked out over the plains that stretched beneath a gray sky. It was June, the season for winter crutching. For the past week Hugh and his men had been out in the paddocks shearing the tails and hind legs of ewes who would soon be giving birth. It was done for cleanliness purposes, especially where lambing was concerned, but also to protect the sheep from blowfly and infections. It was a difficult job, the men struggling with frightened ewes and trying not to cut the animals or themselves, and such a backbreaking task that the men had looked forward all week to their Saturday-night rum. But now, because of the threat of a storm, they were out riding watch over the nervous flocks.

When Joanna entered the kitchen, she found a fire blazing in the hearth, filling the room with heat and a cozy glow. Peony, Jacko's daughter, was sitting at the table cleaning the glass chimneys of the oil lamps, while Adam sat at the table eating buttered bread dipped in egg. "Mama!" he said, running to her.

Joanna took Adam into her arms and hugged him. Then she removed her hat and hung it up. "Where is Mr. Westbrook?" she asked.

"Down by the river with Mr. McNeal," the girl said. "Mr. Westbrook came home. He says a big storm is coming."

"I shan't be long," Joanna said, drawing her shawl tightly around her and heading out the door.

"Can I come too?" Adam said.

But Joanna said, "You stay here and keep Sarah and Peony company."

As she followed the path to the river, Joanna saw flashes of lightning on the horizon. She looked up at the gray winter sky, and marveled that this was June. In India, the British women would have already made the journey to the mountain resorts in their annual escape from the summer heat. But here, on the western plains of Victoria, it was the dead of winter.

Joanna entered the clearing, where the billabong reflected a pewter sky, and looked for Hugh and Philip McNeal. In the gloom Joanna could see them walking through the trees, examining the cement footings that were going to be the foundation for the new house. Hugh and Joanna and McNeal had together agreed upon a site that was far from the sacred ruins, where neither the spirits would be disturbed nor the house threatened by river floods. And they had not torn down a single tree to clear a place for it. Maude Reed had once said to Joanna, "When we built our house, we tore out all those filthy gum trees and planted sensible English willows and elms."

Joanna paused for a moment to watch her husband as he talked with McNeal.

Hugh was bareheaded, his hair ruffling in the wind. His boots and trousers were caked with mud; his shirtsleeves were rolled up and there was mud on his bare arms. How different Hugh was from other graziers, Joanna thought, men who seemed to need to show the world how prosperous they were. Even when they were out riding their paddocks, or showing prize stock at the Graziers' Show, John Reed and Colin MacGregor and all the rest looked like English country gentlemen who got about as close to the land as a game of croquet.

Did these feelings ever go away? Joanna wondered as she watched him. The thrill of suddenly seeing him, the jolt that went through her each time she encountered him, when he came in at night from the paddocks, when he appeared unexpectedly in the kitchen doorway, when she caught his voice on the wind. Did the excitement ever fade? she wondered. Did the electricity die? No, she prayed. I want it to always be like this.

Joanna called out his name, but her voice was drowned by distant thunder rolling down from the mountains. A few seconds later lightning flashed.

"Hugh!" she called again.

He turned, his smile broadening; and Philip McNeal raised a hand in greeting.

"Be careful," Hugh said, as Joanna stepped over the bare cement threshold. He held out his arms and Joanna went into them. Please, she thought as he kissed her. Let it always be like this.

"I'm glad you're home," he said. "I was getting worried. Another few minutes and I would have sent someone out on the road to get you. Philip and I were just making sure everything was secure here. I don't like the look of that sky. Watch your step here." He took Joanna's hand. The concrete floor was littered with tools, rubble, and the sawed-off ends of lumber. One of the workers had left a billycan in a corner, half filled with tea.

Finally they stood in what was going to be the drawing room. A dark shadow was spreading across the plains. Hugh said, "What did Poll Gramercy say?"

"She said we're fine, and that I am about five months along."

"Was there anything in the mail?" he asked.

Joanna thought of the letter that had arrived from Aunt Millicent, a reply to Joanna's request for more information about her mother's childhood. It was very simple and direct. "Your poor mother is dead," Millicent had written. "Leave her in peace."

The wind began to rise, rippling the surface of the billabong. Hugh looked up at the sky and murmured, "Storm's going to hit any time now. It's going to be a long night for the men, out in the paddocks."

"Hoy!" came a voice on the wind. "Hoy there! Hugh!"

The three turned to see a station hand named Half-Caste Eddie riding up at a fast gallop, waving his hat. "Hugh! You gotta come quickly!"

Hugh went to him. "What is it, Eddie?"

"Cripes, Hugh, it's terrible! Lightning struck a tree near three-mile! The sheep have bolted!"

"Get the men on it then."

"Hugh," Half-Caste Eddie said, his face drawn and white, "the mob's broken through the north fence and we can't contain them! They're runnin' wild! Hugh, they're heading toward the river!"

"Get back to the house, Joanna," Hugh said as he went to his horse. "Mr. McNeal, will you please escort my wife back to the yard?"

As they watched, Hugh rode off into the turbulent night.

———————— • ————————

Hugh and Eddie rode across plains exploding with lightning. Their horses jumped creeks that had been dry but which now ran deep with water; they flew past trees bent nearly in half beneath the force of the wind. By the time they reached the northern boundary, the rain was coming down in slanting sheets, and Hugh looked down on a sight that made his blood freeze.

Thousands of sheep, panicked and stampeding, were racing over the stormy landscape, with men on horseback riding back and forth, trying to control them. Sheepdogs were barking frantically, while lightning continued to fork down, splitting earth and sky with great fiery swords.

"How the hell did that fence get down?" Hugh shouted as he rode up to Stringy Larry.

"The mob didn't do it, Hugh!" Larry shouted back, his voice barely heard over the wind. "Look, it's fallen down *this* way!"

Hugh rode along the broken fence and saw that Larry was right. The posts and wire were lying toward the oncoming sheep. It had already been down when they got here. The storm hadn't done it.

"But these five thousand acres belong to Frank Downs!" Hugh said. "He's always kept this fence in good repair!"

A man named Tom Watkins rode up then, the brim of his hat overflowing with rain and running onto his oilcloth coat. "Jesus, Hugh! The mob's in the river!"

And then the real nightmare began.

Back at the house, Joanna and Philip McNeal hurriedly fixed storm shutters over the windows while Peony sat in frozen terror, listening to the thunder crash overhead, and Sarah quietly tried to distract Adam. The cabin seemed to tremble as great gusts came down the chimney, shooting sparks and cinders into the kitchen. The hearth rug caught fire and Joanna rushed to stamp it out. "Peony," she said. "Get the spare billycans out of the pantry. We'll need lots of water for tea."

Philip said, "Will your husband be able to save the sheep?"

"I don't know," Joanna said, recalling stories she had heard about men who had drowned while trying to pull sheep from a river.

She looked at the faces of her companions, white with terror. Sarah held Adam, and Philip hovered close to them. They'll be all right, Joanna thought. I haven't had any nightmares, no premonitions about this. But the next crack of thunder reminded her of Hugh out there in the elements, trying to save sheep in the storm.

Sarah came up to her and, glancing over her shoulder to be sure the others didn't hear, said, "There is bad magic tonight."

Joanna felt a familiar stab of terror. She had experienced it before—in nightmares, and during the typhoid epidemic. She had hoped then that her fears—that she was the cause of the trouble—might only have been her imagination, but she could tell by the look in Sarah's eyes that the poison was back; the curse was striking again.

"Bad things happen tonight," Sarah said quietly. "Men get hurt. Someone dies. The Rainbow Serpent is angry."

Joanna stared at her. "Why the Rainbow Serpent, Sarah?"

"Because the Serpent created the rivers in the Dreamtime, and guides them now."

Joanna thought of her mother's dreams, and her own, of the giant snake, and its single, terrifying eye. Had Lady Emily overheard something about the curse of the Rainbow Serpent? Was this fear based on something that really happened, involving a snake?

"Yes," Joanna said, as she and Sarah looked at each other. "I understand. And if that's the case, then we had better be prepared." She reached into the cupboard for her medicine kit. "Mr. McNeal, would you please go to the bunkhouse and get some spare blankets? And fetch the large billycans from the cookhouse, please."

There was a sudden pounding on the door, and it flew open to admit wind and rain and a station hand named Banjo. He was holding a blood-soaked rag over his left arm.

Joanna and Philip helped him inside, while Sarah took Adam into the other room.

"Cripes, missus!" Banjo said, as he gratefully accepted a glass of whiskey. "It's bad out there—by the river! Lotsa blokes getting hurt and no one to take care of them."

After Joanna cleaned and bandaged his arm, she hurriedly gathered together a healing kit, bandages and whiskey, and went to the door, where an oilskin coat hung on a hook. Putting it on, she said, "Mr. McNeal, will you please stay with Sarah and Adam?"

"You're not going out in this, Mrs. Westbrook," he said. "I mean, considering the baby and all."

"I shall be all right, Mr. McNeal. I'll take Matthew with me."

He watched as Joanna pulled the door open, and he thought to call her back, but Joanna was already going down the veranda steps and vanishing into the night.

In the stable, Matthew, whose eyes were popped wide with fear, hitched the horse to the wagon. While he did so, trying to steady the nervous animal, Joanna threw blankets into the back, a lantern, a box of matches, and the medical kit, covering it all with a canvas sheet. Finally, she climbed onto the seat, and Matthew climbed up next to her.

Joanna knew where the three-mile well was. Hugh had taken her all over Merinda's seventeen thousand acres, showing her the tracks and the gates and the wells and the out-stations where the boundary riders and musterers camped. But it was one thing to take a leisurely ride over sunny pastures, with the nearby mountains a tranquil and reassuring landmark, and another to plunge headlong into a stormy night, praying that luck and guessing would get her to where she needed to be.

She and Matthew rode through the storm, holding tight to the reins; the rain came down hard, and Joanna was soon soaked. The horse reared when lightning struck nearby. Twice Joanna thought the wagon was going to go over onto its side.

They passed a flock of sheep—the wethers and ewes not in lamb, over a thousand of them, being herded into a tight, nervous flock by men on horseback and quick-footed sheepdogs. As Joanna sped by, a flash of lightning briefly illuminated the scene, and she recognized one of the men on horseback. He was giving her a startled look and shouting something at her.

Finally, Joanna and Matthew arrived at the crest of land that divided the southwest paddock from the one where she knew the in-lamb ewes were being pastured. She urged the horse to climb the muddy incline, and then she was over the top and her gaze fell upon a horrific scene.

A flat plain stretched before her, black with night and rain. Directly ahead, the mountains looked mighty and wrathful, frequent flashes of lightning creating the illusion that the stony summits were moving, rolling toward her like a giant rocky sea. To her left Joanna saw the river, which was normally peaceful but which now seemed to boil down from the mountains in a furious tide, sweeping everything out of its path, the gum trees along its banks whipping in the wind, and sheep, hundreds of them, tumbling into the raging water.

Joanna stared, unable to move.

Sheep were running all over the landscape, while men and dogs tried to control them. They swarmed like a white tide, a thousand at a time, bolting, suddenly turning as if one body, like schools of fish. The men on their horses shouted and whistled and the sheep came together; then lightning would flash, and part of the mob would break off. It was mesmerizing and terrifying.

And at the river—

The men had managed to head off the major part of the stampeding flock, creating a wedge with their horses, making the frightened sheep veer away from the river. But many had already made it to the muddy banks and were slipping, sliding, plunging into the rampaging current. Men were frantically chopping down trees, trying to create a dam, a way of stopping the sheep from being carried away.

Joanna shouted, "Geeyap!" and snapped the reins and her horse began to run. The wagon flew down the hillock, bouncing crazily, nearly spilling over, while Matthew clung to his seat. When they finally came to a stop and climbed down, their feet sank into ankle-deep mud. The rain came in such punishing gusts that they could hardly see. But they saw enough: sheep trapped in the muck, bleating and struggling, dropping their premature lambs, tiny dead things that lay in the ooze; men with ropes were trying to save some of them, their horses rearing and whinnying; a sheepdog lying still, his head submerged in a deep puddle; the men at the river, up to their waists in the rushing water, working furiously with axes and ropes, felling trees, trying to lasso ewes that had fallen into the river.

Joanna could barely find anyone in the rain. Where was Hugh? While Matthew ran to the river to help with the ropes, she picked up her soaked skirts, and struggled over the muddy ground. She saw Larry, and recognized another man, Tom Watkins. They were both hatless, their hair plastered to their heads; they were wearing long oilskin coats, standing on a fallen eucalyptus, throwing ropes out to drowning sheep.

The thunder was almost constant as the heavy clouds clashed and rolled overhead. The rain came down harder.

Finally Joanna saw Hugh. He was down on the river bank, hauling in a ewe. The animal was struggling against the lines, its head disappearing under the water and then emerging again while men waded out and tried to seize it with their bare hands.

One of the men slipped and fell, the rope snaring the ewe gave way, and she swirled helplessly on the current. She crashed against a rock and rolled over like a log, her legs sticking up out of the water, kicking furiously. And then she was gone.

Joanna scrambled down the bank. "Hugh!" she cried.

He turned and squinted through the downpour. "Joanna! What are you doing here!"

"I want to help!"

"Get back to the house!"

"Hoy there, Hugh!" Larry shouted from his makeshift eucalyptus bridge. "Caught another one!"

Three men waded out into the water and grabbed hold of Larry's ropes. They pulled the lifeless animal in and dragged her up onto the river bank. Joanna stared in shock. The sheep was dead. Her half-born lamb, only its head showing, was also dead.

Suddenly there was a shout, and Hugh and Joanna looked up to see Larry disappear into the river.

"Oh God!" cried Tommie Watkins, jumping in after him.

"Freddo!" shouted Hugh, signaling to one of the men. "Tie that rope around me. Come on! Hurry!"

Joanna watched in horror as Hugh, securing the rope around his waist, dived into the water and vanished.

"Hugh!" she screamed. "*No!*"

She ran to the two men who were holding onto the other end of the rope, their heels dug into the mud, leaning back with all their might against the pull of the river. But they were sliding down the bank, losing their foothold. Joanna got behind Freddo, seized the rope, and started to pull, but he shouted for her to get away.

Through the storm they caught glimpses of Hugh as he tried to swim against the powerful current. Several times he disappeared in the foaming water, only to reemerge, still swimming, trying to reach Larry and Tommie.

Joanna sobbed and grabbed again for the rope. Freddo lost his balance, fell back against her, and they ended up in the mud. The man left on the rope nearly lost it, but two other men came running down the river bank to take up the loose end.

As Joanna held on, she felt the sickening dance of the rope in her hands and thought of Hugh on the other end of it, out there in that ferocious river. And suddenly she hated the river—this same river which, only four miles away, branched out into the creek and billabong that she had once thought so peaceful and beautiful. And then she hated Merinda and Victoria and the whole continent of Australia. She swore that if Hugh died tonight she would never forgive this land for killing him.

And then the men closer to the water were suddenly backing up; Joanna was pushed out of the way by Freddo as they hauled Hugh out of the water. He had hold of someone—a man who was dragged up onto the muddy bank as limply and lifelessly as the sheep had been, and Joanna saw that it was Larry.

She dropped the rope and ran to them. "I'm all right," Hugh managed to say. "Look after Larry. The boy's still out there."

He dived in again, and Joanna watched in the rain as he swam out among the swirling debris and sheep carcasses. She left the men to hold onto his rope, and turned her attention to Stringy Larry who was, she discovered, barely alive. There was a bad gash on his forehead, and she saw in horror that his leg was badly broken, the bone jutting up through the fabric of his trousers. It was bleeding furiously. Joanna removed his belt and tied it around the leg as a tourniquet, then she got Half-Caste Eddie to help her carry him to the wagon.

"I need a board!" she shouted above the wind, as Larry was placed in the wagon bed. "I have to set his leg."

Eddie picked up a rock and pounded it furiously against the side of the wagon until one of the boards came away. He climbed up next to

Stringy Larry and watched with frightened eyes as Joanna worked in the rain, trying to clean the wound and staunch the bleeding.

She felt the river behind her, mighty and awesome as it thundered along its course, carrying trees and debris and animal carcasses with it, and two men—fifteen-year-old Tommie Watkins, and Hugh.

"Help me," she cried, as the wind threatened to topple the wagon. Eddie slipped the board under Larry's leg.

"Take hold of his ankle," Joanna said. "Pull hard and steady. Don't yank it! Slowly!"

Eddie leaned his weight away from the unconscious Larry, his eyes fixed on the bone protruding through torn flesh.

"Steady," Joanna said, as she carefully guided the ends of the broken bones together.

There was a sickening grating sound, the bone slipped beneath the skin, and Joanna quickly lashed Larry's foot to the end of the board.

"Go on, Eddie," she shouted. "Go and help the others."

Joanna wanted to look back, she wanted to see what was happening at the river, but she knew she didn't dare. As she worked over Larry, she prayed with all her might. She felt the pulse at his neck, then she lifted his eyelids. He was shockingly white.

Joanna returned to his leg wound, cleaning it again, and sewing it up with silk thread. Then she applied potassium permanganate, and wrapped the leg in a bandage that soon became sodden. Making a pillow of one of the blankets, she placed it under his head, then looked toward the river, but couldn't see Hugh. She took a second blanket and rigged a makeshift tent, to keep the rain off Larry's face, then checked his pulse again.

She looked back at the river. The men were still on the bank, holding lines that led into the water. Still no sign of Hugh.

She looked down at Stringy Larry. His eyes were open, glassy and staring.

She felt his pulse. He was dead.

———————————— • ————————————

Dawn broke over a scene of devastation.

For miles in every direction the face of the land had changed. Murray River gums—massive old trees that had stood in these pastures since before the white man came—lay on their sides, roots torn up from the earth and pointing to the sky. Sheds and fences and water tanks lay scattered about like a child's toys. Great pools of water buried grazing grasses, mockingly reflecting a blue sky and warm sun.

And there were sheep carcasses as far as the eye could see.

Joanna stood by the wagon, shivering inside a borrowed coat, frantic, exhausted. She hadn't slept—no one had.

Philip McNeal was there, plodding through the mud, helping with the hauling of carcasses into a newly dug trench. Dead sheep lay everywhere, many of them with lambs at their sides, still connected to their mothers by umbilical cords. Huge scavenger birds circled overhead, casting shadows on the ground, while the men went silently about their grim burials.

Everyone suddenly stirred to life as a rider on horseback appeared. He was riding from the direction of downstream, and as he came near, they saw that he had a body slung across the front of his saddle. Joanna rushed forward with the others, and when the body was laid on the ground and she felt for signs of life, one of the men took her by the shoulders and said gently, "It ain't no use, missus. He's dead."

She stared down at what was left of Tommie Watson's young face. His head had been bashed against the rocks.

"Was there any sign of Hugh?" she asked the rider, already knowing the answer, before he shook his head, no. Hugh had come loose from the line that held him, and he had been carried downstream. Eight men on horseback were searching the river.

Philip came up to Joanna and laid a hand on her shoulder. "Why don't you go back to the homestead?" he said. "You need to have something to eat. Lie down."

She shook her head. Hugh was still out there.

All of a sudden they heard, "Hoy! Look there!"

Joanna turned and saw a figure limping along the river bank.

"Hugh!" she cried, and ran to him.

He looked awful. His clothes were torn and mud-caked, his face haggard and drawn. He had aged ten years.

"Joanna," he said, taking her into his arms and kissing her. "Are you all right?"

"What happened, my darling?" she said, holding onto him, tears running down her face. "My God, we thought you were dead."

"The last thing I remember was climbing out of the river. I tried heading back this way, but I must have gone too far. How's Larry?"

"He's dead, Hugh. And they found Tommie Watkins—"

Hugh was silent for a moment, then he said, "Larry."

The others crowded around, regarding Hugh with stark faces, some of them reaching out to touch him to be sure their eyes weren't deceiving them. "Thank God you're all right, Hugh," one of the older station hands said. His voice sounded as if he were on the verge of crying.

"I'm all right, Joe," Hugh said. "See that the others are taken care of. Has anyone sent for Ping-Li and the cook wagon?"

"Hugh," Joanna said. "Let's go back to the homestead. You need to be taken care of."

"Wait," he said, looking around at the scene of destruction.

Joanna tightened her arms around him and rested her head on his shoulder. She felt him draw a deep breath and let it out with a shudder.

"Looks like we lost most of the lambs," he said.

"It'll be all right, Hugh," she said. "We still have Zeus and his ewes. They survived the storm."

"Yes," Hugh said in a flat voice. "But we won't have a clip this year, or any lanolin. And I lent money to Jacko. Joanna, I'm sorry. I'm afraid the house will have to wait."

"I know," she said, wondering when her inheritance money was going to come from India. "All that matters is that you're all right. I can live wherever you live. We don't need a big house, not yet. We have each other, that is what is important. And we have Adam and Sarah. And we'll have the baby."

He held her close and kissed her almost desperately, holding her tightly against him as if hungry for the life her body promised in the midst of so much death.

CHAPTER 16

M y dear Joanna," Frank wrote, "I have just received a communication from my friend at the Sydney *Bulletin*. He has gone through their archives, and I regret to report that he has found no mention of a ship bearing the name of a mythical beast in the years that you are interested in. I found mention of a ship called the *Unicorn*. Unfortunately, inquiry disclosed that it was a convict ship between 1780 and 1810, and it did not carry paying passengers. But I maintain hope, and I will keep up the search.

"On another subject—I do wish you would talk your stubborn husband into accepting a loan from me. I cannot help but feel somehow responsible for your catastrophic loss. I gave those five thousand acres to my sister's new husband, and although I cannot believe Colin is responsible for the terrible thing that happened, I cannot divorce myself totally from the possibility. Please, Joanna, try and see if you can persuade Hugh to accept a loan."

Frank sat back in his chair, wishing he could escape the bad feeling he had about the whole thing. It was all too coincidental—as soon as

Colin had obtained possession of the five thousand acres, disaster had befallen Merinda. There were whispered rumors around the district that MacGregor blamed Westbrook for his wife's death, and that he was seeking revenge. Was it possible? It seemed too crazy, but Frank wondered. Unfortunately, there was no way he could ask Colin about it. He and Pauline had left for their honeymoon right after the wedding reception and were, at this moment, on a ship bound for Scotland, and Colin's ancestral home on the island of Skye.

Frank thought about the wedding, and how happy Pauline had seemed, even if it had turned out to be a much smaller affair than the one she had planned with Westbrook. Because this was Colin's second marriage, the ceremony had been modest, with just a few close friends in attendance. It struck Frank as ironic, however, that Pauline was now stepmother to nine-year-old Judd, whereas she had once claimed to have broken her engagement to Hugh because she didn't want to inherit another woman's child!

But Frank didn't try to fathom it; he decided that he had given up trying to understand women. Whenever he thought he knew a woman, she seemed to turn him upside down. As Ivy Dearborn had done, at first refusing his attentions and then accepting them, only to vanish. He was glad he had finally gotten over her. Frank didn't like the feeling of being distracted, or tied emotionally to a woman.

"So when are you going to get married, Frank?" Maude Reed had asked him at Pauline's wedding reception. And Frank knew that it wasn't only Mrs. Reed who was interested in his plans. Now that Lismore had lost its mistress, every mother in the district had her eye on it for her daughter. No sooner had the minister pronounced Pauline and Colin married, than Frank had become the center of feminine attention, from young Verity Campbell to the elderly, matchmaking Constance McCloud. "You can't intend to stay a bachelor *forever*, Frank," Louisa Hamilton had teased. "It isn't good for a man to be alone." It was just like Louisa, Frank thought, to consider herself to be too much of a lady to utter the word "celibate." But that was clearly what she had been implying.

But Frank wasn't celibate, not by any means. No man with money living in Melbourne needed to deny himself whatever sexual indulgences he wanted, whenever he wanted. Frank had lady friends all over town who were more than accommodating—ladies who gladly took his money and his gifts without making demands on him, and certainly without matrimony on their minds. And that was just the way he wanted it. Being only thirty-six, Frank reckoned that he had plenty of time left to enjoy life before committing himself to one woman, and to getting down to the business of producing an heir.

"Frank?" said a voice from the open doorway.

He looked up to see Eric Graham, the *Times* reporter who prowled the harbor for news. He was a tall, bowler-hatted young man who, Frank knew, was eager to make a name for himself in the newspaper business. Eric was one of Frank's most valued reporters; it was he who had scooped the story on the capture of Dan Sullivan, the notorious outlaw, getting it into the *Times* while the fellows over at the *Age* and *Argus* were still asleep. "Come in, Eric," he said. "I hope you've got something lively for tomorrow's edition." It was Frank's policy to review all copy before it went to the editorial desks.

"I'm afraid there's not much going on down at the waterfront today, Frank," Graham said, removing his hat and revealing carefully oiled, slicked-down hair. "Let me see," he said as he flipped through his notes. "An American clipper came in, rather impressive—"

"Clippers are old news by now."

"I suppose so. Here's one: a killer whale was sighted offshore."

"How far offshore?"

"I couldn't find that out."

"Was it sighted from the beach?"

"No."

Frank shook his head.

"Well then," Graham said, riffling his notes, "the SS *Orion* is due to arrive tomorrow, the fifth ship to arrive at Melbourne after going through the Suez Canal."

"The first ship was news, Eric, the fifth isn't," Frank said, as a copy boy came into his office and handed him a stack of page proofs. While Graham continued with his report, Frank sorted through the papers.

"All right then," Eric said, "here's an amusing piece: A group of satisfied pub patrons were seeing a barmaid off. She's sailing to England and apparently they took up a collection . . ."

But Frank wasn't listening. The first story in the pile of papers was about the man the police had been bringing in from Cooper's Creek, the survivor of the ill-fated 1871 expedition. Apparently he had committed suicide before they could get him to Melbourne. "Damn," Frank murmured. He had planned on running a special edition on just that story alone—the survivor's personal account of the expedition from the minute it had departed Melbourne, through the mass killing, right up to the moment the police found him living with the Aborigines. Now, it was just another news item.

Eric reached the end of his report, and was frustrated to see that he wasn't going to be getting a byline in tomorrow's edition. If only the American clipper ship had panned out, like the one that arrived last month, bringing a team of explorers who intended to go in search of the South Pole. The only thing this morning's clipper had brought, as far as Graham could determine, was a new edible treat from America called Cracker Jack. He personally liked the story about the pub patrons seeing their favorite barmaid off. It might not be news, but there was an interesting angle to the story: The woman was some kind of artist. She had stood there at the ship making sketches and handing them out as good-by mementos. Eric had managed to get one—he had asked her if she could do the premier of Victoria. The resulting caricature was a remarkable likeness of the man, and a comical one, too.

"Well, Frank?" Graham said.

Frank was thinking about the survivor of the 1871 expedition, and that the story might not be lost after all. It could be written up as an "as-told-to," getting one of the policemen to claim that, just before the poor man took his life, he had told all. In fact, Frank thought, it would probably make an even better story than the real one, since a certain amount of creativity would be involved.

"Frank?" Eric said. "Can you use any of this?"

"I need something political for tomorrow's edition, Eric. People are beginning to think that everyone in Parliament has died."

"Sorry, there's nothing political on my beat."

"All right. Run the whale story. But *say* that it was coming dangerously close to a fishing boat or something. And change it to a gray whale."

"But grays don't swim in southern waters."

"I don't care. They're bigger."

After Graham left, Frank went through the rest of the proofs, doing some quick editing, pulling a few, and adding comments on others. Then he went through a small pile of personal communications—letters from readers, interoffice memos, invitations to various functions. He came upon a note that had been sent up from the research desk: "Examined most recent government maps and land surveys of Queensland, New South Wales, Victoria, South Australia and Western Australia. Sorry to report no places named Bowman's Creek or Durrebar."

Frank frowned. It was strange. Hugh had said that Miss Tallhill was certain of her analysis of the writing on the deed, but clearly she had made a mistake, and Frank now had the unpleasant task of reporting it to Joanna. Frank had hoped that, when Joanna went to Karra Karra, he could send a reporter along with her to describe her journey for *Times* readers.

Frank consulted his watch and saw that it was nearly time for lunch. He was in the mood for a beer and a meat pie, and the company of his fellow newsmen down at the Coach and Four. As he was reaching for his coat, Eric Graham materialized in the doorway again.

"It just occurred to me, Frank," he said eagerly. "I know we don't run illustrations in the *Times*, but you said you needed something political. What do you think of this?" He held out the sketch he had picked up at the harbor.

Frank looked at it. "My God," he said. "It's the premier himself! This is marvelous! Why, if you didn't know the man, you could tell everything about him by just looking at this picture. Where did you get it?"

"I told you. There was some kind of a party going on down at the dock, pub patrons seeing a barmaid off. I hung around, thinking it might make a good human-interest story. A barmaid who does sketches of the customers."

Frank stared at him. "What? Where?"

"Down at the harbor. She was going back to England—"

"Good God, man. Why didn't you tell me!" Frank seized his coat and rushed to the door. "What boat was she leaving on?"

"I believe it was the *Princess Julianna*. But I think it's already sailed—"

Frank jumped down from the cab before it stopped, handed a bank note to the driver, who protested that he didn't have the change for such a large bill, and disappeared into the crowd.

He searched the wharf, going from pier to pier, reading the names of ships at anchor, pushing through the busy throng. Finally he waylaid a customs official. "Where is the *Princess Julianna?*"

"The *Princess Julianna?* She's just sailed, sir," the man said, and he pointed toward the sea, where Frank saw white sails receding toward the horizon.

"I'll hire a boat then, and go out to her." When Frank started off in the direction of a small pier, where a faded sign advertised boats for rent, the official caught his arm and said, "There aren't any boats left. Someone said a whale had been seen out there, and everyone's gone to look at it."

Frank swore under his breath and surveyed the chaos on the dock. Two large ships had just arrived, and there was the usual band playing

"God Save the Queen," the usual crowd greeting the disembarking passengers, the usual opportunists on the prowl, looking for pockets to pick, victims to fleece.

And, in a deserted corner of the pier, away from the mob, a well-dressed red-haired woman was sitting on a large trunk, gazing out at sea, the feathers of her bonnet fluttering in the wind.

He walked up to her, and when his shadow fell across her, she looked up.

"Hello, Ivy," Frank said.

She smiled and shook her head. "I must be out of my mind," she said. "After all my careful planning, and saving up for the ticket, and letting my friends throw a party for me and saying good-by, I couldn't walk up that gangway."

"Why?"

"A reporter from your newspaper asked me to give him a drawing. I knew you would see it.

"My God," Frank said, sitting down next to her. "I thought you had died of typhoid. Why did you leave? Where did you go?"

"During the epidemic, I heard that your sister had organized the women in the district to put together food and supplies for stricken families. I went to your house; I went to Lismore and offered help. But they didn't want me. As hard up as they were for volunteers, they didn't think I was good enough to help. And that was when I saw the reality of our situation. Church services and Sunday picnics could never completely cover up the fact of what I really am—a barmaid."

"I ran notices in the *Times*, searching for you."

"I know. I saw them."

"Then why didn't you get in touch with me? Why have you been hiding from me?"

"Because my feelings for you are so confused! And because I have to be careful."

"About what?"

She turned and looked at him. He was sitting close to her; Ivy could see the details of his face, the soft brown eyes, the early shadow of beard on his jaw, and she realized that this was the first time they had ever seen each other outside in daylight. Now that he was here again, in person and not just in her thoughts, and now that they sat in open sunlight, so close together that they almost touched, Ivy explored her feelings for him once more. And she realized that they weren't confused at all. "Frank," she said, "when an unmarried woman fights to maintain her respectability, she must cut herself off from intimate relationships with men. A man on his own, like you, is free to have such relationships. But a woman cannot. And you can ask any man—I am respectable."

"I never thought you weren't respectable," he said. Frank couldn't believe his eyes. Here she was, in the flesh, sitting so close to him that he saw the tiny flecks of black in her green eyes, the pinpoints of glitter on her earrings, the wispy strands of red hair that were stirred by the ocean breeze. When she smiled, small wrinkles appeared at the corners of her eyes, and Frank recalled Finnegan telling him once that Ivy was nearly forty.

"Tell me," he said quietly, "why didn't you sail on the *Julianna*? Where were you going?"

"I don't know really. Just . . . away."

"Away from me?"

"Perhaps."

"But you stayed."

"Yes."

"Come back with me, Ivy. Give me a chance."

"You don't know anything about me," she said. "My mother—"

"And my father," he said, "was the tenth son of a penniless Manchester factory worker. I don't care about a person's background. I only know that when I think about you, or look at you, I feel good. Please allow me into your life. Please, Ivy." He held out his hand. "You still owe me a picnic, at least," he said.

CHAPTER 17

S arah knew which room in the boardinghouse was Philip McNeal's, and as she waited unseen near the back door listening to the kitchen maids prepare breakfast, she looked up at his window and felt her anxiety mount. She prayed she had not come too late.

The maids finally left with their trays of tea and toast, and Sarah slipped inside. She crept along a hall, making sure no one saw her, and when she came to the foot of the stairs, she ran up on silent, bare feet.

When she reached Philip's room, she found the door standing open. She looked inside and saw an empty wardrobe, a table covered with blueprints and draughtsman's tools and a bed with rumpled sheets.

Philip was standing at the dresser, emptying the drawers and folding clothes into a valise. When he looked up, his eyebrows arched. "Sarah! What a pleasant surprise," he said, coming up to her. He looked out into the hall. "Did you come alone?" he said.

When she didn't answer, he said, "How did you get here? Did you walk, all by yourself from Merinda?"

"Yes."

"Why?"

Sarah was silent for a moment, then she said, "To say good-by."

"You walked all those miles," he said, "with no shoes, just to say good-by?"

Sarah looked down at her dusty bare feet.

"You know, Sarah," he said, going back to the dresser. "I think that in all the time I've known you—how long has it been? Six months? In all that time, I haven't heard you say much. I guess they told you I was leaving. Since Mr. Westbrook can't afford to build his house right now, and since I got a letter from my brother in America saying that my mother isn't well, I decided it would be a good time to go home." He looked at her. "I'll miss you."

As he regarded the tall, dark-skinned girl in the doorway, he noticed that her hair was tied back with a ribbon, something he had never seen her do before. He thought about how she had been down at the river every morning when he had arrived with the work crew. She would hover nearby, almost invisible among the ghost gums, and watch him as he worked, staying until sunset, when he would pack up his tools and leave.

"I'm sorry," she said.

He gave her a questioning look.

"Your mother is not well."

"It's kind of you to say that." As he folded a shirt into the valise, he said, "What about your parents, Sarah? You've never spoken of them."

He looked at her as she lingered uncertainly in the doorway, as if she were afraid to cross the threshold.

"Did you know your parents?" he asked.

"My father was a white man," Sarah said quietly. "He had a farm. They say that he wanted a woman. They say he stole my mother from her camp. He kept her with him at his farm, and then he let her go."

Sarah's voice moved quietly on the morning air. Philip stood very still, a half-folded shirt in his hands.

"My mother returned to her people," Sarah continued. "But the clan said she was taboo. They drove her out of the camp. So she came to the Aboriginal Mission. That was where I was born."

"What became of her?"

"She went walkabout. She never came back."

He looked at Sarah a moment longer, then, dropping the shirt onto the bed, he said, "Come on. I'll take you home."

They went down to the stable where his horse was already saddled.

McNeal mounted the mare, then he held a hand down to Sarah. She hesitated.

"Have you never been on a horse before?" he asked.

She shook her head.

"It's all right," he said with a smile. "I'll make sure you don't get hurt. Put your foot on top of mine in the stirrup. That's it." He pulled her up. "Now put your arms around my waist," he said.

She held on to him as they rode through the morning sunlight, past green pastures and fields of white, woolly sheep. She closed her eyes and rested her face against his back. She felt the wind blow through her hair; she felt Philip's heart beat beneath her hands. Soon they were galloping; Sarah flung her head back, felt the power of the horse between her legs. Her arms tightened around Philip; she wanted to ride with him past Merinda, toward the horizon and over the edge, and never look back.

But eventually they arrived at Merinda's yard. Philip jumped down first, then helped Sarah dismount.

"I want to give you this," he said, and he removed the silver-and-turquoise bracelet from his wrist. "To remember me by." He handed it to her.

Sarah looked at the bracelet. "When will you come back, Philip McNeal?"

He gave her a surprised look; he had never heard her speak his name before. "Six months, maybe," he said. "A year at the most. But I will come back. By the time I return you'll be all grown up and you'll have a line of young men waiting to court you, and you won't have time for an old man like me."

He drew her into his arms, and embraced her. "God be with you, Sarah," he said. And he kissed her on the forehead.

She watched him ride out of the yard, and she thought of the day she had first met him, down by the river, when he had agreed to build the house away from the ancient ruins. She looked back over the past six months, recalling how Philip had told her about a people across the ocean who also lived in clans and who descended from totem ancestors. She pictured the way he had laughed with his workmen when they had dug trenches or poured concrete, and how he had sat on the grass and eaten with them, telling them stories about his travels in America. She thought of how intently she had seen him keep to the task of building the house, studying the blueprints, conferring with Hugh Westbrook, examining every inch of ground, making the workmen do something over again if it wasn't right, never criticizing them, but guiding them, and how every so often his glance would return to Sarah, to smile at her occasionally as she watched him through the trees.

Finally, as she watched him disappear down the drive, it was quite clear to fifteen-year-old Sarah King what she had to do.

———————————◆———————————

Joanna had a strange feeling, a new kind of feeling. She had had it all day, and it kept her from concentrating on her work by the river, where she was tending the rare ginger. She had been at it all afternoon, cutting fresh roots and planting the pieces in the moist earth. Ginger had to be planted in the spring to be ready for harvesting the following autumn, when the leaves died down. The cuttings had to be especially young, distinguishable by a pale green color; they had to have eyes, the same as potatoes did, and, since it was important that each piece have at least three eyes, the task of cutting and planting the roots required care.

Joanna tried to concentrate, but it was hard. Her thoughts and emotions were confused; she was both very happy and yet troubled.

A cloud passed over the sun, and she paused in her work to look up.

It was a hot September day, just early spring, and she was eight months pregnant. She felt slow and full and languid. The hum of bees filled the air, along with the drone of flies and the chatter of birds. But the disquiet that had followed her like a shadow for the past few days was with her, too.

Finally, she laid aside her spade and sat back.

Joanna knew that part of what troubled her was that tomorrow marked two years since her arrival in Australia. Then, she had stood on the deck of the *Estella* and had expected to find out something about her legacy, about Karra Karra, within days. But now, twenty-four months and a great deal of searching—and a great deal of happiness—later, she felt no closer to Karra Karra than when she had left India. Bowman's Creek and Durrebar were proving to be elusive. The only explanation Hugh and Frank had been able to come up with was that, in the forty-three years since her grandparents had been in Australia, those place names had changed. Patrick Lathrop had written to say that he had so far been unable to decode John Makepeace's notes; and Buchanan & Co., the shipping line in London, had reported that their ships the *Pegasus* and the *Minotaur* had been constructed in 1836—six years after Joanna's grandparents had sailed for Australia.

But Joanna knew that this was not the sole cause of her uneasiness.

There was something more, something deeper, she thought, and it had to do with the baby, and the poison-song.

She felt the baby move. She wondered if it sensed her unrest. From the day Joanna had found out she was pregnant, her joy had been clouded by misgivings and fears. And as the day of delivery had drawn closer, her anxiety had grown. Had a poison-song been sung on her family, and did it still have power, after so many years? She thought of her grandfather's cryptic papers, and she felt a cold chill go through her. Were *they* the poison-song, and would it be passed on to her baby?

Joanna settled back against a large boulder, drawing a measure of relief from the heat in the rock. She reached into her workbasket and took out her mother's diary. Just the feel of it in her hands brought a sense of comfort and solace. She turned the pages and read, "February 23, 1848: Gathering dandelion roots—darling Petronius tells me that the name comes from the French *dent de lion,* which means 'lion's tooth,' because of the jagged edges of the leaves." On May 14, 1850, Lady Emily had written, "Old Jaswaran is proving to be a treasure trove of healing knowledge. Today he has shown me how to make eyedrops from licorice root. They are an excellent treatment for inflammation of the eyes." Lastly, Joanna came upon an entry dated January 30, 1871—three months before Lady Emily died: "I pray that the poison will not be passed on to Joanna."

The wind suddenly picked up, carrying with it the distant bleating of sheep on the plains.

Joanna thought of Hugh, who was in the special paddock that had been set up for his lambing ewes. Even though the storm had destroyed much of Merinda's stock, there were still the nearly three hundred ewes which his new ram, Zeus, had serviced. They were close to lambing, and Hugh was holding vigil over them. There were many dangers when lambs were born—from eagles and hawks that swooped down and carried them off at the instant of birth, to the scavenging crows that came along and pecked the newborn lambs' eyes out. Joanna knew how important those lambs were to Hugh. They were going to be the first step along the way to the fulfillment of his dream, and to the recovery of Merinda.

But, Joanna wondered as she gazed out over the green pastures, what if Zeus's offspring turned out to be inferior? In the past few months, graziers had dropped by to look the ram over and speculate upon Hugh's chances of success. "I think you're making a mistake, Hugh," Ian Hamilton had said as he had stood at the fence rail with a toothpick in his mouth. "You'll never get superfine wool out of that fellow's offspring. And superfine is all anyone is interested in." John Reed had shaken his head and said, "Some blokes in New Zealand tried the same thing. They crossed Lincoln rams with large-framed merino ewes and got disastrous results. The lambs all had weak shoulders and tail drop. I'd give it up if I were you, Westbrook. It's a waste of money."

Frank Downs was the only one who gave Hugh any encouragement. He owned fifty thousand acres up in New South Wales that so far had been unable to support sheep, and he had promised Hugh he would buy the first of Zeus's rams, if they turned out the way Hugh was expecting. Any day now, the results of Hugh's experiment would be known.

Joanna prayed that he would be successful. She looked at the concrete footings Mr. McNeal had put in. There were only four of them—half the number needed for the house. She thought about Frank's offer of a loan, and Hugh's adamant refusal to accept money from anyone. Joanna had even offered to sell the fire opal, but Hugh would not hear of it. And unfortunately her inheritance had become caught up in a legal tangle because, as Mr. Drexler had reported in his last letter, a relative of Joanna's father had appeared unexpectedly to claim some of the money. Although Drexler had assured her that it would work out in her favor in the end, the money would be slow in coming. And the loss from the storm had been enormous; Hugh was deeply in debt.

Joanna wondered if Colin MacGregor was truly responsible for their catastrophic loss, as some people were whispering. She couldn't imagine why Mr. MacGregor would do such a thing. What reason would he have for despising Hugh so? And yet Poll Gramercy, the midwife, had hinted at revenge—revenge for what, Joanna wondered? She also suspected that a few of the Aborigines still wondered if bad things came from her. But at least Ezekiel no longer seemed to be poisoning people, turning them against her.

Joanna longed for the new house, but she also understood the pride behind Hugh's decision to remain at the homestead until he could afford to resume construction of the house on his own. The cabin had been enlarged and made comfortable. In time, Joanna knew, they would have their big, beautiful house down here by the river.

As the fragrance of ginger blossoms filled her head, Joanna wondered again about the puzzling uneasiness that seemed to be following her. She had not told Hugh about her troubled state; he was so happy about the coming child that she didn't want to dampen his joy. And then there was the new development with his poetry. Frank Downs had taken it upon himself to publish Hugh's latest ballad under the author's real name, and when everyone in the Western District had discovered that the "Old Drover" of the poetry that occasionally appeared in the *Times* was their own Hugh Westbrook, he had been the center of attention.

Joanna understood why everyone loved Hugh's poetry, especially his latest and, all of his friends declared, his best ballad, "The Dreaming"—"Out in the backblocks of the wild country/Where the ghosts of blackfellow shine. . . ." It was all there, people said—Australia—in Hugh's shearers and graziers, his drovers and outlaws, in the emus and the hawks, and the Rainbow Serpent "whose body is yellow and red in stripe," and who "strolls curved against the body of his wife," who was "blue from head to tail." People recognized the fact that Hugh Westbrook saw how times were changing, and that someday all that remained of the old Australia might be found only in his verse.

The hot sun was making Joanna sleepy. She looked up to see a pale-yellow cockatoo land briefly on an overhead branch. She regarded the tall ginger stalks, their sword-like leaves and pink flowers quivering in the mist of the waterfall. The wind fluttered the pages of the diary. Joanna read her mother's delicate, swirling handwriting: "The baby was born at dawn. We are going to call her Joanna. I am no longer a girl. I am a woman."

As the diary slipped from Joanna's hands, she thought vaguely, perhaps that is all that is troubling me, the fact that I am changing. Does every girl feel this way when she has her first child? Is this what it is like to pass from girlhood to womanhood? Joanna had thought her passing into womanhood had come when she had first made love with Hugh. Or perhaps when she celebrated her twenty-first birthday the following year. But the true affirmation of her femininity, she realized, lay with the creation of a child.

She closed her eyes and tried to shrug off the uneasiness that continued to trouble her. She laid her hands on her abdomen and felt the baby's restless slumber. Joanna wanted to be happy; she wanted to experience only the pure joy and exhilaration that comes with the momentous passage into motherhood. But perhaps there was always a kind of fear that accompanied such a change. Perhaps, she thought as she drifted off to sleep, the shedding of the old self and the embracing of the new was something that both excited and frightened every girl who experienced it. She wished her own mother were here to guide her through the miracle, and to share it with her.

Joanna tried to recall something Sarah had once said about Aboriginal initiations—about mothers and daughters and songlines—but she fell asleep before it came to her.

As Sarah followed the river, she walked with great care so as not to disturb the Dreaming Sites she passed. Each time she came upon a site she recognized—the Diamond Dove Dreaming, the Golden Cockatoo Dreaming—she softly sang it to show respect.

She carried a small bundle that contained the clay and ocher and cockatoo feathers she had been collecting for the ritual she had planned to perform when Joanna's baby was born, to ensure the child health and good magic, and to bind it to the land into which it had been born. But Sarah was going to use the objects for another purpose now, because the bundle also contained emu fat stolen from the cookhouse, a hair-string headband she had made for herself and a pair of shoes Joanna had bought for her long ago and which Sarah had never worn.

She walked with the sun in her face, steadily, with a long stride, and with her eyes always ahead. She had to make sure she was far away from buildings and flocks and men. She had to go to a private place. And as she walked, she sang the songline of the Fur Seal Ancestor—the song-line of her mother and her grandmothers.

Presently she came to a place on the river that was protected by a screen of trees and boulders. She listened to the wind and heard no voices riding it. She turned in a slow circle and saw no farms, no fences, no riders on horseback. White people, Sarah knew, feared Aboriginal magic. Mr. Simms had once locked her away for three days without food and water for doing what he called "a heathen practice." She had only been trying to call down the rain because the mission's crops were dying.

She undressed slowly and folded her clothes into a neat pile. She untied the bundle and took out each object, whispering its song as she placed it on the river bank: the ocher, the fat, the feathers, the hair-string, the shoes. Then she walked into the river and washed herself in its cold water. She gathered stones and grass and made a small fire on the bank, singing as she fanned the flames, inviting the spirit of the All-Mother to give power to the fire. Then she proceeded to make paint out of the clay and ocher.

When the paint was ready, Sarah greased her body all over with the emu fat. She rubbed it into her skin until she glowed red-brown in the dying sun. She massaged it into her hair, she mixed it into the ash of the fire, singing the songs of the All-Mother. Finally she began to paint her naked body.

First she highlighted the contours in red and black paint, calling upon the Bush Berry Dreaming from which the black had been made, and the River Clay Dreaming from which the red had come, bringing their power into the designs she created. The white paint she applied with a stick, tracing stripes from her shoulders down her arms, and circles on her breasts, and dots on her abdomen. Her thighs received stars and suns, and the great swells of ocean currents, and symbols which stood for a rocky beach that lay far to the south and was the original home of the fur seal. She sang all the while, validating the paint and the symbols, giving them power. She sang her mother's songline.

Sarah was aware as she sang that her range of songs was limited, because her secret initiation at the mission had been interrupted, but she was confident that she knew enough of the ritual to draw the power into herself.

When she was done, she drew the hairstring over her head as a headband, then she sat down and faced the setting sun.

She breathed in the smoke from the fire, smelling the charred kangaroo grass, the fat-enriched ashes, the burnt feathers—a magic smoke that possessed the spirits of the powerful Kangaroo, Emu and Cockatoo Dreamings. She swayed as she sang. She closed her eyes and felt the rays of the sun pierce her flesh. Colors and shapes moved behind her eyelids. Then she was on her feet, and she began to dance the reenactment of the long journey of the fur seal from antarctic waters to warmer ones.

She felt her body begin to change. She felt the mighty ocean move around her, she tasted its salty waters, she saw shimmering green sunlight stream through swirling kelp forests.

Sarah felt power move through her body. She felt strength and magic course through her veins. She sang and danced the Dreaming of her clan; and by her singing and dancing she was continuing the songline, as her mothers had done before her, each in her own time.

She should not have had to go through this alone; the law of the People dictated that her mother be there, leading her through the sacred rites, passing the songline on to her daughter. But Sarah had no mother; she was alone.

Joanna was dreaming.

She was watching the entrance to a cave; she was very little, and being held in someone's arms.

Women were coming out of the cave, and the little girl Joanna was happy to see them. Then she saw a white woman, who was so beautiful as she walked with the others, singing with them. Joanna thought that the woman must be her mother, and yet she didn't recognize her. And then into Joanna's dream came the thought: Am I dreaming my mother's dream?

The child in the dream asked the woman who was holding her, "Can I go into the cave?"

But she was told, No, only girls who have become women can go in there. And they must go with their mothers.

Can daddies go in? Joanna asked.

No, taboo for daddies. Very bad magic for men to be there.

And then Joanna saw a man coming out of the cave, behind the women, moving among the rocks. And she cried out, "There is he is! There's Daddy!"

And she reached out for him.

But then the dream began to change. The sky grew dark; the landscape took on ominous shapes. The people became angry; they began to chase the man who had come out of the mountain. And suddenly there were dogs, and Joanna was running toward the man, whom she thought of as "Father," but whom she didn't recognize. And the dogs came closer.

The man's arms seemed to be reaching for her and she wanted to go to him, but she saw that he was starting to change shape. He grew tall; he collapsed onto the ground; his body seemed to flow over the red sand. He writhed in the shadows until Joanna saw that he had turned into an enormous rainbow-colored snake.

Joanna tried to scream, but she had no voice. She wanted to run, but her feet wouldn't move. The snake inched slowly toward her, and then suddenly Lady Emily was there. Joanna stood frozen in fear as she saw the giant serpent draw closer and closer to them, its slitted golden eye fixed upon her.

Now the dogs were running toward Lady Emily. They started to spring. But just then the snake opened up its jaws and swallowed Lady Emily whole.

Joanna saw her disappear into the snake. She screamed. Suddenly, the snake was upon her; it curled around her waist, it began to crush her. There was sudden, unbearable pain.

Joanna awoke with a start. She lay still. Night had fallen; the river was black. As she lay in the darkness of the woods, still in the grip of the terrifying dream, barely aware of the sharp pains in her abdomen, Joanna thought how extraordinary it was. Had she in fact been able to dream her mother's dream? She tried to go back over it, to fathom its meaning. She recalled her mother's lifelong fear of dogs, and she wondered if the dream had somehow been a memory of an incident she had once witnessed. Had the poison-song something to do with dogs? Was it some form of a curse, placed perhaps upon the Makepeaces and their future generations? A curse involving dogs?

Suddenly, another memory came to Joanna: two years ago, on the road to Emu Creek camp, the Aborigines at the side of the road, the old woman telling Joanna's fortune—"I see the shadow of a dog following you"—and Joanna thinking the woman had been speaking of the past, while Hugh had said that he thought the old woman had been referring to the future. Did the curse, then, somehow involve death by dogs, either imaginary or real?

But why? Joanna silently asked the river darkness. What was it her grandparents had done to bring such a terrible punishment upon themselves and their descendants? Lady Emily had described in her diary a dream in which she saw her father emerge from the cave. Had such an incident actually taken place? In another entry, she had written: "Something is buried, and I must unearth it. I feel compelled to return to Karra Karra and claim a legacy." What legacy? What did it all mean?

Joanna looked around and felt the power of the Aborigines in this place. The people might be gone, but here their presence remained, their spirits, energies and passions. She understood now the nature of the uneasiness that had haunted her pregnancy: Some deep part of her was afraid that the mother-daughter legacy of fear—was somehow going to be passed along to her unborn child.

Joanna tried to pull herself to her feet, but a hot pain suddenly shot around her waist. *The Rainbow Serpent strangling her.*

No, she thought in fear as she sank back to the ground. No, it was the baby, coming too soon.

Sarah bathed in the river. She washed off the sacred symbols and the emu fat, giving their power to the river, watching them float away to a secret place. On the river bank she erased the symbols she had drawn in the dirt, and smothered the fire, singing the Dreaming back into the land. It was over. Sarah had done her own initiation; she had done it by herself. Her mother had not led her through the mysteries, nor taught her the secrets. There had been no grandmother to pass down ancestral wisdom, no sisters or female cousins to celebrate her passage, no clan to receive her into its loving embrace. And so Sarah had gone through her initiation alone, and she knew that that was now how it must be.

She also knew that it might be the last ritual of her people that she would ever perform.

As she thought of Philip McNeal and how it had felt to ride behind him on his horse with her arms around him, feeling the reassuring beat of his strong heart, she carefully removed the leather thong from her neck. She tucked the bone from the Fur Seal Dreaming into the pocket of her dress. Then she put on the shoes for the first time. Finally she slipped Philip McNeal's bracelet onto her wrist.

And she turned her back on the vanished sun.

———————————

Pain struck again, a band of fire encircling Joanna's waist. Her legs gave way beneath her and she collapsed to the ground. She lay against the rock and forced her breathing to come more easily. She closed her eyes and tried to examine herself internally. Something was wrong. She knew about childbearing; she had helped her mother in midwifery. The baby was supposed to turn before it emerged, but Joanna felt the head still high up. And the pains were coming too close together.

Joanna listened to the night, but all she heard was the gurgling of the waterfall, the rustling of the wind in the trees. She thought of the Rainbow Serpent, whom every Aborigine revered and feared, and which even her own mother, Lady Emily, had feared too—and which, revealed by the dream she had just had, Joanna also feared. She felt the spirits in the rocks and branches stir to life around her, as if her presence in the woods were waking them from an old sleep. She heard Sarah, telling her again that terrible things befell the person who desecrated a sacred site. It was taboo to step on a stone that was inhabited by a spirit, or to brush aside a ghost-inhabited branch. In the old days, Sarah had explained, the People had known where it was safe to walk, and which rocks and trees to treat with respect. But Joanna didn't know about this place; no one had taught her.

She struggled to her feet and paused while another circle of fire shot around her waist. She tried to take a step, but walking increased the pain. The child was coming.

And then she heard a sound that chilled her: the hungry wail of a dingo.

And the nightmare came back to her, and she realized that she was suddenly afraid of dogs.

She had to get away from the river, away from the wild dogs. So she moved slowly, going from tree to tree, stopping when the pain was too great. Perspiration broke out on her face. Bands of pain flew down her legs.

The woods were dark, it was difficult to see, there was only a sliver of moon in the sky. Joanna looked around at the darkness and thought of stories that Sarah had told her of the spirits that came out at night. When the sun set, ghosts and phantoms walked the land, Sarah had said, stealing babies, killing the old ones. The People knew never to go abroad at night, but to stay by the fire, close together, watchful.

Joanna was immobilized with pain. Her breath came in quick gasps. She wished Sarah were there. There was comfort in knowing that Sarah was familiar with the forces that walked the land at night; that she knew how to deal with them.

Someone had to be coming soon. Surely they were all wondering where she was, and were out searching for her. Or were Sarah and Adam thinking that she was with Hugh, at the lambing pens? What if it was hours before anyone missed her?

Something black and shapeless suddenly loomed in Joanna's path—a low, moss-covered wall that was part of the Aboriginal ruins. Centuries ago, it had been someone's home.

Thinking of the kangaroo with the joey, and what Sarah had said to her about her being a member of that clan, Joanna drew comfort from the thought that the Kangaroo Ancestress might be here, in these ancient stones. She crawled inside and lay back against the wall. She put her hands on her abdomen and felt the baby move.

Another pain, and then a rustling sound, and heavy breathing.

It was Sarah. "I went to the house," the girl said anxiously. "Adam said you had not come home. I came looking for you."

"The baby is coming, Sarah."

"I'll go for help."

"No," Joanna said, catching her wrist. "There's no time. Sarah—you will have to help me. My shawl . . . spread it beneath me."

Sarah looked back through the trees. She couldn't see the homestead. It was too far—if she called out, no one would hear.

"Hurry!" Joanna said.

Sarah moved quickly.

When Joanna suddenly cried out, Sarah lifted Joanna's skirt. She froze.

Two tiny feet, pale and unmoving, had emerged.

Joanna cried out again; Sarah stared with wide eyes. The baby's feet had protruded a little and then receded.

"Take hold of it," Joanna said. "The next time . . . take hold of the baby."

Sarah tried to remember births she had witnessed at the mission, and others she had heard about. She reached down and took careful hold of the tiny feet.

With the next contraction, Sarah gave a gentle pull, but the baby didn't move. Sarah thought there was too much blood.

Her mind raced. She should run to the homestead, she told herself, and get help. But from whom? Hugh was away in the lambing paddock, and it would be useless to try sending someone to fetch Poll Gramercy, who lived miles away in Cameron Town.

Joanna gave another sharp cry, and when Sarah saw that the baby made no progress, she remembered the Aboriginal Mission, and how the women gave birth there—in the Aboriginal way.

Suddenly she was on her feet, searching frantically in the darkness until she found a large stick. Then she dropped to the ground and began to dig.

"Sarah—" Joanna gasped. "What—"

The girl attacked the damp soil, sending dirt and clods flying, prizing up rocks and throwing them aside. She dug until her body ran with sweat, she clawed away at the earth until her arms were caked to the elbows in mud. Then she pulled off her shawl and spread it inside the wide, deep hole.

She went back to Joanna and helped her to her feet. "Over here," she said. "Quickly."

They staggered together to the place Sarah had dug. Sarah steadied Joanna as she knelt over the hole. "Now," she said.

Joanna's thighs rippled with strength as the next powerful contraction gathered momentum. Sarah watched for the baby.

"Again," she said.

Joanna's fingers dug into the girl's shoulders as she pushed.

And two tiny legs appeared.

Letting go of Joanna, Sarah quickly reached down and took hold of the cold limbs. "Again," she said. "It's coming!"

It took several more pushes, and then finally the baby was out. Sarah caught it and she saw that it was a red and wrinkled little girl, who shivered but did not cry.

As Joanna sank to the ground, Sarah quickly seized handfuls of kangaroo grass and rubbed them over the baby's body. She sucked the mucus out of its nose and mouth, and finally it cried. She laid it on Joanna's breast.

Joanna looked at the baby in her arms. A girl! She thought of Naomi Makepeace giving birth to her baby, to Emily, somewhere in the Australian wilderness. She thought of Lady Emily giving birth to Joanna

at a remote outpost in India. And she saw the thread connecting them—
the songline—as if it were a bright silver filament traveling from grandmother to mother to granddaughter. Joanna looked at the beautiful
baby and thought: my daughter.

As she laughed weakly, Sarah frowned. She lay down next to Joanna
and put an arm across her, to warm her and the child.

"Keep the Rainbow Serpent away from her, Sarah," Joanna whispered.

"Yes," Sarah said, "yes," hoping that she could, hoping that she had
the power now, the power of women's songlines. That she could sing
the poison away from Merinda, and away from this woman and this
child, once and for all time.

PART THREE

1880

CHAPTER 18

H ey, Mrs. Westbrook," the boy in the doorway said. "What's
wrong with Mum?"

What is wrong with your mother, Joanna thought as she
secured the bandage, is that she married the wrong man.
"She just had a little accident," she said, glancing at Sarah, who stood
at the foot of the bed. Fanny had asked that no one be told the truth
of her injuries. "She'll be all right."

It was still early morning. A few hours ago, shortly before dawn, the
Merinda household had been awakened by a banging at the front door,
and the frantic shouts of a boy, calling, "Missus, you gotta come quick!
Mum's awful crook!" Such sudden emergencies, often interrupting
sleep or meals, were not uncommon at Merinda, because the women
of the Western District had gotten into the habit of calling for Joanna
Westbrook whenever they needed doctoring, rather than summoning
the male doctor in Cameron Town. Mrs. Westbrook might not have
the formal schooling, but everyone from Maude Reed to the poorest of
squatter's wives declared she had a gentler touch and more understanding than most medical men.

So Joanna and Sarah had dressed quickly, and driven through the predawn light in a buggy, following the boy on his horse. The Drummond homestead was located twelve miles away on a hardscrabble farm; it consisted of bark cabin, a falling-down barn, and the bare remains of a shearing shed. Mike Drummond was struggling to support thirty acres of wheat and eight raggedy children ranging from ten years to four months. Joanna had been here before, the last time Drummond had gotten drunk and beaten his wife.

"Fanny, why don't you report him to Constable McManus?" Joanna said as she washed her hands and rolled down her sleeves. She spoke quietly so as not to alarm the children, who were gathered in the doorway, barefooted, with running noses and bewildered expressions on their faces.

"It's not his fault," Fanny said with swollen, cracked lips. "I deserved it."

Joanna shook her head. It was what Fanny always said—that she deserved it.

Joanna thought it ironic that, with these outback men being so desperate for wives, and newly arriving single girls being desperate for husbands, the matches seemed rarely to work out well. The problem was that the young men came to Australia with unrealistic visions of getting rich quick, and when they saw their dreams slowly crumble as farms failed, gold mines dried up or a lifetime's savings was lost at gambling, they took their frustrations out on the innocent bystander— the wife. And the young girls who arrived from England, ignorant and uneducated, knowing little about life, let alone being equipped with what it took to survive on a bare-existence farm, took up with the first man who made big promises. Many of the girls were so innocent when they accepted the marriage proposal of a stranger, usually as soon as they got off the boat, that the wedding night was a shock, sometimes tantamount to rape. And life afterward became an inescapable treadmill of babies, debts, poverty and drunkenness.

Joanna looked at Fanny's bruised face. Mike had used his fists on her this time, something he had never done before. "Fanny," she said, "you don't have to put up with this."

"Where am I going to go? Me, with eight kids." The young woman tried to smile. "It'll be all right from now on," she said. "He's promised to stay away from drink."

Joanna rose from the bed and tied the handles of her medical kit. She no longer used the small box that had belonged to her mother. She carried so much with her now that when she made house calls she used a stringybark basket that had been made by one of the women at the Aboriginal Mission.

"I'm afraid I can't pay you," Fanny said.

Joanna looked around the cabin, at the mattress on the floor for the children, the table that hadn't seen soap and water in weeks, the half loaf of bread, the opened tin of tea, nearly empty. "It's all right. I know you'll pay me when you can," she said, knowing that payment would never come.

Joanna and Sarah stepped out into the sharp dawn light, ducking their heads through the sagging doorway, while the children fell back, staring. Joanna saw the dusty yard, the wagon without wheels, tipped on its side, the tethered cow, its ribs so sharply defined that she wondered that it was still alive. She looked at the children. These would be among the ones, she knew, that missionaries and government workers had tried to rescue by requiring they attend the local outback school. But invariably they never went, because they had no shoes, or no inclination, or their father said he needed them to help on the farm. They would grow up to be like their parents, illiterate and uneducated, and the cycle would begin again.

Joanna reached into the deep pockets of her skirt and drew out a handful of hard candy. She held it out, and the children grabbed for it.

As Joanna climbed into the buggy after Sarah, Fanny Drummond appeared in the doorway, an anxious look on her face. "What is it?" Joanna said, going back to her.

"I was wondering, Missus," the young woman said, her eyes nervously avoiding Joanna's. She lowered her voice. "I was wondering if you could help me. It's about babies. I've got eight now, and I asked Poll Gramercy, but as Poll's Catholic, she wouldn't—"

"I understand," Joanna said quietly. It was a familiar request. "Do you have a sea sponge, Fanny? For washing?"

"Yes, I think so."

"Cut a piece off about the size of an egg. Tie a length of strong sewing thread around it—about this long." She gestured with her hands. "Make sure it's tied securely. Keep the sponge in vinegar. When you think your husband will want relations with you, put the sponge inside you first, making sure you can feel the string, so you can pull it out afterward. And be sure to remove it as soon as possible when he's finished."

Fanny regarded her with terrified eyes. "He'll know it's there! He'd kill me for sure if—"

"He won't be aware of it, Fanny," Joanna said. "Just don't let him see you putting it in or taking it out. It isn't completely effective, but it will help."

As Joanna and Sarah rode away from the Drummond homestead, Sarah said, "Next time it will be worse. Next time it'll be a broken arm or a leg. And there is nothing anyone can do about it."

"I'll tell Constable McManus. He'll drive over and take a look around, and give Mike Drummond a stern lecture. Sometimes it helps."

They rode through the morning sunshine, two young women wearing practical cotton blouses, long brown skirts and wide-brimmed hats on their upswept hair. A passerby might at first glance take them for sisters, as they both sat smartly upright in the buggy, shooing flies away, their voices soft. But the similarity ended with Sarah's dusky skin and exotic features. When Joanna had first started taking Sarah with her on calls, to deliver a baby or treat a wound, people had thought it odd. But over time, as Sarah's own skills had grown, she had gradually come to be accepted, even at the large houses such as Barrow Downs or Williams Grange, where Aboriginal servants were restricted to the kitchen, and by station hands who had overcome their resistance to being treated by a woman or an Aborigine. At twenty-one, Sarah King was regarded as another Westbrook, and only strangers raised an eyebrow now and then.

When they had driven a few miles from the farm, Joanna brought the buggy to a halt, took out her diary, and wrote by the light of the morning sun, "March 12, 1880: Fanny Drummond battered again by her husband. This time required stitches." The rest she did not record. The dissemination of information on anti-conception was illegal and punishable under the law. Should the diary fall into the wrong hands, Joanna knew that both she and Fanny could be in serious trouble.

Joanna looked out over the vista. It was almost time for the autumn rains. But the sky was as clear as a new china plate, deep and cloudless. The air was uncommonly dry, even at this early hour, as if the countryside were in the grip of a summer heat wave, and for as far as the eye could see, the grass was yellow. She could just make out, in the distance, a small flock of sheep moving slowly. Joanna added to the diary entry: "I fear the predicted drought will indeed soon be upon us, and then Fanny Drummond will have something far more serious to worry about. I judge Mike to be one of those types who will abandon his family when harder times hit."

The diary, handsomely bound in moroccan leather, was Joanna's own, a gift from Hugh the day after their first child, Beth, was born, six-and-a-half years ago. Joanna recorded everything in it—events, observations, reflections, every time she took care of someone. It contained the history of the Westbrook family, including the birth of their second child, Edward, in 1874, and his death the following summer; through two miscarriages and up to the birth of Joanna's last child, a boy who also had not survived, and who was now buried beneath a headstone that read, "SIMON WESTBROOK died 1878, aged three months." The larger story of the Western District had also been carefully recorded, and included such entries as:

January 14, 1874—Diphtheria has claimed fourteen more children in Cameron Town; I spoke out in favor of creating an underground sewage system, and to divert the raw sewage that currently runs down the town's main street.

November 10, 1876—Bush fires swept over a hundred thousand acres. Gracemere and Strathfield suffered heavy damage.

May 30, 1877—Attended wedding of Verity Campbell to Constable McManus. It was a beautiful affair, with over two hundred people attending.

November 12, 1878—Jacko Jackson's run has finally failed and he has relinquished his 7,000 acres to Hugh, in repayment of the debt he owed. Jacko and his family have moved to Merinda, where he will be Hugh's station manager and Mrs. Jackson will be our cook.

The diary was also a chronicle of her search for her mother's past. Joanna kept a meticulous record of whom she had contacted, when, and the results. When Bowman's Creek and Durrebar continued to elude her, she wrote again to Miss Tallhill in Melbourne, saying that she wondered if a mistake had been made. But Joanna had been informed that Miss Tallhill had been taken north for her health, and she was never heard from again. An entry dated July 25, 1877 read, "I have received another letter from Patrick Lathrop in San Francisco. He regrets that ill health is preventing him from devoting as much time to studying my grandfather's notes as he would like, but that he will persist." This was followed by: "My last letter to Patrick Lathrop has been returned, marked, 'Addressee Deceased.'" The diary contained copies of letters Joanna had written to missionary societies, shipping companies, and, as always, to Aunt Millicent in England who, although always responding to Joanna's letters, never spoke of her sister, Naomi, or Joanna's mother, whom she had raised, or the subject of Karra Karra and what had happened there.

Finally, the diary contained maps Joanna had drawn, using the information on the deed, trying to locate Durrebar and Bowman's Creek in relation to each other. She had shown the maps to Hugh and Frank Downs, hoping they might recognize something familiar in one of them, but all they had been able to determine was that it looked as if the deed were for a large piece of property, and that it could be quite valuable should she ever find it. Joanna had then made tracings of different points along Australia's twelve-thousand-mile coastline, and juxtaposed her maps next to them, hoping to stumble upon a match. But in the end, one vital key—her grandparents' place of disembarkation—was always needed.

She had also filled pages of the diary with her own attempts at deciphering John Makepeace's shorthand, all of which resulted in gibberish. And lastly there was a systematic categorizing of all the clues she had been able to glean from her mother's diary and other sources, but the list was scanty and so far had come to nothing.

When she put her diary back into the basket, she realized that Sarah was watching her. "What's the matter?" Joanna said.

"I was going to ask you that. You've been rubbing your forehead."

"Have I? I wasn't aware of it."

"You're having headaches, aren't you?" Sarah said. "And you haven't been sleeping well lately. I've heard you out on the veranda in the middle of the night. What is it, Joanna? What's keeping you from sleeping?"

Joanna looked at the sky, which was turning from yellow to robin's-egg blue over the eastern mountains, and she thought of the joy she had known for the past few years—her life with Hugh and Beth; seeing Adam grow up to be a normal boy. In those years, Joanna had not forgotten the legacy she had inherited—the poison-song, the fear that disaster could strike at any time—but her nightmares had gradually abated, and some of the urgency had gone out of her search for Karra Karra. But now the dreams were back, and with them, the old fears.

"The nightmares have started again, Sarah," she said. "Just like before—the wild dogs, the Rainbow Serpent, the cave in the red mountain. When I wake up I'm not only frightened, but I feel a strong compulsion to go there, wherever those things are taking place, and face something—I don't know what. It's the same compulsion that gripped my mother at the end of her life."

"When did the nightmares start?" Sarah asked.

Joanna thought for a moment. "It was just before shearing, I think. Yes, about six months ago."

"Can you think what could be causing them now?"

"I don't know. I think I recorded the first time it happened—" She drew out her diary and flipped through the pages. "Yes, here it is. Oh, it was the night of Beth's birthday party." She frowned. "That's strange. . . ."

"What is it?"

"I seem to recall something . . ." She looked at Sarah. "My mother's nightmares began when *I* turned six. Well, clearly, my unconscious mind must have picked up the suggestion. I read about my mother's dreams and perhaps now my mind is re-creating them."

They sat in silence for a moment, as the countryside around them began to stir, and a kookaburra flew by overhead, laughing at the dawn. "Sarah," Joanna said, "how can I dream of things that never happened to me? Have I somehow inherited my mother's memories? Or are my dreams the remembrances of things my mother told me long ago?"

"Whether they are real or not," Sarah said, "whether the poison-song exists or not, doesn't matter. It seems to me that the effects are the same. If your mind is convinced something bad is going to happen, then it is more likely to happen."

Joanna stared at her friend. "And is history going to be repeated? Is Beth going to have to go through what I went through with my mother? I am beginning to see a pattern forming, Sarah. I never used to be afraid of dogs, but now I am. I never used to have nightmares, but now I do. What comes next? And what can I do to stop it? I won't let my daughter become a victim of this madness."

"What are the nightmares about, Joanna? What are they telling you?"

"They're telling me that I have to be afraid," she said. "I keep thinking that the opal is an important part of it, that it might in fact be a key to all of this. But I don't know in what way."

"What are you going to do?"

An event was taking place in Melbourne called the International Exhibition, which Joanna had been planning on taking Beth and Adam to see. All the Australian colonies were represented there, as well as most of the nations of the world—all in one place, under one roof, at the same time—colonial officials, newspaper people, explorers, scientists, missionaries and various assortments of experts in all fields . "I'm going to take the opal to Melbourne with me," Joanna said. "Surely someone, among such a population, will be able to tell me where it came from."

———————————

Joanna guided the buggy past the main homestead and down the newly graded drive that led toward the river, where the building of the new house, begun nearly seven years ago but halted for various reasons, was once again under way, and she was struck as she always was by how the countryside had changed. She remembered how it had been when she had first come here, nearly nine years ago. There had been fewer homesteads then, and more trees; the roads had been little more than dirt tracks. But the railway now reached Cameron Town from Melbourne, and with it people had come. The main road was paved; and telegraph lines followed it. More homesteads dotted the landscape. There were more wells, more windmills, more fences.

And Merinda was growing, too. Despite threats of a coming drought, the Westbrook station was doing well, due to Hugh's vigilant management and some good financial investments, plus the rising price of lanolin.

And Zeus's first experimental lambs had been a success. When the new lambs had grown to maturity, Hugh had crossbred them with large-framed Saxony ewes, and the resulting offspring had proved to be big-boned and strong-wooled—sheep that everyone declared ought to do well in the drier areas. The new sheep did not produce the superfine wool that the Western District was so proud of, but a sturdy, practical wool that went into the making of blankets and carpets. At a time when the demand for expensive superfine wool was beginning to decline around the world, the market for coarser wool was rising. Frank Downs was the first to put the new Merinda strain to a test on his fifty thousand acres in New South Wales, and everyone watched to see how they would do. Seeing that they might thrive on those arid plains, other graziers, willing to take a risk, purchased Westbrook's new stock until, by this spring of 1880, six-and-a-half years after the birth of the first lamb, the new Merinda breed was being run experimentally on several stations in Victoria and New South Wales.

Merinda's prosperity was evident in the homeyard. Buildings had been added, and pens and livestock. The yard was busier and noisier than ever, with new lambs bleating, stud rams running with ewes in the breeding paddock, and station hands working at their myriad tasks. The original cabin was still there, but it was larger now. Rooms had been added over the years; the walls were freshly painted, a new veranda had been constructed all the way around it, with giant sunflowers and brilliant oleanders nodding against the railings, and a patch of lawn lay on either side of a stone walkway. And now that the new house was once again under construction, Joanna realized she would miss living in the old homestead.

When she reached the clearing, she brought the buggy to a halt under the shade of some trees—her trees, grown tall and strong from baby saplings that she had planted with her own hands nine years ago. She paused to watch Beth, as brown as bark, paddle in the billabong with poor old half-blind Button, one of the sheepdogs, splashing after her. Joanna and Hugh had christened the child Elizabeth, for Hugh's mother. But Joanna and Sarah called her Beth; to Hugh and Adam, she was Lizzie. She was a sturdy child, as tough and resilient, Joanna sometimes thought, as the Australian eucalypts that grew around Merinda. And she was never seen without Button. Two years ago, Beth had spared the dog from the customary sheepdog's fate—a single bullet to the head—once he was past usefulness by pleading for his life. Hugh had relented, and now Button was Beth's constant companion.

Adam, who had just turned thirteen, was sitting in the shade of a tree, painting a watercolor. He was growing into a handsome boy, Joanna thought, with the Westbrook eyes and that serious, attractive furrow between his brows. He hadn't the Westbrook robustness, but rather, Joanna often thought, the gentle mien of a scholar. Everything in nature fascinated Adam—fossils and insects, rocks and plants. When he had read Darwin's *Origin of Species,* he had declared that he wanted to be a naturalist. And so he was enrolled in a special science program at the Cameron Town Secondary School, which he would begin next month.

Not a day went by in which Joanna did not marvel at these two children. And the love, the overpowering love! When Joanna had been pregnant with Beth, she had expected to feel a mother's love for her child. But when she had taken the baby in her arms for the first time, Joanna had been thunderstruck by the intensity and swiftness of that love. And how could it grow? she often wondered when she would watch Beth asleep, or frowning over a book. How could a human heart possibly hold such a volume of growing love? And yet it did. And now Joanna understood the other side of the mother-daughter bond. Now she knew the love Lady Emily must have felt for her.

But something threatened that happiness. Watching Beth splash and play in the billabong, with Button splashing blindly after her, Joanna was rocked by another strong emotion: the determination to protect her daughter from the legacy of fear and death she had inherited from Lady Emily. No Rainbow Serpent or poison-song was going to harm this beautiful child.

Joanna saw Hugh coming through the trees, in conversation with another man.

Hugh did not look as if he were a year away from forty. He looked in fact, Joanna could not help thinking, in his dusty trousers and flannel shirt and wide-brimmed cattleman's hat, like the handsome hero of his most recent ballad, "One Tree Plain."

While Sarah got down from the buggy and went to the children, Joanna watched Hugh talk to the architect, Mr. Hackett. Seeing the tension in her husband's body reminded her of the desire he had expressed recently to take a trip up to Queensland and visit the "tracks of his youth." Although "One Tree Plain" had been received wonderfully, Hugh had written it nearly four years ago; he had written nothing since. "I want to go back to Queensland," he had said suddenly one night. "I don't know why. Maybe it has to do with turning forty soon, and realizing that my youth is gone. But I've been feeling nostalgic for Queensland lately. I want to take you there, Joanna—just the two of us, without the children—and show you where I grew up, the towns, the people, the isolated stations, to see it all before it vanishes forever."

But when could they ever find time to go on such a journey? For it would take weeks at least. It seemed that Hugh was always needed at Merinda; and so, in fact, was she. And now, the house was going to be built at last. It had taken them several years, but they had finally recovered from the financial loss of the storm—recovered so well, in fact, that by the time Joanna's inheritance finally came from India, she was able to put it away for Beth's future, since they agreed that Adam was going to inherit the station.

But when they had been able to start to build again, using Philip McNeal's concrete footings and plans, the river had flooded and the site had been destabilized. They had worked for more than a year preparing the ground and reinforcing the footings, and then an influenza epidemic had swept through Victoria, forcing so many men to their beds that all work in the district, whether it was harvesting, shearing or building, had been brought to a halt. And then a false gold strike up near Horsham had taken many men out of the district, leaving most stations with only the barest and most loyal crew. But men were available to build the house now, and Hugh had the money. But another problem had arisen: Hugh was having difficulty finding an architect who would work with McNeal's plans. No one, it seemed, thought it practical to build on this site. Everyone advised razing the Aboriginal ruins and building there. Which was what Hugh was in the middle of arguing with Mr. Hackett about, when Joanna arrived.

She waited until Mr. Hackett stalked away—angrily, she noticed— then she went up to Hugh, and put an arm around him. He turned to her and asked, "And so how is Fanny Drummond?"

"Not as lucky as I am," she said, and he drew her against him, and the frown vanished from his face. Joanna always made Hugh think of a phrase from the Bible, something about bringing peace like a river. Joanna was like that, he thought, calming, restorative.

A hot wind blew, unusual for March. The rains were not coming, and the summer heat was lingering. As Hugh stood with his arm around Joanna, he felt the dryness and dust in the air; there was not a cloud in the sky. The billabong had shrunk, and the river that fed into it was dwindling to a trickle. In all his years at Merinda he had never known such a severe dry spell. He reached down and scooped up a handful of soil. It felt powdery and lifeless in his hand. He thought of his grazing pastures standing yellow and parched in the sun, and the sheep, trying to find food and water. He looked up at the cloudless sky and thought that if rain didn't come soon, he was going to start losing stock.

Damn Colin MacGregor, he thought, as his eyes stung with dust.

Hugh had clashed with Colin at the last meeting of the Graziers' Association, when Hugh had made a speech about irresponsible destruction of the land. MacGregor was chopping down the trees that grew along the Kilmarnock side of the river to sell as timber for a high price. He had cut down so many trees that he had thinned out the windbreak. Every time Hugh tried to plant, the wind carried away the topsoil and the seeds.

Hugh looked at the place along the river where a forest had once stood when he had first come to Victoria, nearly twenty years ago. Now it was just a plain of tree stumps. The face of the countryside was changing. Hugh remembered more trees being here then, and fewer fences. The animals, too, were becoming scarcer. He couldn't recall the last time he had seen a kangaroo. They were being driven away by human habitation, by the loss of their feeding grounds to sheep, and worst of all, by the massive hunts that the local gentry continued to consider good sport.

The land is being underplanted and overgrazed, Hugh thought. Nature needs to be kept in balance. The Aborigines knew that. If they came upon a waterhole where there was abundant fish and wildlife, they stayed only a while, and then moved on before they cleaned the place out. They didn't return to that spot, even though it was a good one, until they were sure the wildlife and fish were plentiful again. They gave nature time to heal. But the white man doesn't.

"You're very quiet," Joanna said. "How are things going with Mr. Hackett?"

"I just fired him. He insisted we build over there, where the ruins are. I knew I wouldn't be able to work with him."

Joanna regarded the moss-covered walls that stood beside the billabong, glints of broken sunlight playing on its surface. In the six-and-a-half years since Philip McNeal had left, they had heard from him only once, four years ago, a letter informing them of his mother's death.

Hugh said, "They all think we're wrong in the head. They don't want to hear about songlines and the Dreaming. And to tell you the truth, Joanna, I'm not all that sure that I do, either! But the house will be built, I promise you that."

"Without an architect? There are so few competent men available, it seems. They're all in Melbourne, building housing tracts."

Hugh smiled and reached into his pocket. "Well, I happen to have good news," he said, as he brought out an envelope. "This came in the post while you were at the Drummond farm. It's from McNeal."

"*Philip* McNeal?" Joanna said as she opened the letter. Then, "Oh Hugh," she said as she read, "he's coming to Melbourne for the International Exhibition! He says he wants to visit Merinda!"

"I'm going to ask him if he'll stay on for a while and build the house. After all, the foundation is his."

Joanna waved to Sarah and called out, "Come here, there's good news!"

When Sarah read the letter, her face broke into a smile. "Philip is coming back. I knew he would." She read further. "He says he'll be accompanied by his wife and son." Sarah looked at Joanna. "He's married," she said. "I wonder what his wife is like. He doesn't say anything about her, not even her name. All he says is that his wife and son will be coming with him."

Sarah looked at the silver-and-turquoise bracelet, which she often wore, and recalled the day Philip had given it to her. She had been fifteen then, and hopelessly in love. She had often thought about Philip over the years, wondering where he was, what he was doing. She thought now: It will be nice to see him again.

"We'd better go in," Joanna said. "We have a lot to do to get ready for our trip tomorrow." As they walked back to the house, Joanna said to Hugh, "I wish you would come to Melbourne with us."

"I wish I could. But some of the bores are starting to silt up, and the five-mile well has gone completely dry. We have to muster the sheep farther distances to water them. But don't worry," Hugh said as he took her hand, "I'll be all right here. You just make sure you and the children have a good time at the exhibition."

As Beth skipped ahead, chanting, "We're going to Melbourne! We're going to Melbourne!" Joanna found her joy overshadowed once again by the memory of her nightmares, and what they might portend.

They took a suite at the King George Hotel on Elizabeth Street, with Joanna and Sarah sharing one bedroom, Beth and Adam in the other. On the first morning of the exhibition they went directly to the Hall of Art and Architecture, where, after fighting the crowds and making their way to the American booth, they were told that Mr. McNeal had gone up to Sydney, and wasn't expected back until the end of the week.

It was a week of adventures and marvels. As if Melbourne weren't enough—that noisy city with its traffic and sidewalks full of people and tall buildings—the exhibition grounds and buildings were nothing short of miraculous. Foreigners with strange speech and colorful clothes were crammed into the exhibition halls; there were foods from all nations; a constant thumping of music and folksinging; and the pulse of an excited populace dizzied by the new scientific age. There were things to gawk at, exhibits displaying inventions and machines and the mysteries of the universe; and there were entertainments to stare at in wonder, such as the team of young men sitting at machines called typewriters, clacking out marvelous sheets of perfect printing right before your eyes; and a man in a checkered jacket throwing dirt on a perfectly good carpet and then sweeping it clean like magic with something called a carpet sweeper. There was a cooling box from America, called a refrigerator, which somehow kept food cold, and there was a contraption called a vacuum cleaner, demonstrated by a woman in a maid's uniform and a small boy who operated the bellows with his feet. And then there was the "electric candle," which burned without a flame, pure and white and bright, and ran not on oil or kerosene but from something called an electric generator.

Joanna and Sarah had trouble keeping up with the children. Adam and Beth went from exhibit to exhibit, shouting and pointing. In one booth there were demonstrations of the "telephone," and in the next an American was showing off the wonders of what he called a "gramophone." He had a gentleman in the crowd talk into a box while he cranked a handle, and moments later out came that man's voice!

And there were funny things, too, such as the rocking chair with a woman sitting in it and knitting, while the rockers somehow worked a butter churn. And an alarm clock that poured cold water on the sleeper's face and then jerked up the foot of the bed. And a machine with wheels and a seat and a smoking motor that carried one man around in a ring, like a train without a track, and which the rider said was going to be the transportation of the future.

But there were awesome exhibits as well: Adam stood and stared for a long time at the skeleton of a dinosaur that was part of a French science exhibit. There was also a replica of a human ancestor, found in a place in France called Cro-Magnon, and the sign beneath it read: "Believed to be 35,000 years old."

They passed under an enormous arched doorway, and Joanna glimpsed their reflection in a tall, gilt-framed looking glass. My family! she thought with pride. Adam in his first long pants, his tawny hair smartly combed; Beth in a drop-waist dress with a big bow at the back, ringlets dancing on her shoulders. Dusky Sarah, so serene and beautiful, turning men's heads as she walked by in a long, bustled dress with a small waist, and a feathered bonnet set forward on her crown of red-brown braids. And Joanna herself, still slender at twenty-eight, the hem of her blue velvet dress sweeping the marble floor. If only Hugh were here, she thought, then the picture would be perfect.

Their last day arrived all too soon; tomorrow they were going to leave for the Western District. Joanna was looking forward to going home. The visit to the city had been exciting, but she was anxious to be back at Merinda with Hugh.

The nightmare, with its phantoms of Rainbow Serpents and savage dogs, had followed her to Melbourne. Joanna had wakened several times, suddenly, her heart pounding, to look around the hotel room and wonder where she was. She would hear the unfamiliar street sounds outside, and she would feel cut off from Hugh, Merinda and familiar things. Although the dream varied each time, the same basic elements were always present—the dogs, the Rainbow Serpent, the opal—along with a very real terror that did not immediately leave when she woke up. As she lay in bed listening to her galloping pulse, she imagined that she sensed the presence of the Rainbow Serpent lurking nearby in the darkness.

It can't be real, she told herself. It was all in her imagination, the result of reading her mother's diary. But Joanna knew that, as Sarah had suggested, this was beside the point, because the results were the same: a growing fear for her safety and the safety of her daughter. Joanna knew that she either had to find the source of the poison-song and put an end to it, or somehow convince her unconscious mind that the poison-song no longer existed.

The fact that the opal appeared in her dreams had made her wonder if it would lead her to that source. Had the gemstone in fact come from Australia, or had her parents come by it in India? Unfortunately, inquiries around the exhibition, among geologists, gem experts and representatives of various countries, had failed to give her any idea of the opal's origins.

Now, there remained one last thing to do before going home: find Philip McNeal.

"Oh, look!" Beth cried, her voice rising up to join the thousands of other voices echoing beneath the domed ceiling of the rotunda. She took her brother's hand and pulled him toward a large exhibit.

The Westbrook party gathered around to admire the striking tableaux which formed an exhibit entitled, "The Melbourne *Times* Proudly Presents: Melbourne Through the Ages." Four life-sized dioramas had been constructed, and they took up nearly the length of one hall. Visitors were invited to enter by way of a velvet rope, and to walk slowly along and admire the historic phases of Melbourne—"Sylvan Solitude, 1800," which showed nearly naked Aborigines throwing boomerangs and painting their bodies; "Primitive Village, 1830," where a few white men lived in huts; "Modest Town, 1845," with a real reconstructed general store and a live horse tethered out front; and finally "Topsy-Turvy City, 1870," which was a painted backdrop showing the beginnings of a skyline juxtaposed against the masts and ships' funnels of the busy harbor.

A penny guidebook explained that this "expensive exhibit" had been invented and created by Frank Downs, publisher of the *Times*. What the book did not mention, however, was that the idea had really come from an unknown artist named Ivy Dearborn.

After a tea of lemonade and cream puffs, they strolled through the Hall of Health, where the children were astounded to discover that there were commercial medicines to cure what seemed like every ailment known to humankind. Exhibits showed demonstrations of doctors washing their hands with Ivory Soap, and children in hospital beds cheerfully munching Dr. Graham's Crackers. There were demonstrations of electric belts and hernia trusses. Salesmen stood on boxes and shouted over the heads of the audience, defying anyone to step forward and disprove the efficacy of the Kickapoo Indian Cure or Dr. Foote's Cancer Cure. An American named Kellogg had invented a new flaky breakfast cereal that was "guaranteed to lower the sex drive." There were books on sale with such baffling titles as *The Turkish Way of Making Love* and *The Meaning of Dreams*. And free samples were handed out to the adults—packets of "Gono, Man's Friend" for the men, and tubes of "Dr. Cooper's Guaranteed Scalp Food" for the ladies—while the children received colorful trading cards advertising "Mrs. Winslow's Children Quietener" and "Dr. Smiley's Pink Pills for Pale People."

There was a group of French physicians there, giving talks on the new "germ theory," which their countryman, Louis Pasteur, had recently formulated. Joanna listened to explanations about bacteria and bacilli, microbes and cells, and how it had been discovered that they caused disease. The example that was used was the typhoid bacillus, of which there were large diagrams, and Joanna thought of David Ramsey, and how he had given his life for medicine, dying too soon, his ideas later being brought to fruition by men who became famous in medicine.

In the next hall they came upon a series of small booths that were really nothing more than tables and chairs separated by ropes. Banners identified the exhibitors as socially concerned societies, such as the Women's Temperance League and St. Joseph's Lunatic Asylum. Joanna noticed one in particular: the British Indian Mission Society. It was situated between the Ladies' Orphan Relief Aid, a charity to which Joanna sometimes gave money, and the Salvation Army, which she had never heard of. Joanna brought her group to a halt in front of a sign that read, "India Famine Relief Fund," and while she struck up a conversation with the man and woman who were minding the booth, missionaries who had "devoted twenty years to God's service in the Punjab," the children became bored. Adam wished they could go back to the Royal Exploration Society exhibit, where they had real New Guinea headhunters on display.

Joanna was saying to the missionaries, upon hearing their account of the famine in India, "I had no idea. Of course, I shall do what I can to help," while Beth and Adam decided to wander down to the end of the hall, and take a closer look at an exhibit that was set up like a little farm.

A compound had been created, with real post-and-rail fencing, and dirt was spread on the floor. There were bails of hay, a horse and a plow, and dogs running loose. Some boys were shearing sheep and milking cows, and there were demonstrations of wood cutting, wheat threshing and winnowing. There was a long table where boys sat at microscopes examining samples of soil and grain and grass. Another group of boys was studying the large anatomical chart of a ram. And there were gentlemen in black coats who were explaining to onlookers that they were "witnessing the latest and most modern methods of progressive education known in the world." Beth and Adam read the sign over the exhibit—Tongarra Agricultural School. There was a smaller sign that said TAKE ONE. And beneath it was a stack of pamphlets.

Adam picked one up. It was full of illustrations of boys shearing sheep, riding horses and sitting atop modern plows. There was a scene showing boys singing in a chapel, and another showing them playing cricket on a lawn. Finally, there was a page of small, round illustrations, which were photographs of classrooms.

Beth and Adam walked along the fence, fascinated that such an outdoor scene was actually inside a building. "This looks like a wonderful school, Lizzie," Adam said. "Perhaps I should go here, instead of Cameron Town Secondary."

"I'll go here, too!" said Beth.

"You can't go here, silly."

"Why not?"

"Because it's only for boys. See?" Adam pointed out that only boys were involved in the demonstrations, and that there were no pictures of girls or women in the pamphlet. "When you're old enough, you're going to go to a girls' academy," Adam said.

Beth frowned. It didn't seem right.

"Children," Joanna said, as she and Sarah came up. "We've been looking all over for you."

They went along to the Hall of Art and Architecture, and as they neared the American exhibit, Sarah was surprised to feel her heart begin to race. Then, suddenly, she saw him. Although Philip McNeal was conservatively dressed in a green frock coat and gray trousers, he was exactly as she remembered him, tall and slender, and gracefully handsome.

"There is Mr. McNeal!" Joanna said.

"Mrs. Westbrook," he said, coming up and taking her hand. "How wonderful. I was hoping we might meet."

"Yes, we received your letter last week. How nice it is to see you, Mr. McNeal!"

"I'm Beth!" the six-year-old said.

Philip laughed and shook her tiny hand. "How do you do, Beth?"

"She was born the day we said good-by," Sarah said.

He turned and looked at her. "Sarah?" he said, a look of surprise on his face.

"It's nice to see you again," she said.

After a moment, Sarah put her arm around Adam's shoulders and said, "This is Adam. You remember him."

"I remember. You've certainly grown, Adam," Philip said, as they shook hands

"How did the new house turn out, Mrs. Westbrook?" he asked, turning to Joanna.

"I'm afraid it didn't, but it's a long story. We're still building it. You said in your letter that you would be able to come to Merinda for a visit. Hugh would be thrilled to see you again."

"As a matter of fact, I very much plan on coming to Merinda. I am writing a book, Mrs. Westbrook, on Australian architecture. There are certain unique qualities to be found here that are found nowhere else, and I thought I would take advantage of my being here to learn some more. I've studied the city architecture both in Melbourne and in Sydney, and now I would like to take a look at some things in the country."

"You couldn't do better than the Western District, Mr. McNeal. And you're welcome to stay at Merinda if you like. We can even show you around the countryside. When may we expect you?"

He glanced at Sarah—again, a look of surprise and interest, showed briefly on his face. "I have to stay for the duration of the exhibition, but after that my wife and I have no immediate plans to return to America."

"Just let us know, Mr. McNeal," Joanna said. "Until then, good-by."

They left the hall by way of another arched doorway that was flanked by leafy palm trees. Because of the trees, none of them saw the booths on the other side, with signs that read: "St. Mary's Children's Home," "Jewish Relief Fund," and "Karra Karra Aboriginal Mission."

By the time they left the exhibition grounds, the sun was making its way toward the west and the March sky was growing dark. Joanna paused to look up and down the busy street. How Melbourne had changed in the years since her arrival! And how rapidly it was continuing to change even now, making her almost believe that if she were to close her eyes and then open them, she would see a new building before her, or a house torn down, or fifty more carriages rattling down the street. It was not at all like Cameron Town, where the buildings were still only one or two stories tall, and horses clip-clopped in a leisurely fashion down the peaceful streets, and where cowboys and station hands and shepherds all met in the rustic pubs for a beer and a yarn.

Joanna felt herself swept up by Melbourne's pulse. There was so much life here, so much going on, and so much beauty in the new city gardens and bright green horse-trams and statues commemorating anyone who had ever done anything of significance. It was almost impossible to believe that this very spot had once been that "Primitive Village" of only fifty years ago!

"Let's see if we can get a cab," Joanna said.

She stopped and stared down the street, as she saw Pauline MacGregor emerge from a shop.

Joanna stared for a moment at the woman, whom she barely knew. Although Hugh had never been able to prove it, he still blamed Colin MacGregor for the downed fence and the subsequent loss of so many sheep in the river, and as a result, the Westbrooks and the MacGregors, though neighbors, were not friends. When affairs were held at Kilmarnock and Western District society attended, Hugh and Joanna did not. And when Merinda was the site of a social event and the gentry came, the MacGregors were conspicuous by their absence. When the Graziers' Wives Association met in Cameron Town, to discuss philanthropic projects and distribute their special charities, Pauline and Joanna very politely exchanged neither a word nor a glance.

Joanna continued to watch as Pauline came out of the shop and stood hesitantly on the sidewalk, as if undecided which way to turn. At thirty-three, Pauline MacGregor was still slender and attractive, and caught many a male eye in her tight-fitting dress of dark-blue silk.

As Joanna was beginning to wonder why Pauline, who was so careful about doing the right thing and making a respectable appearance, should be all alone on a public street, an elegant carriage drawn by two horses pulled up and stopped. Joanna saw Pauline smile and walk forward, and then a man stepped down from the carriage, his hands held out.

Joanna caught a glimpse of his profile.

It was Hugh!

And then—

She frowned. The gentleman, in taking Pauline's hand, turned his back and Joanna could no longer see his face.

Had it been Hugh?

"Look, Mum," Adam said. "Here's a cab."

But Joanna didn't say anything.

"Mother?"

Joanna looked down the street in time to see the train of Pauline's gown disappear inside the carriage.

It *had been* Hugh, Joanna would swear to it.

"Sarah, did you see—"

Joanna shook her head. Of course it wasn't Hugh! For one thing, that man hadn't been as tall as Hugh, and for another, what on earth would Hugh be doing here in Melbourne?

"Never mind," she said, watching the carriage pull into the street. "I must be tired." That was it. She was tired. It had been a stressful week—and filled with nightmares. She was imagining things.

"All right, everyone," she said. "Let's get into the cab."

When the door closed and the cabman climbed back up to his seat, everyone sighed with relief. It felt good to be sitting down and heading home.

Adam couldn't stop talking about all the marvelous things he had seen: explorers and balloonists and adventurers, men who discovered rivers and named mountains, who took exciting journeys and visited all the exotic places in the world. But most especially, he spoke of the dinosaur exhibit with the relics of the Cro-Magnon man. "I'm going to do that someday!" he said. "I'm going to discover the bones of an ancient race, or an extinct animal. Perhaps I shall find a new plant that no one has ever seen before."

"Name something for me, Adam," Beth said.

"I'll name a flower for you, how would that be? I'll go to New Guinea and I'll come across a rare orchid that no one's ever named. And I'll call it the *Elizabethus officinale*. Would you like that?"

"Adam," Joanna said. "What do you have there?"

He held out the fistful of pamphlets and fliers that he had collected at the exhibition. "They were free," he said. "It was okay to take them. Look," he said, and handed them to her.

Joanna glanced through the brochures Adam had gathered, and found them to be quite a mixture, from advertisements for "Wilson's Electric Belt," and "Black-Boy Chewing Tobacco"; and an invitation to come to "Dr. Snow's Office on Swanson Street and Obtain a Free Treatment of His Genuine Mesmer-Hypnosis Cures"; to a coupon worth sixpence off any hat in "McMahon's Haberdashery for Gentlemen" on Collins Street.

"It was all right to take them, wasn't it?" he said.

"Of course, darling. But I rather suspect that they hoped their advertisements would be picked up by someone who intended to spend money in their establishments!" As Joanna started to hand the papers back, she glimpsed a flyer sticking out from the bottom of the pile. At the top was printed the word "Karra." She took it out, and she saw that it was a pamphlet asking for help to save the Karra Karra Aboriginal Mission in New South Wales.

CHAPTER 19

When the baby started to cry, Mercy Cameron said, holding out her arms, "I'd better take her. She wants her mother."

Pauline said, "Yes, of course," and with reluctance handed the baby over.

"Jane might be only two months old, but she knows who her mother is. Don't you, Janie-dumpling?"

Pauline watched the baby grow quiet in Mercy's arms, then she turned away. There were children lined up at the archery booth waiting to take a turn, but Pauline had left her post to look at Mercy Cameron's new baby. Now she went back to what she had been doing—helping youngsters to shoot at a target and win a prize. As she walked away from Mercy, Pauline glimpsed once again the sign over the tent across the way, and, as always, it gave her a chill: SEE THIS SHOW WHILE YOU LIVE BECAUSE YOU'LL BE DEAD A LONG TIME. It reminded her that her birthday lay just days away. She was going to be thirty-three.

The Cameron Town fairgrounds were crowded on this warm April morning as everyone in the whole Western District, it seemed, had turned out to see such peculiar and exciting sights as the man who swallowed a sword, or the Aborigine who boxed with a kangaroo. There were wood-chopping contests and horse races; men walking on stilts, and clowns riding donkeys; a fortuneteller named Magda, and a magician named Presto. Pauline and Louisa Hamilton were working at a booth where children shot miniature bows and arrows at a target on a hay bale. It was a popular booth, costing a penny for three shots, and the proceeds were going to go to the new Cameron Town Orphan Asylum. But Pauline couldn't keep her mind on her work; she was preoccupied with two subjects: babies, and a man she had met in Melbourne last month—John Prior, a businessman from Sydney. A man who bore a strong resemblance to Hugh Westbrook.

"Jane is having trouble with colic," Mercy said, as she watched Pauline assist a little boy with the bow and arrow. "Maude Reed told me to put peppermint in her milk, but it hasn't seemed to help."

Pauline had been reading a book on how to care for infants, written by a prominent Melbourne nanny. She also read articles in ladies' magazines that related to the care of babies, and she always listened when mothers exchanged advice. She wanted to tell Mercy that peppermint was too volatile for infants, that the milder spearmint was preferred. But Pauline knew better than to say anything to Mercy. She had learned long ago that when it came to children no one would take the advice of someone who didn't have any.

It was unfair, Pauline thought as she felt the small, narrow shoulders of the little boy she was helping. She had a lot to offer when it came to the care of children. She couldn't help it that she had yet to have a child of her own. Having a baby, she knew, didn't automatically make one an expert on the subject. But it was a special badge of honor, to have given birth, and women who were childless were somehow considered failures, second-rate. And certainly without anything worthwhile to contribute.

Pauline sometimes so longed for a child that she awoke in the middle of the night to find that she had been crying in her sleep. In the early years of her marriage to Colin, she had waited anxiously for a child that never came. She visited experts in Melbourne, but they had offered no help; she had consulted with local midwives, who had suggested she drink various teas and sleep with certain herbs under her pillow. But nothing had worked.

"It is God's judgment, my dear," Pastor Moorehead had said, when she had confessed her anxiety to him. "There is nothing you can do to change it. For His reasons, God does not wish you to have children."

But it wasn't fair, Pauline wanted to say. Louisa Hamilton had six children. Couldn't God have distributed His bounty a little more equitably?

Finally, Maude Reed had suggested another reason for the barrenness, and Pauline was beginning to wonder now if perhaps she was right. "There must be love present for a child to be conceived," Maude had said bluntly. "I sense coldness between you and Colin. No child will be conceived under such conditions."

Is that it? Pauline wondered. Is it our lack of tenderness that is the root of the problem? Was that, in effect, what Pastor Moorehead had been trying to say? That God did not allow children into loveless lives? If that were the case, then it seemed there was only one solution—to somehow get Colin to love her.

After seven years of marriage, Colin was still more of a stranger than a husband to Pauline. Their lives were like two circles, spinning independently of each other, coming together only when the circles touched, at a ball or a hunt held at Kilmarnock. At such times Pauline and Colin would act the perfect husband and wife, solicitous of each other, laughing at each other's jokes and complementing each other— Colin with his arrogance, Pauline with her beauty. Victoria's rural gentry would pay homage to the pseudo-royalty at Kilmarnock, and then they would go away, envious and admiring and full of expensive champagne.

Then the two circles would spin away from each other again, and Colin would go to his sheep paddocks and men's club in town and shire council politics, Pauline to her charity works, her tennis club, her archery. They addressed each other as Mr. and Mrs. MacGregor. They dined together in the evenings, slept apart at night, and once a week Colin came to her bed and dominated her. Sex was calculated, a rite.

Out of such a union, Pauline decided, no child could ever come.

But there had been a time . . .

As she helped the little boy notch his arrow and take aim at the target, Pauline thought of those early days with Colin. Especially their wedding night aboard the ship bound for Scotland. How he had taken her into his arms, his body hard and electric. She had tried to speak, but he had put his hand over her mouth. "Don't talk," he had said.

Pauline had been stunned by the force of Colin's lovemaking, the roughness of it. He had been voracious, as if he would devour her. She had tried to be a partner, but he had overcome her, dominated her with such violence that it had at first startled her, but soon it had swept her away, as he possessed her completely. Pauline had never known what submission could feel like, never been so totally in another's power. For the first time in her life, she was not the one in control.

And she had loved it.

They had made love this way in the early years of their marriage, and Pauline had thought that surely a child must come of such passion. But the years had passed, no child had come, and their lovemaking had grown mechanical.

Now she was desperate. She was in the last decade of her childbearing years. She dreaded the thought of the future that might lie before her, the lonely, empty years in which she would be reduced to being the "auntie" of other people's children.

Of course there was Judd, who was now nearly sixteen and a very independent-minded young man. He had resisted Pauline's efforts to mother him; and if she really thought about it, she would have to admit that she hadn't tried very hard. He was another woman's child. Being Judd's stepmother was not the same as having a baby from her own body.

She knew what everyone thought, how surprised they had been when, after a few years of marriage, she hadn't produced a baby. Pauline's friends regarded her as someone who won all the competitions, who succeeded in everything she tried. And yet it seemed that she could not accomplish what the most ordinary woman could, what in fact women were created for.

Pauline couldn't bear their pity. She wanted to be able to do what Mercy Cameron had just done—take a baby from another woman's arms and say, "He wants me, he wants his mother."

"This is how you hold the bow," Pauline said to the little boy. She had her arms around him, one hand steadying his bow, the other helping him to draw back the arrow. "You aim below your target in order to hit it. Point the tip of the arrow into the ground in front of the target, bring the arrow back so that the feathers touch your ear— yes, like this . . . now let go."

The arrow flew wildly, hit the canvas wall of the booth, and broke.

"That's better," Pauline said gently. "Keep trying—here's another."

It was supposed to be three tries for a penny, but she allowed him five, and still he couldn't hit the haystack. When his turn was over and tears were brimming in his eyes, Pauline gave him a pick of the prizes anyway, for trying.

"Really, Pauline," Louisa said when the boy ran off to show his prize to his parents, "you can't go giving prizes to every child. How will they learn anything, if they're rewarded for failure?"

"There's no harm in it, Louisa."

"I find that surprising coming from you, Pauline, considering how much you love to compete for trophies yourself."

Pauline regarded her friend, who was so plump that she could hardly maneuver in the small booth. How had Louisa managed to bear six children? Pauline wondered. Were she and her husband so warm and loving to each other? Or was Maude Reed possibly in error when she said that love had to be present in order to conceive a child? It was for this reason that Pauline could not get John Prior, the Sydney businessman, out of her mind.

She had been browsing through Wallach's, Melbourne's largest emporium, which boasted that it sold everything from ribbons to gas stoves, when she had seen, in the menswear department, Hugh Westbrook handing money over for a purchase he had just made. Startled to see him in Melbourne, and feeling the old thrill, the old yearning, Pauline had been unable to turn and walk out as she should have done. Hugh was her husband's rival, but her old love for him had never quite died. And so instead of leaving the emporium, she had gone boldly up to him, laid her hand on his arm and said in her most mocking tone, "How on earth are all those sheep getting along without you, darling?"

He had turned around with an astonished look and said, "I beg your pardon?" And Pauline, too late aware of her mistake, had stared in horror. "Oh! I do apologize!" she had said. "I thought you were someone else!"

But the stranger, who bore an amazing resemblance to Hugh, looked amused and said, "His gain and my loss, madam." And before she could retreat, he had tipped his hat and said, "John Prior, at your service."

What had held her to the spot Pauline never knew. When propriety demanded that she walk away quickly, and with dignity—not even those wretched factory girls had the effrontery to accost a stranger in a public place!—something had kept her there. Perhaps it was his resemblance to Hugh, although the voice wasn't the same and he wasn't quite as tall as Hugh; or perhaps it was the way he was smiling down at her, or the expensive cut of his clothes and the self-confident way he held himself. Whatever it was, Pauline was immobilized long enough to find herself suddenly introduced to a man she had not known a moment before, and, worse, to hear herself continuing to speak to him.

"I truly thought you were an old friend of mine. I assure you I am not in the habit of addressing gentlemen who are unknown to me!"

"Well, you know me now," he said, "and I believe that since you have interrupted this important business transaction of mine you at least owe me the courtesy of telling me your name."

Pauline gazed at his handsome smile and for the moment forgot herself. He was so much like Hugh . . . "Pauline MacGregor," she said.

"So I look like a sheep farmer, do I?"

Pauline was appalled to find herself blushing. She said, "You resemble a friend of mine who owns a sheep station in the west."

He gave her a long, appraising look, and then, apparently liking what he saw, said quietly, "Your friend is very lucky. I believe you called me 'darling.' "

"He's an old friend," she said quickly. "Like a brother."

"I see," he said. "Then perhaps you might consider me an old friend as well and do me the honor of joining me for tea?"

Pauline caught her breath. He was standing too close, his smile was too intimate. "I'm afraid I cannot, Mr. Prior."

"Why not?"

"We don't know each other. And besides, I'm a married woman."

"Invite your husband to join us, by all means."

Pauline glanced at the salesclerk, who seemed to find the conversation amusing, and gave him a look that sent him away. Then she said, "My husband did not come with me to Melbourne, Mr. Prior."

"I'm astonished," he said quietly. "If you were my wife, I would not leave you alone in a city like Melbourne." Then he added, "Or anywhere else for that matter."

"You are entirely too forward, Mr. Prior," she said, and turned to go.

"Please, Mrs. MacGregor. I intended no insult, merely to pay you a compliment. And I assure you my intentions are entirely honorable. I am in Melbourne for a few days on business and as I don't know a single person in this rather overwhelming city, I find myself feeling quite alone and lost. If I have to eat one more meal in the sole company of John Prior I shall go mad."

"Are you so boring?" she said, unable to resist the flirtation.

"All by myself, I suppose I am. But with a charming woman like yourself, Mrs. MacGregor, I believe I could be quite brilliant."

Pauline didn't want to accept, but found herself accepting all the same. And she found also that the prospect of meeting Mr. Prior for tea was rather exciting.

She agreed to meet him in front of the emporium in two hours, during which time Pauline was so shocked by her inexplicable behavior, and so excited by the delicious impropriety of it, that she couldn't concentrate upon her shopping. Mr. Prior's hair wasn't the same shade as Hugh's, nor did he have the ruddy, sunburnt complexion of the outback, but there was a remarkable likeness that she couldn't put from her mind. And when she left the store at the appointed time, and saw Mr. Prior riding up in a handsome brougham drawn by two horses, she found herself offering him her hand.

They spent the afternoon in a tearoom, drinking Darjeeling tea and eating cucumber sandwiches and talking about the wonders that were on display at the exhibition. But as one hour rolled into the next, as the gaslights came on and an air of intimacy settled over them, Pauline began to fall beneath the stranger's spell. She was so used to her husband's coldness that she had forgotten what it was like to be in the company of a warm man. And John Prior was warm. He leaned across the table and looked at Pauline as if she were the only woman in the world, as if she were the only thought on his mind. He mesmerized her with his attention; he charmed her with flattery and deference. He listened to what she had to say and seemed to find her words important. He laughed when she said something funny. He told her he felt as if he had known her forever. And Pauline found that, despite herself, she was captivated by this man who was everything that Colin was not.

When they parted finally and John Prior said, "Please let me take you to the theater tonight, and supper afterward," Pauline knew she should have declined, ending right there and then whatever it was that was starting. But his magic had touched her, and she had agreed.

For an evening, Pauline was young again. She was desirable, as she had once been; she laughed more than she had in years; she felt the cold gloom of Kilmarnock recede. And she was feeling things she had not felt in years: the pleasure of flirtation; the electricity of a man's touch; the giddiness that came with sexual desire. John Prior was discreet and proper at all times, touching Pauline only to remove her cape, to help her descend from a carriage, to pin a corsage to her gown. But he stood close to her, and his eyes looked deep into hers, and Pauline read meaning into his every gesture and facial expression. The thing that both frightened and excited her remained silent and unspoken between them, but, she knew, they both felt it.

When they had parted with a lingering handshake and an exchange of calling cards, Pauline had told herself that she would not see him again.

But she couldn't get him out of her mind.

She was brought out of her thoughts by Louisa Hamilton's youngest daughter, Persephone, who was saying, "Mummy, may I have some fairy floss, please?"

"But Persephone, darling," Louisa said, fanning herself, "the fairy-floss seller is on the other side of the fairground. It's much too hot for such a long walk."

"I'll take her," Pauline said, needing to get away. "We'll get some lemonade, too. Would you like that, Persephone?"

They strolled among the booths and looked at the trinkets and knick-knacks for sale. They saw games of ring toss and pitch-a-penny. They stopped to read posters, such as the one that said: "See the Great Carmine Shoot a Gun While It Is Aimed Down His Throat!" And the best poster of all, the one that was as tall as a man and which had been plastered on every wall and fence in the Western District, telling everyone about THE GREAT AUSTRALIAN CIRCUS: "A Catalogue of Comicalities! The Knights of Palestine! Monster tent, capable of accommodating 600 persons! The best brass band that travels! The Australian Minstrels will pour forth their marvelous melodies during the evening, thereby keeping the arena constantly supplied with a succession of interesting novelties. And we have the only troupe of Japanese wonders! We proudly present the first TRAPEZE act in all of Australia, performed by Monsieur Léotard himself, the actual inventor of the trapeze, who will swing from the bars without any mattress below. The show will positively appear at Cameron Town on Friday, April 10, 1880."

"Oh look, Aunt Pauline!" Persephone said, pointing toward a stage where a man in a checkered jacket was calling out for the attention of passersby. Behind him hung a backdrop that had been painted with a blue sky, clouds and flat, grassy plains. On the stage with him was another man, one so strange that children stopped and stared open-mouthed.

Pauline also stopped and looked, but her attention was not upon Chief Buffalo, a "genuine Red Indian from America," who stood in buckskins and feathered warbonnet, but upon the tent next to it where another barker was also trying to attract attention. His show was of a different nature: For just a penny one could go inside the tent and "actually see," cried the barker, "Miss Sylvia Starr, the Australian Venus, who posed for Lindstrom's famous statue. She will appear exactly as she did while posing for the artist. You will see why her beauty has created a sensation." Behind him was an enormous poster of Miss Starr, depicting her in two ways: on the right, wearing a red gown that had an impossibly narrow waist and a large bustle, and on the left, as a statue of Venus, with flowers placed strategically over her nude body. Between the two pictures was a list of Miss Starr's "remarkable measurements," from her nose down to her feet, concluding with: "Height, 5'5"—Weight, 151 lbs."

It was not the beauty of Miss Starr that caught Pauline's attention, but rather the crowd that had gathered to buy tickets to her show. They were all men, and Pauline saw how they looked at the poster of Sylvia Starr. Pauline remembered when most men had looked at her in the same way. But their numbers were growing fewer, and she was reminded once more of the passing of time.

She thought of John Prior again. She knew that he had desired her, that he had wanted to make love to her. But she didn't want him. Love affairs were available to Pauline; she was not without admirers. More than one man had let it be known that he would be only too pleased to share intimacies with her. And she had had moments, during a ball when she had drunk too much champagne and was being twirled around the dance floor in strong arms while something delicious and exciting was being murmured into her ear, when she found herself wondering what it would be like to succumb, to go to a country inn, or for a long carriage ride. But Pauline was not looking for sex—she got that from Colin. She wanted love, and a baby.

It was Hugh Westbrook she wanted, of course. Even after all these years of trying to bury the painful memories, to deny the desire she felt for him, it had all resurfaced again. That was what meeting Prior had done. It had been, for a while, like being with Hugh. Prior had rekindled her old love for Hugh, had made her start wondering what her life would have been like if she had married him. Would I have children now? she thought.

"Mrs. MacGregor, there you are! I've been looking all over for you."

It was Mrs. Purcell, senior matron of the orphanage. She was carrying two cups of tea and looking very flustered in the heat. "We're having wonderful success at our works-of-art sale. We shall be able to buy five new beds for the orphanage. How is the archery going? I do wish you would come by the asylum some time and visit us. The children so need the love and attention."

But Pauline would not set foot in the asylum. She worked to raise money for it, and she wrote checks, but she would become no more personally involved than that.

Once, a year ago, Mrs. Purcell had had the audacity to hint that Pauline might want to adopt one of the babies. But everyone knew what those babies really were—bastards, abandoned on the asylum steps by unwed mothers who didn't want them. And Pauline didn't want another woman's baby, she wanted her own.

When she returned to the archery booth, she handed a glass of cold lemonade to Louisa who took it thankfully and said, "My, it *is* hot!"

Pauline thought it a wonder that her friend didn't faint from the tight corseting beneath her heavy silk dress. As Louisa moved about the

booth, one could hear the creaking of her whalebone stays. The under-
arms of her sleeves were dark with perspiration.

"I do envy you your slim figure, Pauline," she said, without any envy
in her voice. "You always look so cool, so untouched by the heat. Look
at me. This is what childbearing does to a woman. I do try to reduce,
but it's difficult, what with having to oversee three meals for eight of
us every day!"

Pauline collected the bows and arrows and lined them up on the
wooden counter.

"You're just so lucky," Louisa continued, "having Judd away at
school, and Colin eating at his club so much. You can avoid temptation."

Pauline wasn't listening. She was thinking: I know Colin is capable
of love. When I married him, I realized he was unlikely to love again,
but I also know that inside him, he has the capacity for loving. She had
once witnessed a demonstration of that love, when she had paid a call
on Christina, nine years ago, and she had come upon Colin at his young
wife's side, tender, solicitous, overflowing with devotion. It must still
be there, that deep, hidden wellspring of affection. Perhaps, Pauline
thought, she had been wrong to believe that Colin wouldn't love again,
perhaps because of that she hadn't found a way to tap into it; perhaps
it was still there all the same, waiting for her.

"My," Louisa said, "would you just look at that girl! I swear, she is
growing by the hour!"

Pauline turned to see Minerva Hamilton, Louisa's eldest daughter,
approach the booth. She was a tall, sloe-eyed girl with a handsome head
of hair and a sultry mouth. She was nearly sixteen, and Pauline saw how
male heads turned when she walked by.

"The boys have already started coming around," Louisa said, as she
sat fanning herself. "I tell myself that she's much too young. But then
I have to remind myself that I was eighteen when I married Mr.
Hamilton, and Minerva is only two-and-a-half years away from that.
And when I think of it!" She laughed. "I thought I had finally done
with babies and all that, and now to think that I might soon be a
grandmother!"

Pauline fought down the impulse to tell Louisa Hamilton to be quiet.
Instead she focused on her plan to find a way to get Colin to love her,
and then to conceive a child.

Colin stood at the French doors that opened from his study onto the garden, and inhaled the hot, dry air deeply. It was hard to believe that winter was officially one month away. The night felt more like January than April. Like the rest of the graziers in Victoria, he was praying that the drought wouldn't adversely affect this year's wool clip. Wool prices had fallen in the world market. Twenty years ago the price of wool per pound was twenty-two cents; today it was less than twelve. It was getting harder and harder to increase Kilmarnock's yearly profits. And now there was this drought.

Colin studied his reflection in the windowpane, and saw the face of his father, the twelfth laird of Kilmarnock, a severely handsome man who with but a glance was able to make a man fall silent, a woman tremble. It was the face of the man who was in control, the man with power. Colin's father had had that power, back in his castle on the island of Skye. But Colin knew that his own look was but a façade. His power was spurious; it depended upon rain and droughts, and sheep and grass; his sovereignty over thirty thousand acres was founded not upon bloodline and noble rights, as his father's was, but upon the vagaries of weather and economics. Colin knew that he could lose it all if he weren't constantly vigilant.

He thought of Hugh Westbrook. Despite Merinda's setbacks due to the drought, Westbrook was enjoying success with his new strain of sheep.

When Hugh had introduced a rambouillet ram to his flock seven years ago, Colin had been the first to scoff. "He'll never do it," he had said to John Reed and Angus Hamilton. "Any fool knows you can't run sheep west of Darling Downs." But the new Merinda strain had looked promising. Several graziers had bought Hugh's new rams and tried them on their stations, breeding them to prize ewes, carefully selecting and culling the flock, until the breed began to show itself to be very tough. The third generation was now being run on land that had never supported sheep before, and the Merinda strain was being talked about from Coleraine to the Barcoo.

And Colin despised Hugh for it—and for much else.

When Colin had come into possession of the useless 5,000 acres at the base of the mountains, and knocked the fence down along the Merinda border, he had thought luck was on his side, because much of Westbrook's stock had perished in the river as a result. But then the district began to look askance at Colin, and he had had to put a rein on his thirst for power and revenge. But MacGregor would never forget how Hugh had kept Joanna Drury from coming to his wife's aid when she was dying. He was biding his time. The right moment for repayment would reveal itself, and Colin would be ready. *He will be hurt as I was once hurt,* Colin thought grimly. *And his loss will be as great as mine.*

There was a knock at the door. It was Locky McBean, his former overseer, who entered with cap in hand. "Good evening, Mr. MacGregor. I've just got back."

"I can see that. What do you have for me?"

Locky had been promoted a few years back from the job of overseeing Kilmarnock to being in charge of collecting rents from properties MacGregor owned around the district. Some of the families who worked Colin's holdings rented from him and turned over the profits of whatever they farmed, keeping a small percentage of the sales for themselves. Others were buying small farms and stations from him, making regular mortgage payments plus a percentage of whatever profit they made from their wool crops. It was up to Locky to see that everyone was paid up to date, and that there was no cheating. And when times were hard, as they were right now for some of the smaller farmers, Locky saw to it that they paid just the same, whether they could afford to or not.

He produced a battered ledger and set it on the desk before Colin. Then, pointing with a dirty fingernail, he said, "Yer gonna have to raise the interest rate on Drummond's mortgage, Mr. MacGregor."

"Why? What's the problem?"

"Their wool's bad this year, because of the drought. You're gonna have a loss in profit after shearing."

It was the practice among some of the landlords in the district to have any tenant who couldn't meet the year's wool profit make it up in higher mortgage payments. But the problem was that when squatters like the Drummonds were forced to pay higher interest on their mortgage they had to cut costs in other areas, usually by laying off their hired help, which sent unemployed men into the countryside.

"Give him one month," Colin said. "If he doesn't pay, evict him."

"Drummond's got eight kids."

"They're not my responsibility. What next?"

They spent a few minutes going over the accounts, and Locky suggested several more families for eviction. These were farmers who, far from having problems like the Drummonds, actually expected to make a good profit this year and therefore would have enough to pay off their mortgages, once the wool or wheat was sold. It was Colin's practice in such cases to call the note on the property and demand the whole of it immediately, before shearing or harvesting, forcing the farmer and his family off the land, penniless, with Colin keeping the initial capital that the man had put into the farm. Colin would turn around and sell the farm again, to another hopeful with a bit of money and ideas of owning his own farm, with the expectations of putting *him* off when he got too close to being able to own it outright. To Colin it was a ridiculously simple way of making money, and he had contempt for landlords who didn't use it because it was, after all, entirely legal.

After McBean left, Colin picked up the letter he had received that morning from Scotland, read again the one significant phrase that stood out from the pages of his mother's writing: "Your father is very ill. I wish you would come home."

Home, Colin thought bitterly. He wished he could go home; it was not his desire that he should be estranged from the land that bore him. Colin had tried, in fact, to reconcile with his father when he had taken Pauline to Skye seven years ago, on their honeymoon. But Sir Robert had refused to receive them; he would never forget the words his son had spoken to him years ago, when they had argued over the issue of evicting farmers to make room for the more profitable mutton production, and Colin had turned his back on his heritage and sailed to Australia. Colin and Pauline had spent two weeks exploring Skye, walking among alder and birch woods, and riding over the brooding moors, where black-faced sheep grazed; they had hunted in the forests surrounding the castle, and fished in Loch Kilmarnock; discovered moss-covered Celtic crosses and gravestones, the carving on them no longer readable; they had taken supper with Lady Anne, and then they had left, cutting their visit short, having never once seen Sir Robert.

Colin was distracted by another knock at the door. It was fifteen-year-old Judd, dressed in the school uniform of Tongarra Agricultural College—gray flannel trousers and navy blazer. He was tall and reedy, with silky platinum hair, and disarmingly bright blue eyes. "May I have a word with you, Father?" he said.

Colin was pleased to see him. "Certainly, son. Come in."

Judd closed the door behind himself and hung back. He wished he could talk with his father in another place, the drawing room perhaps, where history and the dead weren't so omnipresent. At almost sixteen, Judd was still cowed by his father's study. He tried not to glance at the latest sampler that Lady Anne had stitched. It hung framed behind glass on the wall, a poem titled, "The Haunted Kirk of Kilmarnock," where "Kilmarnock was drawing nigh, Where ghosties and ghoulies nightly cry." Judd preferred poems about the Australian outback, such as Hugh

Westbrook's ballads, which spoke of golden suns and luminous skies, and men who were alive and vigorous and who weren't afraid of ghosts or legends.

"What is it, Judd?" Colin said as he poured himself a whiskey. He was looking forward to the day when he would introduce Judd to the Men's Club in town, and they would share their first drink together.

"They've asked me to make a decision, Father. I'll be sixteen soon, and my course of study will be ending a year after that. But if I'm to stay on, then they'll enroll me in a special—"

Colin held up a hand. "You already know my feelings on the subject, Judd. I've told you. Why are we discussing it again?"

"I don't think you're being fair to me, Father."

"Judd," Colin said with a patient smile, "you're only fifteen. You don't know yet what you really want."

"I'll be sixteen soon. Didn't you know what you wanted when you were sixteen?"

Colin's smile turned sad and wise. "I thought I did. But I was young and ignorant and I made many mistakes. I want to save you from that."

"I'd rather make my own mistakes, sir."

The thunderous face of Sir Robert flashed across Colin's mind. "Mistakes bring pain," he said to Judd. "I want to spare you the suffering I went through. You know, there are times when I regret the day I gave in to you, when you pestered me to let you go to Tongarra in the first place. I should have sent you away to school in England, as I had planned. But I thought that maybe having you go to an agricultural school would be of benefit to Kilmarnock. I see now that I was wrong."

"But, Father, the school *is* good for me," Judd said eagerly. "And I think that maybe someday I can use what I have learned there to develop a new strain of wheat that will grow under drought conditions."

"Judd, you're a sheepman, not a wheat farmer," Colin said, coming around the desk and placing a hand on his son's shoulder. "I wish we wouldn't quarrel like this. Can't you see that I only have your best interests in mind? I can't allow you to demean yourself by being a teacher."

"I won't be a teacher forever, Father. I want to be a scientist."

Colin shook his head. Where had the boy gotten such obstinacy? And then, suddenly, Colin saw himself standing in a similar study, in a large stone castle much like this one, and confronting a stern-faced man like himself. And he heard his father saying, "You'll be the laird of Kilmarnock someday. I forbid you to go to Australia."

No, Colin thought. That was different. I had to get away. I had to make my own way in the world. "Judd," he said, "I built this station for you. On the day you were born, I made you a promise that I was going to hand an empire over to you. How can you stand there now and tell me that you're willing to settle merely for being a teacher?"

"I won't be settling for anything, Father. There is so much I want to learn, and to do—"

"Judd, you're going to be the laird of Kilmarnock someday—"

"Father, I'm not a Scottish lord, and I never will be. I'm Australian, and proud of it."

Colin sighed impatiently. Where on earth had the boy gotten these notions from? From the very first day he could talk, Colin had taught him about his home in the Hebrides. He had described the stark beauty of Skye, the often turbulent skies, the meadows like thick green velvet, the hard splendor of the Cuillins, the lochs running like liquid pewter, the craggy peaks and tumbled-down crofters' cottages, and the centuries of history imbedded in its soil. Colin had taught Judd love and loyalty for his ancestral home at Kilmarnock, and for Scotland in general. The first song Judd had ever learned was, "My heart's in the Highlands, my heart is not here;/My heart's in the Highlands a-chasing the deer."

Where was that loyalty now? Colin wondered. Where had he gone wrong in instilling in his son a sense of bloodline and Celtic pride? Judd's boyhood heroes should have been William Wallace and Robert the Bruce, but instead he had worshiped a rebel convict named Parkhill and an outlaw named Kelly.

Pauline was passing through the hallway outside Colin's study, when she heard voices coming from behind the closed door. Wondering if this might be a good time to talk to Colin, tell him of her desire to go away on holiday somewhere, the two of them, to someplace romantic, she paused outside the door and listened.

It was another argument with Judd.

There were times when she wished Colin's son were truly her own. Judd was tall and attractive, resembling his mother more than his father, and he was intelligent, with a pleasant personality. Pauline had tried, in the beginning, to be a mother to him, but only with modest success. Neither of them had been able to put from their minds the fact that Judd was another woman's child. She had ultimately been unable to find herself at ease with him. And, in the way of children, Judd had sensed it. He addressed her as "Pauline" and introduced her to his friends as "My father's wife." But she sometimes wished that, in front of others at least, he would address her as "Mother."

Pauline opened the door a crack and watched Colin as he went to the liquor cart and poured himself a whiskey. At forty-eight, he still cut a striking figure. Colin kept himself in excellent physical shape; and the silver in his black hair only added to his good looks. Pauline remembered the intense sexual desire she had felt for him long ago, during their honeymoon, when she had ached for his touch. When had that desire faded away? she wondered. When had he become simply the man she shared a house with?

Then she thought of John Prior, who excited her in a very different way. Prior had brought to the surface all the old feelings she had once had for Hugh Westbrook, feelings of warmth and tenderness as well as passion.

She heard Colin saying to Judd, "No Kilmarnock MacGregor has ever been a teacher, and we are not about to start now."

"But, Father—" Judd said.

"Good God, son, what would your mother think?"

"Pauline doesn't mind—"

"Not her! Your *real* mother!"

Pauline froze, slowly closed the door and stared into the shadows in the hall.

So, there was love in Colin after all, as she had suspected, but it was not for her. Yes, of course—she had always known it. Christina still occupied his heart. And, Pauline realized, she probably always would.

She searched the dim shadows for answers. She wanted a baby out of her body. She thought of John Prior. She thought of Hugh Westbrook.

———————— • ————————

Pauline wanted to look her best for her first visit to Merinda in nine years, and so she dressed with care. She wasn't nervous or anxious; in fact, she found herself quite calm, as she thought: A desperate woman will try desperate measures.

From the moment of that fateful meeting with John Prior a month ago, Pauline had not been able to get Hugh Westbrook out of her mind. She had found herself dwelling on what might have been, had she not so foolishly ceded him to another woman. Pauline would think of Hugh and wonder what her children would have been like, had she married him. She would think of the empty nursery next to her bedroom, the monthly disappointment and the growing desperation to have a baby before her childbearing years were over, and she would associate all of this with Hugh.

She looked at herself in the mirror. "Still beautiful," was how the society pages described her. But Pauline knew it would not be long before the silver strands began to appear among the blond. And she thought: A woman doesn't mind gray hair when she has something to show for her life.

And what, she wondered, did she have to show for her thirty-three years? A cabinet filled with trophies—cups and statues that were shiny but cold, engraved with dates and events and the names of top honors. A trophy could not be cuddled or loved, or express love in return. How much more those awards would mean, Pauline thought, if she had someone to pass them on to. How much more satisfying her achievements in riding and archery, if she could teach her skills to a daughter. To Pauline, her life seemed sterile, pointless.

A recent copy of the *Times* was lying on her dressing table. Pauline had read the letter that was printed on the second page.

"It is time for us to stop thinking of ourselves as Victorians and Queenslanders and New South Welshmen," Hugh Westbrook had written, "but as Australians, one and all. We have to stop thinking of England as home, we have to cease looking across the ocean for protection and security. It is time we came of age, as a united people."

Pauline had heard Hugh speak on the issue of federation of the Australian colonies. In the nearly one hundred years since the first white men arrived, Hugh argued, the continent of Australia had been divided into six independent, self-serving governments, so lacking in cooperation with their neighbors that each colony had its own postal system and set of stamps, its own army and navy with different uniforms; each placed a heavy tax on products imported from another colony; each had a different-gauge railroad. All of which, in Hugh's mind, worked counter to the best interests of all Australians. "It is ludicrous," he had written in the *Times*, "that when a man travels from New South Wales into Victoria, he must alter his pocket watch because the two colonies cannot agree to adopt the same time. Such rivalry among our colonies could put the rivalry between European nations to shame."

Hugh's outspoken patriotism for Australia filled Pauline with pride. And it drew her to him all the more.

As she rose from her dressing table, she felt a grim resolve steal over her. She had no doubts or misgivings about going to Merinda. She had to go. Her seven years of marriage with Colin had produced no child. A tryst with John Prior, a man who excited her but whom she did not love, was, for many reasons, out of the question. The solution lay at Merinda.

Hugh rode into the yard, hastily dismounted and left his horse in the care of a stableboy. What had once been the front veranda of the cabin was now the side veranda of the kitchen, the cabin having been transformed into a cooking station when a newer cabin had been built next to it, the two buildings being connected by a covered walkway. The heavy green canvas shades had been drawn down over the kitchen veranda to block out the westering sun. Hugh went around to the side, through a wall of protective hedges, and into the small garden that had been laid out in front of the newer house. This had been built when the Westbrooks had outgrown the cabin, but had not yet been able to afford to build down by the river. It was a modest dwelling, with a high, pyramidal roof to permit the movement of air on hot days, and a newer, more spacious veranda that was set out with cane furniture and potted plants.

Hugh found Joanna on the lawn, sitting on a stool in the sunlight. She had just washed her hair in a tin tub, and was now brushing it out, rich and brown. The privacy of this little garden, which faced the drive but blocked the house from view, permitted her to undo the top buttons of her blouse and roll up her sleeves. Hugh paused to look at her. Eight years of marriage had not diminished her mystique, or the power such a prosaic sight as her weekly hair-washing had to arouse him. The first time he had come upon Joanna at this ritual, he had swept her into his arms, taken her inside and made love to her, her hair still wet and clinging to her naked shoulders. And he wanted to do so again now. But circumstances had changed in eight years. He and Joanna were not as free to indulge their sexual impulses as they once had been; Hugh could hear the voices of Adam and Beth on the rear veranda, where they were playing. He glimpsed a maid through the parlor window, polishing something. And he had noticed on his way in a station hand out front, not where he could see Joanna, but there all the same.

Hugh called out and waved to her with the packet of mail he had just brought from Cameron Town.

They went to the veranda, and Joanna asked the maid to bring tea. This was their daily ritual: to take a break from their work, read the mail, and catch up on each other's news. It was a quiet hour, reserved just for them.

"Here's something from Karra Karra!" Joanna said, after she had buttoned up her blouse and rolled down her sleeves. But she left her hair loose, to dry in the heat.

On the evening of their last day in Melbourne, just hours after she had discovered the Karra Karra brochure in Adam's possession, Joanna had sat down and written to the mission, which was located on the New South Wales border. She had explained why she was writing, and enquired about any records they might have of someone named Makepeace. While she read the reply from Mr. William Robertson, the director of the mission, Hugh opened his mail.

"This *is* good news!" he said after a moment. "It's from McNeal. He says he'll be free to come out month after next, when the exhibition closes. He says he has no immediate plans to return to America, and will be able to commence right away on our new house. I'll write back and invite him and his wife to stay here with us. We have plenty of room, and a hotel in town would be an unnecessary expense." He looked at Joanna. "Well? What does the mission say?"

"The director doesn't say much," she said, reading the letter again. "It's rather strange. He makes no mention of my grandparents, and he hasn't answered any of my questions. But he has invited us to come to the mission and meet with him at our convenience."

"Maybe he has too much to tell you and prefers to tell it in person."

"Yes," she said, refolding the letter into its envelope. "Perhaps. Oh, Hugh, do you suppose this is the same Karra Karra that I've been looking for? Something doesn't seem right."

"We'll go and find out," Hugh said.

Jacko, Merinda's station manager, appeared at the opening in the hedge. "We've got trouble, Hugh," he said. "Number six and seven bores have silted up."

"All right," Hugh said, rising, and replacing his hat. "Let's go and see what we can do." He kissed Joanna on the cheek and said, "I'll try to be home for dinner. But I might have to stay out tonight."

"I'll send Ping-Li with a hamper if you do."

She watched him go. When she started to reread the cryptic letter from Karra Karra, she was surprised to see someone appear at the break in the tall hedge. She was further surprised to realize it was Pauline MacGregor.

"Pauline," Joanna said. "Goodness, come in. I'm afraid you've just missed my husband."

"I know, I waited until he had left. It was you I came to see."

"Please," Joanna said, mildly baffled. "Come inside. It's cooler in the parlor. May I offer you some tea?"

"No thank you," Pauline said as they entered the dim interior, which smelled of fresh lemon polish and autumn flowers. Pauline recalled the last time she had visited Merinda, when Hugh had been living in that deplorably crude, almost derelict cabin. Now he had a proper house, modest but well taken care of, and graced with vines and shrubs. The parlor, though not grand, was meticulously kept, with new furniture, a brightly colored Turkish carpet, fringed lampshades, framed photographs and lace curtains. And she could not help but wonder "What if . . ." once again.

"What can I do for you?" Joanna asked, and Pauline looked at her. It had been a long time since they had seen each other, and Pauline thought Joanna looked awfully young; she remembered that she was still in her twenties. With her hair falling loose like that, she looked even younger.

"I have come on a very personal errand," she said, "and I don't quite know where to begin."

Joanna sat and waited.

"I have been told," Pauline said, aware that her gloved hands were clasped tightly in her lap. "That you are discreet?"

"You have my word that whatever we say will not go beyond these walls."

"Very well, I will come right to the point. You are no doubt aware that I have been married for seven years, and that I am so far childless. I heard that you were able to help Verity McManus conceive a child, when doctors and Poll Gramercy had told her there was no hope. Can you help me?"

"It is possible that I can," Joanna said. "But first we shall have to try and discern the cause of your childlessness. Very often, it is a simple thing to correct."

"Before you go any further, I first must tell you something," Pauline said. She looked around the parlor that might have been hers, at the portraits of the boy and girl, and the neat little vases of flowers sitting on tidy doilies, the Bible on its stand. In the background, homely sounds drifted from the kitchen, and children's voices called to each other from the veranda. Kilmarnock seemed like a museum compared to this; not a home, not even a house, but a repository of relics and ostentation.

"I have resented you all this time," Pauline said, looking at Joanna, "because I thought you stole Hugh from me. But now I realize that he was probably never mine in the first place. Especially in that year following the typhoid epidemic—I bore particularly hard feelings against you. And that is why I did something of which I am now ashamed."

Joanna regarded Pauline with some mystification. They had been vaguely distant rivals for such a long time that this sudden intimacy, and the confession that she sensed was about to be uttered, perplexed her.

"I am talking about the five thousand acres that my brother used to own," Pauline said, "that edge the northern boundary of Merinda. I knew Colin wanted them as part of his twisted response to Christina's death, his desire for revenge against Hugh. I offered that land to Colin because I wanted him to marry me. I didn't know what he was going to do with it. I'm sorry you and Hugh suffered such a loss in that storm."

Joanna stared at her. "I don't understand," she said. "I had heard rumors of this revenge, but I don't know what it's about."

Pauline told her in a straightforward manner about the night Christina died, and how Hugh had said Joanna would come to Kilmarnock after she woke. "I lied to Colin. I knew then that I had lost Hugh to you, and I hated you both. So I told Colin you had refused to come and help his wife."

"And then, when she died, he blamed both Hugh and me."

"Yes."

"I see," Joanna said, as she rose and went to stand by the fireplace. She ran her finger along the mantle and made a note to tell Peony that she had forgotten to dust it again. "I appreciate your honesty, Pauline," she said after a moment. "It was a terrible tragedy. We lost two men in that storm, and we almost lost Hugh. It set Merinda back severely. But we have recovered, and people can't always help what they feel. I think we should put it all behind us." Although, she thought unhappily, Stringy Larry and a fifteen-year-old boy died because of that vengeful act.

"I shall need to ask you some rather personal questions," Joanna said, returning to her chair. She would think further about Pauline's confession later, when she was alone, and when and how, or even if she was going to tell Hugh about it.

"You may ask me anything you like," Pauline said.

"Do you and your husband make love very often?"

Make love, Pauline thought wryly. We go to bed, we have sex. Love is not involved. "Once a week," she said.

"The position is sometimes important in matters of conception. Do you lie on your back?"

Pauline felt her cheeks redden. Not even the doctors she had gone to had asked her such intimate details. "Yes," she said.

Joanna asked a few more questions—Did Pauline get up immediately afterward? Did she take a bath right away? Was she in the habit of regularly using hygienic douches?—and then she proceeded to explain how little was known about women's bodies and the mysterious process of reproduction.

Joanna had purchased a book in Melbourne called *Modern Gynecology*. It had been written a few years earlier, in 1876, by a well-known American physician, and in it was a reference to the discovery of the human ovum, earlier in the century. The author postulated that the ovum might possibly be subjected to a periodic cycle, and that it might in some way be connected to the menstrual cycle. He went a step further with the radical suggestion that menstruation might not be triggered by the moon after all, as was commonly believed, but by physiological factors within the body.

Although the man's theories were generally snubbed by the medical community, Joanna had been wondering if it was possible that he was right. Was there a regular cycle in women, she asked herself now, that could somehow be predicted? She thought about sheep farmers, and how they had known for centuries that ewes were not fertile all year round, but only at certain times, and that those times could be predicted so that rams could be put with them. Was it possible, therefore, she wondered, that women were also fertile only on certain days in their cycle, and that those days might be determined and then charted?

"I am going to ask you, Pauline, to keep a diary throughout three or four complete cycles," Joanna said. "Write down how you feel every day—every hour, when possible. I will give you a thermometer. Take your temperature daily. Chart it. Note any changes you experience, physical and mental, no matter how slight. Describe your emotions, for instance, or any cravings you might have, or headaches or other problems. Perhaps we will see a pattern. And then perhaps we can determine when you are at your most fertile moment."

"I'll do whatever you suggest."

"I cannot guarantee anything," Joanna said, "but from what I have read about experiments in this cycle theory, which is called 'ovulation,' there have been promising results."

They rose together and regarded each other across a mote-filled beam of sunlight.

"In the meantime," Joanna said. "Remember what I said about a pillow beneath the hips, and to remain on your back for a while afterward. And avoid drinking such teas as pennyroyal or juniper."

As Pauline rode away from Merinda, she thought of what Joanna had suggested: calendars and temperature charts. But where, she wondered, was the love?

CHAPTER 20

S arah stood in front of the mirror and studied her reflection. She was naked, having just finished bathing.

Philip McNeal and his wife were due to arrive at Merinda any time now; Hugh had gone to the railway station to meet them. The household was bustling with last-minute preparations; Sarah could hear them in the hall: Beth instructing Button to behave, Adam asking Joanna if Mr. McNeal was going to tell them stories about America, and Joanna assuring Mrs. Jackson, the cook, that her meringue of peaches was going to be a huge success with the guests. The household had been preparing for days, ever since Hugh and Joanna had offered the McNeals the hospitality of Merinda and they had accepted. Nothing would do for Joanna except a thorough housecleaning. With the hired help of two local girls, they had gone through the rustic rooms with the vigor of people sprucing up a palace. Down came the curtains and up came the rugs; floors were scrubbed and polished; bedding was washed and ironed; and everything that didn't move was dusted, mended, polished and replaced with care. The house smelled of lemon oil and the aromas of Mrs. Jackson's days of baking.

The McNeals were going to be living at Merinda while the new house was being built. Philip would be sleeping here, in Sarah's bedroom, in her bed, with his wife. Sarah would to move into the next room with Beth.

She could hear everyone heading toward the veranda, where they would greet the visitors. She was lagging behind. She had lingered over her bath, and now she lingered before her mirror, studying her large breasts and wide hips with a critical eye. She felt cursed with the voluptuousness of her mother's people; she wished she had Joanna's modest breasts and slender hips.

She thought about Philip. She was surprised that he was married. He had seemed to her to be a rootless spirit, a soul that must always be on the move, following his own private songline. Perhaps that songline had led him to the woman he had married, perhaps she was what he had been looking for. Since the day they met at the exhibition, Sarah had been able to think of little else, and it troubled her. She knew she had once had a girlhood crush on him, but she had not really expected ever to see him again, especially as the years went by and she had no word of him. The sudden rush of emotion she had felt when she saw Philip in Melbourne had startled her, and now she was trying to sort out her feelings. Surely, she thought, she couldn't be falling in love with him.

She wondered what he thought of her. What had gone through his mind when he had seen her for the first time in six-and-a-half years? There had been a look of surprise on his face.

Sarah tried to picture what his wife would be like: She could only imagine Philip marrying someone strong, someone with substance. She thought of Pollen on the Wind. Perhaps that was whom Philip had married. He had spoken often of her.

But his wife's name was Alice. That was what he had written in his latest letter. Her name was Alice.

Despite the closed shutters and the wet sacking that had been hung on the outside walls to cool the house, the room was hot, and late-afternoon sun knifed through the slats of the louvered shutters. Sarah placed her hands on her breasts. Her skin was feverish, damp. She closed her eyes. Philip was married, she told herself.

Hurried footsteps in the hall outside her door reminded Sarah of the hour. And then she heard Beth's voice ringing through the house, "They're here! They're here!"

Sarah dressed hurriedly, her hands shaking as she did up the buttons of her white blouse. The high collar and cuffs were starched; her petticoats were heavy and layered. She suddenly resented the restrictive clothing, which was so impractical in this heat. She often wondered why, when they lived in such a warm climate, Australian women chose to dress as though they were still in cool, misty England. But Sarah complied with the rules. She cinched her waist with a corset; she wore her hair swept up on top of her head; she fastened a cameo brooch at her uncomfortable collar; and she pushed her feet into high-heeled leather boots.

She came out onto the veranda just as the carriage was pulling into the yard. Beth wanted to run down the path and greet the visitors, but Joanna kept a restraining hand on her daughter's shoulder with a murmured, "Act ladylike." Everyone's excitement was palpable in the still afternoon air. Houseguests were not uncommon at Merinda, but they were usually Hugh's grazier friends. An architect from America was quite a different matter.

Hugh got down from the carriage on one side, and Philip on the other. They both raised a hand to help Mrs. McNeal, and the little boy with her.

"She's lovely!" Mrs. Jackson whispered as she stood behind Joanna. "But she's so young. Still a girl, I'd reckon."

Sarah's eyes were fixed on Alice McNeal. She took in the petite figure dressed in a brown velvet traveling suit, the delicate way Alice put her foot to the ground, the graceful bend of her wrist as she accepted Philip's hand, and the demure smile she offered Hugh. When McNeal took the little boy by the hand, Sarah saw that Alice barely came up to her husband's shoulders. Compared to the two men who accompanied her along the walk, Mrs. McNeal appeared almost doll-like. Sarah saw the rich black hair beneath a smart bonnet, a complexion that was even whiter than she had imagined and the kind of heart-shaped face that was currently in vogue in ladies' fashion magazines.

"Mrs. Westbrook," Philip said, "I would like you to meet my wife, Alice. And Daniel."

Joanna went down the steps with her hands out. "I am so pleased to meet you, Mrs. McNeal. Welcome to Merinda. And Daniel, how nice!"

As Alice McNeal walked up the steps, Sarah saw a wan smile and deep-set, shadowed eyes. She was struck by an air of melancholy that had not been apparent at a distance.

"These are my children, Adam and Beth," Joanna said. "And this is Sarah King, who lives with us."

Sarah thought that Alice's eyes rested upon her for a rather long moment. And then everyone was going inside.

They went into the parlor, but Hugh couldn't wait to say to Philip,

"Why don't we go down to the river and have a look at the building site? I'm anxious to hear what you have to say."

"But Hugh darling," Joanna said. "Our guests have only just arrived. Can't it wait until they have rested?"

"Not at all, Mrs. Westbrook," Philip said, as he and Hugh headed for the door. "I'm anxious to get to work. I've come up with some new ideas that I think you will find exciting. Gas lighting, for one thing. I predict that in ten years every household will have gas lighting. If we install gas piping and a shed for the gas machinery now, it will save an expensive conversion later. And indoor plumbing. . . ."

The two men left the room talking, with Beth and the dog and Adam trailing behind. When Joanna offered Mrs. McNeal a chance to freshen up, Alice accepted, saying, "Daniel and I would appreciate it, Mrs. Westbrook. The journey was most exhausting."

Joanna said, "I'll take you to your room," but in the next instant Hugh was in the doorway, saying, "Joanna? Aren't you coming with us?"

"You go ahead, Joanna," Sarah said. "I'll take Mrs. McNeal and Daniel to their room."

As they walked down the hall, with Sarah carrying a suitcase and Alice McNeal leading three-year-old Daniel, Alice said, "It's so warm out. How do you manage to keep the house so cool?"

"We hang wet sacking on the outside walls. As the moisture evaporates, it cools the inside of the house."

Sarah led the way into her bedroom, which had been made ready for the guests by the addition of another bed and a cot for Daniel, and the removal of Sarah's things. "The dresser has been emptied for you," she said as she opened the drawers. "And there is plenty of room in the clothes cupboard. These doors here," she said, going to the shuttered French doors, "open onto the veranda, which will make the room cool at night. There is fresh water in the pitchers on the washstand, and you will find extra towels on the top shelf of the cupboard. If there is anything else you need—"

Daniel suddenly pulled loose from his mother and went running out of the room.

"Daniel!" Alice said, going after him.

She and Sarah found him next door in Beth's bedroom, reaching for the stuffed fur toy that sat on her bed.

"No, no, Daniel," Alice said. "That doesn't belong to you."

But Sarah said, "I don't think there would be any harm in Daniel's holding it."

Alice watched how her little boy clutched the strange toy, and said, "What a curious-looking doll! It looks like a pillow made of fur. What is it supposed to be?"

"We don't know, really. It belonged to Joanna's mother." Sarah bent down and said to Daniel, "His name is Rupert. And he's very old. You will take good care of him, won't you?"

Alice looked around the room and saw how cramped it was, the second bed clearly not belonging. "You've given us your room, haven't you, Miss King?" she said. "I'm sorry to put you out. I told Philip that Daniel and I would be perfectly all right at a hotel, but he insisted upon staying here."

"It's all right," Sarah said. "I'll be sleeping with Beth for the time being. It's no inconvenience. And please call me Sarah."

Alice gave her an uncertain look, and it struck Sarah that even the bedposts seemed to diminish her. Sarah guessed her age at around twenty-five, and she spoke, to Sarah's surprise, with a British accent. "I'm afraid I'm a bit baffled by all of this," Alice said, smiling apologetically. "Philip and I have been on the move ever since we got married. We left England to live in America, and then, when we left America to come to the exhibition, I was under the impression that we would not be away for long. I miss my family. They're all in England, and I have been away from them now for such a long time."

She looked down at the little boy who was turning Rupert over and over, as if to determine which was top and which was bottom. Daniel's head was damp with perspiration; black curls were matted to his forehead. "Daniel has never known a real home," she said quietly. "Philip and I have only lived in hotels, because his work calls for us to move around a lot. And then there was the long ocean voyage to Australia, and five months at the exhibition. And now . . ."

She looked at Sarah, and again her smile was apologetic. "Well, I am sure we shall make the best of it. Thank you for giving us your room. It is very kind of you. A house is so welcome after years of hotels. Daniel will be very happy here."

"He'll have Beth to play with, and the animals, of course," Sarah said, realizing that there was a sadness about Alice McNeal that was almost tangible.

Alice regarded Sarah for a long moment. Then she said, "Philip told me about you. You're just as nice as he said you were."

Sarah left and quietly closed the door behind her. She tried to understand her confused emotions—her sudden, unexpected feelings for Philip, and then meeting his wife and experiencing compassion for her, a woman-to-woman feeling; and sadness also for the little boy who had never had a home.

As Sarah carefully measured fennel leaves into the pot of boiling water, she tried not to think about Philip. She was in the solarium, making herbal syrups. It was late evening; Joanna and Alice were in the parlor with Beth and Daniel; Hugh and Philip had gone back to the river to view the foundation of the new house by moonlight. As she worked, Sarah could hear, in the distance, the lonely wail of dingoes.

The night seemed to wrap itself around her like warm velvet. Even the stars looked hot. And the moon was so big and yellow and bright that it might have been another sun. Sarah's skin was damp; she felt her petticoats clinging to her legs. As she watched the fennel leaves simmer in the pot, taking care not to let the water boil down too far, she thought of how she had watched Philip across the dinner table, the way the candlelight had glowed on his face. She had been fascinated by the shine of moisture on his upper lip. She had found herself watching his mouth, mesmerized by it while he spoke.

Occasionally, as the conversation had moved around the table, she thought she had caught Philip glancing at her. Had she seen a silent communication in his eyes? She chided herself for having an overactive imagination. Sarah told herself that it was only in her mind that Philip had seemed to look at her more frequently than he had looked at the others, or that while he had spoken to everyone at the table in general, whether it was to talk about America, or the exhibition, or the ideas he had for the Westbrooks' new house, he had seemed to be looking only at her. Hadn't she herself been guilty of staring? Hadn't she barely glanced at her companions? Could she recall what Joanna or Alice had worn at dinner? She hadn't been able to eat. She had moved the food around her plate. She had listened to Alice McNeal's soft-spoken description of their ocean voyage from San Francisco, and had stared at her wineglass. She had heard Philip's warm laughter fill the room, and she had heard him address his wife as "darling." Afterward, when the others had adjourned to the parlor, Sarah had excused herself, saying that if she let the fennel go for too long, it would lose its potency.

Now, as she paused in her work to look out the window at the moonlit plains, she realized that Philip's presence in the house was going to be very unsettling.

She heard a sound, turned and saw him emerge through the trees. "Oh, hello!" he said, coming to the open doorway. "I was looking for Joanna. Alice has gone to bed, and Hugh thought Joanna might be in here. He said she might be able to help me with a problem I've suddenly developed."

"Joanna is probably reading a story to Beth. Is it something I can help you with, perhaps?"

He smiled self-consciously. "I suppose it's nothing," he said, and he rolled up one of his sleeves. "But something down by the river doesn't agree with me."

When he stepped into the light, she saw the angry rash on his forearm. "You must be allergic to something here," she said. "But I don't recall this happening the last time you were with us."

"It didn't. But I think I know what it is. I've had this rash before, back home. Has Joanna by any chance added a poplar tree to her garden? I'm allergic to poplars."

"We imported several trees from America a few years ago, poplars among them. Here, let me take care of this for you."

"I have it on both arms, I'm afraid," Philip said, as he rolled up the other sleeve and took a seat on one of the stools by the workbench. "And it burns like fire." He looked around the room that, by day, was open to sunlight. It was crowded with plants in pots, or hanging from the ceiling, flats of seedlings, trays of leaves and stems drying out. The workbench was cluttered with bottles and phials and jars; and the air was thick with the mingled fragrances of fennel and honey.

But it was Sarah who was the focus of his attention. Sarah, who had caused such a startling rush of emotion when he had seen her at the exhibition, and whom he had not been able to put out of his mind since.

"All right," she said, coming back to him. "This should make the rash feel better." She unstoppered a jar, scooped a creamy mixture onto her fingers and gently applied it to his arms.

"What is that?" Philip asked, as he watched her hand move slowly back and forth over his arm, noticing how her olive skin contrasted with the white cuff of her sleeve; feeling her nearness, detecting her faint perfume.

"This is calendula," she said. "It won't cure the rash, but it will help the itching. The only way to get rid of the rash altogether is to stay away from the poplar tree."

He was silent for a moment, then he said, "It certainly is a hot night."

"I'm afraid we're in the middle of an autumn drought."

"In America, May is a spring month, not autumn. What I couldn't get used to the last time I was here was the reversal of the seasons. I discovered something else, too. Did you know, Sarah, that water going down a drain runs in the opposite direction here than it does in the northern hemisphere? Very difficult for a person to adjust to."

She smiled and said, "There now. That should give you some relief for a while. Keep this jar, and apply the cream whenever the rash flares up, or when it is particularly bothersome."

As Philip rolled down his sleeves, Sarah went back to the workbench to check on the simmering fennel. It was time to add the honey and allow the mixture to cool.

"It's nice to see you again, Sarah," he said. "To tell you the truth, I hadn't expected you to still be here at Merinda. I thought you would be married by now, and living somewhere else."

"No," she said quietly, "I'm not married."

He wanted to ask her why; and then he realized that it wasn't a fair question. Sarah was what some people in America would call a half-breed, not a kindly term. He suspected that the same prejudices that pervaded society back home were also at work here in Australia.

"Do you still know things, Sarah?"

She looked at him. "What do you mean?"

"I remember that you used to have premonitions, or second sight. Remember the night of the storm, when Hugh lost so many sheep? You knew then that something bad was going to happen. Do you still know things like that?"

"Sometimes, but not often." She smiled.

Sarah returned her attention to the fennel syrup. She brought down some earthenware jars from the shelf over the workbench, lined them up and poured small amounts of fennel syrup into each.

"What will you use that for?" Philip asked.

"It settles the stomach, and it also works as a diuretic."

They fell silent again. Philip looked at the jar in his hand—it was made of opaque purple glass, heavy and smooth, and it was stoppered with a large round cork. A label had been pasted on the side: CALENDULA CREAM: FEBRUARY 1880.

"Alice seems to be very nice," Sarah said when the syrup was measured out. "How did you meet her?"

"I was traveling in England, and we met through a mutual friend."

"You do travel a lot."

"Yes, I do. I suppose I'm restless."

She looked at him again, her hands pausing over her work. "I remember that you were searching for answers the last time you were here. Are you still searching for them?"

"I don't know if there are any answers, Sarah. I work; that's mostly what I do."

"Building other people's houses, without having one of your own."

He stared at her, at the high cheekbones and full mouth, and the stray curls from her upswept hair that caressed her bare neck. And he was stunned by her raw sexuality; a sensualness that was only barely tempered by the carefully cultivated delicacy of her tiny pearl-drop earrings, the modest cameo brooch at her throat and the tortoiseshell combs holding the thick brown hair in place.

"You know, Philip," she said, as she stoppered the jars, "if you were an Aborigine I would say that you go walkabout a lot. I would say that you were following your songline."

"Following it," he said, "or maybe just searching for it? Can a songline go all the way around the world, Sarah?"

"Yes. But it must end sometime, somewhere. Just as there was a beginning Dreaming, there is an ending Dreaming."

"I know, they're called birth and death. Maybe my life is my songline, and I don't know where it's leading me."

She smiled. "You cut your hair."

He touched the back of his neck. "A couple of years ago. Alice didn't like it long. For me, it was a reminder of the time I spent living with the Navahos. I sometimes think that that was the happiest period of my life. That," he said, "and the six months I spent here."

A large moth suddenly flew against the window above the workbench. It fluttered desperately against the glass, beating its wings to get inside to where the light was. Sarah stared at it, aware of Philip sitting close to her, watching her. Something was starting to happen between them, something that she knew he also felt; and she sensed that they were both afraid of it.

"Tell me about the book you're writing," Sarah said.

"I want to make drawings of Australian country houses, and I'd like to get started on it as soon as I can. I want to go around the district and choose the most typical examples of Australian architecture. Perhaps you could go with me, and show me around?"

"Joanna and I are leaving for New South Wales tomorrow. We have been invited to pay a visit to an Aboriginal mission there."

"When you come back then?"

"Perhaps," she said, noticing that the moth had flown away.

———————————

Joanna tossed in her sleep. *"Where are we, Mother? What are we doing here?"*

Lady Emily's voice came from far away: "Hush, little one. We're hiding."

"What are we hiding from, Mother?"

"From the dogs—"

Joanna sat bolt upright in bed. "No!" she cried.

Hugh was suddenly awake. "Joanna," he said, sitting up. "What is it? Another bad dream?"

She was shaking so badly she could hardly speak. "It was awful," she said. "It was so . . . so real."

"Why don't I get you some milk. We can sit up and talk about it."

She laid a hand along his cheek, feeling the rough stubble. Hugh had come to bed late, and he had to get up early again and ride out to the distant flocks to make sure they had water. "Really," she said, "I'll be all right. I just want to sit up and read for a while."

She put on her dressing gown and slipped out of the bedroom, quietly closing the door behind her. She went into the parlor, lit a lamp, sat down in one of the easy chairs and laid her head back. She closed her eyes, trying to will the headache away. She knew that none of her medicines would help. The headache had no physical origin; only mental effort would ease the dull throb that was always brought on by the nightmare.

If only she could stop these dreams. She had brought her mother's diary into the parlor with her, and she opened it, turning to pages she had read many times before, but which she read again, hoping to find some hint, some hidden clue that she might have missed.

The clock over the mantel ticked softly; something rustled in the brush outside the house. A night bird perched briefly on the windowsill, then flew away in a whispered flapping of wings.

Joanna slowly turned the pages until she came to the end of her mother's handwriting and the beginning of her own—her first days at Merinda, her early worries over Adam, her first stirrings of love for Hugh. And then she came to the day when Sarah had taken her down to the river and told her about the Kangaroo Dreaming. "Sarah told me that I am following a songline," Joanna had written nearly nine years ago, "and that I am singing up creation as I go. What did she mean, that I am singing up creation? I am not aware of doing this."

Joanna stared at the page and suddenly remembered something Sarah had also said long ago, about the diary being a kind of songline.

If this book is my songline, she thought, then perhaps the act of writing in it is the same as singing up creation. Is that what Sarah had meant? And if this is my songline, then it is also my mother's because it was her book before it was mine—but I am continuing it, just as I am now experiencing the nightmares she suffered, and feeling the same sense of fear and dread that haunted her final days.

Songlines, Joanna thought wearily. Rainbow Serpents and wild dogs. What did it all mean? She was sick of it, and yet obsessed with it. Why couldn't she unravel the mystery here? There had to be a way of changing a songline, altering its course. She refused to let her mother's fate become hers—or hers become Beth's.

Laying the book aside, Joanna went to the small desk where she took care of correspondence; she lit the lamp, took out a fresh piece of paper and a pen, and sat down and wrote: "Dear Aunt Millicent, I know that I have asked you in the past to please fill in for me certain blanks in my mother's life, and out of respect for the pain of grief that you said such recollections would bring back—grief for the loss of your sister—I did not press for that information. But now I must insist. I have begun to suffer from a certain affliction that troubled my mother in the months before she died—nightmares and headaches, and a increasing feeling of dread. It is urgent that I determine the cause, which I believe lies somewhere in her childhood, the details of which you alone can supply for me. I entreat you, Aunt Millicent, for the sake of my health, and for my daughter's also, as I fear she too will fall victim to this legacy, to please tell me what you know about the circumstances surrounding my mother's departure from Australia. *Is there something I should know?*"

———————————•———————————

The coachman was obstinate. "I'm sorry, missus," he said. "I don't give rides to blacks. I gotta think of the other passengers. They paid their money. They got rights."

Joanna couldn't believe it. To have come this far, after so many hours of traveling, and to be this close to Karra Karra, only to have the driver of the overland coach refuse to take Sarah because she was an Aborigine.

"Surely you can't mean that," she said. "You aren't seriously going to leave us here!"

He lowered his voice. "It's not me, you understand, missus. I got nothing against niggers. If it was up to me I'd let her on board. But the other passengers—"

Joanna looked at the five people who had gotten off the train with her and Sarah—three men and two women—seated inside the coach and pointedly looking the other way.

"What do you expect us to do?" Joanna said to the coachman.

"There is nothing here!" The train stop consisted of a small shack and nothing else. A few yards from the railroad tracks, dense forest grew. This was the end of the line for anyone not continuing on to Sydney. Those going to other towns and settlements disembarked here and took the overland coach the rest of the way.

"I'm sorry, missus. But it's company rules. No Aborigines." He shrugged apologetically and climbed up into the driver's seat of the coach.

"Please, Joanna," Sarah said. "Go with him. I'll be all right here."

"But I might be spending the night at the mission, Sarah. Where will you sleep? In that shack?" Joanna turned to the driver and said, "Can you at least tell me how far it is to the Karra Karra Mission?"

"Ten miles up the road. But it's uphill all the way. And it looks like it's gonna rain. You might want to do as the girl says, and ride with me."

"I have no intention of riding with you. And you can be sure that I shall be writing a letter of complaint to your company."

"Suit y'self," he said and snapped the reins.

As the coach rattled away down the road, disappearing into the towering pine trees, Joanna sensed the threat of rain. The western plains might be crippled by drought, but here in the lush mountains near the border of New South Wales, a light rain was common. "Well, Sarah," she said as she picked up her valise, "I suppose we had better start walking."

The brisk mountain air invigorated them as they walked. The smell of pine trees and loamy earth was almost intoxicating. As she followed the forest track, Joanna felt her excitement mount. Could this really be Karra Karra after all these years? Was there a creek nearby named Bowman's? And another place called Durrebar? Were she and Sarah, in fact, walking over the ground that was designated in the deed— property that was rightfully hers?

Joanna had written to William Robertson, the director of the mission, asking if he knew anything about her grandparents, but he had sent back the hasty reply of a busy man: "I don't know what I can tell you, Mrs. Westbrook. But if you come and visit us, we shall offer you the extent of our modest hospitality."

Whenever rain threatened, Joanna and Sarah stopped frequently and sought shelter under the trees. Their wool coats became heavy with the dampness, and their boots were soon caked with mud. But their spirits remained high. Joanna had been excited ever since reading the handout Adam had picked up at the exhibition. And now here she was, high in the mountains, about to visit the place where perhaps her mother had been born.

They trudged along the road, listening to the forest silence. Occasionally they saw a flash of blue and red among the trees, as a parrot flew by. Animal sounds came from deep within the forest; and flowers unlike any they had ever seen grew in profusion. They were both starting to get tired, being unused to the altitude and feeling the effects of an uphill walk. They paused every so often to switch bags from one hand to another, and to catch their breath.

Joanna began to worry. How far had they walked? How much longer before they reached the mission? With the sky so cloudy, it was impossible to guess what time it was.

Finally, they followed a curve in the road and came upon a strange sight.

Up ahead, the way was blocked by a bullock team. Twelve massive animals, harnessed in pairs, were drawing an enormous dray loaded with logs. It was driven by a man who stood on the dray cursing the bullocks, flicking their hides with a fourteen-foot whip. Hugh had written ballads about the bullock teams and their colorful drivers—bullockies—most of whom had been convicts. The teams had been a common sight in his youth, when the country was being opened up, but now they were vanishing, because they were expensive to operate and slow moving. Horse teams were replacing the bullocks, and so was the new railway. To preserve their memory, Hugh had written the immensely popular ballad, "The Bullockies."

What made Joanna and Sarah stop and stare now, however, was not the bullock team, but rather the overland coach, which had come to a halt behind it. The passengers were leaning out of the coach, complaining loudly, and the coachman was shouting at the bullock driver, who ignored him.

Joanna and Sarah walked by them all, feeling small next to the monstrous dray and its load. It creaked along at an impossibly slow pace, the wheels, which were taller than Joanna and Sarah, digging into the mud, the animals straining in their harnesses. When the bullocky saw the two women, he smiled and waved. Joanna waved back and called out, "Do you know how far it is to Karra Karra Mission?"

"Eight miles," he said. "Just follow the road."

Eight miles! That meant she and Sarah had only gone two. It had seemed so much longer.

They continued on past the bullocks, trudging through the muck and praying that the rain would hold off. They had gone only a few yards, and Joanna was saying, "Perhaps we can find a homestead," when she saw a wagon coming down the road toward them.

"Hoy there!" called the driver as he pulled up. "Are you Mrs. Westbrook? I'm William Robertson, superintendent of Karra Karra."

As he helped them into the wagon, he said, "When it started to get late and the coach hadn't come by, I decided to come looking for you. This happens sometimes, the bullocks taking up the road. It'll be hours before that coach even gets to the first stop."

Robertson turned his wagon around and headed back up the road. Joanna and Sarah glanced behind them at the coachman, red-faced and still shouting at the bullocky, while the passengers sat miserably in the stalled coach. After a few minutes they were left far behind.

Robertson was a Scot with long red hair and a bushy red beard. Joanna was surprised when he told her that he was a minister, because he was dressed like a lumberjack. "I can't tell you how pleased I was to get your letter, Mrs. Westbrook," he said. "We receive so little attention at our mission. You asked about a couple named Makepeace. I found no mention of them in our records, but then some of our early superintendents were not efficient record-keepers. But I thought maybe if you talked to some of our older members, they might remember something."

"How old is the mission, Mr. Robertson?" Joanna asked, looking straight ahead, anxious for a glimpse of Karra Karra.

"Very old. It was one of the first missions in the colonies."

Joanna's excitement grew. "Why is it being closed down?"

Robertson's face darkened. "The Aborigines were granted this land years ago, because the government didn't consider it to be of any value. But since then, white settlements have gotten closer, and timber has become more in demand. Especially now, with the building boom."

Joanna and Sarah had seen evidence of that building boom: As their train had passed through Melbourne, they had glimpsed the tracts of new housing springing up in the suburbs, going up as fast as possible to meet the needs of a burgeoning population. And then later, as the train headed north toward New South Wales, they had noticed miles and miles of cleared forests, where all that remained were tree stumps as far as one could see.

"This is rich timberland, Mrs. Westbrook," Robertson said. "A lot of men want to get their hands on it, and so they're putting pressure on the board to move the natives."

"What board is that?"

"It's called the Aborigines' Rights Protection Board. But I'll tell you, they do anything but protect them."

"How can the government make your people move? Have they the legal right?"

"They can if they make it look like they've got the Aborigines' best interests in mind. They're using our high rate of tuberculosis as an excuse. They're saying that it's the cold and damp here that's causing the illness. So they want to move the Aborigines to a warmer and drier climate—for their health, so the board says! But these people belong here. Their ancestors lived here."

"But Mr. Robertson, science has recently proven that tuberculosis is caused by a germ, not by cold and damp. Surely the board is aware of this?"

"They're aware of it all right, because I told them so. But they're clinging to the old thinking. They've even got some respected physicians in Melbourne who'll attest to it."

And then, suddenly, there it was.

As Robertson guided the wagon off the road, Joanna stared at the archway over the entrance. Carved into the rough timber were the words KARRA KARRA ABORIGINAL MISSION. She filled her eyes with the sight of the trees, the gray sky, the stone buildings, the pigs and chickens in the yard. She tried to imagine how it had looked to her grandmother so many years ago, when there had been nothing here, except possibly for the crude dwellings of the Aborigines. She tried to feel, in the bracing air, the zeal and faith that John Makepeace had brought to this forest in his search for the Second Eden. And she thought about the young black woman Lady Emily had believed she remembered—Reenadeena—and wondered if by any chance she or her descendants were still alive.

"We'll have a cup of tea first," Robertson said. "And then I'll show you around."

The superintendent's residence was a small stone cottage consisting of two rooms and a veranda. A half-caste Aboriginal woman named Nellie served tea to the guests in Robertson's small parlor, giving Sarah a curious look every now and then.

"Now then, Mrs. Westbrook," Robertson said, "what is your interest in Karra Karra?"

Joanna told him about John and Naomi Makepeace, her mother's unexplained departure from Australia, and her own subsequent search. But when she was finished, Robertson said, "Oh dear, I'm afraid this couldn't possibly be the same place!"

"Why not?"

"For one thing, this mission wasn't founded until 1860."

She and Sarah exchanged a look. "But you said it was very old!"

"Yes, relatively speaking. In colonies that are themselves less than a century old, twenty years seems a long time. But for another thing, Mrs. Westbrook, Karra Karra was not our original name. Until I came to work here a year ago, it was called St. Joseph's Asylum for Natives."

"I see," Joanna said. "That explains why I was unable to find it on the map."

"I didn't think the former name was appropriate for a home for Aborigines. So I asked them to choose a name of their own. They got together and decided upon *karra karra*, which is the name of a flower that grows in great profusion here. You've seen it—the trumpet-shaped one with white and lavender petals."

Joanna's disappointment was acute. She didn't know what to say.

"I'm sorry, Mrs. Westbrook," Robertson said. "I truly wish this was the place you had been looking for."

"Would you happen to know," she said at last, "if the word *karra karra* means the same thing among all Aborigines?"

"It is believed that there are over two hundred separate and distinct languages among the Aborigines spread out over this continent, Mrs. Westbrook. A word in one dialect might mean something else in another."

"I see," she said.

"Would you like to take a look around the mission now?"

Joanna and Sarah were taken first to the chapel where, with Mr. Robertson, they said a prayer. Then they were shown around the main compound, which consisted of private houses, communal buildings and pens for the farm animals. Joanna was shown how the women made baskets, using the same methods their ancestors had used. The women traveled a great distance to collect the right variety of rush, Robertson explained. The rushes were then split, the strands tied together, soaked in water for some hours and then hung up to dry until they were ready to use. The baskets, Joanna was told, were in high demand in the nearby towns.

She and Sarah watched men cure and tan possum hides, which they made into rugs and sold. She saw the vegetable gardens being tended and harvested; cows being milked; and children singing their lessons in a rudimentary schoolhouse. Everywhere she and Sarah went, they were met with smiles and politeness. But Joanna saw a difference between these people and those of the Western District Mission, where

Sarah had lived as a child. The Karra Karra people seemed to stand taller, and to carry themselves with a kind of pride that was not apparent in some of the others. Simms's Aborigines were servile; Robertson's people had dignity.

"We have reached the point, Mrs. Westbrook," Robertson said, "where we are completely self-sufficient. The mission no longer receives government aid. We grow our own wheat, hops and vegetables. We make baskets and possum-skin rugs, for which there is a steady market. We have seventy head of cattle, fifteen milking cows, and enough pigs to keep us in bacon for years. You see, unlike other mission superintendents, who feel that the natives should be treated like children—guided, so to speak—I believe the Aborigines do better when left to govern themselves. By being denied their own initiative, they lose their feeling of self-worth."

Joanna recalled the times she had visited the Western District Mission, of which Reverend Simms was still the superintendent. The Aborigines there were generally unhappy, often unruly. Simms's answer was to tighten discipline, which seemed to Joanna only to make matters worse.

"Are your people happy here?" she asked.

"They are quite content, Mrs. Westbrook. Of course, the majority of them are half-caste, and they feel more secure in a place such as this than out on their own in society, where they are accepted by neither the blacks nor the whites." He cast a quick glance at Sarah, in her smart velvet traveling suit and feathered hat, with a gold crucifix at her throat. "We have very few full-bloods, and they are very old."

Joanna thought about the Aborigines she had seen at the Western District Mission, when she had last made a tour of it with Reverend Simms. They had been well dressed and well fed; they had smiled and proudly showed off their baskets and rugs. But underneath, Joanna had sensed a kind of perplexity. She had looked into their tidy little huts and had been introduced to Mary and Joseph and Agatha. She had been greeted by smiling mothers who wore European dresses, and proud old gentlemen in frock coats and trousers. But she had been troubled by the feeling that something was wrong. In the midst of contentment and obvious prosperity, Joanna had felt a sense of loss. It seemed to her that, rather than growing, the Reverend Simms's people were just biding their time until they died.

As they walked past a long clapboard building, Joanna said, "Do I hear singing, Mr. Robertson?"

"Indeed you do," he said. "That is our infirmary. There is a woman in there who is very sick, and her relatives are trying to cure her. The women are chanting a healing-song."

"What's wrong with her?"

"She has severe pains in her abdomen—they came on quite suddenly last night. The women have been singing over her for quite a while now."

"Is that all they will do for her?"

"They have rubbed her body with emu fat and ash, and tied a hairstring belt around her waist. But the singing is the main part of their cure."

"Shouldn't she be seen by a doctor?"

"It wouldn't do any good, Mrs. Westbrook. The district doctor did come by to have a look at her, and he said there's nothing he can do for her. She isn't sick from any real physical cause. From the way I understand it, she ran off with another woman's husband. They got as far as the nearest town, where he abandoned her. When she came back, the other woman 'sang' her—by which I mean, cast some sort of spell on her."

Joanna stared at him. "You mean, like a poison-song?"

"Why, yes. You've heard of such things, then?"

"Can nothing be done to help her?"

"Her relatives are trying to drive out the poison by singing their own healing force into her. White man's medicines won't help, perhaps theirs will. It's all a matter of belief."

"Would they mind if I saw her? I have some skill in healing."

"They wouldn't mind at all, Mrs. Westbrook. They would appreciate your trying to help. You go on in, I'll wait out here. I'm forbidden to enter when the women are performing one of their rituals."

Joanna and Sarah stepped through the doorway and found themselves in a long room furnished with eight beds and a few chairs and tables. Seven of the beds were neatly made and unoccupied, but in the eighth a woman lay with her eyes closed. She was clearly ill; her head rolled from side to side, and she was groaning. As Joanna and Sarah watched, a group of women moved in a dance around the bed; they held their hands in a cupped fashion, facing away from their bodies, and as they danced they pushed their hands outward and over the supine woman.

Suddenly, one of them noticed Sarah and Joanna. When she stopped singing, the others also stopped and stared at the newcomers.

"Hello," Joanna said. "I'm sorry to interrupt, but may I take a look at her? I might be able to help."

She had expected to meet resistance, or perhaps resentment, but instead they smiled shyly and gestured for her to come to the bed. Joanna sat at the bedside and examined the patient, checking for certain signs and symptoms. Although the specific nature of the ailment eluded her, she saw the look of fatalism and acceptance in the woman's eyes. Then she noticed, on the table beside the bed, small packets of powder labeled GINGER and YARROW, a bottle of willow extract and a mustard poultice, all of which she herself would have prescribed, and which had no doubt been left here by the district doctor. Clearly, they had not helped.

When Joanna rose from the bed, the women looked at her hopefully, but all she could do was say, "I'm sorry."

They resumed chanting, and the curious dance around the bed, and Sarah and Joanna retreated to the door. "I wonder if they will help her," Joanna said.

"I don't know this ritual," Sarah said. "I don't know how to help someone who has been sung."

"Perhaps it can be any kind of ritual," Joanna said thoughtfully, "perhaps all that is necessary is that the victim believes that the singing and the words will help. I wish I could believe in their power as these women do. I wish I could make up my own song and believe that I could sing the poison away. Perhaps it would in fact go away. Perhaps I would never have another nightmare, and I wouldn't have this terrible feeling of dread whenever I look at Beth."

They joined Robertson outside, and when Joanna commented that such rituals were forbidden at some of the other missions, he said, "I'm rather sad to see these people losing their culture. The Aborigines have been dispossessed of so many of their magic places. Hundreds, perhaps thousands of sacred waterholes and caves are lost to them forever. And the loss, I might add, is more than just a spiritual one. Bear in mind that the Aborigines never wrote down their history. The record of previous generations abides in the sacred landmarks that lie along the songlines. The Aborigines would follow the ancient tracks and repeat the old stories as they went. But cut off from their songlines, they soon lost the record of their ancestors. I have often complained that depriving Aborigines of their sacred sites was the same as burning down a library!"

"Your people seem to be very happy here," Joanna said as they neared Robertson's cottage.

"Unfortunately, Mrs. Westbrook, there are still a few who run away."

"Where do they go?"

"To the towns and settlements, mostly. They've become attracted, even addicted, to alcohol and tobacco, so they go where they can get it. But a few run into the interior, where they hope to find the old way of life, a place where there are no white people."

"Are there many in the interior who are like that?"

"No one knows. There are still parts of Australia that are unexplored."

Unexplored, she thought, by white men. But no doubt they have been heavily explored and were well known to the Aborigines who lived there.

Joanna found herself thinking of the driver of the overland coach, and of his passengers, who hadn't protested his anti-Aborigine policy. And she thought of the natives she had seen in Melbourne, drunk, begging, prostituting themselves. She thought of Sarah, who seemed to know less and less about her people's culture. And Reverend Simms, who had once said to Joanna, "We encourage the Aborigines to marry outside their own race, for then the better qualities of the civilized whites overcome and dispel the black traits."

"Can the rulings of the Aborigines' Rights Protection Board be influenced, Mr. Robertson?" she asked when they were back in his cottage. "Can the board be persuaded to take more of an interest in protecting these people?"

"I have been trying, Mrs. Westbrook, but I am one voice against six. That was why I made up those handouts for the exhibition—I was hoping to catch the attention of others like myself who might offer some help."

"I would like to help, Mr. Robertson. Tell me what I can do."

He went to his desk and said, "I'll give you the names of the board members. You can write to them, protesting their decision to move my people."

While Robertson wrote the list of names, Joanna contemplated a photograph that hung over the fireplace. The caption described it as a portrait of Old Wonga, the last chief of this area. He was naked except for a possum-fur cloak, and he looked stately with his spear. What had he been thinking, Joanna wondered, when he had looked into the camera's lens? Had he heard, in the click of the shutter, the death knell of his people?

"Here you are," Robertson said, handing her the list. "I would be most appreciative of anything you could do. Now then, would you care to stay the night? We do have accommodations for visitors."

Before Joanna could reply, something else on the wall caught her eye. It was a document, very old and yellowed, framed behind glass. Joanna stepped closer. She stared at the familiar dots and swirls and lines, the cryptic symbols she had come to know so well, but which still remained elusive after so many years. "Mr. Robertson," she said, suddenly excited, "what is this?"

"That, Mrs. Westbrook, is my pride and joy. It's a page from Julius Caesar's *The Gallic War*. It's not the real thing, of course, but a rather clever facsimile sent to me by a friend in England. I'm something of a classicist."

"But what *is* it? The writing, Mr. Robertson, what is it?"

"It's a form of shorthand invented by a Roman who lived in the first century B.C., named Marcus Tullius Tiro. He was Cicero's private secretary. Many famous men, including Julius Caesar, used Tironian shorthand. It was in use for about a thousand years, but it disappeared, during the Middle Ages, when shorthand became associated with witchcraft and magic."

"I would like to show you something," Joanna said, and she went to her traveling bag and took out the leather satchel. She handed the papers to Robertson.

"Good heavens!" he said. "This is the very same shorthand! Whoever wrote these must have been a classicist like myself."

"Can you read it?"

"Well, let's see, shall we?" He removed a pair of spectacles from his pocket and seated them on his nose. Bushy red eyebrows came together as he concentrated on the writing. Finally he said, "I'm afraid it's no good, Mrs. Westbrook. My document is in Latin, these papers of yours seem to have been written in English."

"But can't you translate them?"

"I'm not an expert on Tironian shorthand. There are hundreds of symbols, you understand."

"Is there no way the code can be broken?"

"The friend who sent me this facsimile is quite knowledgeable on the subject; in fact it was he who drew this excellent facsimile for me. I shall write to him in England, and send him your grandfather's papers, explaining the problem. Giles owes me a favor anyway."

Joanna hesitated. "I would rather not allow these papers out of my possession, Mr. Robertson. They are very valuable to me."

"Yes, of course. I understand. Well then, I'll ask Giles to send me the Tironian code, with instructions on how to use it. That way, Mrs. Westbrook, you can translate your grandfather's papers yourself. How would that be?"

CHAPTER 21

On the morning of August the eleventh, 1880, at precisely ten o'clock, the colony of Victoria witnessed the end of an era. Seamus Langtree, notorious bushranger who had for so long terrorized decent citizens and eluded the troopers' net, was hanged at Pentridge Jail, Melbourne. With a white cap pulled over his eyes, Langtree danced and struggled at the end of his rope for a full four minutes before death finally claimed him. This grisly and disreputable end to the highwayman marks the end of lawlessness in the Australias."

Thus began Frank Downs's eyewitness account of the most celebrated execution in the colonies. He wrote furiously, taking down all the details and adding a few flourishes of his own—"Five thousand people were gathered outside the jail for the news; many were women who wept for the doomed outlaw." While his competitors, the *Age* and the *Argus,* had sent reporters to cover the sensational event, Frank believed that the hanging was worthy of being written up by the *Times*'s own publisher himself.

"Well, that's that," said one of the newsmen in the gathering of about thirty at the foot of the gallows. "I'm for steak-and-kidney pie at Lucy's. These hangings give you an appetite!"

Frank looked at his watch; he had a luncheon appointment with the president of the First Melbourne Bank, but there was time yet, time enough to get his story over to the office and on the presses for the afternoon edition.

It was a good story, and Frank believed his edition would outsell the others. Especially as it was going to be accompanied by Ivy's imaginative illustrations of the Langtree Gang and the infamous shoot-out at Glenrowan. Frank hadn't seen Ivy in two weeks, and he realized she must be missing him, must be getting lonely. As he filed through the gates of the penitentiary and shook the warden's hand, Frank decided that no matter what came up tonight, he was going to make a point of visiting Ivy.

It wasn't just the newspaper keeping him busy; it was other things too. One morning he had woken up to realize, all of a sudden, that he was forty-three years old. This had gotten him to thinking that it was time to give serious consideration to the future—the future of Lismore, of the *Times,* of the Downs name. It was time to get married and have a family. But it wasn't a prospect he particularly relished facing. He had been so happy with Ivy, and continued to be so. If only they could go on as they were, or if he could marry her—but that was out of the question. The whole purpose of marriage, as far as Frank was concerned, was to produce heirs, and he was sure Ivy couldn't have children.

When he had subtly let it be known that he was, well, looking, the invitations had started to pour in—to this dinner and that, to the such-and-such ball, to the so-and-so's garden fete. He imagined word spreading through Melbourne like fire through dry brush: Frank Downs is looking for a wife! Every mother with a marriageable daughter, it seemed, had found out that an eligible man had put himself on the market. "Jungle tom-toms" was how he thought of it, each time his valet brought in yet another tray of invitations. They whispered, they murmured, they conspired—every mother in Melbourne who was worth her gowns and her husband's bank account.

And so he went to the fetes and balls and dinners and luncheons, an endless round of smiles and being polite and bad whiskey and homely daughters and overbearing, overbosomed mothers anxious to make the publisher of the *Times* their son-in-law. Frank found it tiring, and there were moments when he told himself it wasn't worth it. But then he would look at the new ten-story building he had just put up, and the increasing circulation of his paper, and the graceful gardens at Lismore, and the empty, unlived-in rooms there, and he would think, yes, it was worth it. Besides, it was his duty. It was every man's duty to produce an heir.

But finding a wife was proving to be no easy task. He didn't think his expectations were unreasonable: He just wanted a woman who was smart, nice, pleasant, and who knew how to run a large house and a full staff of servants without running to her husband at every little crisis. But so far he was finding fault with all the young women he was being introduced to, finding himself thinking halfway through supper: She's too talkative, or too short, or too well-read. Frank realized that while he did not know just precisely what he wanted, he knew what he didn't want, and so far the latter was what he was finding in the Melbourne drawing rooms.

Still, he didn't lack prospects. There was no end to the nightly and weekend invitations. He even admitted in some vain masculine part of himself that he rather enjoyed all the fuss being made over him. Nonetheless, he didn't delude himself into thinking that all this sudden romantic attention from Melbourne's unmarried girls came out of a mad passion for Frank himself. He was forty-three and looked it; his appearance was more substantial than ever, his paunch having grown, and his hairline, it had to be admitted, having started to recede. No, Frank knew what they were after. It was what everyone who had a brain in his or her head was after—money and power. And Frank Downs had both.

As Frank made his way along Collins Street, joining countless other Melburnians who seemed undaunted by the August chill, he felt his spirits rise. Despite the threat of rain from black-bellied clouds, the owner of the Melbourne *Times* was in a good mood. Things were going well at the paper, and at Lismore. Circulation of the *Times* was up, and the wool clip and lanolin production at Lismore had brought in the largest profit ever. And he had Ivy.

And that was the reason, Frank knew, why he seemed to find other women lacking. Ivy was so perfect for him—loving and faithful, always there for him, ready for good conversation about what was going on in the world, to laugh with him, even to scold him occasionally. He loved Ivy for her streak of independence, for the way she spoke her mind; she enjoyed sex and rarely shunned his advances.

As Frank paused at the curb, waiting for an opportunity to cross, his attention was caught by a headline on the *Argus,* a rival newspaper: EVIDENCE OF A WILD WHITE MAN FOUND AMONG ABORIGINES.

Frank bought a copy and quickly scanned the story—about explorers in the Great Desert in Western Australia coming across a rock with the letters S.W. and the date, Jan. 14, 1848, carved into it. The article explained that it was known that a man named Sam Wainwright and four others had ventured into the Great Desert in 1848, seeking a route across Australia from Perth to Sydney. They were never heard from again. But the carved rock had been found very near an Aborigine encampment, and the blacks there told the explorers about a white man who had lived with them for fifteen years before dying.

It was usually the *Times* that got good stories such as this, and Frank didn't like the idea of the *Argus* getting ahead of them. He made a mental note to put his reporter, Eric Graham, on it to see if he could find more information.

As he hurried across the street, dodging carriages and horse-drawn trams, Frank thought of Joanna Westbrook and her recent trip to the Karra Karra Mission in New South Wales. The mission director had promised to secure for her the key to the shorthand her grandfather had used, and Frank was placing high hopes on that translation. There was the possibility of a sensational story in all this. Frank could hardly wait to find out what was in those cryptic notes; he could almost see the headline: WHITE WOMAN KILLED BY ABORIGINE CURSE THIRTY-SEVEN YEARS LATER.

A cab rushed by, its wheels plunging into a puddle and sending muddy water everywhere. As Frank jumped back, he cursed this hazard of Melbourne's winters. Still, he thought, as he brushed off his spattered trousers, summers were worse, when armies of flies invaded and diseases broke out, and the dirt streets turned to powdery dust. In the summertime, one could always spot the newly rich of Melbourne, because they rode in their carriages facing forward, coughing, while the seasoned carriage riders always rode "back to horses."

As Frank entered the *Times* building, he decided that the *Argus* wasn't getting such a jump on him after all. Ivy's caricatures continued to boost circulation, and while her cartoons had sparked the *Argus* and the *Age* into following suit with their own series of drawings, theirs didn't come anywhere near the cleverness of Ivy's. Who, everyone wondered, drew those marvelous pictures? But Frank did not reveal the identity of his cartoonist. He and Ivy had agreed that the mystery sold newspapers.

Yes, he thought as he rode up in the trembling hydraulic elevator to the tenth floor, he had to see Ivy tonight. After seven years—exactly seven years, next week, he realized—she remained the only woman in the world who, for some unfathomable reason, seemed to love Frank just for himself. She had never expressed interest in his money; she had never asked for anything.

And Frank's sexual relationship with Ivy had been especially wonderful, ever since the day it had dawned on him that, after nearly twelve months of sleeping with him, Ivy hadn't become pregnant. He hadn't questioned her about it—a gentleman didn't bring up such subjects, not even with his mistress—but he knew it all the same. And now that she was forty-six, he knew her chances of pregnancy were probably over. And that was why, now that he wanted heirs, he couldn't think of marrying her.

When the elevator door opened, Frank heard the racket of the new Remington typewriters in the outer office.

"Here," said Frank, handing the secretary his notebook. "Langtree's execution. Have it transcribed, and fast!"

The *Times*, like its publisher, was getting bigger every day. Frank had listened to several suggestions from Ivy, such as running stories that were about topics other than politics and politicians. When *The Daily Telegraph* of London sent an expedition into Africa to search for the source of the Nile, it was an event that captured the attention of the entire world. Ivy had suggested that perhaps the Melbourne *Times* could finance an expedition into unexplored New Guinea. Frank's star reporter, a flamboyant adventurer named Jameson, got himself speared in the stomach and nearly eaten by cannibals, but he got back with the story, and the circulation of the *Times* doubled.

Then Ivy said, why not report cricket and football scores? Why not get the latest weather predictions from the Astronomical Laboratory and print them in the afternoon edition? And why not have a comical cartoon, to make people laugh over their morning tea? And run a weekly item about a Melburnian of unique interest? And hold a contest every Christmas for free puddings? Frank had tried them all, and with excellent results. The *Times* was now sixteen pages long and boasted being the bulkiest penny daily in the British Empire.

And it was read by every male voter from here to Wagga Wagga, a fact not lost on local political aspirants.

Frank went into his office, sat down and rested his face in his hands, suddenly feeling very tired. The hanging must have gotten to him more than he had thought. The way Langtree's legs had kicked and struggled . . . Frank looked at his watch again. He was supposed to meet the bank president in an hour, but he didn't want to go. What he really wanted to do was to see Ivy, to take her into his arms, to remind himself that he was still alive and that it had been another man's death, not his own, that he had witnessed.

Then he thought of the bank president again, of the unmarried daughter the man was anxious to introduce to Frank, and Frank knew where his first duty lay. To get himself a wife who could provide him with a family.

Ivy was scared.

She knew that she was going to lose Frank. It was just a matter of time.

As she stood before her mirror, making last-minute adjustments to her hat before going out, she was reminded once again that she was forty-six years old—an age when many women were enjoying their grandchildren. And what did she have to show for her life? A room full of paintings that no one wanted.

Forty-six, Ivy thought, with no husband, no children, no family. When Ivy walked down Melbourne's streets, she was sharply aware of the destitute women who lurked in dark doorways. Unwanted, cast-off women who, often through no real fault of their own, were useless to themselves and to society, begging, selling fruit they had stolen, offering their bodies in exchange for a meal. Melbourne was full of them, and although Ivy had been with Frank for seven years, there was no ring on her finger, no marriage certificate that bound him to her. Surely he was going to wake up one morning and decide it was time to start a family. And a wealthy man like Frank was going to look for someone young and respectable to be his wife, and the mother of his heir.

It was time, Ivy had decided, to start thinking of her own future, and to make plans for her survival. But the problem was—how?

How, she wondered, did a woman with no income and no man to support her survive in a city as harsh as Melbourne, where ragged children begged in the streets and finely dressed ladies and gentleman sailed by without noticing? How could a woman on her own, with no skill, no education, her looks and youth vanishing, ensure herself of a comfortable old age?

When the prospect had first presented itself to Ivy, several months back, she had decided to study Melbourne and see just what lay waiting for her. And what she found not only dispirited her but put fear into her as well.

There was not one single person who would hire her.

The pubs wanted young barmaids; wealthy households were looking for governesses and nannies who were respectable; and Ivy wasn't a very good cook, nor did she have references. All other occupations were held by men.

Whenever Ivy's spirit withered, she would remember Frank and his solid, comforting presence, and she would think: He won't let that happen to me. But then, late at night, as she lay awake listening to the city grow quiet, she would hear the anxious thumping of her heart and feel the panic wash over her again: I can't count on him. He's going to leave me. He'll have to.

But if Ivy Dearborn had nothing else, she had one gift: She could paint.

For as long as Ivy could remember, she had cherished the dream of being an artist. Even as far back as her girlhood, when her family was still in England and struggling to survive on her father's coal-mining wages, Ivy had spent whatever spare time she could find scribbling pictures. When they sailed to the Australian colonies, she and her mother and five brothers and sisters, they had all been dazzled by Daniel Dearborn's oratory on the great opportunities that lay waiting for them there. He was going to mine for gold, he said, and they were going to be rich. Little Ivy's head had been filled with new ambitions and dreams: I shall go to art school; I shall become a famous painter. But nothing had come of Daniel Dearborn's dream. He and two sons died of typhoid at Ballarat; a daughter died a year later in childbirth; the second daughter ran off to Tasmania, never to be heard from again. And Ivy was left alone with her mother and younger brother.

They came to Melbourne because they couldn't survive in the outback. Mrs. Dearborn took in sewing in a small flat behind Collins Street, and died before she was fifty. And the brother, embittered and disillusioned, sailed for New Zealand, leaving Ivy alone.

She had tried again to make her dream come true, by taking what jobs she could find, working in middle-class households as a maid-of-all-work. But the pay was barely enough to survive on, and the hours were so long that she never had a moment in which to put pencil to paper. Which was why, when a handsome young gold miner came through and Ivy caught his eye, she believed his ambitious talk and prayed that this was going to be her way out at last.

But pregnancy sent him running. Ivy woke up one morning to find herself deserted, alone with an infant. It was only good fortune that had crossed her path with that of two kindly people, a husband and wife, who could never have children and who wanted to give Ivy's baby a good home. And so Ivy was left free to find employment again. After a few years of unsatisfactory jobs, many of which had carried the condition that continued employment meant special favors to the boss, Ivy left the city and went to the countryside, where no one knew her. A man named Finnegan hired her to work in his pub, and it was only a short time after that that Frank Downs had noticed her.

That was when her dream to be an artist had been rekindled. Once she was seeing Frank, Ivy had found she finally had the time and money to be able to pursue her dream. He paid for this apartment, which consisted of a kitchen, a parlor and a bedroom, and a dining room that she had converted into a studio, where glorious southern sunshine streamed through a curved bay window, illuminating her easel, paints and stacks of canvases. Free from any obligations except to please Frank, she had plunged herself into painting. In the years since, she had discovered that she had talent, and she saw something unique in her work. She also discovered something else: that no one was interested in paintings done by a woman.

Hence Ivy's dilemma as she walked along Melbourne's crowded sidewalks on this cloudy August day. She couldn't get employment that would pay her a wage, and she had very little of her own money saved up. She wondered if she could tolerate still working for Frank, doing drawings for the *Times*, once he had left her. But she didn't see that as an option.

Teatime found Ivy standing in front of one of the many photo-graphic salons that were cropping up all over Melbourne. The new dry-plate process and faster exposure time were creating a boom in the photography business. Where people once sat for portraits, or hired painters to come out and do a picture of the house, now men with boxes and tripods produced facsimiles in less time and for less money.

Most artists, Ivy knew, hated the new photographic science. Fearful of their profession dying out because of modern progress, they com-plained that there was no "soul" in a photograph, and that a picture taken by one man looked much like a picture taken by another. It was true. But Ivy liked photographs. She liked their realism and precision— an artist, no matter how skilled, could never quite capture the details that a photograph did. But on the other hand, she did admit, as she now stood before the plate-glass window of the studio and studied the photo-graphs on display, that there was a kind of flatness to the pictures. For one thing, they seemed static and lifeless; for another, they had no color. And that was a pity. Becaused nothing in nature lacked color. There was color in even the dreariest of things, and sometimes those colors—in storms, in raging seas, in shadows behind doors—could be

THE DREAMING | 309

the most dramatic and moving facet in a picture. And people's faces, Ivy found herself thinking as she stared at a portrait on display, certainly were not black and white. Where was the flesh on that man? What color were his eyes? Were his lips white or gray or pink? Was he robust or in ill health? The photograph left out so much.

"Can I interest you in a portrait, madam?"

Startled, Ivy turned to find a man in a loud, checkered jacket smiling at her. He was hatless; he had just emerged from the shop.

"I noticed that you had been standing here a long time looking at my pictures," he said with a smile. "Are you thinking of having your photograph taken? My name is Al Gernsheim, and I can assure you that my prices are the most competitive in—"

"There is no life in them."

"I beg your pardon?"

"There is no life in your pictures."

He blinked. "How can you say that, madam? They are taken directly from life!"

"What I mean is, they have no color. And life has color, doesn't it?"

He frowned. "No one can take color pictures. Maybe someday, but not yet."

"It's a pity," Ivy said quietly. "That photograph there, of the eucalyptus standing against the outback. It's a lovely picture to be sure, but it would be so much more dramatic if it were in color. But . . . a white sky and white sand and a black tree?" She shook her head. "It needs the blue of the outback sky and the golden tones of the land and the dramatic shadings of eucalyptus bark. Otherwise, it could be a scene taken anywhere, couldn't it?"

"Yes," the photographer said with a sigh. "It could. And it's one of my best pictures. Took it up Tumbarumba way."

"It's lovely," Ivy said, and she realized she was thinking of one of Hugh Westbrook's ballads. This photograph, she thought, had the same kind of spirit.

An idea started to form in her mind. "How long have you had it for sale?"

"Ever since I took it, a year ago. I haven't had even a nibble on it."

She looked at him, feeling herself grow excited. "I should love to have it, if I may. How much is it?"

When he told her the price, Ivy had to think hard. It was a costly gamble, and there were no guarantees. Still, what other chances had she? Sometimes one had to take risks—Frank was always saying so.

So she bought the landscape and took it back to her apartment on

Elizabeth Street where, divested of her outdoor dress, she set the photograph on the easel in her workroom and began to prepare her paints. For once she would be using watercolors, not expensive oils, and she knew before she placed even one brush stroke on the photograph that she was going to be successful.

Three days later, a startled Al Gernsheim stared at a picture so brilliant with color and so alive that he thought he held the Australian outback in his hands.

"This is a miracle!" he declared. "Why, it's ten times what it was before! It's better than a painting!"

"Would you be able to sell it, Mr. Gernsheim?"

"Sell it! My dear woman, this picture will be gone from my shop before the day is out! Why, just look what you've done! You've captured the true colors of the outback! There is such a mood here! You've done far more than my camera ever could!"

Ivy was delirious with joy, but she restrained herself. "But I could not have done nearly as well without your photograph, Mr. Gernsheim. Perhaps we could work together on other photographs? With the precision and exactness of your camera, and my eye for color—"

"By God, you've got something there!" He tore his gaze away from the photograph and gave Ivy a long, thoughtful look. Suddenly, his cramped little shop, filled with the smells of chemicals and dust, was too small for his ambition. There wasn't a photographer in all of Melbourne who could offer pictures the exact color of their subjects. "Better than paintings!" his mind shouted, racing ahead with the slogans that were going to go in his shop window and in magazine advertisements. "More lifelike than mere photographs!"

"Would you be willing to sell this picture back to me?" he asked. "I'll give you twice what you paid me. And at that I will still make a profit."

Ivy laughed. "Of course you may have it back!"

He gave her another long, considering look, then said, "My dear Mrs.—?"

"Dearborn," she said. "Miss Ivy Dearborn."

"My dear Miss Dearborn. Would you pay me the honor of joining me for a cup of tea in my studio? I have a business arrangement I should very much like to discuss with you."

And Ivy, suddenly seeing in the grinning Al Gernsheim her destiny and salvation, slipped her hand through his arm and said, "I should be most happy to, Mr. Gernsheim."

Another dreary luncheon and another anxious mother foisting her daughter on him. This time, the girl was Lucinda Carmichael.

Frank Downs already knew exactly what she was going to be like. Ever since his wife-hunt had started, he had met the same type of girl a thousand times over. She was usually short—the mothers worked very hard not to have the bad taste to point up Frank's own shortness— or she would hunch her shoulders to soften any height she might have over him. Her hair would be done coquettishly; her dress would be outrageously expensive and still smell of the dressmaker's shop. She would be demure and retiring to the point of boring him; she would play the piano like an amateur, and she would sing atrociously.

Whenever his friends or his sister remarked that he seemed to be taking his time about finding a wife, Frank simply said that he was choosy, and that, as it was an important step, he wasn't going to settle for just anyone.

"G'day, Downs," Geoffrey Carmichael said as he came into the parlor. The Carmichael mansion stood on a hill overlooking the Yarra River, in a Melbourne suburb that was available only to the very rich. When he married, Frank intended to build such a house for himself and his wife so that they could divide their residence between the city and the Western District.

"Carmichael," Frank said, shaking his host's hand.

Geoffrey Carmichael, a robust man in his sixties, had made his first fortune in gold mining; his second in boots and saddle manufacturing. He was now about to make his third—in silver. Ostensibly, this was the purpose of their meeting today, to discuss what Frank had found during his visit to a place called Broken Hill. But the real, unspoken purpose of Frank's visit was to have a chance to meet Lucinda, Carmichael's only daughter.

Frank accepted a glass of whiskey and went to stand in front of the fireplace. It was September, the tail end of winter, and a cold day had Melbourne in its grip. Frank was glad to be back in civilization and drinking civilized whiskey. He and Carmichael discussed the merits of investing in the new Broken Hill silver mine, and when, a while later, Carmichael put down his glass, held out his hand and said, "I trust you, Frank. Consider me another partner," Mrs. Carmichael suddenly appeared, as if she had been listening on the other side of the door and waiting for the business to be concluded. "There you are! Mr. Carmichael, don't be greedy and keep our guest all to yourself. Mr. Downs," she said, entering the room, "I would like to present to you my daughter, Lucinda."

Frank put his glass down and drew himself up. When he saw who entered the parlor, he found himself staring.

Lucinda Carmichael was tall—taller even than Ivy. And she had a bold, beautiful smile that was accompanied by an outstretched hand ready for his handshake. She smelled of roses and was not afraid to meet his eyes. And Frank Downs, suddenly finding himself pleasantly surprised, heard himself say—and mean it—"I'm pleased to meet you, Miss Carmichael."

Instead of hurrying back to the Western District to discuss the Broken Hill mine with Hugh, Frank put off his departure from Melbourne. He took luncheon that afternoon at the Carmichael mansion and attended the theater that same evening with Mr. and Mrs. Carmichael and Lucinda. The next day he appeared again at the house, this time to sit on the lawn and discuss business with Geoffrey, while they watched the lovely Lucinda play tennis on the newly laid out tennis court. That evening he dined at the house, and the next day accompanied the family on a ride to the seaside, where they ate lunch at a café in St. Kilda and remarked on the bracing qualities of the sea air. For six days, Frank found himself in the constant company of Miss Lucinda Carmichael, always chaperoned, and by the end of that time, he came to a very practical decision. He could find no better choice for a wife.

In fact, with her father's wealth and connections, Frank would be getting even more of a bargain than he had first anticipated. But more important than that was the fact that Lucinda was a companionable girl, not mincy and false like so many others he had met, girls he was certain would change the minute the marriage vows were spoken. Lucinda was forthright and sure of herself, and honest in a way that actually gave him a sense of what married life with her would be like. And when he imagined the long legs that must be hidden beneath her skirts, and saw the generous swell of her bosom over a narrow waist, Frank decided he need look no further.

There was no need to talk it over, either with the parents or with the girl herself. The Carmichaels had made it clear that they would welcome Frank as a son-in-law, and Lucinda, who was twenty-one and rather too tall, was ready to settle on a husband. Nor was there any reason to wait. Once his mind was made up, Frank was never one to waste time. He need only make the formal proposal, and then they could settle into a comfortable courtship of a decent six to twelve months, at the end of which he would take his bride back to Lismore and get her settled into country life.

Considering the fortune he expected to make on his Broken Hill shares, and the unexpected dividend he had found at the Carmichael house, Frank decided he had done all right for himself. And so as he waited for his valet to bring his coffee and brandy and hot water for shaving, he marveled at his good luck.

And then he thought: I shall stop by and see Ivy tonight, on my way to the Carmichaels'.

Frank presented himself an hour later on Ivy's doorstep, bearing champagne, flowers, and a very expensive diamond bracelet.

"You're back!" she exclaimed, having missed him during his absence in South Australia.

When he saw Ivy's hair, still richly red, and when he smelled the sweet lavender scent she always surrounded herself with, Frank experienced an unexpected pang. He should have come to see her the minute he got back from Broken Hill. But he had been anxious to get Carmichael's commitment, and then Lucinda had appeared, and, well, the week had simply gotten away from him. But he was here now, in Ivy's comfortable flat, handing her his ulster and the gifts.

"Did you miss me, Ivy?" he said.

She had wanted to scold him. She hadn't seen or heard from him in over three weeks. But the sight of him, the sound of his voice, flooded her with love. She went into his embrace and kissed him, and when his arms tightened about her, and she felt his passion, she wondered how she could have ever been afraid that he would abandon her. She would never do or say anything to hurt him.

Which was why she had kept a secret from him.

She knew that Frank believed she couldn't get pregnant. He hadn't actually spoken of it, but she had felt it after their first year together. She had sensed his relief, and she knew it was partly this that gave him such wonderful freedom in their lovemaking. Ivy had decided to allow Frank his illusion, not wanting to tell him about the illegitimate child she had given birth to years ago and whose whereabouts she no longer knew. She suspected, in fact, that it was not she who was unable to produce children, but Frank himself, and this she would never utter.

She took his coat, sparkling with winter mist, and accepted the champagne and the bouquet of rain-forest orchids that ranged from deep blue to brilliant pink. Ivy recognized the rare flowers—they came all the way from the northern tropical coast of Queensland, and were very expensive.

"What a day I've had!" he said, striding to the fireplace to warm the backs of his legs. "Had to run a special edition this afternoon. Got the news off the latest steamship that the Americans are talking of switching to the Australian ballot for their national elections. Can you imagine? They don't have secret ballots over there? I tell you, Ivy, someday Australia is going to be first in everything. By the way," he said, as he reached into his pocket and drew out a small, wrapped package, "this is for you."

"What is it?"

"Open it, Ivy. This is a celebration."

While Frank uncorked the champagne and poured it, he watched her open the jewel case. He could hardly contain himself as he anticipated her reaction to the bracelet. It was by far the most extravagant gift he had ever given her.

"It's lovely," she said, giving him a puzzled look. "But what's the occasion?"

"Put the bracelet on and drink your champagne. I told you, we're celebrating."

While Ivy sipped her wine, the gemstones on her wrist throwing glittering reflections on the walls, Frank told her about his findings at Broken Hill. "We're going to be rich beyond imagining, Ivy!"

She laughed; his mood was infectious.

"I'll get you a bigger flat, Ivy. How's that? And an ermine cape."

"I don't need those things, Frank," she said, laughing. "I've got you. That's enough for me."

He fell silent then, remembering his other news. This wasn't going to be as easy. He cleared his throat and said, "Well, ah, there's something else, too, Ivy. Something I have to tell you."

She waited.

"I've decided to get married."

The flames in the fireplace crackled and sparks shot up the chimney; outside, a solitary carriage drove by, the horse's hooves clip-clopping with a hollow ring on the street.

Ivy stared at Frank and felt herself turn to wood. So . . . it had happened after all. She had been preparing herself for this moment, she had tried to imagine what it was going to be like, how he was going to tell her and how she would react. But now that the moment was here and Frank had spoken the dreaded words, Ivy found herself suddenly unprepared.

"Married?" she heard herself say.

He cleared his throat again and found that he couldn't look directly at her. "Well, Ivy. I've got Lismore to think of. I need an heir. I owe it to my father."

"Who," Ivy said, "who is she?"

"Lucinda Carmichael, the daughter of the man who's buying into Broken Hill with me."

Ivy sat stiffly on the sofa, her hands clasped tightly in her lap.

Frank spoke hurriedly. "I don't want you to think that this will make any difference between us, Ivy. I'll be living right here in Melbourne, just as I always have."

Ivy looked at him. "What are you talking about?"

"About us, Ivy! You didn't think I would leave you, did you?"

She stared at him for a moment, and then her eyes widened in horror. Of all the scenarios she had imagined, this was not one of them. He meant to keep her! "Frank," she said. "You'll be married. You can't go on seeing me after you're married."

"Why not?"

She shot to her feet and began to tremble. Everything was suddenly all wrong. The scene seemed twisted, backward. It wasn't playing out the way it was supposed to, with Frank announcing that he was leaving her. Instead it was Ivy uttering the long-dreaded words, Ivy who was putting an end to their years together. "Don't you know what that would make of you, what it would make of me?"

"I don't see what's different about it."

"Oh, Frank! It was one thing when you were single. But now you'll have a wife! You'd be an adulterer, and I'd be a—" She turned away. "I won't see you any more, Frank," she said quietly. "Not after to-night."

He went up to her and put his hands on her shoulders. "Ivy, believe me, Lucinda Carmichael can never mean to me what you do. My God, do you think I want to do this? I've got the best life any man could want. I've got you—"

She stepped away from him. "You don't have me anymore, Frank. I will not be a married man's mistress."

"But it wouldn't be like that! Not for you and me, Ivy! We've been together for too long. We mean too much to each other."

She turned to face him, and spoke calmly and without anger. "Frank, I have loved you for seven years. Longer, perhaps. I probably even loved you while I worked at Finnegan's. And I shall go on loving you until the day I die. But this is where we come to the parting of the ways. You spoke of duty. You're right. You must get married. I've known it for some time. I knew this night was coming. But from this moment on, we go our separate ways."

He stared at her. "You can't mean it, Ivy."

"I can and I do."

"But how will you live? You have no income. You need me, Ivy!"

"As a matter of fact," she said, her voice growing strong, "I don't need you. At least, not for financial support. I can support myself, and that is exactly what I intend to do."

His distress began to turn to rage. "And just how do you expect to live without my help? This flat—"

"I don't need this flat any more. I've found another place to live."

"And another man to take care of you, I suppose."

Ivy knew that she should have been furious at his words, but all she could feel were sadness and disappointment. "No, Frank," she said. "There is no other man. I shall be taking care of myself from now on."

"And just how do you intend to do that?"

She looked down at her hands and saw that she had been twisting the diamond bracelet Frank had just given her. Judas diamonds, she thought. To salve a guilty conscience. "I shall live in St. Kilda. I have rented a cottage there, by the seaside."

He stared at her.

"It's true, Frank. I've paid a deposit on a small house by the sea. In time, I hope to be able to buy it. I shall move there before the month is out. And we won't see each other again."

He stared at her in disbelief. "But how are you able to do this, Ivy?"

She told him about Al Gernsheim and the work she had started doing at his studio. Her clever tinting of photographs was proving to be popular, and therefore lucrative for both Gernsheim and herself. Ivy suspected that she would soon be so busy with commissions that she would have to start turning down orders.

When she finished talking, Frank continued to stare at her as if he hadn't understood a word she said, so Ivy went into her workroom and brought out a framed picture. It was the one she had done of the eucalyptus in the outback. She was keeping it for sentimental reasons, and she showed it now to Frank for the first time. "I will be able to support myself on this work," she said. "In fact, Mr. Gernsheim predicts that 'Tinting by I. Dearborn' will soon be in demand."

"Why, Ivy?" he whispered. "Why didn't you come to me? You know you would always have a job with the *Times.*"

"Because I knew that someday I would lose you. And I couldn't work for you after that."

"But you aren't losing me! I've told you that. My getting married isn't going to change anything!"

Tears welled up in her eyes. "Oh Frank, this is such a mess. All this time I've been afraid you would abandon me. I was prepared for that. That was something I could understand. But . . . to say that you would still keep me, to make something dirty and deceitful of our love, that I cannot abide."

Frank felt something dark and alien begin to boil inside him. There was Ivy, his precious Ivy, standing there with that colored photograph, showing it to him as if to mock him, telling him that she no longer needed him, that she had gone behind his back and found a job working for another man! He had taken care of her, and now she had the audacity to tell him she didn't need him! It so thoroughly enraged him that he couldn't speak.

Finally, he said in a thin, high voice, "After all I've done for you, this is how you repay me."

"After all you've done for me?" she cried. "How many hours have I sat here, staring at the clock, hoping that this was the evening you would come to see me, only to end up going to bed alone and disappointed? Even on days when I wasn't feeling well, I always placed your comfort and pleasure first. How about everything I have done for *you*?"

"And what do you think *I* have been doing all these years! Keeping you in a fine life-style! You've never lacked for anything, Ivy! You've never gone wanting! All you ever had to do was ask!"

"I never wanted a keeper!" she shot back. "I only wanted a man who loved me and cared about me."

"I've cared about you more than I've ever cared for anyone."

"Did you ever show any real interest in my painting, Frank? Did you ever ask me about my dreams, my worries, my uncertainties? It was always you, never me."

He seized her arm and raised it to the light. "What do you call this, then? A bracelet that cost me two hundred pounds! If this isn't caring, then what is it?"

She drew in a deep breath and, regarding him with pain-filled eyes, said, "Payment for services."

Silence descended on them again, a silence filled with dangerous, ominous overtones. Letting go of Ivy's wrist, Frank turned, snatched up his coat, and walked out the door, letting it slam behind him.

Payment for services! How dare she!

"Stop here," Frank said to the driver of his carriage. He was on Princes Bridge, which spanned a sleepy, mist-shrouded Yarra River. Behind him, Melbourne's gaslit streets twinkled in the night; up ahead, the river disappeared behind dense woodland, with only the occasional light showing from one of the secluded mansions.

Frank was so enraged he could hardly breathe. Looking down at the dark water, he heard Ivy's voice echo again in his head: "Payment for services."

Who was she to say that to him! A barmaid who thought she had talent! A woman no other man wanted. A woman who would have ended up working Collins Street if Frank hadn't come along and taken pity on her. After all these years, this was how she treated him!

Well, good riddance, he decided, trying to control his fury. He had to be at the Carmichaels' house soon. They were expecting him. He was going to make the formal proposal to Lucinda, and then they were going out to supper to celebrate. He couldn't show up in this agitated state. What if they asked him what was wrong? "I'm a bit upset. You see, I've just broken up with my mistress."

Good God, why couldn't things be simple? And why did Ivy have to turn out to be just like the rest of her irritating sex? Of the millions of women in the world, Frank had given her credit for being different. But tonight he had found out otherwise.

Fine then! he decided as he paced up and down the bridge. Let her go off on her own. See how she likes it. Women thought it was so easy being a man. See how she liked having to work for a living, praying that the money kept coming in and that some disaster didn't overtake her. He didn't need her anyway. Frank didn't need any woman. It boggled him now to think he had gone searching for her that day at the harbor. He must have been out of his mind. And then to stay with her for seven years, the same woman, and older than he was at that! By God, it was a good thing he had found Lucinda. She had come along just in time for him to get his eyes opened good and proper. He didn't need Ivy any more, he never really had. He was his own man, and a great deal happier when he was with his friends at the pub than among tiresome female company.

Payment for services!

How dare she say that to him! Frank could have had any woman in the city. But he had stayed with Ivy. And she had become a comfortable habit, like broken-down slippers.

But no more. She was welcome to go her own way, with her painted photographs and notions of thinking she was something more than she was. Frank didn't need the flat on Elizabeth Street; it was time to let go of it and find someone new. Lucinda was young and fresh. He'd mold her into the kind of woman he wanted. And then his life would be his own again.

As he went back to the carriage, Frank paused and looked at the city lights.

He didn't like leaving things this way. If it had been he who had ended their relationship, then he could go to Carmichael's with an easy mind. But it was Ivy who had done the discarding, adding further insult by denigrating his generous gift—"payment for services" indeed!

Ivy had had the last word, the last insulting word. And Frank couldn't allow that. He wasn't finished, not just yet. He couldn't go to the Carmichael house feeling this way. It was *his* right to get the last word in.

And that was exactly what he was going to do. Go back to Elizabeth Street one last time and tell her everything that was on his mind. Ivy wasn't going to get off so easy, just by saying, "We go our separate ways." He wasn't going to make it painless for her. She was going to have to suffer. He was going to go back and insist that she see him; then he was going to tell her exactly what he thought of her; and then he was going to tell her that she had to be out of the flat by tomorrow and not a day later.

———————————◆———————————

He pounded on the door, and when it opened, Ivy stood there framed in the firelight, her eyes red from weeping. Frank, having rehearsed his diatribe on the ride back from Princes Bridge, removed his hat and heard himself say, "Marry me, Ivy."

CHAPTER 22

Suddenly there came a cry from the wool room: "Ducks on the pond!" It was shouted by the wool presser to alert the shearers that a woman had entered the shed. The overseer, having heard it, passed it along the board, shouting above the clamor, "Watch it, mates! The ducks have landed!"

The warning was not meant to offend the intruding female, but to warn the shearers to watch their language and to go easy on nicking the sheep while a lady was present. The "lady" in this case was seven-year-old Beth Westbrook, who loved being treated like a grown-up. Whenever she came into the shearing shed the men whose hands were free tipped their caps to her, and a merry banter ensued for the benefit of the girl.

The noise in the shed was almost deafening—clippers clacking, dogs barking, men shouting and sheep bleating above the din. The shearers, twelve of them, were bent over their animals in deep concentration as they guided their dangerously sharp cutters under the fleeces, peeling them away from writhing rams or ewes. The rouseabouts dashed around the shed, whipping the massive fleeces out from underfoot and running with them to the wool-rolling table, while shearers shouted, "Wool away!" or "Shake that broom, boy!" Outside, the musterers were driving the frightened sheep into pens to get them ready for shearing.

Beth loved shearing time. It was more exciting than Christmas and lasted longer. She loved the yolky smell of the new-shorn wool and the laughter of the men as they wrestled with protesting animals and expertly stripped the wool off them. And most of all she loved shearers.

They seemed to her a romantic band of men, like the kind she read about in adventure stories, like pirates, Beth thought, or highwaymen or knights on chargers. Beth had learned all about shearers from her father, who himself had, years ago, been a shearer. Every year, at the onset of winter, there was a mass exodus of men from towns all over the Australian colonies, men who shouldered their swags, kissed their wives and sweethearts good-by and struck off on the "wallaby track," where they would be gone for months, moving from station to station, following the jobs, passing through places with exotic names like Cunnamulla, Alice Downs, and One Tree Plain. It was something of a glamorous life for a young man with no roots, Hugh had said, heading off into the unknown, on foot or on horseback, never sure of finding work, sleeping under the stars, drinking tea out of a billycan and drawing comfort from the company of mates. And they were a queer bunch, too. Beth thought there must be no one like them anywhere else on the face of the earth, with their sturdy, beefy bodies and rough language, but with hands, because of the lanolin in the fleece, softer than a baby's. And a tighter band of mates never lived, because it took a rare and special spirit, Hugh had told his daughter, to stick to shearing. It was a life that broke your back and ruined your marriage and punished you with illness and injuries and hard labor in sheds where the temperature often reached 120 degrees. It was a dangerous job, with the ever-present threat of being kicked or slashed by a hoof or losing fingers in the clippers. And at the close of each exhausting day, when the bell rang for tea, a shearer was plastered from head to foot in sweat, blood, urine and feces. Then, at the end of the season, it was off to the nearest pub, and waking up three days later with no memory of the binge, followed by the long weary trek home to wife and kids and the vow that this was the last season for sure. Only to feel the call the very next year, when once again the roaming shearers hit the wallaby track.

Beth's father had written a ballad about shearers, "Emu Creek." It was a long poem about men on the move, with names like Crooked

Mick and Smiling Jack, and the sheds they'd shorn, from Gundagai to Moulamein, and about the hardships they'd suffered, in places named Broken River and Winding Swamp, and their mateship and sacrifices, and the sweethearts named Mary and Jane and Lizzie they had left behind. It had been one of the first of her father's poems to be published under his real name, and it made Beth very proud.

The seven-year-old was in love with shearers, in love with the shearing life, and when she grew up, she, too, was going to be a shearer.

"Well now, little miss," said a shearer nicknamed Stinky Lazarus, striding up to Beth as she stood, excited, in the doorway. "What can I do for you?"

"Oh Stinky!" she cried. "Isn't it wonderful?"

He looked around at his weary crew, sweat dripping off their faces, and at the sheep squealing and pissing all over themselves, and he laughed and said, "Yeah, I reckon it's wonderful all right."

Beth thrust her hands into the pockets of her dress and sighed. She was a tomboyish girl with long braids and a dirty face, barefooted more often than not. Stinky had to shake his head at the thought of Beth Westbrook. During shearing she was always hanging around the shed; at other times she could be seen on her pony, riding around the home-yard, with the old sheepdog Button tagging behind, while her brother, Adam, showed more interest in the plants that grew along the river.

Beth adored Stinky Lazarus. He came with his band of shearers year after year, always full of funny yarns and always seeming to have time to spare for her. "They call me Stinky," he had once told her—since it was the rare shearer who did not have a nickname—"because it says in the Bible that Lazarus stunk to high heaven." And it was Stinky who had put up the sign in the shearers' cookhouse that read: SHEARERS MUST HAVE A BATH EVERY TWELVE MONTHS WHETHER THEY NEED IT OR NOT.

Stinky told wonderful stories, such as the one about a shearer named Old Turnip, who had wanted to get out of shearing one day. Shearers didn't shear wet sheep, because it was thought to be dangerous for both men and animals. So Old Turnip, wanting a day off from work, had told the grazier that the sheep were wet, thinking that the man would let him get out of it. But the grazier, being a crafty person, had said, "All right, Turnip, but you still have to shear the lambs, because they're smaller and they dry quicker than grown sheep." But Old Turnip, being even craftier, had said, "No sir. Lambs don't dry faster. They're so little they're farther away from the sun!"

"I'm going to be a shearer when I'm older," Beth declared now, thinking she might faint from the excitement of it all.

"You can't be a shearer, little miss," Stinky said with a laugh.

"Why not?"

"Because sheilas can't be shearers, that's why not. You'll learn cooking and sewing and things like that."

Beth thrust out her chin and said, "Oh, I'll learn those things, but I'm going to be a shearer, too, like my daddy was when he was young, and I'm going to muster and ride the boundaries and mend fences, just like he does now."

Stinky laughed and pushed his hat farther back on his head. For October the day was awfully warm. There was still a drought in the Western District, and it looked like it was going to be another hot, dry summer. "And what about your husband then?" he asked with a grin.

"I'm not going to get married."

"What about when you fall in love?"

"I'll never fall in love. I don't like boys. At least, not in that way. I'm going to own Merinda and then I can do whatever I want."

Stinky's eyebrows rose. "You're going to own Merinda, are you? And who says so?"

"I say so. It's going to be mine someday."

"I don't think so, missy. The property's going to go to your brother, Adam."

Beth stared up at him. "Why?"

"Because he's a boy, that's why. Boys do all the inheriting. Girls don't inherit anything."

"I don't believe you."

"Well," he said, patting her on the head, "you'll see, someday. And by then you won't mind getting married instead of shearing sheep!"

As Stinky Lazarus walked away, bowlegged and stoop-shouldered from years of shearing, Beth felt the wonderful happiness of the morning give way to disappointment. It wasn't fair! She was always being told she couldn't do things that she wanted to do. Like working in the pens at the Annual Agricultural Show. Only boys and men got to do that. Girls and women cooked food and served meals.

Beth knew Adam wasn't interested in Merinda; at least, not in the way she was. He was more interested in his schoolbooks, which were full of pictures of fossils and insects. It was Beth who sometimes rode out with her father when there was work to be done around the station, like during the drought when it had been so hot and dry that the grass was poor and they had had to go "feeding out" to the sheep, and Beth had ridden in the wagon and watched the men distribute grain and hay to hungry sheep. She went out with her father when he set rock salt in the troughs by the river; she helped him oversee the sinking of new bore holes; she watched as fences were mended; she listened to the men's talk of the drought and how far they were going to have to drove the sheep for water; and she sang along when Stinky Lazarus plucked his banjo and the men sang, "We camped at Lazy Harry's on the road to Gundagai . . ."

"I *am* going to be a shearer," she said quietly, leaving the woolshed with Button. She walked across the noisy yard, and headed down the path toward the river. She avoided the new house, which stood fresh and empty and almost ready to be lived in, and wandered among the ghost gums and poplars, tossing pebbles or trailing a stick in the dirt. When Button suddenly stopped and let out a long, low growl, Beth looked through the trees. She heard something moving toward her. "What is it, Button?" she said.

He raised his nose and sniffed the air. In the next instant, he was wagging his tail.

"Oh, hello," Beth said, when she saw Ezekiel emerge through the trees. The old tracker was a familiar sight around the homesteads these days; the drought had caused many itinerant men, both white and black, to stay close to the river. A swag camp had sprouted up a few miles upstream, a collection of tents and huts belonging to men who hired themselves out during shearing season as day laborers. And several miles downstream, a similar camp was home to Aborigines like Ezekiel, men who normally wandered a wide range, but whose movements had been curtailed because of the water shortage.

"You go walkabout today, little girl?" he said.

She kicked a stone and watched it roll away. "They won't let me be a shearer."

"Whitefella got strange ideas," the old man said, as he sat down on a boulder and reached into the pocket of pants that were too large for him. "Now, blackfella, he let the women work. Men sit in the shade, women do all the work."

Beth gave him a cautious look, and when she saw his grin, she smiled. "What do you have there, Ezekiel?" she said, when he drew something out of his pocket.

"I take Mr. MacGregor and other whitefella into the mountains. They go hunting wallaby. Plenty of food. Ezekiel take more than he can eat." He held it out to her, and Beth's eyes widened. "Oh my," she said. "It's chocolate. Thank you very much, Ezekiel. Would it be all right if I gave some to Button?"

"You give him," the old man said, patting Button on the head. "This good dog. Some dogs, not so good. But this dog—" He stopped.

While Beth carefully broke off a small piece of chocolate and gave it to Button, Ezekiel's eyes narrowed; he searched the woods behind her.

"Here you are," she said, handing the rest back to him. "It's awfully good, thank you."

He looked at the outstretched arm, the bright smile. Then he looked past her again, at the shadows that had pooled at the base of the trees. He closed his eyes, and felt something he had felt once before, years ago, when he had met the girl's mother, in this same spot. When he opened his eyes again, he saw that it was still there, the shadow of a dog, lurking behind her.

"What's wrong, Ezekiel?" Beth said when he didn't take the chocolate from her.

Ezekiel looked back over his shoulder, and thought of the pair of dingoes he had seen a few days ago, not too many miles from this spot, a male and a female, their ribs sticking out from starvation. Not the tame dingoes found in the Aborigine camp, but wild ones. Dangerous ones.

He frowned. He had to think. Since the white men came, everything had changed—the songlines, the Dreaming Sites. It was hard to go walkabout now, too many signs had vanished. The grove of gum trees, where the Emu Ancestor had sat on his nest, was gone. How could blackfella keep the world created if he couldn't go walkabout?

And so Ezekiel, and others like him, had simply thought: This is the end of the world, the end of the Dreaming.

But now, as he looked at this little girl, and recalled her mother, to whom the Kangaroo Ancestor had spoken, another thought began to occur to the old man. For months he had watched the new house go up by the river and become part of these woods; he saw new paths laid; new trees brought in. And he hadn't known what to make of it. But now he began to wonder: Instead of this being the end of the Dreaming, mightn't it simply be the beginning of a new Dreaming? And now that the thought was fully formed in his mind, he looked around the countryside again with new eyes, and all of a sudden he saw new songlines, new Dreaming Sites, belonging to a new people.

And here was this little girl, at the beginning of it all, just as the Ancestors had once been at the beginning; and he wondered, therefore, if that made her an Ancestor, too.

Ezekiel wore the same kinds of clothes the mission people had given to him long ago, when his family had been broken up—basically, a shirt and trousers. But underneath these foreign clothes he still wore what he would have been wearing if the white men had never come—a hairstring belt around his waist, and a small possum-skin pouch in which he carried his treasured possessions. In the old days, men carried sharpened stones in such a bag, as well as string, a spearhead, sometimes a lump of beeswax, a hook for fishing, and flint for making fire. But today the men carried matches and tobacco, a small knife, shoelaces, and, if they were lucky, a few coins.

The old man now reached under his shirt and dipped his hand into the pouch concealed there. Then he held his hand out to Beth, saying, "This is for you."

She looked at the curious object lying on his palm. It took her a moment before she realized it was an animal's tooth. "Golly," she said. "What *is* it?"

"Tooth from dingo," he said. "Very old, very powerful magic. I give it to you."

"It's for me?" she said. "But why?"

He didn't want to frighten her by telling her the truth—that she was in danger and needed protection. So he said, "Good-luck piece," with a smile. "Little girl of Merinda always nice to old Ezekiel. Now I give you a present. This will keep you safe and happy."

"Golly," she said again, taking it from him. "Thank you, Ezekiel!"

"Keep it with you all the time," he said. "Very strong magic."

An Aboriginal song suddenly came into Sarah's mind:

> "I climb the high rock,
> I look down,
> I look down,
> And I see the rain falling, falling, falling,
> Falling on my darling."

How strange, she said to herself as she drove the buggy through the tawny countryside, I haven't thought of that song in years. Old Dee-reeree taught it to me when I was little. Why should it suddenly come back now? Sarah had been remembering a lot of things lately: the way Old Deereeree had taught her to make a stringybark basket; a girl named Becky, who had been her best friend at the mission; secret rituals in the woods nearby. The memories were returning because of the questions Philip occasionally asked, usually beginning with, "How do your people do this . . . ?" And Sarah realized how nice it was to think of such things again.

She had gone into Cameron Town this morning to make some purchases: embroidery thread for Alice, baking soda for Mrs. Jackson, pencils for Adam—and to collect the mail as well. There were two letters for Joanna: one from Mr. Robertson and the Karra Karra Mission, and one from England. There were also letters for Alice.

Sarah thought about Philip's wife, so quiet and unobtrusive, baffled, as Alice herself had said, by this frontier life. She seemed to spend a lot of time writing to the many friends and relatives she had in England. She wouldn't be seen or heard from for hours, and then she would emerge from the bedroom with a packet of letters to be mailed. She would receive postcards and photographs and newspaper articles from her family, and she would spend hours carefully pasting them in her scrapbook. It was apparent to everyone that Alice McNeal was terribly homesick. Which was why it had not really come as a surprise last night at dinner when Philip had announced that, now the house was almost finished, he and Alice and Daniel would be leaving for England as soon as possible.

Sarah had known that the moment of his departure must come, but to hear him actually speak of it, to make it real and final, had distressed her. But she also knew that it was best that he was leaving, because what had somehow been born between them, but which both refused to acknowledge, should not have been given life in the first place. Sarah had taken care over the past five months not to allow herself to be alone with Philip. Her feelings for him were growing, intensifying; and she sensed the same feelings in him, which made things worse. It was a dangerous situation.

She had tried to analyze the love she felt for him, had asked herself many times, Why Philip? Sarah was not without admirers. There was Half-Caste Eddie, a lively, intelligent and good-looking station hand who was clearly infatuated with her. And then there was the young Aborigine who worked at Thompson's Store in Cameron Town, who always lingered around Sarah's buggy when she made purchases there. There was even a white man who was interested in her—Arnie Ross, one of the town solicitors, who had seen Sarah at a town picnic and had sent notes to Merinda asking if he could call on her.

But Sarah was interested only in Philip McNeal—more than interested. She was desperately in love. And she wanted to know why. He was attractive, but so was Arnie Ross. Philip was witty and smart and laughed a lot; so did Eddie. He was sensitive and kind; the young man at Thompson's was sensitive and kind. What was it about Philip, then, that made him so very special?

Perhaps it was the way he reminded her of her Aboriginal half. He would refer to it, he seemed to want to bring it out of her—seemed fascinated by it, in fact. If she let him bring that hidden part out of her, she wondered, what would happen to the white part? She couldn't be two people; she could only be one or the other. And yet, after seven years of living like a white woman, emulating Joanna, confining her body in corsets and shoes, and keeping the Aboriginal part of herself private and secret, now the white half seemed to be succumbing to that other, suppressed self. The sudden memories of her past were proof of it. And further proof was that when these remembrances did occur, Sarah welcomed them, they pleased her. Perhaps that was one of the reasons why she loved Philip.

And so now she wondered, as she rode through the morning sunshine, if she were to marry a man like Philip, to marry Philip himself, in fact, would she be allowed to be an Aborigine again?

She recalled how she had watched him a few nights ago, when he had been unaware of being watched. She had been down near the river where, hidden among trees, as she had once been hidden nearly eight years ago, she had watched him in the music room of the new house, running his hands over the carpentry, inspecting the paint, stooping to check the baseboards. Moonlight had slanted into the room, making Philip look as if he were composed of angles. He was tall and slim, with sharp shoulders and hips, and he moved with fluid grace.

She had wanted then to go to him and say good-by. She had wanted to say good-by to him in a passionate and permanent way, with her body and her breath. She had wanted to leave an imprint on him so that he would never forget her, as he had never forgotten Pollen on the Wind. But the wildness that lurked forever within her still alarmed her, she felt that she must always keep it in check. And so she had said good-by to him silently, with the few words she remembered of her own language: *Winjee khwaba.*

As she drove the wagon down the country road, she looked up to see a wedge-tailed eagle come skimming out of the sky toward her. It swooped low, then was up and off again in a bronze flash. She turned her face to the wind. In the distance she could make out the dark remains of a burned-out farmhouse surrounded by charred fields. And then she saw—

Philip, sitting in a meadow, drawing on a sketch pad, his horse tethered nearby.

She brought the buggy to a halt and observed him. She thought of how he had spent late nights poring over the house plans with Hugh and Joanna, proposing a change here, an addition there. Philip had overseen every beam going up, every nail driven in. When he had spotted a flaw no one else seemed able to see, he had ordered it torn out and done over again. He had walked over the construction site with the plans rolled under his arm, inspecting, measuring, checking and rechecking. And when an extra pair of hands had been needed—to raise a wall, to mix cement—Philip had joined the work crew.

The new house at Merinda was a unique house, Sarah thought; Philip had brought daring innovations to his creation. Although very large, it was built on one level, under one roof, the only grazier's house in the district like it. Philip had incorporated the kitchen into the plan instead of sticking it at the end of a long causeway, as was the usual custom. There was a bricked-in laundry copper on the back veranda, with taps for running water, a highly unusual feature. And the house was the first in the district to be lit by gaslight.

The design was beautiful, with a handsome hipped roof and a deep veranda that encircled the house, and tasteful iron lacework on the veranda posts. Visitors had come from all over the district to take a look at this house that Sarah often thought of as having been shaped by spiritual forces. Frank Downs had written about it in the *Times*, with an accompanying illustration drawn by his new wife, showing the Merinda homestead sitting grandly but harmoniously in its setting of eucalypts and native shrubs and grasses.

And Sarah thought now: Only Philip could have done that.

He looked up suddenly. A hot wind blew across the plain, causing the pages of his sketch pad to flutter. He was a hundred feet away from her, and yet Sarah felt something come from him; it rode the hot currents and swirled around her like an embrace—Philip's desire for her. And she wondered, as she waved to him, if he felt the same thing from her, reaching out for him.

He walked up, rather slowly, she thought, as if uncertain perhaps, or giving himself time to think of the right thing to say, because she suddenly realized what it was they both wanted to say, yet knew they could not, had no right, to say it.

"Hello, Sarah. I've been sketching the big house at Tillarrara," he said, holding the pad up to her. "It's a perfect example of Australian architecture. See the concave galvanized roof and the buttressed posts, the rusticated stone dressing. Judging by the use of bluestone and weatherboard, the Georgian influence and the carved bargeboards, I would place the time it was built at around 1840."

"It was built in 1841," Sarah said, handing the sketch pad back to him.

"I didn't expect to see you here," he said.

"I went into town," she said, "for the mail." Sarah recalled how, that morning, she had almost insisted that Joanna stay home and take care of Daniel, who had a bad cold, saying that she didn't mind driving into town for the mail, telling herself at the same time that since she knew Philip had said he was going to be taking a look at Tillarrara, she would avoid going that way, and take the main road instead. And then she thought of how, when she had left Cameron Town and approached the crossroads, she had convinced herself that this way was better because it was shorter, and that she most likely wouldn't run into Philip anyway. But she saw now the deliberateness of her actions, that she had very much intended for this encounter to take place.

"I'm glad you're here," he said. "I was hoping we could have a chance to talk before I leave."

And then Sarah realized, as she looked back over the past months, that Philip must have been avoiding her, just as she had been avoiding him.

He helped her down and they walked for a while.

They walked in silence, feeling their mutual love and desire weave an invisible shell around them, separating them from the rest of the world.

Philip marveled at how calm Sarah always made him feel; how his restless spirit seemed to grow tranquil when she was near him. He thought about the house he had just finished building—the crowning achievement, he thought, of his career as an architect, inspired in part, he suspected, by his feelings for Sarah.

The Westbrook house by the river, in its woodland setting, looked exactly as he had intended—as if it had grown there, naturally, among the eucalyptus trees and kangaroo grass. The sheer simplicity of its hipped roof and deep veranda demonstrated perfection in style. Philip thought of what a joy it had been to design a house that was harmonious with its environment, to work with local timber and native stone, to create lines and angles that complemented nature rather than usurped it, to embody in its design the very spirit of the land it shared. It was almost as if, Philip realized, he had built the house the way the Aborigines would have done, if they had built houses—as an extension of the world around them, not at odds with it. Philip had felt restricted in the many cities in which he had designed and erected houses; his creative instincts had always been suppressed. Which was one of the reasons, he supposed, why he was always on the move, always searching. And he wondered now if he had in fact found what he was looking for after all, here in this remote corner of the world, in Westbrook's house, in the inspiration that the silent girl walking at his side had brought him. Never before had his work brought him such deep satisfaction.

Suddenly a gust of wind came up, and Sarah's bonnet flew off. She cried out, Philip made a grab for it, but the wind carried it away.

"I'll get it!" he said.

Sarah joined him in the chase, and they ran through the brittle grass, darting at the hat as it caught on a bush, only to have it snatched away by the wind again. Soon the loss of the hat ceased to matter; they reveled in the freedom of the wind and the sun and the open plains.

The hat finally came to rest on a low shrub, and Philip stopped suddenly to catch it, causing Sarah to run into him. They stumbled and caught each other, laughing, and then they were standing still, Philip holding Sarah against him, the hat forgotten.

His arms tightened around her. "Sarah," he said.

She buried her face in his neck. They felt the sweet sun on their bodies. He kissed her hair, her cheek. He held her so tightly she could hardly breathe. And then his mouth was on hers.

Sarah held onto him for another moment, then she drew away. He was beautiful, and he was what she wanted, but Sarah knew that Philip must travel on; and that he was married.

"Sarah," he said. "I want to talk to you, I want to explain. There is so much I want to say to you."

"Please don't," she said, tears shimmering in her eyes. "It isn't fair to Alice."

"We can't help what has happened between us, Sarah. Do you deny that it's there? That we love each other?"

"No," she said. "I won't deny it. But we haven't the right."

"Doesn't our love for each other give us some rights?"

"But it isn't just us, Philip. There are other people involved. Your wife—"

"I don't want to talk about Alice. This has nothing to do with her. It isn't her fault. I loved her when I married her, and I still love her, but in a way far different from the way I love you. I was attracted to her quietness, to the way she was rooted to home and family. I thought she would help me to settle down and put an end to my restlessness and wandering. Instead, she has become a victim of it. You were right, I build homes for other people, but none for myself. That isn't fair to her and Daniel. And that's why I'm taking her back to where she belongs, where she'll be happy.

"Walk with me a little while, Sarah. I don't want to leave like this; I want to tell you about myself, and I want to know everything there is to know about you. There is such a wonderful secretiveness in you that I want to explore. When I go away, you'll go with me, in here," he touched his chest. "Let's just talk, Sarah. Just for a little while, and then we'll each do what we have to do."

"Will you come back, Philip?" she said. "Will I ever see you again?"

He wanted to take her into his arms once more, but he let the space between them remain. "To someone else, Sarah, I would say: If it's in my stars, I'll come back. But to you, Sarah, I would say: If my songline brings me back here, then we will see each other again."

———————

Joanna quickly opened the letter from the Karra Karra Mission. It contained a smaller envelope bearing English stamps, and a note from Robertson explaining that he had heard from his friend in London, the expert on Tironian shorthand, and that "enclosed herewith is the code which he sent to me. He has offered, Mrs. Westbrook, that, should you have any difficulty in translating your grandfather's notes, he would be glad to undertake the task for you."

She opened the envelope and withdrew the contents—a letter from Giles Stafford explaining the Tironian code, with a small notebook filled with symbols and their alphabetical, phonetic and whole-word equivalents.

Joanna stared in wonder. This was it. The key at last. Now she would be able to find out if the answers she had been seeking were indeed contained in her grandfather's writings.

But, eager as she was to get started on the translation, Joanna first opened the other letter, from a Mrs. Elsie Dobson, who lived, according to the return address on the envelope, in the same village as Aunt Millicent.

Joanna unfolded pale-blue stationery that still gave off a faintly lavender scent despite the many miles it had traveled, and read the small, precise handwriting. Mrs. Elsie Dobson introduced herself as a widow who lived across the village green from Millicent Barnes, whom she had known for nearly sixty years. She went on to say that it was her sad duty to report that Millicent had died, at the age of seventy, peacefully and in her sleep.

"As I was her closest friend," Mrs. Dobson had written, "and had taken care of her in her final days, when she was bedridden with stroke, she left everything to me, which was very little. When I was finally able to bring myself to go through her things, I came across your letters, Mrs. Westbrook. Millicent had saved them all.

"I am sorry that Millicent caused you and your mother such unhappiness by not answering your queries. She was not a spiteful woman, but she had never quite gotten over 'losing' her sister, as she used to put it, to John Makepeace. And then later, when Emily married Petronius Drury and left England with him to live in India, Millicent felt once again abandoned. But now that she has passed on, I don't think it would do any harm if I were to try to answer your questions.

"Millicent and her sister, though twins, were very unalike. Naomi, your grandmother, was so bright, so optimistic, and she was the stronger of the two. Millicent always seemed to me to be like the other side of the plate, dark, gloomy, and frankly, rather weak. The two were inseparable as girls, but when Naomi fell in love with John Makepeace and sailed off with him, Millicent said she would never forgive her."

Joanna realized that the room was growing dark. The sun had set, and beyond the closed door of her bedroom, she could hear Mrs. Jackson giving orders to Peony to set the table. The French doors to the veranda stood open, and Joanna could catch, on the warm evening wind, sounds from the yard as the shearers packed up their gear for the day.

Lighting a lamp, Joanna resumed reading Mrs. Dobson's letter. "I remember the day your mother was brought here, Mrs. Westbrook," she had written. "I was paying a call on Millicent that day. It would have been forty-five years ago, because I remember that I had brought little Raymond, my first child, to show Millicent. We were having tea, as I recall, and we were interrupted by a knock at the door, and we saw a most extraordinary man standing there. A sea captain, and he had a child with him, and he told us the most fantastic tale."

As she read Mrs. Dobson's words, Joanna pictured the odyssey her mother must have taken—from Australia to Singapore, and from there to Southampton, spending months on the open seas in the company of seamen. The child who had appeared on Millicent's doorstep had been nearly five years old, her skin burnt brown, her hair hanging past her waist, and wearing a pea jacket over her dress, and a sailor's hat. The only thing she had with her, aside from the presents sailors had bought for her, was a leather satchel containing some papers, and a curious toy made of fur, which she had named Rupert.

"The captain couldn't tell us how Emily had gotten to the Australian coast, where the first ship picked her up," Mrs. Dobson wrote. "The letter that came with her didn't explain much. It had been hastily written, we could see that."

Mrs. Dobson described the note as saying merely, "This is Emily

Makepeace, the daughter of John and Naomi Makepeace, and niece of Millicent Barnes. Please deliver her to Crofter's Cottage, Bury St. Edmund's, England. You will be rewarded."

Joanna tried to imagine the circumstances that had surrounded that desperate flight from Australia. Who had taken the little girl to the coast and delivered her to the authorities? Was it someone called Reena? Why hadn't she accompanied Emily to England herself, or had she been unable to do so? And what, then, had happened to John and Naomi?

She returned to the letter: "Millicent was beside herself. After all, this was Naomi's child, and Millicent adored Naomi. But what became of Naomi herself we never did find out. I suspect she died a long time ago, somewhere in Australia.

"As your mother was growing up," Mrs. Dobson continued, "she sometimes wondered why she had no memory of her parents. Whenever she asked Millicent about it, Millicent told her that she had had a fever when she was six, which of course was untrue. What had been the true cause of your mother's memory loss neither Millicent nor I could deduce, but it must have been something terrible, because I remember poor little Emily suffering from nightmares. She had an almost paralyzing fear of dogs and snakes. She had seen something unspeakable, I always thought, when she was in Australia. Millicent would not pursue it. I think she was too afraid of what she might find out.

"I'm sorry, Mrs. Westbrook," Elsie Dobson concluded, "but that is all I can tell you. I have either forgotten the rest, for my memory is not what it used to be, or there simply isn't anything else. Your mother eventually grew into a lovely young lady, and we were all sorry when she went off to India, for we feared we would never see her again. I must tell you this, Mrs. Westbrook: When I heard of her death, I was on the one hand shocked, and yet, strangely, on the other hand I was not. There seemed to me always to have been something about your mother that made me think she was fated for tragedy. I don't know why I should have thought this, but I can only credit it to something I must have heard once, long ago, but have now forgotten."

The letter was signed, "Very sincerely yours, E. Dobson."

Joanna stared at the last line. The one woman who might have filled in so many important blanks was now dead, and the only other person, it seemed, who had had anything to do with Emily as a child was failing in memory.

She read the letter again to see if she had missed anything, and she paused over two phrases: "She had seen something unspeakable . . . when she was in Australia," and ". . . something about your mother that made me think she was fated for tragedy."

So even back then, Joanna thought, among people who had had no idea of Emily's background or circumstances, people who could not have had any knowledge of poison-songs or Aboriginal curses—even Mrs. Dobson of Bury St. Edmund's had sensed the doom that had followed Emily around the world.

As she was about to fold the letter back into its envelope, Joanna realized there was one more page. When she brought it into the light, she saw that Mrs. Dobson had added a postscript.

"After rereading this letter, Mrs. Westbrook, I realized that I left out two things which you might wish to know. You enquired after information concerning where in Australia the Makepeaces had traveled. I do not know that, but if it will help, I do recall that in 1830 they sailed on a ship called the *Beowulf*. Of this I am certain, because I have always been intrigued by the Beowulf saga and thought the name of their ship rather ominous. The other thing you might want to know is that about a year after Emily had been living with Millicent, the strange little fur toy that she had had with her, when she arrived with the sea captain, suffered some sort of damage—I don't recall what. But because the child was hysterical, Millicent restored it by cleaning it and reinforcing its seams. In doing so, she discovered that there was something hidden inside the toy's stuffing, and when she brought it out, she discovered that it was a fairly large, rather dazzling gemstone, which we later learned was an opal. I don't know if this is of any use to you, Mrs. Westbrook, and I don't know what became of the opal. But I do hope that, in my small way, I have been of some help to you."

Joanna stared at the last lines. The opal! Hidden inside Rupert!

She went to her jewelry box, and brought out the stone. As she looked into its fiery red-and-green depths she wondered how it was associated with Karra Karra. Had her grandfather perhaps taken it from there? Was this the cause of her mother's sudden compulsion to go back, because something "else" was there, the "other legacy" which Joanna had never been able to ascertain? Had John Makepeace found an opal mine? Was that what the deed was to? Had Joanna in fact inherited more than just land, but something valuable beyond imagining?

She held the opal in her hand, felt its warmth, felt that it had an energy of its own, and wondered, What are you? Where did you come from? What is your purpose? Are your powers for good or for evil?

It was time now to address her grandfather's notes. Surely the answers were here, in these cryptic papers.

She laid the codebook on the desk before her, then placed the first page of her grandfather's notes next to it, and a blank sheet of paper opposite it. She looked at the first symbol, then located it in Giles Stafford's book.

And then, with one last glance at the opal, which flashed fire in the lamplight even though it lay motionless, she began.

CHAPTER 23

Joanna was puzzled. She had been translating her grandfather's notes for a month now, and so far her efforts had turned up little more than a dry, rather uninspired account of John Makepeace's trek through the wilderness, following the clan of an Aboriginal chief named Djoogal. Joanna had found no clues as to where in Australia they had lived, or the name of the tribe they were a part of. Nor was there, as far as she could determine, anything in the notes that indicated what might have been the cause of her mother's fears. No mention of dogs, other than the dingoes the clan kept as pets, and little mention of snakes beyond the fact that the Aborigines revered the Rainbow Serpent.

The only significant thing she had learned was that the clan's totem was the Kangaroo Ancestor.

She sat back in her chair and rolled her head from side to side, releasing the tension that had been building up in her neck. Every afternoon, when Joanna sat down at her desk with the Tironian code-book and her grandfather's papers, she expected to find something astonishing, a breakthrough. And every evening she was disappointed.

It was late. With the exception of Hugh, who had ridden out to the lambing paddocks to watch over the new lambs, everyone was asleep; the house was still and quiet. Now that the McNeals were gone—they had left two weeks ago—and shearing was over, life at Merinda had settled into a quiet routine. Soon, once the final interior painting was done, Joanna and her family would move into the new house by the river, and say a final good-by to this lovely old place.

But, tonight, peaceful and still as it was, Joanna felt tense and anxious. It was almost as if the very absence of anything startling in the notes was in itself some kind of omen. And then there was this disturbing business about dingoes coming close to Merinda. "Ezekiel said he's seen them just a few miles upriver," Hugh had told Joanna that morning. "I'm not going to take any chances. I've put extra men on dingo watch. Make sure Adam and Beth stay away from the river. The drought is making the dogs bold."

Dingoes, Joanna thought, as she watched insects flit around the chimney of her oil lamp. Wild dogs. They haunted her nights in dreams, and now they plagued her days. And Ezekiel—had he warned the other homesteads of the proximity of the dingoes, or was his warning particularly for Merinda, for her, for Beth? Beth had shown Joanna the dingo tooth the old tracker had given her. Joanna wondered if it had some significance, or if it was simply a good-luck piece, as Ezekiel had said.

She looked at the few pages that remained to be translated; she prayed the key to the mystery lay in them.

Joanna picked up her pen and resumed decoding the odd shorthand. "I am worried about Naomi," John Makepeace had written nearly five decades ago, "I fear that she is starting to change. Something strange seems to be happening to her."

Joanna was startled. After reading pages and pages of description about how the men of Djoogal's clan lived—how the men hunted, how they made spears and boomerangs, the men's rituals, their stories—the tone of John's notes suddenly changed. Joanna read more quickly now.

"Naomi is flourishing in this place, while my own self-doubts have been growing. What is worse, she says that I am leaving out half of the Aboriginal population, half the culture, in my observations, because I am leaving out the women.

"Naomi claims that Aboriginal women hold equal status with their men. I admit to their importance in the clan, for I have observed this myself. Despite the occasional hunted kangaroo brought into camp by the men, it is the women who do all the daily foraging for food. Aboriginal women also have control over their own reproduction and sexuality. The marriage ritual is a simple one—a woman declares a man to be her husband. Nor are the women restricted to childbearing and child rearing, while the men do all the important work. When vital decisions are made concerning the clan as a whole, men and women make them together, equally. When the clan follows the songlines, the men sometimes lead while the women follow, or the women sometimes lead while the men follow. However, I am speaking of the process of daily living. About the women's religious or spiritual importance to the clan, I see nothing significant, because as far as I can determine, it is the men who hold this power.

"Naomi argues this point," Makepeace had added, "saying that women do have rituals of their own, which are forbidden to men. Female rituals do exist, she says, and in many ways they are more important and more powerful than men's in that they involve fertility and giving birth—the life-force that is vital to the continued existence of the clan. For example, she has told me that the rituals revolving around a girl's first menstruation are far more complex, and demand much more secrecy and many more taboos, than the rites governing a boy's coming of age. Naomi says that the Aborigines do not seem to understand that it is the man's seed that starts a child in the womb. Instead, they believe in 'ghost-babies'—a woman walks over a certain spot, and a baby-spirit wanting to be born will jump up inside her. For this reason, the power and magic of procreation are the sole purview of women, and it is these mysteries that are the essence of their secret rites.

"Naomi says that the reason European observers acknowledge only the men's rituals, thus drawing the erroneous conclusion that only Aboriginal men possess spirituality, is because those observers are men like myself, and so are allowed to hear only of men's matters. The result is a one-sided reporting of this culture.

"I suppose I should consider it an advantage having a wife with me who has made friends among the women of the clan, and who has been privileged to witness and even take part in some of their secret rituals. But she is not fully cooperative with me. Naomi will not divulge the nature of these rites; she claims she has promised the women that she would keep the secrets. But she assures me that they are ceremonies of the most solemn and pious nature. She adds that, when the women go off together alone, whether it is to forage for food or to perform a religious rite, it is a time of intense female kinship and spirituality.

"She might be right, I do not know. But it annoys me," he concluded, "that she keeps these secrets from me. I have told her that it is only for the sake of scientific inquiry and intellectual knowledge that I wish to be allowed to observe one of these secret rites."

Joanna stopped writing. She felt the night shift around her; the silent house seemed to stir and move and sigh. She reread the sentence she had just written. She suddenly sensed what was coming.

———

Beth awoke suddenly. It was dark. She was lying in bed, listening to the silence of the house. She wondered what had wakened her. And then she realized: Button wasn't on the bed. She had become so used to his heavy weight against her as she slept that his absence had wakened her. She sat up and looked around. Button was standing at the door to the veranda, scratching at it. "Do you want to go out, Button?" Beth said.

He was an old dog, and sometimes needed to visit the bushes during the night, so she unlatched the French door and opened it a few inches, expecting the blind sheepdog to spend a few minutes on the grass, and then come back in. But, to Beth's surprise, he rushed through the door, flew across the veranda, growling, and disappeared into the darkness.

"Button!" she said. "Come back here!" And she went after him.

———

The night was so silent that the only sound was that of Joanna's pen scratching across the paper. She had memorized the code by now; she hardly needed to consult the codebook. She wrote rapidly.

"The clans have been gathering for days here at Karra Karra," John Makepeace had written. "I had been told that the tribe was large, but I had no idea how large. Clans and families have been following the songlines for weeks, coming from north and south, east and west, to this place which I have learned is their holiest place. Karra Karra—the Mountain of Life. There are hundreds of people here, with still more coming. They light their fires, and they sing and dance. Relatives who have not seen one another in years celebrate reunions; old friendships are rekindled; bargains are made; marriages are arranged; and Djoogal sits in judgment on crimes that have been waiting a year to be judged— usually having to do with taboos being broken. It is a massive, noisy, lively gathering, and I marvel that Naomi and I, and little Emily, are the first white people ever to witness such a display.

"And tomorrow Naomi is going to take part in the most sacred, most secret of rituals. She will tell me very little about it, only that it involves mothers and daughters. Naomi has become increasingly secretive lately. She has been going off with the women, collecting the clay and paint and dyes with which they will paint their bodies. They have been instructing her in the secret songs, in the mysteries of the ritual, the taboos she must observe. She cannot sleep with me tonight, she told me. She must be pure for the ritual."

Joanna noticed that her grandfather's tone intensified here; she could sense his envy, his fretfulness at being left out.

"I have assured Naomi that I would not repeat whatever she told me, that she can be sure the secrets are safe with me, but she refuses to answer my questions about the ritual. I have reminded her that she is my wife, and therefore she must tell me what she is doing. Also, that she can trust me. I don't understand what has happened to her. Living with the natives has done something to her. She obeys me less and less; the authority I once had over her, when we were first married, is gone. Perhaps I made a mistake bringing her here. There is a streak of independence in Naomi now that I find most unattractive and unlady-like. I remind her that I came out here to observe these people and to record their ways. Therefore, it is her duty to report to me everything she learns. My sweet Naomi, once so compliant, so obedient, has now become as headstrong as the women with whom she goes out food-gathering. And Emily, only three years and six months old, is begin-ning to exhibit the same willful tendencies.

"What, I wonder, will the women be doing tomorrow?"

———

Beth walked through the woods, calling Button's name. He had never run off like this before.

When she saw him ahead of her in a clearing, she called out, "Button! You naughty boy. Look, you've made me come out in my nightgown."

She stopped still. Something else was there in the bushes, close by. She strained her eyes to see. It stepped out of the shadows. She saw the squarish body, the erect, triangular ears, the short bushy tail and cream-colored fur. It was the wild, wolf-like dog the Aborigines called dingo.

There were two of them, male and female.

Button, old and blind and going by smell and instincts, placed him-self between the girl and the dingoes. "It's all right," Beth said in a small voice. But she was suddenly very frightened.

———

The night closed in around Joanna. She no longer wrote down her translation, but read her grandfather's notes by the light of the lamp.

"Naomi left our camp early this morning, before dawn, leaving Emily in Reena's care. She has gone to a secret place with the rest of

the women, to prepare for today's ritual. The tribe is in a frenzy of
activity—hunting, preparing food for the great feast tonight, dancing
and singing. The men, strangely, seem to show no resentment at being
left out of this vital rite. There are no priests here, no cardinals or
bishops. The ones who will be performing this most important of the
tribe's ceremonies are ordinary women, with no special status or titles,
simply women who have daughters. Men are forbidden to have any
knowledge of how the ritual is performed. No man has ever witnessed
it. What do the women do, inside that mountain? Having witnessed the
savage circumcision rites that are performed on boys, I can only imagine what unspeakable practices they submit their innocent daughters to,
many of whom have only just left girlhood.

"I came to this place searching for the Second Eden. This new
science that is polluting our age—with its so-called proof that God did
not create and design the world—a science that is supposedly refuting
the Holy Word of God by calling the Bible a book of 'myths and
stories'—the new science in itself demands to be refuted. I came here
to prove that the Holy Bible can withstand empirical analysis, that the
Truth can be proven by the same intellectual examination that sets out
to prove it false.

"I came seeking the Second Eden, a place where God created another Original Pair, who, this time, did not eat of the forbidden Fruit
of Knowledge and so were allowed to continue to live in Innocence.
The Aborigines know not the shame of nakedness, nor of fornication.
They are exactly as God created them.

"But now I see that I was wrong. This is no Second Eden; it is one
of God's mistakes. Here, the Serpent is worshiped, and the knowledge
of the One God is absent. These savages revere stones and rivers and
animals. But of the Lord they are ignorant.

"God forgive me, I was wrong, I was wrong. And now my sweet
Naomi is about to be drawn into their sins, and away from the path of
righteousness. And I fear she will be punished for it. If only we could
go back to England. But how can we? The money is gone. The last of
it went to pay for the land for our farm.

"I must know what the women are going to do inside the mountain,
and protect Naomi from it."

———

Beth watched in fear as the male dingo began to walk toward her.
Button growled. He backed up against Beth, pushing her away from
the dingo. The female moved to the right, circling around. Button
swung his head and growled at her. The fur rose up on his neck. His
lips jerked over white fangs.

The dingoes moved closer.

Button growled, showed his teeth, and pushed Beth back with his hindquarters. She tried to think what to do. She reached for a stick and threw it at the wild dogs.

It landed between them, unheeded.

"Go away!" she said. "Scat!"

Gold eyes remained fixed on her. She saw mouths shiny with saliva.

When the male suddenly made a leap, Button flew up and sank his teeth into the animal. Beth screamed, and then the female turned on Button, seizing him by the tail. Beth stared in horror as the dingoes attacked the sheepdog from opposite sides. She saw fur fly, she heard terrible sounds, there was blood, Button's ear was ripped off, an obscene gash suddenly appeared in his flank. The dingoes fought the way they did when bringing down a kangaroo—one at the head, one at the tail, driving their prey mad with frenzy, reducing him to helplessness.

"Stop it!" Beth cried. She picked up another stick and swung it hard. "Get away!" she screamed, hitting one of them.

The male let go of Button and turned on Beth. He lunged at her; but she fell back and his jaws snapped on air. Button went for him, heedless of the other dingo savaging his flank.

Beth dropped the stick and stared as Button, now covered with blood, his flesh torn, his fur matted, fought blindly, unable even to see his attackers.

Clapping her hands over her ears, Beth spun around and ran.

———

Joanna sat for a long time, staring at the last words her grandfather had written. She was filled with a sense of premonition, a dark and heavy foreboding, as she thought of a young Englishman, cut off from the world and laws he knew, trying to maintain his grip on reality, believing that he was losing his wife to mysteries that were beyond his understanding. Was that what had brought the poison-song upon her family—the breaking of a very sacred taboo, a man spying upon women's ritual? Or was there something more? What had three-year-old Emily witnessed? What terrible maelstrom had swept her up when her father's crime was discovered?

And what, indeed, had the women done inside the mountain?

Joanna looked up. She realized that the woods were suddenly alive with the screeches and cries of birds that were normally silent at night. She heard the frantic *faark* of crows, and even the high-pitched laugh of a kookaburra. Something was wrong. Something was happening.

And then she thought: Beth!

———

Beth plunged through the trees, pushing branches and brush out of her way. She flew through the woods, her heart pounding. She realized that the homestead was in the other direction, behind her—but the dingoes were behind her, too. She ran blindly, in mindless terror, into the darkness, tears burning her eyes. She fell, picked herself up and raced deeper into the woods.

Finally she stopped, her chest heaving, and listened. There were no sounds now, just silence. Even the birds had stopped their noise.

And then she heard the soft patter of paws running steadily through the growth.

She felt them drawing closer and began to run again. She heard the snapping of jaws, she collided with a tree, and scrambled up without thinking. Hungry eyes glinted up at her.

Something sharp clamped down on her ankle, and she screamed.

———

Joanna flew out of the house and down the path toward the woods. She ran into Sarah and Adam, who were in their nightclothes, trying to determine from which direction they had heard the scream.

And then they heard another scream. "That way!" Adam said.

They ran down the path and plunged into the trees.

They came upon something in the grass. It was one of Beth's slippers. Joanna looked around in the darkness. "Beth?" she called. "Where are you?"

She turned in a circle, and then her eyes fell upon something that made her freeze. She ran to it. "My God," she said. It was Button's savaged, bloody body.

"Beth!" Sarah and Adam called.

"*Beth!*" Joanna cried.

They heard another scream, then another.

Beth, screaming . . .

Joanna flew through the trees, knocking branches out of her way, unaware of the stones and twigs that cut her legs and face. "Oh God," she sobbed. "Please. No." Sarah and Adam ran behind Joanna, dashing headlong into the darkness, flailing their arms, their nightclothes snagging on bushes. "Beth!" they called out. "We're coming!"

And then suddenly they heard another sound—a strange whining, a whistle through the air. They heard a sharp *thwack* and a yelp.

"Over there!" Adam said. "It came from over there!"

In the next instant they saw a dingo flash by, torn and bloody, and immediately behind it ran Ezekiel, his arm lifted, holding a boomerang.

They found Beth halfway up a tree, screaming hysterically, her legs covered in blood, a dead dingo lying at her feet, one of Ezekiel's boomerangs lodged in its neck.

"Mama!" Beth screamed. "Mama, Mama!"

Joanna reached for her daughter and held the desperately crying child in her arms. Joanna turned and ran back through the trees, Sarah and Adam following, with Beth screaming for Button, her legs streaming with blood.

———————————◆———————————

The kitchen door crashed open and Hugh came running in. "Joanna!" he shouted.

He found her in the hallway, just closing the door to Beth's room. "How is she?" he said.

"She'll be all right," Joanna said, wearily pushing a strand of hair away from her face. "She suffered some bad bites, but they'll heal. Thank God her legs weren't broken. But she's had a terrible shock, Hugh. I don't know how she'll get over it."

"Ezekiel came and told me. I got here as quickly as I could. Should I go in and say something to her?"

"I've given her something to make her sleep. Hugh, Ezekiel saved Beth's life. I believe he may have been watching her. That dingo tooth he gave her . . . it's as if he knew . . ."

Now Beth is marked, too, Joanna thought. The legacy of Naomi Makepeace has been laid upon her. Joanna thought of her mother, dead at forty from an illness that did not really exist. Did such a fate loom over Joanna and Beth, and possibly Beth's daughters? Would it never end?

"We have to find it, Hugh," she said. "Whatever is causing this, we have to find it and stop it. Before it's too late."

PART FOUR

1885–1886

CHAPTER 24

It was night in the outback, with a hint of distant ridges behind the silhouettes of the eucalypts; and the stars were in the thousands, scattered across the sky. A fire burned golden in the heart of the darkness—a campfire, around which weary men slouched, their faces fixed patiently upon the steaming billycan. The silence was as vast as the sky and the horizon, which one could not see, but the outback spoke all the same, in the lonesome wail of a dingo, the crackle and hiss of the fire. Suddenly, a voice came through the darkness, strong and loud:

> "They were cruel days and trying days,
>   And hard old days as well,
> When we shouldered our swags and set out on the track
>   That we knew would take us to Hell."

The voice went on to tell of the Great Outback, with its dancing kangaroo and stalking blackfella, of huts built of sapling and bark, and of a girl named Ruth, buried somewhere in the Never Never, "with a babe asleep in her arms." While the voice spoke, the men around the campfire went about their tasks, laying out bedrolls, unsaddling horses, lighting pipes and cigarettes, the silence and the stars hanging over them, "cold and honest and clean." They moved like shadows "enacting a familiar play, tired and stooped, broken and broke, but trusting the night to bring the promise of a better day." At the end of it, the fire went out, and the men settled down, "under blankets that were old friends," and the voice said at last, "But for all our pains, and all our curses, we would have those hard old days again."

The stage went dark and the theater seemed for a moment to hang in time and space. Then the lights came on, and a whole new scene dazzled the eyes. Now it was daytime and there was a hut with smoke spiraling out of its chimney, and fields of golden wheat that seemed to stretch for miles beneath a blue sky. A woman toiled in the yard beside the hut, and the voice said, "How wondrous to think all those rough bush tasks one woman's hands could do . . ."

When the ballad of "Hannah's Heart" ended, the homely scene was replaced by a flat red vista out of which the Ayers Rock monolith rose fiery in the sunset, and the unseen narrator recited the famous "The Dreaming: For Joanna."

The scenery continued to change onstage as each poem was read, creating a parade of landscapes and seascapes drawn from the face of Australia. There were few people in the audience who did not see something familiar in at least one of them, for although many who occupied the seats of the Melbourne Music Hall on this night two weeks before Christmas were city dwellers, they were reminded nonetheless of childhoods in the bush, or tales told by their elders. The ballads spoke to their hearts of a way of life that was vanishing, scenes remembered from times long past were being recreated on stage in rich detail, from the twinkling of the desert stars and the laugh of the kookaburra to the crack of the bullocky's whip and the sound of the wind blowing through the mulga.

Joanna and Hugh watched the show from box seats. With them were twelve-year-old Beth, wearing a long white lace dress and flowers in her hair, Sarah, in an emerald evening gown, and eighteen-year-old Adam in black tie. Sharing the theater box with them were Frank and Ivy Downs. They had come to Melbourne to attend the opening night performance of *Living Tales from the Outback*, an imaginative staging of the collection of ballads that had been published three years ago in a book titled *Poems by an Outback Son*. Hugh had invited Ivy Downs to paint color illustrations to accompany them, depicting the pine trees of the Snowy Mountains, "where the dark green gum trees touch the bright blue bowl of the sky," and the desert so large and clear that "a man can shade his eyes and see into tomorrow." The book had been such a success in the Australian colonies that Hugh's most popular ballad, "The Swagman," had been set to music. It was sung in schoolrooms and pubs, on the track and around campfires. The collection was being widely received all over the British Empire, and people everywhere were reading about the convict whose "sins were written before he was born," and the "shearing tracks that were shortcuts to death."

A barn dance was the next setting, with shearers and sheilas flying around the stage in a lively polka while the audience clapped their hands in time to the music and the narrator could barely be heard reciting "Cut Out Time." And when the stage became the scene of a rodeo, and the audience laughed and howled at the antics of "Lachlan Pete" as he chased after a spirited calf, the noise was so deafening that one could hardly hear the speaker. Frank leaned forward and said to Hugh, "You're giving them a show for their money all right, Hugh. There's nothing ruder and noisier on the face of the earth than a satisfied Australian audience!"

The stage went dark for the last time—on the silhouette of an old drover on his horse—and the voice, fading away, said, "For this is the life, the droving life," and the curtain came down.

Joanna held her breath. The theater was silent. And then the applause began, slowly at first, but rising as the newly installed electric chandeliers came brilliantly to life overhead. A man came out onto the stage, recognized by everyone as Richard Hawthorne, one of Melbourne's best-loved actors. It had been his familiar baritone they had heard reading the ballads. He bowed twice, then held his hand up toward Hugh, and all eyes turned to the theater box. One by one people stood, until the entire audience was on its feet, and their applause filled the music hall.

"They're treating you like some sort of hero, Hugh," Frank Downs said later, as they waited on the sidewalk in front of the theater for their carriage. "By God, but you've shown the world that we're not just a bunch of backwater colonists."

"Give credit to your wife, too, Frank. It was her paintings that inspired the show."

"You both deserve credit," Joanna said. The sidewalk was crowded with ladies in evening gowns and gentlemen in opera capes and top hats. It had been a special night for Melburnians. For once, the entertainment they had come to see was not the work of a Frenchman or an Italian or even an Englishman—a reality that, being such a young race of people, they had become resigned to—but rather it was the product of their own Australian-born Hugh Westbrook. Many came up to him to offer congratulations.

"Stupendous show, Hugh," John Reed said, pumping Hugh's arm. "By heavens but it brought tears to my eyes. I may have been born in England, but at heart I'm Australian."

"Why don't you and Maude join us for dinner, John? We've reserved a private dining room at the hotel."

"Thanks for the invitation, Hugh, but we've made some other arrangements, I'm afraid."

Pauline, who had come to the performance with Judd, held out her hand and said, "It was a beautiful evening, Hugh. You should feel proud."

"Are you coming back to the hotel with us?" he asked. "We're going to open as many bottles of champagne as the King George has to offer."

"I'm a little tired, and I have to catch the early train back to Kilmarnock." She took Joanna's hand and said, "My congratulations to you both."

Ian Hamilton was there as well, and Angus McCloud with young Declan. They praised Hugh for the show and for his ballads, which, Harold Ormsby declared, were certain to be treasured by Australians for decades to come.

Louisa Hamilton and her family came by, and while they congratulated Hugh, Joanna noticed that Athena, Louisa's seventeen-year-old daughter, gave Adam a significant look. "Hello, Adam," she said, smiling at him from beneath sable lashes. Joanna had discovered that, at almost nineteen, Adam seemed to have no end of young ladies hoping to catch his eye. He was a handsome youth, whose scholarly ways and seriousness seemed, for some reason, to awaken passion in young female hearts.

Joanna was proud of her adopted son. Next month, shortly after his nineteenth birthday, Adam was going to start attending classes at the University of Sydney, which had awarded him a scholarship for having graduated from Cameron Town Secondary at the top of his class. The university was a school Adam had been passionately striving to enter, since it possessed, as he put it, "a top-notch science department that's recently added a professor of vertebrate paleontology, a man who's a member of the Royal Society in London, and who actually worked with Charles Darwin!"

It was Adam's dream to follow in Darwin's footsteps, to join the Royal Society and explore the world as a naturalist, discovering new species, unearthing dinosaur bones, contributing to the growing evidence for the case for evolution. Joanna saw in the energetic way he carried himself, the enthusiasm with which he spoke, the eagerness shining in his eyes, that he was going to succeed.

"It was a good show, Joanna," Hugh said, "wasn't it?"

She felt the warmth of his hand through her glove and, looking into his smile, recalled the young man she had met fifteen years ago. Hugh at forty-five was just as handsome tonight, she thought, as he had been then, and the years had etched wisdom into his face, as well as a quiet dignity. "Yes, Hugh," she said. "It was a very good show."

He looked at her for a moment, then he said, "Are you all right, Joanna?"

She was not surprised by his question. Even though she hadn't told him about her recent trouble, and had in fact tried to keep it from him, she knew that Hugh would sense it. "Yes," she said. "I'm all right."

"Are you up to having dinner in the dining room? We could go straight to our room, if you prefer."

"I wouldn't think of it. I'm not going to let one of my ridiculous headaches spoil your special night."

But it was more than just a headache this time, more than just the aftermath of another nightmare—Joanna had been troubled by a strange feeling all day, the kind of premonition one gets before a storm. And today was not the first time she had experienced it; she had been unsettled by a vague but growing sense of dread for weeks now.

"Oh, Father!" Beth said, breaking away from a small knot of friends, "everyone is *so* impressed! You're positively marvelous!"

As Joanna watched father and daughter embrace, she looked back to the day when the strange feeling of premonition had begun. It had been two months ago, when Beth had begun to menstruate. While Joanna had been explaining to her daughter the changes that were taking place in her body, and what to expect and how to take care of herself, she had experienced the first vague tremors of dread. She had thought: Beth's no longer a little girl; she's growing up.

That same night, troubled by sleeplessness, Joanna had gone through her mother's diary to see if there was anything significant recorded around the time when Joanna herself had begun to menstruate, when she, too, had just turned twelve. But there was nothing—no mention of the event, and no hint that Lady Emily had felt disquieted afterward.

The future frightened Joanna. She knew that her mother's nightmares had started when Joanna was six, just as her own had started when Beth turned six. Was it simply the power of suggestion, she wondered, or was there something more? Joanna had nearly been attacked by a rabid dog when she was seventeen; did such a fate, therefore, await Beth five years from now? Was the attack by the two dingoes some kind of foreshadowing?

What should she do; what shouldn't she do? She couldn't keep Beth with her always; she didn't want to be a grasping mother, but she wanted to protect her daughter from whatever forces seemed to be following the descendants of Naomi Makepeace. Joanna knew about Beth's violent fear of dogs. It upset her to look at her lively, happy daughter and think of the hard, dark kernel of fear that lay within her. Joanna knew about it because Lady Emily, too, had carried this same fear; and because Joanna herself carried one. It was almost as if a real disease—something like hemophilia—was being passed from generation to generation, an inescapable curse of heredity that caused each generation to feel sympathy for the next, knowing what lay in store for it.

Joanna had purposely avoided telling Beth the details of her past, and about Lady Emily. She had hoped to end the cycle by simply not allowing Beth's imagination to re-create it, as Joanna was certain her own had. Beth had not read her grandmother's diary, she did not know about Lady Emily's afflictions or her strange, unexplained death. And Beth thought Joanna's search for Karra Karra was simply to locate a plot of land.

And yet Joanna, feeling chilled in the hot December night, knew that, despite her careful precautions, the symptoms were starting to manifest themselves in Beth. And this time she could not so easily lay their cause to imagination.

Joanna would never forget the weeks and months that had followed the night the dingoes had attacked Beth. She had taken her daughter to a seaside resort, where she had fought to restore her child, physically and emotionally, through the curative powers of sunlight, ocean air and love. And Beth had indeed recovered. The wounds had healed; the hysteria and grief had become just a memory. But when they had returned to Merinda, Joanna had seen that the cure was not complete— Beth was terrified of even the friendliest sheepdog.

"Oh Mother," Beth said, as they waited for their carriage in front of the theater, "I should think you would want to faint from the excitement of it all! Everyone just *adores* Father! He's positively famous!"

"All right you two," Frank said when the carriages finally arrived, "let's not waste any time. I'm starving!"

The King George Hotel was on fashionable Elizabeth Street, not far, in fact, from the flat where Ivy Dearborn had once lived. As the Downses rode past the familiar green door with its polished brass knocker, Ivy felt Frank's hand squeeze hers, and knew the intimate joy of a shared memory.

In the second carriage, Sarah and Adam talked excitedly about the show, and Beth again told Hugh how proud she was of him. But Joanna stared out the window, trying to will away the headache that had plagued her for days.

The carriage went past a steamship office, and Joanna was reminded of how she and Hugh had searched for the *Beowulf*, the ship her grandparents had taken to Australia. They had finally learned that it had gone down at sea with all hands in 1868. It had been a privately owned vessel; the captain/owner had drowned with his crew, and there were no surviving records or logs or passenger lists. Joanna had written to the Retired Seaman's Association and to various related organizations, hoping to find someone who might have sailed on the *Beowulf* with her grandparents. The few responses had come to nothing.

She felt a hand on her arm, and turned to see Sarah giving her a questioning look.

Joanna smiled to reassure her, then she said, "Which scene did you like best, Sarah?"

"I loved them all," Sarah replied. She was thinking of Philip, how she wished he could have been here, and how he would have enjoyed the show.

She recalled the day in the country when she and Philip had accidentally met, and kissed. They had walked and talked for hours afterward, not touching, sharing themselves in the spiritual rather than the physical sense. He had told her about his boyhood in America, his family, how the War Between the States had changed their lives. And she had told him about growing up at the mission, being neither Aborigine nor white. They had talked about architecture and healing, about music and sheep, Navahos and the Rainbow Serpent. And finally, as he had promised, they had gone their separate ways, he back to Tillarrara to finish his sketch, she to Merinda to deliver mail to his wife.

In the five years since his departure, Sarah had heard from him occasionally—a Christmas card from Germany; a letter from Zanzibar, where he was studying Muslim architecture; a picture postcard from Paris. He had also sent her a copy of his book, with a painting of Merinda on the cover. His communications were always brief and light; he never spoke of love, or of their chance encounter. And Sarah read loneliness in his letters; she sensed his restless, searching spirit. The last letter she received from him had arrived six months ago—"I have asked Alice for a divorce. We are simply too different, and my way of life makes her unhappy. But she will not grant the divorce."

Finally the carriages arrived at the brightly lit King George Hotel. The Westbrooks and the Downses crossed the hotel lobby and entered the small foyer of the restaurant, where maids in uniform took the ladies' coats and the gentlemen's hats. As Frank was saying, "I hope the roast beef is rare tonight," a flustered maître d' came in. "Oh dear," he said. "Mr. Westbrook! There appears to have been some sort of mix-up. We have your party down for tomorrow night. I'm afraid the private room you requested for tonight has already been given to someone else."

"Now see here—" Frank began.

But Hugh said, "It's all right. Mistakes happen. Do you have any tables available?"

"I believe so, Mr. Westbrook. Let me take a look." He disappeared behind the curtain that separated the restaurant from the foyer.

"Imbecile," said Frank.

"What will we do," Joanna said, "if he doesn't have a table?"

Adam said, "We can try Callahan's."

"But the tables there are so small, Adam," said Beth.

"We could try Moffat's Crystal Café," Hugh said.

"It's awfully late," Joanna said. "Doesn't the café close early?"

Frank said, "I don't like the pudding at Moffat's."

The maître d' returned. "We can accommodate your party, Mr. Westbrook," he said. "If you will follow me, please."

As Hugh emerged on the other side of the curtain, the familiar faces did not at first register with him, nor the fact that everyone in the restaurant was standing up. But when they all shouted, "Surprise!" he suddenly realized that the gentleman standing near the orchestra was Ian Hamilton, and that the two men holding up champagne glasses were McCloud and his son, and that the woman with the outrageous osprey feathers in her hair was Maude Reed. And as the musicians struck up the familiar melody of "The Swagman," Hugh saw other faces well known to him—Camerons and McClintocks and more Hamiltons—until he realized with a shock that nearly the entire Western District must be represented here tonight.

When Pauline came up to him and gave him a glass of champagne, he said, "I thought you had an early train to catch," and everyone laughed.

"Surprised?" Joanna said.

"Stunned. Did you know about this?"

"We all did. Come on, there's a special table just for us."

"Good God, the governor is here."

Everyone sang "The Swagman" as Hugh and Joanna passed among the tables, and when the song came to an end, the applause lasted so long that Hugh had to hold up his hands for silence. "Thank you one and all, my dear old friends," he said. "I don't know what to say."

"Never thought I'd see the day!" Ian Hamilton said.

Beth came and stood next to Hugh and said, "Father, we have a surprise for you." She turned to the governor of Victoria, and smiled.

The governor, a man appointed by the British Crown to oversee the management of colonial affairs in Victoria, spoke with great energy and ceremony, addressing the nearly one hundred people in the room as if he were giving a speech before Parliament. "You have given your people," he said to Hugh, "their own culture, separate from the heritage they brought with them from Mother England to these distant shores. And to show her appreciation . . ." He produced a sheet of vellum, tied with ribbon and sealed with wax. "It is my great honor to have been chosen to present to you, Hugh Westbrook, this special commendation from the Queen-Empress herself, Victoria."

Hugh accepted the letter and began to read it out loud, but he had to stop when his voice caught. So Joanna took the letter and read it for the guests. "Through your poetry," the Queen had written, "we are brought to a closer understanding of our subjects so far away, with whom we have had sadly little contact, but who are beloved to us all the same." Joanna paused, then looked at the gathered guests, and said, "It is signed Victoria, R.I."

There was a moment of silence, then Angus McCloud said, "Give us a few words, Hugh."

Hugh cleared his throat. "I'm afraid I wasn't prepared to make speeches tonight. Needless to say, I am deeply honored that Her Majesty has read my poems. I'm reminded of an old friend of mine who has since passed away, by the name of Bill Lovell. He wasn't well educated, he could barely read or write, but he was given to speaking his mind whenever he felt like it. One day, a grazier he worked for said, 'If you don't mend your ways, Lovell, I'll throw you off my station.' And my friend said, 'You can't treat me like that. I'm a British object.'"

When the laughter died down, Hugh said, "My dear old friends. What my poems are about is who we are and where we are." He looked at Joanna and said, "While we might have come from far away, and while we must never forget that Britain is our mother, we know that Australia is our home. And our future."

The applause rolled out through the closed doors of the dining room.

It could be heard in the hotel lobby, where a man in a mariner's uniform was walking toward the desk. He was a weathered-looking gentleman with a neatly clipped white beard and faded blue eyes; he wore a dark-blue naval jacket with brass buttons and an officer's cap; he carried a duffel bag.

"Pardon me," he said to the clerk at the desk. "I understand you have a Mr. and Mrs. Westbrook staying here?"

The clerk said, "One moment, please," and he consulted the registration book. "Ah yes, here we are. But I'm afraid they aren't in. I have their keys, which means they are out of the hotel."

"Do you know when they'll be back?"

"I couldn't say. You're welcome to leave a message, if you like."

The stranger thought a moment. "I don't know that it would do any good," he murmured. "I've got a boat to catch. And where I'm going, there's no forwarding address, no way they can reach me."

Laughter came from the dining room, and the sea captain turned and looked across the lobby. "It sounds like someone's having a good time," he said with a smile.

"Must be a private party," the clerk said. "I was told that the dining room is closed tonight. Would you like me to tell Mr. and Mrs. Westbrook that you were inquiring after them?"

"It wouldn't do any good. They don't know me, and I don't know them." He thought for a moment. Then he shrugged and said, "It's not important. Good night to you then." He picked up his duffel bag and went out into the dark.

While the orchestra played waltzes and polkas and the lively "Click Go the Shears," and waiters passed through the crowd with trays of champagne and hors d'oeuvres, Joanna moved among the guests, thanking them for coming, and accepting praise for her husband's success.

Pauline came up to her and said, "Congratulations, Joanna. The party is a great success."

"Pauline, I'm so glad you and Judd could come."

Pauline looked past Joanna and saw Beth join Adam and her father for a group photograph. She felt a pang of envy—not for Hugh, whom she had long since accepted as having lost, but for Joanna's daughter. Beth was the kind of girl Pauline would have liked to have, smart and pretty and full of life. She was the kind of girl who had occupied Pauline's fantasies when she had still dreamed of having a child before she had finally come to accept the fact that she was one of those women for whom motherhood was never meant to be.

"I'm sorry Colin isn't here," Joanna said.

Pauline looked at her, thinking of the first time she had seen Joanna, fifteen years ago, at the party she had given for Adam. It was strange, Pauline thought, how one's perceptions changed over the years. "Thank you," she said, knowing that Joanna and the whole district knew why Colin had left Australia three months ago.

Kilmarnock was in trouble. When world wool prices fell, Colin's tenant farms failed, and because of an economic depression that struck the colonies, evictions were not succeeded by immediate purchase. MacGregor had then tried turning to Melbourne real estate in an effort to recoup his losses, buying large tracts of new houses in the suburbs with the expectation of selling them at massive profits. But because of the depression, the high flow of immigration of the previous ten years slowed to a trickle, bringing Victoria's building boom to an end. The sound of hammers and chisels that had been a constant feature of Melbourne for as long as anyone could remember finally ceased. Supply exceeded demand; there were no buyers for the new houses, and the auctioneer's raucous cry as he sold the property of bankrupt estates became the new trademark of Melbourne. Colin had been left holding empty houses, and most of his tenant farms and runs continued to stand unoccupied and unworked. It was common knowledge around the district that he had been forced to mortgage Kilmarnock to pay his debts.

Pauline would never forget the look on his face when he had walked into the parlor, stood before her and said, "I'm ruined, Pauline. The bank is going to call in my note. They're going to take Kilmarnock from me."

Pauline had suspected this would happen for some time, but the starkness of Colin's tone, the desparate way in which he had said it, had made it suddenly terrifyingly real. She knew what would happen if the bank took Kilmarnock: It would divide the property into smaller properties and sell them individually. And so when Colin had added that he was going to go to Scotland to see if he could raise the money to save the station, Pauline had known the truth: He was never coming back.

It amazed her now to realize that she, who had always striven for victory and conquest, who thrived on competition and lived for the trophy, had failed, at both motherhood and marriage.

Ivy joined them then, a glass of champagne in one hand and a caviar canapé in the other. "Joanna!" she said. "What a wonderful party!" Ivy was fifty-two, with gray in her red hair, and wearing a long black gown that suited her handsomely. Aside from the illustrations she had done for *Poems by an Outback Son,* Ivy was famous for her paintings. "Mrs. Downs," the Cameron Town *Gazette* had reported, "has somehow managed to capture on her remarkable canvases the blue of Australian skies and the clear transparency of Australian distances. For once, in the opinion of this art critic, we have scenes of the local countryside that are not done up to look like the English countryside, by giving us quaint hedges and low-lying mists. Mrs. Downs gives us in her landscapes the hot north wind and the dry grass and the strong light. She is aware that she lives in Australia, not in Surrey, and that is a very refreshing notion!"

"Yes, it is a wonderful party," Pauline said to Ivy. Her prejudice against Frank's wife was a thing of the past. Disappointments in her own life had led her over the years to temper her judgment of others. She had come to appreciate Ivy as the woman who made Frank happy, and to admire her for being a woman who had, by her own determination, made her way in the world, and in a profession dominated by men.

"Have you heard from Colin?" Ivy asked.

"He said he would write to me when he got to Scotland. I am expecting a letter any day now."

"I wish he would let Frank help him, Pauline," Ivy said.

"I tried to talk to him about it, Ivy, but Colin is stubborn. He said that he will not encumber himself with any more debts, and you know how he feels about accepting charity, even if it is from family. He wouldn't accept a single shilling from Frank."

"Pauline," Ivy said, "is there really a chance you will lose Kilmarnock?"

"Yes."

There was the sudden pop of the photographer's flash powder across the room, as he took a picture of Hugh with the governor. "You know that you always have a home at Lismore, Pauline," Ivy said.

"Thank you, Ivy, but everything will be all right. Colin will find a way. He will come back with the money."

The three fell silent while the noise and music of the party continued to go on around them.

Pauline thought of her last hours with Colin, as they had stood together at the dock, waiting for him to go aboard his ship. Colin had not wanted her to come and see him off, but she had insisted. They had not spoken on the train, and had said little on the dock. Then they had embraced politely, and he had walked up the gangway. Pauline had realized in that moment that she could recall only their good memories—their early days as husband and wife, their nights of passion, their days of competition. She thought of Colin's hard body and the way he had excited her. She thought of the beautiful parties they had presided over at Kilmarnock, and how elegant their life together had been. And she wondered if, had she tried harder, been less selfish, could she have made their marriage a successful one? Was it in fact she, and not he, who was responsible for the lack of love between them? She would never know now. Pauline was on her own at long last, destined after all to become "Poor Pauline."

"I have to warn you, Joanna," Ivy said, "my husband and a few others are trying to talk Hugh into standing for Parliament."

The three women looked over at the group of men gathered at the bar, and they heard Frank saying, "I'm telling you, when we're federated we're going to need men like Hugh Westbrook in government."

And while Hugh protested, his friends all heartily agreed with Frank.

The Melbourne *Times* was now the largest newspaper in Victoria and, like his paper, Frank had also expanded. Since his marriage to Ivy, the watch chain that stretched across his vest had become twice the length of a normal man's. His hair had grown away from his forehead so far that it was only when one looked at Frank from the rear that one noticed he was becoming gray.

"I read your latest editorial on Aborigines, Frank," Ian Hamilton said. "I must say, you said some pretty harsh things about the Aborigines' Rights Protection Board. Recommending that it be abolished and that the blacks be allowed to run their own reservations!"

"Good God, Ian," Frank said as he drank his gin and tonic, and handed the empty glass back to the bartender. "The board is made up of idiots. It was their idea that government reservations should be for full-bloods only, which of course meant driving the half-castes into the cities, where they were supposed to support themselves somehow. You've seen the disastrous consequences. They can't function in our society. They need to be taken care of."

"I don't see why," Hamilton said.

"For God's sake, man, don't you think we owe them something? The latest census has revealed that there are only eight hundred Aborigines left in Victoria, and none of them are full-bloods."

"That's my point exactly, Frank. Everyone knows the Aborigines are going to be extinct in about twenty years. There aren't any left in Tasmania, are there? So why worry about a problem that isn't going to be around much longer?"

"That's asinine thinking," Frank said as he stepped aside for Judd MacGregor, who said, "Pardon me," and reached past the men for a glass of champagne.

Judd turned away from the bar as the conversation moved from Aborigines to sheep, and looked around the crowded room. His gaze settled on young Beth Westbrook, who was laughing at something Declan McCloud had just said. Declan was twelve years old, like Beth, and both were preparing to enter Tongarra School next month.

As Judd watched the Westbrook girl, he recalled again the meeting that had taken place in the office of the school superintendent, Miles Carpenter, between Hugh and Joanna Westbrook, and Carpenter and his assistant, Scott McIntyre. Judd had also been present. Whenever an issue came up involving whether or not to admit a questionable pupil, it was school policy to have the teaching staff represented. Judd had volunteered.

Miles Carpenter had been astonished at first that Westbrook should even consider enrolling his daughter in a boys' academy. "Extraordinary," he had said. "A girl wanting to be a grazier." But he had invited Hugh and his wife to present their case.

"Beth is bright and eager to learn," Westbrook had said, "and she already knows a lot about animals and the running of a sheep station. She would be an asset to your school."

"But Tongarra is a residential school, Mr. Westbrook," Carpenter had explained. "The boys live here, in dormitories. Surely you see the tremendous difficulties in admitting a girl."

But Westbrook had confounded them by saying, "Merinda is only a few miles from here. Beth could be a day pupil, coming in the morning and leaving at night."

Carpenter had tried another tack: "Our course of study involves hard labor. We not only have classroom work, Mr. Westbrook, we also teach saddlery, horseshoeing, husbandry. Cattle branding, even. Labor most unsuitable for a young lady."

When Westbrook had said, "My daughter can learn any of those things," Mr. Carpenter and Mr. McIntyre seemed at a loss for further argument. Seeing that their position was weakening, Judd had spoken up. "Mr. Westbrook is missing the most important point here," he had said. "The impropriety of what he is proposing. The girl would be a distraction to the boys. Her presence would be an impediment to learning. As a teacher, I would certainly find it difficult to have her in my classroom."

It was then that Westbrook had taken out his checkbook and said, "I'm prepared to make a generous gift to the school."

"It has nothing to do with money, Mr. Westbrook," Judd had said quickly, seeing the look that had passed between Carpenter and McIntyre. "It is a question of honor. We have to think of the school's reputation. Tongarra is known for its excellence and high standards. We are one of the finest learning institutions in the colonies. If we were to admit a girl, our prestige would be damaged, not to mention how badly it would discredit our diploma."

But, in the end, Judd had lost. Hugh Westbrook had presented the school with a large endowment, and Beth, with certain restrictions, was to attend in the new term.

When Judd had continued to protest, Carpenter had said, "Mr. MacGregor, don't you think you are taking this rather personally? After all, the girl will be the school's responsibility. You won't be blamed if there is trouble as a result of her being here."

But Judd *had* to take it personally, because it was an issue that related directly to him. The girl's presence at the school was going to weaken the integrity of the very argument that had caused the final break between him and his father.

As he moved away from the bar and the talk of sheep and politics, tasting his champagne, nodding vaguely at Miss Minerva Hamilton, who smiled at him, Judd thought of a conversation that had taken place two months earlier. It had occurred in his father's study at Kilmarnock, and, although Judd hadn't known it at the time, it was to be the last time they would ever speak to each other.

He watched Louisa Hamilton, across the crowded room, suddenly collapse into a chair, with her daughters rushing to her side. Judd heard his own voice, back in September, saying, "You can't seriously mean you're leaving now, Father. Shearing is just two weeks away!"

But Colin had been packing his valise like a man obsessed. Judd had seen the tight set of his father's shoulders, the furious snap of his wrist as papers and documents went into the valise. And Judd had recognized the nature of those papers: original deeds to the old castle and its holdings in Scotland, some of which dated as far back as the reign of Henry VIII. There were also Colin's birth certificate, his passport and a steamship ticket. "This is what a man can count on, Judd," MacGregor had said. "Fortunes might come and go, land can be bought and lost, friends can turn into enemies, and sons into strangers, but one truth remains—the legacy of one's birthright. The bank might take my sheep station from me, and my creditors might strip me of all my possessions, but one thing they cannot take away from me is my bloodline. I am the laird of Kilmarnock."

That was when Judd had known that his father was going to run away and never come back. And so that was when, in a desperate bid to keep him there, Judd had said things he now regretted, angry things, meant to hurt, intended to spark the core of aggression he knew always lurked in his father, hoping that he could waken Colin's fury and make him want to stay and fight for Kilmarnock—this Kilmarnock, not the old, crumbled one that belonged to the ghosts, but this one that stood in the sunshine and that was new and held so much promise.

"You've never appreciated your heritage," Colin had said with much bitterness, and Judd had said, "I am Australian, Father. This is my bloodline, here, in this place."

"As a teacher."

"Yes, as a teacher! I'm not a lord, I don't want to be a lord."

"Then go and live at your agricultural school. Throw away everything I've built for you, everything I've worked to give you. Go and be a common teacher teaching common boys in a common school. Christ, Judd, it's not as though you've been appointed to Oxford, is it? It's a bloody backwater farming school in a bloody backwater colony."

Father and son had regarded each other across the hated study, and the words that had been said on both sides could not be called back; they hung in the air like echoes, and the misery and bitterness and regret that each man felt caused him to hold his tongue and keep him from saying, "I'm sorry."

Judd's fingers curled tightly around his champagne glass as he watched the women cluster around Louisa Hamilton, who was fanning herself furiously. He saw Joanna Westbrook hold a bottle of smelling salts under Louisa's nose. He saw the Hamilton daughters, all spoiled young women, flutter around their mother helplessly. And then he saw how his stepmother stood out in the crowd.

Pauline was thirty-nine, but Judd thought that she was still beautiful. He knew there was pain inside that slender, graceful body; he knew what Colin's desertion was doing to her. And it occurred to him that perhaps he had been unfair to Pauline all these years, distancing himself from her, thinking that she was just like Colin, simply because she had married him. As Judd had watched her these past three months bear up under the strain of Colin's departure, he had found himself starting to admire her.

Judd drained his champagne and went back to the bar.

As Joanna sat with Louisa, she searched the room for Beth, and found her standing beneath a portrait of King George, a glass of lemonade seemingly forgotten in her hand. Joanna followed Beth's line of sight and saw that the object of her attention was Judd MacGregor. And the

look on Beth's face brought Joanna's feelings of anxiousness and premonition to the surface again. She realized how her daughter felt about
the handsome young man—Mr. MacGregor was all Beth could talk
about. "I never knew he was so charming, Mother," Beth had said after
the last Annual Graziers' Show, at which Judd had taken a prize for
a stud ram. "I've seen him hundreds of times, but I only just now
realized how wonderful he is. And just think—he's going to be my
instructor at the new school!"

It had reminded Joanna that it wouldn't be very long before Beth was
married; she would go away and live somewhere else. How would
Joanna be able to protect her then?

"Oh dear," Louisa Hamilton said, the center of sudden female attention. "It's must be the hot night, but I really don't feel well."

As Pauline stood to the side and watched Joanna try to help, she saw
Louisa flash her a fearful, familiar look. And that was when Pauline
knew what Louisa's problem really was: She was expecting another
baby. After thirteen years of managing not to get pregnant.

"Louisa," Joanna said, "you really don't look well. Let me find a
place for you to lie down."

Joanna left the dining room and went to the front desk. She waited
a moment while the clerk sorted through some receipts. When he
looked up, she said, "Hello, I'm Mrs. Westbrook. I was wondering if
there was a room where one of our guests can lie down for a few
minutes. She's not well—"

"Mrs. Westbrook?" the clerk said. "Forgive me, but I wasn't told
when I came on duty that the private party in the dining room was
yours. There was a gentleman in here asking about you. I told him that
you and your husband were out."

"A gentleman? Did he give his name?"

"He said you didn't know him, and that he didn't know you. He was
a sailor of some sort—a sea captain, I think."

"A sea captain! And he left no message?"

"He said he had a boat to catch and that where he was going you
wouldn't be able to contact him."

When the clerk saw the distressed look on her face, he said, "I truly
am sorry, Mrs. Westbrook. Had I known that you were just in the
dining room . . ."

"How long ago did he leave?"

"I'd say about ten minutes—"

She hurried across the lobby and through the doors. She went out
onto the sidewalk and looked up and down the street. She saw two men

standing on the corner beneath a lamp. One was a newspaper vendor, the other a sailor shouldering a duffel bag.

When she approached them, she saw that the sailor was an older man, in his seventies, she judged, with white hair and a white clipped beard, his face etched with hundreds of lines. "Pardon me," she said.

They gave her a startled look.

"Were you in the hotel just now, asking after Mrs. Westbrook?"

"I was."

"I'm Joanna Westbrook."

"Pleased to meet you, Mrs. Westbrook!" he said. "I am Captain Harry Fielding."

Joanna shook a hand that felt as hard as wood. "What was it you wanted to speak to me about, Captain Fielding?"

"I've been away," he said. "In Asia, mostly, and I've only just recently gotten back. I usually spend a week catching up on the news I've missed, so it was some time before I saw your notice in the paper. Well, the paper was so old, I didn't really think anything about it. And then I saw an item in today's *Times* about you and your husband being in town for a show, and that you were staying at this hotel. I'm glad we didn't miss each other."

He smiled expectantly.

"Captain Fielding," she said, "please go on."

He reached into his pocket and drew out a newspaper clipping. "You are Mrs. Joanna Westbrook, are you not? The lady who placed this notice in the paper?"

Joanna looked at the ad which she had put in Frank's paper ages ago. "Yes," she said.

"It says you are looking for information concerning the ship *Beowulf*. I served on her when I was a young man, as bosun's mate. I can try to tell you anything you want to know about her."

"I had just about given up hope!" Joanna said. "Captain Fielding, I'm trying to trace two passengers who sailed on the *Beowulf* in 1830. Were you with the ship at that time?"

"Indeed I was. I was twenty years old and setting off to discover the world."

"Would you remember," she said, trying to contain her excitement, "the passengers who were on board? I know it was a long time ago."

"You'll find, Mrs. Westbrook, that when you reach my age, which is considerable, you can't recall what happened last week, but you can remember in exact detail events that occurred years ago. That was my first real commission. I can even tell you what color the captain's eyes were."

"Do you remember a young couple by the name of Makepeace among the passengers? John and Naomi?"

"Makepeace," he said. "Oh yes, the religious chap. The fellow who said he was searching for the Garden of Eden or something. I do remember him and his pretty wife. I remember thinking their name was rather odd." Fielding's eyebrows came together. "Another odd thing, too, now that I think of it. When I stopped there again, a few years later, I heard the strangest tale about them."

"Where was this, Captain Fielding? Do you remember where they got off the ship?"

She held her breath.

"Indeed I do," he said, "because we all thought it an unlikely place for a pair of newlyweds to start their married life together. I can tell you the exact spot, Mrs. Westbrook. Is it very important?"

CHAPTER 25

By the time Judd MacGregor had read the first few paragraphs of the homework assignment, he knew he was going to write "Excellent" at the top of the page. But when he turned the paper over to see which of his pupils had written it and saw the signature of Beth Westbrook, he hesitated. She must be receiving help at home, he thought. No girl could be this good in biology.

"Girls simply do not have the capacity for learning that boys have," Judd had said to Miles Carpenter back in December, when he had been told that Beth Westbrook had been admitted into the school. "I assure you, Mr. Carpenter, that I will not devote a single extra minute to teaching the girl. She will be given the same assignments, the same amount of teaching time as I give to the boys. She will get no special consideration from me. And when she falls behind in her studies, as I'm sure she will, I will recommend her dismissal from the school. That, Mr. Carpenter, I predict will be one week after the school term begins."

But the term had begun four weeks ago, in January, and the West-brook girl had so far kept up with the boys. In fact, Judd realized, she was doing better than many of them. Which led him to believe that someone must be helping her with her schoolwork at home.

Hearing laughter beyond his window, Judd looked out and saw some boys down on the lawn in front of the Academics Building. They were calling after Beth Westbrook, who had just been left at the school gates by her Aborigine governess, Sarah King. Judd watched how stiffly the girl walked as she tried to ignore the taunts. He knew the boys made things difficult for Beth, but he was not going to interfere. If they were picking on another boy, he wouldn't intervene. The instructors at Tongarra rarely involved themselves with the personal problems of their pupils. The student body had formed its own special code of conduct; they enforced it themselves. And one of the rules was that a student fought his—or, in this case, her—own battles, and didn't go running to a teacher.

It made Judd think of his own early days at the school. He had been small for his age, and the other boys had been merciless with him. His father had said to Carpenter, "Don't give Judd any special consideration because of his size. Treat him like the other boys. It'll make a man of him." Judd had withstood the tests and initiations with the stoicism that the unspoken rules of conduct demanded, and he had emerged strong and self-reliant. He had also won the admiration of his tormentors and ended up becoming one of the most popular boys at the school.

A voice carried on the morning breeze: "We don't want girls here!" one of the boys called after Beth. And Judd remembered his father, years ago, saying, "You have to try harder, son. You don't want everyone to think you're a girl, do you?"

Judd looked up at the February sky. It looked as if the autumn rains were going to come early this year. Judd thought about his father, who had been gone for five months now. Judd imagined Colin sitting in his drafty castle among his Celtic relics, and wondered if he was happy, or troubled by even the slightest regret or feeling of shame.

"What's the matter?" one of the boys called after Beth. "Can't you go anywhere without your wog nanny?"

When Judd saw Beth turn around to reply, he closed his window. The only drawback to living on campus, he decided, were distractions such as these.

He missed the peace and quiet of Kilmarnock, but he had found that he couldn't live there. The constant reminders were too painful. Judd's father was still there, in every brick and board of Kilmarnock, in every suit of armor and teacup and dust mote. Judd thought of the letter of apology he had started, asking his father to come home. He would never finish it; it would never be sent.

As Judd returned to reading Beth's paper, he pictured the girl who had appeared in his classroom early one morning in January, not shy and hesitant, but just standing there, as if waiting for something to happen. She had been wearing a long white dress, her hair shining, and Judd had been reminded of times in the past when he had seen Beth Westbrook, at the Annual Graziers' Show or in Cameron Town. She had been a tomboyish girl in braids and a pinafore, running in and out of the exhibits with a group of boys. But the girl who had presented herself at his classroom, before the rest of the pupils had arrived, was not a tomboy. Judd knew from Beth's records that she had turned twelve last September. And he could already see the signs that, over the months, were going to make Beth more and more of a distraction in his class. Perhaps for now the boys might treat her as one of themselves—they certainly picked on her the way another group of boys had once picked on a puny Judd MacGregor—but soon, Judd knew, the boys were going to start looking at her in a different way, and she was going to make it increasingly difficult for them to concentrate on their studies.

As he watched the boys taunt her, Judd decided that she might not be at Tongarra for long. The students were making it very hard for her at the school. They resented her presence, which was understandable, especially since she was doing so well. And Judd knew of one instructor who refused to call on Beth if she raised her hand. One teacher had even talked of resigning out of protest. And some of the parents were protesting. Four boys had been removed from the school when their fathers had learned that a girl was attending. When Judd had confronted Miles Carpenter on the issue, and he had reminded the superintendent of the damage the girl's presence was going to do to the school, Carpenter's reply had come in the form of pounds and shillings. "Westbrook's endowment more than makes up for those lost tuitions, Mr. MacGregor. And we have his promise that the endowment will be renewed each year that his daughter attends this school."

But Judd maintained that it was more a matter of honor than money. Just look, he had pointed out, at the troubles being caused by new legislation in the colonies permitting females to attend institutions of higher learning. Massive protests at the University of Melbourne, because of the recent admission of female students, had caused a cessation of classes that lasted for days. And the teachers who had walked out refused to return. Judd was proud of Tongarra. He hated to think what effect this new lowering of standards was eventually going to have on the school's reputation.

With luck, he decided, the girl would leave on her own accord. And certainly if she ever came running to him to complain about the way the boys were treating her, Judd would ask for her dismissal from the school.

He looked at Beth's paper again, and, deciding that he was spending too much time dwelling upon a minor problem, he wrote the word "Excellent" across the top of the page.

"What's the matter?" a boy named Randolph Carey called out to Beth. "Can't come to school without your wog nanny?"

Beth had had enough. The boys had taunted her all the way from the campus gates, where the Merinda carriage had dropped her off and she had said good-by to Sarah. Beth had ignored their insults and jeers, but this was too much. She turned around and said, "Sarah's not a wog. And she isn't my nanny. She's my friend."

"Everyone knows your mother is a nigger lover," thirteen-year-old Michael Callahan said. "My father says she should go and live with the Abos, if she's so keen on them."

"And your father writes poetry," Randolph said. "What is he, a nancy-boy?"

"A lot of men write poetry!"

At that moment, Beth caught a glint of sunlight. She looked up and saw Judd MacGregor close the window of his second-story room. Had he heard? she wondered.

She decided that he had not, because Beth knew Mr. MacGregor was a gentleman. If he had heard what the boys were saying to her, he would have made them stop.

Beth liked the way Judd MacGregor didn't give her special treatment. He never singled her out, or made fun of her, or treated her as if she might break, like old Mr. Carmichael, who didn't give her hard work or make her stand at attention when he entered the classroom. And if she gave an incorrect answer in class and the boys laughed, Mr. MacGregor never laughed with them, the way Mr. Tyler did. In fact, Mr. MacGregor treated Beth with a kind of indifference that she was certain was a sign of his confidence in her. She suspected that he knew she would rather succeed on her own merits than with special help. And that made her fall all the more desperately in love with him.

Randolph Carey, a tall boy with red hair and freckles, said, "Whyncha go back to England, you bloody pom!"

"I'm not a pom!"

"Your mother is. My father says she's a pommie bi—"

Mr. Edgeware, the Latin professor, appeared at that moment from the Academics Building. The boys fell silent. Then they said, "Good morning, sir," as he hurried by.

"Why don't you leave me alone?" Beth said to her taunters when Edgeware was out of hearing.

"Listen, Westbrook," Randolph Carey said, "if you want us to leave you alone, then you've got to become one of us, you have to join us."

She gave him a wary look. "How do I do that?"

"You gotta pass a test. Anyone who wants to be one of us, has to go through the initiation."

"What sort of initiation?"

"I can't tell you ahead of time. That would make it too easy. But if you don't think you can do it—"

"I can do it," she said.

"All right then. This is what you have to do."

The student body was getting ready to put on its yearly entertainment—an evening of skits, songs and recitals, all written, staged and performed by the pupils without help from the teachers. "There's going to be a rehearsal in the auditorium tomorrow night," Randolph said. "Tell your Abo nanny that you'll be staying for it."

"But my parents know I'm not in the show."

"Tell them you're going to watch the rehearsal. It finishes at nine o'clock. But don't go to the auditorium. Be at the dipping paddock at seven o'clock. You'll get your instructions then. Unless, of course, you're too scared to come."

Beth hesitated. She looked at the boys who surrounded her. She saw the smile playing on Randolph's lips. Then she remembered a snake he had hidden in her desk. "I'll be there," she said.

When Randolph and his friends walked away, Billie Addison said to Beth, "Be careful. Carey's up to something."

But Beth already knew that what was going to happen tomorrow night was going to be some sort of test. The dead snake in her desk today had been only one of a series of pranks that had been played on her—ink on her chair; her desk top glued shut; her lunch stolen—small trials to see if she would run to the teachers or to her parents. But Randolph and his friends had yet to receive any satisfaction.

"If you go," Billie said, "they might do something bad to you."

"Will you help me?"

When Billie hesitated, Beth said, "That's all right. I understand."

"I'm not a coward," Billie said. "It's just that my father says if I get into one more fight, he'll take me out of school and make me work the farm. You should just stay away from the dipping paddock tomorrow night and go home like you always do."

But Beth knew she couldn't walk away from Carey's challenge. She had played with boys all her life, she knew their rituals, the tests they put one another to. And she knew that she would eventually have to face Randolph, or she would never be happy at the school.

"It's something I have to do, Billie. I'll never be accepted if I don't prove myself. But I'll be all right. You'll see."

———————————————

Joanna knocked on the door to Beth's room. "Is something the matter, darling?" she said when Beth let her in. "You hardly touched your dinner."

"I'm all right, Mother," she said. "Just a little tired."

Joanna searched her daughter's face, then she smoothed back Beth's hair. "Is everything all right at school?"

"Oh yes. I'm having a marvelous time at school. And by the time you and Father return, I shall have passed my winter exams with honors!"

Joanna had not wanted to leave Beth at home, but Captain Fielding had advised against taking her with them to Western Australia, saying that it was no place for a young girl. Beth had further assured her parents that she would be all right, that she was grown-up enough to be on her own, and besides, Sarah would be there with her. Hugh and Joanna and Captain Fielding were planning on leaving within the week, departing from Melbourne on a coastal steamer that would take them to Perth. Adam was already away, attending his first term at the University of Sydney.

"Would you rather that we didn't go, Beth?" Joanna said.

"Oh no, you must go, Mother. You have to find the place where Grandmother was born."

Whenever Joanna was beset by doubts about her decision to go to Western Australia, she reminded herself that she was going as much for Beth's sake as for her own. Although she had tried to help Beth overcome her new fear of dogs, she had found it nearly impossible, since she herself had the same fear. And Lady Emily, who had also been terrified of dogs, had believed that the cause of that fear, and perhaps therefore its remedy, lay at Karra Karra.

Joanna thought of the journey she and her mother had almost made fifteen years ago, before the poison had claimed Lady Emily. She wondered if she was near the end of that journey now, if she was close to fulfilling this quest that she had inherited from her mother. What had started out as a duty to her mother, and had changed into a duty to herself, had now become something she must do for Beth. It was like a songline, Joanna thought, whose terminus lay somewhere in Western Australia.

Joanna looked at Beth and wanted to say, "I'm going for you, darling, to find a way to stop the poison from claiming you." Instead, she said, "I'm worried that you'll miss us, that you'll be lonely."

"I'll be fine, Mother. I'm making lots of friends at school. And I am so enjoying my studies."

Besides, Beth thought now, her confidence returning, the boys couldn't keep it up forever; eventually they would get tired of the tricks they played on her and finally accept her. And it wasn't all the boys who tormented her—just the few who followed Randolph Carey. Soon, he too, she decided, would see the futility of his pranks, and leave her alone. Because Beth was determined not to give him the satisfaction of seeing her break down.

The next day, the carriage from Merinda did not appear at the school gates at the usual hour, and at seven o'clock Beth was at the dipping paddock.

The boys showed up five minutes later, carrying a long, narrow plank, which they laid across the large trough that was used for teaching sheep dipping. The trough was twenty feet wide and filled with muddy water that reflected the moon as it came out from behind the clouds. "You gotta walk all the way across it," Randolph said. "And then you can be one of us."

Beth chewed her lip as she eyed the plank. It was easy to see when the moon came out, but when the clouds drifted over the moon, the plank and the trough were hidden in darkness. And it was a very narrow plank, standing only inches above the muddy water.

Beth suddenly questioned the wisdom of her decision to accept Randolph's dare. She looked around the quiet school campus; most of the buildings were dark, the pathways lighted by gas lamps. Boys' voices drifted over from the auditorium, and the smell of cows and sheep filled the night.

"Well?" said Randolph. "Too scared to try?"

She thought of the snake she had found in her desk, and wondered what Mr. MacGregor would have done had he seen it. She believed Mr. MacGregor was fair and would take her side.

"Well?" Randolph said, and Beth saw all the boys were watching her.

"If I walk all the way across the plank then I can be one of you?" she said.

"Fair dinkum."

Beth went to one end of the plank, and saw it was even narrower than she had thought, and that it sagged in the middle. She also realized in dismay that, when she looked down, her skirt hid her feet. She couldn't watch where she stepped.

"Go on," Randolph said.

She looked at Billie Addison, who didn't meet her eyes. Then she proceeded to walk out onto the plank.

The boys stood in a circle around the trough, watching in silence as Beth made shaky but careful progress over the water. The moon came out and disappeared again. Laughter came from the auditorium. A cow lowed softly in the nearby barn.

Beth walked with her arms out, cautiously placing one foot in front of the other, her eyes on the plank and the water, just inches from her hem. A cold wind blew from the south, rippling the water. Beth held her breath as she moved along the board.

"She's doing it," one of the boys said.

"Shut up," Randolph said.

Beth felt her mouth go dry as the board sagged beneath her. The night suddenly seemed colder. She started to shiver.

"You're halfway, Beth," Billie said.

She stopped for a moment. The trough seemed too wide; the water, deep and cold. When the moon winked from behind the clouds, Beth saw insects floating on the water's surface.

"Go on," Billie said softly. "You can do it."

She continued. The wind picked up, and tugged at her skirt. The plank wobbled beneath her feet.

"She's doing okay!" Declan McCloud said.

"Go on, Beth," another boy said.

When she realized she was nearing the other side, she raised her head and saw Randolph Carey standing there, waiting for her. She smiled.

And then she froze.

She saw the dog at his side. One of the school's sheepdogs.

"C'mon, Westbrook," Carey said. "What's the matter? You're not afraid of an old dog, are you?"

She began to tremble. She felt her mouth go dry; her stomach rose up. She tried not to look at the dog, tried not to think about it. Just put one foot in front of the other, then another, and another—and she would reach the end.

But she looked at the dog's eyes, golden in the moonlight. He wasn't menacing, or growling or threatening in any way. She knew his name, too: Wizard. A friendly old kelpie. But his eyes were fixed on her.

And then she saw dingoes—chasing her—and Button, desperately trying to protect her.

Beth felt the world suddenly swing around her, and then suddenly there was nothing beneath her feet. She hit the water with a tremendous splash, and went under. For an instant she panicked, as the icy water closed over her head and she felt the weight of her skirts pull her down. Then her feet touched the bottom. She tried to stand up, but the mud was too slippery. She flailed her arms and gasped for air. Then all of a sudden she was being lifted up and out by Billie Addison and Declan McCloud.

Randolph Carey roared with laughter, and a few of the others joined him. But as she struggled out of the water, her hair streaming down her face, Beth caught the uncertain looks on the other boys' faces.

"That wasn't fair, Carey," Billie Addison said.

But Randolph only laughed harder. "Yer all a bunch of sissies!" he said. "I reckon you can't be one of us after all, Miss High-and-Mighty. You didn't pass the test. Not if you're gonna be afraid of an old dog!" He turned and walked away, leading the dog, a few of the other boys following.

"Cripes," Declan McCloud said as he helped Beth out of the water. "You're a mess."

Beth was shivering so badly that her teeth chattered.

"What're you going to do?" Billie said. "Are you going to tell old man Carpenter?"

"You'd better go home," said Declan. "You can't let any of the blokes see you like this."

But Beth couldn't go home; the carriage wasn't due for another two hours.

She tried to keep from shaking. She looked around the dark campus and wondered what she was going to do. She couldn't remember having ever been this cold.

"You'll catch pneumonia," Declan said. "People die from that."

"You can sit in the barn," Billie said. "You might get warm in there."

But Beth said, "No. I'm all right. You can go."

"What are you going to do? You're a mess!"

Beth looked at a lighted window in the second story of the staff residence. She knew the person she could go to for help.

When Judd opened the door and saw Beth standing there, he said, "Good Lord, what happened to you?"

"I fell."

He took in the drenched hair and dress, the pool of water collecting at her feet. Then he said, "Come in," quickly looking up and down the hall before closing the door.

He took Beth over to the fire. "Tell me what happened."

"I was walking by the dipping trough, and I fell in."

"The dipping trough! What were you doing over there—and what are you doing at school at this hour?"

When she didn't reply, Judd tried to think of what to do. Beth was a sight, with her wet hair hanging down, her skirt clinging to her legs. And she was shaking badly.

Judd removed a blanket from his bed and handed it to her. "Here. Take off those wet things and wrap this around yourself. Stay close to the fire. I'll find someone to go to Merinda and tell your parents."

When he came back a short while later, he found her sitting by the fire wrapped in the blanket, her clothes spread on the hearth.

"Someone has gone to Merinda," he said, looking down at her. "Beth, who did this to you?"

When she didn't answer, he said, "This is serious. You understand that, don't you? You have to tell me who did this to you."

"I just fell, that's all."

Judd looked at his watch. How long would it be before her parents got there? He knew what to do for boys who got into trouble, but Beth confounded him. There was a small spirit lamp on his worktable. He heated some water on it and stirred in some tea, keeping an eye on the silent girl.

"Beth," he said when he came back with the tea. "I want to help you. You won't get into any trouble, I promise. Just tell me what happened."

She continued to watch the flames, her eyes shimmering with tears. A few strands of wet hair lay across her cheek.

"The boys have been teasing you, haven't they?" he said.

"It's all right," she said. "They don't bother me."

He watched a tear roll down her cheek. And Judd suddenly felt inexplicably uncomfortable.

"If you tell me who did this to you, Beth, I'll see that they're punished."

But she said nothing.

There was a knock at the door, and Mr. Carpenter came in with Hugh and Joanna.

Joanna took Beth into the next room, dried her off and helped her into the clothes she had brought. "Are you all right, darling?" she said. "Tell me what happened."

"Oh, Mother," Beth said, trying not to cry, but sobbing all the same. "It was a dare. They made me walk a plank. And there was a dog—"

Joanna took her daughter into her arms and held her close, as if to draw Beth's pain into herself. It is going to go on, she thought—on and on.

When they came back into the room, Joanna said, "She'll be all right, Mr. Carpenter. I want to know who is responsible for this."

"I assure you, Mrs. Westbrook," the superintendent said, "we are trying to get to the bottom of it."

Hugh said, "Beth, tell us who pushed you into the trough."

But Beth sat close to her mother and said nothing.

"Has anything like this happened before, Beth?" Hugh said. "Have the boys been cruel to you?"

"I warned you, Mr. Westbrook," Judd said. "I told you there would be problems. It is not easy for a girl to be accepted in a boys' school."

"Did you do anything to help her?" Hugh shouted.

"It's not Mr. MacGregor's fault, Father," Beth said.

Miles Carpenter said, "I'll instruct the staff to be more watchful in the future. And I assure you, Mr. Westbrook, that this won't happen again."

"Mr. Carpenter," Joanna said, putting an arm around Beth. "Our family is leaving on a trip in a few days, we're going to Western Australia, and Beth is coming with us."

"But Mother—" Beth began.

Carpenter said, "Oh dear. Mrs. Westbrook, I wish you wouldn't withdraw your daughter from the school. I can assure you—"

"I am not withdrawing her from the school. We shall be back in a few months, in time for the beginning of the next term. I trust that by that time you will have found out who is responsible for this incident and have dealt with him."

Judd said, "I have an idea who is behind it, Mrs. Westbrook. In fact, I'll go and have a word with the boy right now."

As Miles Carpenter hastened to reassure Hugh and Joanna that everything was going to be all right, Beth suddenly jumped up and ran out after Judd.

"Mr. MacGregor, please wait," she called, stopping him on the steps.

"I'm sorry, Beth, but we have to get to the bottom of this."

"That's not what I wanted to say. I just wanted to tell you how sorry I am that I let you down."

"What are you talking about?"

"I know you had faith in me, and I so badly wanted to show you that you were right to have it. You must be very disappointed. I'm sorry."

He stared at her. The clouds shifted, and moonlight swept across Beth's face. For an instant Judd had the curious sensation that he was looking not at a girl of twelve, but at a woman the same age as he, and that they were standing on the steps for a very different reason.

"I don't want to leave Tongarra," she said quietly. "I will come back."

"Is it so important to you to be here?" he said, as he watched how the night breeze stirred her damp hair.

"It's more important than anything." she said.

The Westbrooks came out of the building. "Come along, darling," Joanna said. "Let's go home."

"Mrs. Westbrook," Judd said, "I'll talk to the boys. They'll listen to me. I'm confident that once I have made things very clear to them, they will leave your daughter alone." He looked at the girl and smiled. "We want to see Beth here with us in the second term."

CHAPTER 26

D o you suppose there are songlines out there, Mother?" Beth
asked, as she peered through the window of their train com-
partment.

"I imagine we're following one right now, darling," Joanna said. "They told us in Perth that the railway follows the old
migratory routes of the Aborigines."

Beth was so excited she could hardly sit still. She pressed her face to
the window and looked out at the wilderness and wondered about the
people who had walked this way, long ago.

Joanna, too, could hardly contain her excitement. When Captain
Fielding had said, "Western Australia, that's where the Makepeaces
went," she had been afraid to let herself believe it, to get her hopes up
again. He could have been another Miss Tallhill, who had apparently
been mistaken about Bowman's Creek and Durrebar, or he could have
been like so many others over the years, who had responded to Joanna's
letters and advertisements, offering information for money. But Fielding had told Joanna things that he could not possibly have known if

he were a fraud: "Young Makepeace was searching for the Garden of Eden. . . . His wife, so pretty, pregnant at the end of the voyage . . . had the baby at Perth . . . a girl, I think it was . . ."

And so they had left, a small group consisting of Hugh and Joanna and Beth, as well as the old sea captain, who had entertained them during their four-week voyage around the southern coast of Australia with stories of his adventures. And, as a favor to Frank Downs, there was also Eric Graham from the *Times,* to cover what he hoped was going to be an interesting story. Sarah was not with them. "I'd better stay here," she had said, "so that someone will be home when Adam comes back from school on holiday. And I'll take care of the garden. Who'll look after things if we all go?"

Just before they had left, however, Jacko had raised some concern by reporting early signs of fly-strike among one of the flocks—a condition where flies infest the wool and live off the sheep, causing sickness and ultimately death. Nonetheless, Hugh had insisted that they make the journey. "There will be no better time than this, Joanna," he had said. "Captain Fielding is willing to take us there, and everything is quiet here at Merinda. Adam is away at school. And Jacko can take care of the fly-strike."

But when they had landed at Perth, Hugh had found a telegram waiting for him from Jacko: FLY-STRIKE SERIOUS. CAN'T STOP IT. COULD LOSE ENTIRE STOCK. URGENT YOU COME HOME.

"Oh Hugh," Joanna had said. "What are we going to do?"

"This telegram is a week old," he had said. "The situation might have improved. I'll send Jacko a wire at once."

But the next morning, another telegram had arrived from Jacko: HUGH, it read, EMERGENCY AT MERINDA. DO NOT THINK I CAN SAVE STOCK.

"You had better go home," Joanna had said to Hugh. "Beth and I will stay here."

"I don't like us being separated like this, Joanna," he had said. "We've never been apart. But I'll make it as quick as I can. I reckon it'll take me four weeks to get home, a week to take care of the fly-strike, and then I'll be on the first coastal steamer back. You should be all right," he said. "You have Mr. Graham and Captain Fielding and Beth with you. And I'll be back before you know it."

But now, three days later, Joanna was on a train out of Perth on the west coast of Australia, accompanied by Beth, Captain Fielding and the reporter from the *Times,* and heading toward a town in the interior, a gold-mining town called Kalagandra.

After Hugh had left, Joanna and Beth had searched for traces of her grandparents in Perth. She had conducted a search of the town, whose population was less than eight thousand, going through records, talking to people, exploring the graveyards. But, in the end, she had found no trace of the Makepeaces having ever been in Perth. "After all," Captain Fielding said, "it was over fifty years ago. When the *Beowulf* landed here, there were only a few tents on Garden Island, where the first settlers who had come the year before were camped. There weren't any immigration officials checking papers!" Nor had anyone heard of Karra Karra, or Bowman's Creek and Durrebar.

But Joanna did hear stories about a "crazy white man" who had taken his wife out into the desert many years ago to live with a clan of Aborigines. The story had many variations, depending upon whom Joanna spoke to. The head of a local missionary group had said, "I remember hearing about it when I was a boy. Scandalous it was. The Aborigines ate the man and his wife. They were cannibals then." The official at the Colonial Land Office, who had examined Joanna's deed, had said, "I heard that story when I first arrived here. The white man went crazy, they say. He married a native woman and ran off into the desert with her, abandoning his white wife and baby." In the end, after hearing several outrageous versions, Joanna had come to the conclusion that the true story of the Makepeaces was not known, and that the legend of the "white man who had gone searching for Eden" was just another in the store of legends and myths about Western Australia's colorful past.

However, after three days of searching, Joanna did learn two things: that, if they were looking for the tribe that had once occupied the Perth region, they should search eastward, approximately following the railway line, because that was the old migratory path of the tribe whenever they went walkabout; and that the man they needed to see was Commissioner Fox, who knew "everything there is to know about this area." Fox was currently in Kalagandra on one of his official biannual visits to the interior.

They were on their way to the gold-mining town now. Eric Graham was writing in his notebook, glancing out the window every now and then, laying the groundwork for his story; Beth was next to him, excitement in her eyes and posture, the thrill of adventure glowing on her young face; Captain Fielding, in the next seat, was dozing. Joanna sat opposite her daughter, facing forward, watching the terrain slowly change from coastal forest to farmland to desert. The train was crowded and noisy, filled with men on their way to the goldfields—the hopeful diggers and fossickers, with their swags and shovels and pickaxes. Everyone was covered with soot and cinders. The meticulous Eric Graham continually brushed himself off, frowning now and then over the state of his brand-new bowler, while Joanna's hat was up in the overhead rack, in the brown-paper bag the railway company provided for ladies.

Because Kalagandra was three hundred and fifty miles inland, Joanna and her companions had left Perth the night before and had slept sitting up as the train chuffed through the night. Now it was nearly noon and the goldfields lay just ahead. Kalagandra was the terminus. Beyond it, she had been told, there was nothing except scrub and kangaroos.

"Do you suppose there are songlines out there?" Beth had asked, and as Joanna looked through the window, trying to see through the black smoke that belched from the train's engine, she imagined in the barren wilderness the songlines that an Aboriginal woman, Reenadeena, and the little English girl, Emily, might have followed as they made their way through the wasteland toward the river where the black swans arched their fine necks. A woman and a small child, Joanna thought, trying to picture them, all alone out there, with the sun pounding down upon a waterless land, a beige landscape broken only by mulga and dry scrub.

Joanna looked at Beth, at how excitedly she stared out the window. And she noticed for the first time new dimples in Beth's cheeks— unusual dimples, high on the cheeks, just below the eyes. Joanna remembered that her mother had had the same dimples; she recalled how people had remarked on Lady Emily's compelling smile. And as she watched her daughter, Joanna began to think that it was almost as if her mother were making this journey with her after all.

She thought of what she had read in her grandfather's notes about the ritual that took place inside the sacred mountain—a pilgrimage that was made periodically by mothers and daughters.

Was that what impelled her now? she wondered. Was her quest perhaps motivated by more than just fear for her daughter and the future? Were she and Beth under some sort of compulsion that had been dictated long ago by an ancient race and their beliefs? And might this journey, in fact, be a quest motivated not solely by fear, as Joanna had always thought, but by positive forces as well?

Joanna suddenly thought: It is as if Beth and I are on our way to finish some important business.

The time was coming, she knew, when she was going to have to tell Beth the truth, the real reason why they had come here. She closed her eyes and the wheels of the train seemed to whisper: *Hurry-up, hurry-up, hurry-up* . . .

With a great hissing of brakes, the train pulled into the station. Men were jumping off even before it had come to a halt, and, gathered on the platform, the Westbrook party was immediately engulfed by a milling crowd of shouting, excited people, running in all directions.

Joanna looked about her in the smoky afternoon haze. Kalagandra seemed to have sprung up in a hostile, arid region. To the west of the town there were a few wheat farms, to the east was the Great Desert. Trees had been cut down for as far as Joanna could see, leaving a sandy plain stretching for miles, scarred with hundreds of pits like a lunar landscape, the earth turned up as if an invasion of moles had passed through. Joanna saw men's heads everywhere bobbing up and down in the holes, she heard the ring of pickaxes, the rattle of gold cradles and the constant thud of steam-driven quartz crushers.

There were so many people! A shanty town and tent camp surrounded the goldfields, where crude lodgings had been hastily erected to accommodate the thousands of men who came pouring into the district with shovels on their shoulders. A kind of panicked prosperity was seen in the log-cabin saloons and the open-air theaters with canvas walls, the makeshift bowling alleys and boxing booths, the gin sellers, their bottles displayed on just a board laid across two barrels, and the inevitable women beckoning from open doorways. There were thousands of tents, Joanna guessed, with flags of every nation flying over them—she could even identify the Russian eagle snapping over one sagging hut. The town itself, Joanna saw, was rough and crude, filled with wooden storefronts, hastily erected stone buildings and creaking sidewalks.

"I remember another time when gold fever struck," Captain Fielding said as they made their way to the hotel. "It was back in 1850. You could go down to Melbourne Harbor and see ships at the piers loading up with passengers bound for San Francisco. Shortly after that, of course, gold was discovered in Victoria and the great exodus to California came to an end."

"They seem to be prosperous here," Joanna said, looking into windows at the various goods for sale, from digger's boots to solid-gold watches.

"Yes, but the people who are making their fortunes here weren't born here," Fielding said, "nor had they had even heard of Kalagandra before a year ago. They come from all over Australia, all over the world, even. They get rich and they leave. And when the gold is gone, the town will die."

"Where are the Aborigines?" Joanna asked.

"I'm sure they're here somewhere. I suppose they live on the edge of town, like they do everywhere else, on the fringe so to speak. This used to be their land—they called this area *galagandra*, after a common local shrub—but they don't live in the town or benefit from its prosperity."

They arrived at the Golden Age Hotel and had to wait while the clerks tried to handle customers demanding rooms, even though a NO VACANCY sign had been posted. Joanna looked around the crowded lobby, where people were sleeping in chairs and camping out on sofas.

She secured their room keys, and went upstairs with Beth, who was anxious to get started writing letters to her father, Sarah and Adam. After Joanna was certain her daughter was settled, she met Captain Fielding in the lobby. Eric Graham had already gone off to the nearest newspaper office to see what he could find out about the Makepeaces. Joanna and the captain went across the street to the police station, where they asked for Commissioner Fox.

A man emerged a moment later from the inner office. "Mrs. Westbrook? I'm Paul Fox, the police commissioner for this district. I understand you wanted to see me."

Commissioner Fox was a handsome man in his late forties, with a curiously attractive scar down one cheek. His khaki uniform with its Sam Browne belt and holstered gun, though dusty and sweat-stained, was worn with all the correctness of a man who maintained personal standards against impossible odds.

"I hope you can help me, Commissioner," Joanna said, and offered him her hand.

When Fox had been told that a Mrs. Westbrook was asking after him, searching for lost relatives, he had expected to find one of the two types of women found in Kalagandra—those who came to break the law, and those who came to spread the gospel. He was pleasantly surprised, however, to find himself in the company of neither. Mrs. Westbrook was pretty, in her mid-thirties, and she carried herself with the poise of a lady. She wore a smartly tailored dress and a stylish hat. Her gloves, he noticed, were of the softest chamois.

Joanna introduced him to Captain Fielding, and then said, "Mr. Fox, I came to Western Australia to see if I could find traces of my grandparents. I was told in Perth that you were the man who knew everything there was to know about this area."

He smiled. "I don't know if I know everything, Mrs. Westbrook. But

I shall help in any way I can. When did your grandparents arrive here?"

"They disembarked at Perth in 1830, but I don't know where they went after that. I have reason to believe they came to this area."

"That was fifty-six years ago, Mrs. Westbrook. I doubt you'll find any trace of them." He couldn't help staring at her and thinking what an attractive and refined woman she was, such a rarity in Kalagandra. He wondered where the husband was. "My deputy told me you came from Melbourne," he said. "That's a long way to come, Mrs. Westbrook, just to find traces of your grandparents."

"I am here for other reasons as well, Mr. Fox. I believe that my mother might have been born somewhere near here. If so, and if I can determine for certain that she was, then it will fill in an important blank in my family's history. Also, I inherited a deed for some land I believe is near here, but so far, I have been unable to locate it."

"I see. Do you have anything to go on besides your grandparents' names? Any details that might be of help?"

"They lived for a while with an Aborigine clan—for about three years. And, in fact, I believe they were adopted by that clan."

"Indeed," he said. "Do you know the tribe's name?"

"Unfortunately no. But they lived near a place called Karra Karra."

"Karra Karra," he said. "I'm not familiar with it."

"Mr. Fox, I was told at the hotel that there are a lot of displaced Aborigines living outside the town limits. Do you know if any of them came originally from the Perth area?"

"It would be hard to say, Mrs. Westbrook. They've come from all over. After their tribes were broken up, they dispersed to the white settlements, hoping to be taken care of. In doing so, they crossed over traditional tribal boundaries that, at one time, they would never have dreamed of crossing. So we have natives living here who are far from their tribal grounds."

"Would you mind taking me to see them and speak with them?"

"I'd be delighted to, Mrs. Westbrook," Fox said. "It isn't often I get a break from my usual chores of rounding up drunks and thieves to escort a lady around the town. Shall we say, in two hours? I'll meet you at your hotel."

The late-afternoon sun slanted across the sandy plains from a cloudless sky. Although Kalagandra was getting ready for the coming evening, the men kept at their work in the gold pits.

Commissioner Fox and Joanna walked along the wooden sidewalk, with Captain Fielding and Beth behind, and Eric Graham following in the company of a black trooper named Michael. The air was filled with the aromas of coffee and dust, and men continued to tramp down the street carrying shovels and pickaxes, their eyes fixed on the goldfields ahead.

"Mr. Fox," Joanna said, "besides gold, is anything mined here as well? Opals, perhaps?"

He shook his head. "I've never heard of opals being found in Western Australia. If there were, it would cause another rush!"

They came to the north end of the town, to a rocky hillside scarred with abandoned mining pits. It was a bleak, waterless area where no plants or trees grew, and the only relief from the sun was in the shade of rocky outcroppings, or in the crude man-made shelters that littered the hillside and gully below.

Joanna stopped and stared.

Hundreds of Aborigines occupied the area. Aside from a few stone huts, the majority of the dwellings were lean-tos constructed from hammered-out kerosene cans, oddly matched pieces of wood, scraps of cardboard and cloth and even bottles and cans. Smoke rose from the many campfires, filling the gully with a thick pall. Flies buzzed in the air, and half-tame dingoes, their ribs showing, scavenged among garbage and debris.

There was a curious listlessness to the scene. It seemed to Joanna as if the inhabitants moved in a dream-like way, their gestures slow, their faces strangely blank. The adults sat on chairs or on the ground, murmuring among themselves, while children played in the dirt. They were all poorly dressed, the women in ill-fitting dresses, the men in mismatched coats and trousers. The children were for the most part immodestly clad. Some of the elders wore blankets around their shoulders; Joanna saw a few draped in kangaroo or possum skins.

"Mr. Fox," she said quietly, as they walked along the edge of the shanty town, "how did these people come to this?"

"They tried to fight us, years ago, when the first white people arrived and settled on Aboriginal land. The settlers retaliated by burning the blacks' camping grounds and driving away their food supply. Having nothing to hunt, the blacks resorted to stealing food from the farmers, for which they were punished. Finally, they capitulated. They decided that the way to survive was to join us, to imitate us. But they have no idea of how to go about doing it. They wear cast-off clothing donated by churches, they struggle to speak English, they drink alcohol and smoke tobacco, but they never really succeed in becoming like us."

They paused to watch a woman cook bread over hot coals. She was barefoot, and her dress hung on her. The shelter behind her had been made out of crates, and the words "Adelaide Produce Co." could be plainly seen. The lean-to was large enough to accommodate only one person; inside was a mattress with stuffing spilling out. The woman looked at the visitors, and then away.

As Joanna continued to walk slowly along, she noticed that few of the blacks seemed to care about the group of white people strolling in their midst. "Mother," Beth said quietly, "is there no one to help these poor people?"

"Actually, there is," Fox said. "The government takes care of the natives through the Aborigines' Rights Protection Board, which provides food and clothing, and looks after their general interests. But it is difficult to correct problems that were begun a long time ago. Many of the original missionaries who came here came not to minister to the needs of the settlers, but to take care of the blacks. But I'm afraid their good intentions went awry. For example, they insisted that the blacks give up their kangaroo cloaks and dress like Europeans. But the Aborigine used his kangaroo skin for many things—one of them was shelter from the elements. Rain will run off a kangaroo hide, while the man under it remains warm and dry. Frock coats in the rain, however, become sodden. As a result, a lot of blacks came down with pneumonia and died. Good intentions, Mrs. Westbrook, can sometimes result in negative consequences."

But there was more to this deplorable scene, Joanna thought, than good intentions gone awry. She saw in the blank faces of the people she passed a kind of surrender, as if they had simply given up. Joanna thought of John and Naomi Makepeace, and wondered if the inhabitants of this wretched gully were somehow the far-reaching result of her grandfather's crime, fifty-two years ago. Worse, were some of these people once members of the very clan the Makepeaces had lived with?

"Surely something can be done for these people. Couldn't they perhaps be relocated on their ancestral land?"

"Even if that land was available, Mrs. Westbrook," Fox said as he shooed flies away from his face, "most of them no longer know where they belong. They wouldn't be able to recognize the songlines—that is, the tracks that connect the sacred sites."

"Can we find out if any of these people came from Perth?"

"We could try asking. Otherwise, there is no way of knowing. We don't keep records of these people. Their numbers are always changing. They come and go at will. Some might be here one day, and gone the next. And tomorrow morning you might find a hundred new ones squatting in their place."

"I'm looking for a tribe with a kangaroo totem. Surely they would remember their totem."

He shook his head. "Many of them here wouldn't even be able to tell you the name of their tribe."

"I want to talk to them," she said. "I want to know if any of them are from Perth."

"I must warn you, Mrs. Westbrook," Fox said, "these people have a habit of telling you what they think you want to hear. And that is not necessarily the truth."

They approached an old man who was sitting beneath the one tree in the gully. His white beard reached down to his waist, and he was smoking a pipe. Joanna thought he bore a strong resemblance to Ezekiel. Eric Graham brought out his notebook and pencil and began to write.

Commissioner Fox said, "Do you speak English?"

"I speak," the elder said.

"What tribe are you from?"

Small piercing eyes regarded the commissioner from beneath heavy brows. When the Aborigine didn't say anything, Fox said, "I'm not here in an official capacity, old man. We merely want some information. Do you know anything about the Karra Karra clan?"

"Yeah," he said. "I know Karra Karra."

"Mr. Fox," Joanna said, suddenly excited. "Ask him where—"

"Just a moment, please, Mrs. Westbrook. Old man, do you know the place where the dish ran away with the spoon?"

"Yeah, I know. I take you there."

Fox muttered, "For a price, of course," and turned away. "Do you see now what you are up against, Mrs. Westbrook? Perhaps," Fox said, "you should talk to Sister Veronica. She's lived in this area for decades. She might know something."

"Sister Veronica?"

"She's one of the Catholic nuns who run a school and infirmary at the edge of town. She's been here for ages. I can take you there right now, if you like."

As they headed away from the encampment, with Eric Graham wondering if he was going to be getting a story out of this after all, and Captain Fielding pausing to light his pipe, Beth saw a signpost that caught her attention. It was a pole stuck in the sand and tilted to one side, with several crudely written signs nailed to it, pointing in different directions. One of them read, "Bustard Creek, 20 km. south." Beth smiled. A prankster had gone over the letter "U" with a paintbrush and changed it to an "A."

The other signs read: "Johnson's Well," "Durrakai," and "Laverton."

Beth gave it a puzzled look. As far as she could tell, they were pointing to nowhere.

The convent came as a surprise to Joanna. Expecting to find a plain wooden building set in the middle of arid scrub, she found instead a collection of stone buildings clustered at the edge of what must have been the only water source for miles around. It was like an oasis, Joanna thought, when she saw the stand of trees, the grass growing down the bank of a clear running creek. Fox led her to a large clapboard house with a deep veranda and a tin drum on the roof to catch rainwater. A faded sign over the front door read: ST. ALBAN'S CATHOLIC CHURCH, FATHER MCGILL, PASTOR, MASS EVERY FOURTH SUNDAY OF THE MONTH. Beneath it, another sign had been added: SCHOOL AND INFIRMARY.

"The nuns live in that house over there," Fox said as they went up the veranda steps. "But I'm sure we'll find Sister Veronica in here. She seems to live in the infirmary."

Joanna was further surprised to find herself entering a cool, quiet foyer that smelled of lemon polish and fresh flowers. The dust and flies of the goldfields and the Aborigine camp seemed not to reach this religious outpost that was tended, Fox explained, by twelve very dedicated nuns.

Sister Veronica was a robust woman in her late sixties. She wore a white habit that accentuated her tanned skin, and although her face betrayed her years of hardship beneath the desert sun, she spoke with a surprisingly refined British accent.

"Paul," she said to the commissioner, taking his hand. "How nice to see you again. You don't visit us often enough."

Fox introduced Joanna and Captain Fielding, and young Beth. Eric Graham tried to remain unobvious, his pad and pencil ready. The commissioner explained, "Mrs. Westbrook is looking for traces of her grandparents, who might have come through the area years ago. Their names were John and Naomi Makepeace, and they lived for a while with a family of Aborigines in a place called Karra Karra."

"I'm sorry," the nun said, after a moment of searching her memory. "I have never heard the name Makepeace, and I do not know Karra Karra. Perhaps if you inquired among the Aborigines who live outside of town . . ."

"We already have," Joanna said. "I'm afraid I found nothing there."

When Sister Veronica saw the disappointment on her visitor's face, she said, "Perhaps if you told me a little more, it might jog my memory. I was just on my way to relieve Sister Agatha in the sick ward. If you care to come with me, we can talk along the way."

They left through the rear of the building and followed a path that cut through surprisingly green lawns. The bottlebrush trees heavy with red blooms and the branches of tall eucalypts rustling high overhead reminded Joanna of Merinda.

"What a beautiful setting," she said. "When one sees the town and the goldfields, one can't imagine that such a lovely spot as this could be nearby."

"We have a good water supply here. Bustard Creek, which is twenty miles to the south, is fed by an underground river that flows through limestone caverns, far beneath the earth. There is very little here that we cannot grow."

"You're very fortunate to have this land, Sister."

"Oh, we don't own the land, Mrs. Westbrook," Veronica said. "The colonial government allowed us to set up our hospital here a few years ago, in order to take care of the few gold diggers who had staked claims in the area. And then when the gold rush hit, we suddenly had our hands full. We treat many banged heads and injured feet. The men seem to be so careless with their shovels and pickaxes!"

"I'm sure the men are thankful that you and the other sisters are here."

"We are kept very busy, I assure you. But we have run into a problem, Mrs. Westbrook. The authorities are being pressured to move us off this land, because gold-mining companies want to take it over. We are not a rich order, Mrs. Westbrook. The little money that does come our way is just enough to purchase medicines and supplies. If we are forced to move, I have no idea where we will go."

They passed a carefully tended cemetery; a greenhouse, where more nuns in white habits were working; a vegetable garden; a yard with farm animals. "We try to be self-sufficient," Veronica said. "But we are getting on in years. Our youngest sister is fifty years old. We are having difficulty attracting new members because we are so poor."

They came to the steps of a wooden bungalow, with a sign over the door that read SICK WARD.

"Mrs. Westbrook," Veronica said, "what years were your grandparents here?"

"Between 1830 and 1834."

"And you say they lived with the Aborigines, somewhere around here?"

"Possibly, I'm not sure."

Sister Veronica stopped and looked at Joanna. "If they were here at that time, Mrs. Westbrook, they would have come through Perth at the same time that I was there. I came to Australia as a novice when I was seventeen. I and two other sisters arrived with the first settlers. We lived in the Perth settlement for three years, and then we moved eastward, where we established a farm and a school for the settlers' children. Wait a minute, something is coming back to me . . ."

Joanna waited, as the sun dropped behind the trees and the constant noise from the nearby goldfield seemed suddenly to grow subdued.

"It was in 1834," Sister Veronica said. "I remember the date because I had just taken my final vows. A little girl was brought out of the desert, Mrs. Westbrook. A white child. She was about four years old and in a terrible state. Physically, she was all right, she had been well taken care of, but when questioned about her parents, she became hysterical. We could hardly make sense of what she was trying to say—she was so frightened. I seem to recall that she was trying to tell us about dogs—wild dogs—and a large serpent. And the most baffling thing of all, Mrs. Westbrook, was that she didn't speak English; she spoke an Aboriginal dialect!

"The authorities brought her to us, to take care her of until she could be put on a ship bound for England. There were relatives there, we were told. Mrs. Westbrook, could that child possibly have something to do with your grandparents?"

Joanna stared at the woman. "She was their daughter," she said. "My mother." She became suddenly excited. "Then they *were* near here. They *did* come this way. And if so, then Karra Karra has to be nearby."

"What will you do now, Mrs. Westbrook?"

"I have to find out where they went, where they lived."

"Why? I doubt you'll find anything out there after all these years."

"Something *is* out there, Sister. My mother believed that it was waiting for her, and now, in a way, I feel it is waiting for me."

Veronica's eyes, small and lively, searched Joanna's face. "It is a spiritual journey then?" she said. "I thought I felt that when we shook hands. I get a strong sense of purpose about you, Mrs. Westbrook, a feeling of destiny, perhaps." She looked at Beth. "And your daughter as well. I wonder if God has brought you here for a reason."

"Something brought me here," Joanna said, "because I have been on this journey for years. And it has not totally been of my own choosing. I have felt compelled to come here. My mother did, too."

"I understand," Veronica said with a smile. "I, too, was compelled to come here, many years ago. I came from a rich family, Mrs. Westbrook. And I was, if I may say so, a very pretty young woman. I had all the advantages, as it were. But I was 'called.' I had no choice but to come here, to bring God's goodness and love into this wilderness."

"What will you do if they make you move off this land?"

"We'll find another place. We always have." She took Joanna's hand and said, "God go with you on your journey, my dear. I pray that you find what you are looking for."

CHAPTER 27

"I don't like the look of this, Jacko," Hugh said as he examined a dead sheep. He knelt and studied the wounds on the animal. The nature of the sores on the body and the tattered condition of the fleece showed him he was dealing with fly-strike. Finally, he stood up, stripped off his gloves and surveyed the scene. Sheep carcasses lay everywhere. The sheep that were still alive looked as if they weren't going to last much longer.

It had taken Hugh five weeks to get from Kalagandra to Merinda, and as soon as he had arrived at the homestead, he had saddled up a horse and ridden out to talk to Jacko. And now, an hour later, he realized that the situation was much worse than he had thought. All over the district, sheep were dying in the hundreds. They dropped where they stood, their wool hanging in tatters, their bodies covered with sores and maggots. Entire flocks were affected, from Williams Grange to as far away as Barrow Downs. The weather was cool now, but Hugh suspected that when the warm weather broke and a new generation of flies hatched, there would be a stronger, bigger wave of blowfly sweeping across the plains.

He threw down the gloves and ran his hand through his hair. He was tired. He had traveled almost nonstop from Kalagandra, taking the train to Perth, then spending four-and-a-half weeks on the coastal steamer, and another two days getting from Melbourne to the Western District. And he knew now that he wasn't going to be rejoining Joanna as quickly as he had hoped.

"This is no ordinary fly-strike, Jacko," he said. "There's something odd about this one. The sheep are dying a lot quicker than with the usual strike."

"That was why I decided to send for you, Hugh. I knew that I couldn't handle it myself."

As Hugh walked slowly among the carcasses, looking at each one, his mystification grew. The time seemed to be too short between the initial infestation of an animal and its death. He was glad now that he had left Kalagandra when he did. He suspected that every single day was going to count in finding the cause and a way to prevent more sheep from dying. He walked over to a ewe that was still alive. She lay on her side, her body swarming with maggots. Hugh picked up his rifle and shot the animal through the head.

"Have the men dig a pit, Jacko," he said. "Bury these carcasses."

"And then what?"

"We'll examine every flock. We'll quarantine the infested ones. The clean ones will be crutched right away. I don't know, Jacko. This is serious. I've never known fly-strike to be so swift and so deadly. The incubation period is too short. Maybe it's a new strain."

"We've only got four months until shearing," Jacko said gloomily. "I reckon we oughta get started on the dipping."

"I have a feeling, Jacko, that the usual insecticidal dip isn't going to work this time. Have this carcass hauled back to the homestead for me. I'm going to do an autopsy on it. Maybe I can come up with something. In the meantime, I'm going to ride around to the other stations and see what they're doing."

———————————

When Hugh finally returned home, he was exhausted. He was alone in the house, except for Mrs. Jackson, who was cooking dinner.

As he wearily changed out of his traveling clothes and poured himself a whiskey in the parlor, he found a special comfort from being within the familiar walls. The beauty of the house at Merinda calmed a troubled soul: its polished floors, the modern tile bathrooms, the stained-glass panels in the front door and the finely made furniture and gaslights. It was a peaceful house, solid and large and reassuring—a sanctuary, Hugh thought.

But even more reassuring than Merinda's simple elegance was the presence of familiar objects, each with its special significance, in particular the many photographs of all sizes and shapes, in silver or wooden frames or no frames at all, covering tables and walls: Adam, at nine, proudly holding up a fish he had caught in the river; Beth dressed up for a children's costume party; Sarah and Joanna working in the greenhouse, captured unaware by the camera as they stood with their heads bent over herbs and flowers, sunlight washing over them. There were knickknacks that brought back happy memories, souvenirs from the International Exhibition, a ribbon Beth had won for a pet sheep at the Graziers' Show, certificates of scholastic merit from the Cameron Town Secondary School that Adam had attended.

Hugh slowly sipped his whiskey and tried not to think of the terrible sights of the past few hours—sheep rotting while they were still alive, the hopelessness in the eyes of men who knew they were going to lose their stations, everything they had worked for. Tomorrow, he thought, he would roll up his sleeves and get to work on finding a way to combat yet another scourge besetting the sheep farmers of western Victoria. But for now, tonight, he sought the comfort of his family.

He missed Joanna, and wished she had come home with him, or that he could have stayed with her. Had she found anything, he wondered, in the five weeks he had spent traveling? A telegram had been waiting for him when he'd arrived at Merinda, dated four-and-a-half weeks ago: HAVE CONTINUED ON TO KALAGANDRA. STAYING AT GOLDEN AGE HOTEL. LOVE YOU AND MISS YOU. JOANNA. There had been nothing since.

Hugh heard footsteps in the hall, and turned to see Sarah in the doorway.

"You're back!" she said.

They embraced. "How is Joanna?" Sarah asked. "Has she found anything?"

"Nothing yet, I'm afraid. At least, not when I left. I was hoping there would be more news waiting for me here."

"I'm sorry, there's nothing," Sarah said. "But if I know Joanna, whatever she is doing, she isn't idle! But there is something from Adam." She went to the desk and brought back an envelope. "It will take you an hour to read this, he's so happy at the university!"

Hugh looked at the familiar handwriting, and read the first words: "Dear Family, Greetings from your very brilliant and worldly son!"

Hugh smiled, and an image flashed into his mind of a little boy with a bandage on his head, his eyes full of confusion and fear.

"What about the sheep?" Sarah said. "Do you know what's wrong with them? I've heard people saying it's a new strain of blowfly."

"I think they're right. This time there are complications with mycotic dermatitis as well, which I've never seen in fly-strike before."

"What will you do?"

"First we'll crutch all the stock, and take as much wool off the withers as we can. Then I'm going to quarantine the in-lamb ewes—we have over two thousand of them. If they get fly-struck, then we stand to lose all the stock. And then we'll start dipping them, and see what works."

"Hugh," Sarah said. "If there is anything I can do to help—"

"Thank you, Sarah," he said. And then he thought: but first, a trip into Cameron Town for the unhappy task of sending a telegram to Joanna, telling her that he would not, after all, be joining her in Kalagandra right away.

Sarah couldn't sleep, she was restless. Perhaps, she thought, it had something to do with this new trouble afflicting the sheep station, and her worry for Hugh. Or did it have nothing at all to do with Merinda, was it rooted in events taking place over a thousand miles away, on the western coast of the continent?

Sarah pulled a shawl around her shoulders and slipped out of the house. It was midnight; the Western District slumbered beneath an uncertain autumn moon. As she went down to the river, where she had been tending a new crop of basil and mint, she wondered where Joanna was at that moment—what she and Beth were doing, what they had found. Sarah wished now she had gone to Western Australia with them. Joanna had said, "Mrs. Jackson will look after the garden," but Sarah had feared Mrs. Jackson would not give the garden the care it needed. And then, too, she had she wanted to be here if Adam came home. But he had written to say that he had made so many friends and had been invited to visit a number of them in Sydney, that he was going to stay there rather than make the journey back to Merinda.

I should have gone with Joanna, Sarah thought as she knelt to inspect the first tentative flowerheads on the new mint by the light of her lantern. And when, in the next instant, she thought again, more strongly this time, I *should* have gone with Joanna, she decided that this must be the cause of her strange restlessness. Was Joanna in some sort of trouble? Was she in need of help? Was Joanna, so far away in an alien land, wishing that Sarah were there with her?

Seeing that the mint and basil weren't as leafy as they should be, she very carefully trimmed off the flowers in order to stimulate leaf growth. And as she worked, surrounded by night sounds, watching shadows move through the woods as clouds brushed the face of the moon, Sarah tried to send herself out over the great distance that stood between her and Joanna, tried to sense what was happening in the Western Australian wasteland.

When she heard a sound behind her, she thought at first that it was an animal, pausing to assess the human intruder before hurrying on to its burrow. But then something else—a sudden knowing—brought Sarah to her feet. She peered through the trees. She held her breath.

And then she saw him, walking along the path that led from the main road to the house, a suitcase in his hand.

"Philip!" she cried, running to him.

"Sarah!" He dropped the case and ran to her; they flew into each other's arms, into a tight embrace. Philip's mouth found hers. They kissed for a long moment, then he said, "Sarah, Sarah."

"You're here! You're really here!"

"Didn't you get my letter? Oh Sarah, my God, my lovely Sarah." He kissed her again, driving his hands into her hair. She held on to him, unbelieving, giddy with the feel of him, the warmth, the smell of him.

"Sarah, my God I've missed you," he said, taking her face between his hands. "But Sarah, I wrote to you—I'm still married—"

She kissed him again. Then she pressed her face into his neck and said, "You're here. Philip, you're here."

"I have to explain, tell you. I had to come back. I've traveled all over, Sarah, and wherever I went, you were there with me. I tried to live with Alice, in one place, in the way she wanted. But I couldn't. I don't belong anywhere else. I felt my spirit wasting away. All I could think of was you, and Australia, how at peace I am when I am here with you, how belonging I feel. I asked her to give me my freedom. She said I could go. We aren't the same kind of people. She has her family, Daniel, her home in England. She doesn't need me. But she said she couldn't give me a divorce, not yet. Sarah, my love," he said, "I just want to be with you."

"Yes, Philip," she said, suddenly understanding the restlessness that had invaded her soul, and feeling it suddenly gone. She looked at his mouth—the mouth she had so often wondered about, dreamed about. She touched his lips; she kissed him again, lightly. And then passionately.

"Whatever we face, Philip," she said, "we face together. We'll work it out somehow."

He drew her down into the damp grass, into the privacy of the tall eucalyptus trees, the shrubs and the vines. She saw the Southern Cross glitter in the branches overhead as he covered her with his hard body, and felt the woods swirl around her as he murmured, "I should never have left you . . ." And then no more words were needed.

CHAPTER 28

E ven before Captain Fielding came back to her after conferring with Sammy, the black tracker they had hired in Kalagandra, Joanna knew that something was wrong.

She and her party were in a semi-arid wilderness called the mallee, an expanse of scrubby wasteland that lay on the edge of the Great Victoria Desert. They had left Kalagandra four weeks ago, traveling by camel through the desert wilderness, and they had been following this particular track for the last nine days. But so far they had found no Aborigines, no traces of camps, nothing that could be taken for Karra Karra. Joanna, sitting atop her camel, looked around at the desert that seemed to stretch into infinity, a monotony broken only by gray-green mulga, stunted eucalyptus, and desert oaks with peculiar, needle-like leaves.

She had a clearer understanding, now, of the harsh, stark face of Australia. Maps showed a thin coastal strip encircling the continent, where towns and cities grew, lush forests and grassy plains. But inside that rim sprawled the great dusty heart of Australia, which was why camels had been imported for use there for some time. Joanna and her party had traveled among twisted trees that grew amid sand-plains and miniature salt lakes, where lizards and flies and snakes were numerous; occasionally they saw a wallaby or an emu, but these were infrequent. And there was not a single human habitation in sight; no sign of civilization for miles.

The June day was hot, and ominous black clouds floated on the distant horizon.

Joanna thought of the thousands of years that had gone into sculpting the sandy ridges that were held together by spinifex and scrub, and of what an uninviting place it was. It seemed impossible that a young Aboriginal woman and a little girl could have come across this, alone, on foot. She herself was accompanied by four men, eight camels, water and food rations, guns, tents, a medical kit, and a compass—and still it was very hard going. Joanna wondered if perhaps the Aboriginal woman and child had had some kind of help.

Joanna saw Sammy, the tracker, go off with a rifle and a boomerang, and then Fielding came up on his camel, his face shaded by the wide-brimmed hat he had exchanged for his seaman's cap. "I've sent him off to look for water. Our supply is getting low," he said.

"There's something else bothering you, Captain. What is it?"

"I'm sorry, Mrs. Westbrook. But I'm afraid it appears that we are lost."

"Lost? But how can that be?"

He handed her his compass and said, "Watch what this does."

Joanna held the instrument in the flat of her palm. The needle quivered on "north," and then suddenly snapped down to "south."

"It's been doing that for days," Fielding said. "It wasn't so bad at first. Sammy and I thought we could make our own adjustments. But it's been getting worse. And now I'm afraid the compass is useless."

"What is causing it?" Joanna asked, watching in amazement as the needle suddenly snapped to north again.

"We have no idea. I've never seen a compass do that before."

"Could it be broken?"

"Well, I wondered that myself. But a good mariner never goes to sea with only one compass." He dug into his saddlebag and brought out a sphere the size of a large orange; the bottom half was metal and the top was glass. In it, a compass floated. "We use these on ships," he said. "The needle floats in the alcohol, see? It's more reliable than the hand-held variety. Now watch what it does."

Joanna stared at the needle floating in the sphere. It sailed over the "north" reading, and then slowly swam down to the "south" point.

"If you ask me," Fielding said, looking at the desolation surrounding them, "there are strange forces at work out here."

"Is there no way of telling where we are?"

"Mrs. Westbrook, we don't even have any way of determining what direction we're facing. Usually a watch can tell you—" He took out his pocket watch and showed it to her. "Normally, all you have to do is point twelve o'clock toward the sun, and the north-south line runs halfway between twelve and the hour hand. But I haven't been able to get a fix on the sun."

Joanna squinted up at the flat, white plate of sky. High clouds were stretched over the earth, like cheesecloth over the mouth of a jar. There was no single source of sunlight; it seemed to come from everywhere at once. The only break in the strange whiteness was the black clouds that hung on the horizon and that they had been watching for days. Fielding had said that it was storming where those clouds were, but it was impossible to tell if the storm was to the north, south, east or west, or how many miles away it was.

"What about Sammy? Can't he lead us out of here?"

"Sammy's a Pilbara Aborigine, Mrs. Westbrook. This area is not his ancestral home. He says he can't read the songlines here."

Beth came up on her camel. After a few lessons in Kalagandra on how to ride one, she had become quite good at it. Like her companions, she wore a scarf over her nose and mouth to prevent the dust from getting into her lungs, and a wide-brimmed hat to keep the sun off. Her long divided skirt was tucked into the tops of her boots. "What's wrong, Mother?" she asked.

When Joanna explained about the compass, Beth said, "Are we going to turn back?"

Joanna thought of Hugh, who she felt certain was on his way to Western Australia at that moment. When he had left for Merinda six weeks ago, he had promised that it would take him a week at the most to contain the fly-strike, and then he would return at once to Western Australia. Which meant he would be back at Kalagandra in the next two weeks or so. Joanna had left him a letter at the Golden Age Hotel, explaining what she had done and why, and in which direction her small party had headed. She had also told him she would be back at Kalagandra by the middle of June, which was only a few days away.

She turned to Captain Fielding. "Can we find our way back?" she said.

"First we have to determine in what direction the town is, Mrs.

Westbrook. If we make a mistake and go in the wrong direction, we'll end up in the Great Victoria Desert and then we will most surely perish."

Beth said, "What is in the Great Victoria Desert, Captain?"

"No one knows. It hasn't been explored. Men go in, they don't come out. But I imagine it must be a lot worse than what we have been traveling through in the past four weeks. We don't want to end up in there, I can tell you that."

Eric Graham got down from his camel and rubbed his sore back, muttering something about "bloody insane way to get about."

Sammy appeared then, grinning broadly beneath his battered hat. "She plenty water over there, Captain," he said, pointing.

"Is it a large waterhole?" Joanna said.

"She plenty big, missus," the Aborigine said, holding his arms far apart.

Thank God, Joanna thought as she looked at her companions. It had been six days since their last visit to a waterhole; their clothes were dirty and sweaty, their faces matted with grime. And the dishes they had been eating from had been cleaned only with sand. Joanna looked forward to giving everything a good washing.

"I suggest we stop here, Captain," she said. She was thinking that, if her party was indeed lost and they did not return to Kalagandra in a week, Hugh would surely set out to look for them.

"Aye, I agree with you," he said, bringing his camel to its knees, and sliding stiffly to the ground.

"Captain Fielding," Beth said, "how far do you suppose Kalagandra is from here?"

"I couldn't say, lassie. I think we've been traveling in circles for the past week. In fact, I recommend we stay at this camp until we can get directional bearings. The sky might clear up in a day or two. To keep going would be dangerous."

They set up camp the way they had done every night for the past four weeks, with Sammy going off in search of food, Graham and Fielding putting up the tents and Beth collecting firewood. Joanna retired to her tent to freshen up before joining the others for dinner.

She lit the lantern and pulled the pins out of her hair. She brushed it vigorously and put it up with care, being meticulous with the placement of the pins. She washed her hands and face with the water Sammy had provided, and applied a little lavender cologne. And, since there was a waterhole nearby, she changed into her last clean blouse. Tomorrow, she told herself, would be laundry day.

Outside, she found the table and chairs in place, and the dishes ready.

Sammy was the cook, but Joanna always inspected the food before they ate it. Tonight he was making a stew of a wallaby he had trapped. "Be sure it is well cooked, Sammy," she said. Then she pulled the flour-and-water loaves the Australians called "damper" out of the coals, brushed them off, and put them on a plate.

By choice, Sammy sat by the fire, eating with his fingers, but Joanna and her companions sat on chairs and ate with knives and forks. "Captain Fielding," she said, "those black clouds we've been watching for days, would they be over the Great Victoria Desert? I mean, would it rain there?"

"Aye, it rains in the desert, Mrs. Westbrook," Fielding said, dispensing rum from a bottle he had brought along. He gave the nearly empty bottle a morose look, and added, "But since it rains only rarely there, when it does it's torrential. We want to be sure to keep a distance between us and those clouds."

"What I was wondering is, if the storm is in the desert, then mightn't we determine from that that Kalagandra lies in the other direction?"

"Not necessarily. It could be raining in Kalagandra, in which case the desert is that way," he said, and he pointed over his shoulder.

"What I don't understand," Eric Graham said, "is how the Aborigines manage to survive out here. How do they get around on days when you can't see the sun? They don't have compasses."

"They have a system of roads, Mr. Graham," Joanna said. "Not roads such as we know, but invisible tracks that crisscross the continent. The Aborigines travel along them the same way we would follow a city street or a country lane."

"But if the tracks are invisible, how do they know where they are?"

"By memorizing landmarks," Captain Fielding said. "They might look at that tree over there and think, Here's where we turn to the right. Or a pile of rocks might remind them that they're halfway to a waterhole. We could be sitting smack in the middle of a major highway, and not know it!"

Graham looked around in the darkness, skepticism in his eyes. "So you're saying, then, that if we could identify one of these invisible roads, we might be able to find our way back to town?"

"If we could identify the proper songline," Joanna said, "we could follow it directly to Karra Karra instead of roaming around the wilderness hoping to stumble upon something." Recalling how Sarah had once pointed out the songline of the Kangaroo Ancestor that ran through Merinda, Joanna wondered if she might try the same thing here. Sarah had looked at a pile of stones, a grouping of trees, and she had been able to read the signposts in them.

After dinner, while Sammy washed the dishes, the others gathered around the campfire for tea. Although it was boiled in a billycan, Joanna had brought along a ceramic sugar bowl, teacups and saucers and small spoons. Eric Graham took out his notebook and began writing in it, as he did every night, while Captain Fielding produced a pipe and filled it. Beth settled down to read.

Joanna studied her companions' faces. Eric Graham seemed to be doing fairly well, she thought, despite a problem with insects. She had had to treat him several times for bites and stings that didn't seem to be afflicting the others. And Beth, too, seemed to be fine. Her biggest concern, however, was for Captain Fielding. Joanna wondered if he should be subjecting himself to such harsh conditions at his age. He did not complain, but she saw the fatigue in his posture, and the grayness that had invaded his cheeks.

She was beginning to wonder if perhaps she should have heeded Commissioner Fox's warning against going into the desert. "Wait for your husband, Mrs. Westbrook," Fox had said. "Take more men and provisions with you." But Joanna had felt desperate about time passing quickly; and Sister Veronica had said that Emily Makepeace had come this way, which meant that Karra Karra must be somewhere near here, and possibly remnants of Djoogal's clan. As it was, it had taken two weeks in Kalagandra just to get their small expedition together, because the camels had had to be brought up from Albany, and a trustworthy native tracker had had to be found. Joanna had been unable to wait any longer—she had come such a long way, it had taken so much time and now she was so close . . . she *had* to find her answer.

When Captain Fielding's pipe was lit and he filled the air with pungent smoke, he said, "Did I ever tell you folks about the time . . . " And he launched into a tale of voyages to distant lands, populated with exotic maidens, cutthroat seamen and sea serpents. His companions listened politely, but without much interest, because they had heard all Fielding's stories in the weeks since leaving Merinda, and he was starting to repeat himself. But it was better than listening to the desert silence, which had become frightening and humbling, and reminded them of their vulnerability. While they half-listened to Fielding talk, his companions kept an alert ear toward the silence, thinking of Commissioner Fox's warnings back in Kalagandra of snakes and scorpions and of Aborigines who would spear a man just for his tobacco. Joanna and Beth had been particularly watchful for wild dingoes, which he had also warned them about.

While Fielding talked, Joanna looked at the compass in her hand. She was mesmerized by the peculiar action of the needle, swinging errati-

cally between north and south. She looked up at the sky. "Strange..."
she murmured. "No moon or stars. Just a peculiar blackness."

Eric Graham was thinking the same thing. His pencil made a scratching sound as it moved across the pages of his notebook: "I have never heard such silence," he wrote. "It makes me wonder if we have somehow been transported to another world, where there are no moon and no stars."

Eric was beginning to feel his spirits flag as the prospect of finding the mysterious Karra Karra grew remote. He was worried about going back to Melbourne with nothing to report. When Frank Downs had asked him if he would like to go along on the expedition, Eric had jumped at it. He was tired of writing human interest stories about whales being spotted off the coast. He longed to make a name for himself in real news reportage. And this was a tremendous opportunity for an ambitious reporter willing to take risks, because, he thought, it would be the first time such a story was reported firsthand by a newsman, instead of it being "as told to." He hoped it would bring him prestige and fame, and a chance to prove himself as the best in the business. It could also change the mind of a certain young lady who had rejected his marriage proposal. But first they had to *find* something.

"Faith!" he said, dropping his pencil and rubbing his hands together. "It gets blessed cold out here at night!"

Captain Fielding suddenly stood up and looked around. "What is it?" Joanna said.

He narrowed his eyes and searched the darkness. "I don't know," he said. "The air—it doesn't feel right."

"Beth," Joanna said, pulling her shawl tightly about her, "are you warm enough?"

"I'm fine, Mother," Beth said, without looking up from her reading.

Joanna had given Lady Emily's diary to Beth on their first day out of Kalagandra, explaining to her daughter that it was time she knew the real reason for their journey into the desert. And as Beth had read a little of it every night, Joanna had seen how absorbed her daughter became in the words from the past, how still she sat, what a faraway look she had in her eyes. Afterward, when they retired for the night, Joanna and Beth would spend time talking about what she had read, and Beth was usually so full of questions that they sometimes talked for an hour before falling asleep. Now, she was near the end of the book, and completely engrossed.

"Gosh," she said, finally looking up. "I wonder what it's all about. I mean, why *are* we afraid of dogs, Mother? I know I am because of what happened with the dingoes and poor Button. But Grandmother was afraid of dogs, and so are you. Do you think there really is a curse on us? How exciting!"

"Exciting?" Joanna said. "Yes, I suppose in a way it is."

"And do you suppose Great-grandfather committed a crime? I wonder what it was. Did he steal the opal, maybe? It's very valuable, I know, but I thought the Aborigines didn't have possessions. They wouldn't have thought an opal was valuable, would they?"

"Perhaps the opal has a different kind of value . . . a religious value, possibly." Joanna had shown the stone to Beth the first night they had made camp. Beth had seen it before, but this time, when Joanna had explained its true significance, she had held it in her hand, feeling its peculiar warmth; she had stared into its depths, mesmerized by the brilliant red and green flashes, and she had said, "Why do you suppose it was hidden inside Rupert?"

Now she said, "I'll bet Great-grandfather Makepeace found an opal mine! Doesn't Grandmother mention another legacy in here?" she said, handing the diary to Joanna. "Something that she felt she had to come back and claim? I'll bet that's what the deed is for!"

But Joanna wasn't sure what the "other legacy" might be. As she carefully replaced the old book inside the leather satchel, with the opal—which, valuable though it was, she had decided to bring with her—her grandfather's notes and the deed, Joanna recalled something Sarah had said to her a long time ago: "The book is your mother's Dreaming. It is your songline, as it was hers. Follow it, and you will find the place you seek."

But how could she follow it, she wondered, if she couldn't read the clues it contained? Perhaps there were signs in the diary that pointed the way, but for some reason Joanna had never been able to see them.

When she saw Fielding walk away from the campfire, she said, "Is there anything wrong, Captain?"

"I've got a bad feeling," he said.

"Hello," Graham said, looking up. "What's that sound?"

They listened. "It sounds like thunder," Beth said.

But Sammy was suddenly on his feet. "Water!" he cried.

They turned in the direction the noise was coming from. They couldn't see anything, but they felt the ground begin to rumble.

"What—" Graham said.

And suddenly it was upon them.

"Mother!" Beth cried.

"*Beth!*"

Joanna opened her eyes and stared up at the sky. She lifted her head, and a wave of nausea swept over her. She lay still for a moment, trying to think, searching her mind for her last memory. What had happened? She touched her head, and sand showered down into her eyes and mouth. She coughed and sat up, and the world seemed to tilt. She put a hand to her forehead; and felt a painful lump.

She looked around. The terrain was not familiar; this was not the place where they had camped the night before; the hills and trees were in all the wrong positions. And the tents weren't there. Nor the camels. Nor the men.

And then it came back to her—the rising wall of water suddenly rushing toward them.

Beth!

She struggled to her feet, and frantically searched the landscape, looking for signs of Beth and the others. But there was nothing, no one. Surely she wasn't the only one here! Surely her companions had made it through the flash flood and were now waking up to this same shocking reality, and would soon be making their way back to her.

Surely, dear God, she thought, Beth hadn't perished!

She hugged herself tightly, thinking, don't panic. Keep your head. Don't lose control.

She tried to remember what had happened. They had been sitting around the campfire, Graham had said, "What's that sound?" And they had turned in time to see a dark wall rushing toward them. Joanna remembered Beth reaching for her. After that—nothing.

When she began to shake suddenly, and the world tilted again, she realized that she was going into shock.

She saw a nearby eucalyptus tree that had somehow escaped the raging water; it still stood upright. She made her way to it and leaned against it, shivering, her teeth chattering. The day went dark and then light again, and she knew she was about to pass out. She quickly sat down and put her head between her knees.

"Oh God," she sobbed. "Let the others still be alive. Beth—"

After a few moments, the vertigo subsided and Joanna was able to take control of herself. She took a more careful look at her surroundings. Judging by the brightness of the day it was about noon. She saw the same brown wilderness dotted with stunted eucalyptus and mulga that she had been traveling through for four weeks, except that now the trees and shrubs were all uprooted, their pale roots pointing toward the sky. There was no sign of her camp. Not a chair, not a saddle. It was as if the face of the world had been washed clean.

And Beth. Where was Beth?

She realized that she had also lost the satchel—the opal, her mother's diary, the deed. Everything.

She stood up again and, holding onto the tree, steadied herself. She saw shadows moving on the ground a short distance away and looked up to see large birds circling in the sky.

And then she saw something. A dark form lying in the sand.

She recognized the naval jacket with brass buttons. "Captain Fielding!" she cried, running to him. "Oh thank God!"

He was lying on his back, his eyes closed, his mouth open. She felt for a pulse at his neck. He was dead.

Joanna wrapped her arms around her knees and fought down panic and hysteria. She could not remember having ever been this frightened. Or this thirsty. Where was she going to find water? Strangely, the ground was dry. How could that be, after such a flood? Had she lain unconscious longer than she thought? She squinted up at a lone eagle circling overhead. She knew that eagles sometimes carried off newborn lambs, and even human babies. Would it attack a helpless woman?

She had to take control of herself. The flash flood had swept everything away, but she had been spared. This might mean the others could also have been spared, and perhaps supplies from the camp.

As the dark bird-shadows moved over the ground, Joanna covered Fielding's body with sand and rocks, and when she was done, she fashioned a cross out of branches and stuck it at the head of the make-shift grave. Then, exhausted, she said a prayer, and stood up. She kept the captain's jacket.

She looked for the sun, but saw only the same mocking whiteness stretching from horizon to horizon. She studied the trees and bushes that had been uprooted, determined the path of the flash flood and began to walk.

As she left the grave behind her, she stayed alert for any strange or suspicious object in the landscape. She was hungry, and an acute thirst told her that she needed to find water soon. She called out as she walked, "Beth! Sammy! Mr. Graham!"

After a few hundred yards, she began to find things: a waterskin, still full of water; a tin of salted beef and another of biscuits; Eric Graham's hat. She drank some of the water as she paused to assess her situation. She decided that she had enough food and water to last a few days if she was careful.

She had to find Beth. But where to look? How far could she go on the few provisions she had? And then she recalled Captain Fielding's warnings about wandering into the Great Victoria Desert, which was most likely an even more hostile terrain than this one, a place where she would surely get lost and die. Hugh was probably already in Perth, she thought, or even on the train to Kalagandra at that very moment, and when she didn't show up there when she had said she would, he would certainly come looking for her. She decided she would make camp where she was, and wait to be rescued.

Joanna took a small sip of water from the waterskin and held it in her mouth for a long time before swallowing. She estimated that she had just over a cup of water left. She had eaten the last of the food that morning.

She stepped out of the crude lean-to she had erected against the eucalyptus tree and surveyed the landscape. In five days, nothing had changed. The sky was still strangely overcast; she was still unable to determine direction. At sunset the whole world seemed to darken at once, so that it was impossible to tell which was west or east, and she never saw the sunrise; bright daylight always wakened her. But now she needed to know where she was, because she had to leave her small camp.

For five days Joanna had survived on the hope that someone from her party would find her, that Beth would suddenly materialize, or Hugh. She had set out each day in a different direction, walking as far from her camp as she dared, always keeping the lean-to in sight, leaving a trail of pebbles as she went. She would explore as far as she could, and then return just before dark, following the pebbles back to the shelter, where she ate a little of the tinned meat and biscuits, and then slept fitfully, wrapped against the cold in Captain Fielding's jacket, wishing she knew how to start a fire without matches. She had awakened in terror many times, as she relived the flash flood in nightmares, or as Beth appeared to her in dreams, dying in many different ways. Joanna awoke to her own screams, and then lay trembling beneath the eucalyptus shelter, praying that this, too, was a bad dream, and that she would soon awaken in her own bed at Merinda.

And she had cried—for Beth, for poor Captain Fielding, for herself.

Now the food was gone, and almost all the water. Joanna faced the hard fact that she would have to leave this place in order to survive. But she didn't know which way to go. She had found the compass, with its erratic needle, and the leather satchel, its precious contents intact. But these would not tell her east from west; they would not lead her to food and water.

As she stared at the bleak landscape, she tried to remember what she had heard over the years about surviving in the wilderness. She knew there was water here, hidden, but one had to know where to find it. And food, if one had cunning and skill, could be plentiful.

She felt the weight of the waterskin in her hand. The first thing she knew she must do was to find water.

But Joanna didn't want to strike off arbitrarily, in just any direction. She had to walk with a purpose, she had to choose the right path. She surveyed the low-lying hills to her right, which she had explored on her first day. She knew there was no water there. To her left lay miles of scattered boulders, as if a mountain, long ago, had exploded. Behind her was a flat, monotonous expanse, and ahead the mallee continued, its saltbush and stunted eucalypts offering the most promise.

And so she chose to head in that direction. But before she went, she left a sign for anyone who might come along, to let them know she had been there. Removing one of her lapis-lazuli earrings, she tied it to a sturdy branch of the tree, and then, with a sharp stone, carved her name into the eucalyptus trunk. She made a large arrow in the sand, using pebbles, pointing in the direction she had gone. Finally she left the relative security and familiarity of her little camp, carrying Fielding's jacket, the leather satchel and the disturbingly light waterskin. She decided she would walk as far as she could, even though she was weak, and put off drinking the water no matter how severe her thirst became.

She trudged through the semi-desert, walking across the sand-plains and dry salt lakes, past mulga and spinifex, and twisted eucalypts that, with their multiple trunks, bore no resemblance to the tall and graceful trees at Merinda.

The hours passed, and she kept up her spirits by thinking of home— she recited Hugh's ballads, she carried on imaginary conversations with Beth and Sarah. She envisioned finding Beth just up ahead, sitting in her own little camp, and of how joyful their reunion would be. And when Joanna realized that the day was growing dark, she looked back and could no longer see the tiny lean-to, nor any recognizable terrain. She had no idea how far she had walked, but she was extremely hungry, and her thirst was like nothing she had ever imagined.

She sat down in the protection of a group of boulders, praying that this wasn't home to deadly snakes, and held the waterskin in her lap for a long time before taking a desperate drink. Panic and fear began to steal over her again. She looked up at the sky, but still there were no stars, no moon. I am going to die here, she thought, and she began to cry.

She awoke to another mocking, milky sky, and a silence that she thought was going to drive her mad. After leaving behind her second earring, and another arrow made of rocks, she continued to walk again, searching the dried creek beds for pockets of water, digging under shrubs, trying to coax some wetness out of this unforgiving land. At noon, she drank her last mouthful of water, but she kept the waterskin. Hunger pangs had turned into genuine pain, and as she forced herself to keep moving toward an inhospitable horizon, she feared the terrible end that was most surely facing her. After an hour or two she had to stop. It was useless, she knew, to keep trudging without knowing where she was going. Water wasn't going to just fall from the sky, or suddenly spring up from the earth. She had to find it, and soon, while she still had her wits about her.

She caught up her straying hair and pinned it tight. She thought of the woman who had passed through this very wilderness with her young husband and little girl. "Naomi was strong," Patrick Lathrop and Elsie Dobson had said. And Joanna realized now just how strong her grandmother must have been, to survive in this place.

I am Naomi's granddaughter, she told herself as she surveyed the unpromising scene. I will be strong, too.

And then she thought of her mother, Lady Emily, coming through this area as a child in the company of an Aboriginal girl, and wondered: How did they do it? How could two such vulnerable creatures, walking on foot, have made it across so many barren miles?

And then it came to her: They knew how to follow the songlines.

Of course, Joanna thought, that was the answer. She had been trying to survive by thinking like a gently bred young Englishwoman, when she should have been thinking like the people who had been born out of this land—the Aborigines. They had survived by following song-lines. Joanna knew that songlines connected dreaming sites, each of which represented a stage of an Ancestor's journey, and that they were usually a day's trek from each other. But how to find one?

She turned in a slow circle, trying to make something of the barren scene. She saw rocks, dwarfed trees, sandy hillocks, dried creek beds, but nothing that resembled a songline. But then, she wondered, what did a songline look like?

Suddenly she was remembering something from years ago, when she and Sarah had gone down to the river and Sarah had told Joanna that the Kangaroo Ancestor had come through Merinda. She had pointed to a grassy hillock and had said, "That is where Kangaroo Ancestress slept. Do you see her great hind legs, her long tail, her very small head?" Joanna remembered how she had stared hard at the hillock and had indeed seen the sleeping kangaroo.

Was that the answer? To look at the wilderness for natural clues, images? To stop looking at the wilderness through English eyes, to try to look at this place as an Aborigine would?

She stared and stared, and the landscape did begin to seem more interesting. Rocks and trees and creek beds began to shift; they remained still but they underwent a metamorphosis. Suddenly Joanna stared at a group of boulders; could it look like the outline of an emu?

She ran to them, giddy with hunger and thirst, and when she reached them she searched for the food or water that should have been there. But it was only a barren group of boulders.

She looked around again. There, just over there, the way that creek bed curved. Did it resemble a snake? Joanna ran to it, fell to her knees and dug into the hard clay. But no water came.

She stood up and searched the wilderness with tear-filled eyes. Nature seemed to be mocking her, showing her Dreaming Sites that weren't really Dreaming Sites at all. Despair rose in her like heat. She thought of Captain Fielding, lying in a poor, unidentified grave, his dream of living out his years beneath the sun of Fiji as dead as he.

"It isn't fair!" Joanna suddenly cried. "Beth! Where are you? Oh God—"

She dropped back to her knees and covered her face with her hands. When the salty tears fell into her mouth, Joanna was startled. At first she thought it had started to rain, and then she saw the dampness on her hands. She licked her palms and thought of the desperate state she had been reduced to. Her eyes settled upon her leather satchel, with its tarnished buckles and the initials "JM." She thought of the papers her grandfather had so carefully and meticulously written in shorthand, how useless they were to her now. Although a fascinating chronicle of his observations of the Aborigines, they contained no practical information. He had written that the women had gathered food, but he had failed to mention how. He had said the clan went to waterholes, but he had omitted to record the manner in which they had found those waterholes. Just a worthless, cursed bunch of papers.

Suddenly, she snatched up the satchel and flung it away from her as hard as she could. It bounced off a boulder and landed with a thud. As Joanna stared miserably at it, she remembered that the deed was in there, and the opal and the diary. She got up to retrieve it. She looked inside to make sure the fire opal wasn't broken, and she saw her own notes—the translation of John Makepeace's papers. Her eye caught on a sentence she had written: *Djoogal's clan belongs to the Kangaroo Totem.*

Joanna wondered suddenly if she had been half right—that she should indeed find a songline and follow it. Perhaps she had been wrong in thinking she could just make one up. The right songline had to be here, not just something that resembled an emu or a snake or whatever symbol she chose; she had to know exactly what songline lay across this country. If she was in the ancestral territory of Djoogal's clan, then she must look for the songline of the Kangaroo Ancestor.

She climbed up the bank of the dried creek bed and slowly searched the landscape again, this time looking for the ancient track that the Kangaroo Ancestor must have taken thousands of years ago, when he had come through here, singing up creation. She tried to lay Joanna Westbrook aside, to turn herself into Djoogal, or a member of his clan, or perhaps the girl named Reenadeena. If they were standing here and looking for the songline of the Kangaroo Dreaming, she wondered, what would they see?

Was that it, over there? A rocky formation, thrust up from the earth millennia ago, and which Joanna would earlier have said was a sleeping lyrebird or a fighting bandicoot, but which now she saw might look like two kangaroos, one large, the other small, bent over as if grazing.

There, she thought. Is that where the Kangaroo Ancestor stopped long ago, to rest and to eat?

She began to walk toward it, barely aware of the darkening day, or that she was growing lightheaded, or that her pulse throbbed unevenly in her temples. And even before she reached the formation, Joanna believed she had found a Dreaming Site of the Kangaroo Ancestor.

Joanna kept track of the days by collecting small twigs. Each morning, before she struck out again, she found a twig and put it into the satchel. Then she left some sort of mark—either her name scratched on a rock, or her initials carved on a tree—with the usual arrow made of pebbles, showing the direction in which she had gone. And by the time she realized that she had left the comparative safety and security of the mallee, and had wandered into the Great Victoria Desert, she had collected fourteen twigs.

She had water now, and food. At the first Dreaming Site she had dug into the soil until she had found brackish but drinkable water. At the next Dreaming Site, where she could see in the outline of a salt pan the place where Kangaroo Ancestor had mated with another kangaroo, Joanna had prized witchetty grubs out of the roots of an acacia and had eaten them raw.

She managed one day to catch a lizard, and that, too, she had eaten raw. And then she remembered that Bill Lovell had told her long ago that the inner bark of a tree is often edible. And this, too, had sustained her.

One Dreaming Site was an enormous hole in the ground which Joanna surmised might have been a meteor crater, caused long ago by some prehistoric celestial shower, because when she checked her compass, the needle spun crazily. The floor of the crater had become a clay pan, and Joanna remembered Sarah telling her about a certain kind of frog that buried itself in clay pans, hiding just beneath the surface between bouts of rain and storing water in its body. She dug into the clay and found frogs, which, when she squeezed them, poured out fresh, drinkable water.

One day, late in the afternoon, she had seen a flock of red-tailed cockatoos fly over, and had thought: They are heading for water. She had followed them and found a waterhole filled with fresh water.

On the fifth day of following the Kangaroo Dreaming, Joanna had come across something that shocked and dismayed her, and caused her spirits to plummet. It was a man's skeleton. The clothes had long since rotted away and the bones had been picked clean, so that she knew it had not been a member of her party. But he had perished alone out here. Joanna found a pair of wire-rimmed spectacles near the skull and kept them. That afternoon, before the day grew dark, she was able to make a fire, using one of the lenses and aiming it at where she imagined the sun to be. Finally, she was able to eat cooked food.

On the eighth day, two eagles flew by, fighting over a baby wallaby which one of them had caught. In their fight, they dropped it, and Joanna ran and grabbed it. She stripped off the hide, skinning it the way she had skinned rabbits for dinner at Merinda, and roasted the flesh in hot coals. The meat lasted for days.

As Joanna followed the ancient songline, she felt herself begin to grow strong, despite her primitive diet and the punishing aspects of the landscape. Instead of growing weaker and more helpless, she felt a curious new strength invade her body. She lost all her hairpins, so that her hair hung down to her waist and she had to push it back over her ears. When the weather began to grow hotter, she undid the top buttons of her blouse, undid the cuffs, and rolled up the long sleeves. She removed her petticoats and, out of some vague sense of modesty, buried them. She mixed water with clay and made a paste that she spread over her face to protect it from sunburn. She tied mulga branches together and wore them as a hat. She bundled the satchel into Captain Fielding's jacket and tied it around her waist so that she could walk with her hands free.

A change came over the terrain. Joanna realized one day that she had entered a wonderland. The desert sparkled. Dried-up water holes formed saucer-shaped depressions in the sand, filled with rainbow-colored mineral deposits that shimmered like ground glass. Salt pans glowed; the sky was incandescent. And Joanna was overcome with a sense of having returned to the beginning of time—the Dreamtime.

The sun finally came out and she established direction by using her watch. The north-south line ran between noon and the hour hand—and she realized that she was walking eastward, deeper into the heart of the Great Victoria Desert. Yet she knew she could not turn back. Behind her lay desolation and the risk of getting lost, but as long as she stayed with the songline, perhaps she would be safe.

She was also aware of being impelled by another force. This was the songline of Djoogal's clan—she was certain of it. This was the way Naomi and John Makepeace had come, with their tents and hopes. This was the track Reenadeena had followed to take little Emily out of danger. Joanna no longer felt as if she were alone. Spirits walked with her.

On the fifteenth day of following Kangaroo Dreaming, as she was starting a fire with the spectacles and preparing to roast some witchetty grubs, a shadow fell across her. She looked up and saw that the sun had been blocked by a man standing over her, a spear in one hand.

Joanna stood up slowly and saw that he was not alone. Several other men stood behind him, also carrying weapons. They were naked, their bodies rubbed with fat and ash; they wore hairstring bands around their heads and waists, similar to the one Sarah had made for Joanna years ago, during the typhoid epidemic. They stared at Joanna with expressionless faces.

"Are you members of Djoogal's clan?" she said.

They did not reply.

So she said, "Karra Karra?"

Still no response.

She felt the heaviness of the hot noon air, the vast expanse of the desert stretching away from her into space. She smelled the grubs roasting in the coals and recalled how they had tasted raw. She remembered catching and eating a lizard, and how she had sucked bitter water from acacia roots, not minding the dirt on them, nor the fact that she hadn't a proper napkin with which to wipe her hands. And so it seemed right, she thought, to be standing here in this alien landscape, staring into these deeply set, reddish-brown eyes and feeling no fear.

Without a word, the men turned and began to walk away.

Joanna stared after them. And then she realized that she was meant to follow. Quickly picking up Captain Fielding's jacket and the leather satchel, she went after them.

When they reached the encampment, the sun was a molten disc on the western horizon. Joanna entered the scattered collection of miamias—small shelters made of eucalyptus boughs—and campfires and marveled at both her own fearlessness and the Aborigines' seeming indifference to her presence. She walked past women who were cooking, skinning animals or nursing babies, and they smiled at her as though this were a common occurrence. They, too, were naked. A few young girls, Joanna saw, wore skirts made of cockatoo feathers, but everyone else—men, women and children—went about completely unclothed. Ironically, Joanna felt embarrassed by her linen blouse, long skirt and boots.

The men stopped walking. They turned, and the leader pointed with his spear. Joanna looked to where he was pointing, and she saw a young white girl lying across an open pit of steaming eucalyptus boughs.

"Beth!" she cried, running to her.

The girl was unconscious, badly sunburnt and, Joanna found when she touched Beth's forehead, fiery hot with fever. And she had seen that shocking, unmistakable pallor before—during the typhoid epidemic and on the dead face of Captain Fielding. As Joanna lifted her daughter in her arms and held her close, the native woman who seemed to be taking care of her said something Joanna could not understand.

I am too late, she thought. Too late.

CHAPTER 29

Sarah was in the solarium, preparing ointments made from comfrey and calendula, surrounded by hanging plants, small trees, creeping vines and bushy little herbs in clay pots; overlying the rich scent of loam and compost were the delicate frangrances of pink rosemary and lemon verbena, and the heady aroma of melted beeswax. When Joanna had departed for Western Australia six months ago, Sarah had promised to take care of the healing garden and to keep up the medicinal stores. She worked here every day, nursing seedlings, pruning and transplanting, harvesting leaves and stems and roots.

She often wondered what Joanna and Beth were doing at a particular moment, and if Joanna might at one point give up waiting for Hugh to return, and come back on her own. He was supposed to have gone back to Kalagandra weeks ago, but he was still here at Merinda, fighting a fly-strike that had reached epidemic proportions.

As Sarah checked the consistency of the melted beeswax, her hands suddenly paused, almost of their own accord. She gazed through the glass wall at the billabong lying flat and silver beyond the trees, and she thought: Philip is coming.

She quickly extinguished the flame beneath the beeswax, removed her apron and hurried through the house to her bedroom, where she tidied her hair and brushed away the leaves and tiny flowers that clung to her dark brown wool skirt. As she hastily changed out of her calico work blouse into a pale blue silk one, she realized that her hands were shaking. She was both excited and apprehensive about seeing Philip. Since his return to Australia, they had been cautious about their time together. Sarah knew that, for the sake of Philip's success as an architect in the district, they must be careful. Servants talked; so did station hands. And everyone knew that he was still married. They had not made love again.

Fortunately, Philip was very busy, having received commissions to build mansions for the Camerons and the McClouds, which called for him to make frequent trips into Melbourne to consult with suppliers and spend days at the brickworks and lumberyards. His spare time was limited; opportunities for Sarah to be alone with him were few. He had come to dinner at Merinda several times, and he and Hugh and Sarah had gone to concerts in the park in Cameron Town. But the one thing they both longed for—the freedom to love each other, and to make love—lay beyond their grasp.

Now he was coming to Merinda, alone and unannounced. She sensed his presence in the drive; Sarah could almost see what he was wearing.

She hurried down the hall and opened the door before Philip could knock.

They stared at each other.

"Hello, Sarah," Philip said, smiling.

"Hello, Philip. Please come in. It's good to see you."

He removed his hat and looked around the foyer. Then he kissed her on the cheek, lingeringly. He looked at her for a long moment before saying quietly, "You look beautiful, Sarah. How are you?"

She took in his handsomeness, his tallness, his slightly crooked nose, and she ached for him. "I'm well," she said. "I think about you all the time."

"I try to stay away. I can't concentrate on my work. All I can think of is you. All I want is to be with you."

"I, too," she said, and touched his arm.

"I came by because I got a letter from Alice today. She still won't give me a divorce. She doesn't want me to go back to her, but she is afraid that a legal divorce will hurt Daniel. When he's older, she said."

Sarah nodded. She understood the social stigma that divorce placed on a woman, just as she was aware of her own situation, the stigma of being a married man's mistress.

"How is it going with Hugh?" Philip said, wishing he could say other things to her.

"Hugh is camped up by the north boundary," she said. "He hasn't been home for three days."

"It's still bad, is it?"

"Yes, I'm afraid so."

"I passed Mr. Ormsby on the way here. He says he thinks he's going to lose Strathfield if the fly-strike goes on much longer."

"Yes," she said. "I had heard that."

They fell silent again. In the nearby parlor, a clock chimed the hour.

"You can go out to the camp if you like," Sarah said. "Hugh would be glad to see you."

"I think I will." Philip reached into his pocket and brought out an envelope. "When I went to the post office this morning to pick up my mail, the postmistress asked me if I would be passing by Merinda, as there was this important-looking letter for Hugh." He showed it to Sarah.

She read the return address—it had come from a Commissioner Fox in Western Australia. "It's from Kalagandra, and it isn't from Joanna. Philip, something's wrong. I can feel it. I've felt it for weeks. We must get this letter to Hugh at once."

———————————————— • ————————————————

Hugh laid aside his pen and peered through the window of the tent. He watched station hands mill around the temporary camp, helping themselves to tea from the billycan that was continually on the boil. Hugh thought of it as a military camp, and of his men as soldiers. They rode out every day to inspect sheep, to shoot them and bury them, to crutch animals that might be saved and run them through highly unpleasant insecticidal dips. They came wearily back into camp, filthy and tired; they drank the strong tea and ate Ping-Li's sandwiches, and then rode off again to face another battle in a frustrating war. Hugh was also weary. He would have liked to take a break, but there was still a tremendous amount of work to be done.

As he had feared three months ago, when the warm weather broke a horrific wave of blowfly had suddenly appeared on the western plains, sweeping over stations like death clouds. All over southeastern Australia sheep were dying in the thousands, while graziers from Adelaide to the Queensland border were racing to find a way to stop the epidemic.

As Hugh picked up his pen to resume writing, he paused to look at Joanna's photograph on the workbench. How he missed her! He wished he could have stayed in Western Australia, or that he had been able to return to her weeks ago. He wrote to her regularly, keeping her up to date on this endless battle with fly-strike, but he hadn't heard from her. Storms had been reported in the Bight—boats had been lost, some of them carrying mail. There had also been a maritime strike, bringing sea travel and shipping around Australia's southern coast to a virtual standstill. And Hugh knew that the telegraph was unreliable. Bush fires burned down the lines, and renegade Aborigines occasionally chopped down the poles.

Soon, my darling, Hugh thought, as he imagined Joanna waiting for him at the Golden Age Hotel.

He went back to his journal, a book that was starting to resemble a chronicle of failures, beginning with the first entry:

Wool of two-tooth ewes, dipped in tobacco and sulphur, still infested with eggs.

Week Three—Flock wethers sick after lime-sulphur dip. John Reed suspects inhalation poisoning. Will discontinue.

Week Five—Experimented with higher water temperature. Found to scour yolk out of wool, thus damaging it. Will next try to lower the water temperature, although Ian Hamilton has tried this without success.

Week Eight—Angus McCloud reported an experimental formula he used on six-month lambs. Found it stained the wool. And blowfly still present.

Week Ten—Frank Downs reports disastrous losses at Lismore.

Week Eleven—Merinda flock rams badly infested now. Must destroy them.

Hugh picked up his pen and wrote: "Week Twelve—Am convinced that the green blowfly breeds almost entirely on living sheep. This, therefore, accounts for the failure of trapping to effectively minimize blowfly strike in sheep. A method must be found to interrupt the life cycle of the blowfly."

He looked at the jars that were lined up on his workbench. They contained specimens he had collected from Merinda flocks that had been treated with the usual insecticidal dips. They were labeled: BLOW-FLY EGGS, ONE DAY OLD, BLOWFLY IN PUPA STAGE and MAGGOTS FOUND ON CRUTCHINGS. These proved that the traditional dips used to keep sheep free from blowfly had not worked against this particular strain.

Hugh resumed writing: "Will now check results of experimentation with arsenic dip."

When he had announced his plan to try the radical arsenic formula on his sheep, some of the graziers had warned him against it. "I don't know," Ian Hamilton had said. "Arsenic is a dangerous thing. It can make your stock sicker than they were with the fly-strike. And then there are the shearers to think of—they won't shear if they think there's poison in the wool."

But Hugh had decided it was time to take risks. In the past three months he had made some remarkable discoveries. Among them was the fact that a single green blowfly produced two thousand eggs. Carrying that statistic out mathematically over several breeding cycles, and assuming that at least half of those young flies then each produced another two thousand eggs, Hugh came up with results that were staggering. When the warm weather broke again and all the eggs hatched, there was going to be a new infestation of blowfly so overwhelming that nothing anyone did was going to prevent a catastrophic loss of sheep.

He looked at the sacks heaped against one wall of the tent. They were tagged with labels that read: STUD RAMS, TOBACCO & SULPHUR, JULY 10, 1886, and WETHERS, CORROSIVE SUBLIMATE, JUNE 30, 1886. Neither had been successful. And so, two weeks ago, Hugh had decided to run the cull ewes through the highly controversial arsenic dip. Jacko had just brought in those wool samples, and Hugh decided to look at them.

He picked up a sack labeled: CULL EWES, NORTH CLOVER PADDOCK, ARSENIC FORMULA #12. Cull ewes were sheep past breeding age, kept on the station as foster mothers to rear orphaned lambs. He removed a few specimens from the sack and went to the workbench, placed some wool fibers on a slide, adjusted the microscope, then looked into the eyepiece.

He frowned, angled the mirror to catch more light and adjusted the fine-focus knob. The magnified wool fibers on the slide filled his view. Moving the slide around, he switched to a higher-powered lens and he studied the fibers.

There was no evidence of blowfly.

He went back to the sack and took out another specimen; this one from another animal but from the same flock.

The fibers under the microscope were all clean. Not a single blowfly egg.

He took out another, and another, until he had examined nearly twenty specimens. And they were all clean.

The arsenic had worked.

He hurried to the doorway of the tent and looked out, expecting to call Jacko over. He was surprised to see a buggy arriving in the camp.

"This came for you today, Hugh," Sarah said, when she and Philip entered the tent. "Philip brought it by. We thought it might be important."

Hugh opened the envelope, unfolded the single sheet of paper, and read: "Dear Mr. Westbrook, We have just been informed that telegraph lines are down near the South Australia border. I have sent messages to you which I realize now must not have gotten through. Therefore, I write this letter. It is my sad duty to inform you, Mr. Westbrook, that your wife, by her own decision, went into the desert on May 6, in the company of her daughter, Mr. Eric Graham, Captain Fielding and a black tracker. Apparently the party were the victims of a flash flood. There was only one survivor, Eric Graham, and he is in critical condition. Mrs. Westbrook and the rest of the party have not been found."

He stared at the letter. He read it again. "My God," he said. "Sarah, my God—"

"What is it?" She took the letter from him and read it. "Oh no . . ."

Sarah laid a hand on Hugh's arm. "Hugh," she said. "Joanna is alive. I sense it. If she were dead, I would know. But Hugh, she is in great danger. We must find her."

———————◆———————

Judd MacGregor was in his father's study, working at the desk. He was no longer afraid of this room; the ghosts had left with his father. There was a knock at the door, and Pauline entered.

"Hello, Mother," Judd said. "I say, you look smashing."

She smiled as she pulled on her gloves. "Thank you, Judd. I'm on my way to Lismore to visit Frank. There are still a few things to iron out before I can take title on Kilmarnock. What are you so hard at work on?"

"Well, I was thinking that, since we can't save the remaining stock because of the blowfly, we might as well boil it down for tallow and clear the grazing land. I have a new idea for Kilmarnock—wheat farming. It's very profitable right now, Mother. Do you recall those shares in the Broken Hill silver mine that Uncle Frank gave me last year, for my twenty-first birthday? Do you think he would mind if I sold them?"

"I shouldn't think so. After all, they are yours. So it's to be wheat farming, is it? I think I rather like the idea."

"It requires less initial financial outlay, far less labor, and ultimately higher profits. Especially since I have been working with an experimental strain of wheat that will grow in drought conditions."

Pauline watched the way his hands moved as he spoke about his plan, the eyebrow that went up slightly whenever he was excited. He was so like Colin, she thought, the Colin of long ago, before years of bitterness and frustration had etched lines into his youthful face. Judd was like his father in many ways, she realized—stubborn, dedicated to a dream, but he also showed the gentling influence of his mother, Christina, who had died fourteen years ago.

"I'll be home in time for dinner," Pauline said, as she bent to kiss him on the cheek. "I've asked Jenny to cook your favorite pudding tonight."

As she was about to go out the door, Judd said, "He never appreciated you, you know."

She smiled sadly. "I think maybe he did, in his own way."

"Do you think he will ever come back to us?"

"I don't know, Judd."

"Kilmarnock will belong to you by then. Will you let him come back?"

"I don't know that either."

Pauline tried not to think of what might be, or what the future possibly held. She was determined to continue living life her own way, despite what she suspected her friends were thinking. She had seen it happen before, Western District society laying the blame on an abandoned woman as if she were somehow at fault because her husband had deserted her. But Pauline refused to regard Colin's actions as abandonment. He had run away because he was ashamed of himself, and because he thought he could salvage some shred of self-respect if he returned to the ancestral castle in Scotland. She could not blame him for wanting to escape both from a marriage that should not have happened in the first place, and from financial ruin. Pauline continued to be seen around the district, to attend social events, and to hold her head high even though people gave her covert looks. And she had refused to give up Kilmarnock. She had used her own inheritance, with additional financial help from Frank, to pay off Colin's debts. This was her home now, and she intended never to leave it.

"Everything is going to be all right from now on, Mother," Judd said. "You'll see."

As Pauline reached for the doorknob, she thought of the miracle that had occurred, somewhere along the way, when she had stopped thinking of Judd as another woman's child. She was about to say something more when a voice came from behind her. "Ah, there you are!"

She turned, startled, and saw Frank standing there. "I was just on my way to Lismore to see you," she said.

"Yes, I know," he said. "But something has come up. I have to go to Merinda at once, and I just dropped by to tell you that we shall have to put off our business meeting."

"What is happening at Merinda?"

"It seems Joanna has run into some serious trouble in Western Australia, and Hugh has asked for my help."

"What sort of trouble?"

"The note that he sent over didn't say. But it's urgent, whatever it is."

"I'll go with you," Pauline said.

Judd reached for his jacket. "I want to come, too."

———————•———————

As they rode down the drive toward the house, Frank said, "That's Reed's horse."

"And isn't that the Hamilton carriage?" Pauline said. "Hugh seems to have asked help from everyone."

"Then it *is* serious," Frank said, as he helped his sister down from the carriage.

They were surprised to find a crowd in the parlor. Even Ezekiel was there, his bushy white beard tucked into his belt. As the three entered, the Aborigine was saying, "Got keen eyes. You take me. I find your missus."

"Thank you, Ezekiel," Hugh said. "I appreciate your willingness to help."

Pauline was startled by Hugh's appearance. His hair was uncombed and he wasn't dressed the way he usually was when receiving visitors. And there was something in his voice and eyes that she had never seen before.

"Hugh," she said, going up to him. "What's wrong? What's happened?"

He explained to her about the letter from Commissioner Fox, and how he had then tried to send a telegram to Western Australia. But when he had been told at the telegraph office in Cameron Town that the lines were still down in the Nullarbor, Hugh had decided to take a rescue expedition into the territory.

"That's right up my alley," Frank said to Hugh. "God knows I've had experience putting together expeditions. And there will be no reporters this time. I'm going to go with you. If Eric Graham dies, I shall never forgive myself."

Judd went up to Hugh and said, "What about your daughter? Beth went to Western Australia, too, didn't she?"

Hugh could hardly speak. "She's missing, too."

"If I may, then," Judd said, "I would like to go with you and search for them."

But Hugh shook his head. "It'll be better for all of us if you stay here, Judd. My experimental arsenic dip worked. Now the rest of the graziers need to be told. Some of them might still stand a chance of saving their stations. You're the best man for that job, Judd. You know the formula I used, and everyone trusts you. They'll listen to you."

Later, when all the plans had been made and the members of the expedition chosen, and Mrs. Jackson's coffeepot emptied many times— after everyone had gone and a waiting, ominous silence had been descended over the house, Sarah went to Hugh and said, "I will go to Western Australia with you. I will help you find Joanna and Beth."

CHAPTER 30

M
other," Beth said, "what is happening? The women are acting strange."

"Yes, I've noticed it, too."

Shielding her eyes, Joanna scanned the western horizon as she had done every day of the five months she and Beth had been with the Aborigines. But, once again, there was nothing out there—no men, no camels, just red desert as far as she could see, disappearing over the edge of the earth. But she would not give up the hope of being rescued. Hugh would find them, she was certain.

"You're not afraid, are you, darling?" she said to Beth, as she looked around at the Aboriginal women who were foraging for food, women who were their friends. Something was clearly agitating them today, making them unusually spirited.

"I don't think so," Beth said. "But I've never seen them like this. They wouldn't leave us out here, would they, Mother? I wish Father would find us. I want to go home."

In their early days with the clan, Joanna had tried to find a way to get back to Kalagandra. As soon as Beth had become stronger, Joanna had conferred with the clan leaders in the hope that they might help the two get back to civilization. But the clan was on a relentless eastward course, heading toward a gathering place where they were to take part in an important corroboree. They could not be persuaded to go westward, back toward Kalagandra, nor could they provide Joanna and Beth with escorts. When Joanna had suggested that she and Beth might head back on their own, the elders had reminded her that Kalagandra was hundreds of miles away, across hostile terrain. Alone they would certainly perish. But the old clever-woman, Naliandrah, whose name meant "butterfly," crouched over her fire, had assured them that once the tribe had held the corroboree the clan would turn westward again, and help return Joanna and Beth to their own people. And they believed her, for Naliandrah was wise: It was to her people came for advice. The elders consulted her before a hunt, young girls in love asked her for love amulets, barren women came to inhale the smoke from her magic fire in hopes of getting pregnant—she even arranged marriages as she squatted there. Her hair was long and white, her small, doll-like body dusty and shrunken, but her eyes were always direct and penetrating, sparked with wisdom and knowing.

Joanna had kept track of the number of days they had lived with the clan, wondering when they would come to the place where they would turn around. It was already late November; Hugh must certainly be searching for them. She had continued to leave a trail as she went, marking each campsite and leaving pebbles pointing in the direction she and the clan had gone. She consulted the compass every day, watching the needle grow more erratic the further eastward the clan went, as if they were heading toward the source of the disturbance. Now the clan was camped at a site they called Woonona, which was Aborigine for "place of the young wallabies," and because it was true to its name, the clan ate well here. While the men trapped the small animals, the women carried out their timeless function of foraging, and, as usual, Joanna and Beth helped them.

A sudden eruption of laughter caused Joanna to turn in time to see Coonawarra, a young widow, do one of her impersonations of old Yolgerup, the chief of the clan. He had a ferocious brow and a menacing growl, but he was as threatening, Joanna had learned, as a lazy old cat. Everyone loved Yolgerup, and the women made fun of him out of affection. Coonawarra, whose name meant "honeysuckle," strutted around with her digging stick, making fierce sounds, as the old chief did whenever he wanted to remind the clan of his status; the next instant she was mimicking the old man sitting on the ground playing with invisible children and laughing his toothless laugh.

The women howled and made comments Joanna could not understand. During her stay with Yolgerup's people, she had learned only a few Aborigine words; the language was highly complex and difficult. And so she was thankful that Naliandrah, who had helped Joanna nurse Beth back to health, had spent her girlhood in a Christian mission, and could speak some English. It was from Naliandrah that Joanna had learned what she knew about the people she was living with.

Once, one of the young men in the clan had come back from a hunt with a broken arm. Old Naliandrah had skinned a wallaby and applied the warm, bloody hide to the arm, wrapping it around snugly and securing it with string. The hide stayed there for many weeks, during which time, Naliandrah had explained to Joanna, the spirit of the wallaby went into the arm and healed the bone. But Joanna observed that, as the skin dried, it stiffened until it was as hard as a board; it had in fact become a splint, immobilizing the broken bone and allowing the ends to knit back together.

It was from Naliandrah, too, that Joanna had learned the many laws and customs that governed the tribe, from the taboo of speaking the names of the dead to the marriage ceremony, which consisted of nothing more than a woman sleeping with a man, and publicly declaring him to be her husband, she, his wife. "Does your husband have other wives?" Naliandrah had asked, explaining that an Aboriginal man can have more than one wife. Then she had asked Joanna, "How many husbands have you had?" and had explained that, since Aborigine girls got married when they were ten years old, and a man didn't have his first wife until he was well into middle age, by the time a woman reached her mid-thirties, as Joanna had, she would have gone through several husbands.

The more complex concepts had been less easy to understand, such as the way the Aborigines regarded time. Everything revolved around the Dreamtime, which, Joanna had discovered, occurred not only in the past, but also in the present and the future. They had no words, in fact, for past, present and future—all was Dreamtime. And the clan had no separate words for yesterday, today and tomorrow, just the word *punjara*, which simply meant "another day."

Everything that governed the Aborigines' lives, Joanna had learned, was derived from nature. The way they counted, for instance. They had no words for individual numbers, but instead referred to animals.

The word "dog" meant the quantity "four," because a dog has four legs; a bird was "two," and a kangaroo, "three."

Joanna had also learned about death, which the Aborigines regarded as just another part of life. One did not die, one "went back." To die was to become an Ancestor. When Naliandrah had asked Joanna what her Dreaming was, and Joanna had said that she didn't know, the old clever-woman had shaken her head sadly and said, "Then what becomes of your soul when you die?"

Finally, Joanna had found that the women did not call themselves women, but "daughters of the Dreamtime."

And they, in turn, had been fascinated by her. They had seen her follow the songline of the Kangaroo Ancestor, and when they had asked her who her totem was, and Joanna, remembering what Sarah had told her years ago, had said, "kangaroo," they had nodded in a knowing way. They decided that she was related to the clan, and that, because her skin was the color of a ghost, she must therefore be possessed by the spirit of an Ancestor.

They had opened up to her then, telling her their secrets, answering her questions about the spiritual links between mothers and daughters, the songlines that bound generations together; the women had spoken freely about their rituals, which involved the land, reading the stars, predicting the future, healing and bringing forth life.

But when Joanna had asked, "Do you know Djoogal's clan? Do you know Karra Karra?" they had suddenly closed up, their faces blank.

While they watched Coonawarra entertain the other women with her antics, Joanna said to Beth, "They seem happier than usual. I don't think there's anything to be afraid of." But Beth kept her eye on them. They seemed happy, she thought, but they were nervous as well. Nervous about what? she wondered.

As Joanna watched a young girl named Winning-Arra join in the antics by throwing her digging stick as if it were a spear, and then hopping up and down on one foot, imitating one of the men in the clan and causing the women to laugh, she looked at the baskets and dilly-bags on their backs and marveled again at their ability to draw such a bounty of food from such a seemingly barren land. She thought of the skeleton she had found, whose spectacles she had taken, and of how the man had starved to death in what he had no doubt thought was a foodless desert. And yet here were Coonawarra and Winning-Arra and all the others, helping themselves to roots and seeds, wild nuts and berries, honey ants, grubs and lizards—all of which would be turned into a tasty feast for the clan. They were in the middle of a vast, boiling desert, where the air was as dry as the sand, and trees grew no higher than one's waist, and yet there was Coonawarra with her hairstring belt strung with hundreds of fat, wriggling witchetty grubs which, when roasted, tasted, Joanna thought, very much like hazelnuts. And Winning-Arra had trapped two of the plump lizards they called goannas, while other women proudly displayed rats and snakes and snared birds, promising a great feast tonight, at which the air would be filled with delicious aromas.

Joanna watched her new "family" in fascination. Except for old Naliandrah, whose job it was to remain at the camp and make sure the fires didn't die out, all the females of the clan were away gathering food, from the very oldest great-grandmother, to the youngest baby at its mother's breast. There were prepubescent girls with gangly arms and legs; lithe adolescents, who moved with fluid grace; and young mothers and older matrons—women shrunken small from lives spent between sand and sun. Their bodies were decorated with tribal scars, and they were adorned with necklaces and belts made of human hair, feathers and dingoes' teeth; sometimes the women were painted, if the food collecting happened to carry a particular religious significance for them.

Joanna saw the powerful bond between these various female relations and the other generations. She saw with envy the stairway she had imagined long ago—the descent of women from great-grandmothers to daughters. The smallest child could look at a white-haired woman bent over her digging stick and see the generations through which she had descended. Perhaps, Joanna thought, that was why these people had no need for words meaning past, present and future. They were all here, now.

Joanna looked at Beth, standing at her side, and wished she could have known her grandmother, Lady Emily, and even her great-grandmother, Naomi. Beth resembled the Makepeace women, Joanna thought. She had the rich brown hair, the same high forehead and thickly lashed eyes. And she was growing tall. Beth had celebrated her thirteenth birthday two months ago; she was developing into a lovely young woman. Like Joanna, Beth still wore European clothes, although her skirt and blouse were starting to show wear. She wore her hair long, Aborigine style, and her complexion, like her mother's, had darkened in the sun.

But although she stood strong and straight now, Beth's convalescence had been slow. Joanna had thought, in the early days, that because Beth had wandered for so long in the desert without food and water before the Aborigines found her, she might not survive. But Naliandrah had worked her magic. When Joanna had inquired about the medicinal properties of the roots and berries that Naliandrah was feeding to Beth, the clever-woman had explained about the Rainbow Serpent, the maker of all rivers and waterholes, and the All-Mother in the sky who was the mother of everyone, and how it was their power, not that of the roots and berries, which healed her daughter. At first it had taken all Beth's strength just to eat and drink and speak; but after a week she had been able to sit up. It had been a long time before she could stand and take her first steps, and Joanna and Naliandrah had helped her walk to the river.

When Joanna saw the look of deep concentration on Beth's face as she watched Coonawarra, she thought again about the women's unusual behavior. Although laughter and clowning were always a part of the daily collection of food, she realized from their high-pitched howls and exaggerated dancing that today was different from the previous one hundred and fifty days she had lived with them. They seemed to be more keyed up, their laughter more spontaneous and shrill. And, in a way, she saw that this could be unsettling.

Finally, the food-gathering came to an end and the women returned to the camp. Joanna and Beth, wearing long dark skirts and white blouses, walked among shorter, black-skinned women, who wore nothing more than a coating of emu fat and ash over their bodies. Like their companions, Joanna carried baskets on their backs, leaving their hands free for digging. The women sang as they went, because the Witchetty Ancestor had provided bounteously today, as had the Goanna Ancestor, and the Galah Ancestor, and one never took without showing appropriate gratitude.

Before they reached the encampment, which was beside a sweet-water well among volcanic boulders, the women could hear the songs of the men as they sang thanks to the Wallaby Ancestor, who had also provided in plenty. Coonawarra danced up and down and talked about how she was going to eat tonight and never have to eat again!

Joanna and her daughter had their own miamia, with their own smoking fire, and a pole on which to hang their possessions. Since Aborigines had very little in the way of personal possessions, the poles outside the other miamias were hung with little more than a dilly-bag, a spear and sacred stones and feathers to keep Yowie the Night Beast away. But the pole outside Joanna's miamia, on which she now slung her basket full of squirming grubs, was draped with Captain Fielding's naval jacket, John Makepeace's leather satchel, two wallaby-skin blankets, which they hung out to air every day, and a collection of combs she and Beth had made out of bone and wood.

"Beth," she said, "go and get some water for washing, and I'll speak to Naliandrah. Maybe she'll tell me what's happening."

Naliandrah was crouched over her fire as usual, stirring the embers and murmuring magic spells.

"Naliandrah," Joanna said, sitting down beside her, "Do my daughter and I have anything to be concerned about tonight? Do we have anything to fear?"

The small sharp eyes, almost invisible beneath heavy brows, and glinting with intelligence, met hers. "You have fear, Jahna," the clever-woman said. "You always have fear."

Joanna had long ago explained to Naliandrah the reason for her journey into the desert; she had told the old woman about her mother, about the poison-song that she believed had been sung and her feeling that something awaited her at Karra Karra. Naliandrah had listened expressionless, her eyes shuttered secretively. And when Joanna had finished telling her story, the clever-woman had said nothing.

Now, she startled Joanna by saying, "You come to the end of your songline, Jahna. Very soon now."

Joanna stared at her. "What do you mean?"

"You see tonight, at corroboree."

The corroboree was held when the moon was high. The feast of roasted wallaby and lizards and birds, accompanied by wild honeycomb and berries, was shared, as it was every night, according to a very complex system of priorities and taboos. There was no grabbing or fighting for the food; portions were handed out according to strict rules: A man who had killed a wallaby first gave servings to his parents and his wife's parents, to his brothers, and to the men who had hunted with him; they in turn shared their portions with their families, or with men to whom they owed a debt, sometimes leaving nothing for themselves. The women then portioned out the fruits of their day's foraging according to family bloodlines, marriage ties and other criteria that Joanna had so far not been able to unravel. The young people observed strict taboos: A boy who had caught a goanna could not eat it himself, but had to give it to his parents; a woman could receive food only from a man who had undergone initiation; a girl who had begun to menstruate was forbidden certain foods.

It seemed to Joanna to be a happy, noisy affair, despite all the rules and taboos, and the clan ate well. But the feeling that tonight was different continued to trouble her. She thought the group was louder than usual, that laughter came too quickly. And when the feast was over, she was surprised to see that not all the food had been eaten, which was contrary to the Aborigines' custom. Joanna had learned that, because they frequently suffered periods of famine, when food was plentiful they gorged themselves until their stomachs stuck out and they could eat no more. But tonight, she noticed, there was a studied curbing of the appetite, as food was gathered and saved—something she had never seen them do.

While the men went off to prepare for the dance, Joanna returned to her miamia for wallaby blankets for herself and Beth. The night was growing chilly and the dance, she knew, could last until dawn. She looked up at the moon, which hung in the sky like a polished silver coin, and wondered if, at that moment, Hugh was looking up and observing the same moon. Was he nearby? she wondered. Would he come soon?

Before returning to the campfire, Joanna checked the compass, as was her habit every night. The needle was now spinning.

She joined Beth in the large circle around the campfire, where the women chattered excitedly, speaking too fast for Joanna to understand. She kept her eye on the empty center of the circle, where the men would soon be dancing. The clan held corroboree most nights; while some dances were of special religious or ritual significance to the men, which women could not witness, or to the women, which men could not witness, some were just for entertainment—telling stories, dancing comic dances, acting out a memorable hunt. Tonight's corroboree, Joanna knew, was going to be different.

While the men and youths were getting ready for the performance—painting themselves, putting feathers in their hair and adorning their bodies with shells and animal teeth—the women chewed on the leaves of a poisonous shrub named *pituri*, which had the strength to kill but which, when taken in small amounts, was a powerful stimulant. Joanna saw their constricted pupils, and heard their rapid speech.

Finally the dancers were ready.

The first time Joanna and Beth had witnessed a corroboree, they had seen a disorganized, madcap kind of dancing, which appeared to have no order, no sense to it. But they had learned that every movement was significant, every gesture, every hop had a place in a story. And now, here in the vast desert beneath the ghostly glow of stars and moon the dancers, their faces illuminated by firelight, came out into the circle.

Naliandrah sat with Joanna and Beth, and they watched the dance begin.

A man named Thumimberie was known to be the best dancer in the area. When the main tribe got together for a massive corroboree, clans from all over came just to see Thumimberie dance. As the dance tonight got under way, he hopped around from foot to foot, bending and swaying, gyrating in the center of the circle. Then another man joined him, his body painted red and blue, with twigs and leaves in his hair. He and Thumimberie performed a frantic kind of a dance, coming together and jumping apart, almost as if they were fighting. The women sitting in the circle picked up spears and boomerangs and began to strike them together in a steady rhythm.

"What story is this?" Joanna asked Naliandrah.

"Very important legend, Jahna," the clever-woman said. "You watch."

The men danced around the fire to the almost deafening beat of the drums and boomerangs. The women began to sing; they lifted their voices high and chanted words Joanna couldn't understand.

"Please, Naliandrah," she said. "Tell me this story."

The old woman explained that this was the legend of the Devil, Makpeej, and how he had once done battle with the Rainbow Serpent.

Joanna watched the two men kick up the dust around the campfire; their dance was both warlike and like a waltz. She heard Naliandrah's papery voice tell the story of Makpeej and his pregnant wife, who were known to be spirits sent by the dead, because their skins were white.

Joanna was stunned and then mesmerized as she watched another dancer join in the ceremony. He wore a long grassy wig, and his body was painted white from head to foot.

"But Makpeej was evil," Naliandrah said, "he made the Rainbow Serpent angry, and so the Rainbow Serpent swallowed Makpeej."

More dancers entered the circle, a line of men weaving in single file, their bodies painted the colors of the rainbow. They encircled the white-painted man and he disappeared.

"But because Makpeej was evil," Naliandrah said, "the Rainbow Serpent vomited, and out came a girl child, white like Makpeej."

A smaller dancer appeared, painted white, reeling and staggering around the campfire, while the clacking of the boomerangs grew louder.

"Now, Rainbow Serpent must destroy white child," Naliandrah went on, "but a young woman of the tribe called upon her totem ancestor, the Black Swan. She and the white child climbed onto the back of the swan and they flew away into the west, into the sunset."

Joanna stared at the twenty or so men who danced and stomped over the dusty ground, their bodies glistening with sweat. She looked at the faces of the women in the circle, their passionate expressions illuminated by the flames. The chanting filled the night in a maddening rhythm.

Joanna felt Beth at her side, stiff and tense. "Mother," she said, "do you *know* what this is?"

Joanna heard urgency in her daughter's voice, saw a mixture of both fear and excitement in her eyes.

Joanna turned to the clever-woman. "So you *do* know," she said. "You've known all along who my grandparents were and what they did here. Naliandrah, please tell me what happened to them."

But the old woman shook her head. "I can tell you nothing, Jahna. The answers are within you. You must find them for yourself."

———————————•———————————

No one slept that night. The dancing continued, and food was again brought out; everyone ate, fires were stoked, emotions ran high. Even the women, stimulated by *pituri* leaves, jumped up to dance their own dances. At dawn, when Joanna expected the tired people to drag themselves off to their own campfires and miamias for a day of sleeping, as they usually did after a corroboree, they surprised her by picking up camp and trekking eastward again.

The clan always traveled very light, needing to be unencumbered in order to survive. Naliandrah had the honor of carrying the precious smoldering firebrand, so that a fire could be struck at the next encampment. The rest of the women carried digging sticks, baskets and grindstones—and their babies. The men carried only their weapons, in case they encountered wallaby or emu along the way. Before they left the Woonona site, they slapped mud on themselves as a protection against insects.

Joanna walked with Naliandrah, who "sang" the landmarks along the ancient route—billabongs, waterholes and queer rock formations, all of which had been created by the ancestral spirit-powers. She showed Joanna a sacred site where the family obtained ocher for their corroboree; it was called the Dog Dreaming. There was a dry gully that was the White Crane Dreaming. And a dead acacia tree that was the Ant Dreaming. Yolgerup's people made salutations to the spirits who dwelled in such spots and were careful that no one walked on the sacred ground, no rock was disturbed, no twig touched.

And as they walked, strung out in a long, scattered line, with the rising sun in their eyes, Joanna noticed that despite the previous night's feasting and dancing, everyone was very energetic and lively.

"What's wrong with everyone?" Beth asked. "They're acting as if they're drunk. Look at Coonawarra. She's so nervous that the slightest sound makes her jump. And Yolgerup—he should be exhausted after last night. But look at him over there, walking with those men, talking, waving his arms. What is going on, Mother?"

Joanna put an arm around her daughter and said, "I'm sure we'll find out soon."

As they walked through the morning, and sunlight crept across the red desert, Joanna thought she heard, on the wind, strange sounds up ahead.

"Mother," Beth said, "do you hear—"

And then, suddenly, Yolgerup brought his people to a halt. When Joanna and Beth caught up with them, they saw that the clan had come to the edge of a great plateau. The world seemed suddenly to drop away from their feet, and they saw, stretching before them a vast plain.

"Oh Mother!" Beth breathed.

Joanna could not believe what she saw: Camped on the sands below were hundreds, perhaps thousands of Aborigines, their campfires creating a smoky pall that hung over the encampment for as far as one could see.

"Beth!" Joanna said, filled with wonder at the sight. "It must be a meeting of the clans!"

"But Mother, I've never seen so many Aborigines. Where did they all come from?"

Joanna gazed out at the breathtaking scene as Yolgerup's people hurried down to the plain. When she saw people from the various camps come running to greet them, when she saw the happy embraces, and people holding babies up and tugging on gray beards and when she heard everyone talking at once, their cries of joy as they pointed at one another and laughed, Joanna understood the clan's agitation over the past few days: It had been because of this enormous event.

"Beth," she said, "it's exactly as my grandfather described it in his notes, fifty-two years ago! They meet like this once every five years: They renew friendships, exchange stories, strengthen clan ties—"

"Look at Coonawarra!" Beth said, pointing to the end of the trail at the bottom of the cliff, where a large group had gathered. "That must be the man she's been talking about, the one she wants to marry. And look at Yolgerup! Is that his mother he's embracing?"

But Joanna didn't respond. She was staring at the huge mountain that dominated the plain.

For as far as she could see, the desert stretched flat all the way to the horizon. But rising abruptly out of it, large and square, was an enormous red mountain. As Joanna felt the hot wind blow against her face, while Yolgerup's people continued to hurry past her and down to the plain below, she felt herself becoming curiously detached. The mountain shimmered in the heat; it seemed to move, to breathe. She felt as if some sort of power were reaching out to her, pulling her toward it.

Beth took the compass out of her pocket. "Look at this needle spin, Mother!" she said. "Could that mountain be causing it? Could the mountain be magnetized somehow?"

Joanna couldn't take her eyes from the mass in front of her. Waves of heat seemed to radiate from the hot red walls; pools of silver appeared at the base, trembled in the sunlight and then disappeared, only to reappear somewhere else. Joanna thought she heard a hum emanating from the mountain like the drone of a million bees.

Naliandrah came and stood at her side. She pointed and said, "Karra Karra."

"Why didn't you tell me we were coming here?" Joanna said. "You've known all along that I was searching for Karra Karra."

"I could not bring you, Jahna. You had to bring yourself. You follow your own songline, no one else can follow it for you."

"Did you know my grandfather then? Were you here when Djoogal was chief?"

"It was long ago, Jahna. I was not here, I was in Christian mission school."

"But do you know about the ceremony that used to take place inside that mountain? I believe my grandmother might have taken part in it."

"Only those who go in know about the secret of the mountain, Jahna. I did not go in. By the time I was old enough, the power of Karra Karra had been stolen."

Stolen by my grandfather, Joanna thought.

"Mother," Beth said, "if that's Karra Karra, then what are we going to do now?"

As Joanna stared at the shimmering mountain, she was filled with awe and a sense of mystery. It was composed of rock, but it had a presence, a spirit. And she thought of what had haunted her mother and visited her in dreams; the unspeakable event that Emily had witnessed and that had caused her to be sent away from her parents; the poison-song; the answers to the mystery of the Rainbow Serpent and the wild dogs; and finally, the "other legacy" that had been awaiting Lady Emily's return—all of these things were here, in this mountain.

Joanna thought of the years she had spent searching for this place, the miles she had covered; she could hardly believe she had found it. But now that she had, a sudden sense of urgency gripped her. She wouldn't wait another day, another hour. "I'm going to go into the mountain, Beth," Joanna said.

Beth stared at her mother. "But Mother, is it safe?" she said.

"Beth, darling," Joanna said. "It's something I must do. But I'll be all right. According to my grandfather, women have been holding rituals inside that mountain for centuries. How dangerous can it be?"

"Then I want to go with you."

"No Beth, you stay with Naliandrah." She turned to the old woman. "Can you show me how to get inside? My grandfather described a cave at the base of the mountain."

"I show you," Naliandrah said. "But, remember, Jahna. Rainbow Serpent still lives in that mountain."

CHAPTER 31

T hat's odd," Frank said, as he tapped his finger on the glass of his compass. "It won't hold steady. Damn needle keeps switching back to south. Have a look at yours, Hugh."

They were sitting around a campfire on a night that marked four weeks since their departure from Kalagandra. Hugh's party had been late getting to Western Australia because of storms in the Bight; the captain of the boat had had constantly to take shelter in coves and bays along the southern Australian coast. And then, once they had reached Kalagandra, they had had difficulty finding men willing to go into the desert to search for a lost woman when there was gold to be found right there. But finally, nearly three months after leaving Merinda, they had the men, camels and supplies, and on the first day of November they had struck off into the unknown.

And now, twenty-eight days later, they estimated that they should be near the place of the flash flood. Hugh and Frank had visited Eric Graham at St. Alban's Infirmary, where Sister Veronica was taking care of him. "We got lost somehow," Graham had said. "The compasses went crazy. And then we got caught by a flash flood. If it weren't for those gold prospectors who found me, I'd have perished like the others."

Hugh took out his compass and looked at it. "Yes," he said to Frank, "there's something wrong with mine, too. And this is just about where Eric said it would happen."

Graham had been able to sketch a crude map of their trek into the wilderness. His notebook had been lost in the flood, but he had been able to locate certain landmarks along the way. Hugh brought the map out now and studied it by the light of the campfire.

"All right," he said. "Eric said they kept to an easterly direction for as long as they could, traveling at an approximate rate of twenty-five miles a day. After four weeks, he said they were about here, where he has drawn a spine of craggy hills. We passed those three days ago, so we must be very near where the flash flood hit."

Frank looked at the map, which ended at that point. "Where do we go from here?" he said.

"This is where we use the skills of Ezekiel and the two trackers," Hugh said, as he rolled up the map and slipped it into his saddlebag. "Tomorrow we'll search the area for signs of Joanna's original camp. If she and Beth—or anyone—survived, they might have been able to salvage supplies from the flood and set up a new camp near here and wait for rescue. They would know better than to go wandering off."

"But what if they were forced to wander off?" Frank said. "I mean, we haven't found any water near here. They might have had to go in search of it."

"Even so, they couldn't have gone far on foot. The first water they came to, they would have stayed with it. There would have been no reason to move on."

Hugh regarded his friend across the flickering flames. "What is it, Frank?" he said. "There's something on your mind."

"I'm only thinking, Hugh, that, knowing Joanna, she might have decided to keep on looking for Karra Karra. Having come this far, she might not just sit and wait to be rescued."

Hugh took a drink from his mug. "Yes," he said, "that had occurred to me, too."

He looked at Sarah, whose red-brown eyes were staring into the fire. She continued to maintain that Joanna and Beth were still alive, her certainty growing the farther east the expedition went.

"Well," Frank said as he pocketed his compass, "at least we have the sun and the stars to guide us. No overcast sky, thank God."

The rescue expedition consisted of ten members: Hugh and Frank and three Merinda station hands, who had traveled from Melbourne to Perth by ship, along with Sarah and old Ezekiel. Constable Ralph Carruthers had volunteered to join the search party at Kalagandra, along with two black trackers named Jacky-Jacky and Tom. They were equipped with fifteen camels, food and water to last for months, medical supplies, compasses, tents and tools, rifles and ammunition.

"Which way do we go tomorrow, Mr. Westbrook?" Constable Carruthers asked. He regarded the journey as an adventure, with endless days of riding in the sun, and nights spent around the campfire. Carruthers was young and unmarried; it had been the lure of adventure that had made him join the frontier police force in the first place. And when he had heard Commissioner Fox talking about this rescue expedition, he had jumped at the chance to join it.

"We'll continue eastward, Mr. Carruthers," Hugh said, as he looked at the black night that encircled them. He wondered if Joanna had indeed come this way, if she was in fact somewhere nearby. He looked up at the white, round moon and wondered if Joanna was looking up at that moment, and seeing the same moon. He thought of their many nights together, their private hours of passion and love; he thought of their laughter and joys and all the things they shared and had created together. He prayed that Joanna and Beth were alive; he refused to believe they were not. And he was determined to find them—he was not leaving this wilderness until he did.

"I wonder where Ezekiel's gone to," Frank said.

Hugh looked at his old friend and tried to calculate how many years they had known each other. He recalled the rather bombastic young owner of Lismore and the Melbourne *Times,* who had befriended him when the other graziers had allowed a green Queenslander to struggle on his own. Hugh suddenly found himself remembering events and conversations from years ago, long forgotten: a graziers' show and Ian Hamilton speaking to him for the first time; a barn dance and Frank saying, "Watch out, Hugh, I think my sister Pauline has her eye on you." It was strange, Hugh thought now, what stars and desert silence did to one's memory.

"He said he was going to scout around, see if he could find traces of a camp. When it comes to seeing in the dark, Ezekiel has the eyes of a cat."

"Well then," Frank said, standing up and rubbing his backside. "I'm going to turn in." Although he had lost weight since leaving Kalagandra, he still had not toughened up sufficiently for such a journey. He now cursed his sedentary life and wished he had heeded Ivy's advice to become more active. Frank was almost fifty, and tonight he felt every year of it. As he made his way to the tent he shared with Hugh, he made a silent promise that, when he returned, he would take up riding and shooting and boating, and even that new outrageous sport, tennis.

Carruthers, too, decided to go to bed, announcing his eagerness to be up early and ready for another long ride. The Aboriginal trackers and the three men from Merinda retired to their bedrolls beside the tethered camels, leaving Hugh and Sarah alone at the campfire.

They sat in silence for a while, watching the tea steaming in the billycan. They looked up at the stars every now and then, as if to make sure they were still there.

Hugh had sensed a change in Sarah over the past weeks. The sun had darkened her skin, the heat had given her a glow. But it was more than that, he thought. She had grown quiet, and more introspective. He thought about how every night, when she thought the others were asleep, she would steal out of camp and go into the desert. Sometimes she was gone for only an hour; at other times she wouldn't return until dawn.

"I think we should turn in," Hugh said. "Tomorrow we start traveling without the aid of a map, and without properly working compasses."

"I'm going to sit up for a little while longer. Good night, Hugh."

She went back to gazing into the glowing embers and thinking about Philip, the way he had kissed her good-by at the harbor, not caring that people stared. These past four weeks in the wilderness had given her time and silence in which to think, in which to examine herself. She thought of Joanna, who had chosen to seek out her own destiny. Joanna had not sat passively waiting for life to happen; she had fixed upon her goal and gone after it, creating her own story rather than having it created for her.

That is how it must be for me, Sarah thought. I must decide what I want, and follow my songline until I have achieved it. But how? Philip is what I want, he is all I want. But so many laws and taboos stand in our way.

When she decided that everyone was asleep, she walked as far away from the encampment as she could, still keeping it in view but making sure that she would not be seen. She came to a place where she stopped and looked up at the stars. She felt the Ancestors all around her. She felt the movements of spirits that had passed this way before her, either as creation-beings or as real people: the young Makepeaces, searching for Eden; Joanna's mother, Emily, and the Aboriginal girl, Reenadeena, escaping from danger. Sarah knew that the passions and dreams of everyone who had ever come this way existed here still. They whispered around Sarah, like tiny fish schooling around a larger one. She felt breaths upon her body; she heard murmurs and heart-flutters. And she thought: I will add my own passion to this place.

She closed her eyes and tried to send her spirit out through the night, imagining that Philip, over a thousand miles away, was waiting to receive it. She felt him reach out and embrace her, she felt the hardness and heat of his body, the pressure of his mouth on hers. She ached for the feel of him, for his presence.

And then another vision flashed into her mind: the looks on the faces of the people at the harbor. A white man kissing an Aboriginal woman in public. And—if they had known—a married man at that.

Oh Philip, she thought. What are we going to do?

She heard footsteps in the darkness. Turning, she saw Ezekiel making his way toward her across the sand. He sat down and turned his face to the stars. "This where we belong," he said softly. "This blackfella country. You and I, we Aborigine."

Sarah waited. After a moment, Ezekiel held out his hand, palm up. She looked and saw that he held a blue earring.

"That's Joanna's!" she said. "Where did you find it?"

"That tree, over there. She mark the place, she leave sign. She goes that way," he said, and pointed eastward. "That is where the missus is."

"You mean she left a trail?"

"She creates songline."

"Ezekiel, this is wonderful! We must tell Hugh!"

But he stayed her with his hand, saying, "I don't go. You find her now."

"What do you mean, Ezekiel?"

"My name is Geerydjine," he said. "Whitefella take my name away from me long ago. They call me Ezekiel. But I am Geerydjine. Today, we pass the Dreaming Site of the Emu Ancestor. I will go back there, and I will stay there. I go back to my ancestors now." He paused, and she saw dampness in his eyes. Then he embraced her. She felt his coarse beard against her face; she was startled to feel frail bones and melted flesh. She had always thought of Ezekiel as being strong and robust; now, he was a tired old man, longing for rest.

She watched him walk away, and eventually he blended into the night. Sarah did not try to stop him, she knew that he was following the custom of his people, seeking to die in privacy and dignity, and in his own time.

She looked at the earring he had given her, and she thought of the songline that Joanna had created. She heard Ezekiel saying, "We are Aborigine."

And then suddenly Sarah saw her way as clearly as if a path had been etched in the moonlit sand. It was a path that cut through Aboriginal land, through white man's land, straight to Philip. And at its end she saw herself, running into the arms of the man she loved, kissing him openly because there *was* nothing to be ashamed of, that they were breaking no laws, because she was Aborigine, as Ezekiel/Geerydjine had said. And according to her people's laws, she could declare a man to be her husband, and he could have more than one wife.

Anxious now to resume their search so that they could return as soon as possible to Merinda, Sarah paused to say a silent farewell to Geery- djine, then she hurried back to the camp to tell Hugh the news—that they were going to find Joanna.

As Joanna stepped from sunlight into the darkness of the cave, making sure the leather satchel was secured to the waistband of her skirt, she paused and held her torch aloft. The mountain hummed all around her. She felt its energy; it was almost as if she were entering a living thing. From the entrance, stretching into the formidable darkness, was a beaten path, worn down, she surmised, by generations of mothers and daughters. As daylight gradually receded behind her and she delivered herself into the heart of the great, throbbing mountain, Joanna won- dered what she would find at the end of this path.

Outside, Beth was waiting anxiously at the cave's entrance, listening to her mother's fading footsteps. She looked at the massive gathering of Aborigines on the plain below, she smelled the smoke from their many campfires, she heard chanting and drums. As the last of her mother's footsteps died in the darkness of the cave, Beth felt herself become afraid. She no longer had the comforting presence of her mother; she was all alone with many hundreds of Aborigines. She stood up and began to pace. She looked at the sun, climbing slowly to its zenith, and she wondered how long her mother would be inside the mountain.

Her nervousness grew. At one of the campfires, men were dancing an enactment of a kangaroo hunt. Their naked bodies were painted; they carried spears and boomerangs; they yelped and shouted fiercely.

Beth stared at the entrance to the cave. Sunlight illuminated the beginning of a path that descended into darkness. She looked back at the noisy, smoky plain, and then, without another thought, slipped inside the mountain.

———————————•———————————

Joanna lost track of time as she followed dark, twisting passages. The flame from her torch cast eerie, dancing shadows on the walls. She saw varicolored striations in the rock, ribbons of bright green running through red and orange and brown. She felt the hairs on her neck prickle, not from fear, but from the power of the mountain, perhaps its magnetism, as Beth had suggested, or possibly from something else. She wondered if a mountain could have a pulse and energy, like a person.

The path narrowed; the walls were so close that they scraped her shoulders; the ceiling was so low that she had to stoop to go through. Down and down she went, deeper into the heart of the earth. She came to passages that were so small she wondered if she dared even try to go through.

Time stretched; the darkness grew darker. She could feel the weight of the massive mountain all around her. She heard her own breath, and it sounded too loud. She thought that if she were to stop, she would hear her pulse thunder and echo off the subterranean walls.

She went deeper. Her ears popped. The air changed and became heavy. Her torch sputtered and flickered and she feared that it would go out. Without the torch, she knew, she would find a darkness that was as final as blindness.

She heard a sound, stopped and listened, straining to make it out. It was a soft, rhythmic tap-tapping sound.

Her eyes widened in the darkness. The light from her torch cast a glow only a foot or two in front of her. Every step she took felt as if she were about to step through solid, black rock. But the path continued, down, deeper.

Joanna paused now and then to listen. The tap-tapping stayed with her, and at times it seemed louder, at other times, fainter.

Strange paintings began to appear on the walls. Joanna examined them by torchlight. As the flame danced and flickered, so the figures on the walls seemed to dance and flicker. She stared at images of men and women and animals and mythical beasts that had existed thousands of years ago. She followed the path and the paintings stayed with her, growing larger and more numerous. They seemed to tell a story, but she couldn't unravel its meaning. Joanna felt the electricity of the creation-mountain, she stared at the ancient paintings, and she walked deeper, farther into the earth.

All of a sudden, a great cavern opened up before her. Joanna drew in her breath. Massive stalactites descended from the ceiling to meet enormous stalagmites rising up out of the floor. Joanna wondered if this was the place to which her grandmother had been brought, where mothers and daughters had conducted their secret rites. The tapping was loud now, and Joanna realized that it was water dripping. She saw a large pool, black and inky, moving in a strange kind of tide. The cavern was as large as a cathedral she had once visited in London. Sounds had echoed in that place as they did here, and the Gothic masonry, Joanna thought, had resembled the belly of this fantastic mountain.

Her eye fell upon something. She bent close to look, and saw the bones of small animals, dried-up fruit skins, seeds and nutshells scattered all around. Was this the dwelling of a spirit-power?

She continued, wondering if the inhabitant of this sepulchral place was watching her. She stepped carefully onto a ledge around the black lake, wondering if something monstrous dwelt beneath the water's surface. The ledge narrowed; she clung to the wall as she made her way slowly along. But the walls and ledge were slippery. She reached for a handhold; her footing gave way. She slipped, caught herself in time, but the torch fell from her hand and tumbled into the inky water.

Joanna stared in horror as the flame went out. And in the next instant, her breath was taken away—the cave was filled suddenly with a pale green luminescence. It came from the walls, from the limestone formations, from the vaulted ceiling far above her—an eerie green glow that cast the cave in further mystery, but which was enough for Joanna to see her way by. She continued along the ledge, and when she came to the other side of the lake, she saw an opening in the far wall, through which the path continued.

She hesitated. The opening yawned on an even deeper blackness than that which she had already passed through, and the path, she saw, continued in a deep, downward descent. She thought of the lost torch. She thought of daylight far behind her, where Beth was waiting. And then she felt the compelling magic of the mountain.

She went in.

———————————•———————————

Beth crept slowly along the dark passage, feeling her way along the walls, cautiously putting one foot in front of the other. She had no idea that darkness could be so absolute. Even on moonless nights at Merinda, when the stars were hidden behind clouds, the darkness was never as deep, as formidable as this. She knew that she was only minutes behind her mother, but she realized that, going at such a slow pace, she might not catch up with her.

As Beth made her way through the blackness, she stretched her eyes wide, as if doing so would help her to see. She prayed that she would see a glimmer of torchlight up ahead.

At one point she stopped and looked back. The same inky depths had swallowed up the cave entrance; the sunlight was gone. Her mouth was dry. Very slowly, one step at a time, she made her way along the path, dreading what her hand might suddenly touch, imagining great yawning pits suddenly opening in front of her.

But Beth told herself that her mother had not been afraid to come into the mountain; she reminded herself that her grandmother had come this same way, and had come out again. She kept the thought in her head that generations of women had followed this same path, and had survived. And she knew it couldn't go on forever.

"Mother!" she called. "Mother, are you there?"

But the only reply was her own voice, calling "Mother" over and over as echoes rained down upon her.

"Mother!" she called again, and swallowed back her fear.

———

Joanna was relieved to discover, moments after going through the opening on the far side of the subterranean lake, that the same green luminescence was here, too. She saw that she had entered a large tunnel, and there were paintings and carvings on the walls. But these drawings, she realized, were not like those she had seen earlier, where men were depicted hunting animals or fighting wars. These pictures, which looked far older than the others, were all of women—crudely drawn figures depicting pregnancy and childbirth, the cycles of life. The air smelled strange; Joanna tried to identify the odors, but she could only think of blood and dust. She continued along the tunnel, passing scene after scene showing women with large breasts and bellies, and babies in wombs, and people traveling, walking along a line that was made up of the familiar swirls and dots and circles Joanna had come to recognize as typical of Aboriginal art. She was reading the records of ancient songlines, she realized, painted long ago by women no longer remembered. And she wondered if they had been created in some distant, forgotten matriarchal age.

She continued to go down, deeper into the womb of the mountain. More odors assailed her—clay and mold, a fleshy, mushroomlike scent, and something sticky-sweet. The green luminosity swam around her like a tropical sea; strangely, she thought she smelled salt water, and the pungency of the ocean.

And then suddenly the tunnel ended and Joanna found herself standing at the edge of an enormous grotto-like cavern, green and glowing and damp.

She stopped and stared. She saw it up ahead—that which had brought her, after so many years and over so many miles, to this place at last.

"Mother!" Beth cried out. "Where are you?"

She tried not to panic. She tried to stay calm. But the darkness was terrifying; it had gone on too long. What if she had taken a wrong turn? What if she was miles away from her mother, what if she was lost forever in this terrible mountain, because she hadn't had the patience or the courage to stay put at the cave's entrance?

Her hands moved over the damp walls; her feet slipped on the slimy path. Blind, she struggled to stay upright. As she held back her sobs, she promised God that, if she was given a second chance, she would never disobey her mother again.

And then suddenly, like an answer to her desperate prayer, she saw light up ahead. Except that it wasn't really light, she realized, as she emerged from the narrow tunnel into a large cavern that contained a black, underground lake. The whole inside of the mountain glowed an astonishing green, and Beth stared at it, forgetting for a moment her fear.

She saw the narrow ledge that skirted the lake. And on the other side, she saw yet another opening, where the path continued.

Feeling a little more confident, now that she could see, and thinking that this was most likely the way her mother had come, that her mother was in fact probably just up ahead, she struck off along the narrow ledge and began to make her way carefully around the formidable black lake.

Joanna had experienced an instant of fear when she first saw the Rainbow Serpent. But as she stared at the beautiful, massive rainbow-colored body, as her eyes focused upon the thousands of details that made up the serpent, and the mystical symbols and images that surrounded it, she saw the breasts and realized that the serpent was female.

She could only guess how many years ago, or even centuries ago, this serpent had been made, or how many hands had helped in its exquisite creation. As she slowly approached it, she realized as she drew near the painting that it was many feet high and so long that she couldn't see where it finished. Joanna marveled at the skill and artistry that had gone into this extraordinary wall painting—at how each scale on the giant creature's body was perfectly drawn and filled in with color; at the way it seemed to glisten and vibrate with life; at the intricate arching and curling of its great length as it wound from one end of the cavern to the other. Generations must have created this, she thought.

As she stared at the wall-serpent, she began to see something beneath the layers of paint—striations in the rock itself, geological layers that swept across the wall in red, orange, brown and green ribbons. And the more she looked at it, the more she realized that the serpent had been there long before any paint had been applied to the wall.

She looked around the grotto, at the high, vaulted ceilings and limestone formations, the primitive drawings on the walls, the soft, halo-like lighting, and she thought: This is like a church.

A stream flowed through the cavern. Joanna saw drinking vessels scattered over the rocky floor—gourds and coconut shells, cups made of bark and clay, hollowed-out stones—all painted with the same mystical symbols that surrounded the Rainbow Serpent, symbols relating to life and birth: feminine symbols, Joanna thought. Here was where the women had held their secret rituals for countless centuries. Here, where this water came up from the center, the womb, of the earth—here, where life began.

She reached for an earthenware cup, and dipped it into the water that ran like crystal. She raised it to her lips, and drank.

As Beth stared at the fantastic wall drawings in the green-lit tunnel, she realized that her eyes were playing tricks on her. She could have sworn she saw some of the figures move. She walked faster, frightened by the illusions, afraid that she might grow dizzy and faint.

When she saw the end of the tunnel, and that it opened into yet another lighted cavern, she ran toward it. She entered the grotto and stopped. Her eyes were filled with the astonishing green light. The air around her felt electrified, as if she stood in the center of a lightning storm. Her senses were sharpened, heightened. She saw the Rainbow Serpent. And then she saw Joanna, standing beside a stream.

"Mother?" Beth said.

Joanna turned around. "Beth!" she said. "What are you doing here?"

"I got frightened, waiting for you. I'm thirsty."

Joanna took Beth's hand and brought her to the edge of the stream. She dipped the earthenware cup into the crystalline water, and handed it to her daughter. Beth drank, and found that the water tasted as it had looked: transparent and pure.

"What is this place, Mother?" she asked.

"This is where generations of women came to celebrate creation, and the re-creation of life."

"What sort of ritual did they perform in here?" Beth asked.

"I don't know," Joanna said. "Maybe it was a passing on of secret knowledge and wisdom. Your grandmother was here . . . many years ago. Perhaps what she witnessed was a passing on of songlines from mothers to daughters."

Beth looked at her in confusion. "But I thought a songline was a road."

"*We* are the songline, Beth—mothers and daughters. And I wonder if this is the other legacy my mother spoke of—perhaps she had been told that she would come back here someday with her own mother, and experience the beauty of this place. But she never did. She died, never knowing."

Beth felt the mysterious power of the mountain all around her. "What do you suppose mothers said to their daughters here?" she asked.

Joanna looked at Beth and thought: You were the daughter I wanted. You are my joy. You are you, so perfectly yourself, and yet you are also a part of me. I will teach you our songline; I will teach you to listen to the music within yourself, the music of your own intuition. And then she thought: Maybe that was what the Aboriginal women had said, in this same grotto, to their daughters, thousands of years ago. Maybe it was as simple as that.

Beth looked up at the Rainbow Serpent and said, "Is this the serpent that my grandmother saw in her dreams?"

"Yes, I believe it is. Look closely, Beth, and you can see the natural layers in the rock beneath the paint. Do you see how they form the body of a giant serpent? I think that long ago, in the distant past, people must have come upon this place, and when they saw what they thought was a serpent captured in stone, they began to revere it. Over the centuries they embellished it, painted it, made it more beautiful."

"Mother!" Beth said, pointing. "Look at the serpent's eye!"

Joanna stared at the rearing head of the Rainbow Serpent. It was painted in profile, so only one eye showed. But the eye was nothing but a hole in the wall, and it looked as if something had been chipped out with a knife.

"The opal!" Beth said. "That must be where the opal came from!"

Joanna opened the satchel and brought out the gemstone. It felt warm in her hand, and it flashed sharply red and green. She looked up at the wall painting. The hole where the eye should have been was the same size and shape as the opal. "Beth," she said, "this must be the crime my grandfather committed! He must have crept into the cave when no one was looking, and stolen the eye of the Rainbow Serpent."

"And look over there!" Beth said, her voice echoing high in the vaulted ceiling.

Joanna looked to where she was pointing, and saw small skeletons scattered around the floor of the cave—the skeletons of dogs.

She looked at the serpent again, and saw something she had not noticed before: crude drawings etched into the rock at the base of the painting. Figures representing dogs.

"My God," she said at last. "Naliandrah was right. Do you remember, Beth, when she told me at the corroboree that the answers were within me? Of course! I understand now. I've known the answers all along, but I just hadn't put them together."

"What do you mean?" Beth said.

"These dogs," Joanna said, indicating the wall figures and the scattered bones, "must have been the guardians of the Rainbow Serpent. And when someone committed a crime against the serpent—as my grandfather had done—then the punishment came from the dogs. Do you remember when Naliandrah was telling us the story of Makpeej? She said the Rainbow Serpent swallowed him whole. Beth, it wasn't the serpent itself that swallowed him, it was the dogs . . ." Joanna closed her eyes for a moment, realizing the enormity of what she had just said. That must have been the tribe's punishment on John Makepeace: They set wild dogs on him. And the three-and-a-half-year-old Emily must have witnessed it.

"I understand it all now," Joanna said, trying to imagine what must have taken place near here over fifty years ago—the young Englishmen unable to resist the temptation of taking the opal, the clan finding out, the dogs . . . And what became of Naomi? Had she been part of the terrible punishment, too?

"The opal belongs here," Joanna said. "We must put it back." And in restoring it, she thought, the curse on my family will end.

Joanna handed the satchel to Beth, then stepped over the narrow stream and reached up to replace the opal. As Joanna turned the stone around, trying to make it fit, Beth looked at the satchel and its contents. She saw the corner of the deed; she pulled it all the way out and read the faded words in the eerie light of the cave. When she came to the passage that read, "Two days' ride from . . . and twenty kilometers from Bo— Creek," she suddenly remembered the signpost she had seen near Sister Veronica's infirmary. *Bustard Creek, 20 km. south.* And *Durrakai.*

"Mother!" Beth said suddenly. "I think I know where the land is—the land in the deed! It's where the nuns live, it's their hospital! I'm sure of it!"

Joanna gave Beth a startled look. Then she said, "If that is the land in the deed, then that must be where my grandparents had planned to build their farm. We found it, and we didn't even know it."

"What will we do with the land, Mother?"

Joanna thought of Sister Veronica, and how she had taken care of little Emily Makepeace in those first early days when the child had come out of the desert. If the deed was still good, and the land could be claimed, Joanna knew what she was going to do.

When the gemstone was in place, flashing red-and-green fire, Beth said, "Do you suppose, Mother, that now that the eye is restored to the serpent, the Aborigines will use this mountain again? Will they perform their ceremonies in here the way they once did?"

"I don't know, Beth. Perhaps not. The cycle was interrupted, and now many years have passed, so much has happened since the last celebrant came through here. Not even Naliandrah knows exactly what kind of ritual was performed in these caves. Maybe it is lost forever, and you and I are the last ones to stand in the presence of the Rainbow Serpent."

Beth thought for a moment. Then she said, "Was there ever really a curse on our family, do you suppose?"

"In a way, I think there was. Certainly my mother believed in it, and so in a way she made it real, if only in her mind. But it is finished now. It's over, and we are free." Joanna thought of Hugh, and how much she needed him. "We can go home now," she said.

After taking one final look at the magnificent Rainbow Serpent, they returned to the path and began the upward ascent toward the light.